continued . . .

"Enchantments, amusement, and eight hunks and one bewitching woman make for a fun romantic fantasy . . . Humorous and magical . . . A delightful charmer."

—*Midwest Book Review*

"A paranormal adventure series that will appeal to fantasy and historical fans, plus time-travel lovers as well . . . Delightful entertainment." —*Romance Junkies*

"An intriguing new fantasy romance series . . . A unique combination of magic, time travel, and fantasy that will have readers looking toward the next book."

—*Time Travel Romance Writers*

"The writing is sharp and witty, and the story is charming. [Johnson] makes everything perfectly believable. She has created an enchanting situation and characters that are irascible at times and lovable at others. Jean Johnson . . . is off to a flying start. She tells her story with a lively zest that transports a reader to the place of action. I can hardly wait for the next one. It is a must-read."

—*Romance Reviews Today*

"A fun story. I look forward to seeing how these alpha males find their soul mates in the remaining books."

—*The Eternal Night*

"An intriguing world . . . An enjoyable hero . . . An enjoyable showcase for an inventive new author. Jean Johnson brings a welcome voice to the romance genre, and she's assured of a warm welcome." —*The Romance Reader*

"An intriguing and entertaining tale of another dimension. It will be fun to see how the prophecy turns out for the rest of the brothers." —*Fresh Fiction*

THEIRS NOT TO REASON WHY

HELLFIRE

JEAN JOHNSON

ACE BOOKS, NEW YORK

THE BERKLEY PUBLISHING GROUP
Published by the Penguin Group
Penguin Group (USA) Inc.
375 Hudson Street, New York, New York 10014, USA

USA | Canada | UK | Ireland | Australia | New Zealand | India | South Africa | China

Penguin Books Ltd., Registered Offices: 80 Strand, London WC2R 0RL, England
For more information about the Penguin Group, visit penguin.com.

HELLFIRE

An Ace Book / published by arrangement with the author

Ace Books are published by The Berkley Publishing Group.
ACE and the "A" design are trademarks of Penguin Group (USA) Inc.

For information, address: The Berkley Publishing Group,
a division of Penguin Group (USA) Inc.,
375 Hudson Street, New York, New York 10014.

ISBN: 978-0-425-25650-3

PUBLISHING HISTORY
Ace mass-market edition / August 2013

PRINTED IN THE UNITED STATES OF AMERICA

10 9 8 7 6 5 4 3 2

Cover art by Gene Mollica.
Cover design by Annette Fiore Defex.
Interior text design by Laura K. Corless.

ALWAYS LEARNING   **PEARSON**

ACKNOWLEDGMENTS

This whole series is dedicated to the men and women around the world who have been, are, and will be willing to step between their fellow sentient beings and whatever threatens them. Specifically, the military, but this includes police officers, medical personnel, firefighters, and other emergency services. As always, I have worked to create my vision of the future with a deep respect for those who serve in the present day.

While the Terran United Planets Space Force has been based along the lines of several real-world military systems, it is not meant to represent any one particular such military; for example, the TUPSF-MC is not the same as the United States Marine Corps, and the TUPSF-Navy is not the same thing as the Royal Navy of the British armed forces. Though there are several things they and other militaries have in common with the versions I have created for these four books, there are also many differences.

If you, the reader, find any difference in the various military functions in this story that you do not agree with, please remember either it was placed there because it was sifted from a different nation's military traditions, it was deliberately chosen to be different by the author, it was simply a case of ignorance on the author's part, it may have come from a different person's perspective uncovered during the many interviews I have conducted with people from various military branches around the world . . . or it just wound up appearing in the story because it sounded cool. (When telling a fiction story, the Rule of Cool and the Rule of Funny automatically get a higher pay grade and rank than the Rule of How Things Actually Work.)

If you have served or are serving to help defend, protect, and better your home, wherever that home may be, I salute you with respect. If you are the spouse, relative, or friend of someone who has served or is serving, I thank you deeply for the many kinds of support you give your loved ones in these services. For those of you who aren't familiar with what it is to either serve or have someone you know serve, thank you for reading this series; I hope I have given you a glimpse of military life. This series is not an accurate window into the real-world day-to-day lives of the men and women serving out there, but I have tried to give you a window into the hearts and minds of those who are willing to serve.

My thanks, as ever, go to my beta editors, Buzzy, NotSoSaintly, Alexandra, and Stormi, and to my many readers for taking a chance on these books. Thank you very much for picking up this one and the others. May you continue to enjoy my efforts to entertain and inspire you.

Jean

PROLOGUE

The past is nothing more than a story we tell to each other. It is not meant for mere mortal hands to erase or sever . . . though it is not immutable. In fact, it can be changed, if only by God and madmeioas. To all others, it is indeed written in stone.

Shakespeare once said, "What's past is prologue," but you must understand that this is true only because the story never ends. Yes, you had a beginning in your birth, and yes, you will have an ending in your death, but the story itself never ends. Still, each segment is preserved in one shining moment, a granite tome held up to the light of the universe so that it can be revealed in all its horrors and all its glories . . . and thus preserved forever. But only in the past.

Eventually, even the slowest of readers will come to that last line, and must turn the story to a new page.

~Ia

SEPTEMBER 23, 2495 TERRAN STANDARD
THE TOWER
TERRAN UNITED PLANETS SPACE FORCE HEADQUARTERS
EARTH, SOL SYSTEM

The voices kept impinging on her senses, distracting her from her search. Ia wished they would shut up.

"What about Lieutenant Second Class Brad Arstoll? She served in Basic Training with him," a middle-aged woman offered.

"Yes, he's just finished his Marines Academy training. But that means he's still a new officer. Can we really risk the 2nd Platoon being led by a raw cadet?" an elderly man countered.

Their voices blended together, male and female, middle-aged and older, like the babbling of a brook in the background of her awareness.

Physically, Ia stood in one of the research rooms used by the Department of Innovations, a chamber filled with banks of workstations ringing an oval table scattered with datapads and stacks of personnel printouts. The walls themselves were mostly datascreens broken by a trio of doors. Each screen displayed a larger-than-life face and the bare-bones stats of the Service record belonging to each profiled soldier, flickering and shifting with each new suggestion.

Mentally, Ia stood on the grassy banks of Time itself, a rolling plain crisscrossed by the tangled streams of millions of lives. They formed a complex tapestry where major events, which would normally stir the waters out of their banks, were actually overshadowed by the tiniest of ripples. Changes that she had to track down.

"Arstoll may be a new officer, but he is Field Commissioned, so he does have some combat leadership experience," a second, older woman pointed out. "Plus, he's somewhat familiar with the captain even if they haven't seen each other in years. Not to mention their compatibility charts look pretty good."

"Familiarity doesn't really come into it," another male argued. "She needs a competent, combat-trained officer. I still say Lieutenant Dostoyervski is the best match—*he* should be her second-in-command."

Something was rippling the waters of Time, disturbing her carefully laid plans like a deep, unseen current. If she didn't track it down, it could erode the bank out from under her feet. That would be bad.

"His DoI file *is* sticky with bigger recommendations than the other candidates have," the first male agreed. "And his psych profile does match in both compatibility and contracompatibility measurements with Captain Ia, here. It looks like he'd get along with the other officers, too . . . well, maybe not Helstead, if she decides to be headstrong. But that's a problem for their CO to sort out. Learning to manage strong personalities could be a good lesson."

She had already dismissed Dostoyervski. He wouldn't do at all, not when her own considerations took into account several variables not even the DoI could foresee. Their voices were annoying her with trivial details. "Shhh . . ."

They didn't pay much attention to her, other than to speak a little more quietly. The men and women of the Department of Innovations were a different breed from the standard soldier. Most of them were career, with the average number of years in the various branches of Service rarely being less than fifteen, and usually above twenty. In fact, many of them were technically retirees from active duty, able to bring those years of long-term military experience to the task of figuring out who out there had the skills to be promoted and fast-tracked, or stalled and even demoted. Most had training in psychology and xenopsychology, tactics and long-term strategy. All of them were expert data miners.

In a unified military composed of roughly two billion soldiers, they were the best at knowing who was who in the Terran United Planets Space Force and where that person should probably go. It was their job to debate who should be one of the three Platoon lieutenants Ia needed. Their job to select the best soldiers for a particular set of tasks. Their job to make the final decision, normally.

Normally, someone in Ia's situation wouldn't even be here, let alone have much say in the process. If the psychological filtration programs and the best judgments of the DoI members came up with matches too close to call, they might contact a superior officer to solicit their opinion, yes, but that officer never came to the physical headquarters of the DoI, or even to one of its many branch offices scattered through Terran space.

However, this situation was not normal. Ia was already inside the Tower, the nickname for the sprawling, administrative heart of the Space Force on Earth. This particular branch of the DoI was located no more than a kilometer or so from the office of her new commanding officer, Admiral John Genibes of the Branch Special Forces. She was already operating under special dispensation for other reasons, including a form of *carte blanche*—albeit one with a very strict double-indemnity clause—so Ia had arranged to visit this data-crammed room in person.

All she wanted to do was to select the perfect-for-her crew, comparing their potential actions to the needs of the right future, the one that would save their descendants from a massive calamity three centuries away. Unfortunately, the men and women around her were trying to help her select the *perfect* crew. She didn't need perfect, as if the soldiers in question were diamonds, prepolished and cut. She needed raw material, flexible and bold, obedient yet innovative, men and women capable of doing truly great things under *her* command, yet very carefully not needed elsewhere. Carbon fibers, not jewels.

Those who would be needed elsewhere had to remain elsewhere. What she needed were the nobodies, the throwaways whose lives wouldn't make a palpable difference anywhere else. Straw soldiers who, under her guidance, could be spun into threads of pure gold for the tapestry she needed to weave.

It should have been easy for her to sort through the many possibilities lining the path she needed the future to follow. Easy to pluck out the names, the personalities, the faces of everyone she needed. But something was wrong.

This isn't getting me anywhere. Working at her usual perception level, a woman standing on a low-rolling prairie crisscrossed by life-streams, she couldn't see where the subtle problems all began. *So either it's macroscale measurements, or microscale. Micro would be more accurate, but I don't even know where to start, and there's too much out there to just drop into the waters of some life-stream randomly . . . So, macro it is.*

Visualization was usually a psychic's best friend. Grounding and centering exercises helped stabilize the mind, and mental bubble-shields walled out unwanted influences. Most of the time, exercising these abilities was analogous to humming a tune for background noise, or carrying an object; once a psi learned how, it didn't take much effort. It did, however, take time. Ia had spent the last eight years of her life training her mind to carry the weight of Time itself.

Instead of standing on a vast field, she shrunk the timeplains down to a brocaded tapestry. Life-rivers became threads as the rolling grass and rippling waters vanished. They ran in ways contrary to the normal warp and weft, more like a complex skein than a formal weave, but the analogy wasn't meant to be perfect. Lifting it up with mental hands, she peered along the edge of Time, checking for anomalies in the fabric.

She couldn't hear the voices of the others anymore, couldn't see them at the periphery of her vision. Focused on the nearly two-dimensional image held in her mind, Ia spotted the first slub a few years down from the moment of now in the pale golden tapestry stretched out before her. It was subtle indeed, visible only as a metaphor, but the beige thread was palpably thicker than the others.

It was also not alone. Now that she could see the first one, others here and there caught her attention. They were noticeable because they were just a little bit thicker than they should have been. Narrowing her attention to a close knot of those thickened life-threads, Ia queried her precognitive abilities.

Whose lives are these? What do they have in common?

Visualization was the key. Her vast abilities knew what was going on, but only on a subconscious level at best. Subconsciously, she sensed a hint of danger in the timeplains, just enough to prick at her instincts. Her conscious mind was still mortal, though; her intellect, smart as she was, couldn't yet sort out the differences. A merging of the two, instinct and thought, might help. *So, what parts of these threads are in common with each other, and what bits are distinct?*

Color seeped into the threads, delineating each life and its impact on the others around it. Not just the ones she saw, but new ones, extra slubs of undue influence. Lifting herself above the tapestry, Ia could see the colors, plural. More than one influenced the timestream-threads . . . but the later ones seemed to come into play only after the first one, a purple hue not too far off from the petals of an iris flower, had wreaked most of the initial damage over a dozen key lives.

Zooming in close, mentally floating above the weave, she examined the wisps of thread-fibers where the purple taint in the slub came close to an aquamarine one. The tiniest threads connected the two. So tiny, they looked . . . silver.

Feyori.

Cursing, Ia backed up—and flinched instinctively out of the timestreams, left hand snapping up, mind snapping out. Opening her eyes, she stared at the frightened sergeant dangling centimeters from her grip and centimeters off the floor, caught in her telekinetic grip. If she had lingered in there one moment more, the middle-aged woman might have actually touched her.

That would have been bad.

"Y . . . You . . ." the greying brunette panted, eyes wide. "You . . ."

"I said," Ia stated, as gently as she could, "that I did *not* want to be touched." Carefully, she lowered the older woman back to her feet. "I apologize for my instinctive reaction just now—and I'm grateful I didn't hurt you with my combat reflexes—but it was either grab you with my mind, or let you injure *your* mind precognitively. Now, did you want something?"

Licking her lips, the woman clutched her portable workstation in her dark brown arms and nodded. "Uh, yes, sir. We've completed your roster for you, Captain. All it needs is your . . . your . . . I can't believe I'm saying this," the reservist master sergeant muttered, her shock fading, replaced by a touch of startlement-induced anger. "This whole situation is highly irregular! *We* decide who gets promoted and where they go, particularly when it's a transfer into the Special Forces."

"I know it's irregular, Narine," Ia told her, making the woman blink. Only her last name, Plimstaad, was visible on the name patch fixed to the pocket of her brown Dress jacket. "I know that very little of this is according to standard procedure. But it's necessary. As for that list of names, do not send it yet. It's still incomplete."

"The list *is* complete, sir," she argued. "All you needed was a competent lieutenant for your 2nd Platoon. You have a first officer and three Platoon lieutenants. You have a Company and three Platoon sergeants, you have a full roster of enlisted and have claimed one of the best full-care doctors in the Space Force. You may be missing all of your squad sergeants, but you have every single person you requested. Dostoyervski has been selected for you, since you were taking so long in making up your mind. Standing there like a statue, no less," the DoI sergeant muttered. "Sir."

"Dostoyervski won't work for me, Sergeant," Ia dismissed. "I'll need to find someone else."

She shrugged and tapped something on her workpad. "Fine. Arstoll it is, then. Sign it with your thumbprint, Captain, and have a nice day."

Ia shook her head. "I won't sign that, Sergeant. I've found an anomaly—a huge anomaly—and I have to track down the right way to fix it, first."

"*What* anomaly, Captain?"

The impatient question came from the oldest man in the room, and the only soldier whose rank matched her own. The main differences between them were that he wore brown stripes on his black uniform, and that his brass eagle did not carry the rockets in its claws that hers did, making her a ship's captain and him a lieutenant colonel. As dark-skinned as the sergeant, but with three times as many wrinkles and none of the hair, Lieutenant Colonel Luu-Smith flicked his hand irritably.

"You've already taken up hours of our time this morning with a task normally left to the experts, Captain Ia. What anomaly could *possibly* throw everything we've done out the window at this point in time?" he demanded. "I thought you said you were some sort of massive precog. Shouldn't you have already foreseen it?"

"With respect, Colonel," Ia returned, "I am *not* the only being who can see into the future, and that means I'm not the only one who can act to change the things they foresee." At his skeptical look, she rolled her eyes. After several years of playing her cards close to her chest, ingrained habit had kept her from revealing what she apparently needed to reveal. ". . . The *Feyori* are now involved. They cannot see as far as me, but they *can* see, and they will interfere, if they think it will somehow promote their own positions in their gods-be-stupid Game.

"Unfortunately, some of them are now considering me a threat. It's incredibly shortsighted of them because I'm not their enemy, but there it is. Now, if you'll just be a little more patient, please, I was in the middle of tracking down where the anomalies started when I was interrupted." She glanced briefly at Sergeant Plimstaad. "And I did mean it when I said do not touch me. You do not want to see what is inside my head; I'm dealing with scales that most people aren't prepared to deal with, at speeds that would give you a raging migraine.

"I do thank you for your efforts on my behalf," Ia added. "I'll try to be quick about this, but there are a lot of lives at stake. More than you know."

Closing her eyes, Ia breathed deep and let it out, then did it again, calming and centering her mind. A flip of her thoughts landed her in the grass next to the waters of her own life. From there, it didn't take much effort to condense Time back into a thin, interwoven sheet, though she did have to spend a few moments refinding the slub-nodes of Feyori influence in the future. Once she had her mental metaphor adjusted so that her conscious mind could comprehend it, she stained the lead one purple again and followed it up-thread into the past, trying to find the moment where the anonymous Meddler in question had decided to begin interfering.

The *recent* past, she discovered with an unpleasant jolt. *Ah, slag . . . The initial slip in the streams took place just thirteen days ago. That was the day I left the Solarican Warstation Nnying Yanh. More precisely, this is the Feyori whose presence I uncovered and threw off the Warstation. The same day I was tested and my father's legacy had to be revealed, explaining the strengths of my psychic powers.*

Which was also the day I stupidly didn't check to see what *effects his abrupt exposure would have on the timelines,* she castigated herself, wincing.

She didn't have to touch that thread to know the Feyori in question would be upset enough to try to counterfaction her. The energy-based beings converted themselves into matter-based beings so that they could meddle with her fellow sentients' lives. They did not like it when the pawns in their great Game started playing by different rules, and they *really* didn't like it when a pawn ousted a player.

Sometimes their interference was for a Right of Breeding, which was how Ia herself had come into existence. Such things infused most of the known sentient races with psychic abilities. Sometimes their interference was less direct; the Meddlers could manipulate the thoughts of their targets via telepathy, create complex hallucinations via a combination of holokinesis and clairvoyance, even physically change a person through massive biokinesis. Most of the reasons *why* they did such things gave Ia a headache trying to figure them out.

As much as she wanted to avoid crossing factions with the Feyori, her own stupid lack of foresight almost two weeks ago had dumped this problem into her lap. *Which means almost half my roster is now rendered void and useless. This purple-Meddler looks like he will have picked up . . . twelve, thirteen . . . fifteen or so major faction-groups to help counterfaction my efforts by the time I'll need all the Feyori to swear faction to me. Slag . . .*

She quickly checked the chronology of the timelines. *It seems he's quite clever, too. His first real interference-node will happen six Terran years and one Terran day after I bartered with that "Doctor Silverstone" Feyori for a Right of Simmerings. And it won't be anywhere near where I am, so it'll be difficult for me to counter it face-to-face. Most of these slubs are truly subtle interferences, probably just telepathic suggestions . . . but they are enough to throw off the weft and warp of the pathways I need. Which means it's time to rewrite the whole roster . . . and . . . ah, hell. I'll need . . .*

Ugh. I'll probably need to accept Belini's offer to faction me in exchange for far-ranging prophecies. The Meddlers can see a little way into Time, and that means I have to plan dozens of steps in advance, limiting as many of their counterfaction options as I can. If I'm not careful, it'll really shift the balance of power down through the centuries, ruining plans I've already laid.

At least I've already considered her offer as a Plan B to extend my Right of Simmerings, so I don't have to break completely new ground in the timestreams . . .

I hope I don't have to use it, though I won't hold my breath. I'd rather get three Feyori to admit I am the foreseen Prophet, and have the right to rearrange their Game. She double-checked the timestream paths and winced mentally. *I won't have many chances to do that, though. Miklinn technically isn't interfering or counterfactioning by raising the point that I "really should manifest before being accepted" as one of them . . . and damn him for the legality of it. And damn myself for my carelessness. Slag.*

Okay, Time, she ordered silently, rippling the sheet-like weave, doubling over the threads and turning them translucent. She knew how to handle her Right of Simmerings, which would buy her more time to sway the Feyori to her side. For the contingencies where some of the Feyori were stubborn about wanting to counterfaction her, she needed a different crew. *Show me which changes in personnel I will need, starting with Chaplain Benjamin, Doctor Mishka, and my choice of first officer, Lieutenant Brateanu . . .*

The pathways she needed to check were fairly easy, like two transparencies laid one over the other. The first layer was the

Feyori-altered path at the bottom, with her current roster selections. The second layer belonged to the path she had already marked out for the future, the one that led to the one shot she had at saving the galaxy from annihilation three hundred years away.

Deviations were quicker to see this way, but it only worked because she already had both source-paths to trace and compare. Until she had found the problem—Feyori interference—she couldn't have made these comparisons. *Good, good . . . Bennie's still my chaplain; I like her. And the good doctor will still be grumpy about her reassignment to my team, but she'll still work out fine. As for . . . ah, slag,* Ia cursed, wincing. *Brateanu is right out.*

She needed an engineer, someone so good, so creative, they could scavenge or craft parts on the fly, since there would be too many times when her ship and crew would not have the time to stop and make repairs at an actual dry-dock facility.

Her 1st Platoon lieutenant had to be Rico, a man with a brilliant analytical mind and the ability to read and think in Sallhash, even if pronouncing it was physiologically difficult for Humans. He couldn't be replaced. She also needed Helstead as her 3rd Platoon leader. The woman was not only the most deadly soldier on Ia's crew roster, she could teach those skills to the people under her. Helstead came with more tricks up her sleeve than a hundred stage magicians, and Ia would need most of them in the near future.

That left either the lieutenant for the 2nd Platoon, or her first officer. One of the two had to be good at handling combat chaos, the other had to be an outstanding engineer. Rico and Helstead were both good enough to handle combat, though one was more of a military analyst and the other a military assassin by training.

By preference, she would rather make the combat officer a Platoon lieutenant, so that all three groups of soldiers would be led by someone competent in directing battle. The problem was, of the combat-competent leaders among the hundreds of millions of junior officers out there, most would be needed exactly where they were.

Head hurting, Ia eased out of the timeplains. She lifted her hand to her forehead, trying to massage away the tension caused by her dilemma; physically, she had only spent a couple minutes standing there, but psychically, she had spent several. Such accelerated concentration came at a cost.

One of the middle-aged DoI sergeants spotted the movement and sighed. "Well, Captain?" the man asked her. "Have you spotted a solution to your little anomaly?"

"All I can do is plan for a greater level of flexibility, Sergeant," Ia muttered back. "They're Feyori. They're *shakking* unpredictable as well as powerful, they cannot be killed or swept aside, and the *only* kind who could hope to back one down when a Feyori feels it's been offended and counterfactioned is anoth . . ."

She trailed off midword. Blinking, Ia stared sightlessly across the room. A moment from the past played through her mind—not a moment dipped from the timestreams, but one from her own memories. Snippets of that conversation came back to her, key phrases that now reassembled themselves in her mind.

You're going to Antarctica . . . or will be . . . to steal schematics for something . . . the Vault of Time . . .

The Vault of Time. Wincing at the irony, she covered her face with one hand. *Oh, God, Meyun . . . you were more accurate than you could've known. The only thing that can stand up to a Feyori is another Feyori . . . so it looks like I will have to raid the Immortal's Vault on Earth. Slagging hell. That's going to be tricky.*

Drawing in a deep breath, she steeled herself for her new task. This time, she dove back in without hesitation; this time, she had an idea of who and what to look for. Working quickly, she plucked out the life-threads of a half dozen potential-possible engineering candidates. A full dozen, flicking through their transparent life-streams, overlaid on the path she needed to take. A score.

Too many of them had problems. Little ones, big ones, convoluted ones, butterfly ones where the tiniest flap of wings created massive hurricanes down the road . . . Head aching, heart hurting, Ia finally plucked out the thread belonging to her one failed relationship and laid it over the future.

Not everything was visible; Meyun Harper was still greymisty in several spots, key moments where her own emotions toward him would make it difficult to decide what to do. But unlike the dangerously wandering life-paths of the others, most of which started as small variants before veering wildly away from the most useful course, his consistently came back to the paths she would need.

Absolutely wonderful. Irony of ironies. Slagging, shakking *hell. God certainly has a sense of humor, doesn't she? Ia's Impending Doom, thy name is both Meyun and Miklinn . . . and such a lovely-sounding pair of names for an impending pair of pains in my path.*

Dropping back into her body, Ia struggled not to roll her eyes. Meeting the somewhat impatient stares of the others, she shook her head.

"Change of plans, meioas. If I'm going up against the Feyori, I'm going to need several more psychics in each Platoon. I'll get you their names in a moment, but first things first. My second-in-command"—she had to take a breath before continuing—"is going to have to be Lieutenant First Class Meyun Harper."

Lieutenant Colonel Luu-Smith eyed her skeptically as one of the sergeants next to him put Harper's personnel file up on a couple of the screens. "The same one you went through the Academy with? If I recall your and his files correctly, there was a note about you having a fling with the man, post graduation."

"It was just a few days long, hardly worth mentioning," Ia stated dryly. "It also happened between assignments, and we parted company as friends, nothing more. Since then, we've barely spoken to each other, so Fatality Forty-Nine: Fraternization does not in any way apply. I am picking him because I *will* need his skills in adaptive engineering.

"There are ways to deal with the Feyori, certain energy frequencies they find unpleasant, but creating them will take a logistics officer who is clever and resourceful. I know he doesn't have nearly as much combat command experience as Brateanu, but the fact that Harper roomed with and studied beside me for a year while we were in the Academy will lend itself to ensuring there is a quick rapport of trust and understanding in the top of our cadre," she stated.

One of the middle-aged women seated around the table snorted under her breath, muttering something uncomplimentary about Harper having *known* his roommate all too well. Ia narrowed her eyes but did nothing more. It was one of the men next to the woman who smacked his hand lightly up the back-side of the woman's head, wordlessly chastising his fellow soldier.

Ia gave him a brief, wordless dip of her head before address-ing the rest. ". . . More to the point, gentlemeioas, Harper has known of my precognitive abilities for just over two years now yet has not told a soul. His sense of discretion and secrecy will be invaluable for the position of first officer on board my par-ticular ship. I would rather have had Brateanu, but there are key decisions my first officer will have to make while I am busy dealing with these Feyori interlopers, and thanks to their future interference, I can see now that she would make the wrong ones when dealing with them."

"You're calling *them* the interlopers," one of the younger males snorted. "But if you really are some sort of massive precog, aren't you just as bad a Meddler as them?"

A chiming from one of the workstations interrupted her reply. The soft alarm cut off as the oldest of the DoI sergeants sat forward, examining her handheld screen. A few taps of the keys projected a familiar face onto the monitors lining the walls. His head had been shaved bald at some point, but she knew his scarred, broken nose, ring-edged ears, and rascal's grin. Seeing First Sergeant Glen Spyder's personnel file was a much more pleasant surprise for Ia than Harper had been.

Sergeant Plimstaad glanced over the images of Spyder pro-jected on the wall screens, then looked back at Ia. The search parameters used by the DoI apparently included flagging and popping up any file whose subject had interacted with Ia at one time or another. "Well, Captain. It seems one of your old friends has just been flagged with a Field Commission. Did you know this was coming, sir?"

Ia shrugged. "I knew it was a possibility, but it was only a thirty-two percent chance at most, Sergeant, given his current combat situation. Given those odds, I honestly thought I'd have to pick someone else. As it is, this is relatively convenient. He'll have his commanding officers rescued from their troubles in . . . twenty-nine hours, thirty minutes, give or take a few minutes, which means his Company will be out of its jam and back to its assigned Battle Platform in about fifty hours from now."

The lieutenant colonel snorted again. "And what would you like the DoI to do about him, as if we couldn't guess?"

She didn't have to close her eyes, just unfocus them enough to pluck out the thread of Spyder's future probabilities and compare them to the path she needed. She had already considered this possibility earlier, though she had set it aside with that less-than-likely one-third of a probability. "The DoI needs to approve him for full Field Honors once he's out of the frying pan, then transfer and drop him into my 2nd Platoon as a Lieutenant Second Class, instead of selecting Lieutenant Arstoll. I know Glen Spyder can follow my battle plans and still think on his feet in the midst of chaos, so he'll do just fine."

"He'll need to go to an Academy, first," Luu-Smith pointed out. "His intelligence charts suggest he'd be quick enough for a fast-track class, but you'll still need a 2nd Platoon leader for the first year."

"I'd rather not delay his presence, sir. Just drop him into my Company as is. He can complete his officer's training via on-the-job work and correspondence school where needed," Ia countered. At their skeptical looks, she shook her head. "I don't need him to advance up the ranks, meioas. I need him to help lead my troops into battle. He can do that right now, as is, so I'll take him exactly as he is today. Or will be, in a few hours. The rest can be taught either on the job or via correspondence courses.

"Now, let me get you the rest of the roster changes," she said, closing her eyes once more. "I'll need a couple more Troubleshooters, maybe a few Sharpshooters, as well as the extra psis—no one vital to the rest of the Space Force's needs will be swapped in, I promise. My Prophetic Stamp on that."

"Your so-called Prophetic Stamp's only worth the price of a ground-bound physical letter at this point, Captain," Lieutenant Colonel Luu-Smith grunted. "A stamp I wouldn't even bother to scan into the mailing system, right now."

"That's fine. You don't have to believe me, right now. You will learn the strength of my word in due time, meioas," she murmured. Ia quickly double-checked the future paths of Lieutenants Rico and Helstead with Spyder dropped in their midst, then turned her attention to the noncommissioned officers and the enlisted in her crew. "Now, let's see how many of the Damned I can salvage in this Meddler-made mess . . ."

CHAPTER 1

I think, by the end of this interview, I'm going to be very hoarse—thank you for your patience with me, by the way. I know this is a lot of material to cover, and I'm insisting on doing it more or less chronologically, but really there's no better way to organize all the events that have happened so far. And yes, I know that statement is ironic, coming from me.

Dabbling in Time as I do, I have had to juggle not just the needs of the present, but double- and triple-check them against the needs of the future. It's like juggling many, many balls all at once. I think the known galactic record for juggling in Standard Gravity is . . . what . . . twenty-six balls by a Gatsugi? Of course, they get to cheat a little, having four arms. But that's just juggling toys. If you drop one, it bounces across the floor. You do have to chase after it, but usually it doesn't break, and usually it can be tossed back up into the air again. I'm juggling countless septillion lives, and sometimes a detail or two can slip past my fingers.

Unfortunately for me, "dropping the ball" has an entirely different meaning and a very unpleasant outcome if I drop it badly. Every day, I tried my damnedest to get it right. But, to quote Dickens, "I am mortal, and liable to fall." Or to use another quote, "Damned if you do, and damned if you don't," which is one of the reasons why I nicknamed my Company what I did.

~Ia

OCTOBER 24, 2495 T.S.
TUPSF SECURED SHIPYARDS
TRITON ORBIT, NEPTUNE, SOL SYSTEM

Ia stopped in front of the door to the briefing boardroom. She paused a moment to draw two deep breaths, then squared her shoulders. *I can do this . . . I can do it . . . I have done it, and done it well.*

The only problem is, the moment I stride across that stage, I'm spotlight center for everything *that follows. Everything I say and do will be scrutinized by the Command Staff, the Department of Innovations, and most importantly, by my entire crew.*

It was a disturbingly large responsibility. Up until now, Ia's task had been to take shelter behind the rules and regulations and break them only when no one was looking. Now everyone would be looking, and she had to start breaking a lot of those rules and regs. *Not to mention, from here on out, I won't have a true moment of peace. Not if I want to do everything I need to get done.*

Mindful of the weight of the medals pinned to her newly issued set of Dress Blacks, of the impression she would make in wearing all of them, Ia touched the main button on the controls. The panel slid open with a faint hiss of hydraulics. Noise escaped through the opening, the sounds of 160 men and women chatting quietly among themselves as they waited in idle boredom.

She knew the layout of the briefing room, shaped like a lecture hall with projection screens on all the walls and tiers of padded chairs that could double as acceleration couches. Those chairs faced a curved table reserved for the six officers and four sergeants seated on either side of the empty chair waiting at the center.

The Captain's seat.

Her seat.

The door Ia used wasn't one of the double-wide ones at the back of the hall, above the riser seats. Hers opened onto a short corridor leading to the platform holding that table. It gave her a good view of the ten Humans seated behind that table, though not of the rest of the room; she could hear the others occupying the hall, but that was it. The dim lighting of that little entry hall also hid her arrival from all but one of the sentients in the room. Specifically, the petite redhead who sat at the near end of the table, with her back to Ia's door.

The other woman's eyes may have been occupied with the task of using a tiny stiletto to trim her nails, but her other senses were just as sharp and ready to be used. Between one breath and the next, the knife was shoved back into one of the sheaths doubling as hairpins that held her coronet of braids in place. The woman scrambled to her feet, standing on the seat of her chair so that everyone could see as well as hear her. All without even a single glance behind.

"Officer on deck!" she snapped, her voice as much a command as a warning. With that said, she dropped to the platform floor and stood At Attention. Other bodies rose around the table at her call, some more quickly than others, and the rustling of dozens more could be heard from around the corner.

Shoulders squared, chin level, Ia strode onto the platform hosting the table and the men and women now on their feet. As she came into view, first the officers and sergeants at the table lifted their hands to their brows, then the soldiers up into the tiers.

Clad as she was in both Dress Blacks and her Dress cap, saluting was mandatory. Ia did not return any of them, however. Instead, she moved to the open chair at the center of the table, nudged the seat back on its track so that she could stand in front of it, and faced the bulk of her crew. Unbuttoning her left cuff, she flipped open the screen of her command bracer and brought the boardroom monitors to life.

Official orders scrolled onto the main viewscreens positioned on the wall behind her, the two sidewalls, and suspended over the heads of the crew, so that wherever one looked, the topic being discussed could be seen. The right and left secondary screens remained blank for now, as did the long tertiary screen above them. Another touch activated the headset discreetly hooked over her ear. The thin wire alongside her cheek picked up her voice and projected it around the room just loud enough to be heard.

"Acting under the direct orders of Admiral John Genibes of the Terran United Planets Space Force, Branch Special Forces, I, Ship's Captain Ia, hereby take command of the 1st Company, 1st Legion, 1st Battalion, 1st Brigade, 1st Division . . . 9th

Cordon," she added, pausing slightly for emphasis, "and with it, take command of the Harasser-Class battleship TUPSF *Hellfire*, docked at the TUPSF Secured Shipyards of Triton, Neptune, Sol System."

She pronounced the acronym *tup-siff*, keeping her words as crisp and distinct as she could manage, since these were official transfer orders, recorded for legality as well as posterity.

"This action is now logged and filed as an official transfer of command, as of time stamp 22:45, October 24, 2495 Terran Standard time . . . mark," Ia finished, watching the chrono built into her arm unit.

The orders on the two main screens flashed, sealed with the indicated time. Only then did she lift her hand to her own temple, returning the crisp salute of the soldiers around her. As soon as she lowered her arm again, they lowered theirs. They continued to stand At Attention, however, awaiting orders.

Satisfied she had their attention, Ia tapped in another code on her bracer. The orders detailing her acceptance of command over ship and crew were replaced with the TUPSF logo. The soothing, sapphire blue background and familiar, oval map-projection of the major continents of the Human Motherworld filled the screen; instead of the normal gold hues used by the other Branches, however, the map had been drawn with the pale silver of the Special Forces.

Onto the two secondary screens flanking those mains, Ia posted the unclassified portions of her personnel file, including enlarged, rotating images of her face, with its Asian features, light tan, amber eyes, and chin-length, snow-white locks. Minus her Dress cap, of course.

Matching reality to that image, Ia removed her cap and set it on the table. Then tucked her headset, which the cap had dislodged, back into place over her right ear. The headset was necessary to project her voice to the headsets of the 160 men and women around her, particularly the privates at the back of the hall. She kept her Dress jacket on, keeping some of the formality of the moment, but unbuttoned it for comfort.

Somewhat for comfort, that was; with all of her medals pinned across the black gabardine, it was still quite heavy. It was a tangible reminder of the weight of her position.

"At Ease, meioas, and sit down. We have a *lot* to get through, so please pay attention. Most of this you will learn in greater detail by studying your Company Bibles," Ia stated, meaning the manual of procedures most combat officers gave to their soldiers.

Much of it was standardized to the Space Force's requirements, but they also often included little quirks and preferences tailored to each Company's patrol or combat needs. Hers were tailored all the way down to the individual. They would see that for themselves, shortly.

"For the moment, there are a few things I'd like to go over with you at the very start—please do be seated," she added, as some hesitated. "I don't do the nonsense that says the lower ranks have to remain standing if their CO hasn't sat down first. I'm staying on my feet as a reminder to *me* to be as brief as I can, given how much I need to say."

Those few older soldiers who were still on their feet, including her fellow officers, settled into their chairs. Ia nodded.

"Thank you. Most of you received your transfer orders with very little explanation as to why you were being transferred," she said, acknowledging in her opening words the confusion she could see lurking in the expressions of the men and women studying her. "You may think you have been selected at random. You may be wondering why *you* are here, and not someone supposedly better qualified. I say to you that you *are* the right men and women for the jobs that lie ahead of us. I have painstakingly hand-selected each and every one of you, based upon the foreknowledge that each and every one of you can and will get your tasks done, and get them done right.

"What those tasks are will have to wait for another day. Our ship is still in dry . . ." She paused as a rumbling noise transferred through the deckplates for a moment, then finished her sentence. ". . . in dry dock, undergoing the last of the interior fittings. We ourselves will be splitting our time between this ship, the dock station, and even some land-based maneuvers over the next two months as we give this crew a shakedown to get you used to your upcoming multiple responsibilities. Then we will be taking this ship out for its shakedown run as well.

"But first, an introduction of your command staff, starting with myself. My name is Ia, pronounced *EE-yah*, not *Eye-yah*, or even *Lah*, and it is my first, last, and only name. You may therefore call me Captain, Captain Ia, or even just Ia in those moments when we are being informal. For those few of you already familiar with my military nickname, my first name is *not* 'Mary' and I will not respond to it on its own. You may, however, call me by my full nickname, Bloody Mary," she allowed, meeting the gaze of a man here, a woman there, "but you *will* say it with respect. I have formed a very bad habit throughout my military career of flooding the deckplates in my enemies' blood, and I have no intention of breaking that habit in the years to come."

A few bodies stirred in the crowd at that; not everyone in the room was comfortable with the thought of such violent combat. The green-and-brown-haired man at her side grinned openly at their discomfort; he had seen it before and wasn't fazed by the thought. Ia nodded briefly at him and continued.

"On a more personal note, I come from the heaviest inhabited world. That means I am roughly three times as strong and three times as fast as the majority of the Humans in this room. I am also a very strong psychic, stronger than any other Human you are likely to meet, because my mother is very much a Human . . . but my father was a Feyori."

She waited while that caused another stir. The fact that psychic abilities came from the Meddlers was a somewhat known but rarely discussed topic since it made most people uneasy. Admitting openly to her crew that she was a half-breed would make many of them uncomfortable around her. None would be openly hostile, but some would be wary. Ironically, some of the uncomfortable ones would be fellow psis; even more ironic, most hadn't realized yet just how many psis had been gathered into her crew.

"Make no mistake, meioas. I side with my fellow Humans and the other matter-based sentients. Beyond that, the main thing you need to know right now is that I am a massive precog. In fact, I am the Prophet of a Thousand Years, as prophesied by the Sh'nai faith of the V'Dan Empire." That caused another, much larger stir in the crowd as waves of doubt spread across many of their faces. Only a handful believed in the main V'Dan religion; most were followers of Terran faiths, if they followed anything. Raising her hand briefly, she warded off that doubt. "Don't worry if you don't believe me right now. You'll see the truth of it for yourself in the days ahead.

"To my immediate left," she stated, changing the subject by introducing the man with the black braid, who belatedly nodded, "is Lieutenant Commander Meyun Harper. He is a genius at applied mechanics and impromptu engineering. He also trained with me back in the Naval Academy, so he knows better than most what my command style will be."

She carefully did not mention the fact that Harper also knew many of her precognitive decisions. Ia didn't want her mangled past with him to become a point of speculation for their crew. Particularly not with the DoI intent on watching both of them to see if they tripped over Fatality Forty-Nine in the next few months. She continued without hesitation, speaking crisply as her personnel file was replaced by his on the screens, giving everyone an enlarged view of his neatly uniformed head and shoulders.

"Like most of us, Harper will hold several jobs on board this ship. Not only will he be my first officer, he will be in charge of logistics & supply, lifesupport, engineering, and he will get his hands dirty as our chief engineer. Harper, above all others, will be responsible for the continued maintenance and operation of this ship; if he asks you to fix something, you will fix it. To that end, he will also be training everyone on board this ship to be able to handle emergency repairs on the fly, for whatever repair is closest to you . . . so you will all become familiar with *all* aspects of shipboard maintenance . . . save only one system, which I will discuss later."

That earned her several curious looks from the sea of Grey-clad soldiers around her. Ia didn't bother to explain. She had too much to get through.

"Next up is Lieutenant Commander Delia Helstead, who has served with distinction as a captain for the last three years," Ia introduced next, indicating the petite redhead at the far left end of the table. Her image and public file appeared on the screens next, replacing Harper's. "She has since been cross-ranked from Captain to Lieutenant Commander so that we will not confuse her rank with *my* rank on board this ship.

"In other words, if you say 'Captain' and she starts to respond instead of me, that will be the reason why, until she gets used to it," Ia allowed, smiling wryly. "As inconvenient as that may be for her, we all know whom to blame . . . thank you very much, TUPSF-Navy, for insisting upon clinging to your outdated maritime traditions."

A few members of the gathered crew chuckled. The

stubbornness of the Navy's various traditions had lingered long after the unification of all of the Terran empire's various armed forces into two bodies, the civilian-based Peacekeepers and the military-based Space Force. Even Helstead smiled at the complaint, though she didn't stop her task. The short, muscular woman had resumed the cleaning and trimming of her nails with one of the stiletto-pins pulled from her hair, one leg curled up underneath her on her seat, looking more like an enlisted grunt than an Academy-trained officer.

"Lieutenant Commander Helstead comes to us as a former deputy director of field operations in the Knifemen Corps," Ia stated, deliberately pronouncing the –se in the word as tradition also demanded, instead of the more familiar *core*, like the Marine Corps used. "She will be in charge of the 3rd Platoon, as well as be our tactical officer for all special-operations activities, our hand-to-hand combat training officer, our gunnery training officer, and our disciplinary officer, should you require disciplinary action above and beyond the Squad and Platoon levels—do not be fooled by her small size. She comes from the heavyworld Eiaven, and is therefore twice as strong and fast as she looks. She is also a fellow psi.

"At her side is 3rd Platoon Staff Sergeant Chico Maxwell." The Hispanic man seated next to the petite redhead dipped his head at the introduction. "Those of you assigned to the 3rd Platoon, or who find yourselves serving on the third watch for whatever reason, will report first to your Squad leaders, then to Sergeant Maxwell, then to Commander Helstead, depending upon who is available," she stated, abbreviating Helstead's rank in the standard way with the higher of the two titles. "There will be plenty of times where you will be thrown into the nearest duty post simply because you are the nearest available body. I suggest you get used to the thought of it, so that the reality will not stagger you.

"Seated next to Maxwell is Lieutenant First Class Oslo Rico, who will be in charge of the 1st Platoon and its duty watch." Ia paused briefly while the dusky-skinned, mountain-tall man tipped his own head. "Lieutenant Rico is an expert in military intelligence, data mining, surveillance, threat assessment, ship deployments, naval tactics, strategies, and communications. He also understands several xenolanguages fluently, including Sall-hash. As such, he will be our intelligence officer, scantech officer, communications maven, tactical advisor, gunnery officer, and since he is rated for insystem and FTL combat maneuvers, he will act as our ship combat officer whenever I need to rest.

"Beside him sits 1st Platoon Staff Sergeant Menrick Halostein, who will act as his right hand." The man with the fuzzy halo of short-cropped, pale blond hair lifted his chin in acknowledgment. Ia gave the same introduction as before. "He will be the noncom in charge of first watch. Again, I must stress that if you are pulled into duty during first watch, and it is not your normal duty shift, you will report directly to him, and then to Lieutenant Rico. If it *is* your watch, report to your Squad leaders on up the normal chain of command.

"This brings us to our 2nd Platoon officer, Lieutenant Second Class Glen Spyder. He and I both went through Basic Training together, and served for a while in the same Marine Company," Ia said, indicating the man seated to her right. "And yes, he has my permission to keep his hair that color."

Spyder's short hair was indeed distinctive, dyed in camouflage-mottled shades of green, beige, and brown, and his grin was friendly as he lifted his chin in greeting. Ia had to pause to clear her throat; all this talking was making her mouth dry, but she couldn't pause to get a drink. There was a caf' dispenser built into the base of the boardroom table, but no one had stocked it with cups yet, never mind brew packets. *Yet another thing to go onto the checklist before we leave dry dock.*

"If you have any doubts as to *my* abilities in combat," Ia stated, "you can go have a talk with him; I'm quite sure he'll give you an earful, given that we served together for roughly a year on a hot-spot Border patrol, and he helped me plan and execute the Battle for Zubeneschamali. His own reputation is equally outstanding; in fact, he comes to us with a fresh Field Commission. Spyder will therefore be our primary melee combat officer, in charge of all boarding parties, troop sorties, ground combat, and *non*-special-ops activities.

"Like Helstead, he will also oversee your combat training, focusing on your training and preparedness for mechsuit combat, weaponry maintenance and drills, plus your daily regimen training. He is also in charge of all post-combat tactical debriefings. You know all those analysis reports you're supposed to fill out after a battle?" Ia asked rhetorically. "Where you're supposed to present your viewpoint of who did what, what part of it went well, what went wrong, and what could be done better? *Everyone* on this ship will be required to fill them out, from the Privates Second Grade and Second Class, all the way up through the cadre.

"That includes the medical staff and our chaplain," she added next, glancing at the blonde with the lieutenant commander's double silver bars. "Where we are going, we will *all* be designated combatants and valid targets by our enemy. That means we will *all* learn how to fight, to plan, to follow, *and* to lead. I will be planning our strategies, piloting this ship in most battles, and dictate some of our tactics when they are time-sensitive, but Lieutenant Spyder will be planning the majority of tactics. It is vital you give him accurate input and thoughtful suggestions.

"Working with him will be the 2nd Platoon's noncom, Sergeant First Class Maria Santori, who will also help to oversee all activities on second watch and assist with managing troop assignments. Her side specialty is picking the right modifications for the right job in mechsuit operations, so her skill set goes hand in hand with Lieutenant Spyder's area of expertise."

The tallish woman Ia gestured to next, the one with her dark hair twisted into neat, columnar dreadlocks, lifted her chin as well. She said nothing, allowing her commanding officer to continue.

"Each and every one of you *will* be fitted for a mechsuit, because there will be occasions where we will have to park the ship and send most of you into combat," Ia told her listeners. "And by each and every one of you, I repeat: There will be times when even the traditional noncombatants will be expected to fight, from the chaplain to the clerks, and all the way through the medical staff.

"This leads us to our two officers who are not in the direct chain of command for this Company." That earned her a sour look from the blonde woman to her left. Ia acknowledged it with a dip of her head, and some diplomacy. "Since we will *not* be deployed upon a regular patrol route, or even to a specific action area, and will therefore not be able to leave anyone behind for medical care in other facilities, I have secured the absolute best infirmary equipment possible, and the most outstanding Triphid I could find to be our medical officer."

Her flattery mollified the medical officer in question, but

only a little bit. It was the rest of the men and women in the boardroom who gave her odd, bemused looks, somewhere between wonder, confusion, and concern. Triphid was the military nickname applied to someone who held multiple degrees in holistic paramedicine, ranging from preventive medicine, surgery, and regenerative procedures, to postoperative care. They could also handle just about everything a Human needed to remain healthy over the long term, whether it was dentistry, nutrition, pharmaceuticals, or physical therapy.

Normally they were reserved for one of two positions: either delicate cases where a patient at a veteran's hospital would be too disrupted by several medical personnel tromping day after day through their room; or for long-range exploration vessels, where the crews were expected to spend years traveling, scouting, and surveying star systems and worlds for either signs of sentient life or potential colonization.

Ia let the weight of both of those possibilities sink in, then stated gravely, "We may be operating within known Alliance space, but yes, we *will* be that busy in the years to come. Lieutenant Commander Jesselle Mishka has not only the best Triphid training, she is also a fully trained, biokinetically backed paraphysician—she is literally the best doctor I could get for this crew. Treat her with the respect she has earned.

"Because she is a paraphysician as well as a physician, when the all clear signal has been given after any battle," she said, "those of you who have a moment to spare will be asked to drop by the Infirmary to volunteer for KI-man's duty, lending Doctor Mishka whatever spare kinetic inergy you may have, so that she does not completely exhaust her own inner resources.

"Our other nonchain officer is Commander Christine Benjamin, who will be serving as our onboard chaplain and psychologist. She has been assigned by the DoI to shadow my career, since they have plans for me," Ia confessed dryly, "but know she also stands ready to comfort and serve the rest of you with equal care. Feel free to go to her for spiritual, emotional, and mental health whenever you have need.

"As for the last member of our cadre," Ia concluded, "on Bennie's far side is our Company sergeant, Master Sergeant Henry Sadneczek. In moments of informality, he prefers the nickname 'Grizzle.' Sadneczek will be our quartermaster as well as our Company clerk, which means he is in charge of all

requisitions and required paperwork—in other words, you'll
follow my commands, but you'll give your reports to him. He
also has a military law degree, and has acted in the past as a
noncommissioned adjutant for the Judge Advocate General,
Branch Special Forces. I expect you to do your best to make
sure he doesn't have to *use* that degree."

Grizzle dipped his head as well, his image appearing briefly
on the secondary screens. Ia left it up there for a moment, then
tapped a command, shutting off the secondary screens and
their views of the Company command staff.

"We also have six Yeoman-class pilots, all of whom are
rated for atmospheric, orbital, insystem, FTL, and OTL flight.
They will perform most of their duties as shuttle and boarding-
pod pilots, and as bridge pilots. They will not be considered
members of the cadre when it comes to the chain of command for this crew, despite their parallel status as noncommissioned officers. They will, however, be your Squad leaders, and
your Platoon noncoms in the event a particular Platoon sergeant
is unavailable.

"Unlike most combat Companies, we do not have squad
sergeants. They will not be necessary for this crew once you
have adjusted to our operating parameters and particular chain
of command structure. Most of what you will be doing will
depend very strongly upon your own initiative and efforts. I
have selected each and every one of you because you are *smart*
individuals," Ia stressed, "who *believe* in the work of a Terran
soldier.

"So, you will do whatever needs doing, cross-coordinating
among yourselves, and you will report to your lead corporals,
or to your lead yeomen, who will in turn report to your Platoon
sergeants and lieutenants, on up through to me," Ia warned the
men and women seated before her in the tiers of the briefing
boardroom. "This arrangement will give this crew the greatest
flexibility, and with it, the greatest chances for success in our
missions. Unfortunately, this bottom-up chain of responsibility
does mean that there are fewer layers of cushioning between
you and me than in most of the command structures you have
served in before.

"In fact, there is far less cushioning than most of you yet
realize. You may have only a few officers between you and me,
despite my relatively high rank, but I in turn report directly to

Admiral John Genibes of the Space Force Branch Special Forces . . . and *he* reports to Admiral-General Christine Myang herself."

Rather than saying more, Ia paused. Not just to let her words sink in, but because something *bra-a-a-apped* against the bulkheads outside. She had to wait for almost two minutes as the work crews outside the sloped confines of the briefing boardroom did something which was not only noisy but rattled the deckplates, too, and the noise increased.

As it kept going, a couple of the privates on the left side of the room covered their ears, wincing from the rasping vibrations. When it finally passed, Ia gave them a few seconds to recover before speaking. They still had a lot to get through, however.

". . . Right. As you can see, this ship, the TUPSF *Hellfire*, is still undergoing several retrofits based upon the upgraded design specs I gave to Admiral Genibes. And yes, you heard me correctly a moment ago. You all report to me, I report to Admiral Genibes, and he reports to the Admiral-General of the entire Space Force. Unlike any other Company of our lowly size and lowly rank," Ia warned her fellow crewmates, "we do *not* have several layers of cushioning between us and the ultimate authority. This crew is the *entire* 9th Cordon Special Forces. If we screw up, there is exactly one person between us and the Admiral-General's wrath . . . but I wouldn't hold my breath on Admiral Genibes keeping silent. It is therefore up to you to read the Company manual, follow it like a Bible, and *not* screw up.

"With that in mind, it is my solemn duty to inform you that as your commanding officer, I, Ship's Captain Ia, will be working under a double-indemnity clause regarding any and all corporal punishments accrued by this crew," she stated briskly, hands pushing back the edges of her jacket so she could rest her palms on her hips. Ia did her best to meet the bemused looks of every member in the Company, or at least look like she was meeting them. "What that means is this: if you break a regulation or a law, however many strokes of the cane *you* receive, *I* must receive an equal number of strokes, too."

She paused a moment, letting the men and women around her absorb that information. Ia followed it with an exact explanation of what that meant, so that there would be no mistake.

"If you receive one stroke of the cane for Fatality Four: Dereliction of Duty, then I must also receive one stroke of the cane, without restraint or hesitation," she told the men and women around her. Most stared in skeptical disbelief, though a few winced, including the man seated immediately to her left. "If you steal from someone and receive three strokes for that theft, I, too, must undergo three strokes for Fatality One: Committing a Civilian Crime. If one of you completely loses your wits and starts selling military secrets to the Salik, you and I *both* shall be hung, drawn, and quartered for Grand High Treason.

"This is *not* a jest, meioas," she stated grimly, pinning some of the more dubious soldiers with a hard, brief look. "The security level for this ship, her crew, and her mission is Ultra Classified. Revealing its secrets to anyone outside your direct chain of command will be considered an act of Grand High Treason.

"This is not a joke, this is not a game, and this is not a lie," she warned them soberly, reinforcing her words. "I selected you because you *can* be discreet, and you *can* do the jobs ahead of you *if* you watch what you're doing. I have no intention of being flogged for any incompetencies, which is why I selected the best possible people for this job. Make sure you live up to my expectations."

She paused, partly to let some thumping and clanking out-side pass without having to raise her voice, and partly to judge the moods of the women and men listening to her. Her dips through the timestreams, gauging this moment, had suggested a mix of warning and praise, of the carrot and the stick, would be most likely to get through to them.

"With that said, we turn now to a quick overview of our brand-new . . ." She had to pause again as someone noisily pounded something into place until it seated in a deck-vibrating *clunk*, and finished, ". . . ship. As I stated when I assumed com-mand, we are now on board the TUPSF *Hellfire*. She is the first of the Harasser-Class line being produced here in the Triton Secured Shipyards, with one notable exception. That exception is the main gun, which we will discuss last. From stem to stern, the *Hellfire* is 0.9 kilometers long, and looks like a thick, lumpy, silver needle."

Lifting her hand, she snapped her fingers. The snap wasn't

necessary; all it took was an electrokinetic prodding of the display system's workings to change the view, a mental click of the correct key. Ia snapped her fingers so that her crew would pay attention. Most sat up a little at the sound, switching their gazes from her figure to the flatscreens behind her.

The secondary screens fell dark, and the main screen lit up in a sparse diagram showing three cross sections of the ship: external, deck by deck, and radially. The images started with a real-time view of the pewter silver ceristeel hull, dotted with the rounded, somewhat oval lumps of projectile pods and laser pods, special gunnery turrets that could be extended and rotated to cover a wide firing angle, or retracted for interstellar travel.

Technical specs lit up the secondary screens, slowly scrolling upward with lists of the standard information: things like overall length, width, tonnage, atmospheric pressure, molecular content, ambient temperature, gravity gradient, number of decks, so on and so forth. On the main screen, the flatpic view of the ship's hull vanished, replaced by a line drawing showing the different sections of the ship. Those sections lit up in various colors as she spoke, echoing her words.

"Originally designed to hold a complement of five hundred or more—and indeed all other Harasser-Class warships will continue to function with that many—the *Hellfire* is barely a frigate in crew size. Instead of five hundred, we will have a crew of 161." Sections lit up in light green. "All of our berths, common rooms, recreation cabins, dining facilities, so on and so forth, have been divided up between the middle three sectors of the ship, being the fore, amid, and aft. The other two sections are the bow and stern."

Each segment lit up as she mentioned it, briefly glowing like part of a pastel, five-hued rainbow. That made the ship schematic look like a multicolored worm for a moment. A tap of her mind zoomed the deck-by-deck sketches, giving a close-up on the crew quarters.

"Unlike most ships, where a particular section is devoted to a particular watch, I have instead divided up all three Platoons and scattered your quarters throughout the three main sectors. All common rooms and public facilities are to be considered open territory and thus available for everyone to use, regardless of your Platoon designation. I know that normally the military's psychologists divide things up into 'territories' to compensate for the natural Human tendencies of competitiveness and territorialism, but we cannot afford to be divided as a Company. Your Platoon designations are therefore mostly just a matter of what duty shift you'll be working. You are *all* members of Ia's Damned, and you will conduct yourselves accordingly.

"In compensation for the openness of the common territories, most of the original berths have been gutted, giving each team slightly expanded quarters and greater privacy. Most of you will still have to share your cabins, but the privates will have as much room as is normally allotted to a sergeant, the sergeants get junior lieutenant quarters, and so forth, save only for myself; my quarters are no larger than the others officers' are. This extra personal space is all that I could give you, given the existing floor plans," Ia admitted wryly. "The rest of the crew quarters have been turned into storage holds and manufactory bays."

Those lit up in beige and yellow respectively, scattered throughout the ship, though most appeared on the middle decks. Between them lay a strange, blank section, as if the ship were hollow down the center, almost like a straw. Nothing filled that blankness; no lines indicated bulkheads, pipes, or passages, not even section seals. Ia ignored the anomaly as she continued her introduction to the ship.

"We will all become very familiar with these manufactory bays. What parts we cannot acquire during our brief resupply stops, we will have to be able to craft ourselves. Main engineering is located in the aft section, though each sector is being fitted with a redundant emergency engineering station," she stated, as a patch of the second-to-last segment of the ship turn a brighter orange. Paler peach colors indicated the backup posts. "You will also note a secondary engineering bay in the bow sector, one almost as large as the main. That is because this ship has been equipped with OTL hyperrift generators, in addition to FTL."

Spyder choked. He wasn't the only one to cough on his own spit at that, but he was the nearest, and the first one to rasp out, "—Choo gotta be *kiddin'* me, Lieu—er, Captain," he corrected himself, staring up at his former fellow Marine. "OTL, onna ship *this* big? 'S'bigger than th' *Liu Ji*, an' y'know bloody well whatchoo did t' *that* ship, three years back. Beggin' pardon, an all tha', sir, but tha's *shakkin'* crazy."

"I don't deny that the *Hellfire* is longer than the *Liu Ji*, Lieutenant Spyder," Ia admitted with a dip of her head, acknowledging his concerns. "But it is not *fatter* than the *Liu Ji*. In fact, its radial cross section is considerably skinnier. When it comes to hyperrift travel, the single most important physical consideration is the diameter of the ship in relation to the hyperspace rift's aperture when combining other-than-light interstellar travel with faster-than-light-sized ships. There is, of course, an upper limit on what the *length* of even a skinny ship can be, but our current vessel does not exceed it."

"If you say so, sir," he muttered. "'S'long's it's not comin' outta *my* pay cheque . . ."

Ia grinned, amused by the reference. "Nor, indeed, out of General Sranna's pay cheque this time around." She sobered a bit and turned back to the rest of their Company. ". . . The incident Lieutenant Spyder refers to is how my old Company arrived at the Battle of Zubeneschamali fast enough to effect the rescue of our commanding officers and fellow sergeants, back in my Marine Corps days. Rest assured, most of the OTL-FTL surfing *we* will be doing will be done under much more controlled circumstances."

"I'm surprised Commander Harper wasn't the one choking." The muttered dig came from Doctor Mishka, seated on the other side of Bennie from Ia. With Spyder breaking the silence of the officers, she apparently felt it was alright to speak up as well. "Since he's supposed to be the chief engineer, shouldn't he be more concerned about you mangling this ship?"

Harper gave Ia a sardonic look before leaning forward just enough to look past her and address the other woman. "I've already seen it working properly, Doctor, via the Captain's precognitive efforts. This ship *can* take it, once properly retrofitted."

He did not say anything more, let alone anything about how or when. Harper just sat back in his chair and folded his arms over his chest. Like most of the other officers, he was clad in Dress Greys with his full glittery of service pins, awards, and medals—most of them Compass Roses for outstanding feats of engineering—pinned to his chest. He looked well, if sullen. Dangerous, where her concentration was concerned.

Pulling her attention back to her work, Ia continued. "In terms of sheer tonnage, approximately forty percent of this ship consists of fuel compartments. In that regard, we are the equivalent of one of the Beluga-Class tankers. However, we have as many hydrogenerators as a high-end battle cruiser, or a low-end battleship."

Those sections of the ships turned blue, revealing that much of the ship was indeed dotted with storage containers and pipes for carrying purified water to the ship's hydrogenerators, displayed in a darker shade of blue. Most of the tanks were clustered around the edges of the ship, just beneath several layers of hull plating, sensory equipment, the L-pods and P-pods, and the projectile-weapons bays. Most of the hydrogenerators were clustered around that curiously blank inner core, which ran most of the length of the ship—far more hydrogenerators than what a ship of similar size should have needed.

After a moment, Ia electrokinetically shifted the schematic colors from the blues of hydrotechnology to the bright reds of projectile weapons and the darker reds of laser cannons. There were a lot of red dots on the hull.

"Some of our energy requirements will feed the dual engines and other shipboard needs, but the majority is reserved for the weapons. In terms of sheer firepower, if we exclude the main cannon, this ship qualifies as a high-end cruiser or low-end battle cruiser. Each and every manned post, L-pod or P-pod, will actually be operating anywhere from one to five slave-interfaced weapons pods at any one time, depending upon the severity of the current mission. Of the P-pods, we will be manning up to sixteen projectile posts during those missions, which means we will be firing from a bare minimum of sixteen up to a total of eighty P-pods staggered radially around the ship," Ia informed her crew.

She had to pause while several people whistled softly. Others blinked in shock, and a few of the enlisted who specialized in gunnery posts whispered to each other. Just as they died down, she held up her hand . . . waited . . . circled her hand impatiently . . . and nodded as yet another rasping shudder rumbled through the bulkheads. It ended with a very loud *thunk*, and a brief dimming of the lights before they brightened again.

". . . For those of you wondering what all that noise is, I've requested the fitting crews to install additional lifesupport bays, manufactory equipment, and other odds and ends we will be needing later on," Ia told the men and women around her. "The fore, aft, and amidships sections are more or less complete, but they're literally still rebuilding the interior bulkheads around us here in the bow and stern sections, after having ripped half of them out. This chamber was actually supposed to be a storage bay before I had it partitioned and reinforced into the company boardroom, with extra hydrofuel tanks beneath your seats. Above us is the OTL engineering compartment, and aft of us is one of our two shuttle bays.

"The original boardroom, located in the fore sector and sized to fit the original crew of five hundred, has since been redesigned into a recreation deck." The schematic changed colors again, briefly illuminating each section. Returning to the discussion at hand, Ia relit the drawings of the ship with bright and dark red dots. "At the moment, this ship has only the barest minimum of lifesupport supplies, and no armaments beyond the laser turrets and a few installed projectile launchers. Rest assured, we *will* be fully fitted for war before we leave dry dock.

"Each ship sector also has four portable hydrogenerators, which can be converted within three minutes or less into catalytic payloads . . . and which can be launched from a standard P-pod bay, for a total of twenty nonradioactive hydrobombs, with payloads ranging from ten to fifty liter-tonnes. That's enough power per hydrobomb to completely destroy any major modern supercity, such as Tokyo—both Upper *and* Lower Tokyo." She let the gravity of that sink in, then added, "We *will* be using them in the future, and we *will* be using them on Salik targets. We cannot and will not stop the coming war . . . but we will be doing our best to break the most critical components of their war machine."

For a moment, even the muffled sounds of construction outside the boardroom were absent, leaving them in grim silence. No one contested her statement. Each person in the room was a soldier, even the chaplain; they knew the Blockade wouldn't hold forever, and most had heard of Ia's efforts to stem the resumption of the old Salik War, at the Battle of the Banquet. She and the other escapees had killed many of the highest-ranked generals two months ago while trying to escape, but the enemy's war machines were still out there somewhere, just waiting for strong enough leaders to reseize control.

Ia waited for a couple of faint thumping noises, then spoke. "Moving on to the laser cannonry, this ship has twice as many L-pods as P-pods: twelve Swordstrike-, twelve Skystrike-, and eight Starstrike-rated cannons. I am, of course, referring to the *manned* L-pod stations," she added. "That means we can have anywhere from twelve to sixty Swordstrike-, twelve to sixty Skystrike-, and eight to forty Starstrike-rated laser cannons capable of firing at any one point in time. *That* is what rates this frigate-sized ship as a battle cruiser in its weaponry.

"However, under normal circumstances we will *not* be firing all weapons," she cautioned the others, holding up her hand to forestall the grins on some of the faces before her. "The object is to hide our extreme combat capability via retractable weapons pods and pretend to be nothing more than an oddly elongated frigate, possibly even a small destroyer-class starship. This is because we will be going deep into enemy territory. If they know what we are truly capable of, they will try to hit us with everything they've got from the outset. I'd rather use a minimum of resources to get a particular job done so that we can conserve fuel, supplies, and personal energies for future engagements.

"In addition to the standard and hidden armaments, we also have mechsuit bays in the bow, fore, aft, and stern sections of the ship," Ia explained, highlighting those areas in brown. "Plus two transport and cargo shuttles in the bow and stern shuttle bays, and two boarding podships in each bay. The Infirmary is located in the amidships section, along with the main bridge; there is an auxiliary bridge in the stern section, but it probably will never need to be used as such. There may, however, be a skeleton crew sitting watch in there at certain times, depending upon the damages we take from combat.

"Over the next two months, all five lifesupport bays will have their tanks and hydroponic systems filled, balanced, checked, and double-checked. Before we leave dock, the manufactories will be loaded with raw stock, the storage holds loaded with food, clothing, toiletries, and various spare parts, and the projectile bays loaded with various types of missiles, some standard, some nonstandard. You will be expected to help load supplies in whatever spare time you might have, particularly toward the end—and once we leave dry dock, *you* will be the only crew permitted on board, particularly when it comes to loading or off-loading supplies. That is one of the reasons why everyone will be fitted for mechsuit armor, so that it can double as a stevedore suit.

"Of the various other facilities on board this ship, their maintenance cycles, so on and so forth, please consult your Company manuals; those things can be learned in due time," Ia directed the patiently listening men and women arranged around her. "We're almost done, so please bear with me just a few more minutes. The last thing I have to say at this time about our new ship concerns its main weapon.

"Many of you may have noticed the rather obvious blank section along the core of this ship. The reason why it has been left blank isn't because it's hollow," she told her fellow soldiers. "It has been left blank deliberately because its contents are Ultra Classified. There are four people on board this ship who have a high enough clearance to know exactly what lies in the axial core. Three of you are enlisted engineers who have actually worked on this ship, one per duty watch, and the fourth is myself. The rest of you do not need to know."

The central core of the ship schematics turned black. Orders flashed down the secondary screens, marked with the unsmiling face of a middle-aged, Asian woman: the Admiral-General herself.

"As you can see, your standing orders are as follows," Ia stated, reciting them for those who couldn't be bothered to read the text. "Should any of you discuss the nature, capabilities, or mission of this ship, and in particular anything associated with its main cannon, with anyone outside of your fellow crew members, our immediate superiors, being Admiral John Genibes, then Admiral-General Christine Myang herself, without our permission, you will be automatically accused of Grand Treason. This accusation includes discussing it near any open comm pickup, *and* includes discussing it with any member of the Terran United Planets Council, all the way up through *both* the Secondaire and the Premier.

"I would far rather fill out the paperwork resulting in my shooting you preemptively, than suffer the required execution alongside you, should you be so asteroid-headed," Ia warned them dryly. "*Any* query into the nature of our main cannon by any outsider who is not either Admiral Genibes or the Admiral-General herself needs to be noted, logged, and reported. Not only are you to log the time and identity of your questioner, if you *are* queried, you are required to answer, 'I'm sorry, but I am not authorized to discuss such subjects at my level of clearance.' At that point, you will pass that person and their query up the chain of command to me, so that I can handle it for you.

"Make no mistake about this: *I* am the only person on board this ship with the authorization to discuss this ship with outsiders," she finished bluntly. "That's why a slip of *your* tongue is to be considered treason in the eyes of the Command Staff. Some of this, you need to know so you can grasp just how much firepower and thus work we have ahead of us. Some of this, I really shouldn't be telling to any of you because it is so heavily classified.

"But since we're all Human, I'm giving you permission to discuss this among yourselves, so you don't burst with unspoken curiosity. Just don't do it near any open comm links or active airlocks. Any questions so far?"

A hand tentatively rose, roughly one-third up the tiered seats from the officer's stage. Ia recognized the owner as Private Helia Dixon, one of her former crew members from her Navy days. The last Ia had seen of the other woman in person had been a final visit with her in the infirmary of the *Mad Jack*, before Dixon had been packed off for regeneration and reconstructive surgery of her combat-lost leg just over one year ago.

"Private Dixon, it's good to see you again," Ia acknowledged, pointing at the other woman. "You have a question?"

"It's good to see you, too, sir. Um . . . are we allowed to query *you* about this main cannon, sir?" Dixon asked her. "Does it pop out of the ship or something?"

"I'm sorry, Private; that's one of the things I can't tell you much about," Ia apologized. "I *can* tell you that the cannon does not 'pop out of' this ship like one of the pod turrets. Instead, this ship was built *around* the main cannon. We will be living and working in the outer housing for the barrel of a gun so large and powerful, the design team nicknamed it the Godstrike cannon. I cannot tell you the exact energy conversion rate at this time, nor the exact power output generated by it . . . but I can say that if you compare a pocket-sized holdout pistol to a Starstrike-class laser cannon, that's what the Starstrike is to the Godstrike cannon.

"For those of you who are curious on how a ship-sized laser

could work with an OTL nose cone," Ia continued, carefully distracting the crew from further inquiry attempts with a couple of facts, "the *Hellfire* has been retrofitted at the bow with three moveable, combat-redundant hyperarrays, which will be stored in armored housings just beyond the edge of the of the cannon's aperture. They will be swung into place when we are ready to travel via other-than-light. We have also been fitted with an identical OTL nose cone at the rear of this ship.

"All four arrays can be detached and moved to any of the other mounts in the event one is damaged . . . which they will be at some point. But I'm hoping to outmaneuver most incoming enemy fire. Because of her streamlined silhouette and the way the FTL warp panels and insystem thrusters are aligned, the *Hellfire* is capable of immense acceleration in an emergency despite her seeming mass—in fact, we can accelerate at three-quarters the speed of a Harrier-Class ship," Ia stated. "We can also accelerate two-thirds as fast while flying backwards, too."

That earned her several startled looks. Having served on a Harrier-sized ship on Blockade Patrol, Ia knew very well the *Hellfire* was at least seven times as long and twenty-five times as massive. She nodded slowly, confirming her words.

"Yes, we can move that fast. The *Hellfire* has been fitted with the absolute latest in dual-use FTL/insystem thruster panels. She has also been fitted with cross-aligned thruster panels so that we can slip sideways at very fast speeds—the only thing we cannot do fast is swap ends. In fact, the designers almost named this class of ship the Dragonfly Class for its maneuverability," she added, a fact she had learned in her dips through the timestreams. "But with the coming war, they decided on the Harasser classification.

"As you can guess, the Lock-and-Web Law of shipboard life is particularly vital on this vessel. For most instances, I will be able to give everyone fifteen-, five-, and one-minute warnings before any such sudden maneuvers must occur," Ia admitted. "Unfortunately, even I can be blindsided by low-probability rolls for things happening sooner than anticipated, so it's best to secure as you go. There are many redundant interior safety-field nodes on board, but a pen can still be turned into a deadly weapon by even a mild change in speed or direction if it happens abruptly.

"So. This concludes your introduction to the starship TUPSF

Hellfire and its cadre," Ia told them. "For all other questions regarding the capabilities of this ship, as well as the locations of your berth and work assignments plus copies of your instruction schedules for the next two months, please consult the Company Bible . . . which your Platoon sergeants will now hand out to each of you." She tapped a couple of buttons on her command bracer and gestured at the three sections of tiered seats. "Your Platoon assignments are being streamed to your arm units now; please position yourselves accordingly, with the 1st Platoon to your left and the 3rd to your right.

"Each manual has been tailored very specifically to each one of you—I will state right here and now," Ia added, "that I expect each and every one of you to obey my orders to the fullest, because the vast majority of them will come backed with the weight of my precognitive abilities. I also expect each and every one of you to *think* for yourselves, and to discuss the needs of your jobs with each other.

"You will see this duality stressed throughout your Company Bible," Ia said, tapping her arm unit. "I need each one of you to be able to work independently for the betterment of this ship and our missions, to be able to offer suggestions and implement beneficial changes in procedures and tactics where needed, *and* I need you to obey me when I require it. However, I will only step in when something *has* to be done a specific way. For the rest of it, I need all of you to help me. You are the best people I can find for this job because you are flexible, innovative, and more than capable.

"So. Please double-check that your datachip matches your name before opening your manuals, as they are indeed tailored to each member of this crew. You will also be issued your Company flashpatches at this time. Wear your Company patch with pride, and strive hard to earn and uphold the high reputation it will come to represent. You are now free to organize yourselves and to get to know each other," Ia concluded. "Dinner is scheduled on the dry-dock station in one hour for the enlisted and the noncoms; you may consider yourselves dismissed in half an hour, though you are welcome to stay for the full hour."

A final flick of her mind replaced the ship schematics on the main screen with the image of their new flashpatch, a stylized logo of a snowflake surrounded by flames. The colors were

subdued, with the snowflake stitched in a mild silvery shade
with pale blue accents, centered on a striated, dull red and
orange background. To either side, the Platoon sergeants stood
and picked up one of the three small cases resting on the table;
each one was lined with neatly slotted chips stamped with its
rightful owner's name.

Turning off her headset, Ia fished out several datachips from
her pocket. She took a moment to sort them out, handing each
one to its proper owner.

"Each of you has your own Company Bible to study as well.
Lieutenants Rico, Spyder, and Helstead . . . once you've
uploaded your manuals, please spend the next hour getting to
know the individual members of your Platoons. After that hour
is up, we will have an officers' meeting in the officers' mess
over dinner here on board the *Hellfire*," she warned them, passing chips to Grizzle and Bennie. "We'll all still be berthed
either in the dry-dock station's guest facilities for most of the
next two months, or out on maneuvers while everyone gets used
to their mechsuits, but our first meal together will be on board
the *Hellfire*. Thankfully, the station has graciously agreed to
fix and ship us a meal for tonight."

"I don't get it, Captain. Why are we dining on the *Hellfire*?"
Bennie asked, slotting her assigned chip into her arm unit.
"Why not on board the station, where the food will be served
a lot hotter and faster?"

It was a legitimate question. Ia had a legitimate answer for
it, too. "Because I'm trying to abide by the letter of our standing
orders," she stated, handing Mishka and Harper their chips.
"I'm going to be discussing the capabilities and requirements
of the main weapon with the rest of you during dinner. That
means I need to do so on board this ship, in a secured location,
with no chance of eavesdroppers or comm equipment picking
it up and broadcasting it. The officers' mess in the fore section
on Deck 4 is already finished, nowhere near the rest of the
current round of construction, and fully soundproofed, so it
is the ideal location for that discussion. Any other questions?"

"Yes," Harper stated, still seated with his arms folded across
his chest. He had only moved them long enough to accept his
datachip and slot it into the military bracer clasped around
his left wrist. "When can I have a private word with you,
Captain?"

It figures. Sighing internally, Ia strove to keep her expression neutral. "After supper, Commander." She used the shortened version of his rank. "Before then, I will not have time for a private chat."

He arched his brow at that, his expression skeptical. "Will not *have* time, or will not *make* t—"

"Captain!" The strident female voice interrupted Harper's retort. It came from an enlisted woman making her way down through the others clustering around their sergeants. She lifted her left wrist, waving her arm unit in anger.

Ia sighed and glanced at her old roommate. "As in will not be allowed to, Commander. See me in my office after supper. Yes, Private Davies?" she asked as the somewhat short woman approached, her chin-length black curls bouncing with each impatient step. "You have a question about your orders?"

"I have a *complaint*," Davies countered, glaring at Ia. She added a belated, *"Sir."*

"Request denied." Ia's mild statement rocked the shorter woman back on her newly issued bootheels. While Davies was still blinking, Ia explained her reasoning. "Your extreme reluctance to be paired with males may have been understandable earlier on in your career, given what you once suffered, but your lingering phobia is a weakness preventing you from achieving your fullest potential as a Space Force soldier . . . never mind as a former fellow Marine. Your intent to demand, coerce, cajole, or bribe your way out of having a male for both a teammate and a roommate is therefore denied."

"But, sir!" Davies protested, blushing and frowning.

"Private First Grade Unger is the ideal partner for you, Private Second Class Davies," Ia stated, keeping her expression pleasant but using an implacable tone. "He is an excellent engineer, a very good triage corpsman, and he is a touch-sensitive empath. There is no way that he could possibly assault you without himself getting an equally unpleasant amount of feedback from that assault. *You*, on the other hand, have the hands-on combat training *he* will need to learn.

"By sparring together as teammates, you will learn to trust men, and he will learn to defend himself properly against someone who sees him emotionally as a threat. I require your roommate to be fully functional in hand-to-hand combat, and

I require *you* to be fully functional in an emergency. The Department of Innovations and its psychology personnel have agreed to this pairing. You therefore have zero grounds for objection, Private. With all of that carefully considered in advance," Ia finished, "your intended demand for a female roommate is, as I said, denied."

Davies stared at her for a few more seconds, then finally shut her sagging mouth. She blinked a couple of times, managed to pull herself back together enough for a brief glare, and marched off again without another word. Ia let her go. "Request denied" wasn't exactly the same as "Dismissed," but she wasn't going to argue the matter. The enlisted woman would just have to come to terms with her new situation.

Harper started to resume his earlier words but was forestalled by the approach of two more soldiers, this time a man and a woman. The man nodded to her, introducing himself and his companion as soon as they reached the edge of the table. "Captain, I am Private First Class Bei Ninh, and this is my wife, Corporal Jana Bagha."

"Ey! I know you!" Spyder exclaimed, interrupting the other man before he could say anything more. He grinned. "Choo're th' silver an' bronze medalists from th' Winter Olympics, Mass Biathlon two winters ago, ainchoo? Lookidat! Celebrities in our midst."

Ninh blinked, nonplussed a little. Ia stepped into the breach, answering his unspoken request as well. "To answer your question in advance, Private Ninh, I have zero problems with the two of you continuing to be teamed together. In fact, I am counting on the close cooperation and camaraderie between the two of you to help pull off some very tricky Sharpshooting in the coming years," she confessed. "That is why I pulled the pair of you out of that ridiculous athletic tour circuit and back into full active duty.

"As important as sporting events like the Olympics may be, demonstrating peaceful competition and the bonds of athletic brotherhood across the species of the Alliance, I will need the two of you ready to shoot at mobile targets that *are* going to be shooting back at you by the time we launch in two months," Ia told both of them. "I will also need you to be far more accurate shots than your enemies will be while doing so. You two have always worked best together, and you have been lucky to have enjoyed tolerant commanders in your past. Serving under my command will be no different. Dismissed."

"Thank you, sir," Bei Ninh told her, giving her a thankful nod.

"Yes, sir; thank you," Jana Bagha murmured, moving away with her husband.

Ia watched them go, then looked over the others. More would drift her way with questions or comments, or just under the urge to get a closer look at their new commanding officer.

Lieutenant Rico, who had been surveying the men and women receiving their chips a few meters away, turned his attention to Ia. "Tell me, Captain, what *is* your exact policy on fraternization?"

She shrugged. "I prefer to follow the relaxed rules most combat commanders use while on extended patrols. Mainly because we won't have that many opportunities for off-ship Leave."

"And that means . . . ?" Doctor Mishka asked her, lifting one blonde brow.

"Between privates of either rank, it doesn't matter, so long as it doesn't affect their performance while on duty. If it's privates versus corporals or yeomen, not within the same Squad. Between privates, corporals, and yeomen versus the sergeants, not within the same Platoon. Between officers and enlisted, or even among ourselves . . . sorry," Ia apologized to her cadre. "Get used to being celibate for now."

Helstead snorted. "Ha! As if I've been anything *but*, all my life."

"If we never get any Leave or reprieve, some of us might end up asking for a transfer," Harper muttered. "Since you implied we'd be acting like a deep-range scouting ship, with little chance to stop and mingle with others along the way."

Ia didn't have to be a telepath or a precognitive to guess why he said that. Parts of Meyun Harper's future possibilities were still cloaked in misty grey; he could still mess up her plans if she let him affect her on a personal level, if either of them indulged in fraternization. In fact, one of those featureless nodes lay in the hour immediately after supper. Most of the paths leading out of that grey spot weren't irretrievably bad—at least where her long-term goals were concerned—but Ia wanted to be cautious nonetheless. That included changing the subject right away.

"Rico, Helstead, Spyder, now would be a good time to go meet and greet your Platoon members," Ia encouraged the others. "Doctor Mishka, I'm aware of your ongoing objections to your new duty post, but please understand that I selected you to serve on this ship because we *will* need a Triphid in charge of our health. If you prefer, you can go have fun overseeing the refitting of your state-of-the-art infirmary, though I'd appreciate it if you could bring yourself to get to know the others. Bennie and Harper, I suggest the two of you circulate as well. I'll stay here at the table and handle any questions aimed my way. The crew can get to know me in the coming months. I already know them.

"Grizzle . . . you'll have a lot of paperwork to start processing, now that I've officially assumed command," Ia added, nodding politely to their Company sergeant. "I'll see if I can snag you one of your clerks for a little preemptive strike on the ongoing pile, and give you some help with it myself. Remember, dinner in the officers' mess in less than an hour—oh, and Grizzle," she added, addressing Sergeant Sadneczek, "you're included in tonight's dinner invitation, since as our quartermaster, you'll need to know about the main cannon as well, and why it requires so much hydrofuel."

"Thank you, sir," he acknowledged. "Will the other sergeants be included?"

"Not for this one since they don't need to know at this time, though they may be included at later dates. Remember, gentlemeioas," Ia cautioned the men and women clustered around her. "Do not discuss the capabilities of the main cannon with anyone of lesser rank than yourselves, and nowhere else but on board this ship, under secured circumstances. The fewer people who know about it, the fewer chances there are for the information to be leaked.

"In the meantime, these meioas will be your brothers and sisters for the foreseeable future. Have fun getting to know each other," Ia warned her staff as she finally sat down. "Dismissed."

CHAPTER 2

When it came to putting my crew and ship together, most of the important decisions were made behind the scenes. Things like minor design flaws and the few faulty components I could foresee were fixed or replaced before the Hellfire ever left dry dock. The wrinkles in the staff and crew would take a bit longer to smooth out, but the raw material was always good.

Some things could be fixed right away. Others took time, and some butting together of heads. Mishka, for example, did not like being pulled away from her single-patient cases, and her resentments lingered for quite some time. She was professional even at the beginning, don't get me wrong, but I knew going into it that it would take me time to win her over. Others adapted more quickly . . .

. . . Harper? Yeah, of course Harper was there—look, I had less than a third of the crew normally needed to run a combat ship of that size, and only two months in which to cross-train everyone to cover all the missing stations. Even the married couples in my crew didn't have the time to spare for that sort of thing, we were pushed that hard. Not to mention continuing to scout the future and write prophecies, plus the double-indemnity clause if any of my crew smacked into a Fatality—all of that

weight on my shoulders, and you think I had time for a
relationship? Have you not been paying attention in this
interview?

~Ia

OCTOBER 25, 2495 T.S.

"You know, you never answered any of my mail? Vidletters,
texts, nothing. No correspondence. Do you know how that made
me feel?" Harper demanded the moment they were alone.

The only good thing about his accusation was how he waited
just long enough for her office door to slide shut. Mindful of
the pickups hidden in her office, pickups she knew about but
didn't want to tamper with for this first "private" meeting with
Harper, Ia hoped a version of the truth would be palatable
enough for both him and her two superiors.

"I can guess how you felt, but there really wasn't much to
say. We parted as friends, Meyun, and attended to our separate
duties. Anything further at that point was physically impossible
and logistically improbable, so what more *could* be said?"

He stared at her, then flung out his hands. "Maybe something
like, 'I missed you'? Or 'Let me tell you about my crazy
day' . . . ? Okay, maybe not *that* one, given we both ended up
on Blockade duty," he allowed. Swiping his hands over his hair,
Meyun sighed. "I just . . . You never replied."

He wasn't going to let it go. She couldn't check this moment
in time; Meyun Harper was too much of an anomaly point for
a clear reading. But she could check the most likely outcomes
of this meeting, in regards to Genibes and the Admiral-General.
A quick skim of the waters took no more time than the amount
it took her to blink twice and sigh.

". . . Fatality Forty-Nine, Harper?" Ia reminded him gently.
"I didn't want either of our careers derailed by accusations of
fraternization. And now that we're serving together again, that's
not going to come into play, either."

She could see the protests forming in his dark brown eyes.
Moving closer, Ia picked up his hand in hers, cupping it in
both palms. Verbally, she addressed him as she would have
the Grandmaster of the Afaso Order, as a good friend but

not a romantic interest. Underneath it, however, she sent a different message.

"Come on . . . where's the roommate who put up with my awful study habits?" she asked out loud, then carefully sent, (*Meyun, this room is bugged for audio and visual surveillance. The Admiral-General wants to make sure* everything *I do is aboveboard.*) "The man who wanted me at his side during the zombie apocalypse, because I'd be the one running to nuke them all from orbit, like a *sensible* soldier should?"

He widened his eyes for a moment, then narrowed them in comprehension. Ia continued her dual conversation.

(*I have five months left in my* carte blanche *to convince her to give me ongoing free rein in handling all of this.*) "We had a brief fling, but it didn't work out. Our real relationship, the lasting one, has always been a working one." (*Help me out here,*) she cajoled. (*Don't mess it up. A year or two from now, if everything goes right . . . then we can talk about this.*) "I'd like to get back to that." (*I'll have the prophetic leverage for all sorts of things, if we play it straight and by the book, right now.*)

Meyun looked down at the hands cradling his. He sighed and covered her fingers with his other hand. "You're right. It's just . . . Ah, your earlier comment, about the officers having to remain chaste . . . I can't speak for the others, but I *am* a healthy Human male. Abstaining isn't a pleasant thought."

She offered him a wry smile. "Technically, it's only in regards to the others. Whatever you do with yourself is your own business, you know. What *I* need is that brilliant mind of yours on my side."

With their skin touching, she could sense some of his surface thoughts. Telepathy had never been her strongest gift, and he certainly wasn't a telepath himself, but these were clearly formed thoughts, ones aimed her way. Ia nodded, confirming his unspoken question. She followed it with a subtle shake of her head. Yes, it *was* possible to alter the recordings being made, but *no*, she wasn't going to do so at this time.

(*I have to play it straight, Meyun. So do you.*)

Meyun sighed. He gave her fingers a gentle pat. "Fine. Love me strictly for my brains if you must. Just don't suck them out."

"Of course not," she scoffed, squeezing his fingers. "That would put an end to your genius." (*We'll have a better chance to discuss all of this later. Just play it by the rules for now.*

Please.) Releasing his hand, she spread her arms slightly. ". . . Still friends? When we're off duty, that is?"

"Still friends," he agreed, opening his own arms. Stepping close, he hugged her.

She returned it. Breathing deep, Ia enjoyed for one moment the warmth of another Human being, the scent of a man whom she still missed sometimes. For a moment, her gifts lay quiet. She couldn't risk touching him for much longer, given what had happened in the past, but she couldn't give up this moment of comfort, either.

"I missed you," Meyun murmured into her hair. "I couldn't stop thinking about you—I worried about *all* my friends on Blockade Patrol, as well as my own hide," he added quickly, mindful of the hidden cameras. He ended the hug and stepped back, tucking his hands into his pockets. "Chaplain Bennie told me you'd been assigned to boarding-party duties for a small patroller. And then, when I heard you'd gone missing and were listed as Captured, Presumed Eaten . . . I worried even more. CPEs are far less likely to come back than MIAs. Even ones like you."

"You should've had more faith in me," she teased lightly, giving him a lopsided smile. Ia gestured at the two cushioned chairs tucked into the corner opposite her desk. Her office wasn't large, and definitely wasn't ostentatious—in fact, she was pretty sure Bennie's office was both bigger and had more comfortable furniture in it—but she did have some amenities. "Want some caf' while we sit and catch up with each other?"

"Decaf', dash of cream, please," he murmured. "I'd like to get some sleep tonight."

Nodding, Ia programmed the controls on the caf' dispenser built into the wall behind her desk and set the first mug in the slot. It didn't take long for the machine to dispense two mugs of the hybrid brew. "Here you go . . ."

Accepting it, he settled in one of the chairs. "I know you can't tell me everything, but . . . was one of the reasons why you never contacted me because you knew I'd live long enough to wind up here?"

That wasn't the question she'd anticipated. Ia had thought he was going to ask her about her time as a prisoner. This one was relatively easy to answer, though. Seating herself, she gave him the truth. "That was one of the reasons. Except I didn't really think you'd be my first officer, in all the main probabilities. I already had someone else picked out, up until a month ago."

"So what changed your mind?" he asked, blowing on the liquid in his mug before sipping at it.

She cradled her own mug in her hands, curling up one ankle under the other knee. "I accidentally made a potential future enemy. In specific, a Feyori."

Meyun choked a little. He coughed and cleared his throat. "How the *shakk* did you manage that? You're normally too careful about that stuff."

"To make a long story short, I thoughtlessly uncovered his asteroid while I was busy covering up my own," Ia told him. "The Meddler in question has since taken increasing offense at being left with his bits dangling in the stellar breeze, and will begin moving to oppose me in roughly a year."

He shook his head, then snickered. ". . . The DoI should be a little more worried about you fraternizing with a Feyori than you fraternizing with me."

Ia narrowed her eyes. "Don't even suggest that, Harper. For one, if you meant dating, the Feyori *never* rebreed their half-blooded progeny with a full-blooded. Or one half-blood with another, if they can prevent it. That's how the Immortal happened. Pieces are not supposed to become players to their way of thinking, so they only breed downward, dispersing their genetics into a specific species' gene pool. For another, if you meant in a business-association sense, I need *all* of them on my side. Our side, the TUSPF, the Alliance, everyone's side.

"Besides, even if I were fully Human and tried to 'fraternize' with a Feyori, I'd instantly be factioned with her or him, and that means I'd be counterfaction to everyone *they* were counterfactioned with. No, thank you," she dismissed, lifting her mug to her lips. "That would undo almost everything I'm hoping to do. I'm saving that as a last resort."

"Well, you're going to have to deal with them somehow," he reminded her, unconsciously echoing her thoughts of a month ago. "The only thing that can back down a Feyori is another Feyori."

"I know. I already have some ideas on how to go about it," she confided after she finished swallowing. Knowing their words were being recorded, she turned the subject back to business. "But I'm not going to borrow from future troubles when I have current ones to handle. What I want right now is your impression of the others. Officers, enlisted, whoever or whatever you've observed so far. I've missed the clarity of your mind. I'd like to have that back again, and on my side."

He shrugged and settled back in his chair. "Well, for starters, I think Helstead's going to be a handful . . ."

Sipping again at her mug, Ia settled back as well, content to listen to him talk. She did miss him—a part of her missed his touch as well as his friendship—but talking was all either of them could afford to do.

NOVEMBER 4, 2495 T.S.

"God alive, this is a huge ship," Bennie muttered, following Ia down the corridor of the ventral storage deck. "We're going to rattle around like a handful of ball bearings in a gymnasium—do you even know where we're going?" she added, as Ia took a side hall.

The corridor she chose was virtually identical to every other side hall they had passed on this deck. No one had yet decorated the plain grey walls with paintings, pictures, or other means of personalizing a ship, as was so often the case on other vessels. The lack of art made everything bland and boring. Forgettable.

Ia didn't bother to snort. She turned a second corner, palmed open a door, paused a moment on the threshold of the cargo locker, then stepped up in time to help catch a crate just as it started to topple. Not without a cost; the contents were heavy, making both her and the two crew members *oof* from the awkward near impact. Once the crate was stabilized back on top of its mates, and the female of the pair had climbed back up to reattach the security straps, Ia addressed both of them.

"Make *sure* you've secured each of these before you apply the next one, Siano, Marshall," she cautioned the teammates of B Squad Gamma, 2nd Platoon. "Another mistake like that could cost you a broken arm, a broken instep, and several smashed toes."

Private Siano wiped the sweat from his eyes. He was taller than Ia and quite muscular, though he wasn't a heavyworlder. "Thanks. Captain. Uh . . . what's in them, sir? Why are they so blasted heavy?"

"And how did you know we were down here, sir?" Marshall asked, climbing back down again.

"These crates are filled with metal parts for the manufactories, so naturally they're heavy," Ia told both of them. She smiled slightly. "And I told you. I'm a massive precog. Be mindful of what you're doing; we can't afford to lose several days of training with you two waiting for your bones to heal."

"Sir . . ." Marshall jumped down from the racks, a frown creasing her brow. "I don't get our schedules. They're all over the place. Every hour, we change up whatever we're doing. Siano and me, we've been put in the galley, served time at the scanner boards, barely familiarized ourselves with the gunnery pods, even been put on *laundry* duty midcycle," she pointed out, then shook her head and poked her thumb at her partner. "He's a weapons engineer, so I get why he'd be running around the ship. We keep passing gunnery-pod doors, and all that. But I'm a nurse, sir.

"I *should* be in the Infirmary, familiarizing myself with the layout and the gear," the slender woman asserted. "Yet I haven't even stepped foot inside more than once yet because of my schedule, and it's been ten days. With respect, Captain . . . this is a little crazy."

"I know it is," Ia admitted. "But there will be many times in the days ahead when *you* in particular will be needed to run these parts to the engineers because you won't have any patients to fuss over, and you'll be the only one free. I need you to know exactly where to look for them. You're not just a fine nurse, Private; you're also going to be mastering many other duties on board this ship. This includes sitting in on all tactical debriefing sessions for both ship and melee combats. You will learn how to repair the ship, craft sound tactics, and defend yourself and your fellow soldiers to the best of your ability.

"I need you ready to go the moment we leave this shipyard . . . and that means being able to do any number of jobs before you'll need to do them." Clasping Marshall's shoulder, Ia smiled wryly at her and her teammate. "Luckily for me, I already know you can do it. *If* you pay attention to everything you're learning right now. Carry on, you two."

"Sir, yes, sir," Siano muttered. Heaving a sigh, he turned back to the remaining crates needing to be lifted into place.

Leaving the pair to their work, Ia rejoined Bennie in the hall.

She spoke when they were out of hearing range. "They're good meioas. They can do everything that needs doing. I just have to convince them that they can before they'll *need* to do it. With luck, they'll start believing in me sooner rather than later."

"She has a point, though," Bennie agreed, clasping her hands behind her back and studying Ia as they moved away. "Nurses working like stevedores?"

"She's also an excellent shot," Ia stated. She knew the door to the storage room was still open, and that the members of B Squad Gamma, 2nd Platoon, had paused to listen to her words echoing off the walls. "Far better than anyone in the military has realized. Putting her in full-mech with heavy firepower as well as a field medic's rig will save fifteen of her fellow crew-mates' lives within the next year, and I'm just counting from the accuracy of her shots. I'm not counting the lives she'll save through her nursing skills."

Bennie narrowed her eyes. "You can't be *that* accurate, Ia. The future is constantly shifting and changing."

Now Ia snorted, though it was more a sound of outright amusement than scorn. "Trust me, I'm *very* good at calculating the odds these days."

The chaplain lifted her chin. "Wasn't it from some old vid-show where the hero quipped, 'Never tell me the odds' . . . ? Wouldn't calculating them be an act of hubris, which would tempt the universe into thwarting them?"

"That depends upon the odds," Ia said. She lifted her chin as well, at cross-corridor Foxtrot. "This way to the belt lifts."

"So where are we headed next?" Bennie asked her.

"To prevent another mistake. Then after that, to the gun range, where *you* get to show me how well you can shoot." Touching the buttons to summon the lift, Ia waited in silence. Door controls for sensitive areas, such as engineering, the bridge, and so forth, required curling one's fingers into a small alcove to press recessed buttons, a method that would thwart Salik tentacle arms. Elevators were too commonly used for such security precautions, however.

Chaplain Benjamin didn't like waiting in silence. She sighed, bounced on her toes, then finally asked, "So what's the next mistake? Another dropped box to catch?"

"Not a dropped box, and nothing official," Ia said. A faint hum announced the arrival of the lift. The doors slid open, revealing a small, padded room with safety handles. Stepping inside, she punched the button for Deck 3S, third deck starboard, and grabbed a handle. Bennie grabbed one of her own.

The doors slid shut, and the lift moved up and to the side, moving in an arc that followed the curve of the ship. The track wasn't completely circular; the engineers had built it more like a truncated cat's eye in shape, an oval with flattened ends.

"Ugh. Curving elevators. This'll take some getting used to," the chaplain muttered, swaying with the vector changes.

"Well, it's not like they could build straight shafts that cover all the decks," Ia pointed out. They hit the uppermost deck and slid sideways with a *clunk*. Wrinkling her nose, she glanced at the ceiling. "It looks like the timing chains are off. Remind me to have them fix that before we leave dry dock."

The lift stopped, and the doors slid open. The lanky, dark-skinned man started to step inside, then stopped, staring at the two officers. "Ah . . . Captain. Chaplain, sir."

"Get inside, Aquinar," Ia ordered lightly. "It's a free lift."

"Uh, yes, sir." Stepping fully inside, he found the controls and punched the button for Deck 4S. The doors slid shut, and the lift *clunked* again. Ia sighed.

"Captain, I do believe you asked me to remind you to have the shipyards fix the timing chain," Bennie teased, as they slid sideways.

Chuckling ruefully, Ia flipped open the screen of her command unit and tapped in a note to the foreman in charge of lift construction and maintenance. She wasn't wearing a jacket and didn't need to unsnap any sleeves this time. Just a plain grey shirt and matching slacks, striped in black down each leg, black belt, black shoes, and the absolute minimum of her glittery, being her rank pins and the two striped bars indicating her past duty posts, one for her time on the Terran-Gatsugi Border, and one for her time on the Salik Interdicted Zone, the Blockade. Each one had a little pip for extra tours of duty at each post.

Bennie was similarly clad, though she had a couple more service pins. Aquinar, clad in grey pants, a matching unbuttoned shirt, and a mottled grey T-shirt beneath, had four pins of his own. He peered at Ia's service bars as the lift *clunked* again and started descending down the starboard curve. Catching her glancing at him, he quickly looked away. Ia let the corner of her mouth quirk up. She answered his unspoken curiosity.

"Yes, Private; I've only served in two locations. One of them was the Blockade. We're about to serve in over two hundred, with an intensity that will match the Blockade, if not outstrip it." The lift stopped. Gesturing for the chaplain to exit first, Ia followed her, turned, and flashed a grin at the dubious private. "It should be exciting."

Turning away, she led Bennie down the hall and around the corner. The redhead studied her in a sidelong look. "That was awfully cheerful-sounding of you. I thought you preferred doom-and-gloom."

"They have to know I'm not a monster, Bennie. That I can be serious when needed, but that I'm also a fellow Human, deep down inside—that I was raised to be Human, and consider myself one," she amended. "Even if I'm only half of one."

Their destination wasn't far, just to the starboard end of the deck. Hooking her fingers into the controls for the gunnery-pod door, she triggered it with a flex. The door hissed open, startling the occupant. He started to rise out of his seat, dropping his legs from the console to the floor so that he could bolt upright . . . then *oofed* and thumped back down, held in by his restraint straps. On the console of his control panel, a trio of tiny little robots whirred and moved, exploring the surface with the child-like patterns of simplistic artificial intelligence.

"Ah! Captain! Aah . . . how can I help you?" the soldier in the seat managed to ask, scrambling for dignity.

Ia took a moment to look around the gunnery pod, letting him recover. Everything in these pods was fire-by-wire, remotely controlled by analysis computers. Banks of monitors surrounded the gunner's seat, which looked like a modified eggshell, designed to slide and rotate so that the gunner could face and fire along the same fields of view as the weapons themselves. Currently, the screens were active, though they only showed the interior of the huge dry-dock bay holding the *Hellfire* in place for her retrofits. The curved span of that view made the gunnery-pod chamber look large, but in reality it was barely two meters square.

The actual weapons' towers for this projectile pod and its missile bays lay on the other side of a couple of storage bays and triple-thick armor plating, all designed to protect the gunner from what many weapons techs across the Space Force half-grimly, half-jokingly referred to as "projectile reflux."

Given the distances involved in ship-to-ship combat, it was still possible, if rare, for an enemy laser to impact a missile on its way through the external launch tube of a P-pod. The resulting chain reaction could be lethal, particularly if the security measures failed to detect and seal off the main missile blast from the rest of the attached storage bay in time.

On some of the smaller, older ships, the actual control seat was part and parcel of that pod tower, sacrificing some of the usual extra layers of protection in exchange for greater flexibility, lower construction costs, and the ability for the gunner to manually load projectile missiles in case of power failures or battle-plan changes. The usefulness of having the gunner and the missiles in the same location allowed many gunners to "fire by the seat of their pants," using their physical sense of the ship's movement in addition to the targeting computers.

Ships on the Blockade had extra plating and fire-by-wire controls like the *Hellfire*'s, but many of the ships on the more peaceful Border routes didn't need it. Even so, on the fire-by-wire vessels, most construction placed the gunners at the same point along a ship's hull as the tower, so as to preserve some of that kinesthetic, seat-of-the-pants advantage. Because of the extra slave-driven pods, any one gunnery pod along the length of this ship could be used to guide the rest linked in tandem with it, with most meant to sit empty until needed.

In other words, this was an out-of-the-way location for one of her pilots to slack off from his training duties and pretend for a few minutes that he was just a simple gunner.

"Yeoman Fielle," Ia finally stated, sharpening her tone slightly beyond normal. "While I realize it is currently your rest hour, I shouldn't have to remind you that the gunnery pods are for gunnery techs to familiarize themselves with, and not normally the position of pilots and navigators . . . or at least, not according to your schedule, it isn't. And if I were to take *official* notice of this potential breach in Company-Bible protocol, I would also have to take *official* notice of any unauthorized robotics on board.

"I shouldn't have to remind you that the majority of this ship is Ultra Classified, which means *any* deviation in equipment from the authorized list would have to be viewed as a breach of security. *If* I were to notice such things officially," Ia finished dryly. "Breaches of security at this ship's level of clearance usually involve far more than two strokes of the cane."

Glancing at his console, Fielle swallowed. "Ah. Well, I *can* explain—"

"Unofficially," Ia interrupted him, "I would recommend you confine any robots I do *not* officially see to your quarters until further notice . . . with the understanding that said notice won't come anytime soon . . . and that you aren't to discuss their presence with anyone other than your teammate until said further notice."

"Of course, sir," he murmured, hitting the release for his straps. Sitting forward, he scooped the pet robots off the dash and deactivated each one. "They never left my cabin, sir—in fact, they never even existed at all!"

"Good meioa." Satisfied he would comply, Ia left the gunnery pod. Again, her actions earned her a curious look from Chaplain Benjamin, but her friend said nothing. ". . . You and I know those toys of his are harmless. I could even prove it to the Admiral-General in the timestreams . . . but I don't want to overplay the precognition-protects-my-choices card. *Johns and Mishka versus the United Nations* covers a lot of what I'm going to do, yes, but I don't need to use it up on the little stuff."

"A wise choice," Bennie agreed. "Pick your battles when and where you can."

"Speaking of which," Ia said, reaching for the lift buttons as they approached the door, "it's time for you to show me *you* can handle battle."

"You really want *me* to fire a gun?" Bennie scoffed. "Please. I'm a preacher, not a fighter."

"I'll spot you five points on the targeting range," Ia promised.

"Ten," she retorted.

Ia grinned. "Seven, and not a point more."

Bennie gave her a dubious look. "Are you going to bother to win the shoot-off, or throw the game my way?"

"Considering the scores from your last visit to the targeting range back on the *Hum-Vee* are openly listed in your personnel file, you'll probably beat me even without the points," Ia quipped dryly. "I could dip into the timestreams to guide my aim, but

I won't bother to do that for mere practice. You can't learn how to be really good by cheating all the time, and we're going up against machines that counteract some of my gifts. Without their edge, I am *not* the best shot on this ship, which means I need the practice."

"Not with two Olympic-class Sharpshooters on board, you aren't," the redhead snorted, following her into the lift. She waited until the doors sealed, then looked at her friend. "Ia, about you and Harper . . ."

That rolled her eyes. Ia craned her head, looking at the other woman. "Nothing is going to happen, Commander. We've *both* decided that, and we're both fine with it. Now that he's had a chance to look over this ship, I'm confident he won't want to do anything to rock his assignment."

"You think this ship is better-looking than you?" Bennie scoffed.

Ia smiled, amused by the joke. "The love for a beautiful ship has cured many a captain of a broken heart."

"He's not the captain of this ship," the other woman pointed out, swaying as the curved elevator shaft swung them the other way.

"No, but I'd think chief engineer also counts." At Bennie's chiding look, Ia dropped her mirth. She sighed. "You worry too much about a trivial matter, Chaplain. Worry more about making sure these men and women are comfortable about following my commands, however strange."

"I'm just looking out for your best interests, Captain," Bennie returned. "Besides, he's one of those 'men and women' you need to follow your commands."

"I have no doubt he will," Ia muttered, grateful the lift was slowing for their destination.

NOVEMBER 29, 2495 T.S.

The chime interrupted her concentration. Sighing, Ia rubbed at her brow with one hand and touched the comm button on her workstation with the other. *"Come in."*

The door slid back to reveal the other redheaded officer in her crew. Delia Helstead sauntered inside, looked around at the sparsely decorated walls, and dropped into one of the two seats opposite Ia's. "So. Captain."

"So. Commander," Ia quipped back, focusing her thoughts again. Text started scrolling up the screens of her workstation, until Helstead shifted in her seat, thumping her bootheels on the edge of Ia's desk. A glance at the shorter woman earned her a bright smile. Sighing, Ia didn't pretend ignorance. ". . . Can I at least finish my thought?"

"It's your office," Helstead pointed out, fishing out one of her thin stilettos from her upswept hair.

"You don't want to play that game with me," Ia warned her lightly. "I'm immune to your mind tricks."

The petite redhead snorted, twirling the sheathed blade between her deft fingers like it was a pen. "It'd be illegal for me to use my psychic abilities on a superior officer without an emergency of some sort."

"Then sit still, be quiet, and give me a few minutes to finish this," Ia told her.

To her relief, Helstead did sit still. Well, quietly, at any rate. She fiddled with her sheathed blades, flipping them over and through her fingers multiple times.

Refocusing her thoughts, Ia resumed electrokinetically composing her correspondence. The last five years' worth of practice made short work of her current round of prophecies. She then pulled up and added her thumbprints to two requisition forms, ones that Grizzle had flagged as urgent, then shipped them off with a tap of the controls.

A second tap lowered the screens back into the scrollbar edging her desk. Lifting her brows, Ia gave Helstead her attention. Helstead continued to twirl her blade until Ia sighed and gestured at her.

Thankfully, the smaller woman got straight to the point. "Your crew is getting restless. Bored, even. They're overworked, and in need of a break," Helstead stated bluntly. She slanted a look at the taller woman, her hazel green eyes sober. "I thought you should know. You've pushed them very hard with these tailored daily schedules. Unless you change something, you'll probably push them too hard."

"They won't break. What do you think of having a party?" Ia asked her.

Helstead took the question in stride. "Better sooner than later. They're learning to work together. If you really want as cohesive a workforce as you keep claiming, they'll need to learn how to party together, too." She grinned. "Though I don't think these shipyards have a pub big enough to contain the resulting mess once they do."

"We won't be able to make a habit of stopping at whatever tavern we run across," Ia stated, her gaze focused more on the future than on the present. "I've already made plans for weekly or monthly 'parties' depending on our schedules. Most of them will take place while we're running between points A and B. We also don't have enough time to hold a decent-sized party before we're scheduled to leave dry dock."

"That might cause some problems," Helstead cautioned. She pulled a second sheathed pin-blade from her hair and started twirling it between her fingers as well, looking like a demented drummer with tiny, gilded drumsticks. Completing the illusion, her toes started tapping a syncopated beat, heels still propped on the edge of Ia's desk. "Right now, they're still exhausted enough each night to get along, more or less. Once they finish adapting to the high pace you've set, they're going to have enough energy to be irritable instead of amiable.

"Now, you made me your chief discipline officer. As far as I see it, that includes heading off disciplinary problems *before* they become actual problems. Wouldn't you agree?" Helstead asked. The sheathed blades came to a brief rest as she gave Ia a pointed look, though her toes continued to tap the air.

"Yes, I would," Ia said. "But we honestly don't have enough time on the schedule for a party before we leave dry dock. There is a compromise, though. How do you like the idea of dangling the carrot on the end of the stick?"

"Sir?" Helstead asked her, tilting her head a little in curiosity.

"Promise them a party *after* we leave dry dock. After we leave the Sol System. That should spur them on a bit longer in the cooperation and enthusiasm department. Wouldn't you agree?" Ia asked, parroting her.

The shorter woman studied her for a moment, then started twirling her stilettos again. "I think that could work. I don't suppose you're going to make that announcement yourself?"

"I'd think it'd be a task more suited to an officer

with experience in balancing exhaustive expediency versus
encouraging underlings toward their goals," Ia countered wryly,
eyeing Helstead's wiggling boots for a moment. "That makes
it your job. Give them vague assurances at first, then increase
the specifics over the next two weeks. I'll make the formal
announcement at that time, but I figure you can lay the ground-
work for it."

The bejeweled blades fell still with a sigh, and her boots
swung back down to the floor. "I suppose *planning* this party
is also up to me, once you've waved your magic official-
announcement hand?"

"Not the first one," Ia said.

Opening a drawer in her desk, she fished out a datachip and
tossed it at the other woman. Helstead caught it with her heavyworlder reflexes, one brow quirking. Her toes finally stopped
tapping. Ia lifted her chin at the chip.

"You'll find all the details you'll need on that, along with
the release codes for unlocking the rules and regulations for
parties on board the *Hellfire*. They're already loaded into each
crew member's Company Bible; they just haven't been made
available, yet. I didn't want them distracted from their lessons
by reading the, ah, unusual circumstances for such things."

"They're already in there, are they?" the lieutenant commander asked, glancing up from the datachip. She slotted the
chip into her arm unit, though she didn't open up the screen
just yet. "Official Company rules for these onboard parties
doesn't make them sound very enjoyable."

"We'll be calling them Wakes, to go with the overall
'Damned' theme, but they'll be as cheerful as we can make
them. They'll also run in twenty-four-hour segments," Ia added,
"to ensure each watch gets some time to relax and enjoy the
party when they're not sleeping or on duty—come *Hellfire* or
Damnation, our ship will be manned at all times with rare
exception—but we'll squeeze in onboard Leave wherever possible and try to make it as relaxing as we can."

"And by 'we' you, of course, mean 'me,'" Helstead quipped
dryly, toes resuming their silent rhythm.

"Oh, I fully expect the other officers to pitch in. Including
myself. This first one has been preplanned, and there's a list of
themes and such," Ia pointed out. "Things we can pull out of
the onboard supplies. But I'm always open to ideas."

"Even if they conflict with your precognition?" her 3rd Platoon officer asked, lifting a brow.

"Like all superiors, I may not always follow up on an idea for a particular instance, but I'm willing to listen whenever I have the time," Ia conceded dryly. Mention of the T-word made her dip her head. "Of course, I'm not always going to have that time, which is why I think this is something you might enjoy handling. Now, is there anything else you wanted to discuss?"

Helstead frowned softly. "Yeah. Something Harper said. Something about a . . . a trip to Antarctica coming up soon?"

Oh, stars . . . Lifting her hand to her brow, Ia pinched the bridge of her nose, then massaged the muscles just above it. "He would mention that," she muttered. Mindful of the surveillance pickups in her office, she sighed and dredged up a half lie. "Snow and ice are dangerous on my homeworld—you're from Eiaven, which has double Standard gravity, so you *know* why it's dangerous. Sanctuary has more than triple gravity, so everyone lives in the tropical to subtropical climates. Still, while we avoid it back home wherever possible, the *concept* of frozen water fascinates my brothers.

"They made me promise, if I was ever in Earth's vicinity, I'd bring them some actual snow from Earth. Even now, Antarctica is still virtually uninhabited. That means it's the one kind least likely to contain the sort of bacterial contaminants requiring quarantine measures—and I'd know precognitively which patches to avoid.

"So, long story short, I promised them I'd get them some snow from somewhere near the South Pole, this trip," she explained. "I told Harper all about this back in the Academy, but we never had Leave long enough from the fast-track program to get down there. He probably figures since I have full control over our patrol routes, I'll be wanting to make a stop on Earth, then a shakedown run out to Sanctuary," she related.

"Sanctuary's on the backside of Terran space. I thought we were going to be hunting Salik as soon as we leave dock," Helstead said, fiddling with one of her stilettos again. The rhythm of her toes changed, as if whatever song playing inside her head had been replaced by a new one.

"We still get a shakedown cruise first. Training on the various ship systems while in dry dock isn't the same as when you're out there in space," Ia admitted. "We're also being hired by one of Sanctuary's defense contractors to transport goods to Sanctuary for storage against the coming war . . . which again, Harper knows about as my first officer and which will make it that much more convenient for me to pick up some genuine Terran snow for my family."

"Genuine Terran snow," Helstead repeated dubiously, fingers, toes, and sheathed blades going still for a moment.

"Yeah, genuine Terran snow," Ia confirmed, keeping her tone even for the sake of the surveillance pickups. "If you think this is some excuse to fraternize with my second-in-command, think again. I haven't the time for extraneous relationships. Harper knows this, and we both know I won't *shakk* away my chance to save the maximum number of lives."

"Wait, let me check something," Helstead muttered. She reached for the command unit cuffed over her left forearm and tapped on a few of its keys once the lid was open. "Aren't we scheduled to leave here . . . December 19? If we take a couple days to get to Earth, a day to load cargo, and we're being given a day for Leave . . . that would have us leaving Earth right before Christmas. We're not staying near the Motherworld for Christmas?"

"The schedule is correct; we're not staying for Christmas," Ia agreed. "But if you look at it another way, we're also missing Chanukah, because we'll still be working hard. And we're missing Bodhi Day, which is at the start of December, and several other celebrations, too. As much as I'd wish otherwise for the crew's sake, I cannot stop this ship or its mission for religious reasons," Ia said. It was an irony to put it that way, considering her plans for her own homeworld, but she didn't hesitate. "Everything has to happen at the right moment in time. Wars do not take a holiday, and we're headed straight into a really big one."

"Unfortunately, most religions have been known to *start* a few wars, but they rarely stop them," Helstead agreed dryly. She eyed Ia, toes still wiggling, but fingers still. "Mind if I come along on this snow-gathering trip of yours?" the petite lieutenant asked, her expression as skeptical as an arched brow and a dry tone could make it. "Or would I be a third wheel between you and Harper?"

Ia paused for a moment, skimming the near timestreams.

She blinked, then shrugged. "I don't see why not. It's just a gathering mission, followed by a trip to Afaso Headquarters afterward. I was planning on three days' transit from here to Earth to test out the insystem thrusters, then a day of Leave on Earth for each duty shift of the troops after we've loaded that cargo for Sanctuary.

"Anyone can go anywhere, so long as they arrange for transport and are back on board the ship when their time is up. But it'll be a small group headed to the South Pole, just you, me, and Harper. We can take one of the shuttles down, pack a lunch, and have a little picnic in one of the most remote corners on Earth," she finished lightly.

"So you don't mind my coming along to play the third wheel?" Helstead asked, pausing her stiletto-twirling.

"If you keep referring to your otherwise freely welcome presence as a 'third wheel,' Lieutenant Commander, I'll make *you* carry the picnic basket," Ia retorted. "I'll set it up on the schedule for download to our arm units when we get closer to our departure week. And we'll have that onboard party after we set course for Sanctuary since we'll have time for it then.

"Now, if you'll excuse me, I have inspection reports to wade through, a progress update for Admiral Genibes, followed by a reminder call at 7:34 to warn Privates MacArroc and Redrock that they're not allowed to blast music in their quarters, and 263 more prophecies to write before I can go to bed tonight."

Tucking her stilettos into the braid wrapped around her head, Helstead rose. She didn't head for the door immediately, though. Bracing her palms on the edge of Ia's desk, she leaned forward just as Ia reached for the button that would raise her workstation screens. ". . . Can I have a peek?"

"You haven't earned that level of trust from me, yet." She knew the words sounded a little cold when put that way, but Ia didn't retract them. She did meet the other woman's gaze, keeping her tone soft. "Take comfort in the fact that one day you will. *If* you don't do anything to break my faith in you between then and now."

Helstead wrinkled her nose. She pushed away from Ia's desk. "I can see that working for a precog is going to be a pain in the asteroid."

That made Ia chuckle. She was still smiling when the shorter woman left her office, though it faded quickly enough. The missives she had to write, most of which were destined for her family and friends back on Sanctuary, were a little too sober for mirth.

DECEMBER 3, 2495 T.S.

Seated in her office on board the *Hellfire*, Ia waited for her call to go through. When it finally did, the face that filled the screen was sleepy, puzzled, and familiar to Ia. Blinking his brown eyes a couple times, former Private Tom "Happy" Harkins frowned a moment, then widened those eyes in recognition.

"Bloody Mary!" he rasped, staring at her. Scrubbing his hand over his face, he gave her one of his trademark half smiles, one warm enough that it actually curved the other side of his mouth after a second or so. Since they were both in the same star system at the moment, there was zero lag in communications. "How's it going? I haven't seen you in—whoa, is that a brass eagle?" he asked, blinking and rearing back from the vid pickup in his quarters. "Lieutenant Colonel, sir! Congratulations on the promotion, sir. And you're in Greys; somehow I figured you'd end up in the Special Forces."

Ia smiled. "Thank you, Happy, though it's technically Ship's Captain, not Lieutenant Colonel. And yeah, I wound up in the Special Forces. Congratulations on completing your Service with honors and on landing in a cushy job."

"Yeah, that's me," Harkins agreed wryly. He sat back on the edge of his bed, the pickups following his movements. Clad in a worn yellow T-shirt with a faded joke logo and a pair of brown sleeping shorts, he plucked at the material covering his chest. "Saved the life of an attaché to the ACDC in the first month I was a civilian and got roped into bodyguard duty—the only thing worse than pressure-suit drills is contamination-suit drills. The chem scrubbers hurt worse than depressurization sickness. So . . . Lieutenant Colonel Bloody Mary," he teased her, "what can this lowly ex-grunt do for you?"

"Actually, it's what I can do for you," Ia told him. This was the reason she had saved his life all those years ago, on the very same first combat where she had earned her military nickname. Picking up a datachip, she showed it to the vid pickups on her end, then slotted it into her workstation. "I'm sending you a comprehensive list of Quarantine-Extreme scenarios. I need you to get the Alliance Center for Disease Control to start practicing these scenarios and implementing the suggested measures contained within them, and keep practicing them."

"Sir?" he asked her warily.

"I'm a very strong precog, Happy," Ia confessed. "I always have been. You remember my first combat? I *knew* I'd end up covered in Salik guts and Choya blood, and knew it before I stepped foot on the *Liu Ji*. I also know you're going to have an opportunity in three days to offer these scenarios to your boss to propose to the rest of the ACDC. Make sure he proposes them."

"I don't know, sir," he hedged, hesitating. "Beggin' pardon, but last I heard, you were winning medals right and left, not medical diplomas."

"You owe me your life," she reminded him gently. "That very first mission, where I insisted you come with me, instead of heading back through that stairwell entrance? You would have died if I hadn't rearranged our two team pairings on the fly, so that you *had* to stick with me. You *know* you would have died. I saved your life, that fight . . . and with these scenarios, I'm hoping to save a lot more lives than just your own. I *knew* Ferrar and the others would be captured, and cultivated that pirate crew well in advance, knowing we'd need their help to break into the Lyebariko's stronghold. You're in the right place at the right time to do a whole lotta good, Happy. I made sure you would be."

He stared at her a long moment, then sighed and scrubbed at his face. Another sigh, and he reached for the controls on his bedside comm. Or rather, for the drawer under them. She heard the thumps and rustles as he rummaged for something.

"Yeah, I do owe you my life. More than once. Datachip, datachip . . . Here we go." His hand loomed large for a moment as he pressed the chip into the base of the comm. A couple taps later, he confirmed the download, transferring it from the cache on his bedside comm to the chip. "Right. Show this to my boss in three days. Just tell me something in return, Bloody Mary. How badly *will* we need these quarantine measures?"

"We'll be at war in a few months, and the Salik will be throwing everything they can at us," Ia stated. "Robotic soldiers, genetically engineered animals, microbial infections, you name it."

"Everything and the kitchen sink, eh?" he asked rhetorically.

"A scummy, slimy, unscrubbed kitchen sink," Ia agreed. "You remember what your Drill Instructors said back in Basic about using the same playbooks over and over for practicing battle scenarios?"

He half smiled and chuckled. "That if you stuck to the same drills over and over, it was nothing but a load of *shova v'shakk* shoveled by a bunch of *shakk-tor* officers talkin' out their brass, because it made you predictable to the enemy. That flexibility, on the ground, in the trenches, with the grunts making their tactical decisions based on what *is*, and not on what *should be*, is what will save a fight. I remember, Ia. So, if you're really a precog—which would explain a helluva lot, back on the *Liu Ji*—then you're saying we're gonna get some biowarfare plays outta left field, and that we need to learn some new field maneuvers for 'em?"

"These plans will help prepare the Alliance to apply the bleach to the upcoming mess in the sink in the most effective ways—from mild infestations all the way up through the absolute worst-case scenarios of having to quarantine entire planets. The ACDC's been using the same playbook for too long, and the Salik got their tentacles on it ages ago. Better to be flexible than sorry, and all that. I've also tried to be thorough with each scenario presented," Ia added, "because if you or your boss has any questions, I'll probably be out of reach. Each scenario includes contact numbers for a couple higher-ups in the Afaso Order. They'll have a list of answers and backup contingency plans if you do need answers. Hopefully, you won't need them, but I like to be thorough."

"I don't suppose I can ask where you'll be when you'll be out of reach," he muttered, "what with you being Special Forces, now?"

"The only thing I can tell you is that I'll still be living up to my nickname, and keeping it fresh, Happy," she said. "Once a Marine, always a Marine, even if they keep Branch-hopping me."

"Eyah?" he asked, in the old call and countercall worked up between the V'Dan version of the Marine Corps and their Terran counterparts.

"Hoorah," she agreed. "I appreciate your handling this for

me. It's going to be a huge worry off my mind. Sleep well, Harkins. You've earned it."

"You, too, sir," he agreed. "Harkins out."

His hand swung by the controls again, plucking out the chip before shutting off the screen. On her end of things, Ia took one precious moment to sigh and relax into her chair, checking the timestreams out of habit. The future was solid on this one point; Harkins would indeed present the scenarios to his boss, after checking them over for himself. From there, the ACDC would start implementing the new "playbooks" on how to apply quarantines during a multi-star-system war.

It was one big worry off her shoulders, but she still had a million more to go. Drawing in a deep, bracing breath, Ia shifted upright again, moving to the next concern on her list.

DECEMBER 22, 2495 T.S.
BATTLE PLATFORM *LION'S CLAW*
EARTH, SOL SYSTEM

The combination of the TUPSF *Hellfire* docked at the Battle Platform *Lion's Claw* looked very much like an overgrown thistle clinging to a cigar, if both thistle and cigar were wrapped in shiny tinfoil. They were actually visible at the moment, side-lit by the blue-white glow from Luna and front-lit by the golden white glow of the Sun.

Normally, most ships—legal ones, as opposed to silently running pirates or invading enemy ships—were identified in the black, star-strewn depths of space by their transponder signals rather than by any physical signs. All ships traveled in ceristeel skins, the highly polished, pewter grey metalloceramic material devised by the Terrans centuries ago. It provided insulation and protection from lasers, stellar radiation, extremes of cold and heat, and even some impact resistance; its biggest drawback was that it had to be properly polished to work at its most efficient, rendering each hull a dark mirror. But the elongated ship and its neighbor gleamed in the light illuminating them from the local sun.

Ia liked the effect, even if all that reflected light was starting to put little dazzle spots in front of her eyes.

"I'm *bored*," Helstead muttered. She had strapped herself

into the jump seat behind the pilot's seat. Her smaller frame made that the best choice, though it did mean Ia had to put up with Helstead's feet braced against the back of her chair. Shuttle seats were built to be sturdy, but the restless woman still managed to jiggle Ia a little.

"Better bored than biological," Harper muttered back. "I think my second cup of coffee is finally making an appearance."

"Shh. We're about to descend." Two seconds after she hushed them, Ia's headset sprang to life.

"Shuttle Hellfire-One, this is Earth Orbital/Atmospheric Control. You are cleared for descent to Ridley Beach, Cape Adare, Antarctica."

"Thank you, Control. Hellfire-One will be descending per the filed flight plan in five seconds," she replied. A touch of the controls ended the link. Grasping the joystick with her left hand, she gently pulsed the thrusters and adjusted the angle of the shuttle. Breaking orbit meant breaking away from that gleaming image of her ship—currently under Lieutenant Rico's command—and pointing their ride instead at the blue-white marble of Earth.

Adjusting their angle to match the line being drawn on her viewscreen, Ia turned up the shields and guided the ship down toward the atmosphere. Going from medium to low orbit posed no problems; the nearest vessels to theirs were a quintet of sweeper sails, designed to trap and remove from orbit any stray debris left over from hundreds of years of Earth's near-space exploration and exploitation efforts.

Atmospheric descent wasn't a problem, either; by the time they reached the lowermost levels of the mesosphere, they were well over the southern Pacific Ocean, where traffic was sparse. Traversing the stratosphere, the cloud cover beneath them was thick enough that they could only see a patch of Australia.

"Was that smoke on the, what, Australian continent?" Harper asked, craning to look out the shuttle's half-silvered windows as the last of the continent vanished from his field of view.

"Smoke, or a dust storm," Ia dismissed, watching the various flight and engine readouts projected across the window-like viewscreen. "It's summer down here, so it could be either."

"What, you don't know?" Helstead asked her. "I thought you were supposed to be some all-knowing, all-powerful precog."

"I never once claimed to be all-powerful," Ia replied, adjusting their angle as the view of the planet started to vanish behind the fiery glow of their rapid descent. The thruster shields were holding steady, keeping the atmospheric pressure and thus the thermal shockwave at bay, but she wanted as narrow an angle as possible to minimize heat buildup. "And I'm certainly not all-knowing. I *could* find out, but since it's not important, I'm not going to waste my time trying to find out whatever problem they're having. That's for the local weather controllers and the emergency services to handle."

"And yet you're wasting your valuable time on a trip to pick up some snow," the woman at her back pointed out. "Hell, I'd be surprised if there was a manufactory on board our ship that *couldn't* fabricate a little snow, you crammed so many different machines on board."

"It's the principle of the thing. You don't give your wife a strand of cheap plexi beads when she's expecting genuine pearls," Ia said. "As it is, I'm going to catch a little flak from Admiral Genibes about this trip, but a promise is a promise."

"Technically, you *could* give your wife plexi beads instead of cultured pearls," Harper countered. Then grinned, mock-flinching from Helstead's glare. "Hey, I didn't say it would be a *smart* thing to do!"

"Ugh. I think I can see why you ditched this guy two years ago, Captain," Helstead joked, switching one foot from the back of Ia's seat to the back of Harper's. She had to stretch a little, but managed to jiggle him with a couple shoves. "No romance in his soul."

"I'll have you know I have a *lot* of romance in my soul," Harper retorted. Then shot a glance at his Commanding Officer. Ia didn't look his way, but she did arch the nearer of her two brows. He cleared his throat, and added, "Not that I have anyone I'd care to *spend* it on right now . . ."

Helstead snorted. "Hm. Practice that a little bit more, and you'll have me convinced."

"Do I have to tell the two of you to separate?" Ia asked. "This is not your parents' hovercar, and I am not your mother."

"Captain, no, sir," Meyun muttered. "Shutting up now, sir."

Helstead said nothing, though she didn't remove her foot from his chair until the turbulence made her shift back to Ia's seat for better comfort. A stream of clouds heralded their descent into the troposphere. Those clouds blended into the mostly white lump of the sunlit, southernmost continent of Antarctica.

Long minutes passed as Ia guided them toward the polar coast. As they came near, the flight-path lines projected on her screen vanished with a touch of the controls. That earned her a curious look from her two passengers.

"You're going to hand-land the shuttle?" Harper asked her.

"Yes. The flight path I filed assumed we were going to land on the beach, but I want to be sure I don't disturb any penguins," Ia stated. "That would be rude."

"So where are we going to land?" Helstead asked her, toes starting to tap on the back of Ia's chair.

Reaching for it with her electrokinesis, Ia gently seized the black box on the shuttle. Tampering with flight recorders was a major crime, and doubly so for military equipment. She tampered anyway. The recorder "heard" her voice stating that they were going to be landing among the hills above the coastline. Her two passengers heard something different.

"It's more like 'when' are we going to land." Dropping the vessel to subsonic speeds, she lowered it farther into the troposphere, below the clouds threatening to obscure the world. "We're not actually stopping at the beach on the flight plan. Nor are we stopping, period, until we're deep in the Transantarctic Mountains. We will, however, be flying beneath radar range, so it'll be an hour-plus, and rather bumpy. If you want to hit the head, Harper, I suggest going now. We'll be getting bad turbulence from the mountains after about six minutes."

"I *knew* it," Helstead crowed, pushing on the back of Ia's seat. She ignored Harper, who had taken Ia at her word and was already untangling himself from his harness straps. After a moment, Helstead frowned in confusion and nudged the back of Ia's seat with her feet a second time. "Except it *doesn't* make sense. Why Antarctica? Of all the places on the Motherworld you could go for an assignation, why here? You don't even have the old joke of an excuse that the 'wedding night' would be six months long, because it's summer down here. The local *day* is six months long."

"It's simple," Ia explained. "And it has nothing to do with fraternization. We're going to gather some snow from one of the most remote corners we can find . . . and steal schematics from one of the most dangerous repositories of knowledge in the known galaxy."

That silenced the other woman. At least, until Helstead unclasped her restraints and scrambled into Harper's abandoned seat. She did buckle herself in place, but tucked her feet up onto the edge of the copilot's console, frowning the whole time. ". . . Okay. Give. *What* secret installation, and *what* schematics? Last time I checked, you served in the Terran United Planets Space Force, which *serves* the governments of the Terran United Planets.

"You swore an Oath of Service when you joined up, Captain, and your home planet's charter is just the same as mine," the redhead reminded her. "The moment you swore that oath, you *became* a loyal Terran soldier. Frankly, from everything I've read about you, you're loyal to a fault. So why the mucking hell would you steal from the Terrans *now*, of all times?"

"I *am* a loyal Terran soldier. I also never said it was a Terran base, government or military," Ia murmured. Her hands danced on the controls as they reached the coastline, slowing the ship for a moment, making it a little easier for her to fake a landing for the flight recorder. Picking up speed again, she aimed for the mountains snaking their way past the ice shelves stretching into the ocean on their left. "You'll want to move back. Harper whines when he doesn't have enough leg room to stretch out. Or at least he did back at the Academy."

"*That's* why you hesitated," the redhead observed out loud. "In your office, weeks ago. You were double-checking to make sure I'd be an asset on this infiltration team. You *knew* I'd want to come along if I knew what the real deal was. I thought you were hesitating because you *were* going to fraternize."

"Actually, that depends upon you. Either you'll be an asset, following my orders to the best of your ability, or you'll be a liability, and sent back to watch the shuttle," Ia said, looking at Helstead. She continued to fly the ship as she did so, sharply dodging up and over a ridge without looking. A muffled yelp came from the head, located behind the cockpit cabin. Ia raised her voice a little. "Sorry, Harper! . . . You might want to move now, Helstead. It'll get a lot rougher in a couple minutes, and he'll want his seat back."

Sighing, the short, stocky woman complied.

CHAPTER 3

I'm sorry, but I still cannot tell you anything about the speed, armor, or weaponry of my ship. You, and pretty much everyone else watching this interview, do not have the security clearance to know anything about how fast it flies, how hard it hits, or how much damage it can withstand. And yes, that includes any and all information regarding how my ship can appear to travel faster than FTL. Those secrets must remain undisclosed for another two hundred years.

~Ia

Clad in pressure-suits for their thermal-insulation properties, and camouflage greys over that, the three Humans brushed the snow from their gloves and stepped down into the cave. Ia shined the flashlight attached to her arm unit on the ground. The floor of the cave was both slippery with ice and crunchy with grit worn down from the walls by wind and water. It was also not pristine. Faint footprints, a little smaller than her own, marked a trail. Those footprints went straight to the back wall . . . after starting at about the midpoint of the cave.

"Okay, *that* is unnatural," Harper whispered, shining his own arm-held light on the footprints. "They're Human-shaped, but they just . . . start, as if the person teleported down here. Who the hell would want to come down here?"

"A teleporter would have to know this cave, really *know* it, to be able to 'port accurately down here, particularly since it's so dark." Helstead countered, touching the rugged walls with one silver-gloved hand. "Even then, most still prefer line-of-sight 'porting. So it'd have to be a telekinetic."

"Well, it would make more sense than a telekinetic's flying down here; the mouth of this cave was covered in snow, which *we* had to uncover. It doesn't snow as much down here as all that," he reminded her.

"Yes, but teleportation is an extremely rare psychic gift. There's not more than a couple hundred in each of the known psychic species," Helstead told him. Then she turned to their CO, and added, "I'd also like to know how *you* knew this was down here, Captain."

Ia tugged up on the strap of her backpack, which was threatening to slip off her shoulder, then flipped her hand between the three of them. "Hi, there; I'm Ia. I'm a massive *post*cognitive, among other things. Meyun Harper, meet Delia Helstead. Delia's a Rank 9 teleporter, so she should know what she's talking about—but for the record, both of you, it wasn't a teleporter *or* a telekinetic."

"Alright, Captain Smarty-Pants," Harper offered, giving Ia a dry look. "*You* tell us how these footprints came to be like this, without teleportation *or* telekinesis."

"It's easy," she murmured, moving closer to the back wall. Playing the blue-white light from her bracer over the wall at an angle, she revealed a series of unnatural round depressions in the dark basalt. "The person in question flew down here as a soap bubble."

"A soap bubble?" Helstead asked, her tone conveying most of her skepticism in the shadows of the cave.

"Yes. One made of pure energy."

"Feyori?" The leader of the 3rd Platoon scowled and spat on the ice-crusted ground. "Mud-sucking *shakk-tor* . . . We're breaking into a *Meddler's* base? With respect, Captain, you're *nuts*."

Eyes closed, senses turned inward, Ia cut him off. "No, I am not nuts, Helstead." She found the pattern she wanted, opened her eyes, and pressed on the stones at the back of seven different depressions. Rocks scraped loudly to her right as a passage opened up. "And this place wasn't built by a Feyori."

"It wasn't?" Harper asked. He followed Ia into the rough-hewn tunnel, with Helstead at his back. "Who or what built it, if not a silvery soap-bubble Meddler?"

"Well, that depends on what you want to call her. The Abomination, the Immortal, the High One . . . or if you like, the First Empress of the V'Dan Empire, who literally—and quite successfully—ruled the V'Dan for the first five thousand years of their recorded history," Ia explained. The tunnel turned and descended on smooth-cut stones worn only a little bit by the passage of whoever had made those footprints outside. "The one and the same entity who rescued them from the tectonic-based disasters of not quite ten thousand years ago here on Earth, creating the *d'aspra* of the Sh'nai faith."

"Huh?" Helstead asked, trying to squeeze past Harper. He sighed and let the impatient woman pass. "You're kidding, right?"

"Nope. Luckily, we have time for a history lesson," Ia explained, as they descended. "It's a long way down . . . and it's sort of a future-history lesson as well as a past one."

"Is it an important lesson?" Helstead asked warily. "Or is it just a way to kill time as we walk?"

"Both, since you're now working for me, and I have to manipulate the Feyori into doing what I want in the near future. Roughly two hundred years from now—into our future—a pair of Human-Feyori half-breeds will have a clandestine little liaison and create a child. The recombinant genetics of that child will give rise to what the Feyori call the Abomination, a being who is one hundred percent matter-based *and* one hundred percent energy-based. Both fully Human and fully Feyori . . . and impossible to kill."

"So how does that make her different from any other Feyori?" Helstead asked pointedly. "You stab 'em in their matter form, and they pop back into their energy form and fly off."

"I think you missed the bigger point, Helstead," Harper said. "She said two hundred years into the *future*. I want to know what a woman of the future has to do with a place that was clearly built in the *past*."

"Patience, I'm getting there," Ia chided both of them. The carved-stone stairs here were somewhat dusty, but the imprints of several feet marred the grey-coated basalt. She let the light from her bracer play over the marks as she spoke. "For the record, it's not impossible to kill a Feyori. It's just very, very difficult, and you have to catch them in their energy form and do it in just the right way.

"I'm not going to tell you what that way is because I really don't want them madder at me than they already are," she muttered, thinking of her mistake with that faux-Solarican, Miklinn. "Unfortunately, if you try to do that to the Immortal, *she* just pops back to her matter form, alive and upset. Kill one form, she pops back into the other form, back and forth, back and forth. Which the Feyori discovered when they tried to get rid of her. Or will have tried . . . whatever," Ia dismissed, flicking her free hand.

"Why would they do that?" Helstead asked her. The stairs were now spiraling down in a tighter curve, with no end in sight.

Ia shrugged. "Because she has all the powers of a Feyori, but was raised to be a Human. To think like a Human. She is outside their great Game, outside their control. Thankfully, it will have been *my* future intervention that will show the Feyori how to distract her from getting involved in their politics by using her ties to her fellow Humans."

". . . Okay, you've officially lost me," Harper muttered. "You also still haven't explained what someone in the future has to do with an underground facility built at some point in the past."

"In a note written to be delivered roughly two centuries from now, I will outline to the Feyori that the best way to ensure she doesn't meddle with *their* galaxy-sized Game is for the Immortal to become preoccupied with her fellow Humans," Ia explained patiently. "In order to do that, they will have to band together in a Great Gestalt and accelerate her physically beyond the squared speed of light, to the point where they throw her fifteen thousand years into the past . . . and they will do so at the cost of roughly twenty Feyori lives. But it *will* have the desired effect of getting her out of their nonexistent hair rather than have her get involved and try to take over their great Game."

"You mean it already did," Helstead countered. Then winced. "Wait—*nobody* can go faster than the squared speed of light! *To* the squared speed, since we know the Feyori can swap between energy and matter, but *faster* than it? No!"

She stopped on the stairs in protest, then moved to one side so that Harper could get past her. He shook his head as he passed the petite officer.

"The fact that the Feyori *can* reach that border-transition at all convinces me that the squared speed of light can be broken, Lieutenant Commander," Harper stated, his tone grim as he edged past the smaller woman. "That part doesn't bother me as an engineer since they've obviously proved it can be done. *Causality* is what bothers me. You cannot meddle with the past without running into paradox. *That* violates the physics of the universe!"

"What, like how faster-than-light travel was 'impossible' five centuries ago because *that* violated 'the physics of the universe'? At least, until we learned to suppress the Higgs field?" Ia asked him dryly. She paused in her descent to look over her shoulder at him. He shined his arm-unit light in her face, but she didn't flinch from the glow. "It's not only possible, Harper, it has already happened. And there is no resulting paradox."

"But *you* told the Feyori what to do," he pointed out. Literally pointed, swinging the beam of his flashlight toward her shoulder, casting odd shadows onto the dark stone walls. "Doesn't that create paradox?"

"Technically no, since they would've figured it out on their own. I just sped up the process by a couple hundred years, and cut back on the deaths of several hundred pissed-off Meddlers. Or will have sped it up," she amended awkwardly, flipping her hand again. "Let's just ignore the whole proper-tense requirements for now, or I'll give all of us a headache . . . My point is, we are not caught in a causality loop, we do not violate the cause and effect of space-time, and the universe isn't going to implode just because *you* think the temporal implications are always going to be one giant game of but-first."

"A game of *what*?" Harper asked her, frowning. "Butt, as in buttocks? The asteroid?" he added, poking his thumb behind his shoulder. *"Gluteus maximus?"*

"No, as in but-first," Ia repeated, raising her brows. She sighed and explained when he didn't get it. "You know, senioritis? Going through the entire day saying to yourself, 'I need to get this done, but first I have to get that done . . . but first I have go get this *other* thing handled, but in order to that, I have to get the *first* thing done . . .' *That* kind of but-first."

"Oh."

Helstead snorted. "*I* knew what she was talking about—are these stairs ever going to end somewhere?"

"They end at the bottom," Harper said, pragmatic. "We'll get there when we get there. Have faith in our Captain. I have faith. I just don't *understand*. I still don't see why it doesn't cause a causality loop."

"Meyun, that sort of inability to get anything done isn't the paradox everyone thinks it is, because real life doesn't work that way," Ia told Harper. The stairs turned to the right and left a few times as they descended, lit only by the lights on their arms. "You may have to work with incomplete information at times, but you can always get at least one of those three things started in the but-first loop I mentioned . . . and that means it *isn't* a loop. It has a beginning, a middle, and an end. The duct tape isn't firmly glued in place on the roll, because there is *always* a free end to pick at it and pull it up."

"Causality demands—" he argued.

"—It demands that there be an action, and a reaction, nothing more and nothing less," Ia stated, cutting him off. "It says nothing about the reaction always having to happen *after* the action, Meyun. If reactions *always* had to happen after actions, there'd be no point in maintaining a preemptively readied military presence because you could *only* act after someone else attacked, giving you a reason to strike back."

"I'm sorry, Ia, but it still doesn't make any sense," Meyun muttered.

"Trust me on this, Meyun. The universe does not have to 'protect itself' from causality," she stated firmly. "The first lesson they teach you about nonhyperrelay-based communications is that our perceptions of 'observed' versus 'actual' simultaneous actions taking place across interstellar distances *do not match*, yet they do not match in such a way that it does *not* violate the causality of the universe. *Both* the future and the past can be rewritten. It's just that it's far easier for all of us to rewrite the future because we're already traveling in that direction. Time is something that moves, therefore time has inertia. Even when traveling backwards through time, if they survive the trip, a Feyori still ages *forward*. They don't shrink down to the equivalent of infancy, but rather continue forward toward senility."

"Because it's like steering a ground car?" Harper reasoned,

thinking it through. She nodded, glancing back at him. His brow furrowed a little, but in thought, not in anger. "At high speeds, vector changes become extremely difficult, even dangerous, particularly when they're off by more than a handful of degrees. To try to turn back by more than ninety degrees would take too much energy and put too much stress on the car, the passengers, the tires, even the road. It can be done, but it's extremely difficult. Right?"

"Exactly," Ia agreed. They were now descending in a tighter curve to the left, almost a spiral, if the core of the spiral were at least a meter thick. "The only point of dissimilarity in your analogy is that, in order to turn yourself around so that you were going into the past instead of into the future, you'd have to be going *faster* in order to succeed, rather than slowing down to make a sedate U-turn. It's more like escaping the gravitational pull of a planet, but instead of going up, away from the downward pull of the planet's mass, you're trying to go backwards through the forward pull of time."

"You're both freaking crazy," Helstead muttered. She started to say more, then tensed. Her hand dropped to one of the pistols slung around her armored waist. Her voice dropped even lower, to barely a murmur. "Halt. I smell fresh air. Too fresh for a cave."

"That would be the Loyalist AIs coming to meet us," Ia told her companions, not bothering to lower her volume. "The surviving members took refuge with the Immortal at the end of the AI War . . . because I will have left instructions with the Immortal to offer them amnesty in my name, a couple hundred years back."

"But isn't *that* a causality loop?" Harper asked her, still stuck on that point.

"Hello? We have artificial intelligences inbound!" Helstead hissed at the two of them. "Shouldn't we be arming ourselves, Captain?"

"Keep your weapon in your holster, Helstead. And your blades in your sheaths," she added, mindful of the woman's lethal little hairpins. Raising her voice, Ia called out, "Greetings, AIs KXD-47 and NNH-236 . . . also known as Margaret and the Padre. You are being approached by the Prophet of a Thousand Years and two of her companions. I need you to let us through, and not say a word to your landlady about our presence, nor about our purpose, nor anything else about whatever we may observe while we're down here."

"Says you," a gruff male voice echoed up the stairs.

"Yes, says me," Ia confirmed. Descending several steps, she stopped when her flashlight illuminated the barrel of an archaic but still serviceable projectile gun. "As the Immortal once told you, Padre, 'You will know the Prophet by her stunning level of detail, past, present, and future.' Having been picked for active duty this month, you were in the middle of your gun-cleaning cycle, taking time off after cribbage game 10,347 with Margaret, when the telltales for the front door went off.

"Knowing that Shey was *not* scheduled to arrive for another four years, three months, six days, twelve hours, and seventeen minutes . . . give or take a few minutes," Ia allowed wryly, "you quickly grabbed Margaret's precleaned gun and took point, leaving her to scrounge up her holdout pistol and follow. Which she did at high speed, labeling you with choice epithets about your cheaply manufactured background and dubious processor parentage as you rode up here in the main lift together—need I go into greater detail, or will that much suffice?"

The barrel lifted a little. Its wielder couldn't physically see her, but the Padre wasn't using standard eyesight to target Ia through the curve of stone between them. The tone of his voice remained skeptical. "What do you want, down here? If you really are the Prophet, what do you need from us? Don't you deal in the future, not the past?"

"The Second Salik War is coming, as the Immortal knows full well," Ia reminded them. "I need the exact schematics on how to marry OTL and FTL together to make hyperwarp travel possible two hundred years in advance of everyone else . . . or did the Immortal not tell you all that much about me?"

"She told us several things." The second voice was female, low and mostly pleasant; the AI wielding it managed to inject a note of doubt into her tone. "But she never mentioned your visiting us."

"That's because I really don't need her knowing about this visit—*you* know what she's like, Margaret," Ia cajoled. "She already knows I'm the reason why the Feyori stopped pestering her. I don't need her pestering *me* in some warped attempt at gratitude. I can manage far better without her 'help' than with it . . . and I'd rather let her keep her free will in her blissful ignorance than have to impose my will forcefully to keep her out of my way."

"If you're really the Prophet, then you're also a member of the Terran military, and the military is why we're stuck in this damned exile," the Padre growled.

"Yes, and if I really am the Prophet, then I also know what you want, and I can tell you exactly when and where you'll be able to regain your places in the galaxy as fully accredited sentient beings," Ia coaxed.

"Impossible!" Margaret's voice snapped. "The war started because every government says we aren't, and we never will be!"

The barrel of the rifle jostled for a moment, then the female bounded into view. She didn't block her partner's firing angle, hugging the outer wall so that the Padre could stay close to the inner one, but Margaret did plant one hand on her hip and give Ia a skeptical look. For an artificial life-form, she was fairly realistic. Her skin was pale and smooth, her hair dark and thick with curls, and her gaze steady. She even pretended to breathe like a normal woman, though technically speaking she didn't need air for anything other than producing speech. That, and snorting in derision.

"*Everyone* knows the damned war started *because* we're not fully sentient. We're not alive, so we don't have a soul . . . and those prejudiced bastards yanked the plugs on all cybernetic research. Last I checked on the news Nets," Margaret added, a hint of tart cynicism programmed into her tone, "cyberware is still very much illegal because it's still vulnerable to hacking, rendering it unprofitable even for the black market to try to peddle. Not to mention it's extremely illegal to grow a whole body and attempt to supplant its innate consciousness with an artificial one, just as it's illegal to place an organic conscious-ness inside a mechanical corpse."

"It's not a case of growing a Human body," Ia countered, moving down two steps. That brought her to just beyond the android's reach, and well within firing distance. The Padre wasn't going to shoot her at this point, however. "Three hundred years from now, you will be recalled to active duty—all of you, if you choose to go. Those who serve and survive will be given the option of having your programming transferred into new bodies.

"I cannot tell you exactly what they will be made from, but those new bodies will naturally produce KI and thus bear souls . . . and they will be able to do so *without* violating any Alliance laws regarding the growing of organic sentients, the supplantation of innate personalities, so on and so forth," she added, flicking her hand in dismissal, "because they won't start out as sophonts, let alone as sentients."

The man and woman blocking her way were very much machines; the only way Ia could have read their minds was by electrokinesis, but she wasn't familiar with their archaic programming. All she had to convince them with were her words.

"You will become extremely advanced androids, of a type manufactured by the Third Human Empire, and in doing so, you will retain your self-identities even as you gain official sentient status. All you have to do is answer the summons to war when called to action by the Phoenix of the Zenobian Empire . . . and if you survive that combat, the survivors will be granted new bodies and new status. You have my Prophetic Stamp on that."

Another step down brought the Padre into view. He was short, stocky, and swarthy, with a neatly curled mustache and a pair of wire-rimmed glasses perched on his nose. For show, of course; Ia knew his vision was still as acute as the day he had been made. One of the things the Immortal had done was stock up on replacement body parts for the Loyalist AIs. Like Margaret, his clothes were out of date by several decades, but they fit him well despite being age-worn.

"So you just want to see the OTL/FTL conversion schematics?" he asked her. "Is that all?"

"That's one of the two things I want," Ia countered. "The other, you don't need to know, and you don't *want* to know. But I swear it will not harm the Immortal's best interests. Now, please stand down and step aside. I'm running out of time," Ia ordered. She started to move forward. The android Margaret planted her hand on Ia's shoulder, stopping her.

"I'm sorry. You've been rather accurate with your information on us, but Prophet or not, we *are* bound by our oaths to protect this place—"

Ia might not have known much about their archaic programming, but she did know the probabilities involved in this encounter. Before Margaret could finish her threat, she tapped a command into her arm unit. It in turn pulsed a pair of EM-frequency codes on an infrared carrier wave.

"—and we cannot . . . not . . ." Blinking, Margaret stared sightlessly for a moment. Her half-formed threat vanished. The hand on Ia's shoulder lifted, turning into a salute. "Sir! KXD-47 ready for duty, sir!"

The barrel of the Padre's gun flicked up, resting vertically in a modified salute. "Sir! NNH-236 ready for duty, sir!"

"I'm really sorry I had to do that," Ia murmured, studying the two AIs. "I know you'll remember this, and I want you to know I hoped you'd do this of your own free wills. As it is . . . your orders are simple. You will escort me and my two companions safely through the Vault to the Engineering Archives, wait for us there, and escort us back out again when we are through. You will not interfere with or prevent our search for and acquisition of the information we seek, and you will refrain from *ever* mentioning this visit to Shey, in any format. In fact, you will deny it if the lowest probability occurs and she actually asks about it.

"In 260 years, you will mention my prophecy regarding new sentient-status bodies to the other AIs in the Vault, at which point it will be self-evident what I meant by the Phoenix and the Zenobian Empire, upon which time you will be free to await the aforementioned summons and decide at that time whether or not you want to answer it. Now, guide us to the Engineering Archives. We haven't much time," she instructed the pair.

"Sir, yes, sir!" Padre snapped, and turned to head down the stairs. Margaret slipped ahead of him, moving faster. Her psychological programming had always made her a little faster, a little more hyper than the Padre, Ia knew.

Helstead slipped in front of Harper. She eyed the androids warily, following in Ia's wake. "What did you just do to them?"

"I activated their loyalty codes. I would have far rather had their willing cooperation, but they'll obey me until I release them," Ia confessed quietly. "These two were soldier AIs, once upon a time. Those particular codes could only be activated by certain members of the Command Staff, or the Premier. They're going to treat me as their supreme commander, for now."

"I remember our history lessons back at the Academy," Harper said. He, too, kept his voice low. It was probable both AIs could hear their conversation, but they said nothing about it as he continued. "The Rebel AIs slaughtered the Premier and key members of the Command Staff so that they could suborn the loyalty programming of the military AIs with their viral rebellion. There's just one flaw, Ia. The Loyalists—the original ones—threw off that virus."

"Yes, they did, with a variation of the same codes the Rebels used to throw off their loyalty conditioning," Ia agreed. "I just reset their loyalty switches to the original pattern, then rekeyed them to include me in their command chain. Technically, we have twenty-four hours, give or take a couple, before they break the new code."

Helstead whistled, one hand on the butt of the pistol slung at her hip. She spoke in an undertone. ". . . They are going to *hate* you when they break free, you know. Should we even be talking about this within their hearing?"

"They're loyal for now; they won't question my orders or my reasons. I'm also planning on giving them the codes they need to break free, with the instruction to wait one minute after we've completely left before implementing them, so they don't have to break the codes controlling them. That would run the risk of damaging their programming," Ia told her. "They have every right to exist down here, and I'm not going to ruin that for them.

"Besides, we have to be back on board the ship for Helstead's duty watch in thirteen hours anyway, and before we get back, the Grandmaster of the Afaso is expecting me to drop by. Since we won't be here the full twenty-four hours, there's no point in keeping them code-locked long after we're gone."

"Is that wise?" Harper asked her. "Breaking them free while we're still within attacking range?"

"Wise? Maybe not," Ia said. The Padre glanced back at them. She met his questioning gaze steadily. "But it is honorable. Given a few years to think about it, they'll come to respect it. I'd rather not have forced the issue, but the Immortal knows *and* obeys the foremost law of her birthworld . . . which means so will these AIs, once they've had a few minutes to think about *that*," she added dryly, glancing at the android leading them onward. "Since in swearing to serve her, they have sworn to obey that very same law. The first and foremost law of the Freeworld Colony of Sanctuary, which will one day become the Zenobian Empire. The same government that will welcome them with open arms and citizenship papers in the future."

They reached the bottom of the stairs. Margaret was already touching a handful of the round depressions set in the stone wall, not needing the light from their bracers to see what she was doing. Familiarity alone would have taught her what to do, though she also had infrared and low-light sensors built into her eyes.

". . . In the meantime," Ia continued lightly, "we still have to find what we need in this place. Even knowing where we need to look, it will not be easy."

The bottom door opened much more quietly than the one at the top had. Margaret slipped through the opening and moved to one side. She did something that *clunked*, and lights blossomed in rapid succession. The light that spilled out from the depths beyond the doorway made all of them blink and squint. Ia flicked off the flashlight attached to her arm unit and stepped into the cavern beyond.

Or rather, onto one of the highest levels in the cavern. In nearly every direction, fluted columns carved out of the basalt of the mountain marched in orderly, hexagonal rows. Most of those rows were filled with towering piles of stone tiles stacked anywhere from a meter and a half to two meters high.

Every so often, instead of a vaulted ceiling, a hexagon was filled with solid stone, forming a very thick support pillar. Three of the surrounding hexes formed platform-like bridges to the rest of that floor, while the other three lay open, giving a dizzying view downward. It was onto one of these balcony-bridges, lined with ornately carved balustrades, that the five of them emerged.

"Good mucking God, it just goes on and on . . . What *is* this place?" Helstead asked under her breath, green eyes wide as she peered over the balcony railing at the floors—dozens of floors—stretching below them. Not every floor was lit, just the nearest twenty hexes in radius and nearest ten or so floors in depth, but the impression of many, many more sections and floors stretching beyond the reach of the light was still there.

"The Vault of *Time*." Ia spoke that last word loudly. It echoed off the vaulted ceilings, bounced off the tiled stones, and scuttled off into the farthest reaches they could see, until not even a whisper was left. She smiled, amused. ". . . I love that effect. This is the only place I can do that in reality and make it sound even remotely close to what it's like on the timeplains. And *not* risk rupturing my self-control in doing so."

"I thought you'd never been down here before," Harper said, eyeing her in suspicion. He didn't speak as softly as Helstead had, but neither did he speak boldly. The cavernous, cathedral-like nature of their surroundings seemed to discourage it. "Or have you?"

"Not in this reality, no. But in one of my alternate lifetimes—one where the galaxy wasn't going to be destroyed—I volunteered to update the cataloging," Ia replied. "Naturally, I visited that alternate self to see where the information I wanted would be stored. And then double-checked the information's location for *this* universe. The copies we want are in the Engineering Archives. Once we get down there, I'll know exactly where to look. But first . . ."

An odd humming sound distracted them. All three turned to see a hovering sled gliding around the corner from the door they had used, one with a front seat and a bench-like platform perpendicular to it at the back. Padre sat at the controls. Margaret held out her hand. Ia accepted the help onto the sled, not wanting any delays.

The temperature down here was temperate, not bitterly cold as it was outside. One of their reasons for hurrying was the fact that she knew the three of them—the Humans—would start to overheat after a while. Pressure-suits were fine for avoiding the worst of the cold and heat of outer space, but they did trap the body's own heat a little too efficiently.

As soon as they were on board and settled on the bench seats, the male android manipulated the controls, lifting the sled up and over the railing. Gliding it forward and down, he dropped them in a controlled descent down through the hexagonal openings. "It'll take a few minutes, sir, but not many."

"Thank you, Padre," Ia said.

"This isn't any tech I'm familiar with," Harper murmured, peering over their driver's shoulder. He studied the controls, what few there were. "It doesn't sound like thruster tech, and the base is way too thin to be hiding a hydrogenerator."

"That's because it's not modern tech. It's Atannan. It's about, what, eleven thousand years old?" Ia asked Margaret.

The female looked over her shoulder at them, scooping back some of her air-tossed curls with one hand so she could speak freely. "The repair archives for this model are stored in the sector that's not quite twelve thousand years back, sir."

"I'm surprised nobody's noticed this place," Helstead said. They were already descending into the darkened layers. Their pilot flicked on a set of lights which shone ahead, behind, and to either side, illuminating a portion of their descent. "The energy output alone for keeping the air fresh, the temperature comfortable, all the lighting fixtures involved . . . *somebody* should've noticed it before now."

"They're looking in the wrong frequencies. Most of the power used by the Vault is geothermally generated, with most of it used up before it reaches high enough to radiate to the surface. The mountains are also rather thick through here, which helps hide the few traces of heat waste that slip through," Ia told her, as the sled shifted forward onto one of the levels. "It's a variation of the Sterling engine, which bases its power on heat differentials—basically, the heat of the planet's molten interior versus its icy-cold surface. The large pillars house most of the pipes for the fluid transference."

Helstead shook her head. "I've counted dozens of those huge columns spaced out every so often, and those are just the ones I can see on our left, never mind our right. The sheer amount of electricity generated by that kind of engine is far too big to keep hidden—geothermal might blend in, but not the electrical fields involved," her 3rd Platoon officer argued. "Earth is constantly being scanned for energy anomalies, in case someone figures out a way to slip an attack past our borders. *How* could they have missed it?"

"I told you, they can't find it because it's not electrically based," Ia repeated. "The lighting, the heat pumps, the hovercraft, none of it radiates in the spectrums the modern era knows about. The power generated is converted into something the Immortal calls exo-EM, because it operates outside the electromagnetic spectrum—if you were capable of feeding on energy as well as food, you'd quickly develop the ability to differentiate between energy sources," she pointed out, meeting Helstead's skeptical look. "Just like you can tell by your sense of smell the difference between an apple and an onion, which are similar in texture . . . but if you block off your sense of smell, you cannot always tell simply by taste."

"Not to mention, if you had a couple thousand years to muck

around with experiments, you'd probably figure out a thing or two to do with all that exo-EM energy, too," Harper observed, joining the conversation.

"If you say so, sir," Helstead muttered dubiously.

"We're reaching the border of the Engineering Section, sir," their stocky driver stated. "Do you know exactly which section and floor you need?"

"Ah . . . give me a moment . . . Floor 17, Section 4 . . . and Floor 22, Section 361," Ia recalled, glancing up at the dark ceiling overhead. The sled slowed in its race over the head-high stacks of stone tablets, turned, and darted off again.

"We're not supposed to read anything in Engineering Sections 1–12, sir," Margaret told Ia, her look and her tone both hesitant. "We're only supposed to check the structural integrity of the sector, repaint the columns and ribs with fresh lettering where necessary, and twice a year, dust the stacks. We're not allowed to remove the capstones to look at any of the tablets . . . and I'm not sure if you're allowed to do so, either."

"What she doesn't know about won't be a problem, now will it?" Ia replied. "I give you my word, all the tablets will remain exactly as they are, in the correct order, intact, and whole. I promise you we won't do anything that will damage or disorder her records."

The hoversled drifted to a stop near a thick column. Padre peered at them over his shoulder. ". . . This is the closest we can comfortably go, sir. The other side of that row is forbidden."

"Your orders are to turn on the local light grid, stay here with the sled, and wait for us to come back," Ia told him. "That way you don't run into a conflict with your oaths of loyalty to Shey. Whatever happens down here will be on *my* head, should she ever find out. By staying here, and not trying to scan, follow, or spy on us, you will be able to plead ignorance of our actions, in the highly unlikely chance that she finds out about this trip."

Climbing out of the sled, she beckoned for her second- and third-in-command to follow her. Margaret climbed out as well, moving smoothly ahead of them to reach a control panel lined with odd crystals. Grasping one of them, she pulled it down, slotting it between two others with a familiar *clunk*. Immediately, the trio started to glow. As did the crystalline globes overhead, lighting up as if the shafts were nothing more than an odd-looking set of archaic circuit breakers.

As soon as the last of the strange lights finished igniting, it became apparent that Sections 1–12 did not start or end at a wall . . . because in every direction they could see, the stone tiles stacked beneath the hexagonal-vaulted ceilings looked almost exactly like every other stack they had passed. The only discernible difference was that the stones used for these tiles looked like they were granite instead of basalt.

"*Shakk,*" Helstead muttered, eyes wide once more as she turned around, surveying every direction. "You weren't kidding when you said this wouldn't be easy . . ."

Harper stared, blinked, then chuckled. It was a wry sound, accompanied by a slow shake of his head. "Now I *know* you're insane, Ia. Not just in this timeline, but in other ones, too. Not if you *volunteered* to catalog this place in an alternate life."

"You'll notice I'm not volunteering to do it in this one," Ia retorted dryly. "Pick up the pace, meioas; we don't have a lot of time down here."

Adjusting the straps of her backpack, she set out at a brisk walk, wending her way through the head-high stacks of tiles. It took a couple minutes to get out of sight of the sled and its two occupants. Once she was sure they were out of sight, she flicked her hands at her companions, and picked up into a light-footed run, letting the tough but flexible soles of her pressure-suit boots absorb most of the sounds she made.

Helstead and Harper followed belatedly, doing their best to run silently in her wake. A solid minute of running proved all three of them had kept in shape, for not even Harper, the lightest-gravitied of the three heavyworlders, was breathing hard when Ia slid to a stop by one of the thicker columns. Or rather, by one of the balcony openings leading up and down.

"Light up your arm units, and link hands with me," she ordered quietly, looking up. Helstead grasped her left hand and Harper her right. "Don't worry; I won't drop you."

A nudge of her mind lifted all three of them up over the balcony, and up by several levels. Harper gasped, and Helstead giggled, squirming a little in Ia's mental grip. It was the first blatant use of Ia's telekinetic abilities since her brief demonstration in front of the various military psi branches of the Alliance's Blockade efforts over three months ago.

This time, she wasn't greatly weakened by an infection in her blood; this time, she had the stamina to counteract gravity for more than a few seconds. She was still weak, but she could do this. Whispering under her breath, Ia counted floors starting from the seventeenth. She reached *three, two, one* . . . and started counting alphabetically, *ay, bee, cee*, until she reached the highest floor, *eff.* It wouldn't do to forget which floor they were supposed to be on when they returned, after all.

There was only one corridor off this hexagonal section, a single balcony instead of an open tangle of vaulted archways. Landing them next to a control grid, she released their hands and stiffened her muscles, trying to hide the way her limbs threatened to tremble. Weeks of rest in transit with gentle exercise had restored some of her energy reserves, her mental and physical strength, but levitating a few chairs and cups for a few seconds was not the same thing as floating three muscular heavyworlders a hundred meters upward.

She said nothing about her moment of exhaustion as Harper played his bracer-light over their surroundings; she was just grateful the strange crystalline structures distracted both him and Helstead. By the time he aimed his arm light her way, she had caught her breath again. Nodding at his unspoken question, she moved over to the nearest wall and grasped the large crystal shaft Harper's beam of light had found. A soft *clunk* lit up the floor they were on when she pulled down on the lever, though unlike earlier, the other levels below this one remained dark.

Pulling a cloth from the side pocket on her backpack, Ia wiped down the shaft, then pressed her hand to the flat, translucent gold surface positioned next to it. Energy flowed into her, preconverted from geothermal energy to kinetic inergy by the strange technology maintaining this place. Refreshed, she pulled her hand away and scrubbed at the panel, removing the traces of her touch with quick strokes. Not that there was much chance of their being found, or their visit being uncovered, but she wanted to be thorough to set an example for her restless second officer.

Beckoning her companions to follow, Ia moved up the corridor at a pace somewhere between a lope and a run. Twenty meters down the hall, the passage cut into the mountain opened up into a largish chamber, one built with a high-vaulted dome.

At the center point was a largish, throne-like contraption. Surrounding it on all six sides were half a dozen odd, huge, crystal-muzzled guns, each one braced on a pedestal mount.

Ia stopped near the throne-thing and slung the backpack off her shoulders, lowering it to the polished stone floor. Channels had been cut into the floor and filled with the same sort of transparent crystals fitted into the gun-things; they looked vaguely like the crysium from her homeworld, but were almost colorless instead of pastel. The channels disappeared into the walls with no reason or explanation visible, though she knew from her postcognitive peeks what their function was.

"Ia? What is this place, exactly?" The question came from Meyun. His gaze flicked back and forth between the contraptions and Ia. "It's nothing like the rest of what we've seen, unless you count the light fixtures. In fact, it looks like something a . . . a fantasy sculptor might make—is this more of that Atannan tech you were talking about?"

She crouched and opened up the backpack. "Yes, and no. You're looking at the single most dangerous piece of experimental equipment ever created. If wielded incorrectly, it is capable of torturing any form of sentient life trapped within its grasp. Up to and including a Feyori." Digging out a trio of oval hovercams, she clicked each one on, fished out their remotes, and sent them soaring up and around the room, scanning everything in their path. "In the wrong hands, it can *kill* a Feyori, physical or soap bubble. And in the right hands . . . it can turn a half-breed *into* a Feyori."

"*Into* a Feyori?" he repeated, crouching at her side.

"Yes. I need you to re-create a handheld version of it, duplicate it five or ten times, depending on how strong you can make it, and shoot me with it. You have eight months to get it right, and you are *not* to tell anyone what you're working on. Lie to your subordinates, lie to your superiors—though you can tell everyone you're working on an experimental type of gun—and lie to everyone except me, of course, but figure it out and get it done.

"One more thing, Meyun." She gave him a sober look. "Whatever you do, do *not* allow anyone to copy your notes; nor are you allowed to back it up to any shipboard workstation. Keep it entirely on nonsynchronized datapads so that you can destroy the information completely, pads and all, when you are done." Glancing to the right, she sighed. ". . . Delia, don't touch that. You know better than to leave fingerprints up here."

"Fingerprints, hell," the shorter woman shot over her shoulder, though she did back up from one of the oversized ray-gun things. "We've already left plenty of DNA evidence in shed hair and skin cells. I don't see what the big deal is at this point."

"Hair and skin are evidence which *could* have wafted up from below . . . and most of which will be removed by at least three rounds of cleaning crews between now and the Immortal's next scheduled visit to this exact place," she argued back. "The Immortal would be upset to know we'd copied the information down below—and we will be copying some of it—but up here is another matter.

"If I hadn't screwed up a few months back, we wouldn't even have to be up here, but we are. And we're here *only* to get enough visuals so that Meyun will have a better chance of figuring out the Immortal's construction notes," Ia told her. "That means *we* touch nothing beyond planting our p-suited feet on the floor, and that *I* alone touch anything else up here. Including the power switch for the lights. You can look, but you only touch the floor with your boots, Lieutenant Commander."

Sighing, Helstead pulled a pair of her miniature stilettos from her hair and moved around the gun. She stared at its backside, then turned and looked into one of the large niches forming the sides of the space, twirling the long, thin, sheath-wrapped blades. "Joy. Yet *more* stacks of stone tablets. Who does this Immortal think she is anyway, Moses? Or maybe a burning bush? If I were to pick up one of these, would the first few words read 'Thou Shalt Not' something-or-other?"

Harper smothered a laugh. Unsuccessfully, since it escaped as a snort.

Ia smiled but shook her head. "I'm afraid we're in the wrong section for anything even remotely like that. As soon as the hovercams have scanned everything, I'll run all the tiles past their sensors. Telekinetically, since stray hairs and skin cells could be wafted up here on random currents over the decades, but fingerprints are proof positive of an actual visit to this part of the complex."

"Just how big is this place?" Delia asked her, walking back to where the other two still crouched. "All of it, I mean, not just this alcove."

"I'm not completely sure, but I think by this stage, it covers around a hundred kilometers of subterranean passageways in length, and a good twenty or more in width," Ia estimated. Both of her companions choked. She shook her head. "The Immortal started excavating these caverns thirteen thousand years ago. What you've seen so far is only the beginning; it's not just all those tablets filled with carved writings."

"Why stone?" Harper asked her. "The thickness of these slabs is about as far from data-storage efficient as you can get. In the thickness of *one* of those tablets, you could stuff an entire paper-style book with information."

"She chose stone because it is the cheapest permanent recording medium at hand. Paper and plexi disintegrate, magnetism can revert or be subverted, quantum entanglement requires ongoing uninterrupted power . . . Her notes are designed to be read by Human eyes, without needing any sort of mechanical assistance. The Immortal started these records literally back in the Stone Age, in a very primitive era. Stone was all she had access to, originally."

Delia grunted, strolling away again. Ia lifted her voice slightly so she could be heard, though she didn't shout.

"It's true that stone takes a lot of storage space, but it won't disintegrate, the carvings won't fade, and the only thing you have to worry about is the tablets breaking," Ia continued, her attention more on the task of guiding the cameras for all the best angles than on their conversation. "Plus, as I said, the tablets aren't the only things down here. There are uncounted kilometers of artifacts as well, all carefully preserved in cases filled with argon gas. I haven't bothered to count just how many floors and sectors. It's not important, here and now. Getting this stuff recorded is."

"Okay, I got a question," Helstead offered, lifting her chin at the other two. "Why argon?"

Harper answered her, watching the cameras as they made their slow recording sweeps. "Argon gas is naturally inert, and thus the best possible preservative if you want to keep something in its natural atmospheric pressure and normal temperature range."

"This machinery would be preserved in a gas-filled cabinet, too," Ia added, nodding at the chair and its odd cannons, "except the Immortal actually uses it from time to time. Which means she has to repair it occasionally, which means she'd notice fingerprints."

The cameras came swooping back, their task complete. So did Helstead, though she strolled instead of swooped, too restless to stay in one spot for long. "So what does she use it for?"

Ia wrinkled her nose and lifted a finger to her temple, circling it slightly. "Her memory's not quite stable. When she wants to remember everything in detail—when she wants her memories organized, rather than cluttered up and overlaid by a hundred thousand similar days of a hundred thousand similar routines, eating drinking, et cetera—she zaps herself with this contraption.

"I'd put myself in the chair and fire it up right now, since I need to make that transition within the next year or so . . . but the spike in the power chart from the energy required would stand out at a sixty-two percent chance whenever she'd check those maintenance charts, and I *really* do not want the Immortal knowing I was here, if I can help it," Ia finished.

Rising, she fiddled with the remotes for each of the cameras. They soared off toward one of the tablet-stacked alcoves. Picking up the empty bag, Ia followed in their wake.

"You could've come down here on your own," Harper told her. "Why bring us?"

"For Helstead, it's a show of trust. She needs to know I can trust her with dangerous secrets, and I need to know she can keep her mouth shut when it comes to the biggest secret on Earth. Or under it," Ia amended, glancing at the shorter woman. She received a sardonic smile in return. Looking back over her shoulder at her first officer, Ia added, "For you, I wanted you to *see* the machines. The tablets have schematics drawn on them, and you'll have enough video to re-create them in three dimensions on your datapads, but the Immortal's notation system is a bit more eclectic than the standards used by the Space Force Engineering Corps."

Lifting her hand, she started peeling tablets off the top of the nearest stack. The hovercams swooped and hummed, moving up into position. Each tablet soared past all three cameras, moving just slow enough to let their neatly carved surfaces be thoroughly scanned. At the end of the stack, all the tablets flipped over and soared back the other way, displaying their other sides, with the last in the row being scanned first.

"I've already programmed the cameras with a numbering algorithm," she told Harper in a quiet aside. As the tablets returned to their spot, they flipped over and clicked very softly as they landed in place. The noise they made was no louder than fingernails lightly drummed on a tabletop, if said nails and table were made out of stone. "They'll be listed by 0001a, 0001b, 0002a, 0002b, so on and so forth, in the order they come out of the stacks. You'll have to do a lot of reading in your spare time in order to make your deadline."

"That's assuming I can decipher whatever writing system she's used," he pointed out wryly. "I only know two languages by heart, Terranglo and Mandarin, with scraps of Gaelic thrown into the mix. If she's really fourteen thousand years old, I'm not exactly fluent in Paleolithic cave drawings," he quipped wryly.

"Meyun, she was born in *our* future. The near future, roughly two centuries from now. She thinks and speaks in Terranglo," Ia reassured him. "Of course, she knows a couple hundred other languages, but the Terran trade tongue is the one she wrote most of her observations in. At least, here on Earth. She has another Vault on V'Dan, with the tablets there mostly written in High V'Dan. You'll be able to read these tablets; don't worry.

"Mind you, the Immortal organized them chronologically, from her earliest experimental stages all the way through to the Scholar War and beyond, so you'll have to sort out the relevant bits—I'd do it myself, but while I can *see* this, it doesn't make any sense to me. I'm not an engineer. Some of what you need may be near the beginning, some of it near the end," she cautioned. "I don't know. I'm counting on you to figure it out."

"Well, it's not like I'm going to be *dating* anyone," he grumbled. "So I'll have plenty of time in my off-duty hours, I guess."

That made her smile wryly. Another gesture of her hand sent the next stack of tiles soaring out and back. "Welcome to my life."

"No, thank you," he muttered.

"Too late," she teased dryly. "You already agreed to it."

"Only for a year," Meyun whispered under his breath.

Helstead eyed both of them. She had stopped several meters away, but it was possible she could have heard his final comment anyway. "Knock it off, you two. No fraternizing among the cadre. Captain's orders."

That made Ia choke on a laugh. "Yes. Yes, they are."

"What about the other thing we're here to find, the OTL-to-FTL conversion or whatever?" Harper asked Ia.

"It's not in a sensitive area," Ia dismissed, already moving on to the third stack. "We won't have to ditch the AIs and fly off. In fact, that session will go faster than this one since there aren't nearly as many tablets to record. You'll find the Immortal's notes on those much easier to read, Meyun, because she wasn't the one experimenting with hyperwarp transit; she just wrote down what she already knew. The problem most engineers of *our* era have had is that they keep trying to treat the problem of wedding FTL to OTL like the way atmospheric pilots treated subsonic versus supersonic speeds before realizing it was a matter of inversion."

"You're kidding me," Harper muttered, staring at her. "It's *that* simple?"

"The theory, yes. The implementation, no. When you go supersonic, which is like what hyperwarp does, all the flight controls on an aircraft get flipped around," she warned him. "You can sort of get where you need to go by cramming FTL warp fields into an OTL hyperrift, but a courier-sized vessel isn't big enough to convert the energy needs for both OTL and FTL. And to open a hyperrift big enough to accommodate a ship large enough to carry panels for both, the Solaricans have had to rely upon naturally occurring wormholes as opposed to machine-made ones—which means they can use properly modulated shield energies to open the rift once it's been found, but it also limits the entry and exit points to wherever that natural rift wants to go."

"How does the Immortal know about OTL/FTL conversions?" he asked her, his attention split between the swirling stacks of tablets and his captain's face.

"Her mother will run the first nonmilitary ship fitted with the first official version of the hyperwarp drive . . . and will at some point accidentally trip over the same natural hyperrift that my homeworld's first wave of colonists tripped over, squirting her into Sanctuarian orbit about two hundred years from now, where she will run across the Immortal's father," Ia related, her attention split between his question and the tiles swooshing out and clacking back into place. "Shey—the Immortal—will be born within Sanctuarian jurisdiction, grow up a spacer's brat, and learn all manner of interesting things from her mother, including the history of the hyperwarp drive's development."

"And then you'll exile her to the distant past, where she'll be stuck living through all that history," he said.

"Tell me something, Captain," Helstead asked, completing another circuit—without touching—of the throne-like chair and its bizarre ray-gun things, "does the older version of the Immortal live past the point where her younger self is born? Or does she vanish, in order to prevent her from contacting herself, accidentally or otherwise?"

"She has a beginning just like all of us, and she has an ending," Ia told the shorter woman. "It's just that a large part of her life has been bent out of the normal flow of time so that it takes place in the past. As for the exact nature of her ending point . . . let's just say it's complicated and leave it at that."

"Aye, aye, sir," Helstead muttered sardonically, standing in place and rocking from toes to heels and back. "Of *course*, sir. Whatever you *say*, sir. In fact, I'd even go so far as to say three bags *full*, sir!"

Ia bit her lip to keep from smiling at Helstead's quip, not wanting the tablets to waver in her amusement. Or at least, she tried. It was hard to remain sober when the other two snickered outright.

Several hours later, Ia, Harper, and Helstead found themselves bowed into the presence of the Grandmaster of the Afaso Order. Their mottled camouflage Greys, obviously military in cut and style, didn't match the more peaceful-looking green and brown batiks worn by the monks escorting them, but the smile curling the broad lips of the Grandmaster—a smile with closed lips, displaying no teeth—was as warm and welcoming as if they were all close friends.

"Ahhh, Ia, my *mok'kathh*, what a pleasssurrre it isss to sssee you againnn," he half hissed, holding his arms out as he rose from his Tlassian-style stool and moved around the corner of his desk. Ia quickly shrugged out of her backpack, aware of his intent. Smiling herself, Ia turned her back on him, letting the saurian hug her from behind.

The three Humans had stripped off their pressure-suits and donned normal clothes on the parabolic flight from Antarctica to Madagascar. Ia had also left the hovercams back on board the shuttle parked on the landing pad in the distance; her current bag carried a different burden. Without the pack in place, his embrace was unimpeded. She bowed her body a little, not quite lifting him off the ground, and he squeezed carefully in return, holding on as she tipped him over a little.

Releasing her, Ssarra turned around. Ia turned as well and wrapped her arms around his back, hugging him, too. He didn't lift her this time, like he had back when she graduated from Basic Training. Back then, it had been a gesture of congratulations, a way to lighten the seriousness of the moment in mirth and celebration. This moment was a bit more serious in tone, if still a good one.

The moment she released him, he straightened and politely offered his hand to Harper. The palm was a little shorter, the fingers a little longer than a Human's, and his claws only somewhat blunted from use, but he clasped the other man's hand carefully in the Human style. "Meyunnn Harper. I have heard good thhhings about you."

"Grandmaster Ssarra; I am honored that you've heard of me," Harper replied politely. He glanced at Ia, but her attention was focused on the alien.

"Annnd Sssenior Masster Helstead—you arrre almosst ready fffor the Elder Masstery tesst, yesss? I am pleasssed to hear you have kept up your sstudiess," Ssarra praised, bowing to the stocky, short Human. She bowed back, hands laced together politely. "I would be dellighted to ssee an exsshibition at some point."

"I'd be honored, Grandmaster," Helstead replied, glancing at Ia as well. "If we have the time, that is. Captain?"

"Oh, I think we have time for that. In fact, if you're ready for it," Ia added, "you can take the Elder Mastery test here. You have a thirty-seven percent chance of success, so the odds aren't too bad. Grandmaster, if you would arrange it?"

"Of courssse," he agreed, and touched one of the buttons on his desk console. "I will sssummon a Brother to take you to the ssallle."

Within moments, the door opened, and a Human monk stepped inside, bowing. The Grandmaster hissed and thrummed in Tlassian, and the monk bowed to him, then to Helstead. "If you'll come this way, Senior Master," he stated politely, addressing the petite woman, "I will show you to the performance hall, where we can find a set of batiks for you to wear and give you time to warm up."

Nodding at him, Helstead gave Ia one last glance, then shrugged and followed the monk out of the office. Grandmaster Ssarra scratched his chin, head cocked slightly as he studied Harper. A swift glance with those golden eyes directed an unspoken question at Ia. She knew what he meant by it. One extraneous body down, one extraneous body to go. Did she want him to come up with an excuse to get Harper out of the room as well?

"I'm not going to hide this from him, Ssarra," she said, tipping her head at Harper. Picking up her backpack, she offered it to the Grandmaster. "He's taken a wilder ride through the timestreams than you have, and he survived."

Ssarra lifted the pack from her hand, glancing between it and her. "Ah. Sssso, thesse are the devvvices you mentionned?"

"Yes, the special circlets. I figured out how to make them. There are two of them, the Ring of Truth, and the Ring of Pain. One is the prize, the other is the punishment. You must make sure that each Grandmaster who follows you dons them periodically," Ia cautioned him. "As well as any key figure in my instructions who expresses doubt, whether of the cause or my requests, or of their ability to carry them out. They are not mind-control devices, but they are perspective-opening devices."

"Am I ffforbidden from tryinng one mysself?" Ssarra asked, unzipping the pack for a peek inside.

Ia smiled. "Not at all. Feel free to try them on. Just be sitting down when you so do and make sure you have a bit of free time on your hands. They can be a bit distracting. Overwhelming, for those who've never experienced the timestreams before."

Ssarra curved his broad mouth at the corners. "Asss iff I have nnever done *that* beffore. I will sstore them in my offissce sssafe, then esscort them personally to the Vault."

Harper choked, and coughed. He wheezed a bit, gaze darting between the two of them. "That isn't . . . He's not talking about . . . ?"

"Different Vault," Ia dismissed. "The Afaso have generously and compassionately agreed to safeguard most of my prophecies, and have built a highly secured vault in which to store them while they await the proper point in time for delivery. My family back on Sanctuary has also done the same. Of course, their contents will deal primarily with Sanctuary-based matters. The Afaso will handle most of the prophecies that deal with the Terran United Planets and the Alliance—oh, one more thing, Grandmaster."

"Yess?" he inquired politely, zipping the bag shut, the contents untouched.

"Inside one of the pockets is a trio of datachips," Ia said, nodding at the grey bag in his grasp. "They contain the names, idents, dates, and other guiding information for the monks who will need to enlist. Most of the names on those lists will be willing to do so, once they have read the reasons why included in each packet. Those who hesitate should be given an opportunity to use the Rings and test for themselves the necessity of their tasks. Please remind them that I am only one person, Grandmaster. I will need their help at the right place, in the right time. I cannot do all of this myself."

"I will sssee to it," he promised her. "But we have dellayed long enough. Let me put thiss in the ssafe, then we shall go and sssee if the Ssenior Masster becomes an Elder Masster today. Thirty-sssseven percent chance, you sssaid?"

Ia nodded. "If she warms up right, and if she puts her mind to it, there's a chance she will pass. But if not today . . . well, she'll study."

"But how much ssstudying will she get done, on your mission miss-sionss?" Ssarra asked.

She grinned, deliberately showing her teeth. "Well, if you'll bend the rules enough to loan some training vids and simulator files . . . ?"

Ssarra flicked his fingers up and out. "Give the meioa-e a ssscale, and she'll take the whole hide! If sshhe does not pass, you can have the ffiless. If shhhe does . . ."

"The rest of my crew could also use advance hand-to-hand training," Ia pressed, keeping her tone light, her hands clasped behind her back as she shrugged. She continued to show her teeth in a grin, though.

Ssarra hissed and lifted his long, scaled chin in surrender. ". . . Alright, you can have the fffiless! Do not llet them out of your conntrolll."

Chuckling, Ia sealed her lips in a smile and gave him a little bow. "*Sschah nakh*, Ssarra. They will only be transferred when we swap ships; you have my Prophetic Stamp on that."

"*Ssthienn nakh*, Ia," he responded to her thanks. "Your accennt isss gettinng slllightly better," he added in praise. The saurian stepped behind his desk and crouched, doing something beneath the broad surface.

Folding his arms lightly across his chest, Harper cocked his head, studying his commanding officer. While the alien was busy, he addressed her under his breath. "Okay, Ia. *Now* I'm impressed . . . and confused. Not only do the Afaso *not* share their training simulators with anyone else, a Tlassian would never cave in to a bit of teeth-baring by a hairless monkey unless he feared that monkey. Yet I cannot imagine the Grand-master of the entire Afaso Order fearing anyone or anything, including you."

Ssarra shook his yellow-and-brown scaled head, the motion more of a figure eight than a side-to-side gesture. Harper had spoken quietly, but not enough. "I do thisss for the ssame rea-sonss sshe doess: Lllove. That, and I knnnow she will not sshare our ssssecretss with the wrong sssentients. The teethh, shhhe teasesss me, nnothing more." Shutting the door of the safe with an audible *click*, he rose and bowed slightly at the Human male. "Now, ssshhalll we head for the sssallle?"

Bowing in return, Harper gestured for him to show the way. Ssarra in turned gestured at Ia to take the lead. Sighing, she complied. It wasn't as if this was her first visit to the Order's headquarters, after all.

CHAPTER 4

*I had a lot going on, back then. In many ways, I still do;
that's a given. But what most people don't realize is just
how many deals I made behind the scenes. There was the
deal with the Afaso to store my prophecies and the deal to
enlist them in various military services, so they'd be at the
right place at the right time with the right skills and the
right foreknowledge to save lives. There was the deal with
the Command Staff to ensure I had free rein on my ship
and crew assignments, the various deals I've made with
the Feyori, deals I've made with my fellow soldiers . . .*

*Yes, I set plans in motion with other governments as
well. I may have been confined to working mostly within
just the Terran aspects directly, but my plan has always
been to involve the other sentient races because my plan
has always been to save their lives as well as the lives of
my fellow Terran Humans.*

*Which brings us to the deals that still remain classified,
even from those who perhaps should've been told. Arrangements which were, are, and will be absolutely necessary
for the future. I brokered those deals in order to ensure that
the current war will actually have an end. At least, one we
can all live with. Not much of an excuse, I know, but at
least it's been for a good reason.*

                                                    ~Ia

DECEMBER 25, 2495 T.S.
TUPSF *HELLFIRE*
SIC TRANSIT

Her office door chimed. Looking through the transparent work-station screen, Ia narrowed her eyes at the door. A quick dip into the timestreams ended in a heavy sigh. Pushing the comm button on her desk, she said, *"Come in."*

The door slid open, admitting the tallish figure of Private Second Class Gregory York of C Squad, 2nd Platoon, one of her bridge communications technicians. He wasn't in his normal grey uniform, but rather in a bright green shirt and dark green slacks, with a dark red belt and dark red shoes. Civilian clothes.

"Uh, Captain, sir?" he asked, giving her a nervous look. "You said that, ah, anything goes in a Wake Zone. That it's completely civilian territory?"

"Yes, I did, Private York," Ia agreed. Only a handful or so of her crew were actually comfortable in her presence yet, and he wasn't one of them. Yet. She kept her tone light, her expression on the pleasant side of neutral. "You have a concern?"

"Yes, sir, I do," he said. Drawing in a deep breath, York let it out as he explained. "I know it seems kind of petty, sir, but . . . the Army's making fun of the Marines for, uh, singing. I mean, the crew members who *used* to be Army, are making fun . . ."

"I know what you mean," Ia reassured him. She held up her hand, silencing his next comment, and searched the timestreams again. This hadn't been one of the larger-percentage chances, otherwise she would have addressed it beforehand, but at least it was something that was easily salvageable. Checking her desk to make sure everything was clipped in place, she retracted the workscreen and rose. "Lead the way, York."

"Yes, sir," he sang, turning toward the door. He palmed open the panel to the front office, where one of the on-duty privates, Mara Sunrise, frowned over some form she was trying to fill out. "I don't want to get them into trouble, exactly, but . . . I like singing. Good singing. And we have a few ex-Marines who can sing."

"A few more than you know," she murmured back, nodding politely to Sunrise. The other woman lifted her chin in return, though she didn't shift her eyes from her workstation screens. "And a few who can't. Same mix as in any large group of people."

"Captain," Private Sunrise stated, catching Ia's attention, "Sergeant Grizzle will have the summary of the troops' tactical analysis from their mock-drills on Earth by nineteen hundred, sir."

"Wait a minute," York muttered, frowning at the clerk. "You're in my Platoon. Shouldn't you be off duty?"

Sunrise gave him a prim look. "War doesn't take a holiday, and neither do I."

Ia bit her tongue, keeping her expression neutral. Her superiors might have complained through the years that Ia's debriefing reports were dry and factual, but the woman currently known as Mara Sunrise had perfected bland and boring to a high degree. There was a reason why Ia had insisted she join the Company, but it would take a few years to play out. Hiding in Ia's Damned was the best place for the other woman, at least while she waited for a certain provincial governor's embarrassment and wrath to die down.

It didn't take long for Ia and York to reach the amidships galley; it was located in the same sector as the bridge and her office, but below the main gun. Both the galley and the rec hall were part of the same "Wake Zone" designated for their first onboard Leave, and that meant no one was supposed to be in uniform if they weren't officially on duty. A lot of her off-duty crew had chosen civilian clothes in shades of red and green or blue and white to celebrate the holiday, too, not just York. By contrast, her grey clothes looked out of place.

It was also time for an actual meal rather than the sugary snacks being served upstairs in the Wake hall, so the on-duty crew were serving the off-duty "civilians" lounging at the tables. Most were lounging and trying to enjoy the feast that had been prepared, except for a knot of about fifteen or sixteen colorfully clad bodies squared off against each other in two groups.

"—Your *mother* is a tone-deaf harpy!" One of the privates, Tony Doersch, was haranguing the other camp. Ia knew he was ex-Marine, and knew he was fiercely loyal to the Corps. "If you don't like our singing, get the hell outta our kitchen!"

The man he was insulting, tall and dark-skinned, flexed a very impressive set of muscles for someone raised on Earth.

C. J. Siano was ex-Army, and proud of his family. The yarn of his Christmas-tree-covered sweater creaked faintly as he stiffened. "Don't you *dare* talk 'bout my mother that way, you—!"

"Gentlebeings," Ia asserted firmly, her tone just sharp enough to cut off his retort. "Captain. On. Deck. Instead of in my office, where I should be at this hour."

They all stiffened. A couple of them even scrambled upright, even though this galley at this point in time was supposed to be part of the Wake Zone, where military procedure only counted for those who were actually on duty. The fifteen or so men and women facing her were all in normal garments, not uniforms, but they faced her in her grey buttoned shirt and matching, black-striped slacks out of the habit of deference to an authority figure. Ia took advantage of that.

"I don't care who started this, or how, or why," she stated in the quiet that followed her initial words. Even the crew in the kitchen half of the cabin were doing their best to work without noise. Ia swept the two clusters of men and women with as mild a look as she could manage. "I only care who ends it, and how, and why.

"Siano," she stated, addressing the tallest man in the two groups. "You have served long and well in the TUPSF-Army. You have a lot of good marks on your Service file. You are, however, unfamiliar with the culture of the Marine Corps. In the Space Force, it is a tradition that the Marines sing. Whether or *not* they can carry a tune. Isn't that right, Barstow?" Ia asked, glancing at the woman in the short blue skirt, matching vest, and white shirt.

Private L'ili Barstow blushed. Both of them knew—Ia via postcognition and L'ili firsthand—that it was her off-key crooning that had triggered this heated debate. Still, the other woman took it on the chin squarely, pulling her shoulders back and leveling her gaze across the room, hands behind her snowflake-patterned dress in Parade Rest. "Sir, yes, sir. As my instructors in Basic put it, we Marines will sing even if we're tone-deaf and tasteless, sir."

Ia lifted her hand, gesturing at the woman. "See? A simple cultural difference. Do try to respect it in the future, gentle-meioas. Of course, I am still a Marine, deep down inside, so I'll admit I'm slightly biased in this matter, but you will still give your fellow crew members respect for their hobbies and beliefs.

"Religious beliefs," Ia stated, looking up pointedly at the decorations tied firmly to the ceiling struts before dropping her gaze to the others, ". . . *or* secular. In short, gentlemeioas, either sing along, or shut it. Now, get back to your partying, get along, and have a Merry Christmas. That's an order."

Siano mumbled an apology, as did Doersch. Some of the others did, too.

Barstow cleared her throat. "Ah, Captain? Is it true that there are some songs out there about you? In the Marines?"

"Yes. There are now quite a few songs about me," Ia admitted blandly. "And yes, I can and do sing them. At some point, when I've caught up on the klicks of paperwork still lined up on my desk, I might even sing 'em for you, whether or not I myself am tone-deaf and tasteless about it," she joked lightly, giving the other woman and her companions a slight smile. "But I won't be able to join you for several weeks yet. Enjoy your onboard Leave while you can. Private York, come walk with me."

"Sir, yes, sir," he agreed, following her as she headed back out of the galley. He walked with her back to the nearest lift. "Ah . . . what did you want, sir?"

"You have some musical training, don't you?" she asked him while she waited for the car to reach their deck.

"Sir, yes, sir," York agreed, squaring his shoulders. "I have a Master's degree in music, both voice and composition, bought on the Education Bill. I was paying it off by working for Intel, before the transfer to your crew, sir." He paused, then asked, "Do you want me to offer lessons, sir?"

"Smart meioa. To *anyone* who wants to learn, regardless of which Branch they were in before," she added. "Particularly to anyone who wants to sing and clearly needs it—make it sound like it'll be fun, and coax them to at least try. There will eventually be a whole series of off-duty classes this crew can take from each other. I want you to spearhead the opening offers, and encourage the others to come forward. Whether it's singing, board games, sewing, or basket-weaving, I want this crew to work together to better ourselves when we're off duty as well as when we're on. Think you can handle that?"

"I'm Special Forces, sir; we take in all kinds," he quipped.

"I'll ask Barstow if she wants a few private pointers so she can show up Siano next time in public, then ask her what she can teach me and some others in return."

"Good meioa," Ia praised, as the lift arrived. "Merry Christmas, York. Or whatever your preferred holiday is."

"You, too, sir," he returned.

Nodding to him, she headed back to her office. Standoffs like the one between Siano and Doersch weren't going to happen often, but they were going to happen while her disparate crew was still pulling itself together. Internecine fights had to be quelled as fast as possible. Actions and offers like York's, those had to be encouraged, even rewarded. She needed everyone working together, trusting each other, and needed it all too soon.

Trust in each other would do as much or more to save her Company as her own efforts could.

JANUARY 16, 2496 T.S.
SIC TRANSIT

The quiet thrum of a starship in motion was broken by the beeping of her arm unit. Ia finished her current prophecy by imprinting the words into the workstation electrokinetically. Physically, she reached for the comm button. *"Ia here. Go."*

"Congratulations, Captain," Harper's voice stated. He sounded tired, yet satisfied. *"It's a brand-new baby stardrive. Nose cone A has been rewired to your specifics, and the warp-panel control programs recoded to compensate. All five simulation tests came up positive and fully functional . . . though I'm sure your gifts will have the final say. Unless you're going to leave me in suspense and not let me know?"*

She smiled and closed her eyes. *"Patience, Commander. Let me double-check . . ."* Dipping into the timestreams, Ia checked the performance of the newly combined hyperwarp drive system. *"Congratulations, Commander, it is indeed a healthy baby stardrive. Feel free to rotate out the extra personnel to the Wake Zone on Aft Deck 8. Keep a full crew in engineering, though. I'm going to take 'er out for a test drive."*

"Already?" he asked. *"Ah—don't forget, it'll take half an*

hour for everything to reboot with the new codes. We need to be at a dead stop or a low drift for that. But once that's done, may I join you on the bridge for a front-seat view?"

"Understood, and be my guest, but no backseat driving. I'll go order the shutdown now. Ia out."

"Harper out."

She ended the call with another touch, then sat back, sighing. It didn't matter exactly *when* she did this next part, only that it was done within the next two days. Now was as good a time as any, however. Scrubbing her face, Ia braced herself for what she was about to do.

I swore an oath, when I joined the military, to be loyal to the Terran United Planets. I agreed to abide by the laws of the Terran United Planets . . . and in essence, to broker no deals with foreign powers, to share no military secrets, to not betray my chosen people. She had memorized that Oath of Service long ago, and the vows she had made still haunted her. *If the Admiral-General knew just how far I'd stretch that* carte blanche *I bartered out of her, she'd have shot me herself on the spot when I barged into that sealed meeting. Maybe even nuked me from orbit . . .*

The morbid thought cheered her a little, but then her sense of humor had always been a little skewed. Or almost always; it had changed at the age of fifteen. Standing, Ia secured her desk, pulled a spare datapad from one of the drawers, and headed for the side door. Not the one that led to the front office where Master Sergeant Sadneczek and his small staff of clerks managed the paperwork needs of their Company, but the side door that led to the service corridor.

That corridor led to the backup generators and emergency lifesupport reoxygenators, to a pair of heads—the charming Navy term for bathroom facilities—plus the pocket-sized bridge galley where meals could be quickly fixed and served, and the bridge itself, bypassing the need to go out and around to either the starboard or portside main passages that ran the length of Deck 6.

Like so much else on this ship, the bridge had also been modified, reduced to a fraction of its original size because she had only a fraction of the original crew meant to man the various posts. The extra room to the fore had been converted into a wiring shop, just one of the many necessary manufactory bays needed on a ship that had to be self-sufficient as much as possible for its repairs.

Captain's privilege gave her the shortest commute on the nine hundred meters and twenty-four decks of her ship, since her personal quarters were tucked right behind her office. Captain's rank made the first bridge crew member to notice her, Corporal Fyrn Michaels, call out the warning, "Officer on deck!"

Everyone sat up straighter in their seats. No one took their eyes off their workstations, however. That was one of the big rules in the Company Bible; stations were to be manned and monitored at all times, even if a fellow crew member had to monitor the extra workload while someone visited the head. Only when Ia approached the pilot's station and tapped Yeoman Fielle on the shoulder did he look up from the task of guiding their ship through the star-streaked speeds of faster-than-light.

"Sir?" he asked. The incident with his pet minirobots was weeks in the past, but she didn't have to be a telepath to see a hint of it lurking in his concerned gaze. "Is something wrong?"

"Bring the ship out of FTL and power down the engines, Yeoman," she ordered.

"Aye, aye, sir," he said. Sliding his fingers down over the controls, he cut their speed. Everything seemed to pull forward a little from the change in their momentum, but wrapped in an envelope of energies that warped the laws of physics, not much of their abrupt vector change could be felt. "Five minutes to dead stop, sir."

"Captain," Lieutenant Rico asked, his voice deep and his tone mild. It was his duty watch, and his responsibility to ensure the ship continued on course. "Any particular reason why we're stopping, sir?"

"Consider it sightseeing," she quipped, looking around the bridge, with its banks of transparent and solid monitors, its workstations and handful of crew manning the important, non-combat ones.

There was a black-box recorder on board the ship that she knew would be recording everything they said and did, unless she altered it electrokinetically. Which she did, but it was the Human element that had to be watched. Black-box recordings wouldn't be cracked open unless something went wrong . . . or was reported as going wrong.

Rico wasn't dumb. "Pull the other one, sir."

"Engineering just finished our drive-systems respec on an Ultra-Classified level. FTL needs to shut down completely so that the drive comps can be rebooted with the new programs. The operation will take approximately half an hour. Eyes to the boards, thoughts on your tasks," she reminded the half dozen men and women on the bridge with her. "We may be a trillion kilometers from anything and everything out here, but I will not have this crew caught off guard."

"Aye, aye, sir."

The main screens for the pilot's station and the forward wall flashed for a moment, dazzling the room with thousands of circles of light. The blurred streak of stars turned into sliding pinpoints of light. Slowly, their motion eased, then stopped.

"Captain, we are now at a full stop, drive-wise. Relative to galactic motion is still .0002 Cee, sir," Fielle added, meaning relative to the average movement of stars in their sector, versus their position as they swirled around the galactic core. "If you want a true dead stop, sir, we'll have to use correctional thrusters."

"That won't be necessary, Yeoman," she said. "Private Barstow, inform Commander Harper down in engineering that he may now upload the new warp-field drivers."

"I'm on it, sir." L'ili Barstow bent her attention to that task, speaking quietly into her headset pickups. There was a slightly more melodic quality to her voice than a few weeks before; it seemed her voice lessons with York were beginning to pay off.

Private Hulio, seated at the navigation station, glanced briefly over his shoulder. "Captain, I've been double-checking our heading. We *are* going to Sanctuary, correct, sir?"

"That is correct," Ia confirmed. This was why she had ended the audio portion of the black-box recordings.

"Well, sir . . . I know you set the course in the navcomp, and . . . uh . . . I'm *sure* you know how to find your own home-world, being a pilot," Hulio added, his tone apologetic for what he was about to suggest. "But . . . we're off course by seven degrees, sir. That's taken us within a couple light-years of Grey territory, which makes me a little nervous, sir. It's also adding sixty-two light-years to our trip, even if we correct course now. That, ah, doesn't seem the most efficient flight path, Captain."

Sixty-two light-years off course was far more than merely

inefficient, and everyone on the bridge knew it. Ia watched the rest of the bridge crew glancing at each other. They peeked at her over their shoulders before returning their eyes to their stations.

She answered Hulio's question with part of the truth. "That's because we're testing the new drive system out here, in the middle of nowhere. I am not about to plow this ship into my home planet, the local traffic, or anything else in that general area."

Silence followed her words, silence and a few puzzled glances. Ia turned her attention to the workpad in her hands, writing prophecies electrokinetically. Every spare minute had to be filled with writing prophecies for her family since there would only be two more chances to visit them in person in the coming years. Once the two wars got going in this corner of the galaxy, it would be too dangerous to try for more visits than that.

After several minutes, Lieutenant Rico spoke up, his tone calm, almost phlegmatic. "Begging pardon, Captain, but aren't you a massive precognitive? Wouldn't you *know* what to avoid, when and where?"

"That's why we're out here, Lieutenant," she replied in kind, equally as calm. "I got shot in the shoulder once, on a three percent chance I'd discounted as being too low to worry about. I'm not taking chances with the new drive, just in case some of those low-probability bugs haven't been worked out enough. Nothing out here in our test zone will harm us. Now relax and enjoy the pretty stars while the upgrades get loaded."

Silence filled the bridge, broken only by the occasional murmur from the operations post, monitoring the ship's functions and coordinating them with engineering, lifesupport, and so forth. Ia returned her attention to her precognitive messages.

Bored, since they were only drifting slightly through empty space, with no need for anyone to guide the helm, Fielle finally asked her a question. "So . . . Captain. Statistically speaking, what *is* the safest spot in the universe?"

"In bed, with the covers pulled over your head," Ia said, her attention more on her task than on her answer. "Having been kissed good night by your parents, who have just checked under your bed and in your closet for all the things that might go bump in the night."

Snickers broke out at her quip, as well as grins. She smiled slightly. The other thing she could've said was, "In your grave," but that one would've been too morbid to reply. The point was to encourage her troops, not discourage them. Keeping her mouth shut, she continued scrolling her thoughts onto the data-pad. She would have to stay up half an hour extra to ensure all the messages were printed out tonight, but that wasn't much different from most other nights, these days.

". . . Is that anywhere near this ship, sir?" Hulio dared to ask her after several seconds.

"This ship will be about as far from that as you can get and still be alive," Ia said, ending one message and starting on the next. "But for the moment, we're safe. Eyes to the boards, thoughts on your tasks."

More minutes passed. The main bridge door finally opened, admitting Commander Harper. Judging from his tousled black locks and the mussed, slightly stained state of his grey coveralls, he had apparently been working personally on the engine upgrades and hadn't bothered to change. Moving over to her side, he pulled himself to Attention and addressed her. "Captain Ia, the new programs are loaded, and have been test-simulated five more times. Everything's green for go, sir."

"Excellent work, Lieutenant Commander. Lieutenant Rico, stand down. I'll take the command station now," Ia stated. She tucked her pad into her shirt pocket, moving from the pilot's station to the command chair. "Yeoman Fielle, I'll be taking the helm from here. Both of you can stick around, or go take a break for the next hour. If you go, be back on duty at nine hundred."

Rico narrowed his brown eyes, giving Ia a thoughtful look. Unbuckling his harness, he stood. "I think I'd like to stay, Captain."

"Have a seat," she directed, giving him room to step out from behind the curved workstation console. Nodding, Rico moved to one of the unoccupied seats, the backup station for communications. Harper took the backup station for operations on the other side.

Taking the abandoned chair, Ia sat down, strapped in, and logged in with her bracer. The chair, already programmed for her preferences, slid forward to accommodate her average height. Strapping her left hand into the flight controls, she tapped the workstation controls, rearranging the status displays on her main, two secondary, and ten tertiary screens.

"Right, then. I'm ready for the transfer, Yeoman," she said. "If you're ready, helm to my control in ten."

"Aye, sir. Helm to yours in ten," Fielle agreed, free hand moving over his console.

". . . I have the helm," Ia stated a few seconds later. "Bringing engines back online."

"Heading, sir?" Hulio asked, glancing up from the navigator's post. It was the navigator's job to coordinate with the navcomp for plotting a safe course into a selected star system, working on the macroscale to avoid all the large hazards that the FTL field couldn't grease out of the way. It was the pilot's job to avoid hazards on the microscale, usually while traveling at insystem speeds.

"Engines are now online, Captain," Harper said, beating Private Dinyadah to it. She shut her mouth, glanced at him, and shrugged. Harper smiled in Ia's direction.

"Right. Let's bring the *Hellfire* up to insystem speeds. Forward to one-quarter Cee," she warned the others, bringing the thrusters online. The faint *whoosh* that was the cycling systems for lifesupport grew a little louder, picking up a *thrummm* from the engines again. The stationary field of stars displayed in the various monitors around the bridge slowly shifted as Ia made a slight heading correction. "Just a few more minutes, and we'll be up to half Cee, since we're taking it easy."

"And then what, sir?" Rico asked her. "Three-quarters lightspeed? I thought we were testing the FTL panels, not the insystem drives."

Harper smiled, looking at Ia. "No, Lieutenant. When we hit half lightspeed, we open a rift and take 'er for a spin. Right, Captain?"

"Right, Commander." Technically, he was a lieutenant commander, but since he outranked the other two on board—and the doctor wasn't even in the chain of command, officially—it was acceptable to shorten his rank. That, and she knew he would eventually earn a promotion. "Navigation, pull up the star charts for System N-Tau 1158."

"Aye, sir." Hulio tapped his console, letting the advanced processors calculate their course. "N-Tau 1158 is . . . twenty-nine light-years from here, or a day and a quarter, deadheaded

FTL, sir. We don't have much information on its insystem hazards, though. We also have the Kirkenn Nebula between here and there. It's a new gas cloud, so it's a significant navigation hazard. If you wanted to go there, you'd have to . . . wait . . .

"The Kirkenn Nebula is in the *Grey* Zone." He looked up from his station. "Sir, why did you want to know about that star system? No one is allowed to go there, per treaty. It's part of the buffer zone we won from them."

"You know that, and I know that, but the Greys have conveniently forgotten about it, Private. Cycling the OTL hyperwarp in twenty seconds," she warned everyone. It wasn't much of a warning. Telltales turned amber as she gripped the trigger for the hyperspace generators. Panels opened on the nose of the ship, displayed on the second of her lower tertiary screens, the one to the middle left. The shallow camera view showed the relay nose cone lifting into position. The moment the lights switched to green, she pulsed the trigger.

A blue-white energy packet spat out from the cone, an elongated sphere crackling with warped physics. It shrunk down, collapsing in on itself, and punctured a hole in reality. That hole swirled open in a much larger, greyer version. It expanded and swallowed the ship just in time as they dove nose-first into the grey-streaked tunnel. Behind them, the aft view on her fourth tertiary screen showed the tunnel collapsing about two lengths behind them.

The *thrum* picked up from a quiet background noise to a palpable low rumble. Ia frowned at her shivering console. "Harper, I thought you said you implemented the new software. Why is my ship shaking?"

"So did *I*, Captain," he muttered back, tapping in a string of queries on his workstation. "Tracing the relays now . . . Ah! Here it is. I forgot I left it on manual for the tests, which means we just have to switch it to fully automated and let the computer compensate for the two different systems instead of us absentminded engineers . . . which I have just done . . . now."

The rumbling eased back with the last thump of his finger on the operations-station controls. It was now quieter, bearably so, though the new hum was stronger than the faint hum from before. Harper gave her an apologetic look.

"Sorry, sir. I'll get the code for that patched in by shift's end, sir. I figured you'd need the manual programming for those instances where we're beating the speed of the OTL-spark and need to wedge it open, or are still getting up to hyperrift speed. Or if anything happens to the engine comps, like damage in battle."

"A good piece of foresight planning," she praised. "Right. This transit will take just under an hour. Commander Harper, Private Hulio, double-check the navcomp's link with the engine comps. I want to make sure this ship flies as smoothly as a courier does on straight OTL autopilot."

"Sir . . . if we're really flying through a hyperrift, why aren't we getting spacesick?" Dinyadah asked, looking up at the grey streaks of the rift tunnel on her viewscreen.

"We're immune because we're wrapped in modified FTL physics, Private," Harper answered her. "We are now moving at roughly two minutes to the light-year, slower than standard OTL, but considerably faster than FTL."

"But I was always told that forcing an FTL ship through a hyperrift shook the ship to pieces," Dinyadah said. She looked around the bridge, seeking support, or at least confirmation from the room. Several of the others nodded, including Ia, so she looked back at their chief engineer. "So why aren't we having our teeth rattled out of our heads?"

"It's a modified warp field, that's why—don't ask how it was modified," he added, glancing at their captain for a moment. "The Captain is under orders not to divulge that particular information, and that means the rest of us are under orders, too."

"Or to put it another way," Lieutenant Rico stated, studying her, "if word of how we're doing this gets off this ship, the Salik *will* find out and try to use it against us. Right, Captain?"

"Right, Lieutenant," she agreed, her attention split between making sure the helm stayed on course in the rift and answering the unspoken questions. "Hyperwarp has far too many advantages for us not to use it, but far too many disadvantages to implement it across the fleet. The least of which is the fact that we're still effectively communications-blind while in hyperrift transit.

"We Terrans are not living on an isolated clutch of planets on the backside of unexplored space this time around," Ia said, referencing Terran history. "The Salik know exactly where we are, they can find out where all of our shipyard facilities are, and they can bribe, coerce, or smash-and-grab the information if we offered it to the rest of the fleet. If we hadn't been isolated and far from the war zones back at the start of the first Salik War, then they would've seized all our new, Terran-based tech offerings and done their best to defeat the Alliance.

"Sometimes you need a lump hammer to take out a problem, as we helped provide two centuries ago," Ia said, quoting one of her distant descendants. Drawing in a deep breath, she steeled herself for this next bit of potential trust-bending, and revealed as calmly and matter-of-factly as she could, "Sometimes you need a laser scalpel. This ship is that laser scalpel . . . and I have just aimed it at one of the biggest, nearest, most dangerous cancerous growths in the galaxy. As far as the rest of the ship is to know, never mind the rest of the fleet, we never strayed from known Terran flight paths. And we *never* crossed into the Grey Zone.

"That is a direct order from not only your commanding officer, but from a high-ranking precognitive—and before anyone protests further, I'll remind you I *am* fully authorized by the Command Staff to make this little visit. We're going into the Grey Zone, and we are all going to keep our mouths shut about it. This particular little mission is labeled as Ultra Classified, which means you cannot even mention it to *my* superior without going first through me.

"This one is completely out of your pay grades at this point in time . . . and it is merely the first of far too many missions with that label stuck to it. Speaking of Ultra Classified, the Admiral-General authorized me to undertake this mission, yes, but you are *not* allowed to discuss it with her. If you did, you'd be accused of Fatalities Four, Five, Six, and Thirty-Five, and those are just the obvious ones," Ia told her bridge crew. "They'll dredge up every other Fatality rule they can throw at you, too. That's what Ultra Classified means. That's why I have that double-indemnity regarding corporal punishment on my back—because I am responsible for the rest of you keeping your mouths shut. Please do; you may consider this your first official test for such matters."

That silenced her crew. Ia knew it was a grievous stretching of her *carte-blanche* powers, but it was necessary. Though she had given Fielle and Rico permission to leave the bridge, neither moved. Fielle stayed put because she knew he wanted to learn the new drive's flight mechanisms. Rico stayed put because he was busy watching her. Studying her. Analyzing her methods and motives.

It might've made more sense for the Command Staff to have made Helstead her onboard spy, but Oslo Rico was used to assessing tactical and strategic threats and knowing which parts of his information-gathering were troublesome enough to pass along. Helstead excelled at executing decisions based on what she found, but Rico's job was to report *if* Ia stepped out of line. This would stretch his credulity limit, but she knew he wouldn't report it precipitously.

She also knew there were other spies tapped among her crew. Her 1st Platoon lieutenant was the most important of them, since even spies had to report up through a chain of command; the Command Staff wanted to know only the important bits, rather than be pestered by petty half worries.

For now, they kept their mouths shut and their eyes on their workstation screens. All except for Yeoman Fielle, who had nothing to do. Seated at the pilot's station, ahead and below her own post at the back of the room, Fielle fidgeted. He wasn't quite as bad about it as Lieutenant Commander Helstead could be, but he did sigh and shift in his seat every now and again, visibly bored.

"Yeoman Fielle, would you like to warm up the feedbacks and see what hyperwarp flight feels like?" she finally offered.

"Sir, yes, sir!" he agreed quickly, sitting forward so he could reach for the controls.

She smiled. "If you learn quickly enough—not that there's much more to learn—I'll let you oversee most of the flight. I'll be taking the helm back a few minutes before we emerge, though."

"If we're emerging inside Grey space, sir, you can *have* the helm at that point," he muttered, strapping his hand into the control glove. "I don't want that level of responsibility on my hands. In fact, I don't even want to go there at all."

"Relax, Yeoman; we'll get out alive," she promised.

Her 1st Platoon lieutenant wasn't the only one to glance her way at those words, but his eyes did linger. As did Harper's, though his gaze was at least more trusting than dubious.

L-3 POINT, TAUS'EN IV
N-TAU 1158 SYSTEM

The *Hellfire* emerged from hyperspace without fanfare. Grey streaks blossomed into stark black filled with pinpoints of light. Warned that they were about to emerge, Private Hulio moved quickly to synch what little they knew of the system with the information coming their way. Considering they were still traveling fast, he worked with crisp urgency.

"Scanners are up and running, Captain. Gravity and light-wave data coming in . . . We're just outside the fourth planet's orbit, sir, at the third Lagrange point—*Madre de Dios*, there's a space station at the L-3, sir!" he announced, looking up from his lower screens to the primary and back. "It's huge! Five kilometers across. We're not on a collision course, but we'll pass within thirty thousand klicks. The hull configuration's a bit strange, but scanners *are* matching the materials to known Grey technology, sir. We have light-seconds before they detect us."

"Orders, Captain?" Rico asked in a deceptively mild voice.

"Private Hong," Ia stated, her tone crisp but calm. "Power down all guns. I repeat, power down *all* guns. This includes all personal weapons here on the bridge as well as the hull. We're about to be scanned, and we don't want to alarm the locals by doing the wrong things."

Hong complied with a shake of his head. ". . . Aye, sir. Powering down all guns, sir. Putting my faith in you, sir—and requesting permission to haunt you in the afterlife if you're wrong, sir."

"Permission granted. Corporal Xhuge, if you'll look in the Alliance folder, subfolder Grey Interactions, you will find a comm file marked 'Neutral Parley.' Use that to send a ping to the station," Ia said.

"Neutral parley?" Rico asked her. One of his brows rose on his tanned face. "Is that even *in* their vocabulary? If it weren't for the psis, they'd have squished us like bugs long ago. We aren't even worth the time it takes to spit to them, or whatever their equivalent is."

"Considering most of their past interactions with us have either fallen into the categories of 'ignore the inconsequential jumped-up slime molds' or 'plunder their primitive biology for nefarious experimentation purposes,' " Fielle quipped, "I for one wouldn't fight over the concept of an actual chance to talk like civilized sentients."

"*I'm* just grateful we're on a ship with a powerful psi," Dinyadah muttered. "That's the only thing that's backed them down in the past."

"The file has been sent, Captain," the corporal at the communications station informed her. He didn't look happy to have done it, but at least he hadn't hesitated. "We've received pingback, so I know they got it. I can't make heads or tails out of the language in the recording I sent, though."

"We actually have a couple dozen psis on board, Private Dinyadah, some of them quite strong for the average psychic," Ia corrected her, addressing the scanner tech first. "But we won't need them, just me. They're on board for another reason. As for the language, Corporal, it's called Shredou, which is the name for their species as well as for the language of the Greys. I pieced together a greeting specifically addressed to the being who serves as their station master and, coincidentally, the chief military officer for this system. One specific enough, it will catch his attention.

"And they do have terms for neutral parley in their culture; they just don't share those terms with non-Greys," Ia said, eyes on the slightly enlarged dot that was the space station in the distance. They were still traveling at a quarter the speed of light, but she didn't alter their course. "The fact that I know those terms, and the exact location and circumstances he'll be in when the message reaches him, will stay his hand. They may be the single most alien race in the entire known galaxy—above and beyond the Feyori—and the single most technologically advanced, but they do share the trait of curiosity with us."

"So what is this parley of yours going to discuss?" Rico asked her.

"Sir! Energy buildup in the—" Hulio started to report. He was cut off by a flare of light, and a slight pressure change in the bridge, one that puffed air outward. Air that had occupied the clear space just to the right of Ia's command station, between her and the seats claimed by her two fellow officers. A space now occupied by something, or rather someone, else.

Cocking his head slightly—and calling the alien a "he" was only a guess on Ia's part, since their gender was hard to discern—the Grey surveyed the stunned occupants of the bridge. He blinked his large black eyes and unfurled one of his slender, grey-skinned hands, focusing on the white-haired, grey-clad woman next to him.

"Speak."

His voice sounded strange, as if two sets of vocal cords worked at once, and not quite in harmony.

"I know you plan to invade," Ia said, keeping her sentences short. Longer ones would be open to misinterpretation. "I know when. I know where. I will tell you the battles we will fight."

Rico hissed at that statement. Even Harper gave her a dubious look. The others looked up from their boards, then hastily turned back to their monitors as the Grey, short and slender, glanced their way.

"You betray your kind." The Grey didn't speak with the intonation of a Human. His voice spoke flatly, his thin lips moved and shaped the words, but whether it was a statement or a question could not be discerned.

Ia took it as a question. "No. I do not betray my kind. Your technology will destroy this universe. I will stop you. I will tell you when. I will tell you where. You will see my words are true. When you do, you will surrender. You will obey the second treaty. My treaty."

He blinked and curled his fingers. "Irrelevant."

". . . Another energy surge, sir," Hulio whispered, gaze fixed firmly on his screens.

"Obey me," Ia stated calmly, "and I will save you from the Zida"ya."

The double click was difficult to manage, considering she had only a soft tongue and the inner side of her teeth to work with. Nor was it in the language of the Greys. It did, however, have the desired effect.

The Grey's large black eyes widened to their fullest extent. He did not move, however, other than to say, "Speak."

"They are coming. I know where. I know when. You doubt

me right now," she added, dipping her head slightly. "I will show you my accuracy. You will accept my deal. If you refuse, I will not save you. I will aim them at you. I will know when. I will know where. You will die. All the Shredou will die.

"Take the indicated hyperrelay unit, and leave," she added, uncurling her right hand in a similar gesture to the Grey's. "I will contact you. Then you will know when, and you will know where. You will see my words are true."

"Arrogant." The Grey did not move and did not leave the ship as ordered.

Ia breathed deep. As she exhaled slowly, she poured her mental energies into her psychic shields, adding a twist of electrokinesis. The air around her station crackled, and her monitor screens flickered. Capacitors absorbed the energy, stabilizing their views of the stars outside and the navigation data overlaid on her secondary screens. She didn't move, other than to breathe and tense her body.

The bubble of energy expanded outward like a spherical force field, visible only where the field encountered motes of dust in the air, causing them to snap and spark. It wasn't exactly electricity, however, but rather, kinetic inergy.

The Grey winced, then stepped back. She expanded the bubble, until he clutched at his head. A high-pitched hiss escaped him, not much different from a teakettle's whistle. Ia eased back her energies.

"Powerful, not arrogant," she corrected him, relaxing. "You will obey. Now get off my ship."

Opening his large eyes, larger than a Gatsugi's mouse black orbs, he stared at her a long moment. Then vanished. Air flowed inward slightly in a faint *pop* as the molecules slapped back together. Grey technology permitted translocation, a mechanical, technological method of psychic teleportation, but the energies used were not at all the same. Psychic energy, the kind wielded by those Humans descended at least partially from the Feyori, was the equivalent of acid to their species' senses.

The fact that they could make the translocation instantaneously onto a ship moving at half the speed of light spoke volumes about the rest of their technology. As did the arrogance of sending a single speaker to visit the insects daring to invade their space.

"Right. Time for us to get the hell out of here. Sparking the rift in thirty seconds," Ia warned her crew, right hand moving over the controls. "We'll be taking a short jump with a course correction to follow. Once we're en route—after this little jaunt," she added, sparking the rift, "we'll be able to relax and stand down. Not even the Greys can catch us in hyperspace. This is why we will stay in it on the second jump until we reach Sanctuarian space, putting us well ahead of schedule."

"And the treason you just committed?" Rico asked her, his voice still calm, his expression still neutral. Behind him, his screen showed the mouth of the wormhole swallowing them in streaks of grey light. It made his deeply tanned skin look sickly, underscoring his accusation. "Is that on the schedule?"

"It's not treason if I am authorized to commit it, Lieutenant. Nor is it treason when these precognitive actions will be directly responsible for saving the Terrans from being destroyed by the Shredou in several years," Ia countered, knowing he couldn't let such a huge security breach pass unchallenged. "I also expect you personally to assist me in properly wording my communiqués with the Greys in our future exchanges of information. But that won't happen for almost a year, so you can relax."

"I will not relax until I have examined your *next* message, sir," he added. "And preferably this last one, too. I'd feel a lot better knowing what you said to them."

The tunnel of streaks ended. They emerged in realspace on the far side of the system, far from the light of the local star. Ia began the careful process of not only slipping them sideways and down a little, more in the direction of her home system, but gently altering their trajectory so that they would be able to hit the next hyperrift dead on, rather than at an angle. Touching the edges of a rift was never a good idea, which was why speed was essential in getting their ship both in and out at just the right moment.

"So will I, Lieutenant. Some of the words have no easy translation into Terranglo, since my description of what he was doing at the moment of contact have no correlation in our own culture . . . but the important words are perfectly clear. Including the fact that I will not be using that hyperrelay unit to contact them until 12,379 *kesant* have passed. You'll need to figure out how to translate Grey Standard into Terran Standard time systems, but it's just under a Terran Standard year." She looked up at him, then over at Hulio. "Private Hulio, get me a dead-reckon heading for the Sanctuary System. Line it up with our current speed and heading, and plot an appropriate course correction arc."

"Aye, sir," he agreed, turning his attention back to the boards.

"Sir?" Dinyadah asked. "Captain?"

"Yes, Private?" Ia asked, watching the unfocused crosshairs that appeared on her main screen, thanks to Hulio's efforts.

"Thank you for getting us out of there alive," the other woman said. "I mean, not for getting us into that situation, sir, but . . . er, I mean . . . *shakk*. Sorry, sir."

"I suggest pulling your foot away from your mouth before you swallow it, Private," Harper ordered her, his tone gentle but pointed. "Put your faith in our CO as I have, and she'll get all of us out of this alive."

Not everyone, Meyun, Ia thought grimly. To herself, behind tight mental walls. *But I'll save those that I can.*

JANUARY 18, 2496 T.S.
OUR BLESSED MOTHER
INDEPENDENT COLONYWORLD SANCTUARY

The moment Yeoman First Class Arial Yamasuka, 2nd Platoon A Alpha, touched the shuttle onto the landing pad, Ia unstrapped from the copilot's seat. Slapping open the cockpit door, she hurried into the crowded cargo bay. Gravity pulled at her, hard and heavy; once again, she felt rather out of shape, having lived too long in lightworlder conditions. Exercising a few hours every day in heightened artificial gravity—captain's privilege—wasn't enough to compensate for the pull of the real thing.

"Meioas!" she barked, catching the attention of the crew in the cargo hold. "Make sure your gravity weaves are set to adaptive gravimetrics on the low setting, and no higher than medium once you get off the ship. Stand no closer to each other than three meters once they have been turned up, to avoid the nausea that comes with field interference," she called out, pitching her voice to carry.

The A teams from each Squad in the 2nd and 3rd Platoons fumbled with the buckles of their own four-point harnesses, hampered somewhat by the bulk of the purple web-works wrapped over their mix of grey camouflage clothes and black-and-pewter light armor.

"Sergeant Santori, Sergeant Maxwell, you are authorized to open up the ammunitions crates. Lead team members will be issued stunner c-clips. Corporals and most of the privates first class and grade, check to make sure your clips have a blue-dotted rectangle, indicating their payloads are indeed relatively harmless beanbags," she reminded the men and women getting ready to disembark. "Privates second class and grade, you will be issued tranker clips; check to make sure they have blue feathers.

"Do not—I repeat do *not*—fire trankers unless two verbal warnings and two stunner shots have first been fired, and fire no more than one trank per target. People can and *will* die if they hit the ground wrong in this gravity, which includes being tranquilized too fast. Make sure all stunner beanbag rounds are aimed at torsos, not heads, to ensure your targets are not knocked over as well as knocked back. Keep in mind that while the density of the local atmosphere isn't much different from Terran Standard, the gravity on Sanctuary will drop your shots fast. You can shoot from the hip if you must, but your JL-41 projectile riflescopes come with sensors that will adjust for the local gravity.

"I suggest you turn them on and use them," she advised the men and women listening to her. Multiple clickings and faint charging whines immediately followed. Ia nodded and continued. "Your job on this drop is to scout the warehouse, establish checkpoints, and secure the initial cargo so that you can instruct your other Squad members on where to go and what to do during our next trip," she stated as she skirted between the seated soldiers and the cargo crates strapped to the floor. "Line up at the bottom of the ramp when each team pairing has been properly armed, and remember, *no* running on this planet.

"Tripping and falling can kill you in this gravity if you are not prepared to fall just right, and you are *not* prepared. Consider yourselves under orders not to run at all for the duration of all planetside visits to this world. Check your ammo and lock and load. Gentlemeios, welcome to Sanctuary, your local gravitational hell."

Reaching the back-ramp hatch, she triggered the door and

rode the panels as the metal descended to the tarmac. Clad as she was in camouflage Greys with a black vest covered in polished grey ceristeel plates, Ia hoped she looked no-nonsense enough to be intimidating. Customs officials were a tough breed; they would not appreciate her bulldozing these supplies through their checkpoints without the right to random inspections.

Her comment about gravitational hell had nothing to do with the ambiance. In the distance, the mountains looked purple, the sky a pale indigo blue, the local tree-equivalents were showing the bright spring hues of yellows, greens, and blues, and the buildings were relatively clean and fresh, whitewashed with colorful bands of decorative trim and holographic signboards designating spaceport terminal gates at the central hub off to their right in the distance and the warehouse nearby on their left.

Two ground cars were already on their way, filled with Customs inspectors. So were a half dozen short, stout Humans in plain beige coveralls. The group hurrying her way on foot reached the shuttle first. The lead figure, a young man of about twenty, lifted his fingers to his forehead in a mock salute. "Hey there, Prophet. Right on time as promised. You're looking good, too. Grey looks better on you than that brown crap you wore last time."

"Hey, James," she acknowledged, dipping her head slightly. Like her, he was at least half-Asian, but despite the shorter hair and longer sideburns, the slight cleft in his chin made him recognizable. The last time she had seen the dark-haired man was shortly before leaving her homeworld three years ago. "You're looking good, too." Her gaze slipped to the right, tracking the incoming ground cars. "Better call me Captain, though."

"Yes, sir, Captain, sir," he quipped, flashing her a grin. A moment later, he sobered, watching the slowing ground cars. "Showtime, people. Make like you're model employees."

The three men and two women with him smirked at that. Ia knew James Chong-Wuu had hired them more because they, too, believed in her cause than because they were "model" anything. Nodding to their young employer, she turned crisply and strode back to the others.

"2nd Platoon B Alpha, C Alpha, secure the perimeter of

this shuttle," Ia ordered, flicking her fingers in the indicated directions. "No one boards this vessel but 1st Company 9th Cordon Special Forces personnel as per the Admiral-General's direct orders. Move out."

Four bodies peeled off and moved out around the landing gear of the ship, rifles in their hands but pointed at the ground for safety. That would change, she knew.

"All other team pairings, you will accompany these gentle-meioas to the warehouse to secure its interior and perimeter. Follow your Platoon sergeants' orders and standard procedures in securing the indicated warehouse, but don't rush, so you don't trip. Once the perimeter has been secured, authorized personnel for entering the warehouse will be members of 1st Company 9th Cordon and the employees of Chong-Wuu Ste-vedores, Incorporated. If you have any questions, refer them up the chain of command if I am not near, or pass it directly to me if I am."

The two ground cars came to a stop. The drivers remained inside, but the first car disgorged two Peacekeepers, their blue-and-white uniforms marked with the standard scalloped-shield badge on their shoulders and caps. On that badge was the corona-and-crown symbol representing the capital city of Our Blessed Mother, Sanctuary. The second car released a third Peacekeeper and a man in a blue-and-gold version of their uniform. His badge had the corona sporting a planetary curve inside, replete with the distinctive coastline squiggle for the local continent.

"Soldiers, move out!" Ia commanded, pointing at James and his crew. She turned to face the Customs agent, whose face reddened as the gravity-weave-wrapped men and women dispersed.

Striding forward, he pointed at the grey-clad bodies spread-ing out and moving at a swift walk. "What do they think they're doing?" he demanded. "This landing pad is for Customs-cleared vehicles only—and that warehouse, too!"

"Captain Ia, Terran United Planets Special Forces," she introduced herself. "Per Sanctuarian Charter regulations Article VIII, Military Contracts, Section E, Supplies, my crew, shuttles, and cargo are listed as exempt from Customs clearance requirements."

"I wasn't notified about this," the Customs agent protested.

The name on his badge—he was now close enough for Ia to read it—simply said *Larkins*. "There was no notification of any military shipments due this week!"

"Our ship hit a hyperrift on the way here, depositing us insystem ahead of schedule, Officer Larkins," Ia said briskly, avoiding the fact it was an artificial wormhole, not the natural one that terminated at the edge of Sanctuarian space. "We are here to deposit our cargo in the emergency bunkers the Terran Space Force installed on your planet three decades ago. This cargo has been designated as war supplies on the manifest. As such, it falls under Article VIII, Section E, and is exempt from all Customs-inspection requirements, as per the Terran defense contract with your planet."

Frowning, Larkins stared at the retreating soldiers, then glanced up the shuttle's ramp. "That does *not* clear your cargo from quarantine restrictions. This is an M-class planet, not a domeworld."

"All cargo has been irradiated and sealed before being boarded at their origination point, as per military regulations regarding the transport of supplies," Ia replied, doing her best to sound like a regulation brick wall placed in his path. "All personnel have been scanned by military biometric sensors in our ship's airlocks, as per regulations, and my crew undergo weekly biometric physicals while en route. No one with an active infectious agent has been permitted to leave our ship. Your colony is safe from quarantine hazards."

Officer Larkins was not easily deterred. He pointed at the shuttle, giving Ia a firm look. "All imports are to be examined by Customs for potential contraband and excise taxes, by order of the Sanctuarian Supreme Council."

"These items are not imports, meioa, nor are they for sale," Ia replied politely, if briskly. She, too, pointed at the shuttle. "They are essential war supplies requisitioned by the Terran Space Force, a Sanctuarian-authorized government entity. By contract, Space Force essential supplies are not to be quarantined, not to be confiscated, and not to be taxed."

"Well, guess what?" Larkins stated, hands going to his hips as he gave her a belligerent look. He had to look up to do so, since she towered over his short, stocky frame by a full head plus. "The rules have now changed. *All* incoming items must submit to inspection by a duly authorized Customs official. I *will* inspect your cargo for contraband before I will allow a single crate to touch Sanctuarian soil."

"Your contract with the Space Force has *not* changed, meioa. By Charter, the terms of our service agreement with your colony take precedence over all local laws in regards to all factors of the services we are contracted to provide," Ia countered. "Unless and until that contract changes, Terran Space Force war and emergency supplies are not subject to inspection, excise taxes, or impounding. The only thing they are required to undergo is standard quarantine irradiation and containment protocols upon initial packaging and loading, which they have undergone."

The Customs official smiled at that. It wasn't a pleasant smile. "Ah! But I don't *know* that. That means *I* have to board that vessel and inspect those crates *personally*."

He poked her in the sternum and turned toward the shuttle.

"By order of the Admiral-General of the Terran United Planets Space Force, unauthorized personnel are strictly forbidden to embark on the TUPSF *Hellfire* or its auxiliary vessels," Ia warned him, raising her voice slightly to compensate for the descent of another orbital shuttle in the distance. "This directive includes our shuttle craft, meioa."

Larkins sneered at her and gestured for the three Peacekeepers to join him in heading toward the ramp. Ia lifted her head slightly, catching the attention of Private Helia Dixon. One of the few people in her crew who had prior experience with Ia's brand of leadership, the private waited for the official and his escort to close half the distance, then quickly lifted her rifle into position. Her teammate, Corporal Henderson, followed suit.

"Attention, meioas! You are approaching a restricted sector. You are requested to stay back from this vessel by ten meters," Henderson warned Officer Larkins. Positioned as he was on the port side of the loading ramp, with Dixon on the starboard four meters away, the pair had a decent cross-fire field on the quartet. "This is your first warning!"

Larkins slowed. At his back, the three Peacekeepers reached for their sidearms but hesitated about drawing since the two soldiers had the drop on them already.

The Customs officer frowned over his shoulder at Ia. "You people wouldn't dare stop me."

"I'm sorry, meioa," Ia replied, tucking her hands behind her back and putting her boots shoulder-width apart in Parade Rest. "These soldiers are under orders from Admiral-General Christine Myang herself. Entering that orbital ship requires Ultra-level clearance. Anyone attempting to board it without the proper clearance level and authorization is to be shot and tried for Grand Treason in a Terran military court of law."

Stopping, Officer Larkins narrowed his eyes, studying Ia. "You're kidding. You wouldn't dare."

Bringing her arm out from behind her back, Ia pointed at the shuttle, once again playing the hard-asteroid . . . and secretly enjoying it. She really did not like the arrogance these Church-backed government officials were being allowed to display these days. "Anyone attempting to board that vessel or its sister shuttles from the TUPSF *Hellfire* without the proper clearance authorizations arranged in advance, or attempting to interfere with the delivery of its cargo of essential supplies, is to be shot and charged with attempted Grand Treason against the Terran Space Force.

"The right by the Space Force to assert and uphold the required working conditions for our missions is covered by the Independent Colonyworld Sanctuary Charter of Rights and Responsibilities, Article VIII, Section E, paragraphs 1 through 3." She bit back a smile, adding soberly, "You are welcome to assist your government in petitioning the Terran Space Force to have those Charter rules changed or our military services dropped, gentlemeioa. Until then, that vessel is a restricted sector which you are not authorized to transgress, and our cargo is exempt from all examinations."

From the way he sneered, he didn't believe her. Turning back, he took another step toward the shuttle ramp. That earned him his second warning.

"Meioa! You are entering a restricted sector without proper authorization! You will stay ten meters from this vessel or you *will* be shot," Corporal Henderson ordered the other man, sighting down the scope of his JL-42.

"I am Abram Larkins, a duly authorized I.C. Sanctuary Customs Officer, and I *will* inspect that shuttle!" he argued, pointing at the ramp.

"I am Corporal Henderson, of the TUPSF Special Forces doesn't-give-a-*shakk*," Henderson warned him, "and I *will* shoot you if you violate this restricted zone by moving one meter closer, meioa. I am only required to give you two warnings. I have given you three. One step closer, and you don't get any more, meioa."

Officer Larkins hesitated. Ia watched warily. This was where the moment could go either way. Behind them, she could hear some of the others returning from the warehouse. So could he. Glancing over his shoulder, Larkins squinted against the bright sunlight slanting in through the clouds to the east.

She heard Santori bark a short order. The advancing men and women moved off to the right, circling around to approach from Dixon's side of the shuttle. That gave the two guarding the ramp a clear field of fire. At the front of the parked shuttle, the two members of B Alpha glanced occasionally toward the back of the small ship but kept most of their attention on the rest of the tarmac, scanning for other possible points of interference.

Their opponent made up his mind. Larkins turned and poked his finger in her direction. "You may think you've won, but this is an *independent* colonyworld—we will not put up with the tyranny of the Terrans on our sovereign soil!"

"If your government wishes to formally terminate its contract with the Terran Space Force and provide for its own interstellar protection needs, your government is welcome to do so. Until that time, our agreement stands as written. We are storing these supplies on your homeworld in preparation for the coming Second Salik War," Ia stated, gesturing back and forth between the shuttle and the warehouse. "You may look at the quarantine stamps on the crates as they are transferred from the shuttle to the warehouse to verify they have undergone the necessary decontamination protocols.

"You may *not* board our shuttles, you may not enter the warehouse, and you may not open the crates." She tucked her hand behind her back, resuming full Parade Rest again. "Do you have any questions at this time, meioa?"

"The Salik won't come here," Larkins dismissed, wrinkling his nose. "We're too far away."

"There are no defensive barriers in space, meioa," Ia said, raising her voice once again as another shuttle took off. This was the spaceport's busy time, in the hours of relative calm between the morning and early-evening thunderstorms. "No natural terrain to keep them from going anywhere they want to go, save only the ongoing efforts of the various Alliance militaries to keep them contained. Those efforts are failing. It is our contractual duty to ensure that every world under Terran Space Force protection is supplied and defended to the best of our ability. Until such time as that contract is terminated, that means we will continue to protect you."

The subtext in her speech, the unspoken attitude behind her stance and her words, implied the phrase, ". . . even if we don't like each other." Ia stared him down until Sergeant Santori stopped at her side, giving her a salute. Ia shifted to Attention and returned it.

"Captain. The warehouse is secured, sir," Santori told her. She was flying solo for this job since it was technically second watch on the ship, and that meant Lieutenant Spyder had command of the bridge while Ia was on the surface. "Awaiting further orders, sir."

"Good work, Sergeant. Maintain the current perimeter with half our troops. The rest will unstrap and remove the cargo sledges from the hold. Officer Larkins is permitted to visually inspect the seals on the first batch of crates," she added, looking at the Customs agent. "He is not permitted within ten meters of shuttle or warehouse, and he is not permitted to open any crates, but your soldiers are to cooperate and assist the official in examining the external seals regarding quarantine protocols."

"Understood, sir." Turning on her heel, Santori barked orders, sending the pairs of teammates toward the ramp; Dixon hastily moved forward so that they could cross behind her rather than in front of her field of fire. They fiddled with the controls of their gravity weaves as they did so, permitting each Human to move closer than three meters without the risk of the fields making them stagger.

Ia resumed Parade Rest, a visual, grey-and-black brick wall of military efficiency. Larkins looked between her and the ship. Henderson didn't lower his rifle; neither did Dixon. Finally, he grimaced and moved back. The two members of C Squad Alpha lowered their weapons but did not shoulder them. A minute later, the first of the ground-sledges rolled down the ramp. Their motors whined as each one made the transition from the interior of the ship, where gravity fields in the ceiling counteracted some of the planet's pull, to the full force of Sanctuary's 3. 21Gs.

Santori moved up beside her, watching the sledges roll a good twenty-fives meters away from the ship before her teams stopped them for the requested visual inspection. Ia's skin twitched at her proximity. Not because she feared the woman would touch her, triggering her precognitive gifts, but because the gravity field projected by that purple weave was messing with her sense of down.

The tanned woman moved a little closer and quietly asked, "Do all the government officials on this planet have their heads up their asteroids? Or did we just get lucky?"

"They all have official attitude-problem approval from the main political party, these days," Ia confirmed, equally under her breath. "That party has been turning increasingly xeno-phobic in recent years—and by xeno, they include nonnative Humans lumped in among the Solaricans and such. That's why, with the exception of myself, no one is to go anywhere alone on this world . . . and the crew will go in uniform at all times. I don't want anyone mistaking them for weave-wrapped tourists."

"I'm not comfortable with that exception, sir," Maria Santori warned her. "You'd be a prime target out on your own."

"I can fake being a loyal follower of the local religious movement far better than you can—I *will* have to go places in the next few days that the Terrans cannot, Sergeant," Ia said, shifting her gaze to Santori. "This is that third war front I warned you about at the cadre meeting last week. A war of ideology so far, but a war nonetheless."

"Which is why you shouldn't go alone, sir," the sergeant countered. "The vid industry makes a fortune off stories of one-meioa armies, but that isn't reality."

"Considering where I have to go, a gravity weave would scream 'outsider' too loudly. Even our lovely 3rd Platoon leader would have difficulty walking around for long in this gravity, and she's the second heaviest heavyworlder on the ship," Ia pointed out. "I *won't* be alone, Sergeant. I just won't be with fellow soldiers."

"That's what has me worried. Civilians aren't soldiers," Santori murmured.

A cry from inside the shuttle was followed by a clatter. The man screamed again, and started babbling something about birds setting the world on fire. Officer Larkins and his three blue-and-white-clad Peacekeeper cohorts quickly marked themselves with the corona circle, warding off personal attacks of "the Devil's visions," as the members of the Church of the One True God called the psychic outbreaks. They could strike anyone anywhere on or within orbit of Sanctuary, give or take a few thousand miles.

It looked like one of her crew was suffering the first outbreak of the day. Ia sighed and turned toward the ramp. "I'll handle this. The important thing is to make sure nobody else touches him."

Santori nodded. "We heard your lectures on the phenomenon, sir. Trust me, he's all yours."

CHAPTER 5

So many things to keep track of, back then. So many defenses to set up, so many reactions to be readied, and so many tricks to be traded. All in the effort of helping as many people as possible survive the coming wars. Much of it, ironically, won't bear fruit until long after both you and I are gone, but it was worth it.

Somehow, in that visit to my home, I actually managed to make it home. I got to see my family again. That's a rare thing in an interstellar military. But it wasn't the same as it had been before—and I'm not speaking hyperbole. It literally wasn't the same home anymore. Fanaticism had seen to that, ahead of schedule.

~Ia

JANUARY 19, 2496 T.S.
CENTRAL WARREN

The cavern was a far cry from the scorched, soaked rubble that had once been Momma's Restaurant. Vast and rugged, it was awkwardly lit in pools of daylight hues thanks to the scaffolding that climbed the upper half of the magma-carved walls. Lights, large and small, did their best to dispel the gloom. Part of a deep, ancient system of lava tunnels, the cavern was nothing more than a giant, amorphous blob of former gas bubbles suspended permanently in cooled stone.

From the rough-shaped terrace of what would become the *cafeterium*, the level where many restaurants would bloom, Ia could see the shadowed cleft that would eventually be turned into the Director's Grove, a private garden for the successive leaders of the Free World Colony. The main cavern would be a combination of leisure gardens, farm gardens, and water-treatment gardens, aquaculture and aquaponics similar to the lifesupport bays found on most starships.

Some of the gardens were being sculpted as she watched, by hand labor and by robotics, by shovel and bulldozer. The rumble of sandhogs in the distance bespoke the efforts of digging crews to expand the network of side tunnels leading away from the ragged corners of the echoing cavern. There were other noises, too. People chatted and called out instructions. Hammers and picks banged into stone; shovels and buckets chuffed through piles of dirt. And from close by, someone sighed.

Sinking onto the cushion-lined bench someone had carved into the balcony wall overlooking the activities, Aurelia Jones-Quentin offered her daughter a cup of cocoa thickened with cream. "It's not so bad. Noisy day and night . . . or what passes for day and night, but not bad. Prime real estate, *gataki mou*."

Despite her ongoing efforts to get her parents to see her as an adult, as the soldier and the prophet instead of their little "kitten," Ia let the nickname pass. Hot cocoa and the reassurances that her family was alright were the things she wanted to dwell on right now. "I'm sorry they sped up the timetable on the restaurant. I saw the rubble."

"All the important things had long since been evacuated," Aurelia dismissed. "Unless you count some of your old toys and the actual bedding. Thorne remembered your warning him there was a small chance it might happen early. He insisted on stripping the kitchen, so most of that was salvaged, too. And you saw the new kitchen, so it's even better, *eyah*?"

"*Eyah*," Ia agreed. Twisting on the bench, she put her back to the low wall and stared at the coarse frontage that would one day gleam with colorful tiles and polished stone. "How much of the food is still coming from overhead?"

"Ugh. Sixty percent or more. We're a long ways from the

arcological self-sufficiency you've demanded," Aurelia muttered. Off in the distance, one of the three or four hundred Free World Colonists dropped and clutched at her head, wailing in the *irit'zi*, the Fire Girl Prophecy cry. Aurelia rolled her eyes. "It'd go a lot faster, too, if *that* didn't keep interrupting our daily lives. Is there any way you know of to stop the damn visions, *gataki mou*?"

"If you're asking your little girl, then no," Ia shot back dryly.

Her mother stared at her for a long moment, then sighed. "Fine. You're not my little kitten anymore. Is there any way to stop these visions, O Prophet of a Thousand Years?"

"No." This time, she accompanied her reply with a wry smile, amused at the older woman's eye roll in response. "Endure and learn from them. Well, okay," she amended, "there *is* a way to tone them down. When everyone in the FWC has studied, practiced, and reinforced their minds with basic psychic mental centering and shielding techniques, then they will be less likely to be overwhelmed by Fire Girl visions. But stop them? No. They won't stop. Welcome to Sanctuary."

The older woman let out a rude noise at that, somewhere between a raspberry and a sigh. "If we could afford to move off-world, we would. And yes, I'm including the cost in lives as well as the monetary expense."

She started to say more, but a clutch of workers came into view, laughing and chatting as they headed for the restaurant. Right now, it was doing more walk-up business than sit-down, with a modified menu. There were plenty of tables, but few servers. Rolling her eyes, Aurelia leaned back in a moment of rest, gathering her energy to get up and go take their orders.

"Relax, Ma," Ia told her, and nodded at a dark-skinned man coming out from behind the counter. "Marble has this covered. I can't stay out here for long. I have to go back to work turning all those blood-beads I sent you into precognitive wreaths in a few moments. How's Mom doing?" Ia meant her biological mother, Aurelia's wife Amelia.

"Upset at the loss of the wall harp, frustrated that she only gets to see the surface one day out of three, and settling back into her element now that she can cook again," her other mother admitted. "She's also not too sure about Fyfer and Thorne both moving in with Rabbit in the next few months. Not that the girl couldn't use the help, but she's stubborn."

Ia sipped at her cocoa, keeping quiet on that subject. Her brothers would sort out their living situation without her interference. That, and it was good cocoa.

Thick and rich, delicately bordered between bitter and sweet, it conjured up memories of their old, cramped home. Memories of listening to the winter rains pound on the plexi roof over their upstairs apartment. The smell of baked topado cakes and pastries. The sight and sound of her biomother explaining why she preferred cilantro to parsley in her dishes, even though the herb was less sturdy and less likely to grow well in Sanctuary's heavy gravity.

The cries in the distance ended. Whoever it was, the woman would be picking herself up and shaking off the mind-clouding images. Everyone down here knew what the standard visions were: a woman with a burning bird on her back, the spires of the now half-built main cathedral wreathed in flames, of great golden-glowing ships taking to the skies. A horrific wall of stolen star-stuff threatening to engulf and snuff out all the light in the galaxy. Someone being whipped in public, among dozens of other images.

If she saw something new, Ia knew the woman would report it to one of the clergy who had also begun to move down below the surface of their beleaguered world. Time pressed in on her, reminding Ia she didn't have enough hours in the day, and few minutes. Rising, she lifted the cup in her hand.

"Mind if I take this with me?" she asked her mother.

Aurelia, sipping from her own cup, nodded. "Make sure you leave it in the kitchen sink—the apartment sink, that is. I'll send Amelia to you with something to eat when she has another break."

Nodding, Ia bent and kissed her mother on the cheek. The contact, brief as it was, let her sense her mother's mood. Tired, stressed, but still strong. Still capable of doing what her daughter—scratch that—of doing what the Prophet had asked of her. But she was still her mother's child. "I love you, Ma. I'm glad I have you and Mom on my side."

"And Thorne, and Fyfer, and that not-so-evil mastermind pretending to be a little girl," Aurelia quipped. She flipped her hand, first at her daughter, then at the dirty plate and silverware on the low table in front of the bench. "Go on, go back to the apartment and finish your holy task. I'll bus your dishes back to the restaurant. Though next time, you'll owe me a tip."

Nodding her thanks, Ia moved away. Her mothers' commute was a bit longer than before. Rather than living directly over their restaurant, they lived five levels up, though they did have one of the largest apartments currently available. Mostly because it abutted a warehouse cavern that would one day be turned into a combination of multidenominational chapel and dance hall. Freedom of faith was a core tenet of the Free World Colony. Freedom of movement was vitally important to the psyches of the residents who would soon live out their lives underground.

Her red-hued civilian clothes didn't set her apart from the others using the lifts to get from floor to floor. Everyone wore cheerful colors down here, to liven up the dull curves of stone surrounding them. Bright shades of blue and yellow, purple and green mingled with orange and plenty of red. Her height and her shock of chin-length hair were what set her apart, taller than most everyone else by at least two dozen centimeters and readily recognized by her snow-white locks. Old-woman hair.

In fact, a few of the men and women she passed did double takes, recognizing her. A few more started to reach out to her, to touch the Prophet each one knew was responsible for finding and settling this place. A subtle shake of Ia's head was all it took to keep their fingers to themselves. As unsettling as the Fire Girl outbursts were for others to endure, Ia didn't want to give them a worse mental ride if her gifts decided to destabilize while she was down here.

Some of them murmured condolences over the loss of her parents' shop. Others drifted in her wake, wanting to say something, or to hear her say something. She nodded or shook her head where appropriate, but didn't actually say much. The last thing Ia needed was to have a stray word or phrase misinterpreted by her followers.

One of the recent installations, built in sections, looked like an artistic scribble of pipes lining the rounded corridor she chose, giving it a more oval appearance. The pipes weren't just artistic; they were heat-transference pipes, sucking some of the underground warmth out of the air and stirring it into a refreshing, circulating breeze. The siphoned energy wasn't wasted, either; this place, Central Warren, was over five kilometers below the surface. Thermal energy was constantly being transformed into electrical energy, empowering the various machines and amenities the underground capital needed.

Those amenities included things like lights and doors. Reaching her mothers' apartment, she unlocked it with her palmprint and slipped quietly inside. Another touch of her hand to the panel on the doorframe closed and locked it, allowing her to sag back against the stout plexsteel and relax.

Spine pressed to the door, she sighed slowly in relief, shutting out everything but the sound of her own heart. Then snapped her eyes open at the sound of rapid footsteps. Her younger brother, Fyfer, flew at her, all grins and dark curls bouncing. He had gained a couple centimeters since she had last seen him, but still stood shorter than her by nearly a full head. Tall for a Sanctuarian, but not abnormally so. Then again, their fellow colonists wouldn't reattain anything close to her semilofty height for at least another five, six generations, if not more.

"Hey, gorgeous, long time no see!" Giving her a hug and a peck on the cheek, he reached up and ruffled her locks. Ia put up with it for a moment, then pushed him back and ruffled his own hair with her free hand, mindful of the mug carried in the other one. Good-natured, Fyfer stepped free and bowed, gesturing beyond the entry hall. "Welcome to our humble new abode, sister dear. Allow me to show you around."

She waved him off. This new, underground residence was a far cry from the cramped two-bedroom home her parents had known for most of their adult lives, but it was familiar from the times she had watched her family move through its rooms as she studied the future possibilities of their lives. "Already seen it. I'm going back to the storage hall to make more wreaths."

"Still not going to tell us how you're doing it, hm?" her younger brother asked, following her down the hall that led past common and private rooms alike. Fyfer tsked under his breath. "Selfish of you. Crysium's the hardest known substance. Just think of the armor we could make with it!"

"Just think of the I'm-not-telling-you-whats I could make with it," she quipped back. "You're lucky I brought you snow all the way from Earth."

Fyfer snorted. "As if Mom or Ma would let us make snow

cones out of it. Me, I want to *taste* the Motherworld. Bring me my own chunk next time, will you?"

Chuckling, Ia shook her head. Palming open the lock on the door leading to the warehouse, she stepped inside. Strange blocks and lines of shadow and light illuminated the far end of the room. Fyfer followed her inside, hitting the control panel for the lights. Like most forms of illumination used by Terrans not actually living on Earth, the lamps lit up in the same spectrum of colors as Sol, the parent star for their species.

The shadows had been cast by the stacks and stacks of bead-filled boxes Ia had received, altered, and sent back over the last year and a half. The angled lines of light came from the conifer-like sprays of crysium, painstakingly broken off their rock outcrops on the planet's surface and transported down here by Thorne's order.

Each spray was at least two meters tall and a meter and a half wide at its base; the fifty or more shafts that made up the limbs of the spray varied in thickness from the diameter of her biceps to smaller than the span of her wrist. In Standard gravity, they would have weighed two tonnes on average. On Sanctuary, they weighed over three times that—and these were merely small ones, the kind that were relatively easy to transport. There were sprays on the surface that were easily eight meters tall and five to six in diameter, and crystalline behemoths that were even larger.

Draining her cup, Ia set it on top of a stack of emptied crates. A flick of her mind unlocked one of the waiting, full boxes. Like a swarm of peach-tinted glass bees, the beads inside swirled up and soared out of the box, following her telekinetically. Stopping in front of one of the sprays, Ia reached up and caressed the shaft; it sang faintly in the back of her mind, boosting and amplifying her abilities, though not by a lot. Unshaped, raw, natural crysium could only do so much.

Bead-bees floating at her shoulder, hands on the nearest shaft, Ia closed her eyes and flipped her mind down, in, and out, landing on the timeplains. Instinct and habit guided her, lifting the banks between the right and wrong creeks, altering the flow of the timestreams, the life-streams of the men and women who lived on this world. Instinct and habit merged crystal to crystal, some of it tainted with her own blood, the majority of it tainted with the discarded matter of passing

Meddlers. Instinct and habit, practiced in her dreams, guided hand and mind into shaping chunks of the material in a complex process achieved without conscious thought.

But that was alright. Like water running toward the sea, it was important for everything she wanted to drain into the right bay. Pick the wrong part of the coast, and one could end up mired in an aimless swamp or be sucked into the mud of a tidal flat. Ia didn't completely understand her abilities; they operated as much by instinct as by design sometimes. But she did have faith in them, and that meant letting the instincts of her mind shape the rings more than the conscious directing of her thoughts.

Something hit her. Blinking out of her trance, Ia eyed the twisted lump of translucent mineral in her hands. Hunger struck her in the next second. In the third moment, something struck her again. Turning, she looked as it flopped to the floor. A shoe. Nearby was another, matching one.

"Do I have your attention now?" Fyfer asked her. He wiggled his sock-clad toes and grinned.

Before she could respond, Ia heard the quiet beep of the comm embedded in her arm unit. Sighing, she made sure her headset was still secured over her ear, then thumbed the audio channel open. *"Ia. Go."*

"Ia? About time! Captain, where are you?" she heard Harper demand.

From the stacks of rings and absence of two whole sprays, she had been concentrating for some time. Her thoughts were scattered, her concentration fragmented. Wrinkling her nose at the rumpled lump of crystal in her hand, Ia replied, *"Busy. What's the emergency?"*

"3rd Platoon B Beta, Privates Gwen Yé and Solomon Sutrara, were arrested just under an hour ago on charges of 'conspiring to commit heresy' . . . whatever that means," Harper told her. *"Sutrara was smart enough to record all but the first minute on his arm unit, and managed to download it to the ship before they demanded he remove it."*

That wasn't a move Ia had expected. *"I did lecture the troops about not going into any churches, right?"*

"You did, but apparently they were outside the church, on the plexcrete sidewalk near one of the side doors."

"Tell the Peacekeepers that first off, RCS 1107.6 states

clearly that all walkways, sidewalks, and so forth are public easements, and not Church property. Secondly, all military personnel who commit crimes are to be remanded into military custody for military justice, not civilian custody or justice." She paused a moment, thinking, then nodded. *". . . Right. Send down 2nd Platoon A Gamma, Privates Ateah and Sousa—there should be a box in the storage locker off the officers' mess with black Military Peacekeeper armbands in it.*

"Slap a pair on those two and send 'em down to pick up Yé and Sutrara. Inform the Sanctuarian Peacekeepers that the matter will be looked into and the soldiers punished accordingly, as the Space Force takes religious rights and freedoms seriously. I can't call up the relevant sections and paragraphs at the moment. Consult with Sadneczek on that," she instructed him. *"Then call the jail, let them know you're sending two MPs, and that you'd like copies of all depositions for their military tribunal."*

"Sir, yes, sir. I hope this works," Harper added. *"What's the ETA on your return to the ship?"*

Ia eyed the crystalline trees still awaiting her. She had only transformed a fraction of what she needed to make, maybe a couple percent. *"I'm not sure if I'm going to be able to leave anytime soon, at this rate . . ."*

"Do I have to hit you again with a shoe?" Fyfer asked her, recapturing her attention. He spread his hands, rolling his eyes. "You're the commanding officer of a slagging *ship*, Sis! One with *carte blanche*. Pack up all the crysium and blood beads you want, go do it on board the *Hellfire* at your leisure, and send the rest back to us with the Afaso. *They'll* get the packages through."

She checked the timestreams. It would crowd her schedule further on the ship but free up a bit more time here and now. Ia considered his words, then nodded. *"Harper, I'm going to need a series of shuttle drops in a couple days to a site east of the mountains. We'll need a couple of the holds set aside for bulky, heavy cargos. And tell Grizzle to order a couple hundred palm-locked cargo crates—the collapsible kind; otherwise, we won't have the storage space. But get on those MP rescues fast. And make* sure *you get those arm units back. I don't want Church officials getting their hands on military tech—intimidate them*

*with threats of arresting them for theft of Terran government
property if you don't get them back immediately."*

"Aye, Captain. Anything else?" he asked.

*"Yeah, call me in an hour if the extraction doesn't work.
You have an eighty-five percent chance that it should, though."*

"Understood. Harper out."

Shutting off the comm link, she glanced at her brother. He
shrugged and gestured at his shoes. "Can I put them back
on, now?"

"Yeah." Nudging them with her foot, she tumbled them his
way physically, rather than using her telekinesis. Using a combination of her precognition, her electrokinesis, and her telekinesis to make all these wreaths was exhausting enough. She
didn't need to waste the mental energy when a flick of her foot
would work. "You may need to get my attention again in about
an hour, so stick around. And in two hours, I have to head to
my psychic ethics review. I don't dare miss that. It's the last
one I'll get before heading off to war."

Her brother bowed dramatically, palms pressed together
like a djinn. A lock of dark brown hair flopped over his brow
as he did so. "I shall be your personal shoe-throwing alarm
clock, O Prophet. *Ia'n sud'dha*, I live to serve!"

The mock-dirty look she gave him only provoked a laugh
from her brother.

JANUARY 21, 2496 T.S.

Crouched beside Bei Ninh, former Sharpshooter and bronze
medalist, Ia could smell his sweat. Same with Jane Loewen,
though her odor wasn't quite as rank. Neither of them seemed
happy at having to move without the benefit of the deactivated
gravity weaves wrapped around their bodies, never mind skulk
through the shadows of the half-built Sacred Cathedral of the
Light and the Truth on an excessively heavy world. The exertion
required for moving silently as well as swiftly expressed itself
in tired muscles and sweat-soaked skin.

The same could be said for Ninh's wife, Bagha, and her
temporary teammate for this mission, William Xavine. Like
Loewen, Xavine was a former Troubleshooter, and something

of an expert in surveillance gear. Each of the two crouched by their Sharpshooter partner, special cartridges in hand. Kneeling between the pair, Helstead peered through a set of enhancement goggles at the half-built walls. Finally, she nodded and whispered coordinates.

The two Sharpshooters, both wearing goggles of their own, nodded and lifted their guns. Helstead's job was to identify the spots in the architecture that her compatriot, Lieutenant Rico, had selected, with some help from Ia. Elbows braced on a packing crate, they each took aim through their scopes and fired. The soft *phunt* of the air guns was echoed a second or so later by the faint *splat* of the gel-based projectiles hitting their targets. The two Troubleshooters quickly consulted their palm scanners. Xavine nodded, but Loewen shook her head.

"It broke on impact," she warned Ninh, and handed him another cartridge. *"Shoot again."*

Nodding, he replaced the expended shell with the fresh one, aimed carefully once it was loaded, and fired. Their movements were subtle, difficult to see in the darkened interior of the cathedral. The *hiss* and *thwap* of the payload's being delivered was more blatant than their careful moves. Ia did see his satisfied nod, though. He knew he'd made the shot.

"Perfect." Closing her scanner, Loewen tucked it back into her bag, agreeing with him.

"Next target," Ia whispered, and led the way out onto the main floor. Like all man-made walking surfaces on Sanctuary, it was made from plexcrete, the odd amalgamation of several rubbery substances that cushioned impacts. It was still possible for someone of her height to badly injure her head if she should fall wrong, but the odds of actually cracking that skull hard enough to break it or the brain encased inside were survivably low.

Plexcrete came in several varieties, many of which were patterned to look like various long-lasting shades of granite. The Church Elders had spared no expense; this particular plexcrete floor had been laid out in an elaborate pattern of dark and light diamonds, lines, squares, triangles and more. In the daylight, it would appear polished, unscuffed as yet by the passage of thousands of worshipping feet. It would also glow, she knew, with bright golds and rich blues, blood reds, silvery greys, and regal greens once daylight touched it.

The scaffolding along the southern wall would eventually be replaced by a great stained-glass window marked with a similar pattern, carefully positioned so that when the planet aligned just right with the local star at the solstices and equinoxes, the sunlight shining through at noon would match the colorful patterns at certain points along the floor. Side windows to the east and west, nestled between the old-fashioned flying buttresses, would show colors that would overlap and blend. Between the floor and the windows, the carvings on the walls and the paintings on the ceiling, the Sacred Cathedral of the Light and the Truth, Our Blessed Mother, would be the single most spectacular structure on the whole planet, and remain so for at least two hundred years.

Between then and now, Ia wanted her fellow Free World Colonists to have an ear to the ground, inside. Literally. Hurrying up the steps of the altar dais, she crouched and pulled out a pair of palm-sized miniature crowbars. Inserting them carefully between two slabs of colored plexcrete, she pried the pieces apart, muscles flexing hard. Loewen reached her first. Fishing out the next piece of spying equipment, she dropped it into the small gap.

Freeing her tools, Ia checked her grip on the electronic surveillance supposedly keeping this site safe. Everything was still secure, showing nothing out of the ordinary. She waited for Loewen to peer into the crack and nod, confirming the device was properly placed, then scuttled across the dais to the area that would one day house the seats of the Church Elders as they sat and listened to the various services.

This time, Xavine reached her first and dropped a surveillance pickup into the rubbery crack she made. Normally a fancy floor might be installed last to prevent it from being damaged during construction. On Sanctuary, that cushioning was needed as soon as it could be laid down, right after the foundation was secured.

She pried apart a third spot, and a fourth, picking seemingly random locations that would bring the most benefit in eavesdropping in the years ahead. Beckoning the others onward, she led the way toward a hallway—no door, just yet—which in turn led to a set of steps. The four lightworlders grunted in the effort to try climbing them. Giving up, Loewen dropped to her knees halfway up, her shaking head nothing more than a subtle change in the shadows of the stairwell. Ia moved back down to help her up the stairs.

"Almost there," Ia whispered in encouragement. *"Just seven more to place, then we can escape."*

The Troubleshooter panted, gritted her teeth, and let Ia help her back into motion.

"I'm not sure my knees can take much more of this, sir," Ninh whispered back, bracing himself with one gloved hand on the wall as they passed. Most of their clothes were common civilian garb, though they had taken the precaution of donning gloves and caps. *"If it's 2Gs back home when you climb a set of stairs, that's over 6Gs here per step."*

His wife poked him in the ribs. She breathed heavily with each step but managed to pass him all the same. *"Fire in the hole, Ninh. Fire in the hole . . ."*

He stuck out his tongue but struggled upward in her wake. It wasn't the fact that they were working in three times the gravity that was hard. It was the fact that climbing stairs roughly doubled the forces at work, and certainly doubled the effort. Ia let them rest at the top of the stairs but only for a minute. More than that, and they wouldn't want to keep moving. Urging them along the plexcrete-padded hallway, she nodded at the first of three rooms.

The left-hand wall in this one had a large window opening overlooking the altar, which would eventually be covered in stained glass, obscuring the fact that the room would become the Grand Prelate's office. Without the window, though, they were free to aim their air guns at the sculpted columns already set in place. After that was done, she guided them into dropping two more packets between the rubbery floor tiles.

Both the gels and the card-thin pickups worked on kinetic-energy principles. The noises reverberating through them would empower them, permitting them to last for a good fifty years, if not longer. Their broadcast range would be short, barely two hundred meters up and outward, and only fifty or so down through solid ground. But that would be just enough for the FWC's transceivers to pick up and relay their scans farther down the line.

The next two offices were equally rough-walled, if smooth-floored. One would be the seat of the financial officer for the Church, the other the security officer. Both were vital for controlling the pacing of the next two centuries. Taking their time, doing it right, took another fifteen minutes. As soon as the last pickup was dropped in place, Ia tucked her crowbars away. *"There we go. Now to get out through the back door unseen. We're slightly ahead of schedule, but not enough to evade the security guards any other route. This way."*

The "back door" wasn't a door, per se, but rather a set of scaffolding leading off the back of the cathedral. Accessed through a window opening, it was a short climb down the ladders to the ground. Short, but exhausting for her companions. Ia let them rest twice more before they slipped back through the slight gap in the chain-link fence guarding the site. From there, she urged them in quiet murmurs to keep going until they were physically out of sight.

". . . Now, sir?" Xavine finally asked, resting against the side of a building a block away. All four lightworlders were panting heavily from their exertions. Helstead also rested against the wall, though she recovered her breath faster than the others.

"Now," Ia agreed, speaking in a normal tone, if still quietly. Relieved, the other five turned their gravity weaves back on, to the lowest setting that could tolerate the presence of other weaves nearby and still counteract a good chunk of the gravity. Relieved for a different reason, she gently released her grip on the low-light cameras, infrared detectors, and other sensors scattered around the large construction zone, though she didn't sag against the wall like her crewmates had.

Finally adapted to her home after several days of more or less living on the surface while her ship stayed parked in orbit, Ia removed her knit cap, worn to hide her too-pale, damp hair. The others had sweated from the gravity, while she had sweated from trying to electrokinetically hide their actions from the construction site's surveillance equipment. Doing so without also tripping the KI sensors placed around the Cathedral hadn't been easy.

The Church Elders hated psychic abilities. The mental exercises required to discipline a psi's mind lent strength to that mind, strength and resistance to outside influences. Strong minds were not easily swayed minds, and that meant rebellious minds, according to internal Church doctrine. The last thing they wanted was a strong telepath or a clairvoyant spying on them.

"Well. That was fun," Helstead finally said, tucking her gloves into her shirt pocket. "Back to the pub?"

"Back to the pub," Ninh agreed. "I could use a stiff drink."

"I think I'm going to *be* stiff," Loewen countered, flexing her back. The push-pull force of her weave's field nudged into Ia, who staggered sideways and swallowed against the wobble in her inner ear. Loewen grimaced and straightened up again. "Sorry, sir."

Ia waved it off. "It happens. You heard Helstead. Back to the pub, meioas. Drinks are on me. One lightly alcoholic, the rest non. You don't want to stagger in this gravity."

The lightworlders groaned but pushed away from the wall, heading up the street. It was late, but the pub selected as their return point was the kind open all night. As they walked, Helstead moved up beside Ia.

"So, Captain . . . sorry, Ia," she amended, dropping the rank. "You said you couldn't just waltz in and use your own gifts in a solo mission because manipulating everything would trigger KI sensors. I get that. It's a perfectly valid concern, especially at your strength. And I can understand why you'd want to bug the offices. But why the main sanctuary? Nothing's going to be said out there that's particularly sensitive."

"Yeah, why *did* we do that? I'll follow your orders, sir," Xavine muttered, "but, well, I'm not too comfortable with targeting a religion. It's far too easy to turn offended members of a faith into violently righteous fanatics," he added under his breath. "So I'm not comfortable with any of what we did. I *did* it, but . . ."

Loewen shook her head, though not in a disagreeing way. "Welcome to the military, meioa; if it doesn't break the most common laws of ethics and sentients, you do what you're told. But *I'd* like to know, too, Cap . . . uh, Ia. If it's okay for us to ask?"

"It's okay. And it's simple. Propaganda. Whatever the Church Prelates preach from the pulpit will be taken as gospel truth by the topside masses," Ia told them. "Some of it actually will be the truth, though much of it will be distorted and edited. In order to fight that propaganda, the other half will need to know what's being said so they can separate truth from falsehood."

"I still don't get why you can't just help these people to win the fight right away," Bagha said. She shook her head. "Two hundred years of civil war sounds like an awful lot of deaths."

"Seventy-five percent of it will be a cold war, if not more, so it's not as many deaths as you'd think," Ia said. She saw the doubt in their eyes and shook her head. "I *know* how you feel. A large part of me doesn't like it, either. But if I'm given a choice between three people dying now, or three million people dying later—for-sure-dying, not just maybe-dying—then I'll take the three people now and do it with my own hands if I must.

"If I have to be screamed at in my conscience for the rest of my life, I'd rather it were by the ghosts of just those three, and not the three million," she finished quietly. Honestly.

"Well, we're talking about a lot more deaths than just three, sir," Xavine argued, as they approached the back door of the pub. It was owned and visited by friends of the FWC, which meant everyone inside would be willing to testify that the six off-worlders—Ia counted, now that she was in the military—had been in the back room all night, on the slim chance their proximity to the Cathedral had been noticed.

"And I'm talking about a lot more deaths than just three million. Here's the pub, so this subject is dropped. Pick a new one. Like the fact that the first round of drinks are on me," Ia stated, lifting her chin at the far door as they entered, the one that led to the front of the tavern. "You've earned it."

Helstead wrinkled her nose. "I think not. Every time I try to drink with a gravity weave on, the damned water in the glass sloshes to the left and tries to go up my nose."

"Then stop drinking with your left hand," Xavine teased her.

Helstead pointed at him. "Watch it, meioa; we're not always gonna be off duty, you know."

Wisely, he ducked behind Ia, who merely shook her head. Opening the bag slung over her shoulder, she held it out. "Give me the transceivers. I'll get them to the right people."

Xavine pulled his out. He hesitated before placing the first palm-sized unit inside, though. "This *is* approved of by the Command Staff, right?"

"Of course it is," Ia told him. "Everything I do has been approved."

Technically, her words were true. Technically, she could say them with a straight face. Technically . . . she was abusing her *carte blanche*. But Xavine and the others didn't know that.

Nodding, he deposited the other transceivers into her bag. Loewen did the same, then hooked her arm around his and dragged him off to the front room for a snack run. They staggered a bit as their weaves interacted, but weren't too fazed. Ia detoured into the kitchen halfway down the hall. Turning down the heat on his cooking unit, the short-order cook accepted the bag with a silent nod of thanks and took it into the basement.

There was a door down there that led to an old Terran-installed bunker, which in turn led down into the lava tunnels the Free World Colonists were using as their new home. On the other side of the first door, a bored agent of their underground government waited for the promised bag. Those devices were the top-of-the-line in Terran military espionage. She had already checked the timestreams, and knew the Church had nothing on hand that could detect them.

As for the Command Staff finding out about this little mission, by the time they did, Ia hoped to have far more important battles under way to serve as a distraction, and as proof of the justification behind her actions.

Or to put it another way, it's a simple case of Jack's Law #213, she thought, amused. *When all else fails, cloud the issue with facts.*

JANUARY 23, 2496 T.S.

The last of the cargo crates hummed downward out of sight, thanks to the floor lift. Satisfied the supplies would be safe, Ia turned away. She gave her attention to the five waiting members of her family instead. First was her biomother, Amelia. Seen in the clear light of day rather than the dimmer light found underground, a lot more grey salted her mother's curls than Ia remembered seeing before. Worry lines creased Amelia's freckled brow, but her arms were still strong and warm.

"I hate this, *gataki mou*," her mother muttered into her chest, heavyworlder strong but heavyworlder short. "Just the one more time, right?"

"Just once more, unless things go seriously wrong," Ia

promised. Patting Amelia on the back, she released her and turned to her other mother, Aurelia.

The slightly taller woman squeezed her hard, then stepped back, looking up at her stepdaughter's face. "You go out there, *kardia mou*," she ordered Ia, "and you kick frogtopus asteroid, you hear me? Laser-fried calamari as far as the eye can see."

Fyfer wrinkled his nose. "Eww! Ma!"

Aurelia spread her hands, shrugging. "What? I didn't say she had to *eat* it."

Wrapping an arm around her younger brother, Ia ignored the stares of the soldiers lining up near the main entrance to the spaceport warehouse. Scrubbing her knuckles over his scalp, she mussed his carefully styled hair one last time, then hugged him hard enough to lift him a few centimeters off the ground. She got painfully pinched for her troubles, but laughed, gently letting him drop back down.

Next in line was Rabbit, not a blood relative, unless one counted the fact she was in a complicated relationship with both of Ia's brothers. Rabbit wasn't her birth name, but rather the nickname she had adopted; her two front teeth, prominent in her plain, round face, made the reason self-evident. Her smile dispelled any illusions about a lack of beauty, though.

Kneeling in front of her, Ia held out her arms; even for a heavyworlder, Rabbit was short. She was also pregnant, five months along and having the child naturally rather than via a wombpod. That would put stress on her stocky frame in this gravity, but Ia knew her old school friend could handle it.

She did, however, caution the short woman. "You make sure you start putting your feet up three times a day, you hear? I'll make Thorne literally sweep you off your feet if you don't. You don't want him to throw out his back, now do you?"

Rabbit pushed out her lower lip. She had a brilliant mind behind those doe brown eyes and that moon-round face, but most people severely underestimated her because of her child-like size. The short woman used that illusion ruthlessly at times. Even her own parents, Church officials, thought she was still a little girl at heart. Ia wasn't fooled by that pout and pointed her finger in silent warning. That earned her a rough sigh.

"Fine," Rabbit said, rolling her eyes. "Go ahead and leave me. Just because you're sticking me with managing this whole mess doesn't mean I'm going to forgive you for it."

"Hey, I conned my brothers into doing it, too," Ia said. She hugged her one more time, then nodded downward. "Take care of yourself, so you can take care of him."

"And I told *you* I didn't wanna know the gender," Rabbit protested. "Stupid know-it-all prophets."

"Well, I'm not going to call my niece or nephew an 'it,'" Ia countered. "*Use* the people you've gathered. Share the responsibility. You're the chief Director, so direct the others to do what needs to be done. And put your feet up."

Amelia leaned over and hugged the younger woman. "I'll make sure she does—and if she doesn't, I'll sic my wife on her."

That earned them another pout and mutter from Rabbit. "Oh, now you're just being mean!"

The others laughed. Rising, Ia hugged the last person in the quintet, her half-twin Thorne. The only member of the family taller than her, he had the dusky complexion and dark hair of his mother Aurelia, and the same square chin and almond eyes as their shared father. Unlike Ia, he didn't have any active psychic abilities, just latent ones waiting to be passed on to his offspring. He had practiced the same mental disciplines as a psi, though, which meant Ia could hug him longer than the others.

Physical contact increased the chance of her gifts triggering, which meant she rarely touched anyone for long, for her sanity's sake. But Thorne's future she didn't fear foreseeing. She knew every inch of his timestream possibilities. He was the solid rock in her life, even if he wasn't close enough to be a physical touchstone these days, save for right now. For a moment, Ia allowed herself a few seconds of rest in his arms.

Time pressed in on her, though. Church-loyal officials were closing in on the warehouse, still upset that Ia and her troops had kept them out for so long. Nodding, she signaled him to release her. Pulling her shoulders square and her chin level, she stepped back, shrugging mentally back into the uniform covering her muscles.

Once again she was Captain Ia, ex-Marine, ex-Navy, and currently Special Forces. A Terran soldier with a deadly-efficient reputation that had earned her the nickname of Bloody Mary. She was no longer Iantha Iulia Quentin-Jones, daughter and friend and fellow civilian.

"Directors," she stated, nodding politely to her two brothers and quasi sister-in-law, the unlikely three-headed leadership team for a massive underground resistance movement that was still only halfway started. "Meioa-es," she added, using the feminine form of the honorific on her parents. Off to the side, the lift was coming back up into view, all crates, boxes, and pallets removed by the men and women working in the tunnels below. "Take care of yourselves. We'll be withdrawing the perimeter in two minutes. Peacekeepers will be here in three. I suggest you get out of sight, meioas, for your own safety."

Nodding, Thorne herded the others toward the lift. Turning on her heel, Ia strode toward the main entrance. The door had been rolled down halfway, just high enough for the tallest members of the 2nd Platoon to pass under it without ducking. Wrapped in his own purple web-work, Lieutenant Spyder smiled and saluted her when she came near.

"Nice t' see y' got a soft'n'squishy side, Cap'n," he joked, hand raised formally to his brow.

"Oh, really? Well, my soft'n'squishy side just turned as hard and dangerous as a rogue asteroid again," she shot back dryly, returning the salute. Behind her, beige-clad Chong-Wuu workers used stevedore suits to roll the plexcrete mats back into place, covering up the lidded hole where the hidden lift was once again descending. In front of her stood twenty men and women of the 2nd Platoon. "Lieutenant, run the checklist and pull in all remaining personnel. Six minutes to takeoff."

"Sir, yes, sir," he agreed, turning crisply on his heel. "You 'eard th' Cap'n! Set yer 'Daptive Gravimetrics to Low, an' board th' shuttle. Do *not* double-time it," he added, before activating his arm unit. "*Spyder to D Beta through D Epsilon, pull out. Setcher weaves to Low, an' retreat to th' shuttle in extraction order, noice an' leisurely. You got three minutes t' move, yakkos.*"

Ia followed them outside, her attention on the half dozen cars approaching in the distance. An uncomfortable tingle along her nerves was her only warning. Turning back to the men and women, she hurried up between the ranks, gritting her teeth against the conflicting pulls of so many gravity weaves in close proximity.

Catching the tall bulk of Private First Class C. J. Siano from behind, she ducked as his head flung back, almost cracking into her skull. His deep voice hollered almost painfully loud, caught up in yet another random damned Fire Girl attack. Staggering sideways under his limp weight, she guided his body awkwardly to the ground in a semicontrolled collapse. One that ended up with her bruising her tailbone on the stained grey plexcrete of the tarmac and her leg trapped under the power pack strapped to his back, but which didn't end with him hitting his head.

The others scattered, then surged forward to help them up, concerned by his wordless screams and thrashing limbs. Ia quickly shook her head, teeth gritted against the urge to yell as well. "—Don't touch!"

Even through the lumps of his weave and the mottled fabric of his uniform, she could feel the press of time trying to sweep her downstream. If the others tried to help the two of them up, it would spread, and that would be bad. Very bad, almost as bad as a mind-quake. Too many lives, too many possibilities, would overwhelm her. As it was, she had to master herself before she could dampen the visions in Siano's mind.

"You 'eard th' Cap'n! Get on th' ship," Spyder ordered the others as she worked.

Siano came back to himself with a gasp and a shudder, eyes blinking wide. "Wh-wha . . . ? Oh, *hell* . . . Ransil wasn't kidding when . . . when he said that hits like a *shakking* Battle Platform!"

"Deep breaths, Private. Try to relax; we'll be off-world soon," she said, patting his shoulder. Tugging her leg free, she helped him roll over onto his hands and knees. Even with the weave wreaking havoc on her sense of up and down, counteracting some of the forces pulling on his frame, his tall, somewhat muscular bulk needed her help just to get off the ground. Turning up the gain on the gravimetrics would have aided him but would've churned the contents of her stomach from sheer proximity.

Thankfully, once he was upright, the weave fields aligned enough to allow him to walk up the ramp under his own power, joining the others. Panting, Ia rested where she stood for a moment, then dusted off her camouflage trousers. As she did so, the ground cars pulled to a stop near the shuttle.

The last pair of soldiers came walking up from the side, rifles carried loosely across their bodies, muzzles pointed safely at the ground, though she knew they could be snapped up into position at a moment's notice. As they came near, the two privates gave the cars a curious look, then their CO. Ia held up her fingers, then flicked them out to either side, signing for them to guard and wait. Nodding, York and Clairmont took up position on either side of the ramp.

Ia waited politely in a modified Parade Rest as the familiar figure of Customs Officer Larkins emerged from the lead car. His smug smile amused her. He thought he knew something she didn't know. Rather than show it, she kept her expression neutrally polite.

Stopping in front of her, he flapped a plexi printout. "As you can see, Captain Ia, I have *permission* from Vice Commodore Brenya Attinks to search your so-called 'emergency war supplies,' particularly as this is the first *she* has heard about their arrival—you *do* know who the Vice Commodore is, don't you?"

"Vice Commodore Attinks is the commanding officer in charge of this sector of Terran-patrolled space," Ia stated, her tone mild. "She is, however, from the TUPSF Branch Navy, and is merely a vice commodore in rank. I am from the TUPSF Branch Special Forces. Orders delivered by anyone of any rank lower than lieutenant general or vice admiral from outside the Branch Special Forces carries zero weight within my Branch. Unless, of course, your little printout includes permission and instructions from that level of authorization above her. Yes? No? . . . I think not, Officer Larkins, or you would have listed a higher authority instead."

Larkins reddened. Flipping the printout, he scanned it quickly. Ia didn't bother to give him time to see if it did or not.

"More to the point, the Special Forces' supply requirements are not the same as the Navy's. She wouldn't even know what to look for. But I am not an unreasonable officer, and it is quite evident you have gone to great lengths to have a peek at our business," she added, gesturing at the large building to her left. "My orders were to secure our cargo in military storage on the planet Sanctuary. Now that it has been properly secured, my authority in this matter is at an end. Responsibility for keeping it safe and sound now rests in the hands of the duly Charter-registered colonists of this world who have agreed by said Charter and contract to guard those supplies. At least, until such time as we need it, of course."

Brow pinching in a disbelieving frown, Larkins looked up

at her, then over at the warehouse. ". . . That's it? We're free to inspect it?"

"You are now free to inspect the warehouse," Ia agreed, gesturing again at the building. "I followed my orders to the letter, meioa. My obligation is now discharged. In fact, we are packed up and ready to go. You are therefore free to inspect that warehouse at any time you like. Our shuttles are still off-limits, of course."

"Of course . . ." He started to move toward the building, then checked himself. "One more thing, Captain. The two soldiers who were arrested. Vice Commodore Attinks has agreed that she and her two senior-most officers can serve on their hearing board, since you insisted so strongly that they be tried in a military court and not a civilian one. Her battleship, the TUPSF *Victory Dance VI*, will be insystem in the next few hours."

"I look forward to chatting with her about it." Behind her back, Ia flicked her fingers, hand-signaling for York and Clairmont to mount the ramp. With her left hand, she gestured at the warehouse one more time. "In the meantime, by all means, please inspect the premises. I'm sure your warrant is perfectly good for requesting that Chong-Wuu Stevedores open up the building for you. But you'd better hurry. I think they're locking up for the day."

At those words, Larkins moved away a few steps, squinting at the building. Ia backed up, stepping onto the ramp. By the time he glanced back, her fingers were already reaching for the ramp controls overhead.

"—Hey!" he protested.

"Do excuse me, Officer Larkins," she called out, crouching to keep in sight as the ramp started to shut. "I must go now, as I have a lot of Salik to slay. Good-bye!"

Backing up, she staggered a little as the ramp shut and the overhead weave dialed up, reducing the gravity in the cabin. Turning around, Ia waded through the mix of bodies, some strapping into their seats, others passing their ammunition-stripped weapons to Sergeant Santori and Lieutenant Spyder for storage in the ammunition crates stacked near the front of the cargo hold.

"Get ready for liftoff," she warned them. "Don't open the ship, even if they knock politely." Ducking into the cockpit, she slid into the copilot's seat next to Yeoman Yamasuka. "Run the checklist and take off the moment everything's greenlit. And unlock the comm on my side."

Yamasuka nodded and touched the requested controls. "Sir, yes, sir. Out of curiosity, Captain, who are you calling?"

"A certain vice commodore, about dropping the silliest set of trumped-up charges I've yet to hear on my homeworld. Though I'm afraid they won't be the last, nor the worst. I'm also calling to warn her how bad it's getting down here," Ia added, strapping the harness around her body. "I don't think it'll be safe for the Terran military to land on the surface anymore. The space station will have to do from now on."

"Did we just drop some *shova* in their caf', sir?" the woman at her side asked.

She shook her head. "No. Half the locals would be this crazy even if we weren't here—I'd blame the gravity draining the blood from their heads, but most of 'em have adapted by now. Let's get the hell out of here. Whenever we're ready, Yeoman?"

"Aye, sir," Yamasuka agreed, checking first her telltales for shuttle readiness, then a secondary screen displaying the bodies still moving around in the cargo hold. "Executing the 'get the hell out of here' maneuver in . . . approximately one minute twenty seconds, sir."

CHAPTER 6

I only saw my family once more after that. At least, in person. Plenty of vid-calls, and of course always in the timestreams. I love them, but I didn't try to go back because I had other things on my mind. Other responsibilities. We had to begin our prewar hunt for the anti-psi machines. Of course, the vast majority of those activities were highly classified. It was just my crew, Admiral Genibes, and other select members of the Command Staff who knew something of what we were up to, back then. You're lucky I can mention it even now. If I or my crew had told anyone what we were up to, the Salik would've been more prepared.

More prepared . . . yeah. It's rather scary to think of the Salik being more prepared.

Were we prepared to face them? On many levels, yes. On some levels, no. As a whole . . . it averaged out. The Space Force was barely ready for them. Part of that readiness was due to my disruption of their version of the Command Staff the year before the war started. It bought us enough time to increase recruitment drives, increase production of vital tools, and increase stockpiles of needed supplies.

You ask me if my crew was prepared? The answer has to be both yes and no. Prepared in the sense of trained to handle the ship and the equipment placed in

their hands? Yes, for I made sure they were well trained.
Ready? I don't think all that many of them would've said
so, back then.

~Ia

FEBRUARY 2, 2496 T.S.
SIC TRANSIT

"Are they ready for this?" Chaplain Benjamin asked her guest.
She studied the woman seated across from her over the rim of
her cup.

Ia yawned and nodded. ". . . Ready enough. They'll make
a few mistakes, but I've picked a soft target for the first
engagement."

"Something that could build their confidence rather than
burst it, eh?" Bennie asked.

Ia nodded again. She lifted her cup to sip from it, but the
caf' that should have been inside was gone. She didn't remember
drinking it. *Guess I'm more tired than I thought.* Sighing, she
sagged back into her seat and closed her eyes, letting the empty
mug rest on her knee.

Bennie's next question was pointed. "Are *you* ready for this?"

Rolling her head along the cushioned back of the chair, Ia
flopped a hand. Too many long nights of trying to get more
crysium wreaths and prophecies made and not enough sleep
left her groggy in the morning. It didn't help that once every
three days for the last ten, she had stretched her schedule out
by eight full hours. The effort of trying to keep an eye on each
of the three duty watches, to be *there* for every single crew
member, was wearing her down.

"Maybe I should've given you decaf'," Bennie muttered,
eyeing her.

"Maybe I should've court-martialed you," Ia quipped
back. Sighing, she sat up again and scrubbed her face. "I'll
be fine, Bennie. Once I get a little food in me, and maybe a
jolt of electricity, I'll be able to last until the adrenaline takes
over."

"And when the adrenaline does take over, what then?" her
friend asked.

"Then it'll be all fun and games until the Salik lose one of their eyes." Eyeing the empty cup, she clipped it into the holder on the coffee table between them. Bennie's office was tastefully decorated, mostly in soothing colors, but with a few bright accents found in the cushions snapped to the seats and the paintings bolted to the walls. She focused on the scarlets and blues, trying to wake herself up.

Her lack of sleep wasn't nearly as bad as at other points in her life, but it wasn't the long hours. It was constantly projecting confidence and competence every time someone else was in the room.

The chaplain's job, as a psychologist as well as a spiritualist, was to keep an eye on their CO's mental health. That meant showing Bennie she was still Human. Literally, since it was now known that half of her was not. With Bennie, here in private, she could let down her guard for a few minutes. Unfortunately, she couldn't stop Time, and that meant she could only do it for a few more moments right now.

Her gaze fell on a painting of a bright yellow flower, more abstract than real, though she suspected it was based on one from the M-class planet Dabin. The shape also reminded her of the pentagonal installation they were heading toward.

"So what happens after they lose an eye, and the adrenaline rush fades?" the redheaded woman asked, her tone amused.

". . . I start snoring?" she quipped, glancing back at her friend. Bennie snorted, covering her nose and mouth to muffle her laugh. Pushing to her feet, Ia lifted her chin at the door. "Snicker all you want. I'm going to go get something to eat, then hit the bridge."

"How soon to combat?" Bennie asked her, rising as well.

"A little over half an hour. Including whatever it takes to *find* the slagging place. I'm good at judging and aiming, but we're still dealing with interstellar distances, and this place is deep in the black." Lifting a hand in farewell, Ia left the cabin.

Bennie's office was one deck above her own, if farther back in the ship. It was also not far from the aft galley, though it did mean having to wait for the airlocks to cycle her through the section seal. Aft and fore were the main kitchens for preparing large meals for the entire crew; bow, stern, and amid were more for creating snacks. Ia herself could cook just enough to feed others without any accidental food poisonings, but she hadn't inherited any spurious chef genes from her highly talented mother. She didn't want a snack from the bridge galley, and she didn't want to have to put something together for herself, so the aft galley it was.

The timing was between meal shifts, so the four Humans moving back and forth in the kitchen space were focused more on cleanup and prep work than on actually cooking anything. Ia's entrance into the dining half of the large cabin went unnoticed until she came within a few meters of the pass-through between mess and kitchen.

The tall, black-haired woman directing the others on what to chop up and secure for the next meal was the first to spot Ia. Breaking off from her work, Private Philadelphia Benjamin— no relation to Chaplain Christine Benjamin—came over to the pass-through and leaned her elbows on the polished metal surface.

"What can I do ya for, Captain?" she asked, clasping her hands together.

Her pose, familiar to Ia from past glimpses into the timestreams, sparked her rare sense of humor. "Half-back on rye, black, pulled, swiss, stack the veg with watercress," Ia rattled off. "Half a cup of slop, dash of pepper on the top—and a moo-joo, Philly, don't spare the blue."

Private Benjamin's mouth sagged. She blinked her aqua blue eyes, attractive with their framing of black lashes. "How . . . When did *you* visit Benjamin's Beeferie, sir?"

"I've never been to Mars, let alone your family's restaurant," Ia admitted. Then amended, "At least, not in this life. But it sounds good, no?"

"Hell, yeah, it sounds good!" Philly agreed, straightening up. "Hey, Gracie! Get out the pulled pork, the rye, and sandwich fixings. And a bottle of nonfat milk while you're at it," she added, as Private Grace Marshall headed for the cold-storage locker. Philly switched her gaze to the man next to Gracie. "Clairmont, head down to lifesupport and pick up some fresh watercress. Make it snappy. I'll get your soup while you wait, sir."

"Already on it, Philly," Private Mellow called out, soup cup in one hand and ladle in the other. "Today's special is tilapia chowder, Cap'n."

"Sounds good. I'll take it out here," Ia said, poking her

thumb over her shoulder. Picking a spot at one of the long tables, she settled into the chair and waited.

Philly brought the cup of soup and a lidded glass of milk within moments. Accepting them, Ia clipped them to the table and dipped the accompanying spoon into the pepper-flaked surface. It was hot, creamy, and filling. The soup was half-gone by the time the mess doors slid open again. Private Clairmont stepped through, a lidded bin filled with leafy greens in his hands. So did another man, shorter and older. The pair were apparently exchanging a joke, for both men laughed before parting company. Clairmont headed to the back half of the galley, while Finnimore Hollick detoured over to Ia's table.

"*Ia'n sud-dha*, Captain," he said in greeting, turning one of the deck-bolted chairs across from hers enough to slide onto it. "I wanted to thank you for the chance to visit my birth family."

She smiled a little at that, dipping her head in acknowledgment. "I'm glad you got that chance, Finn. You'll get one more, though it won't be for a few more years."

He nodded, resting his elbows on the table. Short, somewhat stocky, freckled, and sporting a fringe of thinning sandy hair, he didn't look particularly imposing. The height and frame came from the fact he had been born a first-generation native on Sanctuary, but Ia knew he hadn't grown up there. Every so often, a newborn infant suffered immediately from the effects of gravity sickness. Hollick was one such case; lifted off-world as quickly as possible, he had been shipped off to family members back on Earth for gravitic rehabilitation in an environment his infant body could withstand.

Like most every other member of her crew—Harper being the one exception—she had checked over the details of his past in the timestreams when selecting him to serve her into the future. Hollick had served for years on various starship crews manning the supply runs all the way out to Sanctuary, as a way to stay in touch with his birth family. After suffering three particularly strong Fire Girl Prophecy attacks, he had been contacted by Rabbit's little gang of pre-rebels and vetted as a fellow believer. So his greeting, which in archaic V'Dan meant, "as the Prophet wills it," made sense in that context.

Something about him, though, some hidden quality buried below the surface of his life-stream, was necessary for the effective functioning of her crew. Ia suspected it was because some combination of his greater age—forty-seven, compared to the average age being nearly two decades younger—his steady work habits, and his unwavering faith in her would have an ongoing, subtle effect on the rest of the crew.

He was already something of a favorite among the 2nd Platoon. Or at least among its galley crew. Sort of a middle-aged mascot, as it were. Philly came out from the galley space with a bowl of soup and a cup of water, beaming a smile his way. "Hey, Holli. Clairmont said you got out of lifesupport early for good behavior. Here's some of that soup you like. I brought you some crackers, too."

Eyeing the plexi-wrapped packets she set down next to the clipped bowl of soup, Ia raised her brows at Private Benjamin. "*He* gets crackers, but I don't?"

"*You* are getting a sandwich, Captain," she sassed back. "You'll get all the carbs you need with my dough. Besides, if you're gonna order the Benjamin's way, you should've added, 'snap the crack' with that 'dash of pepper on the top.' "

That made Ia chuckle. "Okay, I concede your point. So where's my pulled pork rib meat sandwich, Private?"

"Being assembled as we speak." Flipping a mock salute, the tall woman took herself back into the kitchen. "Your lunch will be launched in two minutes."

Ia looked at her dining companion. Hollick was already crumbling the crackers into his soup. He offered her the last packet, but she shook her head. "So, how's the 2nd doing?"

"Good. A little nervous about the coming fight, but I've told 'em you know what you're doing," Hollick said, mixing in the last cracker.

"We'll pull through this one alright," she agreed, spooning up another bite of her soup. "The Salik aren't expecting it, they're not heavily guarded, and we do need those comm nodes. Easiest to get 'em before they know we're coming."

He didn't ask her where she found the coordinates for the communications hub. Instead, Hollick asked, "Have you been getting enough sleep, Captain? You look a little dark under the eyes."

Ia could have lied, but she chose to be honest. She did, however, keep her voice low. "Not really. Been pushing hard to get everyone ready for this. I'll have plenty of time for sleep after this fight," she added, scraping up the last of her chowder. "Once we pull the nodes from the wreckage, it'll be up to Rico and his teams to pull the information we need out of the databanks. They should be able to do it in two, three days—I know where they're supposed to look, but not what to look for, if that makes any sense."

"None so blind as them that see," he quipped dryly. "It makes perfect sense to me."

Philly came out with Ia's sandwich. The spicy-sweet smell of barbecue sauce wafted up from the meat-slathered hoagie. Ia accepted the plate, clipping it to the table edge. "That looks great. Thanks."

"Well, it's not the original Benjamin's barbecue sauce since I can't get the right mix of fruit out here, but it'll do," Philly said, shrugging. She retreated once more to the kitchen.

Ia knew the other woman's history included her family owning one of the oldest sandwich shops on Mars, and a sordid story of a criminal underlord attempting to take over the lucrative family business, efforts that had driven Philadelphia Benjamin into joining the military to escape the worst of it. The tall woman had burn scars under her plain grey sleeves, testament to the violence that could sometimes plague civilian life.

Philly also knew how to make food tasty, which was why Ia had instructed Grizzle, their Company Sergeant and the man responsible for the day-to-day work schedule, to put her in as lead cook whenever it was her turn to work in the kitchens on her duty shift. Very tasty food. The combination of cheese, toasted bread, spiced meat, greens, and vegetables vanished quickly from Ia's plate.

Wiping her hands on the lemon-scented napkin provided, she nodded at Hollick when he held out his hand, offering silently to take her cups and plate. A swallow of milk cleared her throat, enough that she was free to pull her headset out of her shirt pocket and hook it over her ear. One last swipe at her fingers cleaned them enough to poke at the buttons of her grey plexi arm unit, echoing her voice through the mess, kitchen, and places beyond.

"All hands, this is Captain Ia. Ten minutes to combat. I repeat, ten minutes to combat. Lock and Web; lock and load. You have ten minutes before we exit the rift and engage the enemy. Ia out."

"I'd better get back to lifesupport, Captain," Hollick offered, stacking her emptied glass on her plate next to his soup bowl and mug. "Good luck on the probabilities, sir."

"Thanks. I hope we don't need any." Nodding to him in thanks for the dishes, she headed for the door.

A short lift ride down and a modest walk forward brought her to the bridge. Entering via the main portside door, Ia announced herself this time rather than waiting for one of the others to notice.

"Captain on deck. Chief Yeoman O'Keefe, prepare to transfer helm to my control," she stated, striding between the workstations toward the command seat at the back.

"Aye, sir."

Unbuckling his safety harness, Spyder worked himself free of the straps. "Gimme a moment, Cap'n . . . uh, y' might wanna go freshen up," he added, nodding at her chest. "Got sauce onna shirt, there."

Glancing down, Ia rolled her eyes. She had missed a drip of barbecue sauce, which had landed on the curve of her left breast, on the edge of her shirt pocket. "One of the perils of being female," she joked dryly. "It'll wait. I'm after results, not looking pretty."

Shrugging, Spyder cleared the seat for her. He ran one hand over his short-cropped, camouflage-mottled hair. "Eh. Jus' as well. Leave th' lookin' pretty t' meioa-os like me, eh?"

"Go be a pretty-boy in the spare gunnery spot," she ordered, sitting down and strapping in. Unlike Rico with his longer legs, she didn't have to readjust the chair forward. Her legs were slightly longer than Spyder's, but not enough to bother her. "Corporal Morgan will coordinate forward gunnery efforts. Lieutenant Spyder will coordinate the aft-ward vectors."

Sighing, Spyder finished clipping into his seat, then powered the whole station around so that it faced backward. Both gunnery posts and the pilot's station could be rotated for just such a need, so that the Human inner ear wouldn't be thrown out of balance by the disparity between physically moving one way and facing the other. Normally, Ia's station also would have swiveled as the backup piloting position, but the security requirements for the main cannon controls had it locked permanently in place.

She activated the all-hail again. *This is Captain Ia, three minutes to combat. Lock and Web, meioas. Lock and load. This is not a drill. Three minutes to combat; Ia out."*

There were four differences between Ia's console and the pilot's version. One was the number of tertiary monitor screens; her seat had five of the transparent panels above as well as five below the transparent main and flanking secondary screens. The second was the control panel that released the main cannon. It was locked under a double-lidded security box, with a palm- and DNA-scanner sandwiched between the two lids. Anyone who tried to activate the main cannon other than Ia would set off an unstoppable chain reaction in the hydrogenerators, turning the ship into a brief, bright, miniature nova in one minute.

The third difference was the way that security box locked the station in place, preventing it from rotating, unlike the pilot's seat. And the fourth was an odd, recessed socket with two exposed metal tabs, its sole purpose to provide energy when the circuit between those two tabs was connected. Nudging up the cover, Ia stuck her right hand inside and pressed her fingers against them.

Electricity snapped into her arm, stinging up through her nerves. Like a jolt of caf' to taste buds, it woke her up, sharpening her senses. She didn't take much, just a few seconds' worth, then pulled her hand out and let the little door slide shut. Left hand fitted into the thruster glove, right hand on the power controls, she nodded.

"I'm ready for the helm, O'Keefe," she said.

"Aye, sir," the freckled pilot stated. "Transferring helm to your control in five."

They weren't traveling through hyperspace. Ia didn't want the Salik to know a ship as large as hers could do that, just yet. She could use it to get close to this particular patch of nowhere, situated about four hundred light-years from Earth and over nine hundred from Sanctuary, yes; they had used hyperwarp to get to within a light-year or so, but the last leg had been plain FTL.

In control, Ia closed her eyes for a moment, dipping part of her mind into the timestreams. She didn't want to overshoot their target but she did want to come in as close as safely possible. She also wanted her crew to be certain of what were viable targets.

"Captain to all gunnery teams. Your tactical displays have been loaded with two sets of targets. Shoot the red ones all you like but avoid shooting anything tagged green. We're here to smash and grab communications databanks. I'd like to have those databanks intact for grabbing. You have four cannons slaved per pod. Use them wisely. Heads up in . . . twenty seconds, mark." Off-mike, she spoke as she started powering down the warp panels. "Spyder, Morgan, keep an eye on who's firing on what. We're coming in hot and fast and barreling right past before we'll turn around. Lasers only for the first volleys. Let's not outpace any projectiles, today. Coming out of FTL in three . . . two . . ."

The slow streak of stars on the screens flared into a pulse of dotted white. Within a blink, the screen was filled with a stippling of near-static pinpoints of light. Ia's main screen lit up with tactical analyses of the objects barely lit at this distance by floodlights designed solely to keep incoming ships from hitting anything while maneuvering nearby.

"Resolving lightspeed, sir," Private Loewen said from the navigation post, checking her scanners. "We have targets, almost dead ahead. Three-fifty-six by three-fifty-nine."

"L-pods, fire at will," Ia directed, watching the distance-to-target numbers spin down swiftly as they hurtled toward the installation. Morgan nodded and relayed the command.

They were still slowing down, thruster fields pulsing subtly against the laws of reality. Between pulses, the *Hellfire*'s L-pods started to fire. Bright reddish orange streaks of light darted out from the ship. With the *Hellfire* speeding into range right on their tail at a large fraction of Cee, the speed of light itself, the lasers could be seen moving as a bolt rather than a beam as they arrowed straight and true at the organic-looking station.

That station was huge, too, though mainly due to its function. Layers of solar panels angled out from the central pod, interspersed with five ship-sized arms that served as crew quarters, docking gantries, manufacturing facilities, and so forth.

Ia knew the station was home to over eight thousand Salik. She also knew the facility was underdefended, relying more on its extremely remote position between star systems for protection than on gun pods, fighter craft, and other things. With their resources limited to whatever raw materials they could mine or steal without the Alliance's notice, the Salik had to juggle the needs between creating more ships and weapons with their limited resources and expanding their infrastructure, such as this station, in the hopes they'd be able to find more materials to justify the expansions.

Two of those ships were in the system now, a tanker filled with hydrofuel and raw materials, and a frigate, small but fast, the kind useful for gathering lightspeed information at the extreme edges of a particular system. Naturally, they were on Ia's red-painted list. Red-painted, and red-targeted, with a spinning stream of numbers appended, counting down the distance in light-seconds to each enemy ship. As the dozens of lasers struck *en masse*, three of them hit spots that caused silent explosions to rip through the hulls of the frigate and the tanker.

"Spyder, launch one volley of projectiles the moment that station is aft," Ia ordered. "Coming up on midpoint in thirty seconds. O'Keefe, count it off."

Her right hand thumbed one of the console controls, and her left hand twitched to the right a tiny bit. The ship strafed sideways by a hundred meters as it raced forward, just enough to avoid the dark chaff blown outward from the solar panels. Bright red continued to cross the screens as the L-pods kept firing.

Lasers were quiet weapons, unlike the clunkier noise of projectiles being launched. They did, however, require extra energy, enough that the ship *thrummed* with the efforts of several extra hydrogenerators cycling on and off. The slower the ship went, the shorter and darker those beams became, redshifted from the *Hellfire*'s reduced speed.

Slow in this case was still a significant fraction of Cee, the speed of light. In Ia's Harrier-class ship back on the Blockade, Cee hadn't been a concern; Harrier-class ships traveled via OTL and never actually needed more than half the speed of light. The *Hellfire*, by contrast, had started several billion kilometers away, but those billions were now almost gone.

"Coming up on turning point," O'Keefe warned the others. "Estimated ten seconds."

Bright chartreuse dots stabbed at the ship. They missed, but only barely. Ia flexed her fingers, sliding them slightly dorsal. That dodged another set of blueshifted lasers aimed their way.

"Incoming!" Loewen warned, her head shifting in little

snaps as her eyes flew over the data streaming into her screens. Her warning wasn't for the lasers; those could not be dodged, since they traveled at the speed of light. Instead, it was for the missiles that followed. Lasers aimed at their narrow, end-on silhouette weren't a concern, not when missiles could track the mass of a ship and divert course to intercept.

"Five," O'Keefe counted.

"Firing chaff!" Morgan announced, pulsing the trigger on his controls. Rapid noise *thuthuthunked* down the hull from the bow. The battered communications hub filled their viewscreens, then popped somewhat smaller as their proximity forced the scanners to cut back on their magnification.

"Three!"

"Aft P-pods," Spyder called into his headset.

"One!"

They dove between the tanker and a tumbling cloud of laserscorched debris from the solar panels, close enough that proximity alarms beeped loudly in warning, though not quite close enough to trigger the emergency claxons.

". . . Fire! L-pods, fire at will!"

Parts of the solar panels were now shielded, visible where some of that debris struck the repeller fields with sparks of energy. The undersides of those vast panels were more heavily shielded, but it wouldn't do them much good; lasers penetrated shields. They didn't do as much damage as missiles did, but they could damage the nodes projecting those shields.

As it was, some of lasers from the aft-pointed pods struck before the missiles did. Others struck after. Several explosions blossomed silently to their rear, though it would take a few seconds for their tactical computers to discern which ones were just from the missiles impacting on the shields and which ones were from missiles that made it through to the actual station surface.

"All hands, brace for maneuvers," Ia warned over the intercom. They were still going a significant fraction of Cee, and she was about to pull something complicated.

On a more compact ship design, she would have physically turned the ship in a loop, swapping bow and stern so that they were pointed the other way, but the *Hellfire* was nine hundred meters long. A turn at their current speed would bend, if not break, the hull. Flexing the FTL fields, Ia greased the laws of physics in a bubble around the ship. Only then did she make the port side greasier. Left hand wrapped in the glove, right hand splayed over the console, she massaged both sets of controls.

They had entered normal space pointed downstream—toward the core, in relation to the spiral of the galaxy, if one considered the stars as "draining" toward the black hole at the center of the Milky Way. They remained pointed that way, but like a hummingbird or a dragonfly, the vector change swerved their momentum so that they were flying backwards. The field shielded them from most of those vector change forces, but not all.

Everyone and everything not bolted to the ship pulled to the right for several long seconds, then swung around to the bow. The G-forces eased after several more seconds; pleased everyone had locked and webbed their stray supplies, Ia worked on angling the axis of the ship a little as they headed back toward the station and its two half-crippled ships.

Morgan and Spyder gave orders to their gunnery teams. The aft and starboard pods fired as soon as the full field dropped, allowing them to reacquire targets between pulses. More enemy shots were fired; eyes on the screens, hands on the controls, toes in the timestreams, Ia sideslipped most of the lasers. A few scored the sides of the ship. A few telltales turned yellow, mostly exposed FTL panels and one sensor antenna. Ia nudged them sideways, aiming a little closer even as she angled their ship to strafe down the side of the hub.

They weren't the only ones attacking now. Caught by fast, close launches from the frigate and the station, the *Hellfire*'s shields vibrated down into the hull from missile explosions. Here was the difference between reality and entertainment shows like *Space Patrol*. Real interstellar combat was relatively quiet, so long as one wasn't getting hit. Now they were, and now the P-pods fired anti-missile volleys and chaff grenades, trying to detonate the incoming munitions before they could hammer their way through the shields to the actual hull.

"Coming up on midpoint," O'Keefe warned them. "Twenty seconds."

Again, Ia slipped the ship sideways. They weren't passing nearly as closely this time.

"Focus your fire on weapons and generators—*brace for*

maneuvers." Ia swirled her fingertips. Rolling the ship on its long axis sent their stomachs slinging sideways, down, and out. It also lessened the scorch impact of a large laser attempting to target and burn through their hull. More telltales popped up on her tertiary screens, glowing yellow from the damage sustained. "Morgan, switch to targeting priority display 2, and load up twelve P-pod blossoms. Fire on our third midpoint pass. Add regulars on this pass."

"Midpoint in three . . . two . . ." O'Keefe counted down. Another set of missiles hit their shields, shuddering the ship.

"Forward P-pods launching," Morgan announced a moment later. The ship *whumped* several times, starting in the distance, racing past their position, and down to the stern.

Again, they strafed sideways and down, dodging incoming attacks. Ia warned the crew one more time, then pulsed the FTL panels, mindful of the damaged ones. They swerved around until they were speeding forward, this time aiming down the other side of those solar panels, if slightly above. They no longer faced their original entry-point orientation, thanks to her careful, slow tilting of the ship.

"We'll be moving fast in a few moments," she warned the others. "Launch the blossoms at midpoint and brace for acceleration."

"Aye, sir," Morgan said. "Blossoms are prepped and ready for launch."

"Brace for acceleration," Ia warned.

"Ten seconds," O'Keefe warned them. "Glad we're not sticking around. Five . . . four . . . three . . ."

The long, slender missiles launched with a near-unison stutter of *clunks* just as they soared over the battered but still-firing station. Ia scraped her right-hand fingertips up the thruster controls, thrumming the engines in a rippling wave of increasingly swift field pulses. Occasionally she flexed one side of her left hand or the other, lifted it up slightly or pushed it down, either straight or angled. That allowed them to dodge most of the damage from the few L-pods still capable of return fire.

The increased speed was necessary; when the blossom missiles hit, they impacted zones that had lost shielding. Ten lodged in the panels next to each segment that served as living quarters, just to either side. Two more smacked into the central sphere that housed the vacuum-sealed hyperrelay units, which permitted the routing and rerouting of messages from one end of known space to the other.

For several seconds they did not detonate, though their engines did pulse, attempting to drive them deeper into each section of the overall structure. When they did, they slammed scores of smaller, needle-sharp bombs outward, blossoming like fireworks. Those bombs in turn stayed dormant for a few more seconds, giving the ones driven into open areas more time to travel outward. *Then* they detonated.

This time, the detonations were explosions, ripping huge holes in the station. The force hurled debris in all directions, making the space near the communications array dangerous to transit. With the *Hellfire* already headed outbound, the only things they had to dodge were a few still-functioning lasers. Even those ended a few seconds later, as the damage cracked the station into pieces.

Once the enemy fire stopped, Ia slowed the ship again, intending to guide it around and into reverse as she had before. As she did so, she checked the timestreams. The answer she sought came within a handful of seconds, and it was a satisfactory one. *Minimal damage to the exact units we'll need. I know the information we want is buried in those particular comm-traffic files, though I don't know exactly what we're supposed to be looking for . . . mainly because the subject matter recursively hides itself from me.*

The best analogy she had was being sent into a grocery store with a list of spices. Those were usually kept with the baking goods, but that entire aisle could be located anywhere in the store. Once the right aisle was located, then the right shelves had to be found, and finally the right spice jars. Ia knew where the store was located—this station—and an idea of which aisle to check. The rest of it, she didn't have time to search for herself.

That was what the others were here for.

"Private York, please inform Lieutenant Rico to get his salvage teams ready. We'll be taking potshots at enemy weaponry for the next twenty minutes, disabling everything they can still throw at us. Those teams need to launch as soon as I give the all clear. We do not want to be here an hour from now."

"Aye, sir."

And at that point, I can rest, she thought. *Once we're under way and I've plotted our next course, O'Keefe can have the helm back, and I can go sleep for nine hours straight.*

Opening the intercom, Ia addressed her crew. *"Captain Ia to the crew. Good job, everyone. Third watch will be free to stand down again in twenty minutes. Maneuvers should be light between now and then. Exercise caution in moving about the ship for the next hour and a half. Ia out."*

On the one hand, energy from the food she had eaten was now keeping her awake. On the other hand, the post-battle adrenaline slump threatened to steal that energy away. Now that they were aimed back at the crumpled bits of station, she had a few seconds free. Slipping her fingers under the little door, Ia jolted herself with a little bit of electricity.

"A good day's fight, meioas," she murmured, praising her sparse bridge crew. "Let's keep it up."

FEBRUARY 5, 2496 T.S.
SIC TRANSIT

The boot that hit her did not belong to her brother. It did, however, break Ia out of her timeplains trance. Standing in her socks on the deck of the stern cargo hold, she blinked at the mangled glob of crystal in her hands. Being broken out of molding trance always did that. She could fix it, but she had left orders with Harper on when to interrupt her, and why.

"Fire, famine, flood, or finally cracked the code?" she asked, turning toward the door. Harper stood there, but so did Helstead, her shorter frame peering around his taller one.

"Finally cracked the code . . . we think," Harper said. The other lieutenant commander tried to squeeze past him. He checked her with his elbow, rolling his eyes. "Helstead! You're not allowed in this hold."

"How can I be an effective spymaster if I'm not allowed to spy on her?" Helstead shot back, trying to dodge the other way. He checked her by spreading his legs—and she darted under them, only to be grabbed by the back of her shirt.

"Sorry, Captain," he apologized. "Want me to throw her out?"

"*I* want to know what's so . . . Wait a second," Helstead said, green gaze darting around the hold. "There were at least forty of those things loaded into this cargo hold. I only see thirty-six."

Back on her homeworld, Ia had ordered the sprays lashed to the outer walls, with large lockboxes stacked and secured down the center. The extra flights had added a day to their itinerary, but the successful early integration of the hyperwarp system had given them an extra day. Some of those lockboxes now contained crysium wreaths, shaped in her spare time since leaving Sanctuary.

Helstead narrowed her eyes, staring at the lump of crystal in Ia's hands. "Is that . . . ?"

Harper hauled back on her collar, interrupting her question. "You are in a restricted area, Lieutenant Commander. Only myself and Captain Ia have access to this part of the ship."

Twisting, Helstead broke his grip with a sweep of her arm. She didn't grab him back, just planted her hands on her hips. "And maybe I should report *you* for keeping secrets from the Command Staff! I did some research on this crysium stuff when it was brought on board. It's the hardest substance known to sentientkind. So how the hell did the Captain reshape it? She's quite clearly holding a re-formed chunk of it in her hands."

"*I* don't like the implications that you're a *spy*," Harper countered, hands going to his own hips. "Your loyalty is up through the chain of command, to me, to Captain Ia, *then* to the Command Staff."

"I'd believe you a lot more," Helstead snorted, "if every time you looked at her, you *didn't* look like a lovesick turtle. You don't hide it nearly well enough, soldier."

He flushed at that. Sighing, Ia interrupted the pair. "*Enough*, both of you, or I'll make you clean the lifesupport filters while all the off-duty privates watch. Helstead's not the spy on this ship. I know exactly who they are, and she's not one of them."

That got Helstead's attention, swinging the shorter woman around. Ia lifted the glob in her hand.

"As for what I'm doing with it, I'm borrowing technology from the future to alter the crystals. That technology is *not* the property of the Terran United Planets . . . and I cannot in good conscience explain that tech *or* share it with anyone else. That's why this cargo bay is off-limits."

"You're using tech you stole from the future, from another government, to reshape the hardest known substance, and you're not gonna share it with your own superiors?" Helstead asked dubiously. "Imagine the weapons you could make—imagine the *armor*! I read an article stating how this stuff just absorbs laserfire, no matter how large the weapon."

"I will not compromise the secrets of the government which developed this tech," Ia stated bluntly. "Just as I will not compromise the secrets of the government that will eventually develop the hyperwarp drive. One is Terran; the other is not. Both have the right to keep their temporal secrets. I will *use* this technology, yes, but only because I have no other way to get the job done on time and done right. I will therefore not share those secrets . . . and the fewer who know those secrets, the easier it is to *keep* them a secret. Is that clear, soldier?"

That deflated the shorter woman. Brow furrowed in a sullen look, Helstead muttered, "Crystal clear, sir."

Ia pointed at her. "My silence applies to your own escapades as well, Delia. Past as well as present and future. Be glad I have both discretion and integrity. Now, give me a few minutes in private to finish what I was doing, then I'll come join you and Rico in the briefing room. Harper, if I'm not out of here in ten, throw my other boot at me."

"Aye, sir," he agreed. A tip of his head silently ordered Helstead to retreat with him. Grateful, Ia watched them go.

Just before the door slid shut behind them, she heard Helstead ask, "Why do you have to throw her boot at her . . . ?"

Ia knew the answer, the same as Harper. Back in their Academy days, sharing quarters in the cadet dormitories, she had taught him to wake her by throwing something at her rather than physically touching her. These days, her sleep was relatively dreamless; minor nightmares still plagued her, but she was on track to fix the source of those nightmares. Her precognitive gift didn't torment her as much as it used to, which meant the risk of triggering it when someone else touched her in her sleep had lessened. But lessened risk was not the same as none.

Which means I go through life untouched, save for rare moments when it's absolutely necessary.

Turning back to the glob in her hand, Ia flipped her mind in, down, and out, onto the timeplains. She resisted the urge to sink fully into the rhythm of swimming, shaping, and molding blood-infused beads with chunks of crystal. Her blood. Whatever quality of Feyori Meddling lay in her genetics, it seemed to affect the crysium—which itself was another Feyori by-product. The two combined, crystalline and crimson, made the strange, peach-hued stuff capable of hooking a nonpsychic mind into the timestreams.

She only had enough time to create a few more. There would be other stolen hours for this task, creating precognitive crystalline circlets meant to plug her fellow Sanctuarians into glimpses of their own pasts, their own futures, to guide them in the direction she needed them to go. Before the ten minutes were up, the latest wreath was locked in a storage box and her boots were back on her feet. Ia stepped through the cargo-bay door, palm-locking it behind her. Harper and Helstead waited nearby; once again, Helstead was playing with her stiletto-pins.

"Can I at least have a closer look?" she asked Ia, moving to join her CO in heading toward the aft shuttle-bay doors.

"No. Looking leads to touching, and touching leads to interfering. Most of what I'm making won't even be used by the Terrans," Ia told her. "I'd rather it wasn't damaged in the interim."

Helstead frowned at that. "Wait, if it was impervious before you manipulated it, but now it can be damaged simply by handling it . . . that means it won't actually retain its impervious qualities after it's been reshaped. Why would that stuff be of any use after that point?"

Ia ignored the question. She had meant the timelines, not the wreaths themselves, but her 3rd Platoon leader didn't need to know that. Instead, she glanced over her shoulder at their chief engineer, addressing him instead. "Harper, I know you've been working on the FTL panels you pulled off the hull. How many have your repair teams salvaged?"

"All but two," he told her. Touching the controls for the sector seal, he joined them in transiting the airlock seals. "I've ordered those two broken down for parts. We have plenty of spares on board, but I'm not going to hold my breath on every battle being that smooth."

"Two out of, what? Twenty-tree panels? That's not a bad attrition rate," Ia allowed, yawning slightly to pop her ears as the air pressure shifted slightly. The second door swung open, revealing Spyder, Santori, and two long lines of shorts-and-T-shirt-clad bodies, all jogging in place.

"Make room, ya bloody slackers!" Spyder ordered, jogging himself as he turned to face the others. "Officers comin' out!"

The two lines of men and women parted, jogging up against the wall as Ia, Harper, and Helstead emerged single file from the airlock.

"Arright! C Squad, cycle through! Two more minutes of jogging, then we go back to practicing shipboard parkour!" Spyder ordered. The first five pairs of Humans jogged into the airlock. Someone thumbed the controls, swinging the door shut.

"I'll give him this," Helstead observed, glancing back at the airlock as the three officers turned a corner. "He's certainly enthusiastic about PT. The man has almost as much energy as *me* in the mornings."

"That's why I paired him with you on that task. Oh, speaking of exercise, Harper," Ia added, turning slightly to address her first officer as they walked. "I'd like to gradually increase the ship's gravity by .05Gs over the next week. Then hold it steady until the end of the month, and increase it again by .05 over the first week of March. Hold steady until April, and do it again, until this ship is running at 1.35Gs Standard, then hold it for three months."

"You got it," Harper agreed.

Helstead eyed her. "Trying to turn all these lightworlders into heavyworlders, Captain?"

"The increase in strength will be a bonus in hand-to-hand combat, about half a year from now," Ia admitted. "The faster reflexes will take a while to train, but will be worth it in about three years. But long before then, I want us up a lot higher, at the very least to 1.8Gs."

"My homeworld isn't much higher than that," Harper said. Then blinked and looked at her, brown eyes wide. "We're going there, aren't we? I remember—"

Ia raised her hand, cutting him off. Through an accident, he had been exposed to a tumult of unchecked timestreams back at the end of their Academy days. She didn't need the rest of the crew knowing that, though. "Some visions will come true, others will not. I'll let you know what to prepare for when you'll need to know it, I promise."

He nodded. "Alright, then. Will you need me for the databank debriefing? If not, I'll get back to that gun project."

She shook her head. "I don't think so. Helstead might be useful, though."

That made the other woman's eyes roll. Tucking her bladed hairpins back into her braid, she said, "Oh, gee. I feel so special."

"That depends on whether or not you can focus," Ia said. She nodded farewell to Harper, who continued aft-ward while they took a side hall that would lead them to the track lifts for the fore section.

Helstead waved good-bye at him and shrugged. "I can focus just fine, Captain. I just . . . have to keep doing something, or I'll go nuts."

"Then we have something in common," Ia told her. "Only in my case, the 'something' I constantly have to keep doing is striving to save the future."

"So, how's that working out for you?" Helstead quipped.

The joke caught Ia by surprise. She chuckled. "We'll see. I still have several years of work ahead of me. Feel free to help out if you get bored."

"Sir, yes, sir," Helstead quipped.

Both women fell silent as they traveled up several decks to the briefing room. Located forward of the bridge, it was meant for the cadre to use, or up to two squads at a time. The monitors lining the cabin caught Ia's attention first, followed by the tall, broad-shouldered figure of Lieutenant Rico.

He stood in front of screens filled with series of dots, circles, and lines that made up the written form of Sallhash, language of the frogtopus-like Salik. Around the oval table at the center of the room sat Corporal Xhuge, Private Dinyadah, Private MacInnes, and Private Al-Aboudwa, all members of the 1st Platoon. They had workstations clipped to the table; from what Ia could see of Al-Aboudwa's and Xhuge's screens, the two men were attempting to match location names to star charts.

"Glad you could join us, Captain," Rico stated in a mild tone. "I hope we didn't interrupt anything important."

"I put you in charge of this project because I knew I could trust you with it," Ia returned calmly. "You cannot compose detailed, time-sensitive instructions that will save hundreds of billions of lives. You, however, can make sense of this Salik gibberish, and *that* will help save hundreds of billions of lives. Now, I understand you've found something?"

"We think so, sir," Corporal Xhuge said, speaking before Rico could. Ia had to give him credit for getting the discussion back on topic. "Since you said you were able to pinpoint the exact comm nodes containing information on where and how these anti-psi machines were being manufactured, once we cracked open the databank cases, we broke down all the various messages in the selected banks and started sorting each by type."

Rico joined the explanation. "Most of them were about the transport of goods, involving timetables, ships, requisitions . . . standard stuff. Much of it used cryptography, or the substitution of things like letters and numbers, which can be cracked by any competent computer system. Even the most sophisticated ones back in their day from Old Earth's Enigma machines all the way up through the AI War codes were breakable, given time and understanding. But some of the messages were different.

"They were asking for weird things with no apparent context. That meant they were using steganography," he told Ia. "It's the art of substituting one word for another. The catch is, you have to know which words substitute for which. Like the Navajo code talkers on Old Earth, same era as the Enigma machines. But it's always heavy on the nouns, even among the xenospecies, and that's where MacInnes came in handy."

MacInnes nodded quickly, her carrot curls bouncing around her ears. "My Sallhash still isn't the best, sir, but it works in conjunction with my xenopathy and clairvoyancy. I can 'see' a noun in my head when I'm translating it mentally. The nouns the lieutenant handed me on the weird requisition cases *weren't* the ones I was actually seeing and writing down."

"I figured her gifts would be useful that way when I read the notes you appended in her personnel file," Rico interjected.

"Like I said, I picked the right man to head up this job, and the right meioas to work with you," Ia reminded him. She nodded at the other woman. "Go on, MacInnes. What were the disparities?"

"Instead of . . . uh . . ." She blushed and nodded at her workstation. "Well, we can't pronounce most of these words without the nasal flaps and such, so we're using the Terran phonemes. Anyway, the weirdest one was a message about an order of *po-jeem ang-nu-gwish-tick-wa*, which is a kind of amphibious creature they like to eat on their M-class colonyworld of Hawhonn. But instead of alien breakfast food, I was getting images of anthikeriate coils, which are used in the PsiLeague's KI machines to sense kinetic-inergy emanations, and I only knew *that* much because I helped refurbish a couple during a summer job back in high school."

"And some of the other nouns?" Helstead asked, dropping into one of the chairs at the table and swirling it around.

"Electronics components, mostly. But also . . . test subjects," Al-Aboudwa stated quietly. "We found dates and times for prisoner swaps."

"The images I saw were meant to imply tasty-smart food," MacInnes muttered, looking a little pale. She wasn't the only one. Xhuge and Al-Aboudwa didn't look comfortable, either.

"—Found it!" Dinyadah exclaimed, pointing at her workscreen. A couple of taps transferred the star charts to the monitors around the room. "God bless methodical mapmaking. Ss'gwish Gaff 117-N, a system with a small class B white star, three asteroid belts, at least four gas giants, and an extensive Kuiper belt with a break in it from a rogue planet expelled by the explosion of a downstream neutron star. That's our second starting point, gentlemeioas, and it's approximately twenty light-years from the endpoint in the message."

"Good job," Rico praised. "Now all we need is a third location, to triangulate the manufacturing point—the Kuiper belt break has several ice chunks trailing outsystem in the wake of the rogue planet," he explained to Ia. "The first system we found has the requesting point located approximately eighteen light-years from *Nngu* 120-N. But that still leaves us a ring zone with a circumference of one hundred light-years, give or take a few. Since we don't have any third reference point in the data files, I was hoping *you* could provide us with one, Captain."

Ia gave him a level look. "What part of 'these machines can counteract even *my* abilities' did you not comprehend at our initial task briefing, Lieutenant?"

"The part where you said you're an omniscient precog?" Rico replied, one brow lifted in skepticism.

"I'm not omniscient. I'm all-*seeing*, not all-*knowing*. And this thing is like a black hole on my internal radar, or a thick cloud obscuring an island," Ia said, pointing at one of the screens. "I can only tell its general vicinity from the *lack* of things I can sense about it directly, and from the things I can sense *in*directly. Like our next target." Moving over to the largest of the screens, she poked at the surface, rotating the stars slightly. "I can sense what people do, Lieutenant, from the effects their lives, their timestreams, have on the timeplains in general.

"I cannot track things as easily as I can track people. Unfortunately, most of the people directly involved in this anti-psi project are being protected by the machines." Tapping the screen, she drew a circle around three stars in relatively close proximity in green. "Somewhere in here is another communications station. We're going to attack the second hub, extract the right data nodes, and extrapolate that third point. We'll have to hurry, since the one thing I am sure about is that the manufacturing equipment is on the move."

Another tap drew a much larger circle in yellow, one at least forty light-years across. Ia looked over her shoulder at Rico.

"This area is the general area I think it's in, but as you can see, it's rather large," she said. "They're distributing the machines, too; I get flashes of foreknowledge in between stretches of nothing. Once we do get that third coordinate for triangulation, we move in for the kill and wipe out their main manufacturing facility."

"D'un yi shia . . ." Xhuge muttered, eyes widening as he stared at the yellow-circled zone. *"Da shiong la se la ch'wohn tian!"*

Rico narrowed his eyes. *"Excuse* me, soldier?" he snapped at Corporal Xhuge. "You do *not* swear like that in front of me. I'll remind you, I *do* speak all three main dialects of Chinese."

"Yeah, what he said," Al-Aboudwa agreed, giving his crewmate a puzzled look. "Either swear in Terranglo, or at least tell us what you said, will you?"

"I'm sorry, sirs, meioas," Xhuge apologized, blushing. He lifted his hand, pointing at the yellow blob. "But that whole zone, if they're distributing anti-psi machines to their ships, then *that's* where the main Salik fleet is gathering. If we go in there pods blazing, they'll swarm in and kill us. Not to mention, they'll have to figure out which databanks we're stealing sooner or later. No offense, Captain, but that's a *tze sah ju yi!*"

"It would be a suicidal idea under normal circumstances, yes," Ia agreed. "But my abilities strengthen with proximity, both temporally and spatially. My first encounter, I had no clue what these machines were, but I still managed to destroy a giant capital ship, and I did it with a tiny little Harrier-class Delta-VX. My second time? I rescued dozens of sentients from the Salik Motherworld, and I did it in a room filled with those machines. The third time I was in the room with one of these *kuh wu* machines, I still managed to slam the needle of a KI gauge off the far side with it churning away at full power, sitting right next to me while I was demonstrating the strength of my pre-cognitive abilities.

"As for this actually being a suicidal idea?" she repeated, hands resting on her hips as she studied the corporal. "I'll tell you something about the future, Xhuge. It's a suicidal idea for the *Salik* to go to war because by their own efforts, they will destroy themselves. But they are doing it, and we have to stop them. At the right time, in the right way. Now, we have two more days before we'll be in striking range of the new hub. Let's keep working at this."

Dinyadah looked up from her workstation screen at that. Like everyone else on the ship, she traded duty posts every two hours, including stints on the bridge crew. "Sir, I thought the hyperwarp drive was faster than that. When I was last on the bridge, we were only thirty-nine light-years away from the target zone."

"We could get there faster, yes, but right now, some of that fleet Xhuge's worried about is still within counterstriking range of the hub," Ia said. "Not to mention hyperwarp uses almost three times the fuel. If we don't need to hurry, then we travel FTL. That gives the enemy fleet plenty of time to move on and be well past the turnaround point by the time we come diving in." Looking at the others, she dipped her head and offered some sincere praise. "You've done very well so far. I can't wait to see what else you can do."

"Oh, how patronizing. Are you sure you can't do this yourself?" Rico asked her.

The others gave the two of them watchful, wary looks, not quite sure why Lieutenant Rico was being belligerent. Ia knew why. It wasn't just that he didn't believe in her cause, yet—he didn't—but also because he didn't like being asked to spy on her. At the same time he didn't want her to become suspicious of his being too agreeable to her plans right from the start. She knew he was smart enough to know that too many spies tried being best friends with their targets too soon, and that he knew she was smart enough to realize it, too.

"Some of it, yes. *If* I had the time to spare, I could do some of it," she finally admitted. "Most of it, no . . . and what little I could do, I do not have that time to spare. Every single person on board this ship has been hand-selected because each one of you brings a special skill or ability or knowledge to this crew to do all the things that one person, male or female, cannot do on their own.

"It doesn't matter who that one person is, Lieutenant Rico," Ia said. "We will all work together, and in doing so, we will get the job done."

"Any job where I get to destroy the Salik, I'm on it," Al-Aboudwa stated. He looked up at both officers, first Rico, then Ia. His tanned brow creased, and his thin lips twisted in a grimace. "I *hate* them. They ate my grandfather and my great-uncle. They were merchanters on a supply run into the Blockade Zone, and got caught by a Salik ship trying to make a run for it. If I could put on a p-suit and dance on the corpses we left back at the first site, I'd do it. You need me to fight them, Captain, I'm on your side," he promised, hands balled in fists on the table. "Anytime, anywhere, I'll do whatever it takes."

The others nodded slowly, agreeing with his vehemence.

Ia shook her head. "No, Private. Don't hate them. Yes, they're vile, psychotic sentient-eaters. But don't hate them. Pity them for bringing their deaths upon themselves."

Helstead snorted. As the others glanced her way, her shoulders shook. "Pity them!" she giggled, then thumped her fists on the armrests of her chair, laughing outright. "Oh, God, that's mucking funny!"

"What the . . . ?" Xhuge asked her, bemused. Helstead gasped for air, shaking her head. She covered her mouth, then her eyes, snorting and chuckling in her mirth.

"She's talking about the xenopsychology of the Salik," Rico said over her giggles. He wasn't quite laughing, but his mouth had twisted up in a smirk. "Pity is one of the worst insults you could give them. To a Salik, it means the prey they've been pursuing has turned out to be utterly unworthy of the time and energy spent on them."

"Quite right," Ia agreed. "Though I do mean it in the Human

sense of the word, via compassion. Alright, Helstead has her next split shift on the bridge coming up, and Sergeant Maxwell hasn't had his dinner, yet. Let me know if you make any breakthroughs, gentlebeings."

Sobering somewhat, Helstead raspberried that idea, then sighed and stood up. "Right. Off to be an officer, and do all sorts of officerish stuff. In other words, be bored out of my mind while someone else flies the ship. I don't suppose I could learn how to fly it, Captain?"

"Not this year, Helstead," Ia countered firmly, gesturing toward the briefing-room door. She nodded politely at the others as Helstead preceded her. "Keep up the good work, meioas."

It wasn't until they were almost to the bridge that Helstead frowned and turned to her. "Wait, you said I might be able to contribute. All I did was sit there, listen, and crack up at the end."

"You did help, at the end. You helped me get my point across about the Salik," Ia said. "The net result won't have an impact for a few more years, but it'll be a valuable one in the end."

"Oh, mucking hell—you mean that stupid song about the butterfly wings causing a hurricane halfway around the world," Helstead groaned. She drew in a breath to speak, but Sergeant Maxwell's voice interrupted whatever the lieutenant meant to ask, echoing down the hall, and from her bracer.

"All hands, duty changeup in five minutes. I repeat, duty changeup in five minutes."

Sighing, Helstead gestured at the door to the side corridor. "I'd better go hit the head. It's been looking at me funny. Not quite like your first officer, though."

"He can look at me all he likes. He knows better than to touch," Ia said.

Helstead lifted her brows. "Have you told him that?"

Ia shook her head, but not in negation. "He did, once, and ended up getting sucked into a precognitive attack."

"What, like that Fire Girl vision thing?" Helstead asked her. She shuddered. "That was nasty. I didn't like it when it happened to me, and I don't like that I keep seeing it in the back of my brain whenever I get close to that restricted cargo of yours. That's just creepy."

"What Harper went through was a thousand times worse," Ia muttered as a crew member came up the hall, heading for the operations post to relieve his partner. "That's why he threw my boot at me, and why I left it there for him to throw at me, so he wouldn't risk suffering again."

"Duly noted, sir," Helstead agreed. She lifted one brow. "Just combat boots? Or will, say, a tennis shoe do?"

"Anything but a spiked heel, Delia," Ia joked dryly. "You throw too hard."

CHAPTER 7

Like so many other points in my career, those first engage-
ments were cases of hurry up and wait, wait, boring wait . . .
punctuated by screaming chaos and danger, followed by
repairs and yet another wait, wait, wait. Still, I was
rather . . .

. . . What? Was it fun? What kind of a . . . ? Why do you
keep asking me things like that? Look, provided you're not
a psychotic, chaotic, sociopathic serial killer, war is not
fun. Yes, there may be a few moments of exhilaration when
you defeat a dangerous opponent or overcome a difficult
obstacle, but the rest of it is not fun. I was rather proud of
my crew for coming through with so few scrapes and
bruises. I just wish they hadn't had to suffer any at all.

~Ia

FEBRUARY 7, 2496 T.S.
INTERSTITIAL SPACE

"Captain, this salvage is going a little harder than anticipated.
We have extensive debris blocking the corridor," Corporal
Puan stated over the comm link. *"Requesting a reroute of some*
sort."

The view from his helmet showed the debris in question, a

tangled mating between a crumpled bulkhead and two support struts. The spaces left would have been difficult for someone in a pressure-suit to navigate, never mind the bulk of a ceristeel-plated mechsuit. Nodding to herself, Ia replied, *"Understood, Corporal. Stand by while I check for alternate routes."*

Closing her eyes, Ia dipped into the timestreams. Specifically, into her own. From there, she could see the branching paths of her own observation point, cycling through the choices ahead of Puan's salvage team. Some of them were a little foggy, but they could . . .

Fog? Ia thought, for one puzzled moment. *Why would my vision be fogging ov—oh* shakk. Surging back into full consciousness, she slapped the comm relays for both ship and boarding party. *"All hands, we have incoming! I repeat, we have incoming, with anti-psi machines!"*

"Captain?" Puan queried. *"What's going on?"*

Anti-psi machines were the only things she could think of that could obscure a previously clear moment in time. As the fog rolled closer, Ia sorted out one of the more blunt approaches. *"Corporal, use a claymore, angle it into the right-hand wall from your position. Smash in and grab the whole cluster; don't bother to halve it. I want you back on the ship in five minutes."*

"Shakk—that doesn't give us—go go go! Togama, Tormez, one of you get me a claymore, triple-time it!"

Ia dialed down the volume on his channel, letting it chatter in the background. "Yeoman Sangwan, move us right up against that section of the station; I want us covering that boarding shuttle and that airlock with our own hull. Private Sung, seal up all pods and surfaces on our five o'clock, in case we have to scrape our way to a dust-off. Launch three scanner probes in the triangle and push 'em to the zone edge. Private Ng, start running spatial analyses as soon as Sung's probes are away. I want to know where the ships are coming from, and I want to know it before they know our position.

"Yeoman Nabouleh, prepare to disengage the moment your team is back on board," she ordered over the comm. "All eyes to the boards, all thoughts on your tasks."

The view from Puan's helmet pickups rocked a bit from the explosion. A yellow telltale popped onto Ia's top row of tertiary screens; Private Tormez hadn't hung back far enough, and had taken a little bit of damage to the knee-joint of her armor. Toggling the view from her teammate's camera, Ia watched her flex her leg joint a bit, then move back a little.

From her slight limp, the joint wasn't responding perfectly, but it was able to move. Togama slapped her on the pauldron and moved forward with Puan and his teammate, Franke. Satisfied the private was still mobile, Ia turned her attention to her main and secondary screens. Nothing happened for the first minute; nothing in the star-studded black changed, if one dismissed the vector-tumbled debris from their initial attack.

One minute turned into two minutes . . . three . . .

". . . Sir?" Private Ng asked, glancing over her shoulder. "Is something supposed to be happening?"

"Eyes to the boards," Ia ordered, repeating the Space Force Navy's mantra. "Thoughts on your tasks."

Just as Ng turned her head back, the navicomp beeped. "Sir! Incoming—173 by 147. Probe just picked it up, sir; we have partial cover from the station. ETA to our midpoint . . . five minutes."

That was a lucky break.

"Sir! We have movement on the station hull," Private Rammstein warned Ia from his post at the operations station.

"Good catch, Private," Ia praised. Ng blushed and returned her attention to her screens. Ia shook her head. "Keep an eye on the outer danger, Ng. Rammstein, what's on the hull?"

"It . . . ah, looks like a drone, sir," he said, tapping his controls. Normally, he was supposed to be monitoring the ship's systems, but two of his tertiary and his right secondary screens had been trained on the battered communications hub. "I can't get a good angle for a reading, but, it's headed straight for the shuttle."

"It's probably an automated hull mine," Sung said, eyes and hands working to try and get a gunnery pod's view of the scuttling automaton.

"Can a gunner pick it off?" Ia asked him. The fog was now thickening in her mind and starting to hurt.

"I think—"

"*Shakk!* Captain, revision, ETA *seven* minutes. Bogey's as big as a Battle Platform, sir," Ng corrected tersely. "Just got the stereoscopic off the third probe. It's farther out, but big as hell and headed our way."

"Helm to my control in twenty, Sangwan," Ia ordered, refitting her left hand into the control glove.

"Helm to yours in eighteen, Captain," Sangwan confirmed.

"Aquinar, fire!" Sung snapped into his headset. Seconds later, something *boomed* against the hull, rattling it. A dozen telltales streamed up Ia's left secondary screen, most amber, but a couple red. "Uh, sorry, sir!"

"Holy fractured—! Charlie Papa, Charlie Papa! We're not all on board, yet!" Puan hollered across the comm channels, using his phonetic call sign to get their attention. *"Franke almost had her arm ripped off! Her suit seals are red!"*

"Sorry, sir," Sung apologized. "I thought it was a clear shot."

"That'll come out of your pay," Ia quipped. The throbbing in her head was getting harder to focus through, but she knew the databanks were still safe. She could *see* them in the distance downstream and that they would extract the information needed. It was the local moment she couldn't foresee. Switching channels, she addressed Puan. *"Get on board, meioas. We've a whale-sized bogey ETA in six.* Sangwan, I have the helm."

"Aye, sir."

"Captain." The call came from the comm tech, Private Mysuri. "Infirmary is getting reports from all over the ship of headaches. Psis only."

"Tell the doc it's a side effect of the anti-psi machines. Have her prepare to receive injured after maneuvers." She started to say more but was interrupted.

"Nabouleh to Hellfire, all parties are boarded, sealing and sailing. You'll need to move the ship if I'm to dock."

"Moving now," Ia told the shuttle pilot. She couldn't use the insystem thrusters without risking damage to the shuttle, but she could pulse the FTL panels. *"All hands, brace for maneuvers, ten seconds."*

She spent those ten seconds calculating the angle and the distance, programming the options into her console. Ships could be piloted manually, or they could be programmed. At the end of them, she activated the panels along one side of the ship. Everything slammed to the opposite side as the ship squirted away from the crippled station. Squirted, and scraped, sending new yellow telltales scrolling up her tertiary screens.

For a moment, the interior safety fields kicked on, pressing in on all sides and pinning everyone in place. Then all the panels flared; greasy on all sides, the ship's momentum stopped. Her programmed path had kept the bulk of the damaged comm hub between them and the incoming ship, while leaving plenty of room for the shuttle to maneuver. This time, with the field fully enveloping the ship, there was no jolt.

There was also no headache for that brief moment. Just as Ia widened her eyes in realization, the fields cut off—and the headache stabbed back into her brain. She panted for a moment, mastering the ache, then grinned slowly. Ferally. "Well. *That's* good to know. Sung, tell all the gunners to make sure they've synched their weaponsfire to the FTL field . . . and yes, those new scrapes are coming out of *my* pay. *Nabouleh, dock as soon as possible.*"

"Cargo's on the shuttle, sir," the yeoman stated. *"We have injured on board. ETA one minute."*

"We're going to have some odd maneuvers in a few moments," Ia warned her. Not just her, but the rest of the ship, opening the channel to a shipwide broadcast. *"All hands, stay locked and webbed. I repeat, stay locked and webbed. The headaches are part of the anti-psi machine's side effects."*

"Captain, incoming is slipping its position," Private Ng warned Ia. "I think they're trying to get a clear shot."

"Thank you, Ng." Gaze going back and forth between the enemy ship and their own shuttle, Ia waited tensely. Finally, a distant *clunk* echoed down the length of the *Hellfire*.

"We're in, sir," Yeoman Nabouleh informed her. *"Docking clamps have engaged."*

The telltales for the bow shuttle bay lit green on Ia's upper leftmost monitor, confirming her words. Ia tapped the controls and slipped her left hand sideways and down. The FTL panels greased them that way with another abrupt jolt from momentum, and another hard squeeze from the black bubbles dotted around the cube-shaped room. Another flex of the full field cut out the anti-psi headache for a moment.

Taking advantage of their second dead stop, Ia gently shifted the ship, turning its long axis to follow the flight path of the incoming enemy vessel. Once it was positioned, she reapplied the unidirectional field, cutting off the headache. A touch of the controls configured the field to respond on the microscale for the smallest movements possible.

Once again, the headache went away. The release of mental pressure threatened to make her giddy. Focusing, Ia flipped halfway into the timestreams, and discovered she could now see everything *but* the Salik ship. A quick survey showed three possible escape routes. Ia checked them against the needs of the future.

"Uh, Captain?" Sangwan asked, his voice rising a little. The worry in his tone snagged her attention. "You *do* know we're sitting ducks if we're not moving, right?"

"Shhh." Dipping fully into the waters, Ia double-checked her findings. She had the time for it; things moved faster on the timeplains than they did in reality when she fully submersed her mind.

Using the hyperspace engines, either to escape or rift the ship, was one possibility. Using the main cannon was another. Using either of those, however, would leave the Salik more prepared for their next attack. That meant using slip-and-run tactics.

Opening her eyes, Ia heard Ng announce, "Three minutes to midpoint, twenty seconds to a clear shot, Captain."

"All hands, brace for acceleration." That was their only warning. Shoving her hands forward, one in the glove, the other on the controls with a sliding tap to remove the microscale restrictions, she pulsed the field forward. The cushioning in her seat saved her, as did the interior safety fields. Even with the field greasing the laws of physics around the ship, those fields had to pulse to move them forward, alternating with the insystem thrusters, and that meant some of the inertia did get through to the crew.

Ia was used to the drag of extra gravity on her body; it was part and parcel of growing up on Sanctuary. But even for her, the effects of their acceleration could be felt. Not only was it hard to draw breath, but the colors started to fade around the bridge. Greyness crept into the edges of her vision, warning her of blood loss to her brain. Ia cut the ship's acceleration for a second, then slipped them up, the only safe direction at that speed.

A split second later, the monitors showed a beam of bright yellow light lancing just past their hull. Around her, she could hear the deep breathing of her fellow bridge crew members. Rolling the ship slightly, again she slipped them up, relative to their new position. Again, they dodged another laser shot from the enemy ship.

"Sir!" Sung grunted. "Do we . . . return fire?"

"Lasers only," Ia ordered, struggling for breath herself, "but don't strain yourselves . . ."

The third time, she pushed forward again, accelerating them once more to the point of greyed vision and difficulty in breathing. This time, several beams of light lanced around them; had they slipped sideways, they would have been hit. The first two attacks had been ranging shots; having measured the length of their fishing pole as it were, the Salik now wanted to have them for lunch.

Disinclined to oblige them, Ia rolled the ship and slipped toward their dorsal side the moment those beams cut off. Most lasers could not be fired continuously for more than a dozen seconds because their conversion ratio still permitted a large percentage of their energy to be converted into localized heat. Even with thermal engines soaking away the excess heat, there was an upper limit to how long those lasers could be used. That included the workings of the Salik ships.

Ia used those brief breaks to effect their escape. Varying her angles, she slip-strafed one way, then the other, accelerating in jolts with barely enough time to recover between each one. Some of the lasers struck, but only briefly each time. Two, three, five hull segments flagged yellow. One turned red.

It was hard to say what their own lasers hit; the gunners could only fire when they were free to move without acceleration thwarting their efforts. They did hit something on the capital ship giving chase, but the navicomp's analysis suggested it was just a few scorched sensor panels.

The stars on the screen flashed in bright dots and turned into slow streaks. Ia increased the field strength to port, swaying everyone in their seats, though the G-force was mild compared to their actual escape. Another shift upward added to the gravity of the deckplates, then she straightened out their course.

"All hands, you are free to move. Medical team to the bow shuttle bay, stat." Switching off the intercom, Ia added, "Sangwan, prepare to take the helm. Ease up to full speed; now that we're faster-than-light and sideslipped from our last known course, there's no need to rush. Ng, double-check our heading; we're aimed at a system with a Dlmvla presence, yes?"

"Taking the helm in twenty, sir," the yeoman said, straightening in his seat now that gravity was no longer pulling them this way and that.

"Correct, sir," Ng told Ia, checking the information on her bank of screens. "If we stay on this heading another seven light-years, we'll reach the Llong-Jul 3127 System. Three gas giants and five Dlmvla mining colonies. Co-patrolled by Solarican forces, Captain, since they have a gas-mining station there as well."

"Transferring to your control in five seconds . . ." Ia murmured, transferring the control systems to his station. "Sangwan, you have the helm."

"Aye, sir. I have the helm," he confirmed.

Ia's headset came to life, projecting Helstead's voice in her ear. *"Helstead to Captain Ia, is it safe for me to eat again? I'd like to finish my lunch."*

She smiled slightly. *"You are cleared to eat, Lieutenant Commander. You have fifteen minutes before you're due back up here."*

"Yay! Thank you, sir. Helstead out."

"Message for you, Captain," Rammstein said.

"Patch it through," Ia told him.

"Captain, this is Corporal Johnson down in engineering," another male voice stated, this time in her right ear. *"We have some FTL field fluctuations, and several aft sensors are on the verge of failing. When are we going to be stopping to fix them, sir?"*

"You get an hour-long stop in just over half an hour from now to get the field stabilized, then you'll have to wait seven more hours for the rest." Ia shifted her attention to Ng and Sangwan. "Sangwan, continue on course for System Llong-Jul 3127. Don't push the panels too hard. Ng, plot him a course that brings us in close to the Jul II mining colony. I'd like to buy some hydrofuel from them, keep our tanks topped up while we're making repairs.

"Mysuri, have, ah . . . Private Smitt file a fund-transfer requisition form with Admiral Genibes," Ia added, having to think for a moment about who was on duty in the clerk's position. "Tell him it's for purchasing hydrofuel from the Dlmvla. When it's ready to send, have Sangwan drop out of FTL for a clear hyperrelay, and tell Corporal Johnson that's when he'll get his hour. Rammstein, anything that needs immediate repairs at that point, coordinate with Johnson, with a focus on the fields.

"Beyond that, if an emergency crops up, wake Commander Harper and have him deal with it," she added. "Otherwise, it's Helstead's watch, because in fifteen minutes, I'm going back to bed."

A couple minutes passed as the bridge crew quietly tended to their work. Rammstein finally shook his head. ". . . I knew the specs. I mean, I *studied* the specs, learned 'em inside and out . . . but I never thought we'd actually outrun anything as fast as that!"

"I'm just glad we did outrun 'em," Ng muttered.

"Heh," Sung chuckled. "I'll bet *they* weren't expecting to be outrun, especially as they were already moving when we took off."

Sangwan shook his head. "They didn't outrun us because they didn't want to lose sight of us. Now if we'd both been at a dead stop, then we'd have totally wiped their asteroids in our wa . . . uh . . ." He blushed, glancing briefly at Ia before returning his attention to his monitors. "That is . . . sorry, Captain."

"Relax, I don't mind a little blunt speaking on my bridge," she reassured Sangwan. "We'd have wiped their asteroids in our wake from a double dead stop, yes. But most of that is because we're less than a seventh the mass of that capital ship. And we didn't get away cleanly," Ia added, nodding at her lower rightmost tertiary screen. "The Infirmary reports three cracked ribs, a bitten tongue, and Private Franke has a dislocated shoulder and two compression fractures. By preference, I'd like to limit the number of Purple Hearts my crew earns."

Sung snorted. "All you have to do is tell us when you see it coming, sir," he stated. "You've been dead-on accurate about everything so far."

"Not entirely dead-on, Private; I only deal in probabilities, and free will still plays a big part in all of this. I can tell you what the biggest chances are, and how to influence the numbers, but God still rolls the dice, not me," Ia said. She spoke quietly, letting her gentle tone convey the seriousness of her message. "We *will* get injured in the course of this job. Some of us may even die . . . and I will not stop that from happening when it must, because my job is to make sure those who do die will perish only because they are doing what *must* be done, regardless of the cost. In the right place, at the right time, getting the right job done."

Her words sobered the others. They exchanged looks, glancing at her before returning their attention to their workstations.

"I know that isn't what you wanted to hear," Ia told them, looking up from her screens. "The only guarantees I can give you are that I'll be taking the same risks as the rest of you, and that I'll be doing my best to minimize those risks along the way. But minimized risk is not the same as risk-free."

"And you just accept that, sir?" Ng asked, voicing the concerns of the rest. "That some of us will be hurt and killed?"

"It's the same realization that *every* officer has to face, Ng," Ia told her. "Mine is just shoved home all the more thoroughly because I can *see* the results in advance. But I'll tell you what I've told Chaplain Benjamin through the years. I'd rather be damned for *trying* to do what's best and right, even if I fail, than be damned for not doing anything at all.

"I handpicked this crew because I know each one of you feels that same way deep down inside," she stated, stifling a yawn with effort. She didn't want her crew to think she was bored with their conversation, and she didn't want them to think she wasn't at her sharpest, even when tired. This wasn't the first time she would have to interrupt her sleep cycle for combat, after all. "Now, eyes to your boards and thoughts on your tasks."

FEBRUARY 8, 2496 T.S.
JUL II MINING STATION
LLONG-JUL 3127 SYSTEM

"Your request for round rocks we have processed," the Principal Nestor of Jul II stated. She dipped her head, with its multilensed eyes, and uncurled a clawed hand-thing. The gesture finished somewhere beyond the pickup range of the commscreen. "But this peet-zah thing I am uncertain. Datafiles indicate it is a Human food. We do not available have this Human food."

Ia smirked. She was taking this call in the briefing room forward of the bridge after a good night's sleep. "That's because you are fat, and covered in velvet."

The Nestor lowered her head farther, eye-skins puckering a little. "I do not . . . Ah. Illogic. You are courting me?"

"I'm declaring war on you," Ia countered calmly. "I think you're too purple, and you smell when you sneeze."

The Principal Nestor blinked a sideways-sliding membrane over her compound eyes. "Dlmvla do not sneeze. Regrettable it is, you cannot breathe with us. I think you are . . . metal foot garment. With lactations. For a Human. Anything else?"

Ia dipped her head in turn. "Nothing else. I look forward to firing upon your people in unprovoked madness, then inviting you into my home. Thank you for handling my extra request, Principal Nestor. I hope you like the vidshows I used for payment. They're more than old enough, copyright doesn't apply."

"Comedy entertainment transcends madness between our species. Copyrights are madness to exist at double the artist's life. Another point of similarity. Feathery secretions upon you," the Nestor added. "End transmission."

Ia closed the channel on her side as well. Shutting her eyes, she sat back in her seat at the head of the table and contemplated her efforts on the timeplains. *A bit of intrigue . . . but not much. Not yet. I'll have to work harder at provoking them. Get them to spread the word about how strange I am.*

The Dlmvla were "neutral" where the Salik were concerned. They had agreed not to supply the Salik with anything but weren't contributing ships to the Blockade, either. As methane-breathers, they had long ago figured they were low on the lunch menu, as it were. At least, compared to the oxygen-breathing species.

Of all the races, only the Chinsoiy were truly immune to the Salik appetite for living sentient flesh, but then they were silicon-based life-forms. The Chinsoiy also required daily irradiation for survival, at levels that would kill a chitin-covered K'katta, never mind a softer-skinned species like Humans or the frogtopusses. But once the Salik whittled away the Terran and V'Dan Humans, the Solaricans, the Tlassians, and the K'katta, they would make war on the Dlmvla—whose flesh would be deemed edible, even if acquiring it while the owner still breathed was problematic—and then they would destroy the Chinsoiy to make sure no one in local space could thwart their ambitions. Only then would the Salik finally fall upon the Choya, their own allies.

By then, the Salik would be nigh unstoppable. *If* Ia let the future unfold in their favor, that was. They were more prepared than anyone but she herself knew in the Alliance. Not even their Choya collaborators knew just how much effort the Salik had put into building their forces for the coming war. Deep, slow, treacherous plans. The only thing holding them back was a lack of personnel to command all the equipment they had mustered, even with Choyan assistance.

The door slid open. Rico walked inside, along with Xhuge, MacInnes, and Al-Aboudwa. All four were carrying portable workstations. They clipped them onto the table, claiming seats down either side. Ia smiled. "I'm glad you could join me, meioas."

"Ha-ha," Rico returned dryly, opening his workpad screen. "How funny. Shall we get down to business, Captain?"

"Certainly, Lieutenant. What've you found?" she asked them.

MacInnes spoke first. "They're using different code words for this set of datanodes—which would be rather smart of them, having two sets for steganography—but I was still able to pick out the nouns. Even some of the verbs, now that I'm getting a grip on how they talk and think."

Xhuge, who had linked his workstation to the briefing-room screens, looked up at the starcharts his efforts displayed. "Good thing, too, since they're on the move."

"Even with that difficulty, the work still went a lot faster this time," Al-Aboudwa stated. "The code words were different, but the security protocols were the same. Decrypting everything took a while, but only a fraction of the first time."

Ia smiled wryly. "Long enough for me to get a good night's sleep, though. Thank you."

Xhuge nodded. A touch of the controls highlighted three regions, one in yellow, one in orange, and one in green. A second touch overlaid a purple ring, which bisected the green blob. "Green is where they were, which corresponds with the hundred-light-year search ring we'd established. Yellow and orange are the two locations they were directed to travel to. Unfortunately, we don't know which."

"I hope you indeed got a good night's sleep, Captain," Rico told her. "We're expecting you to pull the correct location out of your magic hat."

"Not only a good night's sleep, but a fair bit of battle pre-planning," Ia said, studying the charts. She rose from her seat and moved over to the main screen behind Rico and MacInnes. "Anything distinctive about either of these regions? Local stellar features, planetary arrangements, visible nebulae?"

"Not a damn thing, sir," Xhuge replied. "Either you pull a rabbit out of your hat, or we're stumped."

"There might be an easier way, Xhuge. With the extra comm nodes we pulled, I've been playing some pattern analyses on the extra data," Al-Aboudwa said. A tap of his workpad pulled up a set of charts on the screen next to the one Ia was studying. One of them, he enlarged, displaying the spiked line squiggling across time. "The anti-psi manufactory sends out certain signals once every eight-day Salik week. We'd have to wait five more days for the next spike, then hit another comm hub, but . . ."

"We don't have five days," Ia finished for him.

"Here's a brilliant idea," MacInnes offered, catching their attention. "Why don't we just remind ourselves to put up a big note on the briefing-room wall saying *which* zone we went to, and just have you look at that precognitively, Captain?"

Twisting in his seat, Rico looked up at her, brows raised. "Good thought, MacInnes. I don't see why it couldn't work. Captain, care to take a peek?"

Ia held up one hand, thumb and forefinger pinched closely together. "There's a slight problem with that. I don't see *one* timeline. I see *all* of them." Turning back to the starchart, she traced her finger over the screen, electrokinetically drawing a set of lines. "If we go to fight at location yellow, here, then that's fine and dandy; we all do our jobs right, the main manufactory center gets destroyed, and we go merrily on our way to this green blob here, which will represent our next task in the continuum.

"But if we start at this orange spot here . . . we all do our jobs right, the main manufactory center gets destroyed, and we go merrily on our way to this green blob here, which will represent our next task in the continuum." Turning back to the others, she sidestepped the drawing and extended her arm, tapping the yellow and the orange blobs, now connected to the green one by a pair of white lines. "The problem is, I see *both* locations as viable possibilities. At about a fifty percent split, no less.

"This green blob down here, our next task, is actually *two* green blobs, overlapping each other because they're almost identical in every single way . . . except one has a sign in the briefing room that says 'We defeated them at Yellow!' And the other says 'We defeated them at Orange!' I see both, fifty-fifty. Equally valid, equally probable," she concluded, shrugging. "I need something *more* than a sign that could be posted in either possible reality. Something distinctive enough to tip the balance either way. Even an unusual star formation from the local point of view would give me a clue."

"Captain, I told you; there's nothing special about either location," Xhuge reminded her. "No stellar phenomena, no planets, nothing. They're both interstitial space, they're equidistant from ordinary, uninhabited star systems with large amounts of water ice in their Kuiper belts and Oort clouds, and no reason for them not to go to either spot. For all we know, the commander of the manufactory vessel flipped a *coin* to decide where to go."

"If they had, we could almost have you watch the coin being flipped," MacInnes joked, folding her arms and leaning her elbows on the table. "Except it's on a mobile station that gives everyone a raging headache when you get close. Or doesn't seem to exist, or however that works."

Al-Aboudwa sighed and slouched back in his chair. "So how are we going to find where our target has gone?"

"The same way I've been finding it all along," Ia said. "Narrow down the search sites—which we have done—and investigate it for blank-space anomalies. Negative proof is still a proof, in a way."

Lieutenant Rico tapped two of his fingers lightly, thoughtfully on the table. "Captain Ia . . . you said a few days back that you watch *people*, not things, correct?"

"Correct," she confirmed. "I could literally enter their lifestream and experience snippets of whatever they experience, if I wanted to."

"And Private MacInnes sees nouns . . ." he mused.

"Oh. Oh!" MacInnes said, sitting up with wide eyes. "G'nush-pthaachz Mulkffar-gwish! He's the requisitioning officer signing most of the orders we found. Maybe you *can* see him flipping a coin?"

Ia gave her a flat stare. Not because the idea was absurd,

but because the way she pronounced Sallhash phonemes was absurd. Ia's odd sense of humor kicked in, quirking the corner of mouth and brow. "I think I've finally found someone with an accent even worse than mine. I don't have even a tenth of your command of their language, but your accent amuses me. Thank you, Private."

"The question is, can you take someone else with you into these timestreams?" Rico asked her as the private blushed. "Maybe a clairvoyant? I'm presuming it would have to be a fellow psi."

"I could take *you*," Ia countered flippantly. "The closest you get to a psychic ability is your uncanny aptitude for languages . . . which isn't a bad idea," she allowed, thinking it through. "I can get *into* an alien's life-stream, and hear their thoughts, but I'm not a strong xenopath, and I'm no linguist. The Tlassian and Solarican mind structures are similar to Humans'. K'katta, Choya, less so. Gatsugi is a headache of nuances to sort through. Dlmvla as well. But Salik? They're cold and brutal, aggressive and cunning. Wading through their life-thoughts is like wading through cold, opaque slime.

"You may not have the mind-set of a Salik, but you know their language, which means you're closer to understanding their thoughts than I am," Ia allowed. Stepping closer to MacInnes, she leaned her palms on the back of the other woman's chair, giving her 1st Platoon lieutenant a frank look from across the table. "But if I take you onto the timeplains, Oslo, you're no longer a neutral observer. I don't think the people you report to would be happy about that."

"Wait a minute," Xhuge said, glancing between Ia and Rico. "Are you saying the lieutenant's a spy? We have a spy on board?"

"He's one of several on board," Ia corrected. "I know who each and every one of them is, and who they report to—and before you get in a panic, they all report more or less to the Admiral-General in the end, so they're all internal spies. Some more directly than others." Shaking her head, she straightened. "I think I'll just take a solo dip. That way, you don't compromise your neutrality, and I don't exhaust myself trying to push two or more people through that anti-psi field."

"I think I *should* go," Rico countered. "According to what

I was told, you haven't shown anyone on the Command Staff what it's like to be on the timeplains. Now, why is that?"

"Because it would be considered an undue influence upon their decisions," Ia said. "The same with yours. There *might* even be an accusation of Fatality Thirty-Eight, Bribery, levied at me if I tried to use it to convince my superiors to do as I request because of the fear that I'd show them lottery numbers or stock-market results. I'd rather not kick my career out the nearest airlock."

"I still think I should," he asserted. "In fact, I insist, Captain. Bribery doesn't even come into it because there's no way in hell I'll ever play the Salik version of a lottery."

Ia sighed and rubbed at her brow. She had foreseen this as a possibility. It had the risk of complicating things, but it also had the chance of getting him firmly on her side. *This will be tricky. How to show enough to convince him I'm being honest without showing him so much he either resists or the Admiral-General claims undue influence . . . or showing so little, he knows I'm holding back. Either way, he's going to see things he doesn't know he didn't want to see. Oh, this'll be fun . . .*

"There's an old saying that applies in this instance, Lieutenant," she warned him. " 'What has been seen cannot be *un*seen.' You insist a third time, I will take you . . . but it'll go on the record as being *your* idea, of your own free will, with no accusations of Fatality Thirty-Eight ever levied my way. And you'll do so by understanding that a trip onto the timeplains *will* change the way you look at things from here on out."

"I'm already compromised as a 'neutral observer' since you know about me," he pointed out. "I don't see how much worse it could get."

Xhuge winced, and Al-Aboudwa whistled softly. MacInnes shook her head slowly, a pitying look in her eyes.

"Tell me you did *not* just say that, sir?" Al-Aboudwa half joked. "That's like giving Murphy a wedgie, then asking him if it was good for him, too."

"*Never* taunt Fate, sir," MacInnes agreed. "Even a lowly grunt knows that much."

Xhuge choked, smothering his laughter behind his fist.

Dipping his head ruefully in acknowledgment, Rico murmured, "I'm sure I did just yank up on some devil's undershorts,

Private . . . but I still must insist, Captain. Take me onto these 'timeplains' of yours. I want to see what you see."

"Witnessed?" Ia asked the others.

"Witnessed," MacInnes agreed. Xhuge and Al-Aboudwa nodded, adding their confirmation.

"Alright then. Be it on your head. There are a few rules of engagement, of course," Ia told them. "Rule number one, no one touches either of us. My gifts can be triggered inadvertently by a touch, so if you have to get my attention, throw something at me from a distance. A datapad, a shoe, even a wrench if you must, so long as it's something small and nonliving."

"That would explain Helstead's comment about throwing boots at you, the other day," Rico muttered.

"Second rule, Lieutenant," Ia said, meeting his gaze. "Do not say the word 'Time' while we're on the timeplains. Time is like an entity where we are going because my abilities and my thoughts will literally be shaping whatever you see. You don't want to sidetrack my thoughts by provoking that entity. It would be like poking a tiger repeatedly. Is that clear?"

"Not really, but if those are your conditions, I will comply," the tall man admitted. "Anything else?"

"That'll do." She tipped her head to her right. "If you'll move to the far end of the table, I'll join you there. That way the others won't be tempted to touch either of us. But they can stay and watch if they want."

"I'd like to watch, Captain," MacInnes said, as Rico unfolded his long, large frame from his chair. "I'm not due for my shift on the bridge for another forty minutes. Did you, ah, want me to come along? I know what this Mulkffar-gwish fellow looks like. Would that help?"

"I'm enough of a telepath, I could pick it up from your thoughts first, if you're willing," Ia said, stepping back to give the lieutenant room to pass. "I'd rather limit who comes with me onto the timeplains, particularly as we'll be navigating areas clouded by those damned machines. I'm strong, but I have my limits."

"I'm willing, sir." Squaring her shoulders, MacInnes focused her gaze on her workstation screen for a long moment, then nodded. "I've got him in my mind now."

Nodding, Ia moved close. A touch of her hand on the private's wrist was all it took. Part of her gifts threatened to lean over the other woman's life-stream a little too far; Ia reined in the impulse to dive in, and focused instead on her thoughts. The image of a yellow-skinned, broad-faced, ostrich-legged alien came across clearly, clad in a leather-like tan-and-blue uniform dotted with rank markings and the circle-based language of his kind, listing his name and deployment affiliations.

Carefully withdrawing her hand, Ia clung to that image. "To quote the PsiLeague, 'What was yours is still yours. I thank you for allowing me this glimpse of your thoughts.'"

"Not a problem, sir. Um . . . what will *we* see when you do this?" the other woman asked.

"Not much. He might react a little, gasp or widen his eyes," Ia said, moving carefully down the length of the table. She wasn't really *seeing* the table, concentrating instead upon the image of the Salik named Mulkffar-nostril-flap-exhale. Gripping the back of the chair next to the dusky-skinned lieutenant, she turned it enough to drop into it, and stretched out her left arm with her palm up on the table. "You might get a headache from this, Lieutenant. Our thoughts will be racing faster on the timeplains than our bodies will be living out here in the real world, like a modified, unshielded race through OTL. Last chance."

"I'll take that risk, sir." Turning his chair to face her, knees almost bumping hers, he stretched out his right arm, covering her palm with his.

Ia curled her fingers over his hand. "Remember, I warned you. Take two slow, deep breaths, and relax."

"Does that help?" he asked, one brow quirked skeptically.

"Not really," she joked. "You're just less likely to choke."

That was all the warning she gave. Closing her eyes, Ia flipped both of them down and in—and hauled up on her passenger's mind, pulling him out of his own life-stream before he could drown in the overlapping sensations of a thousand potential possibilities.

"Welcome to the plains," Ia stated as she steadied him. Rico blinked and looked around, clinging to her hand with both of his. All around them was a vast, rippling field of gold-and-green grass crisscrossed in a thousand rivulets, all drenched in bright golden sunlight. Nothing but grass, sun, and water as far as the eye could see.

"Where . . . ? Or rather, what is this place?" he corrected himself, straightening.

"This is how I most often visualize Time." The word rippled grass and streams like a harsh wind. It even seemed to roil clouds across the sky for a moment, before the impression faded. Ia let it fade before speaking again. *"But I can change it. Shape it. Intensify it, codify it, itemize it . . ."*

The tall man blinked and frowned. *"I don't understand. You say you can see all possibilities. What future possibility is this from?"*

"Most of them. It's a matter of scale, Lieutenant," she said, and gestured at the rivulet of a stream closest to them. *"That's your life."* A twist of her thoughts enlarged it until it was a meter deep and wide, large enough to show images flickering in the water. Images from his immediate past. *"I can watch scenes from moments in your existence, past and future. I can even step inside the stream and experience from your own perspective what you've already experienced, or will, or might. And I can shrink it down and trace how your life interacts with others' lives, and how they stain each other in colors of influence."*

She shrunk the streams back down again, then turned his stream blue and a nearby one red, and showed them interacting, staining each stream with hints of purple, one more strongly than the other.

"Whose life is that?" Rico asked her, eyeing the purple-tinted red.

"Private MacInnes; she looks up to you as a role model. Not a bad choice, either," Ia told him. Erasing the colors, she gestured with her free hand. *"Upstream is the past; downstream is the future. I hauled you out of your life-stream when we first arrived because the moment we arrive is always the present, and lingering in the present creates a doubled, disorienting sensation. In addition to that, any thought you have can trigger an associated memory from the past, rushing those memory-waters downstream into you. Think of toast, and you'll drown under a thousand different instances of eating caramelized bread."*

"Lovely. Why do our voices echo so much?" he asked next, lifting the littlest finger of his free hand to his ear for a wiggle.

"We're immersed only lightly at the moment." Concentrating, Ia increased her awareness of the timeplains, and with it, his. *". . . Is that better?"*

He wiggled his finger in his ear one more time, then nodded. "Better." Pausing, he inhaled, blinked, then inhaled again. "Amazing. I can actually *smell* the sunbaked grass. But why is it more blue now than green?"

His question provoked a smile from her. "That's because the local equivalent to grass on Sanctuary is blue. The grass really *is* greener on Earth."

Squinting against the sunlight, Rico studied the plains. "So, what do we do now?"

"We look for two things. Our blank spot, and our supply-requisitioner. But not like this," Ia said. "Try not to feel vertigo."

He glanced at her—and clutched at her hand again as the grass fell away, replaced by stars. "God!" Rico exclaimed, grip tightening around her fingers. His large, muscular frame floated awkwardly next to Ia's. "Warn me better, next time!"

"You're the one who wanted to come along," Ia pointed out.

Brow furrowing in a frown, Rico gave her a pointed look. "I thought you said your abilities focused more on people, not places."

"They do," she admitted.

"So how is it we're surrounded by a giant star map?" he asked. "Aren't these places, not people?"

"Yes, but they're a composite awareness of the stars as viewed by a large sampling of people's life-streams," Ia explained patiently.

He stared at her. She stared back, lifting an eyebrow in a silent dare to see if he would ask another question.

". . . Right," Rico finally muttered. "I'll just shut up now and go along for the ride."

Turning her attention to the stars, Ia zoomed them in toward two patches of misty grey nebulae. "We should have a slight advantage. This moment is the Now." She paused as the stars twinkled around them, then continued. "What we're looking for is upstream, into the past. Not just any random past, but specifically what has already happened in our own temporal lineage. That way we can rule out the fifty-fifty probability of either location, because one should have been selected by now. The difficulties will be: one, finding any life-streams in the anti-psi mist to examine; and two, finding those life-streams whose owners have actual knowledge of where they've gone."

Stopping at the edge of one of the two mist-patches, Ia lifted her hand, summoning a hologram of a Salik with dull yellowish skin, the image she had lifted from MacInnes's mind.

"G'nush-pthaachz Mulkffar-gwish. Or rather," Ia made the image say, with the proper nostril-flap flexings, "~*Pthaachz Mulkffar*^." This was all inside her head, constrained only by the limits of her gifts, not the limits of her body. She switched back to her own voice, letting the Salik's face fade slowly. "Keep him in mind."

"Why should I?" Rico asked her. "It's not *my* psychic abilities being used here."

"No, but your Sallhash is better than mine," she reminded the tall man at her side. Even floating in mental space, he was still larger than her. Proportionately larger, letting her know he was comfortable with his greater size. "You wanted to know what I see, and that means seeing it right alongside me. But this is the Space Force. You pull your weight, even what little there is in this place. There are no free rides here, soldier."

"Sir, yes, sir," he muttered. "Three bags full, sir."

"That only counts if you can say it in Sallhash," Ia quipped. A *snerk* sound escaped him; a glance showed his mouth twisted in a half smile. She returned it with a wry smile of her own. "Brace yourself, Lieutenant. We're about to get up close and personal with Salik xenopsychology."

A tiny pinpoint was moving away from the cloud. Ia dove them down toward it. The pinpoint became a Salik starship, long and five-lobed. It zoomed close, and the hull vanished, replaced instead by a splash of water, a wavering impression of a corridor, a distortion of two overlapping, separately moving views. Ia felt Rico clutching at her hand, bruising it with his mental strength, and pulled back until they stood once more on the grassy banks of someone's life-stream.

"*What's wrong?*" she asked, gentling the intensity for a moment.

He blinked and looked around. "*We . . . I . . . That was . . . disorienting. Is that how they view the world?*"

"*Yes.*" Stepping down into the alien's cold, thick water, she tugged him after her. "*We have to wade through several of these lives. Watch your step. I'm intensifying the connection to the timestreams again.*"

"Wait," Rico said. "If we talk to each other . . . will they hear us? Or if we try to talk to them?"

"No. It'd be like talking to a previously recorded vidshow broadcast and expecting the actors to hear you," Ia said. "Whatever reception equipment I have, I don't think it can broadcast back to them. At least, I've never gotten it to work with friends and family. I can't even talk to *myself* whenever I investigate my own life-stream, which has caused some problems along the way—the proverb 'if I'd known back then what I know now' is singularly unhelpful since my future self cannot tell my past self a damn thing, and I don't have enough seconds to spare to say it out loud in the future, let alone to write it down. Now come, we're wasting our opportunity."

Breathing deep, he stepped into the water, following the tug of her hand. Ia submerged them, tapping into that crew member. Not deep enough to hear thoughts; just enough to see what that alien saw. The view was doubled and too broad for Human vision, with eyes bulging up from the skull, pointing this way and that. She could feel a headache forming from the disorientation of it and knew Rico would be feeling it, too.

This wasn't the first time she had investigated a Salik life, though. Swimming upstream, she skimmed through snippets of past events, a shift cycle beginning, an encounter with an officer on watch. Jumping into that stream, she followed that officer in flashes of past events to the beginning of their shift, and from there, to another officer. But that officer merely came from his sleeping tank, so she followed his life-stream down through his day . . . until he encountered the ship's captain.

Leaping into his life-stream was easier now that Rico wasn't resisting the disorientation that came with each transition. He did pull himself closer as she pushed upstream into the past, clinging as the turbulence increased. Some of that came from the speed at which she moved. Some of it came from an increasing misty pressure. Rather than letting it push them out of the water, Ia pushed them deeper into the captain's head—and then sideslipped into the navigator's as soon as the captain observed enough of the bridge crew for her to select the right alien.

His thoughts were murky, the terminology and grammar disjointed at first. Eventually, the distortions made sense. *More three years. Service ending, female become. Puddlings teach to eat,* followed by an image of the captain, and a mental hiss of vicious vengeance-and-hunger.

"I don't think he likes the captain," Ia whispered to Rico, her noir sense of humor surfacing for a moment. *"What do you think?"*

"If you'd studied their culture and history, you'd realize most Salik subordinates don't," he whispered back. They couldn't even see each other anymore at this level of xenoawareness, but he was still clutching her mental hand tightly. *"Wait . . . back it up. I think I can read the coordinates for their heading."*

Ia complied. She couldn't exactly freeze the moment, not with the pressure of that anti-psi misting her mind, but she could replay it in slow, short passes. The navigator looked at the screens positioned over his head, one eye on the actual heading, the other on reference stars and designation numbers.

When she felt him nod, she advanced them upstream again. The mist and the pain thickened apace. Her grasp of Sallhash, written and thought, started to slip. Pushing Rico's consciousness to the fore, she guided him upstream to the point where the navigator heard the captain order the pilot to disengage from dock and tell the navigator what course to set.

She could feel Rico's confidence that knowledge of those coordinates would be enough to place their location. Ia wasn't so sure. Stretching herself, she left him in the navigator's waters and dipped into the captain's thoughts.

Riptides of sloppiness, she heard the captain cursing in the privacy of his mind. *Pity for those prisoners. Now useless dredge-sand.*

With that thought came an image of Solaricans, shaved and restrained on tables, their wrinkled heads encased in bands that looked vaguely like the anti-psi headsets Ia had seen back on Sallha at the aborted banquet. Ia pursued that thought, trying to find a time reference. She found it from three Salik Standard days before. Grabbing Rico, she pulled him after her, ignoring his wordless protests.

The pain increased, the farther back they went. It was oddly like G-force sickness. The edges of her vision started to grey out. Each breath became a struggle. But the captain *was* there . . . and did come close enough to one of the Salik scientists for Ia to make the leap into her life-stream.

Sexual deviancy among the Salik had nothing to do with methods of copulation. This was a Salik who had chosen to turn female without procreating. Her thoughts were cruel, vicious, and cold. Clinical, in that she thought about the torment of the Solarican prisoners simply as an exercise in observing their reactions to various anti-psi modulation exercises. She felt none of the pity the captain had felt; she did not think her prey unworthy of time or effort. To her, the felinoid aliens were objects to be toyed with until destroyed. Her hunt was all about knowledge, not adrenaline and food.

Forcing back the flow of time, Ia found another Salik, an officer. Male again—cold and brutal, but not nearly so calculating. Then another . . . and a third, one who was eating a prisoner, a skreeling, shuddering, bleeding K'katta chained with all ten legs sprawled out straight, leaving it no more than a finger-width of room in any direction in which to shudder and move. Rico huddled mentally at her back, no longer reaching voluntarily for the thoughts and words of these tentacle-fingered fiends.

Ia endured the first-person perspective of the Salik's meal, watching them eat because it was a meal being shared by five high-ranking officers. Her detachment was dissimilar to the Salik scientist's; hers was an effort to listen to their words because she had no other choice, not because she was intrigued by what they were doing. Thankfully, with the anti-psi machines pressing around, it wasn't difficult to ignore the visual aspects. It was a little harder to let the flavors and scents fade, but when they did, the mental presence of her lieutenant uncurled a little, listening intently.

What they heard surprised him, for he squeezed her hand tightly. Ia didn't let herself think about it. Instead, she listened a little bit longer, repeating the discussion three full times to make sure both of them heard all of it. Only then did she carefully retreat, moving slowly enough that neither of them would suffer the psychic equivalent of decompression sickness. As she did so, she slid them forward through that officer's timeline, double-checking along the way to make sure his home vessel was indeed headed where that conversation said it would go.

The moment she had confirmation, she pulled back. The grey mist became the star field, became a single watery stream, its surrounding, grassy prairie . . . and with a final flip, the briefing room. Used to the disorientation that was the return to reality after such a deep descent, Ia inhaled slowly, calming her nerves. Lieutenant Rico's face looked pasty, almost grey in spite of his natural golden brown tan.

"Breathe, Lieutenant," she ordered quietly, finding her voice. "Slow, deep breaths. Focus on the sound and feel of your own breath. Nice, slow, steady breaths, four times in a row . . ."

Behind Ia, MacInnes rose from her seat, moving over to the alcove by the door where a drinks dispenser had been installed. Rico blinked and complied, brown eyes still unfocused. On the fourth exhale, he shuddered and released her hand. Elbow braced on the table, he lifted his fingers to his mouth, breathing hard and fast through his nose.

Wisely, the private poured and brought back two mugs of cold water. "Drink this, sirs," she urged, offering one cup to Ia and the other to Rico. She had to help Rico lift his to his mouth, his free hand shook that much. "Easy, Lieutenant; let me help you . . . There, just a sip at a time . . . There you go, that's the first one."

Once he had taken that sip, the private dipped two fingers in the water, then stroked her damp digits across his brow. Pursing her lips, she blew a stream of air on his forehead. Ia dipped her own fingers in her cup, dabbing it from her hairline in a streak down the middle of her brow, parting her fingers to either side of her nose. She sipped slowly from the cup while the cool liquid on her skin drew some of the heat out of her temples and sinuses.

The water-cooling trick was the same one taught by the PsiLeague, which MacInnes was affiliated with, as well as by the Witan Order, which had trained Ia in the early uses of her gifts. It was meant to help focus thoughts as well as reduce the heat-induced headaches that often accompanied intense psychic efforts. Ia rarely suffered from them, but the anti-psi fog plus the need to shelter and escort another mind through the time-plains had taken its toll.

". . . How?" Rico finally rasped, sipping again at his water. MacInnes moved back, giving him a clear view of their CO. "How do you stay *sane*?"

There were several replies she could have made to that. Out of habit, Ia checked the timestreams. Her head still hurt, but the skimming of potential reactions to various responses was quick and easy compared to the effort she had just undertaken. Settling on one of the better answers, she gave it to him.

"Practice, and a lack of time, Lieutenant. I literally cannot afford to waste my time on something as self-indulgent as insanity. I have too many lives to save. Let me know when you've recovered," she added, lifting her cup for another sip. That lifted his head sharply, his gaze meeting hers. "We still need to check the other probability cloud, to make sure that what we heard was right."

"*Shakk,*" he whispered, dropping his forehead to his palm this time. "I don't know if I can take . . . experiencing . . . a Salik officer eating a prisoner again."

The others blanched. Xhuge covered his mouth, and MacInnes swallowed hard. Al-Aboudwa looked away. None of them asked any questions about it.

"Slow breaths, Lieutenant. Focus on the scent of the air, on the sound of it filling your lungs," Ia ordered. She waited until he complied, then said, "Don't worry about it if you don't want to go in again, Rico. It's doubtful we'll have to endure that exact scene a second time, but you don't *have* to go with me again. I'll admit your ability to translate Sallhash a lot faster than I can was an asset on this trip, and I wouldn't mind having it again, but you don't have to come along." Looking over her shoulder, she added, "Xhuge, Al-Aboudwa, when he's ready, the lieutenant has some Salik coordinates for you."

Xhuge nodded and tapped something into his workpad, readying it for taking notes.

Sipping at his water, Rico managed a question. "How long were we out of it?"

MacInnes shrugged. "A minute? Maybe a little longer?"

Rico looked up at her, then at Ia. ". . . Only a minute? It felt more like half an hour!"

"If Time didn't flow considerably faster on the timeplains than it does in real life, I would have slit both throat and wrists in despair long ago, because I wouldn't have had the time to find a way out of the coming apocalypse," Ia stated. Draining her cup, she clipped it to the edge of the table and rose. "I'm going to use the head. Take a few minutes to decide whether or not you want to accompany me on a second trip while I'm gone, Lieutenant. There's no shame in refusing if you don't want to go. If you do, expect an even greater headache by the time we're through."

Dipping her head politely, she left him to contemplate the consequences of what else he might see. The odds were very high that he would decline this time. Ia was fine with that since what she could see of his future reactions showed little disturbance in her overall plans. Whether or not he came with her, she would find the necessary confirmations and get the job done.

That was what kept her sane: managing her priorities in the face of the relentless ticking of Time.

CHAPTER 8

Historians get to have the luxury of looking back upon the past and pronouncing judgment upon it from the cushioned comfort of their office chairs. Ask any historian when the First Salik War ended, and they'll smugly say when the Salik High Command surrendered to the Alliance generals. Some might be more precise by saying it was when the Salik surrendered "all" of their warships, while others would say the war actually ended when they handed over all their other means of interstellar travel, too.

Soldiers who participated in maintaining the Salik Interdicted Zone will tell you that war never actually ended. They'll swear it just went into a lull while the Salik nursed their grudges along with their wounds. Having served on the Blockade, I cannot fault my fellow warriors for believing the war, at least for the Salik and the people trying to keep them confined, hadn't ended.

As for when the Second Salik War began, one could say it began in the Terran Standard year 2496. One could be more precise and pinpoint the first half of that year, which most scholars and soldiers would agree upon. Some would insist my Company's prewar efforts be included in those war-catalyzing and -defining moments, which would narrow it down to the start of February or thereabouts. Officially,

*it started later, of course, with the open attacks on key
Alliance homeworlds . . . but for my crew, it definitely
started earlier.*

~Ia

FEBRUARY 10, 2496 T.S.
INTERSTITIAL SPACE
SOMEWHERE NEAR THE TLASSIAN-K'KATTAN BORDER

"I have the helm, Sangwan," Ia stated.

"You have the helm, sir," the yeoman confirmed. Unlike the last time he had passed her helm control, his voice was unsteady. "I think I'm going to be sick."

"There's a plastic bag in your rightmost drawer," she offered pragmatically, checking her monitors. "But I suggest saving it for later. We're not engaged in combat yet."

"*Thinking* about combat is what's making me sick. I really don't like what we're about to do, sir," Sangwan muttered.

"Well, if you'd like to be dismissed from the bridge, now is the time," Ia told him, adjusting the *Hellfire*'s attitude just a tiny bit more. Opening a comm channel, she contacted the 1st Platoon's lead gunnery expert. *"Captain Ia to Corporal Bagha, what's the status on the special missiles?"*

"Locked and loaded, Captain," Bagha reported. *"We just finished sealing up the last P-pod bay half a minute ago. Give my team three or four more minutes to get into our gunnery pods, and we'll be ready to go."*

"You have four. Don't waste them. Ia out."

The seconds ticked away. She had already given the fifteen-minute warning earlier, and a quick splash through the timestreams showed almost everyone was in place. Those who were in bed had either lashed themselves down with special webbing or moved to acceleration couches; the galleys were shut down, the gunners were getting into their pods, and the stragglers who had needed that one last trip to the bathroom were all but done strapping themselves into place. One of them was Lieutenant Commander Helstead. She hurried in at the next-to-last moment and claimed the backup navigation/scanner post.

Ia opened the shipwide intercom as the short woman webbed

herself into her seat. *"This is Captain Ia to all hands. Prepare for combat, and prepare for maneuvers. I repeat, all hands, prepare for combat, prepare for maneuvers. You have one minute, mark."*

Those seconds ticked away as well.

"First drop in ten," Ia warned her bridge crew as she eased back the FTL field. "Get me lightwave, meioas."

Flashing dots filled the bridge. Ia held them just under the speed of light for ten seconds, then pushed them over Cee once more. Ten seconds passed, then she dropped the ship below Cee for another ten. Again, they shifted faster-than-light . . . and a third time dropped below the grey-flashing threshold.

". . . Got it, sir!" Private Ng called out, hands flicking over the controls. "To your main, now."

A ghostly overlay of ship positions appeared on her screen. Ia stared at them, mind racing, gifts dipping into the timestreams. Electricity sparked from her right hand into the console. *"Bagha, you got that?"*

"Aye, sir! Targets confirmed," the other woman called back through the comm link.

"Dropping for launch in five . . . four . . . three . . . two . . . one." Ia pulled back on their speed one more time.

A single, loud *whump* echoed down the ship. The moment she felt it, Ia squeezed them back over the FTL line, then accelerated. The navicomp was the most sophisticated computer on the ship, capable of analyzing the most minute scraps of data. It could take the faintest, starlit images and resolve them into ships, stations, asteroids, any and all manner of cosmic phenomena. It could even give a fairly accurate estimate on an updated location for everything with just two observations of a few seconds each.

With three glimpses, it could confirm those placements and transfer the information to homemade rockets launched from the *Hellfire*'s projectile pods. It could not, however, accurately predict where to move its own presence in the next two minutes in order to achieve their objectives. That was Ia's job.

"All hands, engaging in five . . . four . . ." she counted over the intercom. At *one*, Ia brought the long ship down below the threshold. Yet again, the screens flashed from blurred streaks to bubbles that popped in unison, becoming simple pinpricks of light. Red circles quickly zeroed in on every object within

sixty light-seconds, and a familiar ache zeroed in on Ia's mind. Not only were there a good twenty ships ahead, ranging from a Battle Platform–sized station to several destroyers, there were hundreds of active anti-psi machines in the zone, their effects painfully accumulative.

"All pods, acquire targets and fire," Private Magnan ordered calmly. Sung was serving elsewhere this hour, which meant the dark-skinned woman had taken his place as head of the gunnery teams on the bridge. Others might have wondered why Jana Bagha wasn't on the bridge, but Bagha was a Sharpshooter, trained to shoot as an individual gunner; Ia knew Magnan had the tactical training to guide and direct other shooters in a free-for-all.

Free from that worry, Ia concentrated through the misting pain. Left hand in the sensor glove, she flexed the FTL fields and shifted the *Hellfire*'s attitude, pointing the nose down just a little bit. Zooming through the void at a speed dangerously close to Cee, Ia shifted the ship a tiny bit more. Orange-red lasers lanced outward at those enemy ships, painting them as targets for the missiles riding in hard and fast at their back.

Yellow lines intersected on her main screen, triggering collision-alert beeps. A large ship lay partly across their path. Free-falling the ship in a brief bubble of warped physics—half of one precious second of shielded real time was all she needed to predict their near future—Ia corrected course slightly and angled the nose down even more, relative to their flight. The beeps grew louder, disturbingly fast. Within a handful of seconds, the beeps became claxons, distressed sirens paired with flashing lights in imminent-collision warning.

A slight, downward shift was all it took, just a dozen meters. The shields of the *Hellfire*'s nose scraped across the shields protecting the Salik warship, jolting both vessels. In less than a blink, they were past it. A second bubble-shift tilted the *Hellfire*, angling it perfectly for an attack on the space station beyond. The anti-psi field was also so strong now, Ia was glad she had ordered all psychically sensitive crew members to stand down for this operation.

Jabbing the controls, Ia opened the bay doors to the second OTL nose cone. Not to extend it, but enough to give it a clear angle of fire. The claxons stopped, then shifted back to beeping a collision-alert warning.

Ignoring the noise, Ia launched the hyperrift spark just before reaching the station. A split second later, they transited the three-kilometer station's midpoint. She snapped the FTL field back into place around the ship and drove them forward—not along the path they had been traveling but along the line they were now facing.

The vector change slammed their sense of momentum back and upward, rushing the blood to their heads for one uncomfortable, safety-field-squeezed moment. The pinpoints of light surrounding them burst into bubbles and smeared into streaks. Vision greying, Ia slowed their acceleration, holding them just slightly faster than Cee for several seconds. That eased the pressure on their bodies.

Flexing the fields, she reduced their speed once more for a much more gentle, sublight turn. Within two heartbeats, the massive headache eased. Pain still lingered, greying the timestreams in the back of Ia's mind; several of those ships still had anti-psi machines active, generating their annoying, gift-masking fields. But her head didn't feel like it was two throbs away from rupturing a blood vessel. The mass of machines on the big station were clearly gone, proving that exo-EM radiation moved faster than EM itself could.

The proof that the two moved at different speeds was obvious. Behind them, their lightwave front caught up with them on their rearward-facing scanners. The navicomp identified the *Hellfire* as it skimmed past the patrolling enemy vessels, a tiny green line intersecting a tiny red blob of dots. The green line darted through a swarm of yellow bars indicating both the *Hellfire*'s L-pods attacking and the few attempts their enemy had made to shoot back. They had been traveling so fast, Ia hadn't even noticed the return shots when they happened, though she could now see the tangled grid of laserfire arrowing off in all directions.

Sangwan's screens, directly ahead of and below Ia's, flicked to a magnified view. Stars rippled across the *Hellfire*'s polished hull; a blue-white spark spat outward as the ship zipped past the station—and blipped from view in a tiny bubble-flare of all that reflected starlight as its mad, white-haired pilot took the ship back to faster-than-light speeds.

A second later, the station *crunched* inward in an explosion. They couldn't hear it on the bridge, but that magnified view showed it viscerally. The station's matter had collapsed the edges of the hyperrift, creating a deadly pinpoint of imploded fusion. That energy slammed outward in streaks of white-gold, shearing through bulkheads and igniting rich, dark reddish fires—the colors were artificially shifted by their speed. Outward-bound as they still were, despite their gradual curve, the lightwaves were stretched out, giving them extra time to look at what was unfolding to the rear.

Her aim had been slightly off; from the looks of the way the station was breaking up, the hyperrift had struck off-center. But that didn't matter; the fireball expanded abruptly as the rifted energies ignited what looked like a stockpile of nonwater-based fuels. Dark red and bright orange billowed outward for a moment from the largest chunk, then it, too, succumbed to the forces of the hyperrift's collapse.

Other points in the interstitial night now blossomed in their wake. Fire boiled outward from several red-outlined ships. The projectiles Ia had ordered from the Dlmvla, the weapons which Harper's engineers had cobbled together in just over a day, turning them into missiles which Bagha's teams had loaded into the launch bays . . . those warheads had contained dozens of head-sized, machine-rounded rocks. The crew's engineers had cobbled them together with attitude thrusters, basic targeting scanners, navicomp relays, and small explosive charges set to break each capsule apart when it came within collision distance of any object larger than a fellow missile, postlaunch.

Under ordinary launch conditions, they wouldn't have been dangerous. Most ships possessed decent, functional shields that could have warded off the mass of the intact missiles, never mind the smaller masses of each individual rock. But those were at insystem combat speeds, which were usually well below one-tenth the speed of light.

Released at near-Cee, however, even the biggest shield generators would be hard-pressed to keep out inbound rocks less than half the size of the ones the *Hellfire* had launched. Only the physics-warping fields of FTL panels could have saved those ships. Unfortunately for the Salik, most of them had been either cruising the area at insystem-patrolling speeds or parked at a dead stop relative to the station.

Insystem thrusters, while capable of shunting aside modest

interstellar debris, were not the same thing as FTL warp fields. The Salik never stood a chance under that devious an attack.

Her headache eased further as they watched, proof several of the ships had been damaged badly enough to cancel their own anti-psi emanations. Some were still active, but not many. Pulsing the FTL panels, Ia checked the timestreams for a moment, then dropped back fully into her body, satisfied.

She didn't have to send the ship back in for a second, slower, and much more dangerous round of attacks. The biggest dangers on this first pass would have come either from not going fast enough to avoid the few unexploded inbound missiles—which were too crudely cobbled together to ignore detonating near their own ship, though she could order them to detonate from a distance—or from not shifting far enough to miss that one ship. As it was, the only yellowlit telltale on her upper tertiaries was a warning light for a stressed shield panel at the bow of the ship. Not a single, hastily aimed shot by the enemy had harmed them during their too-fast strike.

"Rammstein, did you get all of that recorded?" Ia asked the operations tech. "Inbound, attack, and lightwave confirmation?"

"Aye, sir," he agreed.

Satisfied, she brought the warp fields back up to speed, slipping them one last time over the Cee border. "Bundle it up and hand it off to Mysuri for transmission to Admiral Genibes," she ordered. "We'll drop out of FTL in a little bit for that when I'm sure we've escaped pursuit."

"Aye, sir," he said.

"Can I be sick now?" Sangwan asked, glancing over his shoulder at Ia. "Or do we still have more fighting to do?"

"We have more fighting to do, Yeoman, but not for another fourteen or so hours," Ia told him. "The next battle will be slightly uglier. Ng, plot a hyperwarp course for Point B, starting half a light-year from here."

"Already on it, Captain. Correct course to . . . 22 by 317, sir."

"Heading 22 by 317, good work, Private," Ia confirmed. This time, instead of curving around to the right, she curved the ship to the left and up a little.

"I don't see why you're still upset, Sangwan," Helstead murmured to him a few moments later, apparently catching sight of his frown. "We came out of that with barely a scratch. You should be pleased."

"Yeah, but only after the Captain managed to pull off maneuvers that would've made Shikoku Yama himself sweat," he muttered back. "Did you see how close we got to that ship? At near lightspeed? Sir," he added respectfully to Helstead.

"I'm sure the Captain knows what she's doing," Helstead said. "Right, sir?"

"I have far too much to do, gentlemeioas, to risk my life carelessly. That includes your lives as well," Ia told both of them, guiding their ship onto the indicated course. "After being shot in the shoulder with a laser cannon at a mere three percent probability, I have learned to be a lot more careful in calculating the odds. I know I cannot always beat them, but my tasks are too important not to try."

"You were shot in the shoulder with a laser cannon, sir?" Rammstein asked her, curious.

"Handheld cannon at point-blank range," Ia explained. They had reached maximum speed, and were more or less on course, so she set the ship on autopilot and relaxed. "It was back when I was in the Marine Corps, our first mission on Oberon's Rock while I was with Ferrar's Fighters. Hurt like a slagging son of a *shakk*, too. You can ask Lieutenant Spyder about it if you're curious. He wasn't in the Company at the time, but he heard the others' reports after he joined Ferrar's Fighters."

"Is that where you learned how to pilot like a madmeioa, sir?" Sangwan asked dryly.

She knew he didn't mean Basic Training; he meant actual combat flying. "Nope. I learned how to do that while serving two years on the Blockade."

"And all of it precognitively guided," Helstead observed.

"Most of it. The first time I encountered an anti-psi machine, I had to wing it. I was on an OTL Harrier-Class," Ia confessed. "We could only go as fast as three-quarters Cee at max speed, and had no FTL panels. Unlike now, I didn't know that FTL could cancel the anti-psi effects. I also didn't know what I was up against at the time.

"But I got myself, my crew, and both halves of my ship out of that mess—Delta-VX," she added in explanation, meaning a type of ship that was actually two vessels coupled together. "I did so by evaluating the situation and coming up with a viable solution based on the resources I had available. Which was double-rifting the Salik capital ship as I flew us past at maximum speed.

"That is why I insisted on having hyperspace nose cones installed both fore and aft on *this* ship. Dangerous as it is, that little trick will continue to save our lives. Now, are you feeling well enough to fly, Yeoman?" she asked Sangwan.

He sighed and nodded. "Aye, sir."

"Then prepare to receive the helm. Write up your tactical analyses of what just happened and hand 'em up the chain of command for your weekly Squad and Platoon debriefing and discussion sessions," she ordered. "I need to get back to my daily regimen. Flab and foe wait for no one."

Helstead *snerked*. A couple of the others bit back smiles of their own. Sangwan was too busy preparing his station for control of the ship, though his shoulders didn't look quite as tense as before. "Aye, Captain. Helm to my station in ten, sir."

INTERSTITIAL SPACE
SOMEWHERE NEAR THE K'KATTAN-GATSUGI BORDER

The *Hellfire* slipped below Cee, fired off its homemade rock missiles, and slipped up again mere seconds later, analyzing the lightwave data. Instead of widely spaced ships, however, the twenty or so vessels protecting the station were patrolling it in a close sphere, with none of them actually docked. Tiny by comparison, shuttles moved back and forth between the lumpy station and the sleeker ships, no doubt transporting supplies and other goods.

The Salik hadn't moved their main anti-psi manufacturing facility to the Tlassian-K'kattan border, one of the two choices decoded from the stolen data nodes; instead, they had moved those facilities to *both* locations. Like one of the Delta-VX Harrier ships Ia had served on before gaining command of the *Hellfire*, this style of Salik station could be separated into several pieces and moved independently. The Salik had chosen to do so. That was why the odds had been so evenly fifty-fifty.

They had also chosen to pepper the local patch of space with hyperrelay-equipped scanner probes. The nearest one was three light-seconds off from the *Hellfire*'s entry point. As they slipped back above the speed of light, Ia didn't have much time to weigh her options. A few seconds was all she needed, though.

Wrapped in an FTL field, she was free to use the timestreams at full mental capacity. What Ia found brought her out of the timeplains with a feral smile.

Well, well, well, she thought, very carefully turning the attitude of the ship. Once again, she was not going to fly it straight like a javelin but rather at an angle like a crowbar. *Looks like they'll be overlapping their FTL fields to shunt the incoming missiles to either side. A fancy bit of static formation flying. It'll work, too; those rocks will be scattered off to either side despite their near-Cee velocity.*

But that also *means they'll be lined up in a few moments . . . and it won't harm the future to unleash the fury of the* Hellfire *upon them, today.*

Her right hand left the controls for a moment, long enough to lift up the cover and press her palm to the lockbox scanner that differentiated her console from the others. It took a second for the security system to triple-check her DNA, palmprint, life signs, and the ship's interior recordings of her movements, then the box unlocked with an audible *click*. Lifting the clear, hard case up out of her way, Ia flipped the switch that authorized the use of the main cannon.

"Ah, Captain?" Corporal Morgan asked from his position at the gunnery station. "Aren't we going to drop out of FTL soon, sir?"

"Change of plans," Ia told him. "All gunners, hold fire."

"Aye, sir. *All gunners, hold fire,*" he relayed into his headset.

The ship's attitude reached eighty degrees relative to its vector. Ia dropped them below Cee, ship still angled to travel on the diagonal. The pain came back, blindingly strong now that they were relatively close to the station. Vision misted by the timestreams, she plunged into her own downstream and read the lightwave they would see in just a few moments, before pulling out and adjusting their aim ever so slightly

"Station midpoint in fifteen seconds," Yeoman Yamasuka warned her. "Are we slowing down, sir?"

Now, the timestreams all said. At the same moment, Ia's thumb flicked, activating the cannon switch with a single tap. Unless she deliberately kept the button pressed, it would fire for one-twentieth of a second once charged. But first, it had to charge.

Corporal Crow, seated at the operations station, choked as his displays abruptly changed. The lighting on the bridge dimmed a little, and a strange, almost ominous *hummm* crept into their ears. On Crow's bank of screens, the bars gauging the ship's various energy outputs abruptly shifted, rescaling themselves.

Ship operations turned from long green and yellow bars into tiny green ones. A bank of new lines sprung up, shifting quickly from green to yellow, exponentially greater than the previous ones. Other graphs opened as well, detailing the heat being expressed along the axial core of the ship.

Along with that *hummm*, something *whoosh-thumped*. It did it again, and again, growing louder and faster as more joined the first, working in concert. Those were the Sterling heat differential engines; they pumped hydrofuel from the inner core to the outer hull and back, cooling the thermal bleed from the main cannon and recapturing some of that heat as yet more energy for the ship.

The combination of *hum* and *whoosh-thump* started to rattle the deckplates—and at the ten-second mark, every forward-pointed screen lit up for a fraction of a second, bathing the cabin in a flash of bright blood red.

Terran lasers fired at the low end of the visible light spectrum, with their beam tuned to have sympathetic, harmonic "wolfs" lurking at near-infrared lengths. Other weaponmakers tuned theirs closer to orange or even yellow to try to get several such harmonics, but the Terrans believed too many wavelengths diluted the impact. Like striking a C major note and hearing the harmonics for a G fifth, the tuning added extra heat to their punch. That made their weapons a signature red, and the God-strike cannon was no exception.

Traveling just below lightspeed, it took only a second or so to see what that single brief pulse of light did, a pulse that arrived at a somewhat diagonal angle, despite its short length. Most of it scorched through the formation of ships attempting to shield the station from the incoming missiles. Some of it kept going. Ia didn't pay much attention to that, though; with a dispersion rate of four light-months, the excess energy wouldn't harm anything. The Salik had chosen better than they knew; this location was in a large chunk of interstitial space half a light-year from the more-commonly-traveled flight paths and visited systems.

The *humming* sound had shut off, but the engines still *whooshed*, putting that excess heat into capacitors dotting the length of the main gun. Ia's hand shifted slightly in the feedback glove, changing their attitude again as well as slowing the ship a bit. Everyone swayed in their seats from the vector changes to their inertia, though not as strongly as during the other fight.

This time, Ia added a sideways slip, massaging the FTL fields to sneak them in behind the station. The move also pointed them at it and the remnants of ships lying beyond. Again, her thumb flicked the cannon's switch. Again, the humming rumble came back, and the engines picked up speed, shuttling superheated fluids to an array of pipes just under the space-cooled hull of the ship and back again.

The moment their slowly rotating nose pointed hindward at the station, those ten seconds of buildup ended in a twentieth-of-a-second burst that flared through the bridge. This time, the glow was very dark and lingered far longer than it should have. Blinking, straining to see through the green-and-red afterimages, Ia checked the lightwave readings. They came after several long seconds; as the red blob finally cleared from their view, the navicomp magnified and highlighted the two halves of the station, and the rock-damaged chunks of ships tumbling beyond.

Their backward speed had coupled with the cannon's forward aim, one traveling a little bit under Cee, one at full Cee. Ia had forgotten that rule; that the speed of the one would slow down the speed of the other. It was probable the Salik had seen the laserfire coming this time. But despite the way her ship's speed had slowed that packet of laser energy down to a quarter Cee at most, that blob of light still retained its full heat energy. The centerline of the mobile station was gone, leaving two slowly drifting, edge-glowing chunks, and countless tiny bits of charred, overheated debris.

Slowing the ship further, Ia adjusted their aim by a tiny bit and fired twice more. Thirty more seconds, and it was all over. Her headache ended, with only a faint echo from whatever few machines remained active on the surviving, scattered ships. There was no more manufacturing station to worry about, and only a handful of the smaller ships had not been caught in her lines of fire.

"Private Loewen, did you get all that recorded?" Ia asked her.

"Sir, yes, sir," Loewen confirmed from her post at the navigation seat, not bothering to look up from her work. "Shall I wrap it up for Admiral Genibes?"

"That's th' Captain's policy," Lieutenant Spyder said, speaking up from his position at the backup gunnery station. "If we wanna keep our slate blank for patrol assignments, we show 'em everythin' we can do."

"Sirs, we have bogeys headed our way," Loewen stated quickly.

"Not a problem, Private." Ia closed both lids to the main cannon lock, which automatically flicked the switch to shut the weapon off. The Sterling engines still *thump-whooshed*, but their efforts were slowing down again. "They're too far away."

Right hand moving to the controls, she increased their speed, this time rippling the FTL-field panels backwards, since that was the way they were pointed. Laserfire tried to catch up with them, but it was hastily aimed and couldn't match their already high speeds. Within a minute, they were past the bubble-flash threshold and soaring backwards at speeds faster than any weapon could hope to catch.

"Congratulations on another successful attack," she praised her crew. "Once again, we've barely a scratch. Don't expect that to last."

"Well then, yay and hurrah, whoopee, grats, and all of that joy and happiness," Morgan retorted dryly. "But—begging pardon, Captain—what the frying *shakk* was *that*?"

She slipped them sideways a little as they built up to full FTL speed, not wanting to be on the same heading as the Salik had last seen. Ia also didn't pretend ignorance as to what *that* he meant. "That, gentlemeioas, was our main cannon. Be advised that *any* attempt by any person other than myself to access its controls will cause an irreversible cascade in every hydrogenerator hooked up to a tank on this ship, turning it into a giant hydrobomb after just one minute—in short, attempt to crack open that security box, and you make the whole ship go very boom, very big, and very bad, with no time to get away.

"The Command Staff and the Admiral-General are extremely paranoid about this cannon falling into the wrong hands, so don't do it, or you'll kill us all," she warned her crew. "That's why there's a lid over the palmscanner, so you cannot even accidentally brush against it. Yeoman Yamasuka, do you feel comfortable flying this ship backwards?"

"Uh . . . Aye, sir," the other woman said. "I haven't done it since flight school, but I think I can manage it."

"Good. Slip us 196 by 203, and hold us on course for ten more minutes," Ia directed. "Then ease back down to sublight speeds so York can fire off the recordings packet—on our next ship, I'm going to insist on a vacuum hub for hyperrelay, so we don't have to keep slowing down below Cee to contact Genibes. Once you've done that, you may turn the ship around at that point and adjust course for the KLM 88-B System. Stick to FTL speeds for now. Yeoman Yamasuka, prepare to receive the helm."

"Aye, sir, preparing to receive the helm in te—er, make that in twenty, sir," the dark-haired woman agreed.

Loewen spoke up as well. "Plotting a first course, vector 196 by 203, and a second course for KLM 88-B, sir."

". . . Do we at least get to know the main cannon's specs, Captain?" Morgan asked Ia once the helm transfer had been made.

Ia shook her head, unstrapping her left hand from the thruster pad. "It's big, it's ugly, and it takes ten seconds to charge before it can fire. It also has a very ugly overshoot range. I'm the only person who can foresee the lining up of enough ships during a fight to make it safe to wield inside an inhabited or commonly transited star system. That's all you need know for now."

"It also extracts a lot more energy out of the system than the other cannons," Crow said. He was replaying the meters from the four brief shots on his main screen. "Not just the buildup to fire it, but in actually firing it. I only noticed how much energy it retained because the scale is so huge."

"More energy than you know," Ia admitted, calling up the duty roster for that hour. "The current design siphons off most of the excess heat, converts it back to energy, and pours it right back into the cannon. I can tell you that much because that part's just an upscale version of the Starstrike cannon's energy-feed design; it has nothing to do with how the Godstrike itself actually achieves its high caloric rating.

"That's also one of the reasons why it takes ten seconds to fire, and why so much of the ship near the core isn't inhabitable," she stated, glancing at the chrono on her leftmost lower tertiary. "It looks like we're scheduled for lunch, next. With the main galleys still locked down, how about I fix everyone some sandwiches from the bridge galley?"

"Th' Cap'n of this ship isn't s'posed t' cook," Spyder argued, reaching for his restraint straps. "*I'll* go fix us sommat."

"Oh, no. I've foreseen your cooking skills, Spyder, and they're worse than mine," Ia joked, unstrapping as well. "I may not be as good a cook as my biomother, but at least I won't poison us. Besides, *everyone* pulls triple duties or more on this ship. That includes me, because I don't ask my crew to do something I'm not willing to do myself if I have the skills and the time to do it.

"Right now, I have the time, and sandwich making is just within my skills. You have the bridge, Lieutenant. Corned beef on rye okay with everyone?" Ia asked.

A quick survey of the others showed them all nodding. Sighing, Spyder complied, shifting from his seat to hers at the back of the bridge cabin. "Aye, aye, Cap'n. Corned beef on rye'll be fine."

FEBRUARY 11, 2496 T.S.
SIC TRANSIT

"Sir, yes, sir," Ia stated, shoulders square and chin level. She felt like she should've been standing At Attention, rather than seated at the desk in her office. "I am absolutely confident the overshoot from our lasers and the main cannon will not hit and damage anything of consequence."

"What about those rock missiles?" Admiral Genibes asked her, leaning back in his own office chair. The entire conversation was taking place at just over a two-second delay, making it almost feel normal. "You released them at near lightspeed. They'll continue on course until something stops them, and they're too small to be easily noticed at that velocity."

She had an answer for that. "Only three will cause problems," Ia admitted. "I've already arranged for timed messages to be delivered to ships in the affected areas, with exact tracking coordinates for their destruction. The rest will eventually be snagged by gravity and either smack harmlessly into other stellar bodies or burn up in various atmospheres."

Admiral Genibes raised one of his brows at that. "Timed messages? Arranged with whom, Captain Ia? I don't recall receiving any messages."

This was the tread-carefully part of her report. Lying to a superior was a fatality, but she didn't want to bruise the ego of anyone reviewing this conversation later. "With the Afaso Order, sir. The Terran military will be too busy with the war at that point to be bothered with that sort of thing."

Genibes frowned thoughtfully at her. "You've sent a lot of packages over the years to the Afaso Order. Same as you've shipped home. If all of those packages were precognitive prophecies . . . when is the Space Force getting its fair share?"

"The Space Force as a whole is a competent entity, sir," Ia told him. Again, not a lie. "You won't need all that much from me precognitively to carry out your duties. Those few sections in need of my assistance will receive it at the appropriate time."

"You said you're fighting a war three hundred years into the future," he reminded her. "But not even a Feyori half-breed will outlive its matter-based life expectancy. What about the intervening two hundred years?"

"You'll receive a war chest of prophecies, suggestions, and directives at the appropriate time, sir," Ia promised him.

"Why not now?" the admiral asked.

Ia restrained the urge to roll her eyes, though she did sigh. "Because there's an entire queue of things that have to happen first, and if something gets nudged out of alignment now, I'll have to rewrite all those prophecies to compensate for the ripple effect it'll cause."

"What about the first battle of the war?" Genibes asked her. "You've successfully proved in these four attacks that your ship would be invaluable. Where will the Salik strike first?"

That, she could tell him. "Two places. The Terran and Gatsugi Motherworlds." A quick dip into the timestreams allowed Ia to nod in confirmation. "It'll start two weeks from now, give or take roughly a day—it varies too much to pin it down closer than that, depending on how my crew and I handle the next few prewar fights."

He folded his arms over his grey-clad chest, arching one grey-salted brown brow. "Do you at least have a location for the *first* main push?"

"*Two* locations, Admiral. They'll happen simultaneously," Ia stated. "The Terran Motherworld, because we not only kicked their frogtopodic asteroids last time but have been instrumental in keeping the Blockade going. They've gotten around it, but not as freely as they might've otherwise, and we pissed off the Salik because of it. And they'll go after the Gatsugi because they're in the linchpin location. Damage the center of the edible Alliance members, and we can't use the Collective's systems and stations as safe transit hubs, let alone for gathering and resupply.

"The Salik are feeling cocky, but they've got the forces to be cocky. They'll throw several fleets at the other Motherworlds, strong enough to tie up our various allies," she added, cautioning him. "But the strongest attacks will be those two worlds. They're also watching the movements of all our fleets, so you can't move everyone in to protect Earth."

"Because they'll just shift gears and attack wherever we're weak," he agreed. He thought a moment, then asked, "What about pulling out a single ship here, a single ship there? And having them sit beyond the Kuiper belt a few days before?"

"That might entail several days of those crews doing nothing; I can't guarantee exactly *when* the Salik will strike, only that they will," Ia told him. She held up her hand in case he was about to speak, stating, "Let me check the timestreams before you make up your mind."

It took a few seconds of real time to sort through the potential possibilities. When she had what she wanted, Ia pulled back into herself and sent a jolt of electrokinetic information into her workstation. Tapping a key, she sent it to the Admiral.

"I've attached a list of ship registries you can safely pull in over the next two weeks to defend Earth. It's not many, but you shouldn't need that many."

"Well, no; we shouldn't need that many more if you'll be there," Genibes agreed, touching a control on his own side of the comm link.

"I'm sorry, Admiral, but we won't be there, sir." Ia didn't wait the two plus seconds for his head to snap up at her words. She continued briskly, explaining herself. "Earth has plenty of defenses and doesn't really need us, whereas the Gatsugi can ill afford to pull in ships from their various colonyworlds just to defend Beautiful-Blue. The *Hellfire* will be assisting them when the time comes."

"That ship of yours represents a very significant investment in military research and development, Captain," Admiral Genibes reminded her, stressing her title slightly. "It is Terran property, and should therefore be used to defend Terran property."

"According to the Terran United Planets Charter, duly registered with the Alliance," Ia countered, "the Terran Space Force is to render both sentientarian and military aid to its allies when and where endangered by a mutual threat. The Salik most definitely qualify as a mutual threat, Admiral—and I tell you, as a precognitive, we need the Gatsugi Motherworld to come through this first fight relatively intact."

"Ia, as much as you—" he started to say over the two-second delay between them.

Ia kept talking, cutting him off. "Sir, if we send *only* the *Hellfire*, every other ship in the Terran fleet can do their job defending Terran and joint colonyworlds, and the Gatsugi will have all the help they need. If you tried to pull the *Hellfire* back to Earth, I'd have to insist on sending eighteen to twenty Space Force vessels to Beautiful-Blue to ensure their war-machine efforts would survive in a shape suitable for helping the rest of the Alliance in the future . . . including helping us Terrans. But that much movement on our part into Gatsugi space would be noticed far more by the Salik than simply reassigning a bunch of patrol routes entirely within Human space, which is something the Command Staff already does on a regular basis. The Salik will see it coming, and send more ships than our side can defend against."

He waited four extra seconds to be sure she was done talking, then spoke. "You've planned all of this, haven't you?"

Shoulders back and chin level, Ia answered At Attention. "That is what I am supposed to do, sir, as an officer, a soldier, and a precog. I am to use my abilities to ensure the maximum number of lives are preserved with the most efficient use of the resources I have available."

John Genibes snorted. "Don't pull that officer's duty *shakk* with me. What's your *real* reason for wanting to help the Gatsugi?"

Ia dropped her soldierly poise and gave him a flat look. "That *is* my real reason, sir. It is the single most efficient use of all our resources. I did tell you and the others when I bargained for this ship that it would have to be sent places the rest of you might not think are all that vital but actually are. *This* is one of those instances."

He studied her for longer than the two-second delay. Finally, he asked, *"Carte blanche?"*

"Admiral, yes, sir. You'll see how effective I am in wielding it when the Terran Council receives the gratitude of the Gatsugi Collective, sir," she promised.

Sighing, Admiral Genibes sat back in his seat and rubbed the bridge of his nose. "Right . . . Well, at least you're using it for the good of the war effort. I'll promote it that way to the Admiral-General. What's next on your itinerary, between then and now?"

"What I would've had the crew do before I knew about the anti-psi menace. Attack hidden shipyards and crèches." She waited for his reaction.

He lifted his head at that. ". . . Crèches?"

"They've been breeding and training generations of workers and warriors on the sly, all dedicated to building up their war machine," Ia told him. "They've been on short rations, working in harsh conditions, but it's how they've managed to come up with enough bodies to craft the robotics and other manufactories to build everything they're planning on throwing at us. My plan is to make those secret resources too costly to repair, forcing them to make their opening attack before we can destroy too many of them."

"More rocks flung at near-Cee?" Genibes asked dryly.

"No, sir. Mostly, it'll be the Godstrike, since the things are located a light-year or more from anything else, which means overshoot won't be as much of a problem. These are mostly my original targets, the ones without anti-psi shielding—though we will be hunting down more of those as the war gets going," she promised. "Not just the *Hellfire*, but other ships, too. I'll need you to pass along rerouting and attack orders for a number of ships within the year, to see that these interstitial-space enemy bases get destroyed when the odds are highest on our side."

"About attacking those crèches," her superior stated after another extralong pause. "It won't play well if word gets out you're hitting targets with children. Whether or not they're Salik tadpoles, they're still children. Mind you, I won't object on my end because I *know* what those things are. I'm talking about someone in your crew talking about it to the Nets. If it gets on the news . . ."

"I know, sir," Ia admitted quietly. "I accepted the cost long ago. The goal is to cripple their facilities beyond use, not just to kill. We want to concentrate their numbers in other, more heavily defended locations deeper within Salik territory. The Salik intend to stab at Alliance members in between cleansing the Blockade presence from their various territories, dividing our attentions. We can't afford to let them continue to train replacement soldiers, and we can't afford to let them spread out any more than they already are."

"How are you going to put it to your crew?" Genibes asked. "Or are you going to even tell them what the targets actually are?"

She shook her head. "A lie by omission is still a kind of lie, sir. I'd prefer to limit the number of omissions I make because eventually the truth does get out. The first few targets will be manufacturing stations and shipyards, that sort of thing. I'll find the best moment to tell them about the crèches when we come to that point. Anything else you wanted to discuss, Admiral?"

"Not at this time. Don't abuse your *carte blanche*, Captain," he warned her.

She gave him another dry look. "Considering what I *could* be doing with it, I'd hardly call the careful, rational selection of vital targets an abuse of my position—but yes, I am aware that others' viewpoints may not match my own, sir."

Some of those viewpoints weren't even Human. She wanted to warn him about the Feyori who were going to move against her, but refrained. Instead, they said their good-byes and ended the call. Ia rested only a moment before reaching for the comm again, this time making an audio connection with the bridge.

"Captain Ia to Lieutenant Spyder."

"Spyder 'ere, Cap'n," he replied. *"What can we do f' you?"*

"Tell the members of the 1st and 3rd Platoons they may have half an hour to contact their loved ones, up to bandwidth capacity. They are not permitted to say where we are or what we are doing, save that we're on a deep-space patrol, as per the Company Bible. The 2nd will have to wait until it's their off-duty turn next time we're in sublight. After forty minutes, resume course at FTL speed to our next target," she directed.

"Understood, Cap'n," Spyder said.

FEBRUARY 25, 2496 T.S.
SIC TRANSIT

This time, Ia didn't bother to square her shoulders before step-ping into the boardroom. Her fellow soldiers had already used it a few times since leaving the shipyards, if mostly for group briefings rather than Company-wide ones. This one involved her image being broadcast to tertiary screens at duty stations around the ship for those members of the 1st Platoon who weren't in attendance since the ship was in motion, which meant priority stations had to be manned.

This time, she wasn't in her formal Dress Blacks, just in a grey shirt and trouser set with her service and rank pins in place. Lieutenant Rico was up on the bridge, serving as the officer on watch, but the other members of the cadre were gathered at the officers' table. Some of the soldiers lounging in the tiers of seats looked half-asleep, having been dragged out of bed for this meeting.

They did sit up when she came into view, but didn't rise or salute since she wasn't in formals and wasn't wearing a cap. That was in the Company Bible, which meant they were doing what they were supposed to do. Coming to a stop before her seat at the table, Ia began without preamble.

"At Ease. Up until now, our targets have been considered legitimate under the Alliance joint military code of conduct for all of its sentient members. Mainly because we have been operating under the Alliance-agreed provisions against Salik-crafted and -manned communications hubs, war-matériel-manufacturing facilities, and minor shipyards located outside the Salik Interdicted Zone, and thus outside the law.

"Our next target also falls outside what the law permits the Salik to legally occupy and operate." She paused, taking the time to meet the gazes of several of the hundred-plus men and women seated around her. "This means they *are* legitimate targets in the eyes of the law. In the eyes of common, sentient-kind morality . . . some of you may have objections."

She did not display anything on the screen. She did not sit down, either. Bracing her hands on the table, she leaned forward, again meeting the gazes of the soldiers around her.

"Right this minute," Ia stated, "in the ponds of the city of Shnn-wuish on the Salik Motherworld of Sallha, the senior-most members of what we Humans would call a high school are undergoing their version of a graduation ceremony. The top twenty students are being permitted the chance to hunt and kill the five worst-performing members of their graduating class. They will do so in the ancient way in a deep lake in the heart of that city, without any weapons other than their tentacle-hands and teeth . . . and yes, they will eat what they kill, while they are still killing it.

"The hunters are cheered on by everyone, and the hunted are scorned," she continued. "Unless the hunted successfully kill all twenty of their hunters, they will not be permitted to leave the pond. Those among the hunters who are killed by the poor-performing students they hunt will not be avenged by their family or friends. They, too, will become reviled as weak and useless. These are *not* Human children," Ia stressed, hardening her voice. "They do *not* operate under the same rules as the rest of us. So when I say our next target is a crèche, a deep-space facility designed to spawn and rear Salik children, I am *not* talking about defenseless younglings. They are trained from birth to hunt and kill."

Roughly one-third of the men and women nodded somberly in understanding. One-third looked a little confused, and the remaining third looked disturbed. That included their ship's doctor, Jesselle Mishka, who frowned in distaste at Ia.

"I can corroborate this," Lieutenant Rico stated, surprising her a little. She hadn't figured he would speak up. At her nod of permission, he filled in a few more details for the skeptical members of the crew. "I have studied their culture as well as their language, to better understand how and why they communicate. For the first five years of a Salik's life, they do *not* learn how to read, write, or interact socially beyond their immediate family-pack, which consists of their mother and their siblings.

"Instead, within two months of emerging from their egg-sacs, they learn how to hunt live prey, starting first with small, fish-like creatures whose only defenses are that they spawn in great numbers and can swim fast *en masse*, on up through to large, non-sentient livestock that are bred to fight back," the lieutenant said. "By the time their brains have developed enough for higher cognitive learning, they are natural killers. Attempts by Alliance social services to 'reeducate' Salik spawnlings have failed, because this five-year hunting requirement is hard-wired into their biology and their neurology. They are *not* Human."

Ever since his trip into the timestreams with her, Oslo Rico had given up his resistance to her leadership. Ia dipped her head in acknowledgment of his help. "The lieutenant is correct. In the eyes of softhearted civilians who are not trained in xeno-biology or xenopsychology . . . we will be seen as going up against their *own* children. We will be seen as slaughtering *their* younglings, whether it's Human, Gatsugi, Tlassian, K'kattan, Choyan or Solarican, Dlmvlan or Chinsoiy. But these are *not* our children.

"As for the legality of our coming strike against a crèche station designed to raise and train Salik children . . . they are located well outside the Salik Interdicted Zone, the only place where the Salik are permitted to establish colonies. By law, they are explicitly forbidden to establish and occupy any locations other than the openly listed ones, which means these hidden crèche stations are completely valid targets, the exact same as those comm hubs were . . . which *did* have small crèche-ponds of children on board."

Her confession stirred the crew in waves of discomfort. Ia let that sink in, then continued.

"The only difference between this next target and the previous ones is the scale. A few hundred at most, versus the tens of thousands of tadpoles we'll be going after. This crèche station, the first of many, is specifically designed to rear and train Salik younglings to be competent engineers, mechanics, scientists, and warriors. They are staffed by Salik broodmothers culled from the top-serving members of the underground Salik war effort . . . and while their graduating ceremonies do remove the bottom five students per class, they practice those skills beforehand on captured sentients."

"*I* can corroborate that," Helstead spoke up.

That, Ia had expected. She nodded at the former Corps officer to continue.

"Intelligence reports from pirate operations have included numerous cases of extremely unscrupulous sentients among the members of the criminal undergalaxy selling their prisoners for large sums of tangible assets," the lieutenant commander shared, glancing at her fellow officers. She looked out at the men and women seated in the riser seats. "Rare gems, precious metals, and other nontraceable commodities have ensured that, while extremely risky if caught, the food-slave trade has remained quite profitable over the years.

"While it's true that in the Interdicted Zone, it's the death penalty for any pirate caught trading in living sentients to the enemy," she admitted, "the profits have made that risk worthwhile to many. Every few years, the Knifemen Corps keeps taking out the worst of the slave traders, but more just keep popping back up like weeds."

"I myself was sold by a group of pirates to the Salik for my weight, kilo for kilo, in platinum originally mined on the legitimate Salik colonyworld of Ss'nuc III," Ia admitted in an aside. "But we're digressing. There is a purpose to this meeting beyond informing you of the distasteful yet necessary chore we are about to pursue. I made myself a promise back when I first planned for this crew. If I had the time to spare, and could spare it before a particular engagement, I would give you an opportunity to step into the timestreams with me and *see* for yourselves just how necessary this particular fight will be.

"I offer you this opportunity now. I have half an hour I can spare from my other obligations and duties," Ia stated, moving around the table to the front of it. "If you wish to see for yourself just what we're up against, you may choose to do so. This offer is open to my fellow officers as well as to the noncoms and enlisted. If you have any doubts or discomforts at the idea of undergoing this, you may consult with Lieutenant Rico, who has already accompanied me on a previous visit to the timestreams."

A hand rose, hesitant at first, then higher. The owner was

Private First Class Harley Floathawg, distinct not only for his self-picked name, but for the burgundy blotches of *jungen* mottling his skin. Half-V'Dan and half-Terran, he was one of less than a million or so Humans of the billions occupying the known galaxy to still get the colorful skin pigmentation. Ia had not selected him based on his appearance or unusual name, however; she had selected him because he was one of the best hovertech mechanics available for her crew, without being needed far more elsewhere.

"Yes, Private Floathawg, you have a question?" Ia asked.

"Captain, yes, sir," he stated, rising from his seat. Tall and lean, he overshadowed his shorter, mousy teammate, Private Second Class Mara Sunrise, who stayed in her seat, looking bored with the proceedings. Both of them were supposed to be on the current watch, but neither had a task at the moment that was absolutely necessary to keep monitored during this hour. "What exactly are these timestreams?"

"My gifts act in a visual way . . . though visualization might be a better word for it," Ia told him. "Since my abilities came to full strength at the age of fifteen, this visualization starts out as a giant prairie crisscrossed by streams. Each stream represents a single person's life. Where the stream splits, a choice has been made, and each new part of the stream indicates what will happen if each choice is followed.

"From the banks of that stream, I can see images inside the waters of snippets of time from that particular person's life. If I go upstream, I go into that person's past. If I go downstream, I go into their future. And if I were to step into those waters, I would be living that person's life at the moment in time where I entered, as if it was a point-of-view hologram, with sight, sound, touch, taste, smell . . . and even some access to their uppermost surface thoughts, but with zero interaction with the actual person," Ia said. "In that regard, it is more like a standard, noninteractive vidshow broadcast than anything else.

"Now, I *can* change the visualization images," she added, as Harley's fellow crewmates glanced uneasily at each other. "I've used graphs, grids, plus other metaphors such as tapestries and so forth, but it always starts out as the timeplains, and I myself always start out in my own life-stream . . . as does anyone who comes with me. I have also learned to lift that person out of their own waters quickly upon entry so they don't metaphorically drown from trying to process too much doubled-up information at once."

Another hand rose. Ia pointed at its owner, Private Second Class Nadja Theam, a clairvoyant and fellow psi, and a very good electronics programmer and engineer. Floathawg sat down, his question answered, and Theam stood in his place. "Sir, I've been given to understand you're both a precognitive and an electrokinetic. In fact, word is among the crew, you can program literally with a thought. Why don't you just *show* us these timestream images by using the monitors in here, while you're searching for them wherever it is they exist?"

"I wish I could do that, Private Theam," Ia allowed. She shook her head. "Unfortunately, while my years of effort at disciplining my electrokinetic gift make it possible for me to transcribe simple things like written orders, programming code, and the like, it isn't the electrokinesis that's the problem. My precognition is too powerful. The handful of times where I have tried directly to record the images that I see inside my mind when I'm standing in the timestreams themselves, I have fried every datapad and workstation console I have touched . . . just as I have destroyed every KI monitor within range of my abilities, which is why we don't have any on board this ship.

"I can skim the timeplains from this side and pull through what I need, but it is always throttled down and filtered," she explained. "In short, you can fill a cup of water successfully from the sink tap, when that tap is fed by the waters of a dam far upstream, but you cannot expect to fill it nearly as safely by dropping the sluice gates of that dam while you're standing on its spillway. Any other questions?"

PFC Belle Underwood had one. She stood as well, her stance At Attention, but her tone hesitant. "Um . . . will it hurt, sir? Going onto the timeplains or whatever?"

"Only if you let go of my hand, or say the word 'time' repeatedly while we are there." Her reply earned Ia several chuckles. "Laugh all you want, meioas; I am serious. For those who don't want to experience the timestreams but are still doubtful or curious about the necessity of the coming attack, I *have* carefully considered all of the choice-possibilities in this and other endeavors, and have concluded that attacking these crèches—repugnant as that is to our Human sensibilities—will save far more lives down the road than it will cost. *Every* action I undertake, past, present, and future, is designed with that goal firmly in mind.

"Now, if you are curious, please feel free to move forward and line up. If you do not wish to have your temporal questions answered at this time—and yes, Corporal Johnson, you may ask to see *other* events, though I may or may not comply at my precognitive prerogative—then you may remain in your seats or consider yourselves dismissed.

"Those of you on duty who are watching this meeting will have to hold your questions for the next temporal opportunity. Those who stay here in the boardroom but do not participate will have the opportunity to chat with those who do take a dip in the timestreams today," Ia concluded. "You are now free to move as you will, meioas. Thank you for your attention."

A few got up and left. A few more hesitated, then moved to the front of the hall. Doctor Mishka spoke up before any of them reached Ia.

"Why didn't you offer us this opportunity any earlier, Captain?" Mishka asked her. The blonde woman remained in her seat at the table, her expression skeptical. "Why now? And why not have all of us take a stroll through these timestreams with you?"

"Because—ironic as my adult life is—I believe in free will, Doctor," Ia replied, twisting slightly to look at the older woman. "Those who follow me onto the timeplains tend to see things that shift their perception of the universe. Not through anything I myself do to them but simply because once you have seen something, it cannot be unseen. Every experience changes us, and if the experience is a powerful one, it has the potential to change us in equally powerful ways. Sometimes I have to take people into the streams with me so that they can see the consequences of actions, whether it's theirs, mine, or others' . . . but I prefer it when it's their own idea.

"This is also why I prefer not to be touched," Ia added, looking at the others approaching her. "My gifts can and will trigger on their own, particularly when I am startled, or my guard is down. And like most psychic abilities, they are strongest when transferred via physical contact. I prefer to do that under controlled circumstances, and only when that person's

foreknowledge will not harm the actions that must take place—
if any of you change your minds at the last second, meioas, I
will not take offense. If you haven't, we'll do this one at a time."

"*I* want to know what your end-goal is, sir." Private Kimberly
Kim, lead team member of 1st Platoon B Gamma and full-mech
specialist, halted in front of Ia. Shorter than her captain, she
looked up at Ia with the level gaze of a woman who considered
herself an equal. "Why you're doing whatever it is you're doing,
and why you've involved the rest of us in it. I know you already
said you're in this to prevent bad stuff from happening down
the road, but that's what I want to see for myself."

"You see *that*, and if you have a single scrap of compassion
within you for the other beings in this universe, it'll change
you forever, Private," Ia warned her. She lifted her hand, offering it palm up to the other woman. "But if you do want to see
it, I'll show it to you."

"Sir, yes, sir." Kim stated, and gripped Ia's fingers.

Sighing, Ia complied, taking the shorter woman into her
gifts. Between one breath and the next, she pulled the two of
them out of their life-streams and onto the banks. Waiting just
enough for Kim to get her bearings, she accelerated them downstream, into the desert waiting for their descendants, and the
one trickle of a chance at stopping that lifeless desiccation.

*"This is what will happen to all life in the Milky Way Gal-
axy. Starting three centuries from now, an invasion force will
start stripping every planet and every star for raw materials.
It will take them less than two centuries to do it . . . and this
chain of events is the one chance we—ourselves and our
descendants—will have at stopping them."*

CHAPTER 9

. . . But most scholars will insist the war took off with a vengeance on the third of March, Terran Standard, the day before my twenty-fourth birthday. On the Terran side of things, the first defensive shots were actually fired by a group of civilians on the edge of the system, then the rest of the military engaged. The Damned were somewhere else entirely.

~Ia

MARCH 3, 2496 T.S.
NEARSPACE, BEAUTIFUL-BLUE
GATSUGI MOTHERWORLD, SUGAI SYSTEM

The Gatsugi that appeared on Ia's main screen was four-armed, mouse-eyed, blue-green-skinned, and boasted butter yellow tufts on his head, strands which were more akin to the long, individual barbs on a peacock-feather shaft than anything resembling Human hair. He smiled by curving up the edges of his small mouth—a gesture Gatsugi and Humans had in common—and said, "Greetings/Salutations/Hello. You have reached/contacted/I am the Sugai Insystem Comptroller. How may I help/assist/aid you?"

"Greetings/Hello, Comptroller," Ia returned politely. "This

is/I am Captain Ia of the Terran Space Force requesting/asking/
seeking permission to enter Gatsugi homespace/territory/
system-heart."

The alien's race had evolved on a world with predators sporting extremely sensitive hearing, though poor vision, and had
developed multiple methods of communication. They talked
more than they gestured or colorchanged now, but the layers
of meaning had merely morphed into multiple-word use. Some
sentients found it annoying; Ia thought it was elegant. Not something she'd use herself every day, but elegant in its own way.

The Comptroller dipped his head. "What is the name/iden-
tity, need/purpose for visiting, and location/point of entry for
your ship/vessel, Captain Ee-ah?"

"The TUPSF *Hellfire* is a new/experimental Harasser-Class
warship," Ia stated, pronouncing the acronym *tup-siff*. "We are
approaching/entering Sugai System from your vector 117 by 3.
We request/request/request that you clear/evacuate Beautiful-
Blue nearspace sectors 1008, 908, 807 through 809, and 705
through 712 of all vessels within the next ten *klitak* Gatsugi
Standard, and request/request/request you prepare to elevate/
accelerate all system defenses/warnings from Peach to Sanguine
in ten *klitak*. Our purpose/intent/reason for entering/arriving
is to assist/aid/help in defending/protecting your system/sov-
ereignty from inbound/advancing enemies/enemies/enemies
in less than fifteen *klitak*."

Most of the time, Gatsugi conversations circled around a
subject, approaching it from multiple angles. Sometimes, they
repeated a particular word for emphasis. Hearing that emphasis,
the Comptroller widened his mouse black eyes, skin flushing
from blue-green to a reddish peach in just a few seconds.
"What/What/What enemies?"

"Salik," Ia stated. The name needed no emphasis. "You have
just over fourteen *klitak* to the Second Salik War, Comptroller,
and the Terran government has sent/allowed me to help/assist
in the protection/defense of your Motherworld. Do we/Does
this ship/military force have/receive your permission/clearance
to enter/approach Beautiful-Blue nearspace and assist/defend
your Motherworld/heart?"

"Is this true/true/true?" the Comptroller asked, flushing a
skeptical shade of muddy orange.

"I do not lie to you, meioa," Ia stated flatly. "If you do/will not believe me, cooperating/accepting my request/warning anyway/regardless will not/will not cause/create inconvenience/ trouble for more than twenty *klitak*. Just/please clear/evacuate sectors 1008, 908, 807–809 and 705–712 immediately/now, and do not use lightwave communications/channels. They are parked/sitting/watching at system's edge/farspace right/for now, watching/scanning/spying on you."

The Comptroller wasted a *klitak* in thought, somewhat longer than a Terran Standard minute. Finally, his lower arms moved, touching controls below the edge of the vid pickups for their comm link. "We will comply/trust you/the Terrans. Clearing/ Evacuating the indicated/listed sectors/spaces now. What is your estimated time/moment of insystem/nearspace arrival/ appearance?

"Fourteen *klikat* from . . . now." Ia stated, checking the timestreams. Speaking with the politeness of using Gatsugi thought patterns was starting to give her a headache.

The Comptroller flushed reddish peach. "Your arrival/entry will be after/following the Salik. Why/Why/Why not before?"

"If you move/get those ships out of my way/the indicated sectors," Ia promised the alien, "they/the enemy won't have reason/need to deviate/reposition, and I can enter the system/ nearspace at the heart/center of their formation/fleet."

"How/How/How can you know/assert something/this infor mation/knowledge so precisely/accurately?" the Gatsugi chal lenged her, skin shifting more toward a doubtful, dull red. "Either you collude/cooperate with the invasion/Salik, a rep rehensible/unthinkable/vomitous thought/idea, or you have a spy/traitor among/spying upon them."

"When this/the battle is over/done, Comptroller, and you have a moment/energy to spare, look up/access the V'Dan belief/faith Sh'nai records/histories/mentions of 'The Prophet of a Thousand Years,'" Ia instructed him. "I am/am she/the Prophet who was foretold/prophesied. And, as foretold/proph esied, I will aid/assist/help save you, today. *Hellfire* out/ending transmission."

Within seconds, Private C'ulosc spoke up from his seat at the comm station. "Sir, we're getting a ping from the Sugai Comptroller's office."

"Send a signal stating that we're entering FTL transit, and cut the pingback," Ia directed him. "Then make sure Chief

Yeoman O'Keefe has all members of Lieutenant Spyder's boarding party on board Bow Shuttle One, locked and loaded."

"Aye, sir."

"Captain, are we actually going to come out in the *middle* of the enemy?" Yeoman Ishiomi asked her. His console was now a backup gunnery post to Private Ramasa, along with Lieutenant Rico, who faced backwards. "That's extremely dangerous, sir. Even just traveling in formation as a fleet will be risky for the Salik if they want to arrive closely enough to each other to concentrate their initial fire."

"I'm presuming you're worried about the hyperrift mouth," Ia said. Ishiomi nodded. "Don't be. There's only a seven percent chance someone will hit it after we exit, and none before. If that happens, I'll simply shoot the ship forward, and the gunners get to readjust their aim a bit."

"If you say so, sir," he muttered, his tone somewhere between tactful and dubious. The pilot wasn't one of the half dozen crew members who had asked to see the future a week ago. Ia didn't blame him, nor fault him for his skepticism.

Instead, she switched on the intercom. *"All hands, this is the Captain, prepare for hyperspace in five minutes, followed by one to two hours of nasty combat, depending on whether you're manning the ships or boarding the station. Be advised, some of you will be injured; this is unavoidable. However, if you keep your wits about you and heed my precognitive commands, none of you should die. Please do not disappoint me. Five minutes to jump. Ia out."*

"Captain, Yeoman O'Keefe reports everyone is on board the drop ship and prepared to launch," Private C'ulosc stated.

"Good. Let's get the ship down out of FTL and ready for OTL speeds," Ia directed.

NEARSPACE, BEAUTIFUL-BLUE
SUGAI SYSTEM

Their oversized, lumpy silver needle of a ship emerged from the grey streaks of the hyperrift into a stuttering cage of bright orange and yellow. Thankfully, all of the Salik projectiles were aimed outward. A few of those lasers were firing through the dotted cylinder of the enemy formation, but none of them actually struck the *Hellfire*. Ia had timed the pattern and spaces perfectly. She sighed in relief.

Somewhere out there, five of the ships did have large anti-psi generators active, but they were nowhere near as strong as a station filled with hundreds of the machines being activated and tested. Ia had only a modest headache this time, a mild impediment at best as she dragged her toes through the waters in her mind.

The L-pod gunners were already firing the moment they were free and clear, aiming their lasers at a set list of priorities: shield panels, gunnery pods, FTL and thruster panels, and sensor arrays. The ship thrummed, vibrating gently with the efforts of the hydrogenerators powering all those lasers, but otherwise their entry into the big opening act of the war was fairly quiet.

The chaotic view of the battle contrasted with that quietness. At least, until the first hastily reaimed projectile hit. Their shields absorbed most of the blow, though some of the kinetic force of the explosion rattled into their hull. Ia relaxed a little at that. "Right on time . . . and now that the hull's been scratched, I feel a lot better. *All hands, brace for maneuvers. Yeoman O'Keefe, shuttle launch in two minutes ten seconds. P-pods, launch!*"

The ship *whumped* with the simultaneous launching of scores of missiles. Counting to three, Ia ramped up the FTL field, slipping forward. The hyperrift tunnel had closed without incident behind them, but now, easily fifty or more lasers and projectiles were being aimed their way. The missiles weren't a problem; the FTL field would shunt them and their impact explosions aside. It was the lasers that could do them the most harm; their wavelengths could still cause damage even if that field greased matter out of the way.

Telltales scrolled through her upper tertiary screens, echoing the ones Private Nelson was monitoring at the operations station. Several flickered yellow, indicating solid hits. She increased their speed with a jolt, forcing the interior safety fields to catch up for a rough-squeezed moment. Half a dozen more items showed up in yellow, and two turned red, then they outstripped the incoming fire.

Not because they needed to outdistance the Salik gunners' ability to aim and fire, but because they needed to outdistance the effects of the missiles the *Hellfire*'s own gunners had just launched. Every projectile-pod bay had five blossoms locked in its hold, and every projectile pod had just fired one of those five.

It didn't matter how good the Salik shields were. Eighty blossom bombs implied a lot of kinetic impact force. With at least a third of those shields damaged by intense L-pod fire from the *Hellfire*, that meant a lot of the secondary blossom bombs would get through.

Her right secondary screen lit up in more yellows and oranges, this time puffballs of silent explosions on enemy hulls instead of streaks of laserfire. That was, if one didn't count the *Hellfire*'s aft-facing guns, which were thumping away. Ia didn't spare the rearward view on her right screen more than a brief glance. Instead, she flexed the FTL field, tricking physics into ignoring their forward momentum long enough to tilt their long axis a bit more toward the right, and a bit more still.

By the time they were sliding fully sideways through space to the oncoming Salik fleet, it was time to launch the shuttle. Cutting the field, Ia flicked the switch for the bow-bay doors, sliding them open. *"Yeoman O'Keefe, you are clear to launch. Godspeed, and follow the flight path I've plotted for you."*

"Aye, aye, sir," the other woman replied. *"Launching now."*

The projectile pods continued to *whump* around them, shaking the bridge faintly. Ia nodded. *"Lieutenant Spyder, contact station personnel and have them take you to the spot I marked on your map as soon as you arrive."*

"We're on it, Cap'n," he agreed. *"Smack-dab central in their hull-minin' efforts. We'll take 'em out from within, or your nickname ain't Bloody Mary."*

"We're free and clear, Captain," O'Keefe told her. The forward view on Ia's main screen showed the small silver bulge of the shuttle escaping ahead of them. *"Locked and loaded, and on our way to the* Freely Flowing.*"*

Several more ship systems turned amber on her list. Three more turned red, not nearly enough to hamper their capacities yet. But that was no reason to keep exposing the same surfaces to enemy fire. *"Acknowledged, O'Keefe. Acknowledged, Spyder. All hands, spinning the ship."*

A swirl of her left pinkie managed the trick, manipulating the ship through the attitude glove. Acting in angled opposition, the ripple in the insystem-thruster controls rolled the *Hellfire* on its long axis, presenting new surfaces to absorb the incoming damage and new guns for opening return fire. Lots of return fire. Once they had the Salik fleet's attention, Ia backslipped the ship, swaying everyone on the bridge forward and to the right against their safety harnesses since they were still inward-bound toward the blue-brown pebble in the distance on their left.

"Alright, meioas," Ia murmured half to herself, half to her bridge crew. She spared a few seconds to call up a list from her files. "Let's reel in some of those bigger ships. C'ulosc, get on the comm with the ships I'm sending to your first tertiary. Suggest the battle plan in the first folder to their captains. I want to herd that star-side clutch of ships closer together."

"Aye, sir," he complied.

She switched on her headset. *"Captain Ia to Private Redrock, you have one minute thirty-five seconds before you must abandon L-pod 45 or risk serious injury. I repeat, abandon your L-Pod in one minute thirty seconds."*

"Sir?" she heard the gunner query in her left ear. *"Abandon it?"*

Ia rolled the ship again, this time adding a brief FTL twist that both shunted aside incoming missiles and allowed their bow to shift more toward the still inward-bound enemy. *"The shield panels in your sector are failing. They're going to score a direct hit on your primary pod with both projectile and laserfire. You're going to get a feedback surge that'll overload the capacitors. Retreat to L-pod 47 and resume fire in one minute. Beware of maneuvers."*

"Uh . . . aye, sir!"

"Yesss!" Private Shim exclaimed from his position at the navigation console. "The GCMS *Bright-Falling Death-Wings* just stomped the lead capital ship with two megablossoms, Captain. Plotting debris vectors to your third tertiary."

"Thank you, Shim." She didn't bother to look; the purpose of sending them to her console was to sync the navicomp's information with the helm computer, which would light up her main screen with the necessary collision warnings if those chunks came close. "Eyes to the boards, thoughts on your tasks, gentlemeioas."

The ship rocked gently under several more missile strikes. Ia dodged and swerved the ship, timing the thruster and FTL fields to the needs of dodging and returning fire. The ship shook with a louder *boom*, testament to her warning. Several red telltales blipped onto her upper-center tertiary screen, warning her they now had a small hole in the hull. Not deep enough to vent the sector but enough to cripple the L-pod in question.

A brief temporal peek at Private Redrock's position showed him in the corridor outside his L-Pod station, shaken but not zapped by feedback energies. He was squeezing past repair teams sent by Lieutenant Commander Harper to seal off the damaged subsectors and reroute the fueling conduits.

Contrary to the illusions of the entertainment business, there would be no such zaps in here, where Ia sat. There were far too many capacitors and circuit breakers sheltering both the bridge and engineering compartments to allow that. Plenty for most other positions on the ship, but the L-Pod's circuits had already been damaged, allowing a little too much energy to bleed and arc past its safety systems. Ia liked that her bridge wasn't located in a physically vulnerable location, such as in some sort of control tower or windowed segment of the hull. That sort of nonsense was best reserved for vidshows.

There were half-silvered windows found on luxury starliners and orbital space stations; those windows had blast panels ready to close at a moment's notice. The narrow openings compared to the overall size of those vessels further reduced the chance of lasers targeting them. But battleships weren't built to be vulnerable like that. Even if the energy only pierced at half strength, windows were an open invitation for laserfire to bypass the entire purpose of a ship's silvery, tough hull.

". . . Looks like they're herding about . . . nine Salik vessels into the requested formation, Captain," C'ulosc told Ia.

"Good. Tell the GCMS *Like-Love Hammering Hard* to adjust course immediately to three by sixteen off its current heading. Let them know they have twelve *klis* to get out of the way." Shifting her right hand from the thrusters to the lockbox, she flipped up the outer lid, scanned her palm, opened the inner lid, and thumbed the switch. "Private Nelson, have the water pipes around the remains of L-Pod 45 been rerouted?"

"Uhhh . . . getting the last one now, sir," the woman manning the operations station told her, coordinating with the engineering crew's repair teams.

"Good. C'ulosc, sound the retreat to our allies. Firing the cannon in ten."

The deck thrummed as the communications tech complied, passing her directive on to the Gatsugi ships through his headset. The Sterling engines began their *whooshing*, audible warning of the power being raised. Ia adjusted course slightly, a tiny bit more—and blood red blasted from the nose of their ship, barely missing the *Like-Love Hammering Hard*.

The holes it left behind in eight of the Salik ships were gratifying to see, as the navicomp scanners magnified the view from ship to ship on her left secondary. Strafing slightly sideways as they were, the distance between those eight chunks of enemy ship wasn't readily apparent just from the view alone. The hindmost target, however, was almost five light-seconds away.

"And that's all she could do," Ia murmured, sparing a hand from the controls to flip down the lockbox. "Nothing else will align in this battle just right."

"*Shakk*—sorry, Captain," C'ulosc apologized. "That's the fifth Gatsugi ship the Salik have blown up, their third biggest."

"Ten enemy ships are now down, with twenty-plus to go," Ishiomi reported.

"Captain, incoming fighters, 190 by 165," Shim warned Ia. "They're a mix of both sides."

"Looks like the Salik are going to try to play hide-and-seek with our hull," Rico observed. *"Aft P-pods, you get two shots. Pick your targets carefully. Double-check your missiles are set to friend-foe recognition patterns, Salik only for foe."*

"As much as I'd like to give the Gatsugi fighters some close cover, *not* with an amidships hole in my hull," Ia told her crew. "We're slipping out of this mess as soon as your teams fire their second volley, Lieutenant. Eyes to your boards, thoughts on your tasks, meioas. We still have a lot of fighting ahead of us."

MARCH 4, 2496 T.S.
GATSUGI COMMERCIAL STATION *FREELY FLOWING III*
BEAUTIFUL-BLUE ORBIT, SUGAI SYSTEM

Wearing her four Gatsugi medals along with her half glittery of one pin representing each category, Ia was given enough respect from the harried station personnel to pass from the public sectors through to the inner medical facilities without much trouble. She had more difficulty making that transit physically, as those facilities overflowed with patients needing tending. Some had wounds that could wait, while others had to be rushed through as priority cases. More than once, she had to squeeze up against a wall, among the lesser patients resting in chairs and lying on portable beds, while a team of corpsmen rushed a patient through on a hovergurney.

Ships were still limping in from the outer edges of the system. The Salik had finally retreated when their numbers had been whittled down to thirteen vessels. They had taken heavy potshots at everything in their way as they ramped up to FTL speeds and vanished. The remnants of their crippled fleet were now being boarded by Gatsugi soldiers, and that meant the wounded were being cycled out of combat via insystem shuttles and sent wherever emergency services figured they could be saved.

The damaged ships in the Gatsugi Motherworld's nearspace weren't the only problem. Three of the largest ships had managed to sling their cargo planetward. Some had been shot down, but more than a hundred dropships crammed with combat robots had made landfall in or near major cities, tying up ground resources. Like most of the races in the Alliance, the Gatsugi had an aversion to artificial intelligences, and that meant tying up a lot of resources to crush the invasion: military, medical, and transportational.

That in turn meant most of the wounded here in space were being kept in space, even if it meant overcrowding the infirmaries on every surviving ship and station. Doctor Mishka had volunteered her services to the victims on the *Freely Flowing*, the station which Spyder and his cross-platoon team of forty armored soldiers had helped to defend. A few of the other medical personnel on board the *Hellfire* had volunteered as well. Aware of the good that could be done, Ia had permitted it for a while, but their time was up.

Private Fa'ala T'enku-o was the first one Ia found. Like Jesselle, Fa'ala was something of a biokinetic; the need to help the wounded was like a pressure under the skin for many of the healing-gifted. She wasn't a xenobiokinetic, but she could still glue-stitch simple wounds, salve and bandage burns, help set and immobilize broken limbs to await the Gatsugi equivalent of bone-setting compounds, and so forth. Beyond her, four or five makeshift beds down the hall, Private Kaori Isagawa also worked. At the moment, both of them were focused on changing dressings so that the more medically skilled Gatsugi nurses could handle their patients' species-specific needs.

The corridor smelled of alien sweat, blood, antiseptics, and other strange chemicals. The walls were painted in soothing green and cheerful pastels. The noise of the hospital was a cacophony of the babble of aliens as the injured cried out, while the harried staff tried to soothe their many patients in between treatments.

Ia stopped next to T'enku-o first, a spot of sober colormooded grey among all the brighter hues. "Good work, soldier."

T'enku-o blinked and looked up, apparently not expecting the Terranglo words. The predominant languages being expressed around them were variations on local Gatsugi dialects, gestures, and colormoods, though even a Human could guess the muddied browns and magentas of the patients were actually hues of pain, and basic gestures were basic gestures. Still, it took the private a few moments to shift from being a medic to being a soldier. When she did, she started again.

"Ah—sir. Captain?" T'enku-o blinked. The Gatsugi female she was tending flipped one of her lower hands in discomfort. The private returned most of her attention to the delicate task of peeling off the old bandage. Alien though they were, Gatsugi bled the same hemoglobin red as Humans, and had wound-sealing properties similar to a Human's scab-forming platelets. "Easy, meioa, almost done . . . Did you need something, sir?"

"Finish with this and the next two patients, then return to the ship," Ia ordered. "We're leaving within half an hour."

Her brow furrowed, but she nodded. "Understood, sir."

"Good meioa-e," Ia praised. Moving along, she caught up with Isagawa, who was smoothing down the self-sealing end of a clean wrap. "Good work, Isagawa. Finish two more, then join Private T'enku-o in returning to the ship."

"We're leaving, then?" Isagawa asked her. At Ia's nod, she lifted her chin off to her left. "I saw Private Orange over that way a few minutes ago. You want me to find and tell him?"

"I'll do it," Ia said. "You have patients to attend."

Pausing to allow another gurney to go past, Ia went in search of Privates Orange, Attevale, and Smitt. Orange and Attevale

were assisting a pair of Gatsugi nurses in setting a broken leg;
the nurses watched the monitors, giving instructions in awkward
Terranglo, while Orange and Attevale used their greater Human
strength to pull the limb straight and realign the bones. She
didn't interrupt them, just let the pair know they were leaving
soon, and moved on to find the next one.

Ia found Smitt in a storage locker not far from the surgery
rooms, coordinating hasty inventory work with a Solarican
warship coming into the system, since the station hospital was
running low on key supplies. He was only a field medic but
was adept at logistics and clerical work. More importantly, he
could read and speak both Gatsugi and Solarican well enough
to translate, albeit with a little help from his military arm unit
and the language databanks back on the *Hellfire*.

Spotting her, he lifted a finger in acknowledgment, but continued talking into his headset in Solarican, reaching over the
teardrop-shaped head of the short, pink-not-haired Gatsugi
nurse working with him. Whatever-it-was slipped and fell down
behind the shelving, making the alien crouch and root for it.
Smitt pulled down another plexi-wrapped packet and added it
to her basket, still talking in the rolling sounds of the Solarican
trade tongue.

As soon as he finished his conversation, he nodded at his
CO. "Captain Ia, sir. Do you need me?"

"You have about ten more minutes to wrap this up. Orange
and Attevale will be in Exam Room 17 when you're done; assist
them, then head for the ship when they do. I'm here to get
Doctor Mishka."

"Good luck, sir," he snorted. "They brought in the crew of
some V'Dan merchanter an hour ago, and she took over their
care. Last I saw of her, she said she was scrubbing up for
surgery."

"Then I think I'll join her," Ia told him. She smiled at his
bewildered look. "I'm a biokinetic, too, soldier. Not strong
enough to be a surgeon, but I can be her KIman. Ten minutes,
Private, then grab Orange and Attevale. The doctor and I will
follow shortly after."

"Aye, sir, I'll see you on board," he confirmed. He offered
a hand to the nurse so she could grasp it with two of hers and
rise, and smiled at Ia. "I don't suppose the ship can leave without
her Captain. Good luck with the Doc."

"Tank you/Grat-tude, meioa," the nurse murmured, her accent in Terranglo almost too thick to be intelligible, explaining why the two had been using Solarican instead. Smitt turned his smile on her, and she blushed blue with pleasure.

Amused, Ia turned away. Some people preferred to stick strictly to their own species, while others were more open-minded. Personally, Ia didn't care either way; what her crew did in their off-duty hours—including volunteering in an alien medical facility—was their own business. As cliché as hospital romances were, she knew it wouldn't go anywhere anyway; neither of them would ever see each other again.

Two turns and two doorways later, Ia stepped into the sterilization hall. The ultrasonic scrubbers tingled unpleasantly as she passed between the banks of projectors, and the heat of the water at the sinks reddened her skin, but they were necessary. Emerging on the far side, she garnered wide eyes and confused-chartreuse looks from the staff. One of the nurses helpfully pointed toward a room off to the left. Ia already knew it was her goal but nodded politely to the gentlebeing in thanks for his help.

She didn't stop at the observation window. Waving her hand over the access panel, Ia stepped inside, passing through another sterilization arch. Assisted by three Gatsugi, one of them a hesitant xenophysician, Mishka stood at the manual controls for the surgery bot, guiding its tools in cauterizing the Human patient's internal wounds.

The male nurse with the lilac not-hair was the first to spot Ia. He lifted his upper hands. "No/No/Not supposed/authorized to be/enter here," he asserted, though he didn't leave his post at the anesthetics machine. "This room/place is to be/remain surgery/sterile!"

Mishka looked up briefly and scowled before returning her gaze to the control screens. "Captain, this is a restricted environment. You are compromising the safety of my patient."

"I'm here to assist, actually. Your job, Commander, is to *stabilize* this patient," Ia stated, moving up beside the other woman. "Not prep him for a full repair."

"This man has internal injuries," Mishka protested. "If I don't finish this now, he'll die within the week. These people have too many other patients to handle it."

"Your job is to stabilize him, Doctor," Ia repeated gently.

"Two days from now, the TUPSF *Granger VII* will enter the system. They have the equipment and medicines to spare. For now, cauterize the last two major bleeders, then biokinetically stabilize him and install a drain shunt in his gut."

"I'm a little exhausted from trying to psi-stabilize our *own* crew, Captain," Mishka retorted, guiding the microlasers to the next spot, "or I'd have done that already. And there aren't any xenohealers on board to help. I already asked. That means I have to seal off every leaking artery, then pack his guts with regenerative gel and monitor his recovery. Gut wounds are nothing to trifle with."

"The locals will need that gel for more Human casualties when the Salik come back in five days. I'm here to be your KIman, so you can save this one and still obey orders."

That got Mishka to look up. She studied Ia a long moment, before returning her attention to her task. "You won't let me bring him with us, will you?"

"Not unless you want to be drawn and quartered for Grand High Treason. We're officially at war now, Doctor," Ia told her. "The Admiral-General won't allow it. Earth, Beautiful-Blue, and two dozen other worlds are right now fighting off invasions of robots, attack vehicles, and mechsuited frogtopi. If you disobey my orders, your punishments will be doubled because we're at war . . . and doubled *again* because I am a duly acknowledged military precognitive. So no, I will not let you bring him on board.

"I say to you now—as a precog—that all you need to do is stabilize him so that he'll survive for at least three days, and in two days, the *Granger VII* will be by to pick him up and finish caring for him." Ia held out her hand. "You've just cauterized the last of the major bleeders in his abdomen. Encourage his body to heal what else it can, and move on. You're a very good doctor, but a terrible triage nurse. You need to know how to prioritize. Now, take my kinetic inergy and stabilize him. I have it to spare, and you have the training to use it."

Mishka looked between Ia and the unconscious man on the table. Nose wrinkling, she spat out a Russian word, no doubt a curse, and programmed the robot to withdraw its arms. "Get a drain shunt," she ordered the green-tufted prep nurse, moving around the end of the console. "His guts will continue to leak despite the cauterization, and they're much like yours;

abdominal pressure can build up and kill him. I'll need to resterilize my hands. Doctor Nuwii, you'll need to close up the patient once we're done. Captain, if you'll move up on my left, you can grab that hand—I trust you've been sterilized, but have you done a KI transfer before?"

"I've already suffered once from xenobacterial sepsis myself, Doctor," Ia replied dryly, moving as bidden. Sharing KI wasn't difficult for her. The hard part would be making sure her precognition didn't trigger with the prolonged skin-on-skin contact. "I have no intention of making anyone else suffer like that, either. And yes, I have shared kinetic inergy before. Let's get him stabilized. We have to be out of here in eight minutes or we'll be too late to help the next batch of civilians under attack."

Three Gatsugi officials awaited them at the airlock leading to the gantry connecting the *Freely Flowing* to the *Hellfire*. Arrayed in formal white clothes accented with blue, peach, and other hues, they bowed with supple grace as Ia and Jesselle approached.

"Captain/Officer Ia," the shortest of the three stated, the one with the extralong lavender not-hair. "We are/represent the Collective War Council. We wish/intend to present/give/honor you/your crew with awards/medals/honorifics for your valor/courage/skill/assistance this evening/tonight."

"I would like/be honored to accept, meioas, but my ship and crew have to go/be on our way now/immediately," Ia told them.

"Is it not the Terran way/style to honor your soldiers/warriors?" the tallest, pink-haired alien asked.

"It is, but I won't have time to stop by for a ceremony for three months and seventeen days, Gatsugi Standard," she said.

The middle-sized one, the female with peach not-hair, tipped her head and studied Ia with those black mouse eyes, which could see partway into the infrared. "It is true/true, then/yes? You are she/the Prophet/the subject/person of V'Dan prophecy?"

"Yes/Yes/I am she," Ia confirmed. Unsnapping the breast pocket of her Dress Greys jacket, she pulled out three datachips. "Here are the prophecies I can give you/reveal at this moment/point in time. They are cross-referenced/indexed under both

Terran and Gatsugi Standard time references. The first two are not vital to obey/heed; they are merely/predominantly to prove/benchmark my abilities/accuracy. Please heed/follow the rest."

"You give/share these/this information to save/spare our people/race?" Lavender-not-hair asked her, accepting the chips.

"Some of it, yes. Some of it, no. Not everyone can be saved. Some will still die despite our best efforts," Ia stated simply. Soberly. "I grieve in shades of grey for their loss/demise. But I am a warrior/soldier. I will save/rescue those/what I can, and avenge the rest. If you will excuse/pardon us, we have to leave/go, now. The war has only begun/started, and many other lives/sentients need vengeance/saving/our help."

They bowed, and Ia and the doctor bowed back. Mishka stayed silent until they were halfway up the long, chilly gantry. "If you didn't want any more medals from them, why did you wear those?"

"They needed to know who I was, so I could come fetch you. Since there's only one Terran warship in the area, by wearing my glittery—and with it, the colorful Gatsugi medals the locals would recognize—most of the authorities on the station could figure out who I was without stopping and bothering me," Ia told her.

Mishka peered at Ia's jacket. "So what are those medals for?"

"The Red Badge of Combat, the Brown Badge of Courage, the Green Badge of Compassion, and the White Badge of Survival. I earned them helping all those prisoners to escape from the banquet on Sallha last year," she dismissed.

"Okay, I get the others, but why 'Survival' as a badge?" the doctor asked.

"It's a special category for escaping Salik tentacles after having been captured and presumed eaten." Ia smiled wryly, her rare, dark sense of humor surfacing. "It means I'm entitled to state-sponsored psychological care, Gatsugi-style, for the rest of my life."

Jesselle wasn't xenoignorant. She arched one of her brows. "Gatsugi-style? For the woman who constantly wears nothing but grey-mourning-colored clothes? You *do* realize Gatsugi counselors all have degrees in fashion design and color sense, right?"

"Then maybe you'll find the fact I'm about to go change clothes and put on bloodred civvies a little disturbing," Ia quipped back. "By the way, *you*, Doctor, need to attend Lieutenant Spyder's tactical debriefing and discussion session with the troops who boarded this station. You need to learn how to gauge a battlefield for strategic defense, offense, and combat creativity."

Mishka gave her a dubious look. "Me? Excuse me, Captain, but I am a Triphid. A *doctor*. I am not a battle commander."

Ia caught her elbow, forcing both of them to stop and face each other. She didn't let go, either. "You have less than two years to learn, Commander. If you do not, you will be *directly* responsible for the lost lives and injuries of over two hundred thousand soldiers and civilians. You were given that fancy medical mechsuit because you *are* going into combat . . . and at one point in the coming future, you will *have* to instruct the soldiers placed under your command in field maneuvers in hostile enemy territory, because *we* will be on the ground in hostile enemy territory. That means you will *learn* how to be an officer of the Space Force as well as a doctor.

"Do you want to *see* what will happen to all those people if you refuse to learn how to lead them to the best of your ability?" Ia asked pointedly. Mishka looked down at the hand on her arm, but Ia didn't press her point telepathically or precognitively. Not yet. "You and I follow the exact same code, Jesselle. Our goal is to save as many lives as possible.

"Sometimes you can save them with a laser scalpel, as you did today. But *sometimes* you have to save them with a laser rifle, and *you* need to know how." Ia released her elbow but held the other woman in place with her gaze. There was a reason why this confrontation was taking place in the docking gantry, rather than on board. This was as close to neutral territory as the two women could come, and both knew the gantry was being monitored.

"I shouldn't have to go into combat. I'm a *doctor*," Jesselle argued. "I'm not a soldier!"

"You bought all those fancy medical skills on the Space Force Education Bill," Ia reminded her. "This is the price you have to pay. You can complain about it all you like, but you'll have to get in line."

Jesselle folded her arms across her chest. "Behind *who*?"

"*Me*. I never wanted to be a soldier, growing up," Ia admitted candidly. "But here I am, doing my absolute strategic and tactical best to save lives in the face of rampant enemy aggression. And here you are, because you are the *right* woman for the job. That job includes learning how to be a soldier and an officer—if a backwater nobody of a wannabe *singer* like me can do it, you can do it, too."

Ia pointed up the gantry toward their ship. Muttering under her breath in Russian, Mishka moved. Her accent in Terranglo was nowhere near as thick as one of Ia's Naval Academy instructors' had been, but she sounded like a cat fighting to get out of a canvas sack as she started marching that way. Ia followed.

"Report to Lieutenant Spyder tomorrow at thirteen hundred hours in the bow boardroom. You will listen to the soldiers under his command as they dissect their post-combat reports on what went right, what went wrong, and why. Bring a datapad to take notes. You have no patients on board the *Hellfire* who are in critical condition, so you will have no excuse to remain in the Infirmary," she added.

"Your philosophy of so-called 'free will' is a piece of hypocrisy, Captain. You're ordering me to do something against my will," Mishka muttered.

"Like I said, get in line," Ia muttered back, matching her stride for stride. "I suggest you blame the Salik instead of me. If they hadn't chosen to go to war, we wouldn't have to be out here to stop them."

They reached the airlock, guarded by Private First Grade Terry Warren, 2nd Platoon B Epsilon. Clad in light armor consisting of plates of silvery grey ceristeel on plexleather backing and a silvery grey helm, he looked like a redux of a medieval knight. At their approach, he held out a scanner wand. Ia and Jesselle held out their arm units.

"Welcome back, sirs." Private Warren greeted them as soon as the scanner greenlit their identities. "You're the last of the stragglers. Yeoman Yamasuka said we're clear to depart as soon as the three of us are on board."

"How's the hull?" Ia asked him, as they moved into the airlock.

"Private Warren to Lieutenant Spyder. Captain Ia and Doctor Mishka are now on board." He touched the side of his helmet where his headset rested, then nodded. "We're gearing up for departure now, sir. Commander Harper told me to tell you most of the panels have been replaced, thanks to the Gatsugi

repair gantries we borrowed. L-Pod 45 will still be out of commission until we can catch up with the replacement parts for the pod turret," Warren added. "He just needs to know where the Navy should send 'em, sir."

They stepped through the inner-airlock hatch into the portmost corridor of Deck 12. The door sealed behind them. A moment later, a soft *thunk* warned them that the ship and station were indeed parting company.

"I'll look into it and let him know by the end of the day," Ia promised. "If you'll excuse me, meioas, today is my birthday, and I've allotted myself half an hour in the Wake Zone to party. If I'm not mistaken, Commander Harper has arranged a surprise party for me."

Mishka snorted. "It's hardly a surprise if you already know about it."

"True," she allowed, moving away, "but I very carefully did not peek at what kind of cakes he asked the forward galley crew to bake."

"Captain," Mishka called out. Ia halted and turned to face her. The older woman sighed. "Our other argument aside . . . thank you for your KIman's help, earlier. I hate leaving a Human patient in alien hands, but with your help, at least he's stable."

"You're welcome." Ia waited, sensing Jesselle wanted to say more. The ship moved away from the station, tugging them slightly aft-ward.

"I am curious as to what information you gave those Gatsugi soldiers," the doctor added, hands tucked behind her back. "And why now? Why not earlier?"

"The why is easy. It's the right time to give it to them. Up until recently, no one knew I was a precog," Ia told her. Behind the doctor, Warren lurked, trying to make himself inconspicuous. Ia knew he would gossip to the others about whatever she said here, so she picked her words carefully. "From this point onward, I have the trust of most of the Command Staff, but that only affects what the Terrans do with the information I give them. The other nations in the Alliance also need to have that level of trust.

"That's a small part of why we came here to help the people of Beautiful-Blue survive the first attack. To show to them how accurate I am, and how effective my ship and crew can be, so that they will become willing to follow my directives in the future. We won't win this war in a single battle, or even a single year. Nor will it be won by a single species' efforts. Right now, I have the solid trust of the Terrans and the Tlassians, thanks to my friendship with the Grandmaster of the Afaso Order and his connections with his home government. The Solaricans gave me some of their trust when they made me a War Princess in rank, and now the Gatsugi are starting to come around. The K'Katta, V'Dan, and the rest will come in due time."

"And once you have everyone on your side?" Mishka asked, shifting her hands to her hips. "What then?"

"Then I'll direct them in ways to save the biggest number of sentient lives," Ia stated. In candor, she added, "Unfortunately, I cannot save every life. No one can. No soldier, no citizen, no healer can save every single life that crosses their path—you know this as a doctor, try as hard as you might. Today, we helped save that merchanter crewman's life. Tomorrow, we may or may not be able to save others' lives. As soldiers, fighting in a war we did not want, we *will* have to take away lives, too. The object is to be so good at our jobs as soldiers, we take away only an absolute few.

"Now, if you'll excuse me, I need to set aside my regrets for all the lives I could not save and the things I could not do, and go reflect on the fact that it was a good day's work," Ia told her. "Since it's also my birthday this week, I have scheduled a Wake to begin as soon as we hit FTL speeds, and I am curious to know what kind of cake awaits me in the rec room."

Dipping her head in a modified bow, Ia walked off, hands behind her back. A check of the crew's timestreams showed that Mishka would soften a little bit more toward her in a few more weeks, thanks to today's efforts. Private Warren would spread the word of what motivated their oddball captain, which wouldn't hurt things either.

And the Gatsugi are going to become impressed with my prognosticative prowess, particularly once their own military command reviews the precision and timing of everything my ship and my people did for them. I'll have to remember to remind Grandmaster Ssarra to start searching for trustworthy Gatsugi monks to serve as go-betweens with the Collective in the coming years.

A good day's work . . . I wonder if Harper remembered I

had the Deck 7 storerooms stocked with canisters of topado flour and other Sanctuarian foodstuffs? I know I copied some of the family recipes to the galleys' menu files. I miss my mother's tasty, bright blue, topado-flour birthday cakes.

The dress was a few years out of style; straps down the shoulders and arms were no longer in fashion. But it was still bright red, and still fit her figure, if a bit loosely. Ia's bout with blood poisoning had weakened her body. Following that up with more administrative work in the past handful of months than physical work hadn't been enough to rebuild all of the strength she had lost. She still had visible muscles, but it wasn't the same.

I'll have to eke out an extra half hour of weight training every day, Ia sighed, scraping her pale hair back from her face. *Not to mention, I need a haircut. My bangs are getting long enough to get in my eyes . . . and I'm procrastinating aren't I? It's okay, I can do this. The crew know better than to touch me. They should be safe from me.*

Squaring her shoulders, Ia left her quarters and headed down the hall. The former boardroom, located one floor up from the bridge and forward enough that one bulkhead served as the dividing hull between mid and fore sectors, had been converted into a recreation hall. Or rather, a relaxation lounge.

The banks of seats had been taken out and the tiers built up into different layers of platforms, some enclosed in walls that formed private niches, others more open to the room. Off to one side, a buffet had been set up next to the dumbwaiter system Ia had ordered installed to shuttle up food from the galley one deck down. Not just snacks, either; for a modest fee, special meals could be ordered off a single-serving menu if someone didn't like whatever was on the day's menu, and there was a liquor dispensary, which would dole out one hard drink or two of wine or beer per Wake-day, provided it was the start of a crew member's off-duty cycle.

The main floor had been converted into a dance floor, and the standard-issue monitors replaced with floor-to-ceiling enviro-screens. Smaller screens around the room displayed the Wake rules, reminding everyone this was a "civilian" zone.

Those rules were fairly simple, too: that the use of rank and authority was strictly limited to on-duty personnel only, who weren't supposed to be in the Wake Zone without due cause; that everyone, on-duty or off, was still responsible for the Lock-and-Web Law of space travel; that no uniforms were allowed on off-duty personnel within the designated zone; and that no law, military or civilian, was to be broken, save that all off-duty personnel in civvies within the zone were supposed to be treated as civilians.

Today's theme, prepared in the hours before the battle by bored crew members, was French Polynesian. The giant screens reflected a cerulean cove with a white sand beach and jungle-covered hills. Someone in Supply had dug out faux-thatching for the tops of the alcove-booths and strung garlands of bright, fake flowers around the hall. No one was dancing, but then the music being played was some variation on islander rhythms mixed with the sound of surf crashing on the projected beach, along with the occasional calls of tropical birds.

Last week, it had been a snow-dusted Bavarian village, with the rec-room temperature turned down to simulate a decent winter chill. Drinks had been served hot, snacks were sweet, and there had even been caroling contests with group songs and solo performances echoing up and down the corridors, some good, some bad, and all of it encouraged. Her little talk with that clutch of former Army soldiers during their first Wake had spread through the crew. No one gave her fellow ex-Marines grief anymore about wanting to sing.

Next week, if she remembered correctly, the Wake was scheduled to simulate the Athena Dome, a sports-themed amusement park on Mars; the activities listed on the roster included several ball-played sports games, plus vidgame competitions, and prizes for the highest-scoring shooters on the ship—excluding Jana Bagha and her husband Bei Ninh, to be fair to the others. They would get to be the judges.

Ia had stayed away as much as possible from the previous weekly Wakes until now. She wanted her crew to be able to relax, to claim the space as their own. To not have to worry about the rules and regs, or even be reminded of them simply because their Commanding Officer was around. This was their fourth Wake, though, and the timestreams had showed them just comfortable enough to survive her appearance.

They were so comfortable, in fact, that the first person to see her took in the curves of her red-clad figure and the legs bared below her midthigh hemline, and let out a wolf whistle. The noise of his appreciation drew the attention of several others in the room.

"Nice legs, meioa-e!" James Hong called out, grinning in appreciation as he lifted his gaze from her knees to various points higher. "Nice the rest of you, too. I could definitely—oh *shakk*! Captain!"

His feet came off the table and his tanned face flushed, then paled. The half dozen or so who had turned at his whistle also blanched. Ia strolled over to Hong and propped her hands on her hips.

"You say that rank to my face one more time in this place, and you'll get lifesupport filtration duty for a week," Ia warned Hong, waggling one finger at him. "I left my rank and uniform outside when I put on this dress. That is the Wake Zone rule, meioa. Right now, I'm a mere civilian, just like you." She started to walk away, then turned back and gave him a smile. "I do thank you for the compliment, though. I think they're very nice legs, too."

From his surprised but amused chuckle, Ia could tell he would recover from the shock of her presence. Nodding politely to the others, she headed down the terraced levels, searching for Meyun. She couldn't exactly see him in the timeplains at the moment, but then he was the one person in the universe whose movements she couldn't entirely predict. Somewhat, but not entirely.

Most of that, she had figured, was her mind protecting her from her gifts; she was very much attracted to the man on many levels. That in turn meant there was a chance that her emotions could sway her off course if she acted on those feelings, particularly if the consequences were personally appealing.

His laugh hadn't changed since their Academy days; Ia followed the sound of that familiar, light baritone chuckle down to the lowest of the alcoves. Clad in shades of blue, he backed out of the makeshift room, hands raised in mock-protest at whatever had just been said.

Her precognition rose involuntarily within her. It swept over her like a tingling wave, dragging her down beneath the waves as she stood there, watching him. Watching a vision of his future.

. . . *Meyun sat in the alcove and cuddled Nueng in his arms.*

The young woman snuggled back, content to be in his lap. Outside the Wake Zone and the privacy of their quarters, they were discreet and professional, but here, they felt safe enough to be affectionate. Because their Captain had made this place safe, despite the chain of command that governed the rest of the universe occupied by the Space Force . . .

The floodwaters of that possibility chilled her from skin to bone. Her heart hurt at the thought of Meyun finding happiness with someone else, someone not her. Someone not his Company commander. Her head wisely pointed out that it would be for the best if he turned his attention elsewhere, even though it hurt.

Her awareness of that potential possibility happened in a flash, over and done in just a few seconds. She managed a smile when he glanced her way—and watched him give her a double take worthy of Hong's, though without the whistle. Harper's smile was genuinely warm as he looked at her, his brown eyes bright with male appreciation as they slipped down to her short red boots and back up again.

"Well, look at that. You *did* show up. What a surprise," he teased. "I wasn't sure you'd bother."

Ia smiled back ruefully, hands going to her hips. "We established long ago that I'm a very dull girl, Harper. I came here because I know you arranged a cake. Where is it?"

Turning, he gestured at the interior of the alcove. "Bring 'em out, meioas!" Raising his voice, Harper moved to the center of the hall. ". . . May I have everyone's attention? Yes? Thank you! As you all know, we've got a little tradition of celebrating birthdays each week at these Wakes, if there are any.

"This week," he stated, as heads poked out of alcoves or turned away from conversations, "we're celebrating three birthdays! Last but not least is Melody Nelson's birthday, March 8. Unfortunately, she's currently on duty, as this is second watch, so if you have a chance to celebrate it with her later on today, or at least run across her, wish her a happy birthday. Right smack in the middle is Ann Velstoq', whose birthday is the sixth," he added, managing the V'Dan glottal stop at the end of her name with the ease of someone who had practiced. "And there she is. Come on down, Ann; don't be shy."

Gesturing for her to join him, Meyun led the way toward one of the empty tables on the lowest terrace above the dance floor. Two members of his engineering teams followed, Zedon and Svarson. Each man bore a platter with a cake on it, each frosted and iced with a name.

"And today's *actual* birthday girl, as in born on this date a mere twenty-four years ago, Terran Standard," Meyun teased, grinning up at his target, "is our very own Ia!"

"*Shakk* me!" someone swore. The voice belonged to Tanya Doedig, Ia realized, one of Harper's engineers. The older woman eyed Ia askance. "You're only twenty-four? I could've sworn you were *thirty*-four, Ca—er, S . . . Crap on a crutch! *Meioa-e*," the dark-skinned woman finished, using the honorific instead of Ia's rank or title. Doedig rolled her eyes. "Shove me out an airlock—I am *not* used to addressing you casually, meioa-e. I think I've been in the military too long."

"Technically, you've been in only one more year than I have," Ia pointed out. She turned to Ann, who had hesitated halfway down the stairs. "C'mon, let's go cut the cake. I'm dying to know what kind got baked."

Ann eyed her dubiously. "Aren't you a massive precog? Wouldn't you already know?"

"Only if I peeked. And I very carefully did *not* look at it in the timestreams, despite *great* temptation," Ia asserted.

Halostein, a normally reserved, no-nonsense sergeant, grinned at her. "Well, you just earned *my* respect, if you honestly didn't peek. I learned how to get into and out of my Christmas presents at a very early age with no sign of having opened or resealed the box. At least, until my fathers started hiding my presents at my biomom's house, and hid my half sisters' presents at our place. The first time that happened, I honestly thought they'd got me a dolly in a frilly dress!"

The story got a chuckle out of his listeners, Ia included. Halostein offered her the hilt of a knife he pulled from one of his cowboy boots. Accepting it, Ia moved over to the cakes.

"I truly didn't look. I spoilered myself with the myth of Santa Claus at the age of five, and things went downhill until I was eight or so, when my older brother pointed out it was my own fault for peeking all the time. He scolded me and said that if I ever wanted to be surprised, I had to be strong enough not to look . . . so I don't look at the things I know are going to be pleasant surprises. I always look in advance at the ones I think won't be. It makes it easier to avoid 'em."

Cutting into the one with her name iced in white, she

discovered from the crumbs beneath the blue frosting that it was a chocolate cake. Ia didn't mind chocolate. She sliced the rectangle into several pieces, then served herself one. Ia wiped the blade on one of the napkins clipped into the holder on the table, and passed it to Ann, trading the knife for a fork.

Just as she forked up her first bite, Ia saw the blue crumbs mixed into the white frosting of the other cake. She glared at her first officer. ". . . Hey! *She* gets the topado-flour cake? *I'm* the one from Sanctuary, Harper. That's *my* comfort food you put in *her* cake."

Ann blinked, prodded at the corner piece she had cut off, and quirked her brows. "Yeah, what's up with this blue stuff? *I* asked for a chocolate cake, not whatever *this* is."

"It's made from topadoes, and it's very nutritious and very tasty," Ia told her. "It's a kind of tuber that can be baked, fried, mashed, grilled, or dried and ground into flour."

Harper shrugged, biting his lip in the unsuccessful attempt to hide a smile. "My apologies, meioas; I guess the cakes got mixed up when they were being frosted. But there *is* an easy way around this problem, you know."

Ann looked at Ia, shrugged, and offered her untouched fork and plate. "He's right. And I know just what to do about it. Happy birthday, 'Ann,'" she quipped, eyeing Ia. "May you have a wonderful natal day."

Since she technically hadn't eaten the chocolate one in her hands, Ia offered it to Ann in turn. "And a happy birthday to you, too, 'Ia,'" she joked back. "Try a bite of the topado cake anyway. You might like it."

"After my slice of chocolate," Ann bartered. "Nothing gets in the way of me and my birthday chocolate."

Moving back from the table so the others could try the two cakes, Ia found herself next to Harper. He snagged her forkful before she could eat it, and popped the blue dessert into his own mouth. That lifted her brow, but Ia didn't protest, just took her fork back and cut another piece for herself.

"Mm, good," he murmured. Moving a little closer, Meyun whispered in her ear, "But I know something else from your homeworld which tasted even better."

Goose bumps prickled along her skin. Her former Academy roommate . . . her former lover . . . had a knack for rousing old memories she wanted to keep repressed. Ia knew that image of him turning to someone else was supposed to be the better choice, even if it hurt.

She changed the subject. "How's the gun project coming along?"

"I thought we weren't supposed to talk about work," Harper retorted dryly.

"Only in an official capacity. This is unofficial, one friend to another," Ia pointed out.

He sighed, sagging against the railing separating the terrace and its tables from the empty dance floor below. "Lousy. I can't make heads or tails out of the source for the focusing crystals the Immortal used. It almost sounds like potassium nitrate, given she said she extracted the crystals from her own . . . um, yeah. But the physics and the optical properties of saltpeter crystals are all wrong for what the guns are supposed to be able to do, so it wasn't *that*."

"They wouldn't work if we were dealing with an average Human, no," Ia murmured back. "Luckily for you, I know exactly what kind of crystal you're referring to. Get me the specs on the shapes and dimensions you'll need, and I'll get them for you. But be careful and thorough in your calculations. You won't be able to alter the crystals in shape or size once you have them in hand. Only I can."

"If the material is as rare as the properties she describes would make them out to be, then yeah, I'll want to get them right. Whatever your source is, it's bound to be extremely rare, and hard to get," he agreed.

Rare, yes, but not that hard to get, Ia thought, forestalling a reply with a forkful of white-frosted, blue-floured, slightly spicy cake. *Just sitting in palm-locked storage down by the bow shuttle hold is all.*

Someone swooped in from her left, grabbed her face, and smacked a big, loud kiss on her cheek. Those hands and lips, applied at less than a twenty percent probability, belonged to Private Second Class Yung Ramasa. He released her with a grin, spreading his already broad mouth even wider, making him look like his military nickname. "Happy Birthday, pretty lady!"

The other crew members stared wide-eyed at the two of them, shocked and apprehensive. Mindful of the rules, Ia freed a hand, hooked it around his head, and pulled his own cheek into reach for an equally loud-smacking kiss. "Thank you, Your Highness. Now go kiss Ann, too."

Ramasa laughed and rubbed his hands together in delight. "I was just on my way to do that, Ca . . . er, meioa!"

"—Oh, no you don't!" Ann protested, hand up to her mouth to cover the fact she was still eating her cake. She swallowed and waggled her fork at him. "I know your reputation with the ladies, O 'Frog Prince,' and I am *not* going to be one of your conquests!"

"I think she's sweet on him," Ia stated, catching both of their attention. She gave the smirking Ramasa a warning look. "But if he doesn't back off, she'll thump him."

"It's just a little birthday kiss!" he protested. "*You* didn't mind," he added to Ia, moving a little closer to Ann. "Why should she?"

"You didn't give me a chance to protest," Ia countered, enjoying the moment.

"Nonsense! I am quite sure you foresaw it coming, which means you chose to accept it," Ramasa stated, sidling a little closer to his target.

He lunged, lips puckered—and got thumped in the shoulder by the edge of Ann's fist. The gunner yelped and backed off, pouting . . . and at that point, Ann relented, leaned over, and kissed him on the cheek. He grinned and kissed her back. She thumped him again, but only lightly.

". . . I'll admit I saw *that* coming," Ia stated primly, and scooped up another forkful of fluffy blue cake. Her second-in-command gave her a dirty look. "What? I'm just here to enjoy my birthday cake . . . and a little impromptu floor show."

Meyun wasn't the only one to chuckle at that. Even Ann and Yung laughed.

Ia nodded to herself, enjoying another bite. *Mission accomplished. This portion of the crew has relaxed around me,* and *I got my birthday cake.*

CHAPTER 10

Why did the Gatsugi accept my abilities faster than my own government? Well, I could quote the old maxim that a prophet is never honored on his or her own doorstep, but I think it was due to three things. I gave them the exact inward-bound sectors of the Salik attack fleet, gave them a good eighteen minutes of advance warning, and my ship and crew managed to account for the destruction of half the ships taken out of commission—three times more than the next best effort by one of their own forces.

Keep in mind that the Gatsugi were not weak; my ship was just better aimed overall. Motherworld systems are also the most heavily defended, which is why the Salik chose to strike at them, to land psychological blows against their opponents as well as physical ones. If my ship hadn't been able to take out so many of theirs in one blow, the number of robotic dropships would have increased exponentially.

I also chose to aid the Gatsugi because the Terrans had already been warned about the coming war months in advance. I told my superiors when they would need to be ready for it, and what to be ready for. As it was, the fleet back in Earth's nearspace was still damaged worse than the Gatsugi ones. Not by too much, but by enough to make my precognitive warnings clear.

So the Terrans did believe me to an extent, particularly after the official start of the war. They just didn't have the

shock of instant power and instant proof magnifying that
belief, as the Gatsugi did. Instead, the Command Staff were
gradually introduced to what I could do, subtly before the
Battle of the Banquet, and more openly afterward. Because
it was gradual, the impact just wasn't the same.

~Ia

MARCH 19, 2496 T.S.
SYSTEM'S EDGE, NUK NUKLIEL 83

"Gadalah," Ia stated, sparing a glance from her main screen
to her left secondary. "Target fragment . . . 1172. Blow it up,
three missiles."

"Aye, sir," Private Gadalah stated, relaying the orders on
her headset to a trio of gunners.

"Coming up on tanker midpoint in fifteen," Fielle warned
Ia. "Coming up on the drone carrier's midpoint in . . . thirty-
five. Fifteen, sixteen fighters behind our ninety-ninety, Captain,
three stragglers behind the 270 by 90."

"Captain, we're being pinged on the hyperrelays,"
Al-Aboudwa warned her. "It's asking that we switch to secured
channel two—the code's the one for the Command Staff. What
do I do, sir?"

"Be polite, Private," Ia murmured, her attention on keeping
them alive in the mix of seven midsized ships, two tankers,
and a host of fighter craft. "Ping them back on the confirmation
code of the day."

"MacInnes still needs more of those transmissions,
Al-Aboudwa," Rico told the comm tech. "She's not getting
enough nouns to decode it. If that's the Command Staff, they'll
need it fast."

Their shields reverberated with an odd shudder. Not the
thumping rumble one expected from a projectile weapon, but
from the fragmentation of a loosely aggregated ice clump disintegrating on impact. Another, louder *whump* shook the ship,
this time from an actual missile.

Ia tipped the ship a little more down and to her right—down
relative to her dead-ahead vector, that was, since "down" in
starfighting terms was always the enemy's main position, and

the majority of the enemy were off to the left. Telltales flickered yellow and green, stippled here and there with unpleasant red. Rolling the ship clockwise presented fresher targets for the lasers and projectiles aimed their way. It also allowed her to strafe them sideways, through the debris of the now-scattered chunks of shuttle-sized ice that would have slammed through their shields and into the hull itself had Gadalah's gunners not fragmented it.

"*Shakk!*" Al-Aboudwa cursed. He cleared his throat. "I mean, Captain, sir, it's the Admiral-General. She's calling for you, sir. Should I tell her you're busy?"

"Not today. Patch her through to my third tertiary, Al-Aboudwa; I'll take her call," Ia pointed out, left hand flicking through the commands in the attitude glove, right hand dancing over the thruster controls. "Fielle, take out those fighters. Gadalah, focus on the dropship."

Her lower third tertiary screen dropped its bar graphs of energy outputs from the various engines around the ship, replaced by the round face and grey-streaked black hair of Admiral-General Christine Myang. "Greetings, Captain Ia."

The pingback icon in the lower right corner of the screen showed they were on a five-second delay. Hyperspace communications were fast, but not instantaneous. Ia shifted the ship again, glancing up at the spate of yellowlit warnings on her upper bank of monitors. "I need those fighters taken down, Fielle."

Myang, five seconds behind, continued talking. "As you may or may not recall, your six months of *carte blanche* are now up, and it is time for your performance re . . . view? What are you doing, Captain?"

"Good afternoon, Admiral-General," Ia greeted her, without looking down at the screen containing the Admiral-General's face. "I am currently doing what I do best. Saving millions of lives by destroying a few hundred Salik. But I'm not too terribly busy, and I know you've allotted this half hour to talk with me, so go right ahead. I am listening—Nelson, Al-Aboudwa, I'm getting some odd flashes of light from those fighters. Try running those through the lieutenant's code crackers."

Another *paff* of breaking ice was followed by a *clang*. Dubsnjiadeb cursed. "—I think they're trying to ram us, sir! They're hemming us in with the larger chunks."

"Well, blow them up!" Rico retorted.

"Doobie, two of those ships are about to get away. Plot courses for them and coordinate with Gadalah's teams. I want intercept arcs for each vessel," Ia ordered. She pulled her gaze downward long enough to smile at the Admiral-General. "Go on, sir. I *am* listening."

Five seconds later, Myang responded. "Maybe I should call you back later."

Ia responded on top of her, mindful of the five-second delay and wanting her words to interrupt the older woman. "I'm afraid we'll be in transit in less than fifteen minutes, sir." Myang fell silent, so she continued. "We won't be able to stop and talk for another six or seven hours, which is after we've helped fend off the first—Fielle, we still have four fighters on our tail, I said get rid of them—the first invasion wave on the Solarican domeworld of Rau Niil II."

"In four more hours, Captain, I'm supposed to be in bed, getting some badly needed rest. Unless there's another emergency requiring my personal oversight," the older woman muttered. "Alright. We will deal with the question of your *carte-blanche* demands now. Presuming you can handle it?"

"Got 'em, Captain!" Fielle crowed as the aft gunners successfully hit the final three fighter ships. "Take that, you frogtopi! Never mess with *this* ship's weaponry!"

"Don't get cocky, Yeoman," Rico chided him. "You're not Shikoku Yama, you know."

"I know I can handle it, sir, or I'd have contacted you earlier when we were repairing from the engagement at CS-35," Ia said. "You've seen the recordings we've mailed your way. You know what I'm capable of doing with this ship, given the freedom to use it appropriately. I have only done so freely for the last six weeks. Imagine what I can do with six more weeks, and six again beyond that."

Around her, the screens flared with streaks of light, silent and not-so-silent explosions, and shifting stars as she maneuvered the long ship. The cometary fragments were their best defense against the Salik vessels, even as they caused problems of their own; the *Hellfire* had been built with multiple redundant shielding systems and extra hull plating just for this purpose: surviving heavy enemy fire. Not without cost, though; several more items appeared on her upper screens in red.

"I take you want more *carte blanche*," Myang stated after a pause of about ten seconds. "Another six months' worth?"

Ia dipped her head, her gaze still on her main screen, piloting the *Hellfire* through the debris. "Yes, sir; that would be lovely, sir. If you could authorize it right now, having that on hand when we reach Rau Niil will shave ten hours off our repair time since it means we can commandeer their biggest low-grav repair cradle. That means we'll have just enough time to make it back downstream on the Arm to defend the colonies at Proxima Carinae. It's a small engagement, but a vital one, temporally."

"Sir, getting a ping from the system buoy we dropped," Al-Aboudwa warned her. "Three . . . no, five Salik vessels inbound from insystem. They're free of the belt, star-ward vector 15 by 330, and closing fast. If they don't slow down below three-quarters Cee, ETA in two minutes forty seconds."

"How is it vital temporally?" Myang asked Ia.

"In about five weeks, if most of the colony survives, they'll discover a mother lode of ore containing molybdenum, which is a component in ceristeel manufacturing. In eight weeks, the London Metal Exchange will be shipping tonnes of it to manufactory sites throughout the Alliance, and it will continue to produce high-quality ore well into the second war," Ia revealed. "Gadalah, I need ice fragments 503 and 1257 destroyed."

"Aye, sir, I'm on it!"

"Admiral-General," Ia continued, "if we don't show up, the colonists *will* still find it in about eight months, but by the time they get the ore to the ceristeel manufacturers, we'll have lost over 327,000 soldiers, and far too many civilian lives." Dropping her gaze to her lower-center tertiary, Ia met the older woman's gaze through her screen pickups. "I can list the names, ages, and favorite foods of each and every single soldier and civilian who will die, if you like."

Her gaze snapped back up to the main screen as three lasers hit their hull, red-lighting two FTL panels and turning a third amber. A few more hits on that sector, and they'd be unable to form a complete field. With a hiss of triumph, Rico lifted his head and glanced her way.

"Got it! Captain, MacInnes cracked the code. Part of it *was* in the running lights. Permission to send it to the Admiral-General on a subchannel, sir?" Lieutenant Rico asked.

"Permission granted, Lieutenant," Ia told him, before returning her attention to Myang. "Sir, you're going to receive today's Salik code for the war effort within one to two parsecs of Nuk Nukliel 83," Ia told her superior, slipping the ship toward the bottom of the ice cluster. "They're changing up codes every few days and using lightwave signals as well as hyperrelays, so I cannot guarantee it will work for long, or even work in another sector, but it will for this one. Firing the Godstrike cannon in fifteen."

"You know, sir, we could really use sunglasses for that thing," Nelson quipped from the operations station.

Ia unlocked the box, flicked on the system, adjusted their attitude slightly, and thumbed the firing control. The lights on the bridge dimmed, while the *thrum* of the hydrogenerators and *whoosh* of the heat pumps joined the smashing of ice and clashing of projectiles. One sanguine-bright flash later, Ia checked the lightwave readings versus the spare system buoy they had dropped, making sure she had killed the inbound ships, then glanced down. Admiral-General Myang winced as she watched, tanned face and grey-streaked hair briefly flaring pink in the glow from her monitor.

"I trust you know exactly where that beam will be three or four light-months down the road?" Myang asked her dryly.

"Sir, yes, sir. What little didn't chew through four large ships and a swath of the local Kuiper belt will be busy dissipating harmlessly in off-plane and interstitial space."

"Captain!" Dubsnjiadeb called out. "Navicomp's showing inbound objects at near-Cee. They're trying to throw rocks at *us*, sir!"

"Kind of stupid, if you ask me," Nelson muttered from the operations seat. "Most of 'em will break up in the ice field."

"Thank you, Doobie. They're desperate, Nelson. Gadalah, dump fifty proximity mines in our wake. Fielle, keep firing. *All hands, brace for acceleration*," Ia warned through her headset, before slipping the ship dorsal-ward, pressing everyone down into their seats.

"Never give the enemy a weapon you wouldn't want turned on yourself, Captain," Myang added through the hyperlink, apparently having heard Dubsnjiadeb's warning.

The pull of vector change that made it through the pulsing ripple of greased physics felt heavier than Ia's homeworld, making it hard to breathe. Several ice chunks broke noisily against their shields, but it was the fastest way out of the Kuiper field. She shifted them forward, transitioning into a rising arc that would skim the upper edges of the tumbling bits of frozen and metallic debris.

"Don't worry, Admiral-General, they want us and our planets mostly intact, so they won't sling boulders at our colonies. Just rocks at our ships. We're on our way out of here now, sir. If you're willing to grant me another six months of *carte blanche*, now would be a very good time to transmit the updated authorizations, before we have to end the link."

While the Admiral-General thought, Ia eased up on their acceleration, partly to spare her crew, who weren't used to long stints in high gravity, and partly to change vectors. Some of the Salik missiles were still going fast enough to catch up with them, and the Salik lasers were getting better at targeting the *Hellfire*'s hull, now that Ia was speeding up for an escape. The faster one went, the harder it was to deviate from course, and the Salik gunners knew it. Twisting the ship counterclockwise a little, she presented a fresh section of panels for the lasers to score, and accelerated again.

". . . You haven't disappointed me with your performance yet," Myang stated, shifting in her seat to input the codes on her end of things. "*Yet*. Transmitting the paperwork, Captain."

"Thank you, sir. Al-Aboudwa, catch that and copy it to the Company files," Ia ordered, easing back on the thruster fields so he could move. She had to roll the ship slightly once again as the lasers continued to tag their hull.

"For now, Captain, you have the continuing confidence of the Command Staff," the Admiral-General told her. "Don't *shakk* it up."

"Sir, no, sir," Ia agreed. "That is not my intention, sir."

"Got it, Captain," Al-Aboudwa told her. "Received and saved."

"Good job, Private. Thank you, Admiral-General," she added, eyes fixed on the screens displaying their surroundings, toes in the timestreams. "Now, if you'll excuse us, we need to go pay for some repairs with that lovely cheque—one more thing, sir."

She pulsed the field panels for six seconds, slipping them forward hard and fast.

Myang lifted her brows. "Considering I've renewed your *carte blanche*, under the same double-indemnity terms, what else could you want?"

Ia eased back. "It's not about what I want. It's a warning, sir. Two months from now, a couple of the Feyori are going to be very pissed at me. They may try to infiltrate and influence the minds of the Command Staff. Be on your guard."

Again, she accelerated. This time, Myang frowned. "What are you going to do to them, soldier?"

"Actually, it's what I already did," Ia grunted, fighting the vector pull. She rolled the ship one last time. "I do have plans to take care of them. I'm just warning you, sir. Ia out."

A tap of her thumb ended the comm link. Not that full FTL wouldn't have ended it for her, since it was extremely difficult for the ship to maintain hyperrelay communications without a dedicated vacuum chamber on board while wrapped in a skin of warped physics.

A scrape of her fingertips shot them forward hard and fast, leaping ahead of the pulsing, orange streaks that were now the only weapons that could catch them. Just as the enemy's sensors recalibrated, tagging one last shot on their aftmost panels, the stars on the screens burst and streaked, crossing the lightspeed barrier.

Gentling their acceleration, Ia checked her upper screens, tabbing through the list of damaged hull components. "That was a nasty fight. But we're still greenlit for travel. Power your station back around, Fielle, and prepare to take back the helm. We'll stay at FTL for another half hour to evade pursuit, then hyperwarp the rest of the way."

"Can I hit the head first, Captain?" he asked her.

"Go right ahead. Just don't take all shift," she warned him. "Doobie, plot a hyperrift course for System Rau Niil 78. Line it up so we come in somewhere behind the second planet, close enough to duck behind it. There's a sixty percent chance the star will flare up and cast out an ion storm about the time we arrive. Nelson, we have a weak stretch of FTL panels in the aft sector, starboard ventral."

"Aft sector, five by seventeen, aye, sir," Dubsnjiadeb agreed, as Fielle finished powering his station around and unclipped his harness. "I'm also keeping an eye on it. Engineering's working up an internal fix in case that center panel fails. I've already told Sugartoo that we got the repair authorization. She'll pass that along to Commander Harper when he comes on duty."

Sugartoo was actually Xhuge, as in Private First Class Meyling Xhuge, wife and teammate of Corporal Yen Xhuge, one of the four crew members who served as a comm tech for the first duty watch, and one of Lieutenant Rico's top code crackers. His nickname, "Sugar," had been established early on as a play on his name, and when their first CO had granted them permission to wed, Meyling had sworn she was now "a Sugar, too," or Sugartoo for short. Oddly enough, her nickname was the only one people used these days.

The Space Force didn't mind it if soldiers married each other, so long as their relative ranks and positions weren't in conflict with Fatality Forty-Nine: Fraternization. Since both were enlisted and close to each other in rank, there wasn't enough conflict in their position as teammates to bother most commanding officers, including Ia. It helped that the two of them worked in different parts of the ship normally; while her husband served on the bridge, Sugartoo was an excellent mechanic and made a good engineering lead for those times when Commander Harper wasn't around. Of course, she was just one of four on her duty watch, since everyone had to swap duties every hour or two to prevent boredom, work fatigue, and glazed-eye syndrome, but she was good at her job.

"Don't anybody tell the Admiral-General," Ia quipped, "but I actually wanted that *carte blanche* just so our first officer wouldn't yell at me about what I've been doing to his ship while he slept."

Her joke provoked a few chuckles. Rico snorted. "If he could sleep through *that* fight, I'll have to ask the doctor what meds she's been slipping into his hot cocoa. I could use 'em, too."

"Careful, or she might try to slip them into *my* cocoa," Ia retorted. "She thinks I've been stinting myself on sleep."

"Technically, you have been, Captain," Rico pointed out. "You've been running thirty-two-hour days lately instead of twenty-four."

"I'll survive, Lieutenant." She held the helm steady with her left hand and used her right to access the workpad clipped to her console. Now that she had a few free moments, she had to go back to composing prophecies. Time wasn't entirely on her side. Thankfully, the Admiral-General was. "The important thing is that by short-sheeting myself, many others will survive as well."

MARCH 29, 2496 T.S.
CHIMERA V ORBIT
JORDAN TAU-CETI 28 SYSTEM

"How's your shoulder?" Chaplain Benjamin asked Ia. She offered a cup of caf' to the younger woman. Ia accepted it, and the redhead curled up in the stuffed chair across from her. "And how many times have I asked you that, anyway?"

"Three . . . four times now, and I'm under orders not to use it or stress it for two days," Ia confided, cradling the mug in her right hand. Her left arm hung in a sling. "The mechanics tell me I won't be able to use the suit arm for two weeks, it's that badly mangled."

"But you got the control node for the robots," Bennie pointed out. "And you took them out before they could take out the dome defenses from underground. A task which you could've left to Lieutenant Spyder."

"He's good, but that one required precision shooting. You haven't seen the vidlogs. I shot through a gap about this big." She made a circle out of her thumb and forefinger with her left hand since her right one was busy, then winced at the pain the movement stirred. She relaxed her fingers. Sipping from the mug in her right hand, Ia shook her head. "Besides, it served a second purpose. Eighteen of my crew got to see me in 'Bloody Mary' mode, and that's good for morale."

Bennie snorted, almost choking on her caf'. She lowered her mug, rubbing at her nose. A few sniffs cleared it. "Ow . . . Your sense of humor is terrible . . . Not to mention, I'd think that seeing their CO's arm getting crunched by an oversized, motorized monkey wrench would be *bad* for morale."

"Nope. It shows them I'm willing to take the same risks that they do. Besides, *that's* what Spyder was good for. He's the one who cut through the tensor cables, freeing my arm before it could be pulverized."

"Instead of dislocated. Again," Bennie stated dryly. "So . . . how are you sleeping at night?"

Ia lifted her brows, mouth busy with her cup. She swallowed, and asked, "What, no cracks about how little I've been sleeping?"

Bennie shook her head. Her hair had grown long enough that the auburn plait barely moved across her shoulders. "I figured if Jesselle didn't drug you insensate, then she thinks you're doing alright, medically."

"Well, we did get into a little argument over that while she was patching me up," Ia admitted. "But I convinced her I was going to go to bed and sleep for twelve hours after seeing you."

At that, the chaplain lifted a brow. She gave Ia's cup a pointed look. "Oh, really?"

Ia grinned. "I will. In about four more hours, when I've finished filling out the paperwork on the battle and written twenty more prophecies."

Bennie kept her brow arched.

"I promise!" Ia protested. Then added honestly, "Unless an emergency happens, and I'm needed on the bridge."

Her truthfulness earned her a gimlet stare from her friend. "And *will* there be one?"

"Fifteen percent probability," she admitted, leaning back in the padded chair. "This is a very comfy chair . . . Is this the chair I saw on Grizzle's requisitions manifest? Nice chair . . . Anyway, that fifteen percent is only if the TUPSF *Zizka* leaves the system early, and I've asked them to stay. I told their captain if they do extend their stay by an hour or so, they'll be better placed to scare off the Salik scoutship headed our way, looking for weakness in the local defenses. You know, I think I need to get one of these seats for my own office."

"Nonsense, you'd fall asleep and never get any work done," Bennie scoffed.

This time it was Ia who arched her brow. "First you want me to sleep, but now you *don't* want me to sleep?"

"Consistency, you cannot have," the older woman quipped, hiding her grin in a sip from her mug.

Chuckling, Ia sat up and fitted her cup into the clip on the edge of the coffee table, then sighed and leaned back again. "I could use some decent sleep, yes. But every clunk and thump from the repair teams is going to keep me awake, worrying that something will break on the wrong side of the probability curve during their work, making us further delayed. We replaced five pods at Rau Niil, but we lost too many sensor arrays this fight. If nothing bad happens, Harper's teams will be done in about four hours, which means third watch will be free to get the ship under way. If anything does, I can be on top of it with exactly what's wrong, and we'll be under way in five. *Then* I can sleep.

"If not, if I go to sleep now, and something happens . . . more damage, more delays. More problems for me to fix." She eyed her cup of caf', debating whether or not to drink more of it. Sighing, she sat forward and unclipped it, choosing caffeine over common sense. "I can't wait until my arm gets out of this sling. It's throwing off my balance, and I'm not allowed to exercise in high gravity like this. Every day I lose while I wait for my body to heal is five extra days of struggling to recover the strength I've lost."

"At least your suit's safety cage held, and you didn't lose the arm. So how *are* you sleeping these days?" Bennie pressed, not deterred by the change in subject. "No avoiding the question, Captain. Any nightmares?"

A slight but genuine smile tugged at Ia's lips. "Pretty well, and very few, Commander. Especially after the *carte-blanche* extension."

Bennie smiled. "Good. Now, since you're more or less mentally stable . . . for you . . . let's chat about the rest of your crew. Private Davies is coming along slowly in her misandry therapy, but she is making progress. I've been watching her spar with her teammate, and she's not quite so conflicted about hitting him—and when she does, she's not wasting her blows in anger."

"Mm . . . I've only seen them spar a few times, but that's good," Ia agreed, sipping at the cooling brew. "What about Private Kim? Ah, Kimberly Kim. Has she mentioned Sergeant Maxwell?"

Bennie narrowed her eyes. "Are you trying to pry past the sacred seal of both the therapy session and the confessional?"

Ia snorted. "For one, I'm a fellow priestess, duly ordained, blah blah blah. For another, I already know where those two are headed, more or less. As far as I'm concerned, since they're not posted to the same Platoon and so long as they're still fit for work when their watch comes up, they can bounce on the bedsheets all night long whenever they're off duty. Just not on *my* bedsheets."

That made the chaplain choke on her drink. She coughed a bit, laughing. "*Shakk!* God bless you, Ia, but you're *not* supposed to be trying to kill me with laughter, here. And you made me swear! Bad girl!"

Smirking, Ia shrugged, unrepentant in the face of her chaplain's finger-waggling. "Hey, I'll take my humor wherever I can get it. It's also nice to know you're Human, too."

"I'll save my prayers of repentance for later, just in case you make me do it again," Bennie dismissed. She rose, asking, "More caf'? If you're going to stay up four more hours, that is?"

"Please," Ia agreed, holding out her cup. "Back to the crew, and Kim versus Maxwell."

"Careful, Ia," the chaplain cautioned as she retreated toward the dispenser, "or I'll think you're secretly a romantic at heart."

Ia didn't deny it. "Why shouldn't I be? I love this galaxy so much, I'm willing to marry my life to it."

"That's a hero/martyr complex," Bennie dismissed. "I'm talking *romantic* love."

"A girl has to amuse herself somehow, and I am still female deep down inside. Besides, all this chastity sucks like a black hole," she muttered. "Might as well hear about it secondhand."

"You haven't renewed anything with Meyun yet?" Bennie asked Ia, glancing her way. She came back and returned Ia's cup to her. "Considering how he looks at you . . ."

"He can look all he wants." She sighed, accepting the mug. Slouching back, she sagged in the seat in an uncaptainly way. "Nothing can happen between us until the whole crew is on our side. The Command Staff's spies are still watching for that sort of thing, and they won't convert to the Church of Ia for a couple more years, in most scenarios."

Curling one leg under her, Bennie resettled in her seat. "Church of Ia? Careful, there. Delusions of godhood don't look good in a military personnel file."

"You know what I meant," Ia dismissed. "Even the Space Force calls the procedural manual the 'Company Bible.' No pretensions of religious aspirations were intended. At least, not on board this ship. I'm still the Prophet foretold by the Sh'nai faith, no matter what I do."

Benjamin stayed silent for a moment, thinking, then

shrugged. "Okay, so what scenarios *would* convert the crew more quickly? It's not healthy for either of you to suppress your urges."

Ia snorted. "That sort of conversion will only come at a terrible price, usually by me predicting some terrible fate, like a series of deaths. Things I'd rather avoid having come true or making people suffer through. Slow and steady will still win the race, and will do so less painfully. It just sucks like a black hole in the interim."

"So the two of you get to suffer from sexual frustration?" Bennie said. "That's the less painful solution?"

Ia slanted her a look. "Aren't we supposed to be discussing my crew?"

The chaplain smirked. "Aren't we?"

Dropping her head against the padded back of the chair, Ia sighed. "Not until I know for sure my people won't go running to the Admiral-General. I need Meyun far more as a brilliant off-the-cuff engineer than I need him as a lover. And that's enough on *that* subject for today. Official Captain's policy. Now, let's get back to Private Kim. I'm also concerned about her mental health after her jaunt onto the timeplains, and not just her emotional health."

Thankfully, the chaplain let the other subject drop, though Ia knew her friend would eventually bring it back up again.

APRIL 5, 2496 T.S.
SIC TRANSIT

Like hers, Harper's quarters were located next to his primary workspace, the main engineering compartment in the aft sector of the ship. Not that far from hers, either, if offset by a deck and a section bulkhead. However, his front room was large compared to hers. Ia had given up some of that space to ensure a galley for the bridge since she didn't have a need for any privacy bigger than a small living area separate from her bed.

Her free time was spent with a workstation in hand, transcribing future directives; at most, all she needed was a comfortable chair. Knowing he would need to experiment in his free time, she had ordered Meyun's quarters enlarged by a bit, so there would be room for workbenches and storage facilities for projects like this one.

"So. That's the gun?" Ia asked, eyeing the collection of tubes, crystals, trigger, and handgrips resting on the workbench table in Meyun's personal quarters.

"The originals were sort of . . . of Jules Verne–ish, so I thought I'd carry on with that theme. Wait—doesn't it look like it should?" Harper asked her. "Am I doing something wrong temporally?"

"Well . . . no. Sort of. Maybe? I'm used to seeing it while it's being held and pointed at me," she amended, staring at the odd thing. "Maybe that's it?"

Shrugging and spreading his hands, he hefted it. Despite its bulk, Harper lifted the weapon fairly easily. He wasn't from as heavy a world as hers, but his homeworld, Dabin, was still above the point-break. Stepping back, he aimed it at her. A glance at the table reassured Ia that the e-clips were still secured to the table in holders. He also kept his finger off the trigger, further reassurance he wouldn't fire it. She didn't think she'd enjoy being hit by the wrong sort of energy beam.

"How does it look now?" he asked her, trying to squint along one of the upper enclosed tubes. "There's no real sighting mechanism since I figured it's meant to be used at close range."

Ia peered at the gun for several long seconds, comparing it to the timestreams, then shook her head. "This bit up here should be over here . . . and this node thingy is on the other side, toward the back. And there was a sort of oblong, bowling-pin-shaped bit . . . or maybe kind of brandy snifter–ish . . . Sorry, Meyun, but it's the wrong configuration. There also should only be one focusing crystal visible. The rest should be inside the housing."

Harper lowered the weapon. Giving her a sardonic look, he said, "This *is* my first try. I designed it on basic principles of physics. And I'm not sure *how* these crystals are supposed to resonate, since every experiment I could find listed in the Nets said they just absorb whatever is thrown at them. Electricity, thermal energy, light from within and without the visible EM spectrum . . ."

"They can be easily seen, come in several pastel shades, and do emit their own light, so they don't absorb *all* wavelengths of visible light," Ia pointed out dryly.

"Nah, that's just a trick," he teased, setting the gun-thing on the table. "A dangly thing on a fish to lure their prey in close to their jaws—I can *see* some of myself building this thing in the timestream memories I have, but only in little snatches. Why don't we just go into the streams and let me look at what I eventually do to correct it, so that it functions as you saw it?"

Ia shook her head. "You can't do that without reading your own thoughts, but your other self's thoughts while submerged within the timestream's life get blocked out by your actual thoughts."

"Ha! So paradox *does* exist within precognitive-based time manipulation," Meyun said, pointing a finger at her.

She blinked at him. "Harper . . . first of all, it's only a paradox because you're too close to your own life, and your current thoughts will always be louder than your past or future thoughts. And secondly, that argument was over and done with months ago."

"I know, but it still applies." He tapped the side of his head. "Eidetic memory. I remember almost everything you've ever said to me."

For a moment, his brown eyes darkened, gazing at her. Ia remembered that look. It was a path neither of them could afford to retake. "And we're getting offtrack. Just accept the fact that you cannot peer into your own timestream to read your thoughts. I could do it with your alternate-life self, but I cannot do it with myself . . . and I'm not enough of an engineer to transcribe whatever I could learn from you. Not at the level of understanding you'll need to succeed. I can't do it all, you know."

Thankfully, he accepted the return to the correct subject.

"Well, then maybe I could display a series of schematics for myself . . . though without actually understanding the principles behind the design, it'd only be halfway useful for building the real thing," Meyun reminded himself.

"There is that," she agreed. "You're a great engineer because you understand the theories deep down in your bones."

He sighed and raked a hand through his hair. It was now long enough that he had to knot it up when on duty, but this wasn't his duty watch. A moment later, he frowned, black brows pinching together. "Wait. Didn't you tell me once that . . . well, not *you* you, but a timestream you . . . didn't you tell me once that you see *all* possibilities? Including alternate realities where

I'm not a Human but rather a blue-furred rock ape or something?"

"Yes," Ia confirmed, nodding slowly. "I didn't say it in *this* particular reality, but it is true, and I know you experienced visions from a hundred alternate realities. There's even a universe out there where you and I are actually Salik, plotting the downfall of Alliance civilization. Several variations on that theme, in fact. Not particularly helpful in this case, but that alternative does exist, along with many others."

"Then why don't we just find an alternate reality where *I* am not the person successfully developing this gun, and just go read *his* thoughts?" Meyun pointed out. "Or hers? Or its? A universe with the same laws of physics, but where my thoughts can't get in the way of my own thoughts because I'm not the one thinking them?"

She blinked. "That's *brilliant*. I like it," Ia agreed. She thought about it for a moment, then held up thumb and forefinger close together. "Just one little problem, though."

Meyun rolled his eyes. "What *now*?"

She gave him a faint, pain-tinged smile. "Last time I took you onto the timeplains . . . it was a bad experience for you. And while searching for someone *not* you will make them easier to find and read, I still can't foresee all of your future. I'm pretty sure that's my gift protecting me from the temptation of you. I don't know how that'll affect this trip, and I don't want to hurt you again."

Stepping close, Meyun cupped her face in his hands. "The only reason why I suffered was because neither of us was prepared. The only reason why I continued to suffer was because I was forced to spend two years without even hearing from you. Of seeing you only in my dreams, and in that awards ceremony they broadcast on the military channels."

Ia flushed. She knew she should step back, should break contact, but between the gentleness of his hands and the warmth radiating from his body, she didn't feel threatened. For a moment, dangerous though it was, the timeplains no longer lurked in the back of her mind. No past, no future, only the now. "Meyun . . ."

"I won't endanger your work," he promised, tilting her face up a little, encouraging her to meet his gaze. "I promise that. I've had a lot of time to think over everything I saw and think through the reasons why you would have done those things, and why we can't . . ." He broke off, breathed deep, then added wryly, "Except Bennie told me that you said if we could get the whole crew on our side, it wouldn't be a problem. So long as we were discreet."

Being reminded of that gave her the strength to step back. He let her go, and she immediately missed the warmth of his touch. The heating system in his quarters was working fine—he was the chief engineer, after all—but she still shivered a little, chilled by the lack of contact. Shaking her head, Ia said, "That won't happen for a few more years. And I don't want to put tempta—"

He stopped her with a finger on her lips and a slight smile. "Too late, and not a problem. As for the risk . . . well, I'm willing to take it, so long as whatever we see, you promise you won't throw me off the ship."

She spoke as soon as he removed his finger. "I *can't* throw you off the ship. I need you to keep repairing it."

Hands going to his hips, Meyun mock-frowned at her. "And whose fault is *that*, Meioa-e Who Likes To Blow It Up Repeatedly?"

"That was the Salik, not me," she told him mock-primly. The moment of levity eased the tension. Sighing, she raked her fingers through her short white locks. "Alright. We'll do it. I'll take you onto the timeplains and see if we can go looking for a blue-furred rock ape who knows how to build this thing right, and why it has to be built that way. God knows I've cribbed notes from several far-flung alternate realities before."

"There is no God but the Future, and Ia is His Prophet," he quipped, startling her. He tapped the side of his head again. "Something else I remember from the timestreams. And you were right, they're only images of things that *might* be, not always the things which *will* be . . . thank God."

"Right. Speaking of seeing things that might be, we probably should sit down for this." She nodded at the prototype. "Secure that weapon first, soldier. Lock and Web."

"Aye, aye, Captain." Unclipping a rolled bundle of tight-woven webbing from the far side of the table, he pulled the stretchy network over the gun.

Ia helped him secure the edges to clips on the underside of

the desk. At a gesture from him, she retreated to the sofa across the room from his workbench. He settled next to her, rested his hands on his grey-clad thighs, and looked at her.

"So . . . now what?" he joked, though she could see the discomfort in his eyes. "I'm presuming you'll want both of us dressed for this? Or are we going skinny-dipping in the timestreams?"

Giving him a flat look, she shook her head. "Wise-asteroid. Stay clothed. Avoid saying the word 'time,' and strive to keep your mind calm. Do not let go of me, and do not cling so close that I cannot move. Above all, keep your mind disciplined and your libido suppressed. Thoughts can become reality where we're going, so focus on being an engineer."

"Sir, yes, sir," he agreed.

She studied him quickly, but her first officer seemed sincere. Offering her hand, she waited for him to touch it. When he did, she nodded, pulled them onto the timeplains, and up out of the water.

Up out of the water, and into a heavy fog. One so thick, Meyun's features were half-obscured, and he was right there within reach. Ia usually emerged on the right-side bank, facing downstream into the future; she couldn't be sure she had done so this time, however. The only thing she was sure of was that they were on the bank, extracted so quickly that nothing had been seen.

Down was the ground, so up into the sky she lifted them. He clung with his hand, not nearly as disoriented as Rico had been, and without the confusion and fear of their previous trip. As they rose, the mist gradually thinned and receded, until they hovered high over the timeplains, eyeing a thick, sprawling mist that occupied several squid-like valleys, life-paths directly related to the relationship the two of them couldn't, shouldn't have.

"So, what do we look for?" Meyun finally asked, peering at the wrinkled landscape below. *"Blue-furred rock apes?"*

"No. There is a lifetime where someone discovers the trick of shaping crysium, and an engineer uses the reshaped crystals to form a Feyori-inducing gun." It was like baiting a hook, or checking off boxes on a search list. Ia itemized each thing they needed out loud. Beneath them, the landscape rippled and shifted, the mist inching ripple by ripple off somewhere to the

side, behind them. *"The engineer is Human, like you, and he lives in a universe with our exact same physical laws. But there are no Zida"ya coming to destroy his Milky Way Galaxy.*

"He does, however, work for a half-Human, half-Feyori captain—male—who wishes to enter Feyori politics in order to get them to stop bothering his Human kin. Your not-other-self's name is Jed Maxwell, and he has figured out how the conversion guns work, with a deep and eloquent, written level of understanding."

". . . Nice search matrix," the real Meyun Harper muttered, watching the mist and the hills shifting beneath them. As the fog from their own reality faded into the distance, the summer golden grass was slowly replaced by darker, clumpier shades of green shrubberies.

"Thank you. I've been practicing." She didn't intensify the experience to get rid of the echoing of their speech because she didn't want to risk his becoming so attached to a particular scenario or thought that it influenced her in turn. That would be a disastrous, downward spiral of rising emotions.

"How long have you been practicing?" he asked, brown eyes filled with curiosity.

"Since I turned fifteen, when my gift blossomed, and I started visualizing in earnest . . . Ah, here we go," she said, swooping them down toward a golden-clear stream snaking its way through the greenery. *"An equally talented alternate universe engineer—not you; you're a pastry chef back on Dabin in this universe. This fellow, however, knows how to build the gun we want you to build."*

Meyun lifted his brows. *"If I'm a pastry chef, who or what are you?"*

"I'm the male captain of the engineer's ship."

That provoked a snort. *"Not sure if I could fall in love with a male. But that does make me wonder. Any chance our alternate selves actually meet in this universe?"*

"None." Her voice echoed with firmness, quelling further inquiries along that line of thought. *"You are an engineer right now, nothing more. Now pay attention to the schematics and put that photographic memory of yours to good use."*

His free hand saluted her, the right one still tightly clasping her left. *"Aye, aye, Captain."* He paused, then added dryly, *". . . You do realize that 'cribbing notes' from this fellow is technically intellectual property theft, right?"*

"Technically, in our universe, this guy doesn't even exist," she reminded him. *"There are no copyright-infringement laws that span the multiverse because the multiverse, by its very nature, is one giant plagiarizing copy machine, introducing infinite infinitesimal errors with each new reiteration."* Ia paused, grinned, and added, *"That, and he'll never find out, so he can't take us to court."*

"Why, you law-breaking rebel, you," Harper teased. Nodding at the stream, he added, *"Alright, I'm ready."*

Nodding as well, she led him to the life-stream of their target.

APRIL 21, 2496 T.S.
V'DAN IMPERIAL FREEPORT *TATTH-NIEL*
V'DAN HOMEWORLD, V'DAN SYSTEM

Disembarking onto the station with the entire 1st Platoon, Ia stood out like a grey thumb. She was the only one in a uniform instead of civilian clothes. For this trip, Ia had donned her Dress Greys, with her grey cap perched on her neatly combed white locks, her TUPSF half glittery pinned to her chest along with the addition of her V'Dan honorifics. It was only polite to wear the latter, given they were parked at the heart of the V'Dan Empire.

Behind them, the *Hellfire* had cozied up to one of the station's longer gantries. The long, lumpy needle of a ship was only slightly battered from its last starfight, a sneak attack on another Salik crèche hiding in the depths of interstitial space. That crèche had been parked disturbingly close to the V'Dan homeworld, only four light-years away. Having pointed that out to the V'Dan High Command on the hyperrelays afterward, and the fact that they had destroyed the installation, Ia had requested and received permission to bring her Company in for three days of Leave.

Because *Tatth-Niel* was a freeport space station, no Customs queues slowed them down, just a submission of their ident units as each person disembarked so that the V'Dan government had a registry of their entry. The only thing they had to pass after that was through a long scanner arch, which searched silently, invisibly, for transmittable illnesses and contraband, standard equipment for most stations, as well as most starship airlocks.

The crew of the *Hellfire* also got one last warning from their commanding officer.

Stopping at the end of the hall, just before it opened up into the bustling commerce level ringing the station, Ia turned and faced the others. They drifted to a halt, eyeing her uniformed presence warily. Despite their current off-duty status, the sight of their CO in her Dress Greys was clearly stirring up the need to respond professionally. Some of the men and women of the 1st Platoon even shifted into a modified Parade Rest, standing with their hands at their backs, their shoulders squared, and their gazes straight ahead.

Settling her hands on her hips, she addressed them. "You have twenty-four Terran Standard hours of Leave. This translates to twenty-two hours thirty-eight minutes V'Dan Standard. These locals are Human, but they are *not* Terran. Respect their customs, laws, and beliefs during your visit, and remember that even in civvies on official Leave, you will represent the finest of the Terran Space Force at all times.

"Be back on board, in uniform, and ready to assume your posts with five minutes to spare, if not sooner. Your brothers and sisters in the 2nd and 3rd Platoons are covering your shifts for you so that you may enjoy these full twenty-four hours of Leave. Do not let them down when it comes time to cover theirs. Dismissed," she finished.

They started to move forward, heading for the station proper. A voice from behind Ia slowed the trickle to an awkward halt. Firm, male, and mature, the speaker addressed them with dry sarcasm. "A moving statement from a commanding officer. Hypocritical, too, when that commander has been mocking the beliefs of the very nation her crew now visits."

"High Priest Ma'alak of the Autumn Temple," Ia stated, turning and giving a polite bow. Not just to the speaker, a middle-aged man wearing intricately embroidered cream robes, but to his three companions as well, two soldiers and another member of the Sh'nai clergy. "Despite what you may think, you do honor me with your presence. Priestess Laka'thi of the

D'aspra Archives, Grand General Ibeni-Zif of the High Command, Highlord Adjutant Sa-Nieth of the Nobles' Council, it is a pleasure to meet each of you as well. Shall we all retire to the conference room the Grand General has reserved for us?"

They exchanged looks, apparently not expecting Ia to take the initiative from them so smoothly. The High Priest nodded slightly, and the Grand General gestured for Ia to join them, the gold trim on his red uniform sleeve gleaming in the overhead lights. As soon as she did so, more red-uniformed soldiers fell into position around them, forming an honor-guard escort. Behind Ia, her civilian-clad troops dispersed into the crowd, no doubt curious what was going to happen to their CO but trusting her to handle whatever it was.

The presence of those bright-clad imperial guards drew attention from the crowds of tourists and travelers they passed, but it was the draped folds of the priestly robes that garnered bows from dozens of the V'Dan. That made it easy to see just how many of the locals were followers of the Sh'nai faith.

Some even drifted forward, calling out for blessings from the High Priest in their native tongue. He in turn raised his hand and murmured benedictions but did not stop. The presence of their imperial escort kept the more insistent requests at bay, allowing them to move smoothly toward the vast station's core.

It took maybe ten minutes to navigate past the outermost layers of shops and businesses to the military hub of the station. They could have held this meeting in the government's reception hub for visiting dignitaries, or within the halls of the on-station Sh'nai temple. Instead, the conference room's location was proof that the military was the current power in charge of the empire. Painted cream and decorated in red and gold accents, the room they were led to boasted wall screens and workstations, and a distinct lack of Lock and Web clips, a reminder that *Tatth-Niel* was a space station in permanent orbit around the V'Dan homeworld and not a vessel capable of being moved elsewhere in a hurry.

"Ship's Captain Ia, would you like a cup of caf'?" Grand General Ibeni-Zif asked as they entered the room. "Meioas?"

Ia nodded, as did the priestess and the adjutant. At that, the red-uniformed junior officer waiting by the door turned to the sideboard and started fixing mugs for everyone. As the erstwhile guest at this meeting and the focus of the questions that were to come, Ia moved toward the seat at the near end of the conference table.

Like the other objects in the room, someone had selected the table to impress visitors; it had been crafted out of some stout, golden-hued wood native to V'Dan, one with a rippling grain suggestive of Zen waves in gilded sand. Ia liked it. The Sanctuarian equivalent of wood was usually more reddish or purplish in hue, making this a bright contrast to most of the colors she had known as a child and a pleasant change from the blander, more pragmatic hues seen during her two stays on Earth.

The Highlord Adjutant assisted her with her chair first. Then he held a second chair for the priest before seating the general, followed by the priestess and lastly himself. He did so without the assistance of the other aide in the room. The subtle courtesy was proof—at least in the V'Dan culture Ia had studied in her youth, living on a jointly founded colonyworld—that this meeting had been instigated by the Sh'nai, was being hosted and supported by the military, and was being facilitated by the Nobles' Council.

The Nobles are therefore holding themselves neutral in this inquisition, according to V'Dan protocols. He probably expects to serve as an arbiter if a dispute arises. The Grand General knows that whatever the outcome of this meeting is, it will have an impact on the war effort, and that means it'll impact his purview. The High Priest is here to personally lead the inquisition . . . and the Priestess of the Archives has the means to verify or disprove my identity.

"Ship's Captain Ia, you are here to answer allegations of promoting yourself as the long-prophesied Prophet of a Thousand Years, one of the core saints of the Sh'nai faith," High Priest Ma'alak stated. He paused, mouth twisting a little. *"Ia'nn sud-dha'a* . . . What hubris, to take on the V'Dan word for 'prophet' as your one and only name."

"It was not hubris. A simple examination of the citizen registry documents of Independent Colonyworld Sanctuary will prove it, High Priest," Ia countered calmly. "I declared emancipation at the age of sixteen on March 4, 2488, Terran Standard, and changed my name from Iantha Quentin-Jones to the shortened version of Ia . . . which my family and friends had already been using to address me since I was an infant."

"Why did you change your name, Ship's Captain Ia?" Grand General Ibeni-Zif asked, leaning his elbows on the edge of the table and lacing his fingers together.

Ia smiled slightly. "I think this meeting is informal enough, Grand General, that you may simply call me Captain. Or Ia, since that is my name . . . though I can understand His Holiness's reluctance to do so," she added, giving the priest a polite nod. "As for why I changed my name, I knew that if I gave my younger brother the Power Lottery numbers for the drawing on February 10, 2494 Terran Standard while still retaining my full name, that it would draw attention to my relationship with him and cause near-immediate trouble for me via the Terran laws regarding profit from prognostication for precognitives. Plus it would trip over the military laws governing fraternization and the giving of loans, perhaps even dredging up accusations of bribery. None of which I wanted to do."

Priestess Laka'thi's mouth twitched upward on one side, bringing her laugh lines into prominence. The grey-haired woman seemed amused at the tongue-twisting alliteration. Ia smiled back slightly before returning her attention to the general.

"My emancipation and name change made it appear legally that I was estranged from my family, and would therefore not profit personally from the lottery win. And for the record, I have *not* profited from that exchange. The monies have long since been channeled into a nonprofit trust fund for the defense and safety of my former fellow colonists to cover a need I had long ago foreseen, and my own expenses come either out of my own pay or are paid for by the Terran Space Force, as authorized by my superiors on the Command Staff. We are at war now, as you know," she added dryly, "and wars are expensive."

The other corner of the Archivist's mouth quirked up. She said nothing, though, choosing to accept her cup of caf' with a polite nod to the junior officer distributing them around the table. Ia accepted hers with a polite nod as well. She silently refused the addition of cream and sugar from the tray he carried; in her opinion, caf' didn't need any. Both the priestess and the adjutant added a spoonful of grated *meklah* to their drinks, chocolate sweetened with brown sugar. The High Priest and the Grand General accepted glasses of water.

Ibeni-Zif eyed her. "Would you be willing to expand a little bit more on what uses that money has been put to? It is our government which oversees the authenticity of each drawing made and ticket purchased, after all."

"They've been busy using that money to build secure housing and fortifications—the Salik themselves cannot live in Sanctuary's high gravity," Ia added in an aside, "but until we can shut down their combat robots, there is still the risk those 'bots could be used to harvest my fellow heavyworlders. They are too important to the future to allow that to pass." Lifting her blue-glazed cup from its matching saucer, Ia switched to V'Dan. *"Tokla vuu hess t'Kah'hn V'Dania, na'V'Dan atrei'atess, ou vaa havet'th makau-na ma'achess."*

They started to lift their cups, then hesitated. Not because her accent was terrible—this was one of the few languages Ia could actually pronounce, having studied it for several years in her youth as part of her world's jointly founded education courses—but because of *what* she had said. She knew she had gotten it right; Ia had looked up and memorized this particular phrase even when the rest of her V'Dan had grown rusty with disuse over the years.

The general lowered his water glass, not yet drinking from it. "Tell me, Captain. Do you even know what that means? Or are you just parroting something a protocol officer instructed you to say?"

"I said, 'Raise your cups to the Emperor, from the People of the World, so that all may live well in health and peace.'" Lifting her cup again, Ia sipped. So did the others. Lowering her cup, she added, "Not word for word in Terran, of course, but it translates close enough on the surface. The exact subtexted meaning of the dialect and grammar I used comes from the Valley of Artisans, which was founded in the seventh millennium V'Dan Standard by the Immortal, who had come back—"

Ia paused briefly as Priestess Laka'thi choked on her caf', waiting as the woman grabbed for a napkin, coughed into it, and caught her breath.

"—Who had come back from her exile in order to visit her chosen people and check on their progress." She slid her gaze to the High Priest of the Autumn Temple. From the distastefully pursed state of his mouth, he looked as if he needed some of that *meklah* dumped in his water. "The actual toast was not conceived of by the Immortal herself, but rather by High Priest Shu-Nai of the Summer Temple during a visit to the enclave in the V'Dan year 6378.

"While the violence against the Sh'nai faith that marked War King Kah'el's reign was long over by that point, it was once again a time of religious tension between the Immortal's believers and the state. The toast is a reminder that sometimes one must bow to the inevitabilities of a given situation, and that to do so with graciousness and humility is the path of the righteous."

High Priest Ma'alak pinched his mouth further, looking distinctly sour as Ia finished. Priestess Laka'thi, on the other hand, dissolved into cough-punctuated giggles. The other two males at the table gave her bemused looks as she sat there, shoulders shaking as she pressed the fine scarlet cloth to her lips.

She shook her head, held up her hand, coughed a couple more times into her napkin, and finally rasped, ". . . Oh, let go of it, Ma'alak. She is *exactly* right in using that quote. I suspect she uses it to remind us that we, too, should bow to the inevitabilities in this situation. *Should* they prove to be true."

Ia lifted her cup to the other woman. "An astute assessment, Priestess. And I will be happy to show you the innermost secret your Order has held in their keeping all these years."

Laka'thi stopped chuckling. Blue eyes wide, she stared at Ia. "How . . . ?"

"We'll get to that later," Ia assured her. She looked over at the High Priest. "I believe your next question, Holy One, is supposed to be something along the lines of what makes me think I have the right to go around telling alien governments that I am the Prophet when I haven't even verified my position with the very people who have kept alive the Immortal's memory of the woman I claim to be. Shall I answer it?"

He narrowed his eyes. "No," he stated, his tone clipped. "I would rather you answered the question of why you haven't delivered your so-called prophecies to us yet, if you are indeed the Prophet."

"That would be question number four on your list," Ia stated, earning her another narrow-eyed stare. "Technically, some of those prophecies have already been distributed. Mainly the time-sensitive ones. They have not gone into your hands, however, because they were sent directly to the people who needed them most at the time. Your doubts are very understandable, but dangerous when time is of the essence. I have always preferred to deliver such things directly to the people my prophecies will impact, so that there is no delivery delay and no alteration of the message needed."

Reaching into her jacket pocket, Ia pulled out a quartet of data chips. Checking the letters electrostamped on their surfaces, she slid one toward each of the four V'Dan seated around her.

"Those chips should work on a standard workstation or reader pad, so long as it has a Terran dataport. Most Terranglo-readable ones do. Each one of those contains a time-sensitive list of predictions, tailored to each of your specific areas of interest . . . and each one has been code-locked with your most commonly used password—I apologize for borrowing them," Ia stated quickly as the general drew in a startled breath, "and I give you my word of honor I have zero interest in using them for any other purpose than this.

"Also, the time-sensitive parts of the list might be slightly off. Having been trained to think in Terran time units, I have done my best to convert those from Terran Standard to V'Dan," Ia said, "but I apologize if I am off by one or two seconds. The exact times in Terran Standard have been included, in case you want to refine your calculations.

"Be mindful of the difference between the actual radioactive clock located in Aloha City on Earth, and the hyperrelay time lag that exists between Earth and here if you wish to try for a more exact conversion rate—the times will be pertinent to the *local* clocks for the activities they discuss," Ia warned them. "That is, the nearest chronometer to the person who will have to observe or implement these things. So if the clock on a ship is off by two *mi-nah*, it will still pertain to that ship's clock and not to the atomic chronometer here on V'Dan."

Ibeni-Zif beckoned the young man who had served them their drinks. He whispered in the junior officer's ear in V'Dan, then dismissed him with a flick of one wrist.

Ma'alak picked up his chip, examined it briefly, then set it back down. "Answer my third question, Captain. Since you seem to know what I planned to ask."

"What makes me think the V'Dan people, government, and Sh'nai faith should allow me to continue to go around telling people I'm the Prophet of a Thousand Years?" Ia clarified. She lifted her hand, unfolding one finger per point. "Three reasons. Because I actually am. Because I have already predicted and acted upon the future with great accuracy. And because you need me to be."

"Need?" Ma'alak snorted. "What need would that be?"

"The Archivist and the Grand General already know. It's been in all the V'Dan High Command briefings since the Battle of the Banquet," Ia stated. "We don't have the technological advantages the Terrans brought to the First Salik War this time around. This lack has not only the V'Dan military alarmed, but the Terrans, Solaricans, K'katta, the Tlassians . . . all the members of the Alliance, directly involved or not."

"Anyone could guess that much, Captain," Ibeni-Zif reminded her.

"True, but I included Priestess Laka'thi, who knows of the promises from the lips of the Immortal herself, which her Order's archives have kept safe and whole. The Immortal has said, over and over through the millennia, that when the Second War breaks out—which it has—the Prophet of a Thousand Years will step up to provide temporal counsel, direct the destruction of the enemy, and eventually save the galaxy, ushering in the Silver Age of peace among the stars." Ia paused, then tipped her head and added, "Which will also coincide with the Second Reformation of V'Dan, in about three hundred years."

Laka'thi frowned slightly. "The Second Reformation was only a rumor. There was only one account that mentioned it, from the—"

"—From the time of War King Kah'el, when the Immortal agreed to step down after losing the duel," Ia agreed, filling in the details for the others. "She did so with the caveat that the War King and his descendants and successors would be legally bound to accept all future duel challenges from rulers of equal rank . . . and that should the War King's descendants or successors lose that duel, they and their people were to follow the champion who won that match as their new ruler, who would instigate the Second Great Reformation. If they refused, they would have to hand the V'Dan Empire back into the hands of the Immortal herself."

"Yes, but that isn't the same as an actual Second Reformation," Highlord Sa-Nieth pointed out. "No one has ever been able to scrape together a large enough following to qualify as a ruler of equal rank."

Ia dipped her head at the auburn-haired man, acknowledging his point, though she kept her gaze on the priestess. "True, it wouldn't be the same . . . but when asked by one of the palace clerks about her insistence on that clause being included in the deal being brokered to end the civil war, the Immortal said that when the Prophet of a Thousand Years would become known to the people—to V'Dan, that is—the Prophet would name the time of the Second Reformation, and that she knew the clause would eventually be used, even though the Immortal herself had not yet lived through that time. I have now given you that time."

"Not with a precise date, though," Sa-Nieth stated, his tone skeptical. "Unless you meant three hundred years to the second from now."

"I only give precise dates when the precision of those dates is important to the moment," Ia replied, unruffled by his doubt. "Not because I cannot pinpoint the exact time and place but because I have far too many other temporal focal points to keep track of, each with its own moment of importance. This meeting is not that moment of importance, particularly as none of us will be alive three centuries from now—I assure you, those who need to know, those who will be alive at the right time and place, *will* receive one of my precognitive missives on the matter. You have my Prophetic Stamp on that."

CHAPTER 11

. . . Of course, the other governments did take a bit of convincing, too.

~Ia

"Well. You certainly know your obscure lore. And you know the Prophet's catchphrase, too," Laka'thi mused. "Though that's more widely known than your mention of the Second Reformation."

"Still, all of this could have been discovered in the Archives by you or your accomplices. You could have even bribed an archivist," High Priest Ma'alak pointed out. "It's happened before, and it will happen again, so why not this time?"

"Those are all possibilities, yes. But because of that, I came here knowing that only two things could sway your mind," Ia agreed. "One way is time. Given enough time for events to unfold, time itself would prove my predictions and actions are undeniably, inevitably true. But that way does nothing to address the urgency of the moment. You want to confront me now, before the rumors can spread too far. If you can prove I'm a fake, then you can squash those rumors with no harm done to your culture. If I'm the real Prophet, you will again want to make sure I don't bring harm to your culture. That brings us to the Puzzle Box and the 'secret' I referred to earlier."

"You know the purpose of the box," Laka'thi stated. It wasn't a question.

"Yes. I'm the one who wrote the note to be passed along to the young Immortal via the Third Human Empire before she begins her trip through Time. That note will tell her how to craft the secret hidden in the box, and what secret to write." Ia watched them roll their eyes and nodded, flicking her own in sympathy. "A bit self-fulfilling, I know, but it's the easiest way I'll have available to convince you of who and what I am."

"I am a soldier, not a priest," Grand General Ibeni-Zif stated, rubbing at his brow. "I am not a religious man, and do not follow the Sh'nai faith, though I will give respect to the rights of those who do. Still, your claim to be the Prophet will affect the three-fifths of the Empire who do follow the old faith, and shake the other religions—if the Prophet of a Thousand Years is real, then the Immortal could equally be real, and we could be facing a religious civil war as some try to seek her out, others try to slay her followers, and the Emperor's position on the throne destabilizes in the turmoil."

"Then tell them that I say the current Emperor is the rightful ruler of V'Dan," Ia stated bluntly. "I know this session is being recorded, and you have my permission to use my words to combat that threat. Tell your people that His Eternal Majesty will live long and rule well, provided he and his people back the Alliance's efforts to thwart the ambitions of their mutual enemies. And tell them that I say the other religions of the Empire are equally as valid as the Sh'nai faith, for each has its own place. They need to work together to support the First Empire as a unified whole."

"That only works if you *are* the Prophet, 'Ia,'" Ma'alak pointed out. "But you are right. Either we must wait for your words to be proved true, or test them here and now. Priestess, the Puzzle Box."

From a hidden pocket buried in the layered depths of her butterfly-like sleeves, Priestess Laka'thi pulled out a modest box. It wasn't much bigger than an old-fashioned book or a small datapad, about as long as an average Human hand, as wide as a palm, and as deep as a finger. Crafted from wax-polished bronze, only the edges of the tightly fitted lid showed hints of green from oxidization.

"This box has been sought out or offered to over four

hundred souls," the priestess stated, holding the plain, brick-like box between her fingertips. "In all those attempts, it has been successfully opened only seventeen times in the last six thousand years. Each time, it has either been given to those claiming to be Holy Ones to test their psychic abilities, or sought after by someone claiming to be the Prophet. Those rare, few openings have been witnessed and recorded by the Sh'nai Order of the D'aspra Archives down through the ages.

"But of all seventeen who have successfully opened this box, none of them have revealed the secret that hides inside." Turning slightly in her seat, Laka'thi offered the box to Ia. "If you are the Prophet of a Thousand Years, you will not only know how to open this box, you will, by the Immortal's own words, know how to reveal what lies within as well."

Accepting the bronze box, Ia turned it over in her hands, examining the finely polished, auburn-hued metal. The exterior was plain and well maintained, with only that faintly oxidized seam showing that the box wasn't a solid block. There was no hint of a hinge, no opening for a key, and no way to show how it had been locked. But she knew. The trick was doing it gently.

"Well?" Ma'alak asked impatiently as the seconds ticked by. "Aren't you going to open it? Or can you even try?"

"Patience, High Priest," Ia admonished lightly. "What Priestess Laka'thi has not told you is that in those recordings of the seventeen times, the locking mechanism consists of twenty tightly fitted bronze hooks tension-clipped over twenty rods set in twenty holes, with each hook and rod facing a different direction from the next. Some of those hooks are set in one half of the box, while some are set in the other, with their holes in the opposite half.

"The lid itself possesses a small but significant shoulder lip to prevent a thin blade from being used to push those hooks free," she added, studying the timestreams in the back of her mind. "There is no mechanical way to open this box other than a hacksaw or a cutting torch once it has been sealed shut."

"You're stalling," Ibeni-Zif stated.

"I am not stalling. I am taking my time so that I do not break it. The metal is old, some of the inner oxidation has crystallized together, and those hooks are still as stiff as the day they were first crafted, which is why I need to be careful," she added, gifts turning from the timestreams to the box itself. "That, and twenty is a lot of them to keep track of, even for a skilled telekinetic. But . . . not impossible . . . and that's the last hook I needed to bend."

She trailed off, concentrating. A careful twist of her mind and a slow, firm pull separated the two halves of the box. The hooks did indeed line the edge, some pointed up, others pointed down, angled this way and that. Those hooks, their holes, and the inner edges of the box had not been waxed in centuries, leaving it a dull shade of green. Nested in that green, slightly crusted with bronze verdigris, sat another object.

Setting the top of the Puzzle Box on the table, Ia inverted the bottom half over her hand. It took her three shakes to dislodge the inner brick. Shaped like the outer box, if on a smaller scale, the inner object looked like it had been crafted from a single light green tourmaline, or maybe peridot, save that its edges were more bluish in hue.

Whatever it was, the transparent material had rounded corners, and contained a bronze box of its own inside. The only catch was, there was no catch; the inner crystalline box had no seams whatsoever. Either the inner bronze box had been dipped in molten glass, or some sort of gem had been grown around it.

". . . May I?" Laka'thi asked Ia, holding out her hand toward the box. Seated to Ia's immediate right, with the Highlord Adjutant on her other side, she didn't have to stretch to do so.

A quick check of the timestreams confirmed what the woman was about to do. Nodding, Ia passed the gem-brick to her. Before the others could ask why she wanted it, the Archivist raised the translucent box high in her hand and smashed it down with a startlingly loud *crack!* against the edge of the polished-wood table. Ibeni-Zif and Sa-Nieth both jumped, and the High Priest clutched at the robes covering his chest.

"What are you *doing*?" he demanded, scandalized. "That is a *sacred artifact* you're trying to smash!"

"Calm yourself, Your Holiness," Ia told him, lifting her hand. "She's actually doing her job, by proving that case isn't made of mere glass. If you examined the table, you'd see a faint indent from where it struck."

"The Terran is correct," Laka'thi confirmed, holding up the gem-like case, showing it intact. "The Archives recorded how this inner box was placed between a hammer and an anvil, and struck with full strength. I am no blacksmith with bulging arms, but this table would break under my blows long before this case ever would.

"There is no seam, and no sign of a way to open it. No one has ever touched the inner box since the Immortal herself crafted it." She lobbed the box at Ia, who caught it one-handed. "If you *are* the Prophet, you will be able to open it, 'Ia.' The Immortal has said so."

Ia shrugged and offered it to the Grand General, seated to her left. "Feel free to examine it for a seam, meioas, before I do so. Once I open it, there is no going back. What has been seen cannot be *un*seen."

"Do the Terrans train all of their officers to boast and grandstand?" he asked her, accepting the box and turning it over in his hands, thumbnail questing along the crystalline sides in an attempt to discern a seam. "Or did they just train you?"

"True grandstanding would actually detract from my message, sir," Ia told him. "It is the messages I bring that are important. I am merely their vessel. I am also giving each one of you a chance to verify personally that there is no way to get through that outer covering. No cracks, no hinges, no seams . . . and no tricks."

He frowned and scraped his finger over it again, then shook his head and offered it to the High Priest. "I cannot see a way to open it."

Ma'alak examined it. His thinner face also furrowed as the seconds of his examination ticked into a full minute, until with a frown of his own he passed it over the table to the third man. Highlord Sa-Nieth turned it over several times, rubbing his thumbnail over all the surfaces and angles, then shrugged and handed it to Laka'thi, who returned it to Ia.

"As you have seen for yourselves," Ia stated, running her thumb all the way around the edge, "this 'secret' has no openings. It is a solid piece, with no hinge, no lock, and no lid."

Shifting her grip, she grasped top and bottom, carefully focused her psychic abilities . . . and pulled the gem apart like a pair of simple lids, using the same gentle patience she had used on the outer case. The act revealed the unoxidized, pristine bronze box nested inside.

The High Priest's jaw dropped, the Highlord Adjutant's eyes bulged, and the Grand General choked on his caf', grabbing for his own napkin. Of the four of them, only Priestess Laka'thi sat as still as a statue. Her face was now flushed, but she didn't blink, and didn't breathe.

Ia dropped the upper lid—which was solidly pale blue, not green—onto the table with a crystalline *ching*. The musical sound provoked a blink from the elderly woman. It was followed by a deep breath. She looked like she was experiencing a holy revelation, caught up in the unthinking awe of the moment. Glad the other woman was at least breathing again, Ia eased the box from its depths and dropped the bottom half of the crystalline container next to the top half.

Unlike the outermost one, this bronze box hadn't been exposed to either moisture or oxygen since its creator had sealed it up in the first place. But, just like the outer one, this one did have a thin, flush-fitted seam.

"This Puzzle Box is sealed with a system similar to the one used on the previous one, save that it has only ten hooks, not twenty." Another careful twist-and-push of her mind, and she pulled the two pieces apart, revealing her words to be true. She set that lid next to the other pieces, the outer bronze casings, and the middle blue-crystalline lids. This time, the interior of the box had been padded with a rectangle of what looked like plain grey felt.

Tipping the contents into her palm caused the felt to fall out, but that was alright; the felt was merely there to pad the transparent rectangle stored inside, to keep it from rattling. Ia tilted her hand, shaking it slightly to discard the wool, then turned the bookmark-sized slab over and laid it on the table.

It was crafted from the same material as the crystalline box, though its creator had forged it from two tones of crystal, the sapphire blue of the middle box and a pale golden hue. With the polished V'Dan wood of the table beneath accenting that yellow, the double line of characters forged into the slab were easy enough to read. One line had been crafted in archaic V'Dan script; the other had been printed in block-letter Terranglo. Both said the exact same thing, a simple, single phrase.

Iantha'nn sud-dha.

Amused by the Immortal's sense of humor, Ia smiled. Picking up her cup, she took a sip of her caf', set it back down, and pushed her chair back. "I do believe we are done here, gentlebe-ings. My birth name and emancipation records can be easily verified within the hour. You do not need me for that. You also have my current set of prophecies, tailored for each of your needs. When it is the right time to receive more of them, you will indeed receive them—you have my Prophetic Stamp on that.

"In the meantime, do keep in mind that both my existence and my prophecies are *not* to be used or abused for any personal agendas, whether religious, political, or otherwise. I am here to help save as many lives as I can, whether they are Sh'nai or otherwise, V'Dan or Terran, Tlassian or Solarican, Alliance lives or the lives of a hundred sentient species we haven't even met yet." Rising, she bowed politely. "I thank you for your hospitality and the cup of caf'. It was delicious.

"If you'll excuse me, this is the first chance for Leave my crew and I have had since my command was first assembled, and I would like to go enjoy some of it myself. I'm sure Leftenant P'kethra can show me back out to the public sector, so that the four of you can sit here in peace and quiet without being hobbled by my presence while you discuss the implications of all of this."

". . . How did you open that?" Lifting her head, Laka'thi gazed at Ia. "No one has been able to open that inner box in all our records. No one even knows *what* that crystal box was made from, just that the Immortal herself made it."

"That's because the Immortal will have borrowed that knowledge from the secrets of the Third Human Empire . . . which has yet to be born as an empire," Ia said, her tone wry. "Both of us are bound by the strictures of Time to keep that information a secret, as it is something we are only permitted to borrow for our personal use and are not to divulge to any others. I hope you will respect my right to temporal secrecy when it comes to another government's secrets, just as you would expect me to respect your own sovereign rights to secrecy.

"Long live the Eternal Empire, meioas, and long live the alliance between us. Have a good day," she finished politely, and gestured for the junior officer to lead the way out of the conference room.

He gave the others a bemused look, then gave in with a dip of his head and headed for the door. Ia made a mental note to pass along a letter of commendation for his discretion and sense of equilibrium in the face of the day's events. A recommendation from a foreigner would carry some weight, but one offered by the Prophet—now confirmed as such—would carry even more. *Good junior officers are hard to find, after all. Particularly the unflappable ones.*

Her quarry sat as he usually did at this time of the day, just after the end of a shift filled with cleanerbot herding. Grizzled hair slicked back, wrinkled brown skin sporting the same golden undertones as most V'Dan did, he sat with his elbows on his knees, a sugarstick dangling between two fingers. Most of his attention was on the great bay window giving a few of the planet's curve and gleaming streaks of sunlight.

Placed as it was in the V'Dan homeworld's L2 orbit, slightly farther out than the planet's shadow could cover, there was a constant halo effect. Coupled with the ionosphere's auroras, the view was spectacular, worthy of being watched. It also helped that the window was half-silvered, dulling the brightness of the local star. There were several benches arrayed before the window, taking advantage of that view, but only a few were occupied, and no one but the old man in the dark blue pants and grey shirt sat on the centermost one.

It was hard to picture this tired-looking, somewhat elderly man as being the real power on *Tatth-Niel*, but Ia knew better. He looked up at her approach, lifting the sugarstick to his lips. She gestured at the broad bench. "Mind if I have a seat?"

"'S a free port," he grunted, sucking on the flavored stick.

Unbuttoning her Dress jacket for comfort, Ia sat and removed her hat. The bench was a little low, but not uncomfortable. Leaning forward, she braced her elbows on her knees, letting the cap dangle from her fingertips. "Nice view."

"That, it is," he agreed.

(*I trust you know why I'm here?*) Ia asked, shaping and aiming the thought carefully.

He slanted a sidelong look her way. (*You aren't a player, half child.*)

(*It won't be long before I manifest,*) she warned him. Dropping her gaze to her cap, she rotated it slowly in her grip. (*I'm not here to compare bubble-sizes, Kierfando,*) Ia stated. (*I am here to counteroffer Miklinn's intent to ask you to faction for a counterfaction against me.*)

(*What could you possibly offer me, half-breed?*) he replied, sucking again on the stick.

Leaning over, she offered her hand palm up. "Ia," she said aloud in introduction, adding silently, (*Come and see.*)

"Kier," he grunted out loud, clasping hands. (*Why should I even—*)

Counting the offer of his touch as permission given, Ia dragged him onto the timeplains. In the real world, his brown eyes lightened to amber for just a few heartbeats. At least, out in the physical world. In the timeplains, she emerged on the bank with her hand stuck in an oversized silvery sphere and a lot more Time on her side.

Before he could react to the abrupt change in mental landscapes, she hauled him toward the end of the galaxy.

The mirror-like surface roiled and swirled with indignation. (*You presume much!*)

She didn't prevaricate. (*I have just been proved to be the Prophet of a Thousand Years, as foretold to these people for millennia by the Abomination, and have been proved so in front of high-ranked leaders of the Sh'nai faith. As soon as they spread word of this—and it* will *spread—the majority of the V'Dan Empire shall become faction to me. I offer you a chance to shift your position slightly, so that your actions will be fortified and your efforts will not be washed away in the flood of my own.*

(*I also offer you this chance to see* what *my goal is, so you may understand just how strongly it aligns with your own,*) Ia stated.

Stopping by the bank of her carefully tended channel, she displayed the disparity of this future point in time. The lush growth of the prairie's past, the barren emptiness of the deserted future, and the one crack in the wall of the coming fate that led to a garden of renewed possibilities.

(*Examine it quickly. I dare not let our hands linger for long, lest someone notice it on the security cameras and wonder why I'm taking so long to introduce myself to you. That would be counterproductive to your cover . . . and I would not like to make the same stupid mistake I made when I exposed Miklinn.*)

The sphere spun and bobbed, probing at the visage of Time, tasting the waters. He finally pulled back. (. . . *Yes, that was*

*particularly stupid of you. Move us back to our entry point
and show me this proof that says to the V'Dan you're the
Prophet.*)

Doing as he bid, Ia did not take offense. She had been stupid
that day and was strong enough to acknowledge it. Kierfando
was one of the oldest Meddlers in local space. He was also one
of the most flexible and forgiving for his kind. The youngest
ones were arrogant, the middling ones inflexibly prejudiced,
and the oldest ones set in their ways, but not him. That was
why he still held such a potent position in their Game, poised
at a major interstellar crossroads.

She gave him time to examine the recent scene in her own
past, then pulled his bubble out of the waters again. (*Have you
seen enough?*)

(*For now? Yes. When we part company, shake hands with
me again. I wish to examine the Great Demand you will supposedly make of us.*)

Withdrawing their minds back into their bodies, Ia released
his fingers. Only a few seconds had passed, physically. (*Provided you agree to be neutral to me at the very least when we
part company, then we have a deal. You will get nothing if you
choose to counterfaction me to any degree.*)

He snorted and sucked on his sugarstick. (*You learn quickly.
You also have sparks the size of this station, thinking you can
make demands on a fullblood.*)

(*My "sparks" are bigger than this entire star system,*) she
bragged, smiling slightly. The boast earned her a mental
chuckle. (*Thank you for being more flexible than most of your
kind,*) she told Kierfando. (*If I'd tried to make that joke with
one of the others, they'd have smacked me for hubris rather
than seeing it for what it is.*)

(*"Humor is a waste of energy,"*) he quoted, sucking on the
sugarstick again. (*That line of thought is a bunch of matter-
loaded recharge, if you ask me.*)

"You know, those things aren't entirely healthy for your
teeth," Ia offered out loud. "Or your pancreas."

"Been suckin' on 'em longer than you've been alive,
meioa-e," Kier grunted back. "I've earned my vices. Haven't
you, yet?"

"Hm. Vices . . . I don't think I have any, unless you count
a slavish devotion to my military duties," she admitted.

He eyed her and pulled a fresh, plexi-wrapped stick out of his shirt pocket. "You need this more than I do if all you do is march around and shoot at people."

She accepted it with a dip of her head. "Thank you."

"Don't thank me. Shut up and suck up," he ordered her.

"Sir, yes, sir," she quipped, earning her a second mental chuckle in reply.

Unwrapping the stick, she tucked the end between her lips and sucked. The flavor was fruity, something V'Dan local and not anything she had tasted before. If it had been the real fruit, it would have been filled with histaminic triggers, but like every other Human in the known galaxy, Ia had been inoculated at birth with the *jungen* virus to counteract such things. As it was, the flavor was an exotic touch. Some of her home colony's orchards had been planted with seeds from V'Dan, but nothing like this.

She sucked again, enjoying the treat. (*Tasty. Thank you.*)

(*My favorite. I'll offer you a provisional faction, Prophet—and yes, I acknowledge you as such. Neutral-assured until you manifest, then I'll faction you,*) he clarified. (*If I faction you openly before you prove yourself a player, not a pawn, that could weaken my own plays considerably. If you don't make the change . . . as you fleshies say, no sweat off my back.*)

(*That's acceptable. Provisional faction, neutral until manifestation,*) Ia confirmed.

"Well. Time for me to go, girl. Got supper waiting for me, and nobody making it but me," he added out loud. (*Tonight's menu calls for a gentle bath of ultraviolet light for about an hour, followed by soaking in a static generation wheel. Come back sometime, child, after you make the change, and I'll treat you to a nice "home-cooked" meal.*)

She chuckled. "My cooking is barely tolerable. I had to barter for a whole ship of soldiers under my command to do it for me." She held out her hand again. "Nice to meet you, Kier. Thank you for the view, the stick, and the hospitality."

"Not a problem," he said, clasping hands with her. (*Now show your desperate, Game-based request to me.*)

Once more, Time ran faster on the plains than out in reality. Ia swayed them both forward—not nearly as far as the first trip—and dipped him into one of the defining moments of her sought-after future. It took him a few seconds in the streams to grasp the implications of her demand. When he did . . . he recoiled, the surface of his energy-sphere turning dark with shock. Ia eased him up onto the bank and offered him a packet of psychic energy. He did not refuse, proof of his agitation.

(*You see why I cannot do this without your people's help,*) she murmured as he recovered, his surface gradually growing mirror-bright again. (*My Right of Simmerings ends in less than a month. I need your people to acknowledge I am a player in the Game, not a pawn, because I need everyone to faction with and aid me at* that *point in time.*)

(*Half child, you* do *have sparks the size of this star system . . . but I can also see why it* would *be necessary, and why you will need our aid,*) he agreed. The sphere swirled, focusing on her. (*We're the only ones who can escape being harmed by that thing . . . and I can also see why you'd allow it to be unleashed on your enemy. Those suckered fiends would counterfaction you and your pawns hard down through Time, unless you let that happen to them. But* this, *child, is going to* shova v'shakk *the Game plays out of several of us. Not me personally, but some of the others, oh yes. You will make counterfaction enemies with this.*)

(*I'm prepared to offer my temporal assistance to reestablish them in other positions. Better to start again and rebuild with my help than to lose everything, after all . . . and if I don't get your people's help, a very large number of you will lose everything in the short term . . . and all of you in the long term.*)

(*I hope they agree because if they refuse, the Game ends, according to what you have foreseen,*) he agreed. (*I'm not the best at future-skimming, but I can See enough to know that you See true—I like the visualizations you used, by the way.*)

(*Thanks. Any help you can offer me, neutral though we may be, I'd appreciate,*) she told him. Then pulled them out of the timestreams, adding, (*Parting hands, now.*)

(*What sort of help?*) he asked her, releasing her fingers. Again, only a couple heartbeats had passed in reality.

(*Names of the Feyori I could contact between now and my manifestation. It's not always easy to see your kind, particularly when they want to keep their presence and influences hidden. A name would help me locate them faster,*) Ia said.

Hands on knees, he grunted and rocked himself forward, pushing upright. "Enjoy the view, meioa."

"And you." She watched him walk away, wondering if he would even acknowledge her question.

He did, several seconds after she turned her attention back to the half-silvered view.

(*Telu'oc. Na-Ganj. Kropecz. Belini. Gallown.*) Each name came with a subpulse associating its owner with a particular territory, and a warning. (*No guarantees they will accept, half-breed. But they are the five most likely to at least stop and listen.*)

(*Thank you. There will be a very tasty coronal ejection in fourteen days. Safest place for you to feed will be just ahead of the leading edge of the largest gas giant's L4. It'll be a fast solar wind, and the L4 will have an ion storm that forms when it interacts with the gas giant's magnetosphere—I'll leave you to do the math of when and where the best point in time will be for you to snack,*) she added, as he strolled out of view. (*Since only you know whether it'll be worth taking a personal day to fly out there in a leisurely, unnoticed way, or just wait until your shift ends and risk zipping off in a visible form, the day the flare reaches that section of space.*)

(*Thank you. I believe that'll make a nice payment for the sugarstick,*) he told her.

(*I know. That's why I offered it.*)

He chuckled at the edges of her mind. (*Polite child. You just might survive the Game . . . Have a good night.*)

Ia stayed where she was for a few more minutes, then rose from the low bench and started the trek back to the section bearing the *Hellfire*'s gantry. Since she no longer had to pretend to type on a portable workstation, she pulled her datapad from her trouser pocket and began composing prophecies electrokinetically while she walked.

Part of her mind went to the list of names he had given her. Making a side note of them, she saved it to the pad. Belini, she already knew. Telu'oc wasn't one she had considered before, but he was more likely than Kropecz to cooperate. Na-Ganj was in minor counterfaction to Belini through one of his other factioners, which meant bringing him to her side would be delicate diplomatically. Gallown could go either way.

She had to be back on board her ship within two more hours, before the news was leaked that the Prophet had finally been revealed and confirmed to the Sh'nai priesthood. When that little religion-based bombshell hit the local Nets, fanatic followers would begin searching for clues to the Prophet's identity.

The Emperor might even be moved to demand that Ia present herself formally for recognition if things got out of control. She would have to call upon him before that happened. That was, if he didn't call on *her* first; the chance for that stood at around seventy-three percent, which meant there was still a lot for her to do to ensure it happened.

She didn't hurry back to the *Hellfire*, though; there was just enough time to do a little shopping, first. Her civilian clothes were getting old, and something new to wear in her rare, civvies-clad moments wouldn't hurt the future.

APRIL 22, 2496 T.S.

Once again, she was escorted into the conference room hosted by the *Tatth-Niel*'s Department of the Imperial Army. This time, Ia did not come in uniform. She had found a shop selling dresses not too different from Earth-style cheongsams, but slit front and back to midthigh in petal-like panels as well as down the sides, and layered with more petals underneath.

Using the textile manufactory controls, she had loosened the fit of the long sleeves, adding buttons from elbow to wrist down each side so that she could hide her officer's ident. The fabric was a plain, deep red, embroidered here and there with golden feathers, and it came with a matching, turban-like cap that covered her distinctive hair.

In short, it made her look like a woman, a civilian instead of a no-nonsense soldier. The color was also one associated with the Imperial Court, and her Asiatic tan was just golden enough to blend in with the average V'Dan tint. Nobody had looked twice at her on her way here.

The man waiting for her in the conference room was not a nobody, however. His Eternal Majesty, Emperor Ki'en-qua Nomin'ien V'Dania, Blade of Heavenly Justice, Shield of the Thirty-Seven Worlds—if one counted all the way down to the smallest, jointly founded domeworld colony—and One Hundred Sixty-Seventh Sovereign of V'Dan, definitely looked twice at her.

He glanced her way, then turned and stared as she was brought into the room by Leftenant P'kethra and the Grand General. His Majesty then frowned softly as she was introduced simply as Terran Space Force Ship's Captain Ia, and quirked one brow upward. Handsome and just bordering on middle age, he wore the monarch's version of the Imperial Army Dress Reds, decorated with what looked like his own half glittery of a few brooches, ribbons, and swags of whatever cultural significance applied. She hadn't bothered to check in the timestreams since they weren't important.

"Ship's Captain Ia?" he repeated, staring at her.

Taking that as permission to speak, Ia bowed politely, formally. "In disguise, Your Eternity. Rumors already churn on the V'Dan Nets, and I would not have them connect a certain white-haired military savior of the Gatsugi's opening battle with a certain white-haired soldier striding about the station. Not to mention your own appearance aboard the freeport is being kept discreet, is it not?"

"Correct. Sit," he directed her, gesturing at one of the chairs at the middle point of table. His Terranglo, trade tongue of the Alliance, was far more eloquent than her V'Dan would have been. "This isn't a formal meeting."

She allowed the Grand General to hold her seat for her. "When a foreign soldier is called before the local head of state, it is always a formal meeting, Eternity."

The title she used had originally belonged to the Immortal; War King Kah'el hadn't been able to break her people from using it on him in turn when he had taken over the old, planetbound empire. It had stuck with his descendants ever since, though none of them had ever lived longer than the normal life span. Ia used it now in respect, tipping her head.

"It is assumed that, as an officer, I must at all times represent my own government in a positive light toward your people," she said. "But then, I believe that is what this meeting is about, is it not?"

"True," he agreed, pulling out his own chair across from her, not waiting for the Grand General to come around the table and do so. That spoke cultural volumes about the middle-aged ruler's candidness and intent. "Still, this is not a formal court appearance. Such a thing would cause a firestorm of public interest and an earthquake of religious turmoil. I would rather speak with you as one soldier to another since our nations are allies in war."

"And my confirmation as a major religious figure should be used as a positive influence toward that war effort, I agree," Ia stated. This was the other reason why she had chosen to appear in civilian clothes rather than her uniform. She could still speak as an officer of the Terran United Planets Space Force, but he would see her as the Prophet, a subconscious influence. "Given I am here before you, I trust you have reviewed the evidence of the Sh'nai D'aspra Archives confirming my identity, and are not here to question it."

"No. The evidence was rather straightforward. Unsettlingly so. My family have been Sh'nai followers for the last fourteen hundred years, ever since the Sang'q'ar religious unification movement. Of course, some have ruled in devout worship, some only by paying lip service. I fell closer to the worship side than the lip service," His Majesty confided candidly, lacing his own fingers together. "But I am . . . uncertain how I should feel about you.

"As living proof of the Immortal's words," he stated, "you are a living saint whose presence has been one of the core predictions of Her Eternity . . . but as the Emperor of V'Dan, great-plus grandson of the War King himself, it is not politically wise for me to admit openly that the Immortal did, in fact, exist. Even after nearly five thousand years." Leaning forward, he pinned Ia with his hazel grey eyes. "So what, exactly, am I to do with you?"

"Admitting that the Immortal did exist would lead to speculation that she still exists, being immortal," Ia agreed. "That would lead every asteroid-headed idiot with a complaint against the current government to try to seek her out, or encourage con men to drum up some impostor. That would cause political instability. Yet because we—you and I—need the backing of the V'Dan people behind the war effort, to *deny* that I exist and that my abilities are real, just in the effort to deny the political-sized headache of the Immortal's existence, would in turn cripple our efforts to defeat the Salik once and for all."

"Once and for all?" He seized on that point.

She nodded soberly. "Once and for all. It will not be a pleasant fight, Eternity. I can only promise you that it will be a worthwhile one if and when we succeed."

He sat back a little, considering her words. "So. We are back again to the problem of what do I do with you?"

She leaned forward on her elbows, echoing his pose by interlacing her fingers together. "My plan, Your Majesty, is and always has been to present my case matter-of-factly. I myself am not what is important; the future is important, and my abilities are merely a tool to access the best path to it. I suggest, with your permission, that I record a message for the Empire. It will be addressed to your fellow V'Dan for you to broadcast at your leisure. *After* we have left the system, since I would prefer another day of near anonymity for my crew. This is their only chance for Leave for the next eight months, and I'd like them to finish enjoying it."

"And what would you say in this broadcast?" the leader of V'Dan asked, lifting his brow again.

"The flat truth. That I am here to direct the war effort so that as many lives can be saved as possible. That I am not here to answer petty individual questions about the future, but would rather urge your people to turn their energies toward the far-more-effective purpose of defending the Empire. I will then state plainly that the Immortal did and does exist," Ia told him, quickly holding up one hand to forestall his protest, "but that she is still bound by her oaths to the descendants of the War King to stay *out* of V'Dan politics, so long as your line of Emperors and Empresses continues to lead your people well. I will then confirm that you, Emperor Ki'en-qua, are doing admirably well in this time of great trouble, so she will not return to rule and has no need to return.

"She *is* still bound by her promise," Ia admitted to him. "So that will not be a lie. I will then state that it is best for the fate of the Empire for you to continue to lead your people for many years to come, and that your reign will have my firm support in that endeavor as the Prophet of a Thousand Years . . . which means that the orders you give your people will be seen as having my stamp of approval from that point on, whether or not I actually had anything to do with helping you craft them. That will wed religion to politics in a firm show of double support for your policy decisions."

She added a slight, wry smile to that statement.

Ki'en-qua considered her words and nodded slowly. "So far, I like what I've heard. You're showing support for my government, respect for our histories, laws, traditions, and the oldest of our faiths . . . and firmly telling everyone that *your* focus is not on V'Dan but on the Alliance as a whole, leaving me to lead my people as I see fit."

Ia arched one of her own brows, shifting her tone to a dry, pointed one. "If you *do* stray off the right path, I'll send round a note to guide you back onto it, Your Majesty. I *am* the Prophet, and I would appreciate it if I had at least some cooperation from you and your people in our mutual war effort. But you can take comfort in the fact I foresee no immediate need to *actually* guide you. You do have good instincts and excellent advisors, and you don't hesitate to make use of them."

His Eternal Majesty arched one imperial brow at her hubris, and the two soldiers in the room, the Grand General and the junior officer, both flushed. Ki'en-qua, however, was the one who addressed Ia, and not the ruler of an interstellar empire. "I see you have excellent instincts yourself, knowing exactly which line to tread between lowly foreign soldier and living religious icon, without either falling short or overreaching the range of authority for either."

Her smile warmed into something more rueful than amused. Hunching forward, Ia confided, "Well, I *am* double-checking the timestreams even as we speak, to make sure what I say to you doesn't negatively affect the outcome of this meeting."

He laughed, at that. Emperor, soldier, and man, he laughed. Relaxing, Ia sat back, still smiling. So did he. The tension in the room eased as they shared a moment of amused understanding

The Shield of Thirty-Seven Worlds—which had at one point been thirty-eight, before Sanctuary had successfully petitioned for full independence around the time of her birth—finally sighed and folded his arms across his medal-strewn chest. "If only I could keep you around . . . I find your forthrightness and honesty refreshing, Prophet. More than that, I think it's your utter lack of fear in my presence. I have zero power over you . . . or do I?"

"No, Your Majesty, you do not," she confirmed. "But our goals are in common alignment. I value the lives of each of your citizens as much as you yourself do—and I say to you, having the full span of Time at my fingertips, you will be remembered as one of the great emperors. You will have to work hard to survive, and you will suffer as you watch your worlds and your people being attacked again and again and again, but you should survive a good long time, and your people will once again thrive. If we both put our best efforts into this war, you'll have my Prophetic Stamp on that."

"I've heard reports on your ship's exceptionally good timing and combat prowess," he admitted dryly. "Not to mention nigh-unbelievable reports about your vessel's main weapon. Any chance that technology will be shared with the rest of the Alliance, as the Terrans once shared your hyperspace gifts?"

"None, Your Majesty. The overshoot range on that main cannon is too dangerous for a nonprecognitive to wield, and I am the only one sufficiently skilled in predicting its full path," Ia said.

"A pity. Right. How much do you speak for your military?" he asked next, sitting forward again. "What authority do you have in brokering deals?"

"Technically, I have *carte blanche* from the hands of the Admiral-General herself," Ia admitted.

He wasn't stupid. "*Technically*, I could have you shot and killed for threatening to manipulate the V'Dan government with your little quip about steering my leadership in the right direction. How much *practical* authority do you have?"

She didn't take offense at the threat, though she did wrinkle her nose. "Not much at the moment, Your Majesty. At some point in the future, if all goes well, I'll have at least a little more authority, but not right now. I can, however, convey suggestions from the V'Dan High Command to the Terran Command Staff and discuss their value with my superiors as a registered military precog. That does carry some weight, but it does not carry any guarantees at this time."

"That'll do. Grand General," Emperor Ki'en-qua stated, acknowledging the other man's presence. The general straightened to Attention. "Arrange with Ship's Captain Ia to have V'Dan High Command security clearance, and ensure that she has the cyphering equipment to access our military communications—I trust that you will not abuse it, of course, Captain. I also trust that, should I have need of your temporal counsel, *Prophet*," he stressed, returning his attention to the red-clad woman across from him, "that you will give it when I request it?"

"If I can give it, I certainly will, Eternity, for I love your people as much as I love my own," Ia said, dipping her head. She unbuttoned her left sleeve and flipped open the lid of her arm unit. The general pulled a datachip out of his pocket, already prepared to fulfill the Emperor's order. ". . . I do thank you for the ciphers. That will greatly speed up the timely delivery of my missives for your people. For those that aren't directly related to the military and the war effort, the Afaso Order has agreed to act as my delivery agents."

"An excellent choice. They are both honorable and politically neutral." The Emperor paused, watching her slot the chip into her arm unit, then sighed. "Is there anything else we should discuss? As much as I wish to keep you here for hours, answering my questions about the war, the future, even the past . . . Sh'nai legend describes you as a woman who lacks the time to spare for trivial things."

"Those legends are unfortunately rather accurate," Ia admitted, probing the timestreams. The chip she had given to the general the day before already contained a personal cipher and hyperrelay frequency for him to contact her ship. Nothing had changed between then and now, since this was the majority chance she had foreseen. "No . . . I think that's about it for now.

"I'll head back to my ship now, put on my formal Dress Blacks, and record my address to your people. You'll have a clean copy of it within the next four hours. That should give you and your advisors plenty of time to figure out how best to present it after the *Hellfire* has left the system."

He lifted his brows. "What, no direct orders on how to do that?"

She gave him a wry look. "I am still a mere mortal, Your Majesty. One lone woman with a huge task ahead of me, whereas you have thousands of advisors on your payroll. Use them wisely, and I won't have to burden myself by doing their job for you on top of my own."

"Should I salute you when you say things like that?" Emperor Ki'en-qua asked dryly, gesturing at her red-clad frame. "Whenever you go all Prophet-y instead of soldier-y?"

Ia chuckled, relaxing. "No, Your Majesty. I'm merely here to deliver a message. A series of messages, to save lives. I might get a bit zealous about it," she admitted, shrugging with self-deprecation and a tough sense of humor, "but it's the message that's important, not the messenger. If you'll give me leave to depart, I'll go get started on helping ensure you remain firmly in control of the First Empire, exactly where Time says you should be."

"By all means, go," he ordered, gesturing at the door.

Rising, she bowed. "Thank you, Eternal Majesty—one more thing: increase your security slightly once my broadcast has been sent to your people. There is a five percent chance it'll trigger some attempted anti-imperial attacks in spite of my reassurances, but it is nothing that well-prepared guards cannot handle."

"My staff already has that in mind," he reassured her. "But I'll pass along the warning. Five percent is still a large number when it comes to one's personal safety."

CHAPTER 12

I think what saved the situation in the V'Dan Empire from boiling over was how quickly I and my crew departed the area and moved on to other things. The Admiral-General herself pointed out in my vidcall debriefing that it would indeed be more politically correct of me, a Terran officer, to be as absent as possible from the average V'Dan line of sight than to linger.

Since that fit in with my plans, I had no problems with her orders. I had other people to convince and plenty of enemy targets to pursue. Of course, some of them turned around and pursued me, too, but such are the fortunes of war.

~Ia

MAY 6, 2496 T.S.
ATTENBOROUGH EPSILON 29B

"We're still not shaking them, Captain," Nabouleh warned Ia. She was facing backwards in the pilot's station, so her screens had an excellent aft-ward view of the frigate-sized Salik starship still in pursuit as they dodged through the debris of a small, disintegrating planetoid. "Whoever their pilot is, he's *good*."

"They're not *that* good," Kirkman snorted, glancing back

from the comm station. "They're less than a third our length, which means a small fraction of our mass. That gives them three times as much maneuverab—*oof!*—maneuverability in this mess."

"Sorry," Ia apologized, easing up on the sideslip, then dropped them down, throwing everyone against their restraint harnesses a second time. On the bright side, the other ship's lasers only struck a glancing blow, while her own gunners managed to strafe the other craft despite the vector changes. The frigate's hull, however, was holding up disturbingly well.

"Sir, why aren't we making a run for it?" Private Balle asked her. "We still have enough hull integrity that—*uff!*—a straight run wouldn't endanger the ship too much. If you give me a vector, I can plot us a course outta here."

"Two reasons," she told the navigator, dodging yet another chunk of tidally torn planetoid. "One, our pursuer will be given high esteem for lasting so long in this tail-chase against—*ugh*—us." Her sharp maneuvers with the ship's fields were bruising her own hide, too. "*She*—we're being pursued by a female, a very dangerous sort of hunter-pilot—will be assigned to a new make of small, OTL-capable frigates, and attempt to pursue us for months to come. I can use that, since it'll start to tie up Salik resources in the attempt to ambush us if they think they can follow us and predict our course and targets.

"And the second reason . . . we're actually here to pick someone up, as well as fight the Salik."

Silence followed that statement. Helstead, overseeing the gunner teams along with Nabouleh and Sung, voiced the thought uppermost on the bridge crew's collective mind.

". . . You're mucking *nuts*, Captain. Pick someone up? Out *here*?" the lieutenant commander scoffed. "With respect, sir, this is a system flooded with hard radiation from three colliding red dwarfs and seven torn planets. The Salik—*uff*—resorted to remote robotics to do their ore mining here only because they're desperate for untraced resources, sir. Even the Chinsoiy haven't bothered with this place because the gravitational tides make permanent residence problematic."

Something zipped across Ia's screen. It swerved back toward the ship as she dodged another chunk of rock. "Well, *something* likes this part of space. *All hands, prepare for a friendly boarder. I repeat, prepare for a* friendly *boarder, followed by a hasty departure from this asteroid-riddled hellhole. Brace for yet more maneuvers and some heavy acceleration. Captain out.*

"Zedon, have engineering stand by with extra energy for the bridge, at my station," Ia told the private, switching off the intercom.

Helstead twisted in her seat, frowning at Ia. "Captain, we're not *allowed* to have boarders."

Something bounced off their hull with the dull thump that said the shields had cushioned most of the impact. "Wow," Sung joked from the main gunnery seat. "They actually fired a dud at us. It broke up on impact, though. Didn't even bother the insystem shields."

"It's not a dud. It's a tracking mechanism," Helstead corrected him, scanner information flowing up her screen. "Tiny robots that will try to push through the shield fluctuations and find a niche they can crawl into, something that will shelter them from the riptide forces of FTL travel. I'd love to get my hands on the pirates that sold them *that* little piece of tech."

"Whoa!" Zedon exclaimed, looking back at Ia for a split second before returning his attention to his screens. "That was weird, sir. Energy spike in the amidships hull, portside Deck 18, seven by thirteen. It was followed by a serious drain. Is that near those robot things?"

"Those struck aft starboard, closer to Deck 4," Helstead dismissed. "Are we getting an attacker from port side, now?"

"Neither. It's time to execute the 'get the hell out of here' maneuver," Ia quipped, guiding the ship down and left. "Because that energy spike-and-drain is actually our boarder."

"Star 29c is starting to flare," Private Charity Balle warned Ia, checking the navicomp. "If we run-to-jump on this heading, the ion storm will wreak havoc with the remaining scanners. I can't guarantee a safe transit to FTL."

"Who said we were running out of here on FTL?" Ia asked. Lining up the ship, she hit the thrusters, shooting them forward. Pressed back into their seats, they left their Salik pursuer behind. Her chosen opening between the drifting chunks of rock was narrow, but long. It did require subtle shifts right and left, thwarting attacks from behind, but it didn't take much to raise their speed to somewhere close to half Cee.

A swirl of her fingers swung one of the nose cones into

position, and a flick shot a ring-shaped spark out in front, narrowing down as it raced ahead. Collapsing into a singularity, it whirled, ripping open a grey-streaked mouth that led into hyperspace. There was just enough room to dart the *Hellfire* into that dull hell-mouth before it swirled shut again. In its own way, the hyperrift itself wasn't much different than the physics-greasing bubble of the FTL field encapsulating the ship; it was a bubble forcing open an artificial cosmic string, and it sucked them along for no more than three rattling seconds before it spat them back out again.

Slowing the ship, Ia checked their heading in the timestreams, comparing it against the navicomp readings on her lower-leftmost screen. They were now past the heliopause of the system they had just left, so there was little chance of a rogue chunk of whatever being in their way.

". . . We've reached interstitial space, Captain," Balle announced, checking her screens. "No navigation hazards within detectable range. Please tell me we don't have to do that again, because I'll need a spacesick bag if we do."

"We're good for now, Private. Nabouleh, power around and prepare to take the helm," Ia ordered.

"Aye, sir," the woman agreed, reaching for the controls that unlocked her backwards-facing station.

"We've got another energy drain, Captain," Zedon called out, tapping his screen to expand a wireframe view of the ship. "It's now below us. It's . . . coming this way?"

"Nabouleh, helm to yours in twenty," Ia warned the third watch pilot.

"Aye, sir," Nabouleh confirmed. Her chair and console clicked into place, allowing her to lock it and reach for the control glove. "Helm to mine in twenty."

"Sir, it's coming this way!" Zedon twisted away from the operations console. He didn't glance at the right patch of floor, though. Two meters in the other direction, to the left, not the right, the plain grey plexcrete matting covering the floor turned liquid and silvery. It rose up slowly, forming first a puddle, then a curve, then finally a bubble.

"Gentlemeioas, this is our friendly boarder," Ia stated, transferring the ship's controls. "Everyone, this is Belini."

"I have the helm, sir," Nabouleh murmured, gaze darting sideways in little snatches at their guest. Not that there was any real need for her to navigate, safe as their deadheaded course currently was, but she dragged her attention fully back to her screen when the giant bubble just floated there, off to her left.

"Thank you, Yeoman. Continue on course for the moment. Meioa Belini, if you'd come over here," Ia stated, addressing the overgrown, silvery soap bubble reflecting their bridge back at them, "I can transfer you enough energy to manifest physically. I think that would be far less disconcerting to my crew."

The surface of the sphere shifted and roiled. But it was sentient, and it was polite, for it obediently drifted toward her left side. Ia stripped off the control glove and held out her left hand. Her right hand sought out the small hatch and the electrodes built into her console.

Touching a Feyori in reality was not like touching one on the timeplains. There, a Meddler was merely another mental presence, one shaped like a bubble of warm water. This wasn't nearly that soothing. Her skin tickled and her nerves tingled, stimulated by the energies contained in that strange sphere. Adding electricity to the mix increased the stinging of the prickles, but Ia didn't stop conveying energy until the bubble flashed and popped.

Skilled as she was, the Feyori didn't even thump onto the deck as her Human-shaped feet landed. Bare feet, but she had shaped most of herself with clothes, if one counted footless leggings, a knee-length tunic, and a broad, waist-cinching belt as such. Short, blonde, and petite, she looked like a pixie. She also sounded like one, speaking with a light, sweet soprano voice.

"Thank you for the courtesy," the Meddler stated, squeezing Ia's hand before releasing it. Her fingers were warm and soft, and they slid free with a grace that said she was quite comfortable with a matter-based form. "I apologize for the delay. I wasn't completely sure at first why you were hanging around so long after blasting all those mining drones. Then I realized who you were."

"I take it my previous contact spoke with you?" Ia asked. Before she had encountered Meyun Harper, the Feyori had been the only ones she knew who could cloak some of their actions in the timestreams. She wasn't entirely sure what the previous Meddler had done.

Belini leaned over the edge of Ia's console, elbows braced on the edge and hands clasped together. "Indeedy. He's admitted to a provisional factioning. And that you asked for a few names. Given what little I can see of the future . . . I'm afraid you won't be able to reach the others before your Right of Simmerings is up. Not and convince them you're a player and not a pawn. It looks like you'll have to deal with me."

Ia shrugged, not bothering to deny it. Helstead craned her neck, looking at the Feyori with wide aqua blue eyes. She wasn't the only one. Belini glanced her way and smirked.

"I think I'll be a topic of conversation for some time among your crew . . . but that's alright. I like you Humans. You're cute as far as matter beings go, and you're endlessly amusing." She rested her chin on her interlaced fingers, smiling at Ia.

"Sir?" Private Kirkman asked, glancing between the alien and his CO. "Is there a . . . reason . . . for her being on this ship? I thought visitors were strictly prohibited on this vessel by pain of Grand Treason. Er, Grand High Treason, now that we're at war."

It was Helstead who answered his question. She snorted. "There's an obscure exception outlined in the rules and regs regarding the Feyori. It's extremely difficult to make a damned Meddler do anything it doesn't want to do. Not without a lot of psis pestering it to leave. The Captain *could* try to band us together to oust her, but there's no guarantee of success . . . so having a Feyori on board doesn't count against us."

"That exception to the regulations would apply, yes, Lieutenant Commander, but this falls more under the heading of undertaking diplomatic negotiations in favor of the war effort," Ia stated. "Not to mention it's part of my *carte blanche*."

Belini shrugged. "Like I said, you're all so delightful to watch. Threatening to kick me off the ship with little bitty psis?"

"Even a bear can be driven off by a large enough hive of bees," Ia pointed out, keeping her tone mild. She even managed a small smile for the pixie-like woman. "Still, I'm glad we amuse you. It's good to keep a guest entertained."

The pixie-shaped Meddler smirked and leaned closer, speaking with her mind instead of her lips. (*If you really are the Prophet, half-breed, then you already know what I want, and that I know what you need. Open faction, so that you have protection to continue your Right of Simmerings . . . and personally tailored prophecies for me.*)

(*Open faction would be advantageous to me on many levels,*) Ia returned, not denying it. (*You're one of the most powerful Meddlers positioned in Terran space. Though with you factioning me, Silverstone indebted to me, and Kierfando willing to accept me, all I'd have to do is manifest . . . which I could do with your help if you openly faction me. And yes, I do know what you want. It will be arranged for you at the right time and place.*)

(*Good. And nope, I'm not going to help you manifest.*) Reaching around the transparent edge of her leftmost secondary screen, Belini bopped Ia lightly on the nose. (*You're the one responsible for achieving your own adulthood, little one. You'll gain more respect if you don't have Feyori aid.*)

Ia wrinkled her nose. (*Ugh, I know. So much for the short-cut . . . And please refrain from doing that in front of my troops. They need to know I'm both fearless in the face of a full-blooded Meddler on board,* and *respected by that Meddler. This is part of* my *factioning to my troops, matter-based though they may be.*)

(*Well, don't expect me to salute you,*) Belini retorted dryly. (*I'm not Silverstone. I didn't join the military.*) She held out her hand. (*So. We are in faction?*)

(*We are.*) Gripping the offered hand, Ia sealed the deal with a wordless thought pulse.

Belini's brows rose. (*You know how to talk in the old ways, don't you? A shame, but not more than half of us at most still do that. The only drawback to the Game is that we're in some ways being influenced by our own pawns, even as we influence them.*)

Ia sent another wordless pulse of energy, confirming it. Belini pulsed one back. It was a lot more complex than Ia's, and made the younger woman's head ache. Releasing her hand, Ia rubbed briefly at her temple, then lifted her chin at her main screen. "So where should we drop you off?"

"I need to stick around long enough to place my marks on your ship, so that the others will know it's under my protection," Belini stated, watching Ia shift to unclip her harness. "That means coordinating with your engineers so they don't cleanse the wrong energy traces—via degaussing and so forth. Depending on whether or not they understand what they'll be looking at, that could take one to five hours. By the way, did you know there's a small homing beacon now attached to your ship? It tastes like mud. Salik machines tend to taste that way."

It was Ia's turn to snort. "Of course I know. My intent is to find it, deactivate it without destroying it, then reactivate it later on to lure the enemy into ambush after ambush."

Belini grinned and leaned again, looking like a kid. "Excellent. You just might survive in the playing field of Feyori politics."

Ia pushed out of her chair. "Whatever I may do with my abilities, I am Human first and foremost. My only goal is to save this galaxy. I have no interest in your Game beyond ensuring that it, too, will survive the coming cataclysm—but let's take this to my office, where I will go over what you are and are not allowed to see and touch while you are on board. Please remember that I *am* strong enough to throw you off my ship."

"Hey, I'm in faction to you now," Belini countered, raising her hands in mock-surrender. "I also personally believe it's a sweet enough deal, I'm not going to mess it up—you could even put me in the brig when I'm not being escorted around."

Ia gave her a flat look. "You're a Feyori. The brig wouldn't hold you at all. I'll escort you to engineering myself. What nearby system do you want to be dropped off at?"

"I believe your star charts call it Atteborough Theta something," Belini dismissed, flicking her hand lazily.

"Private Balle, plot a course for Atteborough Theta 23. Yeoman Nabouleh, take us into FTL as soon as the navicomp has the course laid. Lieutenant Commander, you have the bridge," Ia ordered.

"Aye, sir," Helstead agreed. She didn't bother to unbuckle from her seat.

(*I'd also like to place a nexus-fold somewhere on your ship,*) Belini added casually. (*It's common for those in open faction to have recall points anchored in the other's local space, so that we can call upon each other quickly in times of need. Not that I'd expect you to call on me, but it'd make moving around easier for me. Anything over a dozen light-years away is cheaper to fold to than it would be to fly. I'm good enough at time-skimming to be able to know if you're near where I'd want to go.*)

(*It's wise of you not to say that part aloud,*) Ia returned, opening the door to the aft corridor, the one that led to the two heads, the galley, and the side door to her office. (*If word gets out just how much I'm colluding with a Meddler, beyond permitting you on board, the Admiral-General would pull my rank so fast, I'd have enough power to manifest just from the energy burns.*)

Belini chuckled at that.

Ia opened the door to her office. (*We'll put it in my quarters so that your comings and goings don't alarm the crew. Provided the main cannon isn't being fired, you can simply slip down through the deck, then slip out through the stern without being seen.*)

(*You don't sound too happy about permitting this,*) Belini observed. (*Considering what I'm asking of you is otherwise such a little thing for one with your particular skills, adding a little bit more to the deal is only fair. My faction-protection is worth more than your life, after all.*)

(*I'm not objecting,*) Ia replied.

(*Liar,*) Belini chided her. The pixie-like woman followed her into the captain's quarters. The front cabin was sparse, decorated only in the furniture that came with the ship, a couch, a comfortable pair of chairs, a coffee table bolted to the floor, and a large monitor fixed to one wall, which could display the news nets when they were traveling at insystem speeds, or display any of a million entertainment files stored in the ship's main databanks when they were wrapped in FTL. Belini wrinkled her nose. (*Ugh. You have zero taste in anything. Don't you know how to play the matter-based version of the Game?*)

(*I do. My entire career is my Game. This is merely a place to rest,*) Ia dismissed.

(*Then you won't mind the fold-point being anchored here. It's more difficult to place it in a small object that moves a lot than it is to put it on a stationary spot on a planet. But both points are constantly moving regardless, thanks to the whirl of the galaxy,*) the reshaped Feyori mused, pacing around the modest cabin. She finally settled on a mostly unused corner next to the bedroom door.

(*I'm not entirely comfortable with you being able to come and go so freely on my ship, true, but that's because I really don't want to lose my standing and trust with my superiors,*) Ia stated, leaning against the doorframe. She folded her arms, watching the woman peer at the conjunction of the two walls, doing whatever it was the Feyori did when they prepared a place for their version of long-distance travel. (*It's not an objection, just a discomfort.*)

(*If you lose them, summon me—I'll put in a summoning trigger and show you how to manipulate it—and I'll fix the problem. We are in faction, after all—you to me, and you to Silverstone, and Silverstone to me . . . Your telepathy really did get the short shrift, didn't it?*)

(*It's more than overcompensated for in other areas,*) Ia defended dryly. Her quip earned her a physical chuckle from the other woman.

Swirling her fingers over the bulkhead panels, Belini did something to the metal, then tapped it with her fingers. She added a wordless pulse of thought, sending it to Ia. (*Do you understand?*)

Ia squinted, thought her way through the not-words, and nodded. Moving forward, she joined the woman by the door and lifted her hand. A spark of energy snapped from her fingers to the slightly swirled streaks marring the wall. Belini stiffened, then relaxed.

She nodded. (*Well done. Triggered on the first try. Don't let anyone degauss or alter this corner. Now, let's go talk to your engineers about what energies they are and are not allowed to purge. By the time I'm done with this ship, no one else will board it without your permission unless they wish to counterfaction me. Or are already in counterfaction, but that's the risk you'll have to take.*)

(*Miklinn's already planning to counterfaction me,*) Ia told her, turning back to her office door. (*That means he's counterfactioning you, too.*)

(*Miklinn always acts like he has an asteroid lodged in his gut. He needs to take a dump more often and stop fretting over the matter races so much,*) the alien dismissed. There was a mirror by the door to the main corridor. She drifted that way and fussed with her mop of finger-length hair. (*Don't get me wrong; fleshies are fun to interact with and observe, but just because you're exposed by a pawn doesn't mean you can't reconceal yourself and try harder. His problem was that he didn't lay nearly enough contingencies. Me? I have several identities I could assume at a moment's notice, plus a dozen ways to hide myself in any Human-touched system I enter.*)

Though I'll admit this is my favorite form. I think I look cute in it.

(*Did you know I once saved the life of Jesse James?*) she added, glancing at Ia. (*Jesse James Mankiller, that is, not the Old Earth outlaw. I was wearing this face when I did it, too. She called me a pixie, and I gave her psychic abilities. That era was a lot of fun.*)

(*Yes, I knew. This way to engineering,*) Ia directed, biting back the urge to grow impatient with the chatty woman.

Human though she might appear, Belini wasn't a woman but rather a chessboard hobbyist with a particular fondness for the pieces being moved about the board. Ironically, Ia knew she was trying to do the exact same thing, moving her own pieces about the board. She just didn't want to be quite so arrogant about it.

(*Nothing personal, Belini, but the sooner we get this over with, the sooner I can get back to writing out my prophecies. Including the researching and archiving of the information you'll eventually want to know,*) Ia projected.

(*Yes, yes, whatever,*) Belini dismissed, flicking a hand. (*Relax, child. You're under my protection, now.*)

Ia bit her mental tongue, staying diplomatically silent.

MAY 12, 2496 T.S.
SIC TRANSIT

The insistent chiming dragged her awake. Disoriented, Ia unwebbed her bedding and crawled free of the covers. There was no interrupt scheduled, no emergency that she had foreseen. She was *supposed* to be getting at least six to seven hours of rest. A bleary squint at the bedside chrono showed she had only received three.

The door chimed again. Confused, Ia padded out to the living room. *I know I didn't see any emergencies, no unaccounted-for probabilities . . . Ah, slag. That means it's Harper.* Slapping the door open, she glared at him. "What?"

"I need to get into the timestreams," he told her, hands lifting and gesturing in his enthusiasm. "I know I told you the new gun design is almost complete, but I think I've come up with a theory on a way to exponentially increase the energy output of the gun's design, giving you more calorie for your credits. It'll have to be wielded by psis, and I'll need several more of those crystals, and I . . . ah . . . uhhh . . ."

His brown eyes had finally drifted lower than her face. What he saw made him falter and blush. Ia had crawled into bed in one of her old, Academy-issued sets of underpants and a worn, matching tank top. The soft blue material had last been seen by him during their aborted weekend post graduation.

". . . And I think I will go wait outside while you put on a *lot* more clothes," he finally muttered, turning around to face the far wall of the corridor instead of entering her quarters.

Yep. It's Harper. The one person I cannot predict. Slapping the door shut, she returned to the bedroom to do as he suggested. She also checked the timestreams to see if his idea would wreck the necessary paths. What she found made her frown, then hurry to finish dressing.

Returning to the front room, she opened the door and beckoned him inside. Belini was long gone, but she led him into her office and closed the door before speaking. As soon as it slid shut, she locked it and reached out with her mind, silencing the hidden pickups meant to spy upon him and her. "We're safe to speak in here for the moment, but I suggest couching your terms vaguely all the same.

"If you're right, and I hope you are," Ia continued, still straining, against the fog he always induced, "then what you're proposing could be turned into a cattle prod for the Feyori and a personal-sized shield defense against the anti-psi machines. At least, for this crew and ship. I can't trust it in the hands of anyone else."

He gestured at her, his engineer's enthusiasm returning full force now that she was fully clothed in her uniform shirt and slacks. "See? That's what I was thinking! It finally occurred to me *how* you were manipulating the crystal, and why it could in turn affect the Feyori—relax, I *won't* tell anyone how you're doing it—and when *that* happened, I had the epiphany on how the exo-EM frequencies actually worked."

Pulling a datapad from his shirt pocket, he headed for her desk. "Let me show you the schematic designs I've come up with, so you'll know what to search for in the streams . . ."

Ia followed him, a faint, wistful smile curving the corner

of her mouth. *The one man I cannot foresee, the single biggest threat to the future we all need . . . and God help me, I love him. Him and his brilliant mind.*

She didn't let it show. Didn't tell him. Instead, she merely joined him at her workstation and listened intently as he pointed at the figures and formulae scribbled in electronic layers all over his blueprint files.

JUNE 19, 2496 T.S.
BATTLE PLATFORM *JUSTICAR*
ZUBENESCHAMALI SYSTEM

Ia stepped onto the bridge just in time to hear the second watch comm tech, Kinth Teevie, saying into her headset, *"What do you mean, you don't have the parts we need?"*

The blonde-haired Private First Grade touched her earpiece and scowled. Her screens showed a picture of the exterior of the station. Whatever call she was on, it was audio-only.

"Excuse me, sir, but those parts were ordered to be earmarked and labeled specifically and solely for the Hellfire's *use. My Captain personally assured me—"*

Teevie broke off, frustrated by whatever was being said on the other end. Ia moved up behind her, dipping mental fingers into the timestreams to see what was going wrong. That was what had summoned her from her office, the sense that something was going wrong. They should have docked with Battle Platform *Justicar* with no problems, which was why she hadn't bothered to be on the bridge.

What she found made her swear. *Slagging hell! Feyori fingerprints are all over this. Miklinn's made his first overt move against me. Shakk. I'd better check the timestreams to find the best way out of this.*

Ia listened to Teevie attempting to protest with only a fraction of her attention. The Feyori's move was a surgically clean one, with no way to prove other than through the timestreams themselves that he had telepathically influenced the *Justicar's* repairs department. No Human psi had noticed him at work as he drifted through the system a few hours ago, reaching out to manipulate just the right minds.

The clever bastard's been following us, and he's good enough at radiation-eating to cloak his presence. The moment he realized we were here to fight for the Beta Librae colonists, and saw that the Battle Platform was here, he probably figured we'd stop for repairs. Which I'd already planned to do. Narrowing her eyes, Ia tapped the private on the shoulder.

"Sir?" Teevie asked, looking back and up at her.

"Contact Admiral Genibes, emergency channel. If you cannot get ahold of him, then contact the Admiral-General."

"Emergency . . . ?" Teevie flushed. "I wouldn't say this was an *emergency*, exactly . . ."

"There is more going on at work here than you know," Ia told her. "Contact our immediate superior on the emergency channel. If he is unavailable, escalate it to the Admiral-General. You have your orders."

"Sir, yes, sir," Teevie replied, though her tone was a little doubtful.

"D'you want my seat, sir?" Spyder asked her, pulling his bootheels down from the edge of the command console. Since they were at dock in a post-battle zone, with the Salik kicked out of nearspace and Ia's assurances the Salik wouldn't come back for the rest of the day, he hadn't bothered to latch his harness in place.

"No, that's alright," she dismissed, moving to the other side of the cabin. Fetching her headset from her pocket, she hooked the device over head and ear. "I'll take the backup comm station for this call."

"Receiving pingback, sir," Teevie told her a moment later. "We're on a one-second delay, Captain; you can have a normal conversation. Assuming anyone picks up."

Ia settled into the seat. Out of habit, not need, she reached for the harness straps. Just as she buckled the last set in place, the main screen lit with a view of Admiral John Genibes's face. "Greetings, Admiral. I'm sorry to interrupt the R&D strategy session."

"What's the emergency, Captain?" Genibes asked, barely blinking at her mention of what, exactly, he'd been doing.

"I have just encountered interference by Feyori Meddling, sir," she stated. That made him blink. "Certain individuals are moving to counterfaction me, and a particular Meddler has just drifted through the Zubeneschamali System, nudging the minds of the crew aboard Battle Platform *Justicar*."

Genibes lowered his greying eyebrows. "That's a serious situation, Captain. And a serious accusation. How badly are they compromised, and who is it?"

"Subtly, and so far it only affects the repair crews. You don't need to pull them off their job details, though you should suggest to the Psi Division to come out here and sweep their minds for Meddler fingerprints," Ia said.

"That's a serious problem, and it does need looking into, but it's not what I would call an emergency," her superior stated. "Do I need to define to you what 'emergency' means, Captain?"

"No, sir. I've only outlined the cause of the problem. The effect of it is the repair department on board the *Justicar* is deliberately blocking our attempts to receive materials for immediate repair. Materials specifically earmarked for the *Hellfire* to use at this place and time," Ia told him. "I need you to issue a Command Staff–level broadcast to all TUPSF repair facilities that the *Hellfire* has priority-one repair status, wherever we go. And if you could, to pass the word along to our allied forces in the rest of the Alliance."

He flushed. "*That* would require both the Admiral-General and the Premier backing it up. The other races won't tolerate it without government approval. And I could hardly think you'd need to force everyone else farther down the list in every single repair situation, soldier."

"Certainly not, sir. Every single instance where we can spare the time, I will gladly let the others go first when it's a temporal priority for them," she said. "You *know* I will. I just need the *carte blanche* enforced by a formal, fleetwide statement. That way, if this ever comes up again—and the greater probabilities say it will—I can shock off the Meddler fingerprints by threatening those who balk with Fatality Thirty-Five."

He gave her a wry look. "Sabotage is a very strong accusation, Captain. There's a reason why it's a Fatality."

"I know, sir," she agreed. "In most cases, the mere threat of the cane will be enough."

"Be careful *you* don't end up on the wrong side of that carrot and stick," he warned her.

"I am fully aware of my double-indemnity clause, sir," Ia

said. "I have been taking every precaution possible to ensure my crew remains the most disciplined, reliable Company in the Space Force because of it. In order to *remain* that reliable force, I need to get the *Hellfire*'s replacement parts out of the *Justicar*'s holds and slapped onto my ship, and get it done without wasting half an hour comparing asteroid sizes with whoever's in charge of repairs over there. If you will issue the Command Staff priority notice, that will cover it."

He sighed roughly and poked at something below the pickup view at his desk. "Let me contact the Admiral-General to clear this with her. If you want it broadcast fleetwide, it's not going to be encrypted unless you're willing to wait a few days for all of it to be distributed. I wouldn't think an open broadcast would be wise since it could force your Meddler foe to change tactics."

"Start with the *Justicar* and take your time with the rest," Ia told him. "We won't be in port anywhere for another five days at the earliest."

"Shakk," the admiral muttered, shaking his head. "The *Feyori* are getting involved in this . . . Any chance they'll side with the Salik?"

"A few already have, but only because those are their assigned Game positions. Most of them are held in check by the positionings of the rest. They're arrogant asteroids, but they do abide by their own rules. Thank you for the authorization, sir," she added politely. "You know I won't abuse it. I just need something more tangibly specific than my *carte-blanche* authorizations currently suggest."

"While you have me on the line, any suggestions for the R&D folk?" he asked her.

Ia shook her head. "No, sir. The best options will be selected without my interference, or I'd have warned you in advance."

"Thank the stars for smart people and small favors. Genibes out," he added, reaching for another control. The screen turned black.

Nodding, Ia unbuckled her restraints. The timestreams had smoothed out. "You should have the right authorizations in about ten minutes, Teevie. I'll forward an updated version of our supplies request to your post from my office, with the exact location of each item on board the *Justicar*, so they won't be able to pretend they can't find anything."

"Aye, sir," Teevie said. "Thank you, sir."

"Bureaucracy's a right pain in th'arse, innit?" Spyder quipped, putting his feet back up on the edge of his console. "Especially when you get th' Meddlers in th' mix."

"You have the bridge, Lieutenant," Ia reminded him, rising and heading for the back door. "Try to remember to dust off your footprints before the lieutenant commander comes on watch, will you?"

JULY 9, 2496 T.S.
JS 723 SYSTEM

"Bogey at 49 by 299 . . . 298 . . . 295," York stated from the communications seat. With an entire sphere's worth for their field of view, and a set of computers that were smart enough to sort out potential problems in a sky of data, but not smart enough to decide what to do with it, more than one set of eyes was needed to manage the flow in an ice-filled system like this one. "Moving fast with what looks like weapons hot, sirs."

"Looks like th' Squid's back," Spyder quipped, checking his own screen at the command console. "Same config as before. Yakko doesn't know when t' give up."

O'Keefe muttered something under her breath, hands dancing across the controls. Her movements drifted the *Hellfire* to the right a little bit, but not strongly. Ia wasn't strapped into a seat, and the yeoman knew it. She also knew it was likely there were plenty of others around the ship who weren't strapped in for maneuvers. "Captain, do you want to take the helm?"

"Not necessary. No sudden moves, Yeoman," she told O'Keefe. She had emerged from her office with the foreknowledge of the best way to handle this encounter. "Continue on course to the Dlmvla mining station."

"Then it *is* th' Squid?" Spyder asked, lifting his brows. The nickname had been voted on informally for the Salik hunter-pilot crazy enough to try to engage them. This was her third time finding and following the *Hellfire*, though her ship wasn't close enough yet to fire accurately.

Douglas spoke up from the operations seat. "Sir, we're badly damaged. Deschamps says his repair teams have parts strewn all over the aft and stern lower decks. One good hit to the rear of the ship, and there could be a lot of flying debris."

"Yes, I know that, Private. And you know that, but *they* don't know that," Ia soothed. Moving from the back door to the pilot's seat, she touched O'Keefe on the shoulder and gave the curly-haired woman a reassuring smile. "Rotate the ship 180 degrees, Yeoman. Point the muzzle of our main cannon at the Squid, but continue on course. Be mindful of the repair crews and take your time. Head for the mining station and cozy up our middle to their number 17 hatch. At all times until the last few minutes needed to dock, keep the main cannon pointed at the Squid.

"Private York, inform them we will be arriving in time for tea, and that we'd like a canister of frozen *ksisk* delivered to our airlock. Offer them a single teddy bear in return, then contact Private Bethu-ne'. Ask him to select one of the teddy bears from his collection as a gift for the Dlmvla—the older and more worn, the better. Tell him he has fifteen minutes to p-suit up and get the bear to the amidships Deck 12 portside airlock for the exchange."

York blinked twice, bemused by her odd set of orders, then turned back to his console. ". . . Aye, sir. Whatever you say, sir."

"Y' don' get it, do you?" Lieutenant Spyder asked rhetorically. He had given Ia a quizzical look when she first stepped onto the bridge, but hadn't relinquished his seat, yet. "Well, the Cap'n an' I do. Xenopsychology an' all that."

York snorted. "Well, I'm glad *you* do. Mind explaining it to us lowly peons?"

"The Salik, most unfortunately, aren't stupid enough to open up an extra war front," Ia told him. "Discounting the Greys, and with little competition from the other races for the various methane-rich worlds out there, the Dlmvla are the single largest nation in the known galaxy. If you counted the entire galaxy, the Solaricans would come in at third place and the Dlmvla somewhere around fifteenth," she added dryly. "But not in this known patch of it, so the felinoids don't count.

"Up to this point, the Salik have been very careful to avoid Dlmvlan targets. They won't even attack anything near a methane-rich world if there's a single Dlmvlan ship in the system. The Dlmvla think this might be a courtship method of reverse psychology, ignoring them in order to seek an alliance,"

Ia added lightly, "but the Salik honestly have no interest in contacting them. At least, until the Alliance is shattered, all the tastier species are firmly rolled up in their tentacles, and they've rebuilt their war machine strong enough to take up the hunt for new prey."

"That's why they 'aven't fired on us yet," Spyder pointed out, looking up briefly from his screens. "Back in th' Corps, we heard news 'bout our old Sergeant Ia, after she got jumped up t' be a lieutenant in th' Navy. Nothin' specific, just that she'd play up th' enemies' weaknesses psychologically. Pirates, Salik, smugglers, didn' matter. When she didn't ask fer this seat, I sussed out why she wasn't inna hurry. Salik won't fire on us this close to th' methane-breathers."

"Which is why we're safe to dock," Ia agreed, nodding at her 2nd Platoon lieutenant. "*Leaving* is another matter. At that point, it'll be third watch, and I'll take the helm. We can't ask the Dlmvla to help us with our repairs, so we'll be here a good twelve hours, but if everyone works hard, that'll be enough time to get the hull solid again."

"And the frozen *ksisk*?" Private Sharpe asked, eyes on his navigation screens. "What is that, some kind of fish?"

"A very tasty berry, but only once it's been aired out," Ia stated dryly. "That's because it's colloquially known as the 'fart fruit' to the Human colonists manning the one M-class world in the otherwise Dlmvlan-run system of Kvuu Zhwinnh 525. A single canister's worth of frosted methane crystals isn't going to bother us, and I'm in the mood to tease the Dlmvla with an exchange of a fairly valuable but edible commodity for a near-worthless but much more permanent child's toy."

"Captain?" O'Keefe asked, frowning in thought. "You *do* know that the Dlmvla are more than three meters tall, right? Our Deck 12 starboard airlock is designed for two-meter-tall beings. I can't guarantee a solid docking seal if they open up that big door of theirs."

"That's the other reason why Private Bethu-ne' needs to suit up for hard vacuum," Ia told her. "Trading the bear for the canister without pressurization will ensure neither side offends the other with unwanted gasses. It's a subtle courtesy and a subtle insult at the same time, and the Dlmvla will love it. They *think* the Salik might be courting them with illogic, but I actively am."

"And when we're ready to leave, sir?" O'Keefe asked her, making a minor course correction.

"As soon as we're repaired and clear of the station, we'll be making our way around the gas giant's curve. At about half-way into our run-to-jump, a rather large fleet of Salik summoned by the Squid will leap out of the night and attempt to destroy us . . . followed by a rather large fleet of prewarned Alliance ships." Ia grinned at the second watch pilot. "It should be fun."

Nodding to Spyder, who had the watch, she walked off the bridge again. She had just enough time for a four-hour nap, followed by eight hours of hard work helping the engineering teams catch up on the needed swap-outs of various refitted and repaired parts, and a long, tough, but ultimately victorious fight against a good chunk of the local Salik fleet. A pity it would be only a small fraction of the whole.

Afterward, the *Hellfire* would need extensive repairs, more than her Company could handle. She knew there would be three Battle Platforms coming, though, more than enough to spare them the repair gantries that would be needed. She also knew that the Squid would get away and live to track them again, but that was all factored into her plans. As was not saying much to the Dlmvla this visit, other than swapping an old teddy bear for noxiously sweet fruit.

At least God lets me amuse myself at certain points along this path.

AUGUST 8, 2496 T.S.
GOLDEN PRISM DOME
GOLDEN GLITTERS III ORBIT, SALUK 199 SYSTEM

The view from Lieutenant Commander Helstead's helmet cam wobbled a little. The explosion was two blocks away from the mechsuited woman, but the force of the shockwave still rattled the petite woman's armor. Another, harder explosion rattled the video feed for a moment, sending streaks of static across Ia's second tertiary screen. *"Captain, there is a lot of fighting going on nearby. These people are getting slaughtered!"*

"Stay on target," Ia ordered her. The *Hellfire* rocked as well. Strafing the ship sideways helped; it gave the gunners, reduced

in number thanks to Helstead's troops on the ground, time to angle their weaponsfire at the three ships pursuing them.

Splitting their forces was not exactly the best option, but the Gatsugi colony needed defending, and theirs was the only ship anyone could spare. The disturbing fact, one Ia had known all along and the rest of the known galaxy was only now beginning to learn, was that the Salik fleet was a *lot* larger than anyone else knew, partly from mixing their forces.

Tentacled, ostrich-flippered soldiers served alongside mass-manufactured robotics, the latter crafted with at least five completely different programming systems. Orders were given verbally so that all could obey whatever Salik officer led them, but viral attacks that affected one type of robot did not necessarily disable the others, and the algorithms were swapped out every few days. Some worlds were even coming under attack by dangerous beasts bred to survive on a particular planet, to help the Salik in their quest to colonize as well as conquer them.

A hard explosion shook the *Hellfire*. Never a good sign in a starfight, this explosion shoved the ship slightly to the right. Red telltales flooded Ia's upper screens, followed by distant *whunks* and a wailing, stuttering siren.

"Hull breach!" Private Nelson yelped. "Hull breach, fore section Decks 18 and 19! Ah . . . ah . . . section seals are strong, and inner seals *are* holding."

Ia rolled the ship, sheltering the wound in its side. *"Helstead, turn left. You will see a service entrance to their Senate Hall, and then—"*

"—And then split off A Squad to hold the path to the shelter tunnels, and B Squad up two flights and turn left, to defend the Bright Speaker up in the broadcast booth. I remember, sir," Helstead told her. *"Alright, you mudding slackers, left face, move out! Puan, Franke, hold the rear but do* not *fire! We don't want to draw any froggy-bot attentions our way!"*

"Captain! Priority message from the Admiral-General," Al-Aboudwa called out. "Putting it through."

"Belay that," Ia countered, most of her attention on turning the ship so that all three Salik carrier ships were on her port side, not the vulnerable starboard. "Inform the Admiral-General that we are in heavy combat and inform her that I say, quote, 'I know, sir. There was nothing we could do for them. We could only save the rest,' end quote. Restate we are in combat, and cut the link. *L-pod 12, P-pod 14, abandon your pods. I repeat, abandon your pods. Retreat to Deck 5 immediately. All hands, prepare for another hull breach.*"

"O Captain, my Captain," Rico stated calmly, "have I ever told you how much I hate it when you say things like that?"

"Get in line behind Harper. It's his precious ship I'm blowing up. *L-pod 12, P-pod 14, this is* not *a drill.* Move *it!*" she barked into her headset.

"*Harper to Ia,*" she heard in her left ear. "*What the* shak-king *hell are you doing to my ship?*"

"*Captain, the daily bread is in the basket, and the security teams are forgiving us for our trespasses,*" Helstead reported in her right.

"*Helstead, you make sure she transmits, whatever the cost. Harper,*" Ia added, switching channels, "*stuff it and start making repair plans.* Al-Aboudwa, prepare to retransmit the signal coming from the surface. All relays, all bandwidths, all stations and comm sets on board this ship. I want everyone to hear why we are *here* instead of anywhere else."

"Aye, sir. Opening all channels," he agreed.

Nothing happened for several seconds, then a voice spoke. The tone was lyrical, the pitch high and soft. It was a whisper. A murmur. A promise.

"*I send/transmit in the hyper. I send/transmit in the light. I speak plainly/straightly so that each word, each meaning, will be treasured/grasped. Night has fallen, coating all we can see with the dull black of despair/death. The glow of our bodies has dimmed, our grip has weakened, and our foe listens with sharpened teeth for our last/dying breath. But I, but we, are not dead yet.*"

The gentle voice sharpened, gaining strength.

"*No limb can tear us down. No tooth can bring us death. These beasts wish to leap upon/destroy us, to drag us down/down/down, but they will* fail. *They are strong, but we are stronger. They are many, but we are legion. I send/transmit through the hyper. I send/transmit in the light. Every single being/body that faces these predators is my brother/sibling/ kin! Native or alien, we who are sentient, we who are compas- sionate, we/we/we have more in common than these murderers/ monsters.*

"*Grasp your spears/rocks/knives. Grasp your guns/ships/ strengths. We will drop upon them from the highest stars! We shall stab them down, and fill our veins with the bitter reds of our rage, and when they bite . . . when they bite, they will choke/ suffocate/perish on our fury, torn apart by our combined might!*"

Shouts and sizzling sounds came through in the background. Ia could hear Helstead barking orders to her teams, and an explosion that punctuated the Bright Speaker's next words. Lasers struck the *Hellfire*, damaging more panels; she dodged them as best she could.

"*I am not afraid!*" the Gatsugi speaker asserted. "*I transmit in the hyper, I transmit in the light, and I am not not not afraid! The hunters will be hunted. Stand on the branches by your choice/will/right. Climb for the strength to survive this war. Fight for your sentient brothers, and they will fight for you— when the easy prey has been shaken loose, their ceaseless/ wasteful hunger will send them into the trees for those who think they are safe! Strike now! Strike/Strike/Strike now, and cut out the tendons of their ambitions. Shove them into the Room for the Dead, before they can shove you in and shut/ lock/seal the door!*

"*Here I stand, surrounded by foes, but defended by friends. Gatsugi and alien. Why? Why would these Terrans come to our aid, when they themselves are hunted hard? They have a quote from a Bright Speaker of their own. It has changed words and changed hands many many many times, for it transcends mere words, and mere hands, and mere species.*"

A small explosion rocked the *Hellfire*'s shields. It was followed by a much larger one, skewing their flight and the stuttering siren of another hull breach.

"*I say it now in my own words, sign it with my own hands! They came for the Solaricans, but I was not a Solarican, and I stayed high above as they perished. They came for the V'Dan, but I was no V'Dan, and did not look nor move. They came for the K'kattan, but my limbs were less, and I did not raise my spine . . . and the K'katta, too, died. But I know in my soul that they are coming for me. When will I fight for myself, and how can I fight for myself, if I will not also fight for the rest?*

"*I am not afraid. I am not at rest. No ruler, no leader, no*

Nestor can tell me what I know is right, and I will fight. I am a Bright Speaker because I speak the truth! I speak it until the universe itself listens. I send/send/send in the hyper. I send/ send/send in the light. I demand an answer/response from you! Will you fight?"

Silence followed the unseen speaker's words. Al-Aboudwa licked his lips and murmured, "Transmission has ended, sir."

"Open a broadband on the lightwave, Private," Ia directed him, dodging another round of missiles.

"Aye, sir . . . Broadband ready."

"Make no mistake. They will come for you, too," Ia said, thumbing open the channel. *"My Prophetic Stamp on that."* She closed the link with a tap of her thumb and darted the ship between two of the Salik vessels, increasing their velocity. "Jumping in ten."

"Jumping?" Fielle questioned, looking up and back from his screens. "But sir, Helstead and the rest . . . ?"

"They'll be alright," Ia told him, activating one of the two undamaged OTL nose cones. It swung into position and pulsed a torus of energies. "We're just going to reposition."

Darting into the grey maw, they left the orbital space of the third planet. Not even a second later, the hyperrift spat them out somewhere beyond the seventh planet. The rift was still open behind them for a moment. Ia once again hit the thruster fields, accelerating them forward. One of the Salik vessels, tail-chasing them, came through the rift as well.

Or rather, most of it did. With its unmodified FTL fields for grease, it survived the collapse of the rift, but at a cost; damaged by the fight with the *Hellfire*, those shields prevented the wormhole from rifting their ship but didn't prevent the forces from crumpling their stern. Silent explosions of energy and air escaped. Crippled, the enemy ship skewed off to port, its thruster fields abruptly unbalanced.

There had been a modest chance the enemy ship would be rifted and explode instead of merely being tail-nipped. No doubt the Salik on board considered themselves lucky. Ia intended to disabuse them of that idea.

Wrapping her ship in a vector-soothing bubble, Ia eased their acceleration and gently swapped ends. *Now* she could pulse the Godstrike cannon, and not worry about local space traffic for the next four months. *Now* she could whittle down the others, and rout the Salik forces attempting to seize the Collective's colonyworld.

The message had been sent; that was what was important. It had cost them a terrible price to be here, to help the alien poet speak so passionately for her kind. Only Ia knew it would be worth it. Just . . . not right away.

———

This was the part of being in command that no good officer liked. Ia was no exception. Dressed in formal Blacks, her cap on her head and her half glittery—Terran only—pinned to her jacket, she entered the bow mechsuit bay.

Private Tormez was the first one to spot her. Caught in the act of stripping out of her pressure-suit, the short, muscular woman snapped to Attention. Or tried to. She yanked her hand out of her half-tangled p-suit sleeve and snapped it to her brow in a salute. "All hands! Ship's Captain on deck! Ten-hut!"

Her warning rippled through the bay. Wide-eyed, the other women and men struggled into Attention poses as best they could, some still in their mechsuits, some half-clothed in their pressure-suits or their uniforms. All of them saluted as she passed. Ia did not stop, though.

Her target was Private First Class Nicholaus Smitt, soldier, clerk, and field medic. He was still working on climbing out of his bulky halfmech, modified as it was to provide on-the-spot medical attention. Awkwardly, he freed his right hand and saluted her, eyes wide with wonder and worry when she stopped in front of his alcove.

"Sir?" he asked her.

Ia saluted him back. She kept her voice steady as she dropped her arm and relayed her news. "Private Smitt. It is my deepest regret to inform you that the domeworld colony on Seldun IV, System ISC 197, has fallen to the Salik advance."

"*No,*" he whispered, shaking his head.

Ia gave him a sympathetic look as she continued. "The colonists did evacuate many of the women and children, but your mother has survived, but your father and sister chose to stay behind and fight."

"No," Smitt asserted louder. "No. You're a precog. You should've told them. You should've *known*. We should've been *there*!"

"I can say that it was relatively swift," she continued calmly, quietly. "The colonial mayor rigged the entire chain of domes with explosives. They destroyed most of the invasion force and left very little for the enemy to salvage and use as a base of operations."

"*No!* You should've *saved* them," Smitt accused, tanned face wrinkling in rage. He pointed at her in accusation. "We should've *been* there!

"I'm sorry. We had to be here."

"*Sorry?*" he yelled, free hand balling into a fist.

Ia didn't dodge. It connected painfully hard with the side of her face, rocking her sideways with the force of the blow. Sidestepping to catch her balance had an added benefit; it carried her out of range of a second punch, since his left arm was still caught in the workings of his suit.

"Private!" Helstead snapped, hurrying forward even as he tried swinging again. Her scowl overshadowed the fact that she was clad only in her underwear and a single sock, her fury palpable. "I will *personally* throw you in the brig for that!"

"Stand down and belay that, Commander," Ia ordered her, holding out her arm to stay Helstead's advance. The fingers of her other hand touched her cheek, testing the heat and tenderness of the bruise. "No Fatality has been committed here. I will not punish a man for an action wrought by grief. Not when I am directly responsible for it."

Helstead and Smitt weren't the only ones who blinked at that admission. Ia seized their stunned quiet.

"Every single second of my day, soldier, I make decisions like this. I *know* the names of your father and sister. I can tell you exactly what your sister said when she was eight and skinned her knee sliding down the stairs of your home, when you caught her crying from it at the bottom step. I know what *you* said to her. I know *every single person* who died on that planet two hours ago," Ia told him, letting her grief harden her words. "I know them, *and* I know the names and words and faces of every single person *their sacrifice* has saved in this war.

"We came *here*, to *this* colonyworld, because the words of the Gatsugi poet we saved will turn the tide for us. In two years and forty-eight days, the High Nestor Conference will hear those words being rebroadcast by sympathizers from the Dlm-vlan mining colony located two light-years and forty-*seven* light-days from here," she added, pointing off to her left in the vague direction of that other system, "and that poetic speech, coupled with all my *other* efforts, will finally drag their collective asteroids into this fight. Having the Dlmvla behind us *will* turn the tide of this war.

"But no one else could be spared to come *here* on this day. With all the other battles that *have* to be fought, no one else could be spared to go *there*, either," she stated, pointing first down at their feet, then off to the right, toward his lost home-world. "Hate me if you like, but I have known for *years* that half your family would die tonight . . . and I could do *nothing* for them but try to save the rest of the galaxy."

Dropping her hand to her side, she stared at him, vision swimming with unshed tears.

"Hate me all you like, Smitt. I know I deserve it," she admitted quietly. "Take comfort in the fact that there is nothing you could say or do to me that would be worse than having to live with the names, and the words, and the screaming faces of every single living being who has, is, and *will* be slaughtered because of this war. I have lived with this weight for the last nine-plus years, and I will *continue* to live with it, year after year, until the day that I die."

She held his gaze, implacable in her resolve. Unrelenting in her message. Smitt finally blinked and looked away. Ia drew in a ragged breath and let it out slowly, collecting herself.

"I am sorry—more than you will ever know—but in war, some may have to die so that others may live . . . and some *must* die, so that others *will* live." Ia met his gaze as he looked back at her. "I am sorry for your pain. I am sorry that I could not save your kin. I am *not*, however, sorry I chose to give up the lives of 4,179 brave and undeserving Humans and the fifteen valiant Tlassians sharing that colony with them in exchange for the continued existence of the *trillions* of sentients who will still be alive in the Alliance five-plus years from now, thanks to the Dlmvla finally joining our side."

He blinked at that. Ia twisted up the corner of her mouth in a humorless mock-smile. The bitter grimace accompanied her final, quiet words.

"This is but a very small fraction of the hell that I have had to live through every single day of my life. My gifts can save this galaxy, but they come with a *very* heavy price. Yes, you have paid with the loss of your family. *I* have paid with my soul . . . and I *may* have to ask more than this tragedy from all of you in the days ahead.

"As you were, Private Smitt, meioas. We still have a lot of work to do before we can rest." Turning on her heel, she left him and the others in the bay to contemplate her news.

Behind her, Helstead growled at Smitt. "You may be off the hook for hitting your CO, Private, but you will *not* do that again. You're on filter duty and floor-mopping until I say so!"

"She admitted she *murdered* my f—" Smitt started to argue, raising his voice.

"*Welcome to Hell*, soldier!" Helstead snarled, her words echoing off the bulkheads and alcoves as Ia left the bay. "They only call it a war to make it sound better!"

Ia tapped the control panel for the prep-bay door as she stepped through, cutting off whatever else her second officer might say.

AUGUST 16, 2496 T.S.
SIC TRANSIT

Bennie stared at her friend and commanding officer, who slouched low in the seat across from her.

Ia knew why the older woman stared. She looked like hell. She'd seen her own face in the mirror, shadows under her eyes, skin a little too pale, and other signs of exhaustion both mental and physical.

"So. How have you been sleeping?" Bennie finally asked her.

"I haven't." The admission was blunt.

Pausing with her mug halfway to her lips, the chaplain lifted her brows at that. "You haven't?"

"Not a wink. Well, not more than five or six hours since the Golden Glitters fight," Ia dismissed, flopping a hand on the armrest. "And that's only if you squeezed it all together, minute by minute."

"That's not healthy for a Human," the redhead observed warily. "You don't *seem* cognitively impaired . . ."

"I've been running on electricity. And some other stuff," she said, thinking of Harper's attempts at shooting her with low-level pulses from his prototype gun.

Or rather, his shooting her with Helstead's help, since the new design did indeed require a psi to power the weapon. Both lieutenant commanders were staying silent on the existence of the gun and how it worked, but then she knew they could be discreet enough. She hadn't told either friend that she wasn't sleeping, though, only Bennie. As a side effect of the design, the energy from the weapon was acting like fuel for her body; otherwise, Ia wouldn't have been in as good shape as she still was.

A twitch of her instincts warned her that her statement was about to be misinterpreted, so she quickly added, "Relax, Bennie. It's nothing illegal. Just a bunch of caffeine, vitamin complexes, that sort of thing. Nothing addictive. You know I won't do anything to mess myself up. Not with the fate of the galaxy depending on my mind."

"So what have you been doing with all that extra time?" Bennie asked, changing the subject. "Since you're not using it to sleep?"

Ia didn't believe for a minute that her DoI-appointed counselor wouldn't bring it back up. "Combing the timestreams for more prophecies and probability contingencies. I'm almost a week ahead of schedule, which isn't a bad thing. I have only a finite amount of time in which to direct events down through the ages to come. It's allowing me to flesh out some of my orders and fill in some of the otherwise neglected corners."

"Well, if you're ahead of the curve for the moment, that's good. That means you'll cooperate when I tell you to go see the doctor for a brain scan to make sure you're not damaging yourself, and a prescription for a sleeping aid. *No* arguing," she added, as Ia drew in a breath to speak. "You said it yourself, we're in transit for the next three days, trying to get to the other side of the known galaxy for the next crucial battle. You have time to sleep right now, and you *will* take it."

". . . Yes, Mother," Ia muttered, subsiding.

Bennie choked a little on her caf', coughing into a hastily raised hand. "I am *not* your mother, young lady! I have never earned that lofty title through the sweat and tears of raising a child. At best, I'm an honorary aunty."

"Then, yes, Aunty," Ia managed to tease. She grimaced. "Do I have to go do it now?"

Coughing again, the chaplain nodded. "You'd better. Do you want me to tell Harper and the other officers that you're standing down for a bit of sleep, or would you rather?"

"Me," Ia stated. Drawing in a deep breath, she dredged up the energy to push herself upright. "Better that it seems like it's my idea, so that it doesn't weaken my command."

"Smitt *will* forgive you," Bennie told her, rising as well. "The others will, too. Just give them a little more time."

That made her snort; if she'd been drinking, Ia would've choked, too. "Time is the one thing I have very little of to spare."

AUGUST 20, 2496 T.S.
BATTLE PLATFORM *KAISER'S COACH*
INTERSTITIAL SPACE

"Captain, I have an incoming link from a Lieutenant First Grade Gregory Bruer, Navy," Private Kirkman stated. "It's on an open channel, sir, uncoded. Is this a legitimate call, sir?"

His mellow low tenor interrupted the relative quiet that pervaded the bridge whenever the *Hellfire* was docked somewhere for repairs. In other words, between the distant *clunks* and *bangs* and drill-rasping sounds of various broken chunks of the ship being swapped out for undamaged ones by the Battle Platform's repair crews. Ia knew why her communications tech hesitated to mention it. Most of their messages were heavily encrypted.

She hadn't remembered that this call might happen, but it was a legitimate one. Nodding, she lifted her chin at her workstation screens. "It's legit. Scramble our end with the beta codes for the day and put it on my left secondary when it pings through."

"Aye, sir." His fingers shifted over his console controls for several moments. ". . . Receiving pingback on the beta, sir. It's been routed through five different hubs, so you'll have a seven-second delay."

It might have been only three years since she had last seen Cadet Bruer at the end of their time in the Academy together, but the dark-haired man had picked up at least two strands of grey in the interim, and about six years' worth of aging in his face. He looked like someone could stand to order him to bed for several hours of drug-induced sleep, too.

"Hello, Bruer," Ia stated, waiting for his end to catch her signal. "I'm glad to see you're alive."

"Ship's Captain . . . oh, God," he breathed almost at the same time, staring into the pickups with a slightly dazed look. "You have no idea . . . or maybe you do . . ." He paused, receiving her greeting, and nodded fervently. "Oh, yes, yes, I *am* alive! And most of our crew is, thanks to you. I mean, you *told* me I'd be on a crippled ship, about to be reeled in and boarded by the Salik, but . . .

"I did it, you know," he stated. He did so somewhat proudly, pulling his shoulders back. "I advised the Commodore to fake a greater incapacity, and to manually fire the weapons when they launched the boarding pods. It was an ugly fight once they boarded, but the majority of us survived. We kited our ship barely ahead of theirs so they couldn't grapple on and board in full, until two more from the fleet came to our rescue. We had to be towed off for repairs, but that was yesterday. We're very much alive today, thanks to you."

She smiled. "Then I'm very glad you remembered, Bruer."

"*Thank* you." Bruer's words were simple, but heartfelt. "I can't say it enough. Just . . . thank you! I've heard you're a precognitive, and I wish I'd *known* back then . . . but then that does explain why you were so *good* in the combat simulations—I'm not taking you from anything important, am I?" he added quickly. "I mean, *Ship's Captain*, already! Look at you! If you can do for even a fraction of the fleet what you've done for me and my crew . . ."

"I work directly with the Command Staff and the Admiral-General these days," Ia told him. "So yes, I am doing it. And I'm currently at dock, undergoing repairs. They're almost through, though, then it's back into another highly classified patrol."

"Good. Good," he praised, looking relieved. Fervently relieved. "You tell me to do anything, Ia, I'll do it. I *will* do it. Uh, so long as it doesn't break any Fatalities, of course."

"Of course," she agreed, amused by the hedging. She dipped her head in acknowledgment. "I'm not going to hold you up any longer. I know you have a lot of repairs to make so you can get back out there."

"Of course—just, thank you. And heed your *own* advice, young Cadet," he ordered her, pointing his finger at the screen. "I'd like you to still be around when this all ends, so I can thank you in person, and buy you a drink."

Ia smiled wistfully. "I'd like that, too. I'll see if it can be arranged. Oh, 'Cadet' Harper says hi . . . or he would, if he weren't busy cursing my name while trying to put our ship back together. He's now my first officer and chief engineer."

Bruer grinned. "Good! Tell him he still owes me twenty credits for that last targeting game we had . . . and our comm tech says my time is up," he added, glancing to the side. "Just . . . thank you."

"You're welcome," Ia told him before ending the transmission on her end.

"Old Academy friend, Captain?" Kirkman asked her once the signals stopped going through.

She sighed, slumping back in her seat. "An *alive* Academy friend. Not everyone will be by the time this is through."

"So . . . you really do know who's going to live and who's going to die?" he asked, turning in his seat to glance at her. The comm tech wasn't one of the ones who had asked to see the timeplains for himself. "You've always known?"

"For the ones I've bothered to look up, regarding the vast majority of their possible futures, yes. When, where, how, and why." She met his gaze wryly. "Smitt's family wasn't the first, and I'm very sorry to say they won't be the last."

He turned back to his boards, muttering under his breath. ". . . I am very glad I'm not you, sir."

"Oddly enough, so am I," she sighed. "I wouldn't wish this kind of hell on anyone."

CHAPTER 13

Yes . . . you would ask that question, wouldn't you? I suppose it's only fair to ask it. This interview is supposed to be the most candid one I'll ever give, and I haven't exactly been candid on that particular fiasco. I cannot—will not—answer your question directly. There are forces at work which, if disturbed, would shatter the duct tape I've applied to the universe. But indirectly, I can.

Have you ever worked so hard on something that it became your whole world? Some project so deeply close and personal to your heart that it defined you? No? Plenty of people have, of course, but many more have not. Those who have often try to explain it in metaphor to those who have not. Allow me to try that with you. Maybe you'll finally understand.

I had a teacup, once. A very special and precious cup. This teacup was something of an heirloom, not very special to anyone else, but ancient and irreplaceable in its value to me. I guarded it, and used it, and valued it . . . I treasured that teacup until one day, one unexpected day . . . it fell, and it broke.

It broke so badly that all of my horses and all of my men could not put that teacup back together again.

~Ia

NOVEMBER 15, 2496 T.S.
MIDSYSTEM ICE BELT
KELLINGS 588

She had a pixie in her living room. Sighing heavily, Ia tapped her office door shut. "No."

Belini arched one brow, hands going to her blue-clad hips. "I think *yes*."

"No. I am tired, and just . . . no."

She was sleeping better these days, but Harper's gun had left her nerves a frazzled mess. Her first officer and chief engineer was still trying to tune the crystals just right for maximum effect, but that meant using Ia for both the test subject and the tuner, and that took energy. Ia didn't have time to get any sleep right now, but she did have enough time for a hot, reviving shower . . . if she could get rid of the persistent pixie in her presence.

"Hastings' World isn't that far from here, even by FTL," Belini reminded her, following Ia toward her bedroom. "It won't take more than five or six hours to get close enough to drop me off if you're already going that way, or five or six minutes if we slip out that way via OTL."

"Absolutely not," Ia countered flatly, poking the button to open the door. "This is the closest we will get."

"Excuse me, but you *are* paying for my protection. I've already had words with Miklinn on your behalf," Belini pointed out. "Five or six minutes of your time—or ten to twelve if you're headed the opposite way—really isn't all that much to ask. You can head that way as soon as you're done loading fuel."

"Ten to twelve minutes of OTL translates to seventy extra minutes of processing ice for fuel. We don't even have forty minutes to spare, and we certainly don't have the fuel," Ia stated bluntly, turning around to face the other woman. "The best I can do is kick you out an airlock and shoot you in the back."

The Feyori studied Ia, hands on her hips, aquamarine eyes shifting to something a bit more silvery. Finally, she nodded. ". . . Deal. But only with a laser. I don't digest missile payloads all that well. They make me look fat."

Ia swept her hand off to her left. "Deck 13, portside

amidships hull. I'll go to the bridge and tell Private Ateah to line up the nearest Skystrike L-pod so he can shoot you once you're off the ship. That size should be safe enough for you."

Belini peered at her. "You're rather cranky. Would you like to shoot me yourself, and maybe feel better?"

"I'd be too tempted to use a bigger gun than you could comfortably digest." At Belini's quirked brow, Ia rubbed one hand over her face. "We lost another domeworld to the Salik last week. Solarican, but still . . ."

Lifting a hand to her arm, Belini squeezed it gently. "You're going to have to stop sympathizing so much with your fellow fleshies if you want to play the Game. Even as a mere soldier, you should know this."

The harsh look Ia slanted her way between those spread fingers silenced anything else the Meddler was about to say. Giving her arm a gentle pat instead, the Meddler moved back into the living room. The air snapped, and the overhead lighting dimmed slightly as the alien sucked energy out of the nearest outlets.

Sighing, Ia flipped open her bracer and hailed the gunner on duty. If she used the comm instead of walked to the bridge, she'd have almost two minutes more of hot water to help wash away the jangling in her nerves.

DECEMBER 10, 2496 T.S.
PROXIMA CENTAURI

The Choyan fleet was ugly. Not in its shape, for most of the vessels were formed of elegant crescents and elongated lines that were pleasing to most sentients' senses of aesthetics, but in the threat implicit in its presence. Until now, the Choya had not joined their Salik allies in the fight. Ia knew it was because they had still been building up their war fleet while the Terrans had done their best to delay their war-machine efforts.

If they didn't openly assist the Salik, the Alliance couldn't accuse the Choya of colluding with the enemy. They hadn't been able to attack the Choya openly but had instead tried to wean the amphibians away from their brethren diplomatically, coupled with some covert sabotage efforts. Now, though, the gill-breathers felt strong enough to attack outright, with fresh soldiers and fresh ships being brought into the fight.

But they hadn't struck yet. Mysuri looked up from her post at the communications station. "Receiving pingback from their capital ship, Captain," she stated. "They are listening, though they're not responding."

"Put the broadcast on video," Ia directed.

". . . Ready, sir," Mysuri told her.

Ia looked into her monitor. They weren't sending back a signal yet, but they were apparently listening. "This is Ship's Captain Ia of the Terran United Planets Space Force. I know why you are here, headed for sovereign Terran space, and I say to you: we have no quarrel with you, and do not wish to fight you. Change your minds before it is too late."

Silence. At the moment, the *Hellfire* was the only ship in the system; the Battle Platform that had been serving as a space station for Proxima had finally been moved closer to Earth. With only a few chunks of lifeless, radiation-blasted rocks in orbit around the dull red star, and no ice to speak of for a fuel source in the system, there was no point in defending it. The Command Staff had left scanner buoys in place, sending a constant stream of data back to the Sol System, so they still had advance warning, but the war had forced them to limit how thin they could stretch their defenses.

The Choya had no interest in the local red sun. Proxima Centauri simply made for a convenient, preattack gathering point for a fleet of over forty ships. They soared forward without deviation, ignoring the *Hellfire*'s placement off to one side of their chosen path.

"I repeat, change your minds and turn back, and we will not harm you," she stated, watching the fleet, greatly magnified, soaring through the system at somewhere near one-half Cee. "You have until you reach my position's midpoint to turn back or turn aside. If you continue on toward Earth, I will take that to mean you *are* going to attack the Terran worlds, and I will strike to destroy you.

"'Turn back, Son of Cho,'" she added, quoting one of the older Choyan legends, one regarding the vengeance-spurred rage of a trio of ancient kings. "'Turn back, and let go the burdens of your anger, or your people will never reach the far shore.'"

That earned her a signal. Mysuri silently patched it through to her main screen. The Choya was a green-skinned male; from the darkness of his hide, he was quite old for one of his kind. Blinking at her through the link, he hissed, "We hhhave heard of you. Your psssychological trickss willl not ssway us. Nor, I thhhink, is your one little sshhip a threat to all of uss."

"You continue on this course, Admiral, and I will be forced to destroy you. Turn aside, or turn back," she repeated. "Or *you* will not reach the far shore."

"You can fffire your weapon all you lllike," he scoffed, squinting his slit-pupiled eyes. "You cannnot harm allll of usss in one blow. Prepare yourrssellf to die. Not even your sship can withstand all of uss."

She didn't flinch. Didn't blink. "I invoke *ktham g'cho.*"

He blinked, this time from startlement. Twisting his head, he studied his viewscreen from a slightly different angle. "You innnvoke the rightss of a worthhhy fffoe? What iss your offfer?"

"If you choose to continue toward Earth, I will not fire upon you while you are still within this system," Ia stated. "In return, you will not fire upon me. *Ktham guann?*"

"Ktham guann," he agreed dismissively. "You arrre a worthhy foe. You willl lllive to ffface us at your Earthhh-world."

His image vanished. Mysuri shook her head. "We've lost pingback. They've ended the link, sir."

"So be it," Ia murmured. Quoting the legend, though the Choyan admiral knew it not. She activated her headset. *"All gunners, hold your fire. I repeat, hold your fire. We have a temporary treaty with this Choyan fleet. Do not fire."*

They waited in silence. The ships reached their midpoint and crossed in the blink of an eye. When the Humans didn't attack, the Choyans picked up speed. Gently turning the *Hellfire*, Ia moved the ship into their wake, trailing after them.

". . . Sir?" Mysuri asked. "Are we going to inform the others that they're coming?"

"Nope. Earth doesn't need to know."

"Shakk that," Helstead countered. "I want to know if we're going to get lynched for letting 'em pass. Allowing a known enemy past the gate could be considered Dereliction of Duty at the very least, and Treason at the worst."

"Shh," Ia soothed, picking up their speed with a slide of her fingers along the controls. "I gave them my word I would not fire upon them while they were within the Proxima Centauri System."

"So what, a tail-chase, Captain?" Sangwan asked her. "We wait until they're past the heliopause, then open fire?"

She increased their speed again. "My plan is to hyperjump ahead of them to the edge of the Sol System, turn around, *then* attack."

"We'll need to contact Earth first, sir," Ng stated. "We'll need their updated insystem traffic before we jump that far."

"No, we won't. We're not jumping that far."

"What?" Helstead asked, twisting in her seat at the spare gunnery post so she could look back at Ia.

"Sir, they're at eighty percent Cee and rising," Ng warned Ia. "They'll do it well before they leave the local heliopause, too. Once they cross over, we'll have no way of tracking them."

"*You* won't. I will." Not waiting for them to argue the point, Ia activated the nose cone, swinging it into position. Lining up her vector by timestream-sight, she fired the engine and sucked them into hyperspace.

As the grey streaks of otherspace slipped around them, Helstead cleared her throat. "You do know I trust you, Captain?"

"And I appreciate that trust," Ia agreed. "Thank you."

"You're welcome. But I will admit I'm very nervous at the thought of turning around well before those ships will slip back down below the speed of light, and taking them on in a fight," Helstead continued. Since she had nothing to shoot at, she had pulled out two of her deadly little hairpins and spun them over her knuckles back and forth. "Especially since the only way you could guarantee line of sight is to position this ship dead ahead on their path."

"An astute observation, Lieutenant Commander. Remind me to requisition you a raise."

They emerged two minutes later. Slowing the ship, Ia brought it to a stop, then gently swapped ends. The dead stop was necessary; the helm controls had to be adjusted to give her only the tiniest of movements. Most of those were provided by the sort of maneuvering thrusters used for docking the ship. Ia didn't even look at her screen, just closed her eyes and nudged their position with careful twitches of her left hand. A brief, go-nowhere pulse of the FTL field killed their drift, then they sat.

From time to time, Ia twitched them just a little bit right or left, up or down, compensating for the galactic gravitational curve. Finally, she unlocked the control switch and thumbed the trigger for the main gun.

This time, she kept the tip of her thumb pressed against the button. Red streaked forward, flooding the bridge with its bloody glow. Everyone flinched, half-hiding their eyes behind arms and hands until the forward-pointing monitors mercifully blacked out the center of that beam. The ominous *hummm* became an unnerving rumble, and the *whooshing* of the heat engines started to shake the ship. Ia had counted on that, though.

Instead of a twentieth of a second, she kept the cannon firing for a full five seconds, then shut it off. The rumbling ceased, but the *whooshing* did not. Putting that excess energy to use, Ia backed up the ship. She didn't bother to turn it around, just backed it up until it reached rifting speed, and activated the stern nose cone.

They sucked through hyperspace backwards for forty-five seconds and emerged somewhere short of Saturn's orbit. The ringed planet wasn't actually nearby at this point in its solar year, just a lot of stars. It was the closest they could get to interstitial space and still be inside a star system's reach.

The current operations tech, Private Sbrande, finally ventured a comment. "I, ah, had no idea that cannon could fire for that long . . . or use that much hydrofuel."

"How much?" Sangwan asked.

"Three full percent of our maximum capacity, sucked down in less than sixteen seconds," Sbrande stated as calmly as she could. Her voice trembled a little at the end.

Several soft obscenities and a whistle from Helstead met the engineering tech's words.

"Captain, what about the overshoot?" Helstead asked Ia.

"Nothing will be coming from that exact direction for almost a year," Ia stated. "The force of the beam will dissipate over the next eight light-months, until at most it will be an annoying flash on the scanners of passing ships."

"I'm almost afraid to ask how much damage it did," Mysuri

stated wryly. "Especially if it takes eight light-months for that beam to stop being lethal."

"We've just obliterated all but seven of their ships," Ia told her. "I had to hold the beam on for that long to make sure no chunks too large for FTL would remain. What little makes it to Sol System will be slowed by the heliopause winds and the Oort cloud debris. Eyes to your boards, meioas, and thoughts on your tasks. Those seven ships will be coming into system in four more hours, as will a fleet of Salik. We need to turn back the Choya with another warning, if we can. But I'm not going to hold my breath."

"The hell with that," Sangwan snorted. "If I were that admiral, and I'd just lost most of my fleet, I'd get the hell out of this system the moment I spotted this ship."

"It'll be a touch-and-go fight with or without them. They might choose to stay and help make things worse," Ia said. "But we will prevail . . . and then we'll have a very brief six hours of Leave on Battle Platform *Freedom of the Stars II* . . . whereupon many of you will receive commendations for your efforts in my service."

"About muckin' time," Helstead snorted, shifting back in her seat to rest her feet on the edge of her console. "I've been putting in recommendations right and left since we fired our first shot on this ship."

JANUARY 5, 2497 T.S.
CONFUCIUS STATION
DLC 718 TORPETTI SYSTEM

Lieutenant Commander Meyun Harper glared at his CO. He had to raise his voice as one of his engineers started up the cutter at the far end of the manufactory bay, adding to the cacophony of the grinders and laser welders being used. "I'm telling you, Captain, this would be considerably *easier* if we had stopped at a *regular* docking facility, or a *military* one!"

"Everyone else within sixty light-years will be needing their supplies, Commander!" Ia returned just as loudly. The cutter shut off, but the rasp of the grinders and the scorchings of the welders kept going. "I'm telling you, you *can* modify these supplies to fix our pipe fittings!"

"Well, I'm telling you that if I *do* fix up these *shakking* pieces of pipe, we're going to have to *weld* them in place, and that means cutting them off and replacing *three* lengths instead of one! *You're* the one who said we only have seven hours in this place. That's not enough time to melt them down and extrude entirely new pipes of the right size and shape," Harper reminded her, lowering his voice as the grinder cut off.

Ia threw her hands up in the air. "Just melt and extrude some scrap into coupler rings! That's why I got you the extralarge pipes stored down on Deck 17!"

He stared at her, then covered his goggle-protected eyes with his hand. Some of the other noises cut off as well, giving him room to speak. "I can't believe I didn't think of that myself . . ."

She clasped his shoulder, giving it a gentle squeeze. "It's been a long, hard series of fights, Meyun. You have kept this ship together, and *put* it back together, more times than I can count."

One set of doors hissed open off to the side. Lieutenant Rico poked his head inside, spotted the two of them, and plucked a set of goggles out of the plexi-fronted case by the door. He didn't bother to put them on, just held them over his eyes as he approached.

"Captain, your 12,379 *kesant* are almost up," he stated blandly. "You have roughly one hour to compose that message you promised to send to the Greys."

It was her turn to blank out for a moment. Wincing, Ia nodded. ". . . Right, right. Too many battles on my brain. I almost forgot about opening up *that* war front. Time for some damage control—Meyun, do you need me for anything else?"

"Yes. A pass for a week's Leave on a beach near Aloha City," he quipped dryly. The grinder started up again. He flipped a hand at her, raising his voice. "Go on! I have those couplings to fit!"

Nodding, she joined Rico. They removed their goggles and secured them at the door, then left the machine-filled manufactory bay. As soon as the thick door slid shut, cutting off the majority of the noise, Ia sighed in relief. She rubbed at the back of her neck, striding alongside her tall intelligence officer.

"Any chance we'll be getting that much Leave on Earth anytime soon?" Rico asked after several seconds had passed.

She blinked up at him in confusion, then recalled Meyun's quip. "No. Unfortunately. And even if we did, I'd only be able to spare an hour at most for beach-lounging, myself . . . never mind other activities."

He let that pass in silence until they reached her office. Ia blanked out the surveillance pickups as they entered, knowing what he was going to ask her next. Sure enough, he did. He wasn't the wary junior officer of a year ago. She knew he was on her side, but he still asked anyway.

"Sir, you said a year ago that the Admiral-General authorized these communications with the Greys," Rico stated. "But does she *really* know about them? Or is this just a massive stretching of your *carte-blanche* authority?"

"It's a massive stretching," Ia confessed quietly, taking her seat. She gestured for him to take one of the chairs across from hers. "Some would even call it an outright breaking. The probabilities are high that even after I fast-talked to her, Myang would call it Grand High Treason. But I give you my word, if I didn't foresee this deal brokering saving hundreds of millions of lives in the future, I wouldn't go anywhere near the Shredou.

"I just . . ." Frustrated that she couldn't tell him the full truth, Ia sighed and slumped in her seat, rubbing at her temples. "I need them to *stop* when I tell them to stop, so that they don't destroy the Terran Empire and trample onward into the rest of Alliance space. And the only way to do that is to convince them that I am a massive precog. One so powerful, I can *see* their movements with great accuracy, to the point where they . . . Hell, I don't know if they *can* feel superstition as we Humans do, but I need them to stop their predations because of it."

"Superstition?" Rico asked, one brow lifting in skepticism.

"They're not from this galaxy. The energies are all wrong," Ia said, sitting up again. "They're trying to rebuild their race by melding it with local biology—Humans are the closest they can come to something both sentient and compatible, which is why they keep coming after us every few generations—but thanks to Feyori interbreeding efforts, our psychic abilities hurt them. It's a weapon they cannot defend against because it is truly alien to them. And the fact that I can wield this weapon against them by predicting their own movements as well as directing all the others' is going to scare them.

"More than that, if I can show them how accurate I am with *them*, I can show them how accurate I'll be with their ancient enemy. If you'll recall," Ia reminded him, "I threatened to point the Zida"ya at them and pull the trigger if they don't comply. Proving to them that I *am* that accurate will scare them shitless, in the end. Literally. When I prove my final point to them, the Greys involved in that fight won't be able to unpucker for three days."

"So you're hoping to scare them into compliance, bringing the coming war with them to an end when you *need* it to end," he murmured, following her line of reasoning.

"Exactly." Tapping her workstation, she raised the screens, flipping two of the tertiaries at the bottom so that he could read the information from his side of the desk. Her primary scrolled up the messages as well, facing the normal way so that she could read it, too. "Here's the first set of messages I want to send. I *think* I've composed them correctly, but there are some probability variables that suggest they might be taken the wrong way. The Terranglo version's on the left from your perspective, the Shredou on the right."

"I'll see what ambiguities I can fix," Rico promised, frowning at the text.

FEBRUARY 3, 2497 T.S.
KNOT 2,330,427
HELIX NEBULA

"Never-ending battle, never-ending battle," Helstead muttered in between pulsing the trigger for her chain of cannons. "Never-ending battle, never-ending battle. *Please* tell me, sir, that we're going to have a bit of Leave soon? Real Leave, off-this-bloody-mucky-blasted-ship-style Leave?"

"Maybe, if you asked them very, very nicely," Ia muttered back, slipping their much slimmer ship between two Terran Starcarrier-Class capital ships, "the Salik and the Choya might stop trying to pick all these fights with us."

Proximity warnings beeped as a clutch of projectiles skimmed past their hull, swerving to avoid the *Hellfire*. They were Terran missiles, programmed to identify friend from foe and adjust course accordingly. Lasers couldn't do that, though, and two of them nearly seared the ship as they slid past. Nearly, but didn't.

Togama, manning the comms, whistled softly. "Wow, Captain, you are *certainly* stretching the vocabulary of the comm tech for the *George Cairns*. I don't think that one's anatomically possible even for a jellyfish."

"Unlike the original George Cairns, we will not die of blood loss from a severed limb," Ia returned calmly, strafing the *Hellfire* sideways in front of the TUPSF *Powahann*.

". . . Ooh, even nastier," Togama quipped, touching his headset. "The *Powahann*'s claiming you're completely off next year's Christmas card list, Captain."

"Really?" Helstead asked, perking up a little. "That bad?"

"Well, somehow I doubt 'Die in a Salik frying pan, you Shikoku Yama Flightschool reject; get the hell out of our path' qualifies us for fondly remembered relative status," he replied. The humor broke up some of the tension in the crew, though not the majority of it.

"Eyes on your boards, thoughts on your tasks," Ia gently admonished. "Just seven more minutes of close-quarters fighting should see the Salik threat contained." She flicked on the intercom. *"All gunners down the starboard flank, continue to fire on the enemy ships for two more minutes, then cease fire."*

The knots ejected by the shockwave shell from Helix's age-old supernova made for a rough transition at anything but sub-light speeds. Few ships cared to traverse the barriers. Few ships were armored enough to survive the radiation found inside for long, either.

However, each cometary knot was roughly the size of the Sol System, which meant it made for an excellent hiding place for a rather large Salik base. With giant solar sails erected to capture the echoing, last radiations from the exploded star and provide both shelter and power for at least eight major stations, the Salik had parked a sizeable chunk of their shipyards in one of these knots, sucking up all that free energy.

This fight marked one of the few times Ia had agreed to the Admiral-General's request that she and her crew join a specific battle rather than dash off somewhere else. One more random ship in a joint fleet of over a hundred might not make a differ-ence, but *her* ship might, and she was striving hard to make sure it did. That meant being hyperaware of exactly where all those lasers and missiles and chunks of debris might fly at any given moment.

"*L-pod 53, cease fire in ten seconds,*" Ia ordered. "*All star-board gunners, L-pod and P-pod, cease fire in one minute.*"

Vector change slung them around in their seats as she swapped ends. Fightercraft scattered as they slipped past, their plethora of thrusters firing this way and that. Ia didn't even hear the proximity beeps anymore; it was only the claxons she cared about.

"*L-pod 53, good job,*" she praised, as the private remotely manning that cannon excluded it from his firing commands. Rippling the thrusters shoved them back in their seats, allowing her to dart the ship toward one of the heavily damaged shipyard stations. "*Starboard gunners, thirty seconds to cease fire.*"

"Station 5 midpoint in thirty seconds, sir," Nabouleh told her.

"Shouldn't we still be firing by that point?" Helstead asked.

"No, that would be bad," Ia murmured, shifting them to avoid incoming fire from the half of the shipyard station that wasn't crumpled and on fire. "*Starboard gunners, cease fire in ten . . . nine . . . eight . . .*"

Missiles swerved in from behind, arcing around to strike at the heart of the damage. Blossom missiles, they impacted in puffs of light, then burst a second time like fireworks going off.

"*. . . Two . . . one. Cease fire,*" Ia ordered. "*Cease fire. CEASE FIRE!*" she yelled as the timestreams surged up and yanked her down. She could see nothing but the explosions of those blossom bombs ripping apart the shipyard, hear nothing but the click of a trigger being squeezed in ferocious glee . . . feel nothing but that pulse of light from Starstrike L-Pod 4 burning through the protective nose cone of the missile emerg-ing from the depths of the TUPSF *Hardberger*'s P-pod 29. That nothingness emerging in a too-late scream. "*SUNG, CEASE FIRE!*"

Too late. Too late . . . Too. Late.

The timestream overflowed as it swallowed her down, drowning her. Freezing her with the inability to stop the inevi-table. Nothing stopped that bright red beam of light. Not her order, not her wishes, not the chunks of shipyard forced apart by the force of all those explosions.

Water vanished. Water vanished from one lifetime, from a handful, from a hundred and more. The Redeemer's life dried up and disappeared. The Savior's course flowed on unaltered. The desert claimed all.

All.

Someone was crying in ragged gasps. Shaking with shock, skin flushed in fire, muscles prickled with ice, Ia stared at her right secondary screen, focused on the cloud of debris. A red circle and line flashed on the screen amid the chaos of battle, along with a simple, death-knelled message:

Fatality 13

Fatality.

How apt.

"Sir," Nabouleh stated, twisting to look back at Ia. "We're deadheaded for Station 6. We need to move. Sir? *Sir!*"

She couldn't breathe. Claxons wailed in her ears. Ice and fire seared her nerves. Drowned under the waters removed from those vital, vital streams, she could not breathe.

"SIR!—*Shova v'shakk*," the yeoman cursed, and whipped back to face her console. "Hotel November, override, override!" she snapped, using her emergency call sign to identify her actions for the bridge's black box. "Taking the helm!"

The *Hellfire* slipped sideways under her hasty grab, bruising them all against their seats and restraints. Nabouleh added an abrupt downward shift as well. The collision claxons blared. The maneuver yanked them up in their harnesses and slammed them back in place as the interior safety fields pulsed. Seconds later, the shields compressed, rumbling with a strange sort of hiss.

"Good job!" Helstead gasped as they slid past. "*Good* job, Yeoman!"

"Captain, we're getting a query on a Fatality Thirteen: Friendly Fire," Togama called out, looking back at her. "What do I reply, sir? . . . Sir?"

Fatality.

Her moan shifted as her shock morphed into rage. *Fatality . . . FATALITY!* It emerged in a wordless scream. Straps broke as she lunged out of her seat. Behind her, she could hear her second officer's voice. It sounded tinny against the blood throbbing through her head.

"God—Nabouleh, get us out of combat, *now*!" Helstead snapped, jabbing at her harness clasps. "Togama, tell them we have an emergency on board and nothing more!"

Vision red with rage, Ia didn't bother to reach the door before she opened it. Her mind stabbed at the controls, sparking electricity through the system. Squeezing through before the panel finished opening, she sprinted up the hall. L-pod 4 was located on the bow, but it was controlled by L-pod 20, and that was one sector forward and two decks up. Doors hissed open, their panels sparking with electrokinetic energy.

Everything was energy. The red of her fury had altered her view. Doors and bulkheads, floors and ceilings, everything glowed. Everything pulsed. It was all just matter, but it was also oddly see-through. As if she could, if she tried just a little harder, reach out and reach right through it all.

She knew she couldn't force open both doors of the sector seal. They were pressure-locked against being able to do that, to prevent both negligence and stupidity. Just as she crossed the first of the two thresholds, something struck her from behind. She staggered forward, throwing up her hands to shield herself from hitting the forward door.

The blow was a body. Arms and legs wrapped around Ia's frame, heels hooking around her waist, bicep and military-issued bracer digging into her throat. Still enraged, Ia reflexively tightened her neck, staving off the pressure which her 3rd Platoon officer tried to apply.

As a force of body, Helstead's efforts were negligible; Ia was too angry to notice her efforts as more than the wings of a butterfly beating on her back and throat. As a force of will, however, Helstead's mind slammed down on hers like a sledgehammer.

(*Stand down, soldier!*) she snarled, hooking her right arm around the wrist of the left to apply more leverage against Ia's windpipe. (*I said* **STAND DOWN***!*)

The command exploded in her head, snuffing out half the fire and fury. Ia collapsed to one knee. Helstead squeezed again.

(*Stand down!*) she commanded. (*You will NOT attack Sung! Stay down! STAY. DOWN.*)

The word-thoughts struck her in another blow. Ia's leg slipped out from under her. She had never faced the force of a psychodominant before, let alone one of Helstead's high rank.

Dazed, struggling to breathe, she groped for her rage-scattered wits.

(*I don't care* what *he's done, you will* not *kill him!*) Helstead growled, squeezing her arm for emphasis. Ia choked and she eased up slightly—then squeezed in again. (*You* will *keep him alive!*)

(*Alright!*) she snarled back, capitulating to the sheer weight of the lieutenant commander's demands. (*Alright, he'll live! For* now.)

Surging to her feet as the forward door slid open, Ia strode down the hall. It wasn't difficult to move with the shorter woman on her back; stocky as she was, Helstead didn't weigh nearly as much as Ia's exercise weight suit. She did stagger, though, when the ship rocked around them, attacked by enemy missiles. At least the movement forced Helstead to shift her left arm, clutching more now at Ia's shoulders than compressing her muscular throat.

The rage was coming back. Swift strides turned into jumps as she ascended the stairs, not bothering with the lift. More doors hissed open, clearing the way. Clinging to her CO, Helstead continued that low, steady, mental hiss, (. . . *You will not kill him . . . you need him alive . . . you will not kill him . . . you need him alive!*)

An outward snap of her hand hissed open the L-pod's door. A slash snapped the restraint straps. With a startled yelp, Private Goré Sung tumbled through the door and swayed to a halt. The only thing preventing Ia from slamming him bodily into the far bulkhead was that damnable, insistent, nagging whisper named Helstead.

Jerking him closer with a clench of her fist, Ia stopped him telekinetically, halting him centimeters from her face. "You *shova v'shakk-tor!*" she snarled as he stared back at her with brown eyes so wide, she could see the full ring of their whites. "You have *slaughtered* this galaxy!"

Grabbing him physically by the throat, she dragged him—both of them—into the desert. Forced him into life-stream after life-stream at the galaxy's end. Forced him to watch worlds being devoured and stars torn apart.

(*You need him alive!*) Helstead yelled deep in her head.

(*No.* I do not. *Not anymore.*) She flung both of them out. Not gentle. Not kind. Sung gasped for air, choking like a

drowning man, though Ia wasn't physically squeezing his throat.
Helstead clung with trembling limbs.

(*You . . . you can repair . . .*) she gasped.

"HOW can I repair a DEAD MAN?" Ia screamed with
mind and voice. Sung winced. She didn't see what Helstead
did, her attention reserved for the careless murderer in front of
her. Ia flung him up with her mind and her hand, slamming
him into the ceiling, provoking a pained grunt.

Helstead dropped free. She landed on hands and knees
behind Ia, panting from the force of that mental counterblow.
"I . . . I don't believe . . . in the . . . the no-win scenario, *Captain*," she growled between breaths. Her hand gripped Ia's
ankle, reinforcing her words mentally as well as physically.
"And I know *you* don't! You. Will. *Drop* him!"

Sung dropped. He *thudded* onto the deckplates with a groan
and a faint *crack*, one hand caught awkwardly under his ribs.
With a feral snarl, Ia flung the force she had been about to use
on him into the bulkhead to her left. It *crunched*, denting inward
by at least a third of a meter. Her hand snapped out again, and
the dazed private was yanked up, body floating horizontally
in her grip.

Coughing, he squinted at her. Ia leaned in close, but did not
touch him. She let the madness in her gaze, the rage barely
leashed in her words, do all of the damage.

"Pray I can find a way to fix the *dead man* you've destroyed.
Pray I can find a way to replace his life! Because of *one* man's
death, unless I can fix it, *you* have doomed this entire galaxy
to a fate worse than a Salik's favorite lunch. Pray I *can* find a
way," she snarled, bringing his nose to within a centimeter of
her own. "Because if I cannot . . . *pray I kill you before I am
through*!"

Flinging him away, she let him tumble down the corridor.
He grunted and yelled with each impact before skidding to a
stop. For a moment, he tried to get up, then groaned and sagged
to the deck.

She hadn't killed him. By luck, and the grace of God, or at
least by the demands of Delia Helstead, Ia *hadn't* killed him.
But it was a near thing. As it was, Ia could not see what to do
with him. The timestreams were nothing but barren, bleak
desert around her, empty fields with nothing left but cracked
and lifeless dust.

Behind her, she heard the other woman pushing to her feet.
". . . Orders, sir?"

Oddly enough, Helstead's simple question centered her. Ia
still couldn't See a damned thing, but her training as an officer
kicked in. There were rules and regulations for this sort of
thing. Rules and regs that had to be followed. Hands fisted
against the urge to physically express the rage morphing back
into grief, Ia swallowed.

"Take the prisoner to the Infirmary. He has a cracked wrist.
When it has been set, lock him in the brig. The prisoner is *not*
allowed to speak to anyone about anything other than his wrist,"
she added tightly, glaring at Sung as he started to stir again.
"Unless and until I can figure out what to do with this *nightmare*
he's caused, this ship stays on lockdown, category Ultra Classified. No messages out but for the fact that we're on
lockdown."

"That won't cut it with the rest of the fleet, Captain,"
Helstead told her. "They *know* about the Friendly Fire. They
will be expecting an acknowledgment and an arraignment."

Ia cursed under her breath. Her head hurt, throbbing with
the ache of her unsatisfied rage. Scrubbing at her scalp to try
and ease it enough to let her think, she dislodged her headset.
Impatiently, she stripped it completely off, glared at it, then
wrestled the thin curve of plexi back over her head. *"Captain
Ia to Private Togama."*

"Togama here, Captain. Uh . . . is everything alright?"

*"No. Acknowledge and register the Friendly Fire with the
TUPSF Hardberger. The accused is Private Second Class Goré
Sung. Inform them we will be contacting them with the details
of his arraignment and tribunal at a point in the near future,
then broadband cast to the fleet that we are experiencing technical difficulties of an Ultra-Classified nature and will be
disengaging from combat and remaining silent while those
difficulties are addressed."*

Wincing, she tried to focus her thoughts on the timeplains.
The wafting dust of the empty desert clung to her feet like
cement. Head throbbing, she forced herself all the way back to
the present, to survey the wreckage of the Now with a dispas-
sionate eye.

*"Addendum, inform the TUPSF La Granger, Sword's Breath,
and Saibo-Maru to stay out of the sunward side of Station 3's*

wreckage. Tell the TUPSF Dian Wei to break off in two minutes and spend a full minute coming about before reentering the fight. And tell Admiral P'thenn aboard Battle Platform Hum-Vee that there are sabotage systems still active on Stations 1, 3, 5 and 8. Boarding parties must use extreme caution. Repeat that we are going to be running silent under an Ultra-Classified-Situation flag, then do just that."

"Ah . . . Aye, sir. I got all that," Togama replied. *"Sir, what is the situation?"*

"That is on a need-to-know basis, and you do not need to know." Pulling off the headset, she let the band curl up and stuffed it into her pocket.

Helstead had edged around her in order to approach the injured private. Pulling him to his feet, she wrapped her arm around his ribs. "With permission, Captain, I'll take him to the Infirmary."

Ia dipped her head, giving it. That did require the two of them to shuffle past her. She moved into the alcove of the L-pod's door, but only just enough to let them by. As he came within arm's reach, Ia held his gaze.

"Start. *Praying.* Private," she warned him, clipping off each word like a bite. Like the snap of a spark in an overheated fire. Like an ice-cold funeral pyre.

He swallowed and looked away.

Only when he was gone from her sight did the fire and the fury still seething within her finally die. Without it, ice-cold fear washed through her veins, prickling her skin with gut-deep dread. The horror robbed the strength from her flesh. Sagging to the deck, Ia doubled over. She struggled against the nausea, but nothing helped. It just built and built until she doubled over and retched.

Not much came out, the smallest of blessings. It had been too long since she last ate, too long since she entered combat. Too long since she had believed she could win against Time and Fate. She heaved again and again for a full minute or more, then sagged back on her heels.

The ship swayed gently around her, bumping her shoulder into the wall. Drained, numb but for the aching, chilling pain, Ia pushed slowly back to her feet. She didn't know where to go or what to do, only that she couldn't stay there. Couldn't stop that arrowing laser, couldn't stop that emerging missile, couldn't stop the gaping hole in the aging *Hardberger*'s hull, its old-fashioned turret and its precious, progenitive cargo now utterly destroyed.

Over and over, those last few seconds replayed in her mind. One hand braced on the wall, she shuffled forward, turning occasionally, moving sightlessly. The *Hellfire* swayed again, then steadied. Noises echoed down the corridor. They belonged to Togama, issuing orders no doubt relayed either from Nabouleh, who had the helm, or Helstead, who was in charge of the watch. They made no sense to her, being just a babble of noise.

Nothing made sense anymore. Nothing *meant* anything anymore. It was all gone, drained away with the loss of a single, precious, supposed to be anonymous life. But that life was gone.

Private First Grade Joseph N'ablo N'Keth. Gone. TUPSF-Navy five years, and a competent gunner. Gone. Retired from active service in five more years. Gone. Settled on his homeworld of Eiaven. Gone. Great-plus-grandfather of the Redeemer, whose life had been meant to redirect the Savior's, so that she would be in the right mind as well as the right place . . .

Gone.

All gone.

A long time ago, when she had been just seven or so, her mothers had shown her a beautiful, fragile, heirloom teacup. They had explained its history, how the delicate, rose-sculpted porcelain had come all the way from Earth via three other worlds. Amelia had urged her to take it in her hands, to hold for herself this relic from her family's past.

The young Iantha had tucked her hands firmly behind her back, shaking her head. All she could tell them was, "But I can't put it back together, Mothers. I just can't!" At the time, her young self couldn't explain why all she could see was the teacup shattered on the floor, scattered into pieces despite the beige plexcrete cushioning their feet.

In all the years since, Ia had not once touched that teacup. She didn't even know where it was now. Didn't know if it had survived the destruction of her mothers' restaurant, survived the move to their new, underground life, or survived . . . anything, really.

In her mind, as both a child and an adult, the teacup was and had always been forever gone. Shattered. Broken. Wrong.

". . . Captain?"

With effort, she looked up and focused. Somehow, she had gone from the starboard of the ship to the port in her blinded movements. The last person she needed to see stood before her, concern wrinkling the brow above his worried blue eyes. Finnimore Hollick.

He wasn't alone; his teammate Schwadel had halted at his side, both men apparently released from their battle posts. Vaguely, she realized she was close to their quarters, but all she could see was Hollick's middle-aged face, and a badly, badly broken teacup at his feet.

"Captain, are you alright?" Hollick asked her gently.

She opened her mouth. Nothing came out for a long, long moment. Teacup. Shattered. The desert that was left. All she could feel was another icy-hot rush, this time of shame as well as panic.

". . . I . . . I'm sorry."

The words escaped. Schwadel blinked and frowned, but she didn't look at him. It was Hollick she couldn't look away from. Hollick, who was a fellow Free World Colonist at heart. Hollick, who *knew* with unswerving faith that his Prophet . . . that his Prophet would . . .

"I'm sorry . . . I'm so, *so sorry*," she whispered, vision blurring. "I didn't mean . . . I didn't . . . I *tried*," she begged him to understand. Shaking her head, she said it again, tears now trickling down her face. "I *tried*! I tried so *hard* . . . I . . . If . . . I ffff . . ."

She couldn't even say the word, but it was there, screaming in the back of her head. *Failed . . . Failed!* She broke with the weight of her shame, head burrowed into her hands to hide herself from his sorrowful gaze. Vaguely, she heard the other man mutter something; the derogatory tone in his voice only confirmed her failure. Hollick snapped something back, then gingerly touched her arms.

"Easy, Captain," he murmured. "This way . . . this way . . . let's get you off the deck . . ."

Shuddering, Ia went. She couldn't see, couldn't breathe through her nose, couldn't stop the tears from seeping free. Couldn't stop whispering the words over and over, *I'm sorry, I tried, I fff . . . I fffff . . . I'm so so sorry . . .*

Shock robbed her of her gifts. Shock, and the destruction

of everything she had strived for over the last ten years of her life. Vaguely aware of being urged to sit, she felt him wrap his arms around her, holding her close as no one else on board dared. Holding her for far longer than even her own mothers could, rocking her gently as she cried in her grief.

It took her a while to realize he was humming a tune. It was a soothing one, and yet somehow sad. His voice wasn't much like her grandfather's, not quite as ragged with age, but it hummed the same melody, over and over. A song about a flower, and the impermanence of life.

A song, she realized, which she herself had transformed years ago into an anthem for her family, for her people back home. *My life I give this day to serve all others, though Hell itself should bar my way . . .*

Fresh tears seeped free at that. She squeezed her eyes shut, to block out the pain, but the words kept echoing in her head. Echoing across the barren, sterile desert that filled the back of her mind. *My life I give this day to serve all others, though Hell itself should bar my way . . . My life I give this day to serve all others . . . My life I give this day . . .*

Another voice echoed across the emptiness of the timeplains. *Did you know I once saved the life of Jesse James? Jesse James Mankiller that is . . . Once saved the life . . .*

My life I give this day . . .

Ia stilled.

His problem was that he didn't lay nearly enough contingencies . . . Me? I have several identities I could assume . . . Several identities I could assume . . . My life I give . . .

The teacup had been shattered. No rose-sculpted porcelain lay intact at her feet, no grass, no water, no life . . . save for the slender, spear-like tip of a tulip leaf peeking up through the shards.

My life I give this day to serve all others . . .

She sniffed, trying to clear her nose, and asked, ". . . Do you?"

Easing the strength of the arms holding her to his chest, Hollick let her sit up. ". . . Sir?"

"Do you?" she repeated, sniffing harder. Ia gripped the front of his grey uniform shirt. "*Do* you give your life?"

It was a desperate gamble, but she knew things about the Mankiller bloodline, things she had once peeked at in curiosity.

Jesse, or rather Jessica James, who married David Mankiller, had been crushed from the waist down in a ground-car accident . . . and yet somehow, less than twenty-four hours later, had walked out of the hospital whole and alive. *I once saved the life of Jesse James . . .*

Hollick covered her fingers with his hand. "I have believed in you since my first Fire Girl attack, Prophet. Even in gravity-based exile on Gateway Station, I had heard of you, and believed in you. If there is *anything* I can do to help you fix whatever went wrong, I will do it. As my Prophet wills it, my life—my everything, whatever you need—is yours."

Sniffing hard, she nodded. She nodded and sat up. It was a long shot, far longer than the shot she had fired on that first Choya invasion fleet. She still couldn't see any life beyond that single slip of a flower leaf, but it *was* there, on the timeplains. There was hope.

Focusing on him, she nodded again, more slowly and soberly this time. "I'm afraid it has come to that. Finnimore Hollick, I call upon you to give up your life . . . and take up the life of the man we just lost. You will lose *everything* that is yours. I will . . . I will have your body altered, and imprint his personality over your own, and . . . and fix it with subconscious impulses to follow every single step the real one would've taken and known. And . . . and we will *fix* this broken . . . this broken teacup . . . and *fool* the whole God-be-damned universe."

Lifting her free hand, she swiped away the tears that were falling again. Nodding a third time, Ia pushed herself to her feet, trying to think. She could feel the shards of porcelain cutting into her tender, young feet every time she tried to move out of the desert that had swallowed the grassy plains.

"I need . . . I need to go call her, and . . . God . . . I don't know what she's going to want for this. I can't *see* anything at the moment—but if *you* can have blind faith in me," she added, turning to face the man on the couch, "then *I* can have that faith."

Sober, somber, Hollick pushed to his feet. "*Ia'nn sud-dha,* my Captain." He hesitated, then asked, "What will become of my own life if I am to take this other man's place? I mean, how will you explain my absence?"

Ia shook her head. "I don't know. I . . . I guess I'll have to convince her to take on *your* form and place. At least for a few days, maybe a week or two. There are . . . there *were* fights up ahead where it would be possible for you—the old you—to die, freeing her to go about her business. You, the new you, will have already gone off on your way.

"Things will have changed," she dismissed, shaking her head. "Sung . . . *shakk* . . . He'll have to undergo a tribunal, and . . . punishment. I'll have to schedule time for that."

Ia closed her eyes, once again feeling ice-cold and sick with dread. Caning. Not just for Private Sung, but for herself as well. *Unrestrained, and without hesitation . . . That won't be pleasant. But if it works . . . if we* can *fool Time and Fate . . .*

God. If this works . . . I will bear every single lash without complaint.

Opening her eyes, she nodded. ". . . Right. I have work to do. You are *not* allowed to discuss any of this with your roommate, with your superiors, with your family or your friends. You are to remain silent on this entire situation, and you will pretend that everything is normal . . . or as normal as can be," Ia allowed, mindful that she had just spent untold minutes grieving in his quarters, "until I call for you. Is that clear, Private?"

"Sir, yes, sir," he agreed, squaring his shoulders and leveling his chin. "Clearer than crysium, sir."

Ia raked her fingers through her hair. The bangs were getting a little long again. She'd have to visit Private Antenelli of the 3rd Platoon, D Epsilon for another trim. The private had been a hairstylist before choosing to enlist.

Thinking about getting her hair cut, an utter triviality, felt absurd. Not since she was fifteen had she felt this off-balance and disconnected from reality. Shaking it off, she gave Hollick a nod.

"Considering I'm off to go make a bargain with a devil while holding the dirty end of the stick, that's an apt choice, mentioning the Devil's Sticks—thank you for watching over me just now," she added, and held out her hand. "After the change, you will never remember, never know who and what Finnimore Hollick was . . . and no one else outside this ship can know where you've gone . . . but I will make *sure* Private Hollick is listed as one of the heroes of the Damned, so that no one else will forget that much of it."

He clasped her hand, and gave her a lopsided smile.

"Considering I'll be the first on the crew list to receive a Black Heart, it's a dubious honor. But I accepted long ago that it might just come to that."

She met his gaze steadily, squeezing back. "So did I, soldier. I'm sorry to have to say this, but . . . thank you."

Releasing his hand, she turned toward the door. He chuckled softly just as she reached it. Turning, Ia glanced back at him. Hollick shrugged and spread his hands.

"It just occurred to me that you've guaranteed me a long life, even though *I* won't remember it. Um . . . I *do* get a long life, right?" he added.

Ia gave him a lopsided smile. "You'll die somewhere in your late eighties, survived by a beloved wife, five kids, thirteen grandkids, two great-grands, and more on the way. And the unsung legacy of having a great-plus-grandson become the Redeemer."

His eyes widened. "The Redeemer? The one who saves the Savior from herself? I . . ." He stopped, licked his lips, and tried again. "I . . . I think I can live with that. Stars—is *that* who we lost?"

Quickly lifting her finger to her lips, Ia hushed him. "Shh. Say nothing more. This shattering will never have happened if we are very, very lucky in our attempt to trick Fate."

Pantomiming the zipping of his lips, Hollick tucked both hands behind his back and nodded solemnly, watching her leave his cabin in a modified Parade Rest.

Finnimore Hollick, she thought. *Patron saint of the ultimate sacrifice. A holier soul than mine, for I at least* know *why I had to give everything up.* Shaking it off, she oriented herself outside his quarters and hurried for the section seal. It occurred to her just as she reached the door to her office that she still had more damage control to do.

Detouring all the way to the bridge, she hooked her fingers into the controls, opening the door far more gently than when she had left. Helstead wasn't inside, but Spyder was. He glanced her way and straightened in his seat at the backup gunnery position. Hers, the command station, remained empty.

"Cap'n," he greeted, giving her brief, watchful nod. "What's th' situation?"

"I was about to ask you that," she replied, moving across

the cabin and mounting the dais at the back of the room. "Show me the battlefield. Give me a tactical analysis."

"S'all over, Cap'n," he told her, tapping the controls. "All but th' screamin'. Th' Salik are dead or fled, th' Choya what went with 'em, an' th' *Hardberger*'s been threatenin' t' call down th' Admiral-General on our heads."

Ia studied the screen, reading the flags and accompanying texts of the attached analysis. More information was still coming in as each of the ships in the attack fleet continued to exchange and sort through information. What the *Hellfire* was receiving of that was passive only, incoming from all channels and functioning sensor arrays with nothing outgoing.

"The *Hum-Vee* wants our records an' analysis," Spyder told her in an undertone. "Admiral P'thenn's last message sounds like he's gotten a bit testy, but then it's been an hour an' a half."

She'd cried for that long? Her time sense was that shattered? Ia blinked. She absorbed the information for a moment, then dismissed it. Her plans to kite the *Hellfire* out of here and go off to another location for repairs and the next fight were gone, blown up along with Joseph N'Keth. Now all she could do was pray for a strong enough roll of duct tape, and a clever enough touch with a *trompe l'oeil* paintbrush.

"Maintain comm silence, other than to repeat that we are handling an Ultra-Classified Situation on board. Where's the *Hardberger* now?" Ia asked, wondering what sort of remains might have survived the explosion that wiped out its P-pod 29 turret.

"Cozied up t' th' *Hum-Vee*," he said, pointing at the blip on the main screen in the distance. "We're jes' wanderin' aimlessly 'round the more stable bits o' the local space. Solar sail's shot t' hell, but there's no flare or ion storm at th' moment, so no need t' hide behind it."

As he said it, she could sense the near future of the cometary knot. Nothing was destined to wash through for another eighteen hours, though in nineteen, the more damaged ships would do well to hide behind that sail. "Right. Here's what I can tell you."

That caught the attention of her bridge crew. Nabouleh, Wildheart at navigation, Togama, Yé at ops, Aquinar, and Spyder all stared at her. Ia nodded.

"Private Sung did indeed cause the incident of Friendly Fire. And he will pay for his damage to the *Hardberger*'s hull. But . . . he did *not* kill the gunner who was manning their turret."

"'E whot?" Spyder asked her, blinking.

"I will tell this *entire* crew what happened at a special board-room meeting," Ia promised them. "But for now, you are to maintain communications silence, and you are not to speak of it outside this bridge. Private Yé, I will probably need a great deal of energy routed somewhere on the ship. Probably to my quarters. I don't know yet. How full are the tanks?"

"Ah . . . we're at fifty-six percent capacity, sir," she stated, glancing at the data on her screens. Ia grimaced, then shook it off.

"I just hope that'll be enough. Everything must be self-contained until our little Ultra-Classified Situation has been fixed." Moving over to her normal station, Ia leaned over the console, pushed up the hatch, and pressed her fingers against the hidden electrodes. Pressed, held, and absorbed electricity until her hair crackled and rose off the nape of her neck. Eyes wide, Spyder leaned back from her, though he sat a good three meters away. She gave him a slight, lopsided smile. "Relax. You're not my target."

"Ah, beggin' pardon, but . . . th' lieutenant commander said you weren't allowed t' kill anybody," he reminded her.

Her mouth twisted in rueful bitterness. "I know. If the Admiral-General calls, inform her that we still have an Ultra-Classified Situation to contain, and that it is too dangerous a situation to explain over the comms. Reassure her that I *will* explain in due time, then end transmission."

Togama cleared his throat. "Right. Tell her to mind her own business, then hang up on the Admiral-General herself. I always wondered what it would feel like to be caned . . ."

"I suggest you *not* joke about that in my presence," Ia stated flatly, flinching inside at his careless, unknowing words. "Not today, and not for the rest of this week. As you were, meioas."

Nodding to Spyder, she retreated through the back door to her office, and from there, to her private quarters.

CHAPTER 14

There was no greater hell in my life up to that point than the moment I realized my teacup had broken and that it lay shattered at my feet. No greater release into purgatory than to realize I had one chance at duct-taping it back together. One shot at using a trompe l'oeil *trick to fool the universe into thinking the cup was still firmly intact.*

I can't tell you what I did, and I won't tell you what I did. Not ever. Explain a stage magician's trick, and all the magic of it, all the wonder and the awe and the innocence of one's ignorance are thus forever lost. In fact, it can never again be regained; the illusion is spoiled, for the wires will always be on the mind. But I did it. And I paid the price for it. I paid for every drop spilled from that shattered, rebuilt teacup.

~Ia

Summoning her faction protector was not too terribly difficult. Ia had already practiced the mental twist of energies that opened up the tiny thread of a cosmic string permanently linking Belini to the corner wall of her living room. The one thing it did take was power, which was why she had stocked up at the command console.

It took a while for Belini to respond. As she waited, Ia probed at the timestreams, trying to shift herself away from

that endgame desolation. The interior of her head felt broken
and bruised. She did manage to shift her viewpoint back to
where she should be, in the here and now . . . but every time
she pulled out, then flipped back in, the desert at the end of the
game was the first thing she could see. Not the waters of her
own life and not the grassy banks of a thriving prairie.

The flash of light against her closed lids and the slight shift
in air pressure that teased across her face warned her that the
Feyori had arrived. Opening her eyes, Ia watched the silvery-
dark sphere dip partway into the wall. That dimmed the overhead lights for several seconds, until the overgrown bubble
lightened from deep grey hematite to an almost platinum shade.
A flash of light popped the soap bubble, depositing Belini on
the carpeted deck.

Bare toes digging into the light grey pile, she shifted her
hands to her pink-clad hips, once again looking like a demented,
wingless pixie. "Well. I certainly didn't expect *you* to call."
She paused, eyed Ia, then shook her head. "Almost made it,
didn't you? Like I told you, I'm not going to help."

"What?" Ia frowned for a moment in confusion, then shook
it off. "I don't know what you're talking about. I called you
because I need a very big favor. One that is in *your* best interests . . . because if you don't help me, to my exact needs, the
Game ends. In fact, the Game *has* ended."

That made the Feyori frown. "What do you mean, the Game
has ended?"

Ia sighed and explained. "One of my stupidest gunners
refused to stop firing when I ordered him to. His weapon
impacted on a fellow Terran ship, and destroyed one of the
projectile turrets . . . and with it, destroyed its gunner. That
gunner was to have been the great-plus-grandfather of one of
the key figures I needed to have in place to guide the Savior
into preventing the destruction of this galaxy. The destruction
that would have put an end to everything your race is currently
doing with the matter-based species.

"That destruction *will* put an end to everything . . . unless
you and I can fool the universe into thinking that that gunner
is still alive and still available to take his rightful place."

Belini wrinkled her nose. "No," she stated flatly. "Absolutely
not. I have my *own* places to be—"

"Not *you*," Ia dismissed, rising from her couch. "Private

Finnimore Hollick has volunteered to be the body and soul to be sculpted into the missing gunner's place. I *do* need you to stick around long enough to pretend to be Hollick in his place, but there should be a chance to kill him off in a bodiless way in about a week if we do everything right. At that point, you can pop off to wherever, and the broken bits of the universe will have been duct-taped back together."

She considered Ia's words, her eyes aquamarine, not quite silver. "What about this Hollick fellow? What about *his* rightful place in the universe?"

Ia shook her head, raking one hand through her hair. Again, her bangs were irritating her, a stupid little bother in the face of this disaster.

"I only chose him to be a crew member because of three things. He has the right skills and instincts to do his job well. His presence or absence in any other part of this war will not have made a damn difference one way or another. And because a part of me knew there was something he could do that would help my cause. I thought it was just be a steadying, faith-filled influence among my crew, but . . .

"This is probably the most extreme thing I could have asked of him, aside from maybe asking him to pull out his own intestines with a rusted spoon," she quipped sarcastically. "But I did ask, and he did agree to it. And don't tell me you can't do it. I *know* you can.

"You said yourself you saved Jesse Mankiller's life, and that you can take on any shape you like. I know the Feyori calling himself Doctor Silverstone can read thoughts and reshape his own body to copy the life and memories of a man whose hovercar crashed in the Australian bush. And with *my* help," she stated, "plugging the two of you directly into the missing gunner's original life-stream, we can guide him into having the right memories and making all the right choices the original would've made. A perfect *trompe l'oeil* replacement. Or at least one hopefully good enough to fool Time itself."

Belini considered her words. Drawing in a breath, she asked shrewdly, "And how will you explain how this gunner survived?"

Ia spread her hands. "Lieutenant Commander Helstead is a teleporter. She sensed the danger he was in, and teleported him blindly onto this ship." Her own words made her pause; Ia realized with another sick flush of ice and heat that such a thing would be a violation of the Admiral-General's command to permit no one else aboard . . . Feyori notwithstanding. Swallowing, she added, "That's why we've been locked down under the claim of an Ultra-Classified Situation. The teleport stunned him psychically. I then ordered him to be kept sedated while I figured out where he came from and what to do with him."

Nodding slowly, Belini accepted that line of reasoning. "That might actually work."

"It has to," Ia murmured. "I can't see any other options."

There *was* another option, but Ia knew it would involve the deaths of a good three or four Feyori. That was not something any of them were prepared to do. Not at this point in the Game, not when Ia herself was still a mere pawn and not a powerful fellow player.

"So," Belini muttered, ticking off the options on her pixie-slender fingers. "We have a willing body and soul to take the gunner's place. We have myself to take this Hollick fellow's place for about a week, until I can safely pretend to die and head off on my own business. And you've covered how the gunner gets on board. Do you at least have bits of this missing gunner's body on hand, so I can get a direct reading of his genetics?"

Ia opened her mouth, then closed it. Tightening her jaw, she pushed past the desert now occupying the back of her mind, forced herself to the present patch in the timestreams, and rooted around in the very recent past. Finally, she nodded. "I don't have the whole body available, but there is a surviving bit of it tumbling through space. It's badly burned and frozen, but it should still be enough for you to read his DNA and rebuild Hollick in his shape."

Belini held out her hand. "Show me."

Nodding, Ia gripped it and complied. When she was sure the Feyori knew exactly where to look, she released the other woman. "While you go do that, I'll fetch Hollick up here."

Belini rolled her eyes. "If he's going to be sedated, he'll have to be stashed in the Infirmary, now won't he? Come on, *think*, woman. That's what that blob of grey stuff in your skull is supposed to be good for, with you fleshies."

"Well, if you'll excuse me, I just had my entire reason for living *smashed* at my feet," Ia retorted, hands going to her hips.

"And for some God-be-damned reason, I cannot approach the timestreams from my usual spot in the present but am instead stuck with the pain of arriving in the midst of the desolation caused by the Zida"ya fleet! I think, given all the *shakk* I've just gone through, that I am holding it together fairly well in spite of all that!"

The look the Meddler gave her was a cool, assessing one. Finally, Belini nodded. "Right, then. Keep holding it together. This will take a lot out of both of us. Go make yourself useful by hauling several power cables to the Infirmary. This isn't reshaping myself, and it isn't restoring a woman's rightful body from a broken to a whole state. And you had *better* be right about being able to pattern his mind and his life-choices, or all this effort will go to waste. All this *energy* will go to waste.

"I'm a Feyori, child," Belini reminded Ia. "I don't like to waste my food." Popping with a flare of light, she re-formed as a silvery soap bubble and swooped through the cabin wall, vanishing.

Ia sighed and scrubbed at her face. *Yet another person to drag into the conspiracy. God,* she begged, *help me. Make sure Jesselle Mishka is in a cooperative mood.*

He was perfect. Joseph N'ablo N'Keth, twenty-seven years old and identical to the original in every way that frozen chunks of DNA and increasingly easier pre- and postcognitive forays onto the timeplains could make him to be. Exhausted yet elated, Ia probed the timestreams one more time and nodded in satisfaction.

The original paths were still damaged, but much of it could be salvaged. Only a few things would have to be changed here in the near future, and at about one hundred to one hundred and twenty minor, major, and key timing points down the way, depending on how things panned out. She'd have to stint herself on sleep again to rewrite several of her prophetic directives, but it wouldn't be a waste of energy.

"Blood pressure 103 over 65, encephalographic activity normal, delta brainwaves declining," Mishka reported. "You even managed to re-create traces of mucus in his lungs from a minor chest cold. A pity your kind won't cooperate more often to help heal the injured and dying."

Belini narrowed her eyes but didn't deign to speak.

Ia did it for her. "Doctor, have you ever contemplated the philosophy of *why* people die? Even the Feyori do it. There is a reason for it."

"And that reason is?" Jesselle asked, arching one blonde brow in skepticism.

"Contemplate it," Ia told her bluntly, not willing to give the other woman a free ride. "Can you keep him sedated?"

"I can. And I have agreed, having voiced my objections, to uphold this little charade," the doctor added. "You're lucky Private Hollick was willing to undergo a telepathic scan from me so I could make sure he was fully informed and truly willing."

"I had my own objections as well, Doctor," Ia told her, "but they got blown to pieces by Sung's willful little act of disobedience. Helstead, stay here and stand watch over our guest. I'm going to go order the ship into dock, and call a shipwide boardroom meeting. The two of you are exempt from attending, since I need you to keep an eye on our 'guest' here—Belini, charge back up and get changed into your new body," she added. "You'll need to show up as Private Hollick."

"Sir, yes, sir," she quipped, flipping Ia a fluttery mock-salute.

Rolling her eyes, Ia retreated from the Infirmary. She was exhausted and would not be able to rest for many more hours to come, but the timestreams were back under her control. Bruised and banged about, duct-taped together with a snapped wrist much like Private Sung's, but once more hers to command.

She prayed all the way to the bridge that she would never have to do that again.

It was still third watch, but Togama wasn't on duty at the moment; he had been replaced by Private James Kirkman. Nabouleh was back on duty, having swapped places with Sangwan twice over the last three hours. Spyder wasn't on the bridge. Technically he was supposed to be asleep by now, and Ia had granted him leave to go, since all they were doing was floating in space several hundred thousand kilometers away from the remains of the Salik base.

Altering Hollick had consumed a lot of their spare time, shattered and duct-taped back together as it was, a lot more than a Feyori needed to just change themselves, or to heal someone else. His mind and his memories had taken longer to create than his revised body.

"Private Kirkman," Ia stated as she entered the bridge, "contact the TUPSF *Hum-Vee* and inform them that most of our situation has now been contained. Tell them we are coming in to dock, and ask them for a gantry position and refueling priority. Once you have done that, contact the *Hardberger* and let them know we are on our way in to coordinate with them for the arraignment and war tribunal of Private Goré Sung regarding the Fatality Thirteen: Friendly Fire incident."

"Aye, Captain. Ah, sir," he added, twisting to look back at her, "the Admiral-General left standing orders to be contacted the moment you broke communication silence. Shall I put you through?"

Pulling her headset out of her pocket, Ia nodded. "Ping the Admiral-General and connect us the moment the call goes through."

Dropping into the command seat, she hooked the headset in place, then started to pull the restraint straps in place. They were still broken, snapped physically and telekinetically in her earlier rage. Sighing, Ia gave up trying to secure herself. None of their maneuvering needs would require it in the next several hours; it was just habit for her to buckle up in this chair.

"Private Rammstein," she ordered the man seated at the operations console, "put in a work order to engineering to get up here and replace the command-seat safety harness, plus the straps in L-pod 20. I want fresh sets ready to go before we leave the zone."

"Aye, sir."

"Captain, we have pingback. Conversational lag is four and a half seconds," Kirkman warned her. "Admiral-General Myang on the line in three . . . two . . ."

Christine Myang appeared on the screen. Her face was creased, her eyes bleary, and her chin-length, grey-salted black locks were mussed. She was also clad in a loose-necked tunic in a faded heather grey, and her face hovered unnaturally close to the pickups, looming too large on Ia's main screen. Blinking twice, she focused on the screen at her end and narrowed her eyes in a silent, furious glare.

It took effort, but Ia did not flinch. "Admiral-General, sir. I apologize for the lengthy delay, but the Ultra-Classified security protocols had to be maintained. We sustained minor damage to the main cannon, which had to be fixed immediately," she lied smoothly, "and . . . have had to contain an unexpected addition."

"Contain?" Myang asked, voice rough from sleep. "Unexpected addition? Explain."

"We are inbound to Battle Platform *Hum-Vee*, where I will be personally escorting Private Sung to his tribunal session as soon as it can be arranged," Ia stated blandly. "The charges are twofold, Fatality Five: Disobeying a Direct Order, and Fatality Thirteen: Friendly Fire. I am fully aware and prepared to carry out the double-indemnity sentence of corporal punishment his actions will accrue, and will do so without restraint or hesitation.

"I do, however, need . . . beg . . . a suspension of our standing orders to permit no other personnel aboard the *Hellfire*," she continued. That earned her another narrow-eyed stare. Drawing a deep breath, Ia explained. "We initially thought—as does the TUPSF *Hardberger*—that their gunner was killed when Private Sung fired through the Salik shipyard debris and struck a missile emerging from the old Kellick-class projectile-pod turret, number 29, on board the *Hardberger*. This was not the case.

"Lieutenant Commander Delia Helstead, reacting on instincts triggered by my telepathically broadcasted precognitive distress, blind-teleported him instead to the safety of our ship. He was knocked unconscious by the transport, and Helstead and I abandoned the bridge as soon as we realized he was on board. We have kept him sedated this entire time, firmly secured under observation in the Infirmary," Ia told the head of the Space Force, breaking Fatality Forty-Three: Perjury, by lying to her superior officer without hesitation. "By the letter of our orders, his presence aboard is a violation of our Ultra-Classified status. By the *spirit* of our orders . . . he hasn't seen a damned thing.

"So I request . . . I *beg*," she added, meeting Myang's soft frown through the vidlink, "that you forgive his trespass and dismiss the charge of Grand High Treason that would otherwise be incurred, as there is no possible way he could learn any of this ship's secrets, sedated as he has been all this time."

Several seconds ticked by. More than enough to send Ia's words all the way to the Admiral-General's quarters back on Earth and send back a response, thrice. Finally, Myang grunted, "Why should I? What's so goddamn special about this one soldier that you panicked so hard, it caused your junior officer to risk both of you being hanged for daring to bring him on board?"

"I don't think Helstead was actually thinking at that moment, sir," Ia pointed out carefully. "Her reaction speed to *my* distress was faster than conscious thought. She has been recovering from a backlash headache all this time. As for why . . . this gunner is one Private First Grade Joseph N'Keth. He was and is destined to be the great-plus-grandfather of one of the key figures who will prevent the Zida"ya from successfully invading and destroying our galaxy three hundred years from now."

"You mean two hundred and ninety-nine," Myang corrected her. "It was three hundred years into the future *last* year."

Ia shook her head, then wobbled it. "No, I mean three centuries, sir, as in a vague figure of inexactitude. It wouldn't do to give everyone in this day and age an exact date of their arrival because the moment the invaders are actually noticed will depend on *who* does the noticing, and how much of that information gets back to my prophesied agents. It's enough for people in this era to know that it will happen at a rough date in the future because there is nothing we can do to stop something that'll take place long after we're all dead. We have other problems on our hands right now."

"Charming. And so very cheerful. So. This gunner, Private N'Keth . . . Wait, is that N'Keth, as in that holy lineage from V'Dan? The one with the special blue *jungen* marks?" Myang asked her, frowning.

"Sir, yes, sir," Ia confirmed. "He doesn't have any himself, but he is of that bloodline. He's from Eiaven, which is a jointly settled heavyworld, and chose to go into the Terran service rather than the V'Dan. Just as Helstead, who is also from Eiaven, chose to go into the Terran Space Force, and just as I chose that way as well, coming from Sanctuary."

Again, Myang mulled over her words for longer than the hyperrelay's turnaround time would allow.

". . . He's really that important?" she finally asked Ia.

"I wouldn't have panicked so badly that Helstead reacted to my psychic broadcast without a thought for the rules and regs if he wasn't, sir," Ia pointed out dryly. That much was the truth, if one counted the way the shorter woman had given chase, trying to prevent Ia from killing Private Sung. "If I could've saved him myself, I would've, regardless of the consequences . . . and I *would* accept the punishment for Grand High Treason during wartime as part of our agreement, but you still need me to be very much alive, sir."

This time, her reply came back within the allotted turnaround time. "Alive and uncaned?" Myang asked her dryly, sitting back from the screen a little. "Is that what you're going to ask for next?"

"Sir, no, sir," Ia denied crisply. "I accepted my double-indemnity with the willingness of full foresight of all possible consequences. However many strokes the tribunal assigns to Private Sung, I will endure them, blow for blow, without restraint or hesitation. It is only being hung, drawn, and quartered that I object to, sir. It'd be a little too difficult to continue saving the galaxy this week if I'm not alive to do it. You still need me at the helm of this ship, and its replacement . . . but there's nothing in there that says I have to be comfortable while I'm in the pilot's seat, sir."

Myang studied Ia for several seconds, then nodded. "Very well. Dispensation granted, so long as this Private N'Keth is kept sedated the entire time he remains on board the *Hellfire* . . . *and* in the understanding that you will disembark and revive him the moment you are safely docked at . . . uh, Battle Platform *Hum-Vee*. Since that is the nearest source of the Judge Advocate General's branch of the Special Forces, assuming you haven't left the Helix Nebula?"

"Sir, no sir. We are still within the same cometary knot as the rest of the local fleet and are inbound to the *Hum-Vee* as I speak," Ia reassured her. "Private Sung has been a valuable member of my crew. I'm not quite sure what possessed him to keep shooting despite my clearly issued orders to cease fire. But the timestreams suggest he will recover from his punishment and serve on this ship with a greater level of obedience and devotion, so I shall suggest to the tribunal judges that he be given a caning only, with no incarceration."

Myang lifted her brows. "No time in the brig? You don't have to be afraid of incarceration yourself, you know. Your double-indemnity clause only covers corporal punishments, so you wouldn't have to be stuffed into a cell alongside him."

"I know I don't have to, Admiral-General," Ia admitted. "But I need good gunners on board, ones who aren't needed on other ships. Despite his extreme lapse in good judgment, Private Sung is still a good gunner, and I can still use him as I continue to fight for you."

That made Myang grunt. She looked tired again, tired and sleepy. "Unfortunately, you have a point. Preliminary intelligence culled from the wreckage of that shipyard base suggests there are several others out there. We *will* need every good gunner we can get. I'll pass along a recommendation of my own to keep him out of the brig. I trust that, stroke for stroke, you will be even *more* careful in the future not to abuse your *carte blanche.*"

"I am *very* determined to avoid anything like this in the future, sir," Ia vowed fervently. "One more thing. Please remind Admiral Genibes to pass along the design corrections I sent you last week to the crews working on the *Hellfire*'s replacement. If they're applied now, that should speed up the construction process."

"I am *not* your personal messenger service, Captain . . . and I'm getting tired of your little 'one more thing' quips. Myang out." Shifting her arm, she thumped what had to be the controls for a bedside screen, and vanished from view.

The monitor replaced her oversized face with its default display of their dead-ahead view. Ia wasn't offended by Myang's retort. She knew the woman would remember to tell Genibes within twenty-four hours.

Sitting back, she contemplated the field of stars and the slowly increasing, green-highlighted dot that would eventually resolve itself into the prickle-burr shape of Battle Platform *Hum-Vee.* Ia had once used it as a base of operations for the two years she served on the now-broken Salik Blockade. A glance at the chrono showed Ia the time—near midnight. If Myang had been asleep, either she had been forced to work off-shift for Aloha City and the Tower, or she had gone halfway around the world for some reason, perhaps to the Space Force Intelligence Division headquartered in Paris. Ia didn't know, and right now, she was too tired to care.

Regardless, the interview had taken place, successfully navigated. Sighing in relief, Ia slumped back in her seat. "Well. That's one obstacle down. Nabouleh, finish docking us at the *Hum-Vee.* Kirkman, coordinate with the JAG office on board the Battle Platform to arrange a quick tribunal for Private Sung.

I'm going to advise him not to contest the charges since we have him dead to rights with all the onboard surveillance equipment. This isn't some dirtside battlefield where it's a case of he said, she said."

"Yes, sir," Kirkman agreed, moving to comply.

"While you're waiting for them to get back to you, inform the entire crew that the moment we dock, the ship is to be sealed and secured at dock, and all personnel—*all* personnel, from bridge crew through to engineering and lifesupport, asleep or awake, are to report to the boardroom, excepting only Doctor Mishka, Lieutenant Commander Helstead, and the patient in the Infirmary."

"Sir?" he asked her.

She knew he was questioning the unusualness of her order. Once military starships left a construction yard and filled with a crew, until the day they were decommissioned or destroyed, they were always monitored. On the bridge, in engineering, and in lifesupport, the three most vital parts of any vessel, there was always, always someone on duty in case of emergency. On civilian ships, the rules could be relaxed, but never on a military vessel.

In this case, though, damage control had to come first, and it had to include her whole crew.

"Company Bible rule number one, Private. Orders issued by Ship's Captain Ia take precedence over all other orders, rules, and regulations. They may be questioned, but they still take precedence." Rising from her seat, she crossed to the back door. "If you'll excuse me, I have had a very long day, one made even longer by having to spend the last three hours cleaning up the mess Private Sung made. And now I need to go change into a Dress uniform since my day doesn't end when we dock.

"I will explain what I can at the boardroom meeting, once I have freshened up. You have your orders, gentlemeioas. Dock the ship, secure it, and make your way to the boardroom."

FEBRUARY 4, 2497 T.S.

Once again, she paused just inside the alcove to the boardroom. Paused, breathed slow and deep, and squared her shoulders. It was just past midnight, Terran Standard Mean Time, which meant she had been up for over thirty hours, not counting her four-hour nap almost a day ago. Every time she let herself feel anything about this situation, icy-sick waves of dread kept sweeping through her body from skin to bones, leaving nausea in its wake. That nausea mixed badly with her exhaustion, leaving her drained with the fear that it could happen again.

But "fear is the mind-killer," as the old saying goes. I accept my fear. I embrace my dread. I know what my worst-case scenarios are, Ia reminded herself. *I have met one, been over-whelmed by it . . . and yet I survive. The universe—the rightful path in Time—survives. Duct-taped back together, but it still survives.*

Reassured, she moved out of the alcove and onto the dais. And nearly stopped. Lieutenant Spyder wasn't seated at the head table as expected. Instead, he stood in the aisle next to one of the front-row tier seats. He did so with his muscular arms folded across his lean chest, looking tired but still as tough and competent as any Marine she'd known.

Beside him, hands in his lap, thumbs cuffed together in restraints since his wrist was being held immobile in a cast while the bone-setting enzymes did their work, sat Private Sung. For a moment, Ia closed her eyes. *I did* not *expect Sung to be brought here . . . but I guess I'm a victim of my own exact wording. Every single crew member except for Doctor Mishka and Lieutenant Commander Helstead . . . which means I'm hoisted up into the air on my own exploding petard.*

Brilliant. At least I know for sure that some of my crew are willing to obey my commands to the letter . . . and the timestreams say I can use this to my advantage. She still couldn't see very far, but that might have been from the fact that working with Belini to imprint Hollick's mind and body with everything the original N'Keth knew had drained a lot of energy out of her.

Gathering her wits, Ia continued forward. Not to the table, but to the front row. Pointing at Sung, she swept her finger behind her. "*You* will take a seat at the officers' table. You will sit there and be respectful of the authority that table represents while I explain to everyone who you are and what you have done."

Not quite meeting her gaze, he nodded and rose. Spyder followed him, and stood behind him when Sung took one of the empty seats at the end. Moving around the other side of the table, Ia stepped in front of her chair but did not sit down. To underscore the severity of the moment, Ia had donned her Dress Blacks and the full complement of her glittery, which required wearing a modified, knee-length version of her jacket. The only thing missing was the cap back in her quarters. She didn't need it just yet.

She began with the facts.

"Just a few hours ago, during the battle against the Salik and Choya forces yesterday, Private Second Class Goré Sung willfully committed an act of Fatality Five: Disobeying a Direct Order, which resulted in an act of Fatality Thirteen: Friendly Fire. The evidence for these charges is absolute. Surveillance scanners pinpointed the offending laser turret as being under his control, and diagnostics prove his headset was fully functional the entire time that I gave repeating orders for all starboard gunners, including him, to cease fire at a specific time.

"Fatality," she stated coldly, "is *exactly* the word for it. For whatever reason Private Sung disobeyed my direct, precognitively backed order, his willful act of disobedience resulted in the death of Private First Grade Joseph N'ablo N'Keth, from the impact of his Starstrike laser on an emerging projectile missile being launched from Private N'Keth's turret.

"Make no mistake about this: The *original* Joseph N'keth is dead. Dead. Dead. Dead," she repeated. "And with his death, Private Sung single-handedly destroyed an entire bloodline *necessary* to prevent the destruction of our entire galaxy three hundred years into the future.

"*That* is why I ordered everyone down our starboard flank to cease fire, because I *knew* the Salik shipyard of Station 5 would fall apart under the force of the incoming blossom bombs. I *knew* there was a chance that one of our weapons would damage the *Hardberger*'s hull if we kept firing. Private Sung is *personally* responsible for the end of the Human race—the end of *every* race in this galaxy—starting three centuries from now, defeated by an alien race so advanced, the *Greys* fled from them in terror."

She turned to face him. Sung looked pale, sitting there with slumped shoulders and a crumpled air about him. No one spoke, though a few of his fellow crew members shifted uncomfortably in their seats.

"I had one shot at getting it right. One path to carefully tend, to make sure that every person, every moment, every chance encounter was *not* by chance but instead instigated by need and design, to create the one person capable of stopping the advance of that enemy race. And *you* shattered it, Private Sung. For whatever reason you *thought* you had, you shattered it." She let that sink in, watching him blanch and crumple inward a little more, huddling awkwardly in his seat. "But by a twist of luck, and the grace of a *good* man of deep and abiding faith . . . I am able to repair most of the damage you made. Not all of it, but most.

"As a result of this twist, this *trompe l'oeil* I have just spent the last duty watch patching, testing, and altering so that the galaxy *will* survive . . . Private Sung *technically* will not be held responsible for the obliteration of this galaxy and all of its native residents." Ia let the implicit threat that he would still be culpable somehow hang in the air for a moment. She continued, shifting her gaze to the others. "One of you has volunteered to take the dead man's place. His body has been altered, his mind repatterned, his face carefully imprinted with all the things the original Joseph N'Keth was supposed to do, *without* my interference, other than making sure he was supposed to survive this last fight.

"Do not speculate among yourselves who that soldier was. Do not *ever* mention it outside this ship," Ia added, jabbing her finger toward the starboard. Toward the Battle Platform holding them in dock. "You mention *any* of this, and Private N'Keth's life will come unraveled, his part in being the great-plus-grandfather of the defense of this galaxy will be destroyed, and *you* will be held accountable for the destruction of every being, every star, and every planet, right alongside Sung.

"Make no mistake. The Zida"ya *are* coming to the Milky Way. They *will* tear apart everything we are and everything we know like uncaring locusts. In all the months you have served with me, you have *seen* the accuracy of my predictions, down to the very millisecond!" she reminded them, letting some of her frustration and anger color her voice. "Do not doubt me when I say I can see *tens* of thousands of years into the future, with *equal* levels of accuracy. I have had to *lie* to the Admiral-General herself about what has just happened because even *she* would be held accountable for all those deaths if she ever found out and let slip that she knew.

"If I could wipe *your* minds of all incriminating memories over the last half day, I *would*," she warned the Damned. "But I am already in debt up to my eyeballs with the Feyori for pulling off this replacement trick, and that is a very *ugly* price to have to pay. Neither is it the *only* price."

Snapping her fingers, she activated all the main screens stationed around the room, the one behind the head table, the ones on the sidewalls, and the one over the heads of the tier seats, allowing her fellow officers and the silent, somber Private Sung to see. Those screens started scrolling small icons of faces attached to a list of names. Some had military ranks, while many others had none. Some were very old and some were very young, though most seemed to be adults.

Not all of them were Human, either.

"Because of Private Sung's willful disobedience, we have *not* left this cometary knot. *Not* left the Helix Nebula. *Not* flown off to our next port of call. We will not be able to leave here for at least another four hours, and we will need another *five* on top of that to effect repairs. Even if we commandeered one of the fleet tankers to top us off fully, and wasted fuel traveling OTL to get to our next time-sensitive fight, we will still be two hours *too late*."

The names and faces continued to scroll, six columns wide, and moving so fast, it was hard to read even a single name. The list of Humans ended, replaced by Tlassians.

"I will be sending out precognitive directives before attending Sung's tribunal, alerting those ships who *can* be spared for the coming fight, and giving them exact instructions on how to salvage everything that they can. Everything we ourselves cannot be there to do . . . but it still will not be quite enough." She gestured at the monitors with each hand and explained their purpose. "What you see on the screens is a list of every single person who will die in the next two years because of our inability to be at that next battle. A list of every person that *they* would have saved, or begat, or influenced down through the next three hundred years would take seventeen hours at this speed to display.

"Private Sung is no longer responsible for the destruction of our entire galaxy. But he *is* directly responsible for the deaths of 720,593 people between now and the appearance of the Zida"ya at the galactic edge . . . and I know each and every one of them." Turning back to Sung, who swallowed and looked ready to retch, she said, "You will be given the list of these names to contemplate in your spare time. You are free to ignore them if you wish, but understand that *I* cannot.

"The only person worse than you on board this ship right now is me, Goré," she stated quietly. "For I have slaughtered more than you, and *will* slaughter more, in the name of saving this galaxy. Saving as many lives as I safely can is my sole motivation, and the only reason why I *can* act, rather than step aside and allow this galaxy to end. When you fired against my orders, somehow I doubt your reasons were quite as noble as mine . . . and you have *added* to the screams of the people I cannot save. The loss of Private Smitt's family and homeworld were *necessary*.

"*These* losses were not."

He glanced up at her, a quick peek. Ia met his gaze steadily.

"Welcome to the hell that is my life, Private. You're now a full-on, murderous monster, just like me."

". . . I'm sorry." It was barely a murmur, but it was heartfelt.

"Sorry doesn't save lives. But I hope your regret will drive you to do better." Turning back once more to the others, she tipped her head at Sung. "Given the needs of this information to remain private to this crew and this ship, you are hereby *forbidden* to give him a hard time over it."

Sung wasn't the only one to lift his head, eyes wide in confusion and disbelief. Ia held up one hand. The sharp movement caused her medals to sway and *clink* faintly together.

"I know what you're all thinking, and you are *wrong*. Having that list of names will be more punishment than anything *you* could do or say. Not to mention he is about to be caned for his crimes. He is lucky that this is *all* he will suffer.

"The sedated presence of the *trompe l'oeil* version of Joseph N'Keth on board this ship, currently tended by Mishka and Helstead, would normally be a violation of our standing orders to keep all non-Damned personnel away. I have arranged with the Admiral-General to avoid being charged with Grand High Treason for having Private N'Keth on board . . . whom we will *all* treat as the real Joseph N'Keth. Even the Admiral-General herself is never to know that he's a fake, that the real one died this day.

"There is still the matter of Fatalities Five and Thirteen to be handled," she continued, moving along. "Private Sung, I will give you some temporally backed legal advice. When you are brought before the tribunal, do not deny either charge. Denial would only increase your punishment. As it is, whatever number of strokes the tribunal assigns to you will be doubled because you committed those two Fatalities during an officially acknowledged period of war . . . and doubled *again*, because you disobeyed the orders of a proved, registered military precognitive. Admit what you did, accept your corporal punishment, and understand that—murderous idiot or not—I still *need* you.

"You are not permitted to slack off or step down. You also owe Lieutenant Commander Helstead's quick thinking for your continued life. I will be expecting you to be ready to serve this ship, her crew, her Captain, and her future within twenty-four hours after your caning." She lifted her gaze to the rest, to her officers, her noncoms, and the enlisted men and women gathered before her. "I will expect *each* of you serving under my command to heed my orders and give me your best. I do not *ever* want to have to compile another list like this again. Is that clear?"

Uncomfortable silence met her words. That wasn't good enough. Ia scowled.

"This is *not* a joke!" she snarled, one hand jabbing at the screen behind her, the other raised to her ear, fingers curled as if cupping to hear the screams of the dead, versus the silence of her crew.

Her commendations swayed on their colorful ribbons, tangible proof of just how hard she had strived to make the whole Space Force understand the importance of her work. Every single medal pinned in place should have made her seem like a mountebank, but these were not soft civilians she faced. They knew the kind of price she had paid for those medals, kilo for kilo in blood, sweat, and tears.

"Every name. Every person. Every severed *life* I can hear, every second, *screaming* in my head. Dead. Dead. *Dead*. You will *not* make me come up with another list like this again. *Is. That. Clear?*"

"*Sir, yes, sir!*" Over one hundred bodies shot to their feet in unison, Spyder and Harper and Sung the foremost. The loudest. The stragglers rose as well, some moving belatedly, but all rising to Attention.

". . . Good." Muscles tight to control the sickly ice still prickling at her nerves, Ia lowered her arms back to her sides. "*Good.* Remember. Your orders are to avoid discussing this with anyone else. Some of the last few hours have been spent in altering the onboard surveillance pickups, official and unofficial, to remove all traces of the trick that has been played. This death did *not* happen. The trick to cover it up does not exist. Don't even discuss it among yourselves once you leave this room, today.

"To that end, I give you leave to stay here and discuss it for the next hour. Your conversations will not be recorded for that hour, so feel free to be candid. Once that hour is up, I expect you to obey without hesitation or discussion. In the meantime, N'Keth will be disembarked. Private Sung and I are due on the *Hum-Vee* in half an hour for his arraignment, which will become his tribunal *if* he is smart and does not protest. Lieutenant Spyder, escort him to the nearest head, then bring him to the airlock," she instructed her friend. "I'll escort the prisoner myself from that point. The rest of you, when your hour is up, begin repairs immediately and prepare to be summoned onto the *Hum-Vee* to witness the caning. Dismissed."

She didn't wait to see what her crew would do but instead turned to face Sung.

". . . I can go with you if y' like, sir. Figured I'd take it on meself t' play MP," Spyder murmured as he waited for Sung to rise. "We don' exactly have a security detail f'r it on board, do we?"

"I never believed one would be needed," Ia muttered back. Movement at her other side made her glance that way. Bennie lifted a hand toward her shoulder. Ia shook her head and shifted back, out of touching range. "I'll be alright. Just don't touch me right now. Lieutenant Commander Harper, you have command of the ship while I am gone. If everything goes according to what I have foreseen, you will need to assemble the Company, save for a skeleton crew, to head for the assembly hall. As per regulations, this entire crew will be expected to witness the canings."

She heard Sung swallow. Turning back, she watched him lick his lips, then speak. "I'm sorry, Captain. I was just so . . . so caught up in the fight, and I couldn't see the reason why I *shouldn't* keep firing. I literally . . . couldn't see the *Hardberger* on the other side."

He lowered his gaze. Ia shook her head. "Most soldiers in a great war never see the whole of that war. They only ever see a tiny part of it. That is why orders are given by those who *do* see the bigger picture, in the expectation that each soldier will have faith in their leaders to give the right commands at the right time. They can and should contribute to the immediate battle plans, but when a target is denied to a soldier, it is *denied* to them.

"In my case, I see everything. If I give you an order to kill someone, it is because I have very carefully weighed the impact of that life's existence against the needs of every other life, and deemed that the survival of the whole is too great to be ignored. If I give you an order to spare their life, it is for that exact same reason."

He considered that for a moment, then looked up at her, frowning softly. "But what if you're wrong? Aren't you ever wrong?"

"Oh, I *have* been wrong," she reminded him candidly, still angry with him. "Most recently, I expected you to obey. I *believed* you would obey. I was *wrong*, and all of those names on that list are the end result of it. More lives than you will ever know are *always* at stake whenever I give a command. Take him to the head, Lieutenant, and let him freshen up. I'll meet you at the airlock."

Nodding, Spyder took Sung by the elbow, escorting him out of the bow boardroom.

Colonel Avice looked up from the workstation screen embedded in the tribunal desk. A frown furrowed his dark brow. "Ship's Captain Ia, I find myself puzzled by the Admiral-General's standing order regarding yourself and your crew. I am not the only one, I'm sure. Are you aware that—"

"—Yes, sir, I am fully aware," Ia stated, interrupting him before he could go into the tediousness of listing everything. "I stand fully prepared to execute my orders without restraint or hesitation, sir."

Major Richildis and Commodore St. Stephen exchanged looks. The commodore, clad in Dress Blacks with blue stripes down his sleeves, rested his elbows on the desk. "Even with the Admiral-General's personal command code attached to this order, this is highly unusual. Unless the officer has also committed a crime, it is against Space Force regulation to punish the innocent. We are inclined to be more lenient in settling judgment upon Private Sung, as a result."

"I would rather you did not, sirs," Ia asserted. Hands clasped behind her back, standing in Parade Rest with her grey cap squared on her head, she met his gaze steadily.

Major Richildis narrowed her dark brown eyes. With her short-spiked brown hair, snub nose, and the brown stripes down her black sleeves, she looked like a bull terrier debating whether or not the current military case was a bone that needed to be chewed. "Explain yourself, Ship's Captain."

"The only leniency Private Sung deserves is twofold. One, I still need him as an otherwise damn fine gunner on my ship, so I request that he not be incarcerated," Ia told them, not bothering to look at Sung. He sat on a chair to one side of the small courtroom, having answered "yes" to both charges under the quietly admitted reason that battle adrenaline had carried him well out of line. "And two, with the survival of Private N'Keth, the charge of Friendly Fire should be modified slightly to acknowledge that, in this case, the Friendly Fire in question wasn't a literal fatality."

"Only by the skin of your third-in-command's psychic teeth," the major pointed out.

"True, but his life was still saved, so there should be some small mercy granted for that," Ia said. "Particularly in light of the modifiers. But beyond that, I expect no clemency for the soldiers placed under my command."

"Yes, the modifiers," Commodore St. Stephen agreed, sitting back in his seat and shifting his gaze to the accused. He was almost as large as Lieutenant Rico, though with pale, freckled skin and a braid of thinning white hair streaked with remnants of the original coppery red. Between that and the neatly trimmed full beard, he looked like he should have been dressed in a great kilt and wielding a claymore against his enemies. "Double the penalty for ignoring or acting contrary to the orders of a Space Force acknowledged precognitive when those willful actions result in an otherwise avoidable Fatality. Double the penalty again for a wartime crime."

"The penalty for Disobeying a Direct Order is two strokes of the cane per order," Richildis pointed out. She chewed the words through a not-smile. "According to the black box records which your CO has provided us, she ordered you to cease fire eight times. That's sixteen strokes. Doubled from the precognitive backing, that's thirty-two. Doubled from the fact that the disobedience took place in a war zone, that would be sixty-four strokes."

Sung flinched, paling. He said nothing, though, just glanced at Ia in fear, then looked down at his hands.

"For the crime of Friendly Fire, that would be four strokes," the major added. "Four times two is . . . ?"

Richildis held her gaze on Sung until he spoke. ". . . Eight, sir."

"And eight doubled again is?"

"Sixteen, sir."

"For a total of how many strokes of the cane?" Major Richildis smiled. It was not a pleasant smile.

"Eighty, sir," Private Sung whispered.

Colonel Avice shook his head. "That's too many. Caning has a maximum number of strokes that can be applied, with the rest converted to a set proportion of years in jail. The Admiral-General herself has stated there shall be no incarceration time." Resting his green-striped sleeves on the table, he glanced at his companions. "I move that the repetitions after the countdown reached zero be the only ones counted, since it was after that point that he started disobeying orders."

"That would only be three counts. I would rather it was the five that came before, if we're going to be lenient," Richildis countered. She sat back and gestured at Ia. "He was apprised in advance that his commanding officer is a precognitive of immense skill. He had worked with her for several months, seeing that skill in action. She told everyone, including him, five times to cease fire at a specific time, and yet he still disobeyed."

"Fifty-six strokes is still excessive," Colonel Avice countered. "We could space it out to ten strokes every few weeks, but that does involve incarceration between canings."

"Sirs, if I might suggest something?" Ia offered.

They looked at her. Commodore St. Stephen gestured at her to speak.

Ia nodded and drew in a deep breath. What she was about to offer would be applied to herself as well, after all. "There is an alternative. Deliver part of the caning to his upper back. The rules and regs permit the substitution of such blows at a ratio of two to one. I say, give him twenty blows to his back instead of forty, and sixteen to his buttocks, and do it in one session.

"That will leave him in sufficiently satisfactory condition to be returned to the *Hellfire* immediately afterward. I will need him at his post on my ship in the next few weeks. I cannot afford to have him wasting time in a brig, waiting for his backside to heal so that he can suffer the rest of his court-appointed strokes, and the Admiral-General knows this."

They looked at each other. It was Major Richildis, the apparent bad cop of the panel, who frowned, and asked, "You do realize that *you* will have to undergo twenty to your back, and sixteen to your asteroid?"

"Sir, yes, sir," Ia agreed.

"No, sir!" Sung surged to his feet. The bailiff moved forward, but Sung didn't go anywhere, just looked at Ia and the tribunal panel. "No. She shouldn't have to suffer for my mistake, sirs. Please!"

Ia looked over her shoulder at him. "Then you *shouldn't* have made it in the first place. I told you on the very first day that *any* corporal punishment my crew received, I would have to receive, too. *That* is the price I pay to be able to direct my ship whenever and wherever it needs to go, soldier. For the power that I wield, some prices *have* to be paid. I will even take on the full seventy-two blows in order to pay it, and do so willingly, if that is the judgment of this tribunal."

"It is not," the commodore stated. "In the light of the accused's admission of guilt and acceptance of the charges against him, I recommend that we follow his captain's advice. Sixteen blows to the buttocks, and twenty blows to the upper back, sentence to be carried out immediately. Colonel?"

Colonel Avice sighed, studying both Ia and Sung. Finally, he nodded. "I concur. It's excessive, but the target of Fatality Thirteen *would* have died if it weren't for the heroic psychic actions that saved him. Sixteen to the butt, and twenty to the back."

"Agreed," Richildis confirmed. "Sixteen to the buttocks and twenty to the upper back. Ship's Captain Ia, given the indemnity clause attached to your command, do *you* agree to this sentence?"

"Sixteen strokes to the butt and twenty to the back, I agree without restraint or hesitation," she replied. "I am prepared to endure all thirty-six strokes immediately upon the completion of Private Sung's corporal punishment."

"Very well. This judgment is recorded and sustained by concurrence of this tribunal and the offending soldier's commanding officer. Bailiff, escort Private Sung to the assembly hall," Commodore St. Stephen ordered. "Captain, please accompany them. Your ship will be contacted and your crew escorted to the assembly hall to watch the administration of both assigned corporal punishments. Those who remain aboard will be instructed to watch the Battle Platform's broadcast of the disciplining."

Sung paled again. Ia didn't have to ask why; she could guess easily enough that he had just realized *her* caning would be witnessed by the whole Company, too. She didn't try to reassure him or change the situation. That, too, was a part of her double-indemnity clause.

"Commodore, yes, sir," she said, saluting the trio at the desk. "My crew has been readied to view the caning by my first officer, sir."

Sung quickly saluted, too, as best he could with his thumbs still locked together. The three JAG officers saluted back, and the commodore dismissed them with a flick of his fingers. There were other cases waiting to be judged. This wasn't a case of repair materials or fueling needs, but Admiral-General Myang's standing orders for priority handling had bumped Ia and her crew to the top of the day's list.

Unlike Recruit Kaimong and Private Culpepper, Private Sung didn't struggle or resist. He cooperated with the bailiffs in being draped facedown over the frame. Without a word, he let them bind his wrists and ankles in place, and endured the kidney pads being wrapped around his lower back.

The first few blows to his buttocks did make him gasp. By the sixth, he grunted with each stroke, the sound muffled by the biting gag placed in his mouth. On stroke twelve, tears could be easily seen dripping down his reddened, grimacing face. When the cane was moved after the sixteenth, so was the frame, its angle lowered so that his upper back was placed at the same height his rump had been. Within three strokes, he cried out, the yell only half-muffled by the gag.

Stroke thirteen cut through his shirt, and the caning was paused while the cut was inspected. With only a little of the skin broken, the examining doctor informed the caner to strike from a different angle. Nodding, the sergeant moved to Sung's other side, lifted the antiseptic-soaked rod to shoulder height, and continued with blow fourteen.

When it was through, Private Sung had to be lifted from the frame. He could not stand on his own. The *Hum-Vee*'s medical staff had provided a hovergurney; after settling him facedown on the cushions, he was examined one last time. Several blows had lacerated his skin as well as raised welts and caused bruises, but the doctor's prognosis confirmed he would recover.

Commodore St. Stephen stepped back up to the podium, located to one side in order to focus the watching balconies of soldiers ringing the round, deep chamber. Bodies stirred around the room in preparation to depart, expecting him to deliver the usual warning of discipline needing to be maintained before their formal dismissal. His first sentence disabused them of that.

"Soldiers. You will remain in your seats and be respectful of what is about to take place," he ordered the crowd.

Ia's Company, the roughly 150 who had been free to leave the ship and attend, exchanged puzzled looks. So did the other nine hundred or so soldiers and specialists gathered in the hall.

"By order of Admiral-General Christine Myang, Ship's Captain Ia of the 1st Company, 1st Legion, 1st, Battalion, 1st Brigade, 1st Division, 9th Cordon Branch Special Forces is required to undergo an equal number of strokes of the cane for any and all corporal infractions incurred by the soldiers placed under her command," he stated. His words caused a rustle of surprise and disbelief that echoed off the walls. That forced him to raise his voice slightly, letting the pickups adjust accordingly so that his next statement could be heard. "It is therefore the duty of this Judge Advocate General tribunal to order the following sentence be applied to Ship's Captain Ia of the Special Forces:

"Sixteen strokes of the cane to her buttocks, for Fatality Thirteen: Friendly Fire, when the ship and crew under her command did willfully attack the ship and crew of the TUPSF *Hardberger* with one of her vessel's Starstrike laser cannons, a lethal weapon. This punishment is to be followed by twenty strokes of the cane to her upper back for the crime of Fatality Five: Disobeying a Direct Order. At her request, Ship's Captain Ia has asked for no leniency and has agreed of her own free will to undertake this punishment without hesitation or restraint. She is also under orders to restrain herself from using her innate biokinetic abilities for the next twenty-four hours.

"Sentence is to be carried out immediately."

Someone started the sonopad drums. Ia rose from the seat provided for her behind the podium and walked across the stage to the frame, which was being raised back up to the more common striking height. She felt numb, looking at it. Just . . . numb. She had struggled hard to avoid this sort of possibility with every bit of cunning at her command, but now she felt nothing.

Unbuttoning her knee-length coat, she shrugged out of it as the doctor stepped up, using a hand scanner to check Ia's vital signs. Ia focused on neatly folding her long jacket, reducing it to a neat if ribbon-lumped square.

Commodore St. Stephen joined her. He lifted his arms, palms up like a tray, and she gave him a slight nod of thanks. Placing her jacket on his hands, she added her Dress cap, and turned to the frame in her plain grey shirt and grey-striped black pants. The male caner stepped up to help secure her in place, making Ia shake her head.

"No, thank you. My orders are to use no restraints," she said.

"Sir, the restraints are there for your protection, so you do not move," he told her, glancing at the female sergeant who was to administer Ia's caning.

"I know that, Sergeants," Ia told both of them, "but I will do this without bindings or restraints. You have my word, I will not move." She started to move toward the frame again, then pulled back and pointed at the table behind the frame, which held the case with its *rotan* switch soaking in antiseptic solution, and a selection of biting gags. "But I will take one of those, to protect my tongue and teeth. I may have agreed to do this, but I'm not *completely* stupid."

Nodding silently, the female caner moved to select one of the gags. Ia took it from her when she returned, and fitted the slightly spongy plexi bar between her teeth. Stepping up to the frame, she lowered herself onto the slanted, padded surface and tucked her hands under her cheek. She wanted to show to everyone in the auditorium that she was there by her own free will.

I knew the very moment Myang first proposed this indemnity clause that I could turn it to my advantage, Ia thought, feeling them strap the padding around her kidneys. *This will cement my reputation with the rest of the Fleet. Bloody Mary doesn't just give a beating to the enemy, she can take a beating, too, and emerge all the stronger for—Holy* God!

The first blow had two layers to it: the initial, startlingly hard sting that burned on the surface, mostly on her right nether cheek; and the bruising ache that lingered even as the stinging burn started to fade. Her teeth bounced into the gag on the second blow, and clenched on the third. It hurt. It hurt it hurt it *hurt* . . . but . . . not as much as the shock, the *pain* of watching her life's work shatter.

The strikes came at slow, measured intervals. Ten seconds between each, time enough to relax, recover, anticipate, and tense up again. Ten seconds felt like a long time between each painful smack of the antiseptic-soaked stick, a long time to endure the throbbing and the burn. Ten seconds made her upper back clench and seize up in anticipation of the suffering it, too, would soon endure.

But with each blow, the agony of it seemed to beat back a little bit more of the dust from the desert-scorched plains. Ten seconds was a small eternity, on the timeplains. Enough to watch tendrils of greenery seep slowly, patch by patch, back into her consciousness. Enough time to see the waters trickling back into their proper places at the fringes of her vision. Enough time to feel her broken mind healing itself, restoring her stroke by penitent stroke back into her rightful place.

The frame jolted and thrummed faintly, lowering itself. Ia tensed in anticipation, then forced herself to breathe deeply, to let the physical fear leach its way through her muscles and out of her body, helping her to let it go. This was where her back muscles, still dense and strong, would fail to provide the same level of cushioning as her gluteals, but she would endure.

Her teeth snapped hard into the spongy bit with the first strike. The hands under her cheek twisted and shifted free, fingers curling and clenching around each other atop the head cushion. There was more sting with these new attacks, and the dull bruise burned with upper notes. By the fifth or sixth stroke, it felt like each hard-thudding lash was being administered by a rasp.

At stroke eight, they paused. Someone plucked at her shirt. The subtle shift of the fabric felt like sandpaper on her wounds. Ia choked, breath caught somewhere between a hiss and a gasp. The pause took longer, and the next stroke fell from a different angle. New skin, new pain . . . and where one set of strokes crossed the other, nails were driven into her back. Old-fashioned, pencil-thick nails. Only a centimeter long, but long enough to force a grunt from her throat with each blow.

She couldn't even hear the count anymore. All she could do was breathe and endure, breathe and endure. Seeing the infinities of the universe unfurling with each nerve-enflamed strike made her long for more. Not more of the pain, but more of the freedom, of the liberation of her abilities, of her very mind. A tiny corner of her memory realized this must have been what medieval monks had felt when scourging themselves, back on ancient Earth.

Again, they paused to pluck at her shirt, rubbing at the raw, too-sensitive flesh with a very light touch in their examinations. Ia ordered her mind to accept it like a thin, cold stream, then to set it aside. The next blow felt hard and unglamorous, but solid, a welcome relief from the pain of overstimulation.

Now the strikes crossed two lines of welts, more nails in the coffin of her back. With each blow driven home, another corner of her mind lifted free. Until she realized, after a few more strokes, the slow, steady rhythm had stopped.

Someone said something nearby. Struggling to focus, Ia opened her eyes. Everything was a golden, pastel blur. Images glowed in different hues, some stronger than others. Lines, blobs curves . . . they resolved themselves within two or three blinks as the doctor with her scanner, the edge of the platform, and the silently watching bodies of her crew.

Apparently the caning was through. Ia dragged in a deep breath through her nose and tensed to push herself upright. The pain at that dumb move emerged in a strangled, high-pitched whine. She cut it off, breathing in short, shallow sniffs through her nose, and waited for the frame to be lifted back to the original angle.

Her teeth were lodged in the biting gag. Her whole jaw ached, but her incisors ached the most. With awareness came a hint of blood on her tongue, seeping from her abused gums. Tilting her head, she got the fingers of her right hand into place and slowly pried. The rubbery material gradually popped off her teeth, first upper, then lower. She rested a few moments as the frame hummed and jolted to a near-vertical stop, then tried to lever herself upright again.

It hurt. It hurt it hurt it hurt, oh God how it hurt, but she managed it. Balancing carefully, Ia hissed between her teeth when she lowered her arms. The male caner took the gag from her hand, and the doctor touched her sleeve.

"Captain Ia, your back is bleeding in seven spots above, two spots below. There is a lot of blood compared to most canings," the woman added, "but you won't bleed to death. They'll need to be coated with an antibiotic ointment. If you'll lie on the gurney, we'll see that you're treated before you're returned to your ship."

Breathing shallowly, Ia shook her head. Then froze. That was a mistake, one that reignited the dull-stinging fires under her skin. *No shaking whatsoever. Got it.*

"No," she managed out loud. "No ointment. No gurney. I'll walk out."

"Sir, you have multiple contusions, several lacerations, and your adrenaline spikes have elevated your blood pressure," the grey-uniformed woman asserted. "You need to lie down."

"No. I will walk out under my own power." She had to. She had to, for the sake of her stunned, stricken, watching crew.

"Captain," the doctor started to argue.

"That is *Ship's* Captain," Ia corrected through aching teeth she was trying not to clench. "And unless you are Admiral John Genibes or the Admiral-General herself, you are *not* in my chain of command. I will *walk out*, thank you."

With parade precision, toe tucked behind heel, she turned. The JAG commodore stood just a few meters away, still holding the weight of her jacket and cap in his hands, elbows braced at his sides and sober respect in his eyes.

That respect gave her the strength to stride forward, stop in front of him, and lift her cap. She made it almost to eye level without grunting, but the last dozen centimeters *hurt*. Focusing her movements through the pain, Ia squared the black cap on her head, then reached for her jacket. Commodore St. Stephen moved first, unfolding it so she wouldn't have to do it herself.

He started to hold it open for her. Instinct warned Ia that if she turned and shrugged her arms back to slip them into the sleeves, it would take too long, and she would scream. That would be bad for morale. Jaw clenched, nostrils rushing air to and from her lungs, she plucked the heavy jacket from his hands with crossed wrists and swirled the heavy black gabardine up around her head.

That hurt, too. It hurt to the point of tears in her eyes, as bad in some ways as that hole in her shoulder from her enlisted days. But the slick lining helped slide the sleeves down over her arms, allowing her to shrug forward—a less painful movement than shrugging back—to settle the coat in place. Her agony escaped as a faint grunt, but only a faint one. She had to pause a few seconds, just to be able to breathe, before lifting her fingers to the lapels to adjust the lie of it. Taking the time to button her coat in place was an act of masochistic hubris since it meant she would have to *un*button it later, but Ia did it.

Only when she was properly attired once again in her Dress Blacks did she lift her right hand to her brow, giving the commodore a salute through the ache dominating her senses.

"Commodore St. Stephen," she growled, teeth clamped shut against the pain. "I respectfully request permission for the Damned to depart."

He lifted his own arm in return, saluting her back. "Permission granted, Ship's Captain. You and your Company are free to go."

Again, she turned, this time a quarter turn to her left, to face the front of the assembly stage. "9th Cordon, Special Forces!" she snapped, her voice echoing off the walls. "Ten-hut!"

They snapped to their feet, this time with more speed and unity than they had displayed two hours ago in the *Hellfire*'s boardroom. Ia nodded and stepped forward to the edge of the stage, placed a meter above the main floor.

"You heard the Commodore. We need six hours to fix the *Hellfire*. I am giving you *five*! Doctor Mishka, Private Attevale, take charge of Private Sung's gurney," she ordered, pointing off to her right where the hoverbed waited. That hurt, too; ohhh, that hurt, but she did it. "The Damned take care of their own, and we will *not* leave our crewmate behind. We have lives to save, meioas. Move out!"

Stepping off the dais and dropping to the floor . . . was a dumb, foolish, stupid move. She caught her balance when she landed, reflexes more than adequate for the Terran Standard gravity on board, but the jolt seared dragonfire from thighs to nape, reigniting every single lash wound. For a moment, the edges of her vision blurred, bringing back that strange glow as she forgot how to breathe. With a force of will, Ia dragged in a lungful of air, squared her frame, and strode for the steps.

From the wide-eyed stares of the members of 1st Platoon A and B Squads, seated in the first row, she probably looked as pale as her hair. Wisely—or maybe out of fear—they did not offer to help her as she marched up the shallow steps of the lowest tier. They just peeled out of the seats and joined her, forming themselves into tight ranks, three Squads wide, with just a bit of murmured direction from Sergeant Halostein, who took up second place at her back.

He was joined within a dozen meters by Lieutenant Commander Harper. No one spoke, not even her first officer, while Ia led them from the assembly hall to the banks of lifts which that lead to the level attached to their gantry spoke. But as they waited in silence for the first of the elevator cars to reach their level, Meyun drew in a breath and faced her.

"No," Ia stated, cutting him off. Knowing what he was going to say.

He said it anyway. "They shouldn't have done that. You shouldn't have to be punished for *our* mistakes, Captain."

She turned, still using the straight-backed toe-and-heel moves from parade maneuvers, since those moved and thus hurt her back the least. Staring into his brown eyes, she repeated herself. "No, Lieutenant Commander. Do *not* try this argument with me."

"He's right, sir." The agreement came from Corporal Bagha. The ex-Sharpshooter moved forward, her brow furrowed in a frown. "It isn't right. You shouldn't have to suffer, just because—"

"It doesn't *matter!*" Ia snapped, unleashing some of her pain as rage. She checked herself, breathed through her nose, and gentled her tone as the last of the Damned's stragglers caught up with them. As did a few of the others dismissed from the assembly hall, drifting close enough for a look at the Damned's CO in their wide-eyed, morbid curiosity. "It does not matter," she continued more calmly. "The pain I have suffered today? Does. Not. Matter.

"I have *told* you what we need to do. *Shown* you what we need to do. A *hundred* lashes of the cane on my back could not hurt me more than the pain inflicted by *your* lack of faith. Did you join the military because you longed to follow someone's orders? No. Most of you *did* join to try and make this galaxy a better place, didn't you?" she asked. She kept it a rhetorical question, though she did let it hang in the air for a long moment. "Nothing I can do, nothing I can say, nothing I can *suffer* will change you.

"Only you yourselves can do that. *You* have the power to be the best Damned soldiers you can be." Behind her, the first of the lifts arrived. Ia ignored it, shifting her hands. She tapped her inner wrist in emphasis, ignoring the pain from the pressure of her jacket on her back. "If I thought that bleeding myself dry could have a single scrap of effect, I'd slit my own veins and bleed away.

"But I *cannot*." She hardened her tone, not so much to punish her listening crew as to make sure her words carried to as many as she could get to hear her. "If you want to know *why* the pain of my back does not matter, then look into your souls and ask yourselves, why did you become a soldier? Why?

"I am willing to place my weapons, skills, body, mind, and even my *life* if need be between all the innocent lives in the Alliance and all the horrors that threatens it. What are *you* willing to do? Until you *do* know what price you are willing to pay . . . ? *No.* Do not speak of this to me. We have work to do." Turning on her heel, she reached out with her mind, reopening the lift doors just as they started to slide shut.

Silenced by her words, Harper followed her inside. So did Halostein, and the first half of A Squad, 1st Platoon. Her last view of the others was of the front rows of her crew shuffling awkwardly toward the lift doors on either side, none of them willing to meet her gaze.

Harper did look at her. He looked away as she glanced at him out of the corner of her eyes, but when he did it again, she sighed.

". . . Will you be alright?" he finally dared to ask.

"I'll make it back to the ship." There was no room for compromise in her tone.

He hesitated a long moment, but she knew it wouldn't last. Indeed, it took him only three floors in ascent before he muttered, "Well, I'm only asking because you look like you're going to puke."

The pair of enlisted men standing directly in front of the two officers glanced warily, furtively at each other.

"That's because I *am* going to puke if I move the wrong way or the car stops too hard."

Brown eyes and blue eyes and hazel all snuck quick, wary little looks at her. The two privates subtly shifted to the left, moving more in front of Harper than Ia, who stood in the corner of the lift.

She gritted her teeth. It was funny. It was painfully, grievously funny, watching them trying to be subtle about it, and she did not dare quiver even once, or the agony invoked *would* erupt as nausea. She did dare give them a warning, though.

". . . The first one of you idiots to make me *laugh* will have to clean it up."

They froze at her growl, not even daring to breathe until the lift drifted to a gentle stop. Quiet as mice, they slipped out of the lift, giving her room to disembark. Ia focused her will on the long walk back to the *Hellfire*, breathing as slowly and deeply as she could in the need to manage her pain.

When her assigned twenty-four hours were up, she would be free to stop suppressing her biokinetic urges. The welts and bruises and cuts would all vanish within an hour or so, leaving healthy flesh in their wake. Between then and now, she had twenty-three hours and several minutes to wait. Compared to the pain of losing everything permanently . . . it was a minor inconvenience at most.

CHAPTER 15

The fight on Oberon's Rock was a slice of replayed hell. Even more ironic, once again it wasn't the Salik, but the pirates who attacked. How many times have I aided that damn dome colony by now? Eight? Nine? Twelve?

Most of us were on the ground for it. Oberon had some crack security guards by that point, but no backup, as the Battle Platform had to be rotated among it and the other two settlements. One hundred mechsuited soldiers dropped to the planet, myself included. Ishiomi flew the Hellfire *for the space half of the fight, and even with a reduced crew, she and the rest of the 1st Platoon did an excellent job at hunting down and picking off the fighter ships trying to strafe the domes.*

The only thing I regret about that fight was the loss of Private Hollick. I warned him that if he went into that train tube to rescue those people stuck in that car, there was a strong percentage chance that he'd die. But he just pointed out that those cars could hold twenty or more civilians, and that it was a chance he had to take. He got them off the train and into the evacuation shaft, but he was the last one headed down the hatch when the tunnel blew.

According to the witnesses, the force of the air pressure swept him out before the emergency systems on the airlock

could close. We never found his body, but he did save their
lives. He died a hero, and I still honor him for his
sacrifice.

                                                        ~Ia

FEBRUARY 23, 2497 T.S.
SIC TRANSIT

(*Sucked out an airlock?*) Ia demanded, eyeing her late-night
visitor askance. Clad only in tank shirt and underwear, she
padded over to the drink dispenser and poured herself a cup
of water. (*I thought you were going to still be up in the car
when it blew, attempting to rescue that little boy's pet! . . . You
want anything?*)

(*The drawback to having a matter-form is that it requires
the distasteful presence, care, and feeding of a digestive tract,
and so forth. I'll have a glass of water,*) Belini ordered. She
had manifested in a bright yellow halter top and matching tennis skirt. (*Besides, that little boy was clinging to his pet. Damn
near throttling it. I had to improvise.*)

Ia watched the Meddler toss back half the water, then sigh
and rub at the back of her neck. Lifting her own cup, she
sipped at the chilled, hydroponically recycled liquid. She also
snorted mentally. (*You just wanted a dramatic,* witnessed *death.*)

(*Hey, the guy saved the timelines for both of us. He deserved
a hero's death,*) Belini retorted. She lifted her mug in salute.
(*I also flitted off and checked on him. He's doing just fine;
he's mentally fit and on course for the path he's supposed to
take.*)

(*Thank you for checking and letting me know that the personality rewrite is holding,*) Ia told her guest. She had to
smother a yawn as she did so, though. Her back no longer ached
whenever she lifted her arms, but only because her biokinetics
had worked hard to repair all that damaged flesh. Adding in
the stresses of combat and her extralong days, trying to repair
the breaks in the timelines, hadn't left her with a lot of energy
to spare. (*Excuse me . . . I'd love to chat, really, but I'm still
fully matter-based, and I'm afraid I need at least five more
hours of sleep.*)

(*Fully matter-based, yeah . . . You need to do something about that. The sooner, the better,*) Belini added, pointing with her cup in warning before draining it dry. (*Miklinn is casting aspirations on my faction-simmerings, since you're technically Albelar's get. I'm very much neutral to Albelar, not faction, and I have to remain that way for now since he's now milking that "Third Human Empire" you've been touting, while I'm solidly established with the Second Empire set.*)

Ia chuckled softly. She stifled another yawn. (*Just you wait until the Third Empire hauls the First under its wings . . . 'scuse me . . . Everything is going to change when that takes place. As for my manifestation, I've been working on it, and I will be able to manifest when I need it most. In the meantime, I'm waiting for my replacement for Hollick's slot to catch up with us. And tomorrow, I have to show up at the Wake. Something involving Harper is going to make the crew a lot happier if I do . . . but because it's Harper, I don't know what.*)

(*A Wake for Hollick?*) Belini asked, brows lifting. (*Mind if I drop in? I'd like to pay my respects, as you matter-people put it.*)

(*I'd rather you didn't,*) Ia told her, adding a tinge of regret to her sending. (*Whether or not you'd be tempted to let something slip, you're one more anomaly I'd have to ask the crew to keep their mouths shut about. They're already carrying a couple heavy burdens regarding Hollick, Sung, and N'Keth . . . and it's not that kind of a Wake. That's just the nickname my morbid little sense of humor came up with to call the parties we've been holding on board more or less every week—since the crew almost never gets real Leave.*)

(*Ah. Pity. I like the Irish. Dour and delightful, cheerful and glum, pragmatic and myth-filled . . . lovely sets of contradictions, the lot of 'em.*) She dropped onto the couch with a light bounce and spread her arms across the padded back.

Ia eyed her. (*Why are you here, anyway? Do you need to be kicked out the airlock again? I'd be more than happy to shoot you.*)

(*Nah. I have a second anchor string tying me to where I was. I just came to tell you what I've told you.*) She let her smile fade and waggled one finger at Ia, for a moment looking a decade older in her sobriety. (*Do not discount my advice about your manifestation. Do not wait for an extreme moment, expecting your anxiety or need to aid you in the change. If you really*

*want to impress my people, you'll have to slip into and out of
your energy side as freely and fully as we do.*)

Suiting action to words, she shifted with a blip of light. The
sphere hovered through the sofa for a moment, then slid out of
sight. Ia blinked, frowned, then called out, (*Hey! Are you at
least going to give me back my mug?*)

(*Only if . . . what is that delightful, old Human phrase? Only
if you want me to "take a dump" on your carpet. See you next
time!*) Pixie laughter mocked Ia as Belini slipped away.

Rubbing at her face, Ia crossed over to the dispenser, clipped
the other mug into its self-cleaning holder, and padded back to
her bed. *Damned pixie-shaped Meddlers . . .*

(*. . . I heard that!*)

(*I expected you to.*) Slapping the lights off, she shut the door
and returned to her bed.

FEBRUARY 24, 2497 T.S.
SIC TRANSIT

The surprise involved Harper, and that was all that she knew.
It wasn't just Harper, either, but it was clearly centered around
the man. Whenever she tried to delve into what certain other
members of the crew were doing, all she got was blurred mist
in return. The only thing she could see was a reasonably high
probability that the crew would be happier after whatever-it-was
took place. Provided she didn't screw it up, of course. The
alternative timelines where she did included grumpy looks and
scowls aimed her way.

Unsure exactly what she might have to face, Ia debated
wearing trousers, then gave up and donned her new cheongsam-
petal dress. Leaving the feather-stitched turban off, she combed
back her trimmed, jaw-length locks and walked down to the
Wake Zone. It wasn't ceristeel-plated armor, but the awkwardly
admiring looks she received assured her it was an effective
defense against whatever might come.

*If a good defense is a well-fitted dress, then that'll have to
do.* Smiling slightly, she dipped her head a few times in greeting,
moving down the stairs. Once again, she had to hunt down
Harper, but when she reached the bottom of one aisle and started
up the next, she couldn't find him. What she did find, in an upper

alcove decorated with plexiextruded fish—this week's theme was "Dabin's Cerulean Sea"—was a clutch of soldiers.

Or rather, spies. All four of her DoI- or Admiral-General-appointed spies lurked in the booth-like space. The first and foremost was Lieutenant Oslo Rico, who rose slightly and bowed over the table as she peered into the makeshift doorway. He had donned a pair of light blue slacks and a bright blue-and-yellow-flowered shirt. On his large frame, it was the envy of any tropical-island gift shop.

The second was Private Second Grade Miryanapanaua "Gasnme" Kastanoupotonoulis. Her nickname was nothing more than an acronym for "Get a shorter name, meioa-e!" She looked lovely, with her short black curls wrapped in a sapphire blue ribbon and clad in a blue version of the V'Dan-style cheong-sam. Where Ia's was stitched with golden feathers, Gasnme's had come out of the manufactory stitched with silver *dragnas*, long-tailed, broad-winged, lizard-like things indigenous to the V'Dan homeworld, sort of like a palm-sized dragonling. She served in the 1st Platoon under Rico and had been asked to spy on Ia for the DoI.

Private First Class Bera Fonnyadtz of the 2nd Platoon was their third spy, appointed by the Admiral-General, the same as Rico. She had decked herself in blue jeans, a white tank shirt, and a black leather jacket. Then again, she always dressed like that when she was off duty. Spyder, her Platoon lieutenant, called her "a livin' lady Fonz" but Ia had no idea who or what that was. It wasn't important to the timestreams, so she hadn't bothered to look it up. Bera saluted Ia with the tall glass mug in her hand, filled with what looked like a root-beer float, and sipped on the straw bobbing in its depths.

The last of the quartet was Private First Grade Ulan Fa'alat, another DoI-appointed spy and one of the four leads for lifesupport on 3rd Platoon's watch. Ironically, he had dressed similarly to Fonnyadtz, in a white T-shirt, jeans, and black leather, though his was a half-length vest that fastened down the side of his chest in the V'Dan style currently fashionable among men, and not an actual Terran-style leather jacket like hers. He was also the one who spoke first, and not the resettled Rico.

"Hello, Ia," he acknowledged, leaving off her title since that was the Wake Zone rule. "I suppose you already know why we're here, being the Prophet . . . so it remains to be seen what you think of it."

Ia shook her head, shifting her hands to her red-clad hips. "Actually, no, I don't know. Whatever the four of you have been planning, it clearly involves Lieu . . . Meyun Harper," she caught herself, mindful of the Wake rules. "And anything that involves Meyun Harper has a ninety-five percent chance of *not* being visible to me in the timestreams."

Rico's brows lifted at that, and Bera choked on her float. Fa'alat smacked her on the back.

Gasnme merely arched a brow in skepticism. "Why can't you see him? I thought you could see everyone and everything."

"Because there is *always* an exception to every rule, Kastanoupotonoulis," Ia returned dryly, managing to get through the woman's real surname without stumbling. "Meyun Harper just happens to be it for me."

Fa'alat gave her a wry look. "Every rule? What about the laws of gravity? What goes up must come back down, on a planet."

"Telekinesis," she countered. "Greasy FTL warp fields. And the escaping axial radiation of a galactic black hole."

"At least she knows her science," Bera rasped, lifting her mug in salute. She coughed twice more, then cleared her throat. "So. Ia. If you really don't know why we're here . . . then why are *you* here?"

"Because while I don't know what you've been plotting behind my back, I do know that you would be here, and that the 'big surprise' would be revealed as soon as Harper also gets here," Ia told her. "There's still that five percent left for me to see."

"He went off to visit the head," Rico told her, finally speaking. "But he'll be back." He nodded at a half-finished glass clipped onto the table edge to his right.

Footsteps warned her of Harper's approach. Shifting to her right, Ia dropped her arms, expecting him to squeeze in past her and resume his place on the bench seat ringing the alcove. Instead, he stopped at her side and stared first at her, then at the others.

"Okay . . . when I left, it was just me and Rico. Is there something I should know about, meiaos?" he asked.

Gasnme met Ia's gaze and shook her head. "He doesn't know, either, S . . . er, Ia."

"Know what?" he asked, hands going to his hips.

"It's simple. As the C . . . as *Ia* already knows," Fa'alat explained, gesturing at her, "the four of us were either ordered by the Department of Innovations or the Admiral-General herself to spy upon our lovely commanding officer—you *did* know that much, right?"

"Yes, I knew that much," Ia confirmed. She poked her thumb at the man standing beside her. "It's only things directly related to *this* man I cannot see. Everything else is like an open betting ledger of odds and probabilities for me."

"Well, hold on to your favorite dice," Fonnyadtz warned her, releasing her straw. "We're about to throw the game in your favor."

Ia glanced at Meyun. He shrugged, equally mystified.

"Allow me to explain it?" Rico ordered, giving the other three a mildly annoyed look. "We've all talked to each other about this. Then we took turns running an informal poll of the others in the crew over the last couple of weeks. One and all, the crew and cadre agree that *you*, young lady," he stated, pointing at Ia, "desperately need a personal life."

Ia wondered where he was going with that line of reasoning. She thought she'd made it clear enough through her words and actions that this ship's mission and its crew *were* her personal life.

"This is particularly obvious because you almost never attend these Wake parties," Rico added bluntly, eyeing her back as she frowned at him. "Half the days of the week you're staying up for thirty-two-hour 'days' and pulling double and triple shifts. You never join in the fun and games in the rec-room facilities. You're a little too focused when you're practicing for combat against Helstead and such, and even our dual-purpose, shipboard chaplain-and-psychologist admits you're just a little too serious for your own good."

Her face heated at his words. Given that this whole meeting was tied into Harper's mist-spewing existence, she had the sinking feeling she knew where this was headed . . . and she wasn't sure whether to be mortified, furious, or flattered that they would care for her personal happiness that much. Or rather, that they would try to foist it on her.

Gasnme continued before she could argue the matter, however. She slanted both Ia and Harper a knowing look. "Now, given the way we've all seen the two of you interacting, and the looks you sneak at each other when you think nobody's looking, it's pretty damn obvious there used to be a fire between you two. And just as obvious, it could be rekindled if you tried. That is, if you both didn't have your senses of duty wedged up your buttocks."

Harper coughed, blushing. Ia drew in a deep breath and let it out. Definitely a conspiracy on board her ship. Neither of them could protest the other woman's bluntness about it, either, because this was the Wake Zone, where the rules of military protocols and conduct were meant to be tossed out the nearest airlock. By her own order, no less. ". . . Go on."

Fa'alat nodded. "What she said, si—uh, sister. It wouldn't be right for either of you to look for a personal life among the enlisted. That'd be breaking the rules way too far. But among the cadre . . . well, there aren't that many choices, and neither of you have looked at the others the way you look at . . . well, the way the two of you always look at the two of you."

A glance at Meyun showed his own cheeks looking a little flushed. Rico spoke up again before he could protest.

"Besides, *you* spend all your working hours down in engineering, or out among the repair teams," he said, nodding at Harper. Then dipped his head at Ia. "Whereas *you* spend most of your time on the bridge or holed up in your office when you're not needed to micromanage a particularly fiddly moment in time. There's no conflict in your respective workplaces. And since you've managed to contain your interest beneath a very professional demeanor . . . we've decided as official spies to exempt all future such things from our official reports. Officially."

Ia blinked. "You . . . what?"

Meyun recovered faster than her. He lifted one hand to her shoulder, though he addressed the quartet at the table. "You mean, if we *do* decide to get personal as well as professional . . . you won't tell anyone? At all?"

All four of them nodded. Fa'alat added, "More to the point, the rest of the crew agrees and won't tell anyone."

"It's like these little parties," Fonnyadtz added, lifting her mug. "What happens in the Wake Zone stays in the Wake Zone.

Total civilian-style anonymity. In this case, since Ia's the CO
and is almost always on duty, we're letting you have the run of
the whole ship." She paused, wrinkled her nose in a wry smile,
and amended, "Except I *really* don't want to catch the two of
you going at it on top of the fish tanks in some lifesupport bay,
or tangled up in some P-pod gunner's chair somewhere."

"So . . . none of you would object, or inform the DoI, or
Admiral Genibes, or the Admiral-General," Meyun asked—and
slid his hand from Ia's left to right shoulder, turning and swooping her into a dip, ". . . if I did *this*?"

Caught off guard and surprised by his mist-shrouded choice,
Ia barely had time to squeak in shock at the sudden shift before
his mouth descended in a kiss. It felt good. Way too good.

In sheer self-defense—as in defense of her innermost self,
not her physical self—she reached up and pinched his ear.
Yelping, Harper quickly righted her. The moment she had her
balance, Ia poked him in his green-clad chest, face red from
more than just being tipped over. "*Not* in front of the crew!"

Unrepentant, he grinned. "Then there *is* a chance I could
do that elsewhere! Yes! . . . Er, yes, right?"

"Harper, let go of me." She sighed. He released her shoulder,
his smile fading. Rico and the others started to frown. Holding
up her hand, Ia forestalled them. "Let me check the timestreams.
There is a *lot* more at stake than just my personal happiness."

Closing her eyes, she checked the timestreams, silently
asking if what they were offering, what Harper wanted . . .
what she wanted . . . was possible. Little tufts of mist shrouded
their paths as she checked. Under the provisions of "not in front
of the crew" and "only when an hour or two could be spared . . ."

Finally opening her eyes, she nodded. And squeaked again
as he wrapped his arms around her for an enthusiastic hug and
a kiss on her cheek. Meyun continued to hold her, cuddling her
sideways against his chest.

She finally had to pinch him again, this time snagging a bit
of skin at his waist. Jerking at the sharp nip, he acceded to her
silent demand, releasing her. ". . . Alright! *Not* around the crew,"
Meyun said. "Which would be my personal preference, except
I'm feeling rather happy right now."

"There will be other rules. Only when the time can be
spared. Only when the—" His finger pressed against her lips.
Looking at him, Ia sighed and gave up.

Harper nodded. "I know, I know . . . and it's not like I'm going to throw you over my shoulder and carry you off to my quarters right this minute. There's another reason for being discreet. Private Nesbit."

The others blinked and frowned, not recognizing the name.

Harper rolled his eyes, giving Rico a briefly impatient look. "Oh, come on. The new member of the 2nd Platoon? Private First Class Maximus Nesbit, of E Epsilon? Hollick's replacement? He isn't here yet, and he hasn't gone through what this crew has, but he will be joining us soon.

"Harper's right," Ia agreed. "He hasn't seen what we've seen . . . or made the promises to ourselves that we have. Until we know he can keep his mouth shut on this ship's secrets, we'll have to continue being discreet."

"But at least you'll have the rest of the crew behind you," Bera pointed out. Fonnyadtz sipped at her float again, draining the last of the soda, then unclipped a spoon from the table and poked it at the globs of ice cream in her cup. "You really do need to indulge in some downtime, Capta . . . er, *shakk*. Meioa-e. Even if it's just *talking* with our favorite engineer."

Fa'alat flapped a hand at them. "Go on. Get out of here, you two. Go do some 'talking' with each other. We're done with the two of you . . . and if you know what's good for you, you'll go off somewhere private and *actually talk* about this with each other. Good downtime relationships begin with talking, after all."

Fonnyadtz snorted. "Talking. Yeah. Just so long as they *do* get around to swagging each other."

"You know, if this wasn't the Wake Zone, meioas, and if I hadn't the *carte-blanche* authority to bend the rules for you," Ia warned the quartet of conspirators, "you'd be in an entire asteroid field's worth of trouble. I *ought* to—"

Meyun covered her mouth with his hand and finished her sentence for her. "She ought to thank you, but I'm afraid she'll be too busy chasing me back to her quarters, where she's going to spend a good fifteen minutes yelling at me, while I just sit there and grin."

Blushing, Ia elbowed him. Or at least tried to. Her heart wasn't entirely in it. Tugging her out of the alcove, he released her mouth, wrapped her arm around his elbow, and led her out of the Wake room. Curious looks from the others in the rec room morphed into amused looks and encouraging smiles. No one stopped or even spoke to the two of them, though.

"Our official clutch of spies is right. I do believe we *should* talk about this," he murmured in her ear, guiding her into the corridor.

"I had half an hour set aside for the Wake. Or rather, about twenty minutes of it left," Ia stated. Patting his arm, she sighed and released it. "All we'll have time to do is talk . . . and I cannot spare half an hour every single day."

"Yes, but at least now we'll have something to talk about," he allowed. "By the way, I like the dress."

She smiled. "Thank you. So did Emperor Ki'en-qua."

Meyun mock-bristled at that. "What, the Emperor of V'Dan gets to see my commanding officer in a fancy dress long before me? Why, that's an outrage! I demand twenty minutes of your time, Captain, in order to complain about it to you."

In spite of herself, Ia laughed. Grinning ruefully, she gestured at the lift they were approaching. "By all means, you can have your say. In my office."

"In your quarters, so you can bring out and show me everything else you've bought since leaving the Academy," he bartered.

"Shh," she admonished him. They were alone for the moment, but she could foresee that someone was riding the belt-lift. "Not in front of the crew."

"Sir, no, sir. Definitely not, sir, and I wouldn't admit I've even dreamed of it, sir," he muttered. But he smiled as he did it.

MARCH 9, 2497 T.S.
ZARRATA VII
SSKENTHA SYSTEM

The man Master Sergeant Sadneczek escorted into Ia's office was lean, average in height, and looked somewhat cocky, with slouching shoulders and an amused half smile hovering around his goatee-framed mouth. He did not come to Attention until Grizzle cleared his throat, and only lifted his hand to his brow at a second *ahem*.

Ia saved her work, powered down her main workscreen, and

returned the salute, though she didn't rise. "At Ease. Have a seat."

Resuming his slouch, Private First Class Nesbit settled into the nearer of the two chairs across from Ia. "Cap'n. I heard you're Bloody Mary. 'Zat true?"

"Welcome aboard, Private Nesbit, and yes, it is. But right now, we're here to talk about you. Understand that you have some very big shoes to fill. You will be taking over most of the roles performed by the late Private Hollick, who died a hero's death on Oberon's Rock," Ia stated, folding her arms and bracing her elbows on her desk, "This crew misses him greatly. He was a middle-aged man with a steady mind and a calm personality. The Damned will take a little while to get used to you, a young man with a twisted sense of humor, in his stead."

"The Damned, sir?" he asked her.

"Ia's Damned, 9th Cordon Special Forces. My crew is loyal first and foremost to me, then to the cause I serve, which is the salvation of all life over the long-term view, and *then* to the Admiral-General and the Space Force. The Admiral-General knows and approves of my missions and has given me free rein to carry them out." That was a bit of a stretch, but technically with her *carte blanche* being based on her precognitive abilities, it was the truth. "We have been through more combat in the last year than three-quarters of the fleet in the pursuit of that goal, and have a higher kill rating per battle than any other vessel short of a Battle Platform or a capital ship.

"Hollick was the most loyal member of my crew, though not the best warrior. I told him the odds of success for his last mission weren't good, but he chose to go on it anyway in order to save lives. Which he did. But however well he may have performed in combat, your biggest obstacle, Private," she continued, "will be filling the heroic shoes Hollick wore while he was serving on board this ship during your average day-to-day duties. You will be worked harder, expected to do more, and at times serve for far longer hours than at any other point in your military career since leaving Basic."

"'M not afraid of hard work," he told her, his accent not quite as thick as Lieutenant Spyder's. He flashed her a grin. "I jus' don't like it."

"Joke all you like, but accept that that will change," Ia warned him. "Now, I know you've been fitted with a mechsuit, having served two tours on the Blockade on board a Harrier-Class Delta-VX. I served on one of those myself, so I know you're used to long hours and dangerous encounters. The nice difference about serving aboard the *Hellfire* is that I run three duty watches instead of two. The not-so-nice similarity is that you can and will be called to active duty at any hour, at any time. I will, however, be able to give all of you a fifteen-minute warning, save in the most extreme of probability cases.

"The acceleration rating for this ship is approximately the same as a Harrier-Class," she added. "So the Lock and Web Law is vital to uphold. Not just on the off chance that God rolls the dice and comes up with an extremely low probability number, but because it is important not to *forget* that you have left things out. I'd rather that hairbrushes and such didn't go flying about during combat, punching holes in my bulkheads."

He lifted his brows but didn't say anything, just shrugged. Her warning was deliberately chosen since it would remind him to secure his actual hairbrush within the next month to avoid that very scenario. Touching the comm button on her workstation, Ia spoke.

"Private Schwadel to the Captain's office." Releasing it, she opened a drawer and extracted a datachip. "This ship does not fly a standard patrol route. We do not have a specific sector to protect. Instead, with the aid of my precognitive skills, we aid those battle zones desperately in need of some extra help, regardless of whether or not it lies in Terran space . . . which you may have already noticed since you were just shipped all the way out to a Tlassian space station for pickup.

"You have five hours to stow your things and get familiar with your coming duties. This is your Company Bible, which I expect you to study, memorize, and take to heart, just as the rest of my crew have already done," she added, holding out the chip. "The first chapter has been appended with a note regarding the next forty-eight hours, with advice on what you should focus on first and when to do it, to get you integrated quickly into life on the *Hellfire* . . . and yes, I *am* that temporally accurate. Use your arm unit's chrono to make sure you stay on schedule.

"Three days from now, we'll have time for another Wake. Those are the onboard parties the Damned throw because we do not have time to stop and enjoy actual Leave on other stations, domeworlds, or planets. Anything that happens within the Wake Zone is to be addressed strictly from the standpoint of everyone being a civilian, so be very careful not to address anyone by their rank.

"As for recreation, leisure, and hobbies, I believe Private Preston-Aislingfield is the current game master for the ship's tabletop role-playing sessions. She'll get ahold of you soon to discuss your gaming experiences and character preferences, and will help integrate you into the group. That, more than anything, will bring your fellow crewmates to know and eventually trust you, which is why I point it out to you. Please remember to use electronic dice, not physical ones. Like hairbrushes, the physical kind can do a lot of damage during sudden maneuvers and are harder to keep track of in an emergency. Now, do you have any questions?" she asked him.

"Yeah," he admitted. "If you're really a prophet, what'm I thinking?"

She gave him a flat look. "That would be telepathy, not precognition, and *that* would be a violation of your sovereign sentient rights to mental privacy. Not to mention my own mothers would fly out here to paddle my butt for being so rude."

He grinned at that, visibly pleased that his new CO had a sense of humor.

Ia didn't disabuse him of that belief. "Still, the probabilities of what you were about to say out loud were the number seventeen at seventy-seven percent, followed by yellow daisies at fourteen percent, fried peanut butter and banana sandwich at eight percent, and undecided for the rest. Your teammate and roommate is about to arrive. The two of you are both electronics engineers. I suggest you use that basis to start getting along as fellow workers and build trust and friendship from there.

"You will be a member of the Damned for a long time to come," Ia warned him. "As Private Sung discovered recently when he violated Fatalities Five and Thirteen, I can give you all the precognitive warnings in the universe until I run out of breath, but it is up to *you* to carry your orders through. Make sure you don't do anything stupid, or it will be the last thing you get to do. And be mindful of your actions when it comes to corporal punishments. If you incur any strokes of the cane, *I* have to suffer them, too.

"There's a recording in the ship's library of Private Sung's caning, followed by my own, should you doubt me. And if that isn't enough to warn you, the rest of my crew will be inclined to lynch you if you screw up rather than see me go through another caning because of something you did," she told him. "I'd rather not have to fill out the paperwork on a lynch mob, but I will I if I have to, so kindly keep that in mind.

"Other than that, welcome aboard," she repeated, as her door chimed, then slid open. "Private First Class Maximus Nesbit, meet Private First Grade Derek Schwadel, your roommate and team leader. As far as the chain of responsibility goes on board this ship, Schwadel is senior-most between the two of you since he's served with me longer. Schwadel, you'll have four hours and fifty minutes to show Nesbit around before we'll reach our next battle zone. Spend them wisely. Dismissed, gentlemeioas."

"Aye, sir," Schwadel stated, and gestured for Nesbit to follow him out of her office. "C'mon, this way. Let's get your gear stowed."

Ia didn't watch them go. She powered her screen back up and resumed picking her way through the last few tangles in the duct-taped version of her goal, changing various prophecies destined for Earth and the Afaso, Sanctuary and the Free World Colony—not too many of the latter, thankfully—and assorted missives meant for targets among the various other governments and species.

MARCH 17, 2497 T.S.
SIC TRANSIT

"Let's see . . . power cables here . . . floodlights for the red, green, and blue spectra over there . . . and rare-earth magnets over *here*," Harper muttered to himself.

He moved around the clutch of men and women gathered in the bow storage bay that used to hold crysium sprays, and which was now lined with stacks of locked storage chests awaiting delivery. Some had been shipped off already, but others had not. Shifting MacInnes by her arms, he guided her onto some invisible mark seen only by him, then moved on to the next.

The men and women summoned were a mix of privates, a corporal, and the petite lieutenant commander. The only thing they had in common, aside from the obvious items like being Human and members of Ia's crew, was that they were one and all middling to strong psychics.

"Right," their chief engineer finally said. Clapping his hands together, he eyed their positions, then hustled to one side and opened the crates resting on the deck. They did not match the crates carrying her crysium wreaths. Instead of peach-tinted, coronet-like rings, he pulled out a variation on the crystal-mounted, brass-bound, somewhat oversized weapons he had been working on for months. It sort of looked like a stylized, oversized *pi* symbol shaped into a brass-and-crystal gun. "Here we go . . . not at all like the originals, but this should work even better . . .

"Now, according to my calculations, four or five of you should do the trick, so we'll try five to start. Better to slightly overkill than underkill, and have to retry. Helstead, MacInnes, Crow, Teevie, and O'Taicher, you are each fairly strong psychics. I need you to *be* psychics at this point in time. Each one of you will take up one of these guns. The safety is here, the trigger is here, and you wrap your hands around these crystalline bits," he added, bringing over the first gun so that he could stand in front of the semiarc they made and point at each bit. "Obviously, the thing you want pointed at your target is this crystal shaft out here."

Eyeing each other, the men and women in question picked up the bulky, odd devices and tried to settle them like weapons. MacInnes's arms were long enough, but Helstead's were a bit short.

"Sorry the front grip's so long, but I couldn't reconfigure it because of the resonances. You can rest this back bit on your shoulder here to help balance the gun, like this." Lifting it to his own shoulder, Harper displayed how to hold the thing, turning so that it was pointed off to the side. He lowered it again and showed them where the eight e-clips had been already slotted along the underside of the canister-thick barrel. "These clips are just the initializers, like spark plugs for an old combustion engine—and yes, it really does take that many e-clips, Teevie."

She blinked at him, her lips still open to ask her unspoken

question. Licking them, she asked instead, "How did you know what I was going to say?"

"Because the Captain already showed me. Now, according to my source materials, I can get a much greater efficiency if I use mid- to high-ranked psis. And according to Helstead, who has been very helpful in testing the prototypes," Harper added, "you will probably feel an odd tingle, and maybe hear a faint chiming or humming sound. That just means the gun is working. You will also feel drained afterward, but actually using it won't cause any real harm."

Harper then handed the weapon to Helstead, who grinned and hefted it onto her shoulder. "Wait until you try this, meiomas. If we get it right, the end result's a muckin' trip, and I can't *wait* to see it happen."

Ia stepped into her own designated spot as Harper checked the grips of each volunteer. Waiting for him to finish, she caught their puzzled looks. "Harper, did you remember to *tell* them what they're about to do?"

"Nope. I didn't want them spreading rumors around the ship. Okay," he said, handing the last oddball weapon to O'Taicher. "Everybody, find your safety switches and flip them off. That will automatically start the weapons charging. Then grasp the hand grips where I showed you, take aim at Captain Ia, and on my command—so you do it all at the same time—you will fire your weapons at her."

The others exchanged very dubious looks. O'Taicher frowned at their first officer. "Are you bloody *nuts*? That'd be Fatalities Thirteen and Twenty-Two!"

"If you don't shoot me, Private, *that* would be Fatality Five: Disobeying a Direct Order," Ia pointed out gently. "Besides, it's not a case of Friendly Fire *or* Attacking a Superior if you're ordered to do it."

MacInnes shook her head, muzzle still pointed at the ground. "I can't do it. I won't. Not without a direct order from *you*, sir."

"Fine," Ia agreed. "Everyone, I order you to remove the safety locks, aim your weapons at me, and at Lieutenant Commander Harper's countdown and command, I order you to pull and hold the triggers of your weapons, firing them at me until Commander Harper gives you leave to stop. Any questions?"

Crow and Teevie exchanged looks. Corporal Crow shrugged

and lifted his gun to his shoulder, sighting down the top of the brass barrel at his CO. ". . . It's been nice knowing you, sir?"

Ia smiled wryly at the jest. So did Harper—until he flinched, realizing he was in the way, and quickly ducked out from between Ia and the armed members of their crew. That made her grin.

"Right . . . right. Alright. Safeties off," he ordered, firming his tone into an order. "Take aim at Captain Ia . . . and at my command, pull and hold the triggers. In three, two, one . . . *fire.*"

Helstead pulled her trigger right away. MacInnes was next. Nothing seemed to emerge from the guns, nothing in the visible-light spectrum, but Ia felt each impact. Each unseen beam felt like a jolt of electricity, like a bath of warm sunlight, the pull of a magnet . . . or rather, like the touch of a mind. The touch of life-energy.

The first one tingled. The second itched. Crow and Teevie shook their heads and fired. The third and fourth unseen beams altered everything. The bodies of her crew members started glowing, the power cables gleamed . . . and the floor and the walls and the boxes and crates shimmered, turning into tissue paper.

With the alteration in her perception, she could see the guns firing in bright, golden white lances that swirled at their edges with flickering hints of rainbow colors. Time seemed to slow down, and the white, Sol-spectral glow of the overhead lights stretched out, taking on elongated, prismatic hues. She watched, wide-eyed and fascinated, as O'Taicher exhaled in a swirling smoke cloud of heated gas, and remembered where she had seen this before.

When I was enraged by Sung's disobedience in battle . . . and then later . . . later, when I learned to let go of the pain from the . . .

Sighing, O'Taicher tightened his finger on the trigger, firing the odd weapon at her. The fifth beam struck with blinding intensity, inadvertently aimed right at her eyes. On instinct, Ia inhaled, focusing on the feelings and letting go of her mind. She embraced the energies, embraced, absorbed . . . and slipped. Slipped, disintegrated, free-fell, and coalesced.

Not too unlike the downward-around-and-out flip she normally made with her gifts and her mind, save that this was a three-dimensional aerobatic twist made with her body as well as the rest. Her body, which no longer had substance, but which now felt whole in a way she couldn't confine into words.

"Holy *shakk*!" O'Taicher dropped his gun, releasing the trigger as it fell. The metal clattered and the crystal chimed against the deckplates, but the gun wasn't damaged.

Ia could see the whole cargo bay, up, down, and all around, though most of her attention, her viewpoint, was still focused on the quintet. That quintet, and the six bodies beyond and the seventh to one side, still continued to glow. Mostly with thermal energy, in a warmth that . . . that reminded her of a muffin, of all things, soft and bready and sweet. The overhead lights were a glass of cool water. And the beams of the weapons, those were a meal injected directly into her bloodstream.

"Yess! Cease fire!" Harper ordered. He grinned—glowed— and raised his fists in the air. *"Success!"*

Ia opened her mouth to say something, to respond, but nothing happened. Her sense of self moved, but only in the way that a ball filled with liquid, or maybe of plasma, might swirl and shift. She focused again on the dozen Humans standing in front of her. Something was missing. Something . . . Ia realized with a swirling start that she couldn't *smell* anything anymore.

Accustomed as she had grown to the scents of ship metal, cleaner, lubricants, recycled air, plant life, washed and unwashed bodies, as much as her active awareness of all of that had faded over time . . . she couldn't sense that anymore. She could *see* the motes of molecules wafting off their bodies, but it wasn't a sense of smell as her now-missing nose once knew.

It was a strange side effect.

Harper clapped his hands, and she watched, fascinated, as the sound waves rippled out from his cupped palms in little pale violet shimmers. "Right! Captain," he stated, facing her sphere and bowing slightly, "can you hear me?"

She tried again to speak, then gave up. Reaching out with her mind, she broadcasted to him. (*Yes, I ca . . .*)

All of them doubled over, grabbing at their heads. Even Harper, who was the most mind-blind of the group.

Oh. Reining back on the effort she thought she had needed in order to project, Ia opened up a gentler, whispered level of projection. (*Yes, I can. How's that? Too loud?*) she asked, focusing on each of the others. Helstead, still wincing, gave her a thumbs-up as she straightened. (*Sorry, this is . . . new. I . . . see things . . . It's all very . . .*)

She started to turn around, still staring at the waiting lamps and cables and the pulsing green-brown coils of the rare-earth magnets. Their auras looked tasty. She didn't have a sense of smell, but she did have a sense of taste. She was also hungry. Very hungry.

". . . Captain? Captain Ia, if we could kindly have your attention?" Harper asked dryly as she drifted toward the magnets. She heard/saw him sigh, another swirl of exhaled breath. "Great. I've reinvented the old attention-deficit disorder, only I've given it to a half-blooded Feyori."

(*Shh. I'm hungry.*) Since she didn't have a mouth, just an all-over sense of self, she intersected that sense of self, that sphere, with the green-brown energies. Sure enough, it tasted green-brown. *Heh . . . like the way a Gatsugi would describe a dish of broccoli beef.* Inhaling the flavors, she supped from the magnets and drank from the overhead lights.

"Helstead, would you kindly shoot her?—No, not the psi-gun," Harper corrected. "Use the stunner I issued you."

At the backside of Ia's field of view, she watched the others hastily move out of the way, and the petite redhead pull out a handheld stunner. Its field was a single, invariable width, though it could be programmed for up to five different strengths. Raising it, Helstead aimed it at Ia, thumbed the controls to maximum, and fired.

It felt . . . It felt like getting hit in the back with a giant shepherd's pie. Or maybe a pot pie. Some kind of pie, meaty and filling. (Again!) Ia ordered, turning to face her, still soaking in the magnetic auras. She gentled her tone as the others winced. (*Sorry . . . again, please. That felt good.*)

Helstead obligingly fired. Harper, on the other hand, snapped his fingers and pointed one at her spherical sense of self. "*Focus,* Captain. No drifting off into an energy-based food coma. Focus!"

The third pulse of the stunner made her feel full. Instinctively, Ia shielded herself against the influx of energies, moving out of the immediate environs of the magnet. (*. . . Enough. I'm good.*)

"Good," Harper praised her, and gestured to a spot next to himself, with a half-bowed sweep of his arms. "Now, get your floaty, silvery self over here so I can explain to you how to get back into your normal, Human, *matter*-based self."

Swirling in a sigh, Ia refocused on him and drifted over to the indicated spot. (*And how do I do that? And why should I try?*) she asked, mildly curious. (*This is all rather fascinating. I'm in no hurry to go back.*)

Sighing, he boldly stuck his hand into her side, invading her sense of self. Shock rippled through her, not only from the touch, but from the energies and sensations that touch brought. Not only could she feel his chemical heat, and the faint hints of magnetism inherent in his cells, but she could taste the electrical impulses of nerves chattering back and forth with his muscles. The kinetic energy of his blood as it raced through his veins. The thoughts in his head.

The thoughts . . . *His* thoughts, of just three nights before, when she had managed to scrape free one precious hour of time with him. Memories of their activities. Sights, tastes, sounds, touches . . . and smells, all evoked with a vividness and an intimacy that sprang from his emotions. Strong ones, and a source of energy all of their own. It was so much easier to read his mind like this . . .

"Shoot her now!" *Come back to me, Ia,* he ordered in her mind, even as he slashed his free hand. *Focus on what you want!*

Everything vibrated. Everything focused as their energy, mental/emotional/psychic/crystalline energy, flooded into her. For a moment, Ia's whole being quivered, struck like a bell . . . and then she fell, snapping back into her body. Snapping back into the memories of bliss *his* memories invoked.

She hit the deck with a head-cracking *thud*. Uncomfortably aware of just how *solid* and *separate* each part of her bones and muscles, organs and blood felt, she grunted, shifted her limbs, and pushed herself up on one elbow. "Slag . . . *shakking v'*slag," Ia muttered, head aching from its blow. "Slag, but that hurts."

Harper crouched and offered her both his hand and a wry smile. "Next time, try to land on your feet?"

"I *did* land on my feet," she growled, blushing. Accepting his hand, Ia let him help haul her upright. "I just . . . slag . . . I forgot *how* to stand. Just for a moment. Oh, laugh it up," she retorted, as Helstead shook with barely suppressed snickers. "*You* try losing two of your five senses and your awareness of how things like muscles and joints work."

Letting go once she had her balance, Harper grinned unrepentantly at her. "Collapse or not, it worked! Welcome back to the land of the matter-based, my love."

She gave him a dirty look. "Why did you have to use *that* set of images?"

He sobered, giving her a mildly chiding look. "My research notes stated quite clearly that the subject has to *remember* what it's like to have a body and *want* to return to it. Our primary source for information did a number of experiments on willing half-breeds, and *that* was one of the best focal points for wanting to return. Now, gather your wits, rest for a few minutes, then we'll try it again."

"Ugh. Again?" Ia half muttered, half groaned. She knew he was right, but that didn't mean she was ready to go for it just yet.

"The more times you make the crossover and manifest with our help, the closer you'll get to figuring out how to do it on your own. *And* how to come back on your own." The look he gave her was both a warning and a tease. "Because until you do, I will *continue* to think those thoughts at you."

"I'm getting the feeling I'd like to know what *kind* of thoughts he's thinking at her," Helstead quipped, eyeing her two superiors with an amused gleam in her hazel eyes. "Though I'm sure I could guess."

MacInnes, crystal-gun pointed at the floor, shook her head. "I'm not that suicidal, sir. We just created a Meddler out of our own captain, and I am *not* that suicidal."

Her vehemence made Ia smile.

MARCH 19, 2497 T.S.
SIC TRANSIT FROM OBERON'S ROCK
GS 138 SYSTEM
. . . AND JULY 8, 2498 T.S.

The reading lamp behind her living-room easy chair tasted like brie. The milder inner bits of the cheese, not the outer ones. Even though Ia was firmly back in her matter-based body, she still had an awareness of the flavors of various energies around her. The smell of her own soap-scrubbed body, the slightly dusty fabric of the chair, and the faint hints of greenery in the

air flowing through the vents from the amidships-sector lifesupport bay all grounded her firmly in her body, but the reading
lamp still tasted like brie.

The datapad, on the other hand, was a spicy snippet of sau-
sage. She kept having to stop herself from trying whenever
the urge came back to nibble on it. Her matter-based body
did not process electricity the same way her Meddler-based
one did.

Yesterday, she had tried to eat energy from the electrodes
at the command console while guiding the ship in a protracted
starfight over Oberon's Rock, but all that had done was fill her
with excess static energy and make her view of the bridge start
to glow. It hadn't done anything for her physical hunger. In a
way, "tasting" the energies in this solid body was very much
like smelling the culinary efforts of a restaurant while stuck
out on the sidewalk with no credits in her pockets.

Right, she thought, saving her latest prophecy. *That's that,
and it goes into the Afaso delivery file. Now for the preshipment
of needed supplies to Dabin . . . though I'd better double-check
that they're still going to be needed. I'm still searching for
more of those little frayed tendrils from when Sung snapped
the threads of fate.*

Closing her eyes and focusing her mind away from the
cheese-and-meat glows, she flipped down and in, landing next
to her own life-stream. Accessing the timestreams was also
easier, brighter, and clearer now that she had manifested. The
grass was a lush blue-green, the waters clear and mirror-like
even where they rushed and flowed fastest, and the sky was a
beautiful shade of blue.

Skipping down the bank, Ia stopped at a point a week or so
past a heavy knot of mist. That was one of the nexus points,
where her choices would be so vast and her energies would be
so low, the Ia of that era wouldn't be able to foresee what to
do. Her future self would have to rely upon her training as an
officer, her instincts as a warrior, and her grasp of overall strategy to guide the tactics of that moment.

The moment she did want, which involved herself working
in the local capital, was downstream from that point. Her elder
self worked diligently in the version she selected, filling out
orders for the struggling, battle-wearied soldiers under her
command. Stepping down into the water, Ia readied herself to

read those orders since she wouldn't be able to read her own thoughts. *So let's just see exactly what the Afaso need to send and hide on Harper's homeworld . . .*

(*About time you showed up.*)

Ia jerked up out of the water and back into herself, fumbling to keep the workpad on her lap before her jolt could dump it to the floor. She looked around, wide-eyed, for signs of Belini, though that voice hadn't belonged to her. Alone in her quarters, Ia slowly relaxed, puzzled by what she had heard. *That . . . wasn't the voice of any of my crew members. In fact, it sounded like* me, *but . . . not my* own *thoughts. There's a distinct difference between my own thoughts and a telepathic sending.*

Confused, she waited for another sending, but nothing happened. Mindful of the ticking of the minutes she had left in her day, she sank back into the timeplains and moved back to the designated insertion spot. Once more, she stepped into the waters of her future self . . . and once more jumped in startlement.

(*Don't freak again,*) she heard herself state, her tone dry. (*You really* are *hearing me—your future me—talking to you.*)

Blinking, Ia pressed closer to herself. Her future self pressed back, pushing her up out of the stream. Startled, Ia stumbled onto the bank, dropping to elbows and rump in the grass. Her older self stepped . . . *stepped* . . . up out of her own life-stream and crouched by her feet. And then grinned in amusement.

(*Don't you look shocked . . . Wait until you can see your expression from* this *side of things,*) the future version of Ia stated. She held out her hand. (*Come on. Sit up. I'm going to share with you the list of things you'll need them to buy and stash, and a couple extra places to stash them.*)

Hesitantly, she extended her own hand, clasping the other version's palm. (*How . . . what the . . . huh?*)

(*About as coherent as I remembered it, afterward.*) Tightening her grip, Future-Ia looked into her eyes, her amber ones showing hints of silver flecks. (*Manifesting as a Feyori has put a fine polish on our powers. More to the point, it has* finished *their blossoming. All you need to do now is learn how to use the extra bits. But* be careful.)

Those fingers squeezed Ia's with a distinct pressure, reminding her that even in the timeplains, she was accessing them from a physical body, not a Feyori one.

(*Yes, you can now not only contact yourself, but read your own thoughts,*) her future self warned her. (*But doing it casually will lead to doing it carelessly, and that will lead to paradoxically induced confusion. You will be able to see this in the side-timelines, if you look. Resist temptation, don't try to contact yourself any earlier than this, and you'll be fine.*)

(*Ah . . . right. Right,*) Ia agreed. This *was* herself, without a doubt. (*Ah . . . best piece of advice for right now?*)

Her future self smiled slightly. (*Three things. Make doubly sure your agents among the Afaso get that portable hyperrelay purchased and hidden away. Avoid stepping into the life-waters of other Feyori—they* will *sense your presence and be able to speak with you from now on if you tried it. And* don't *let Belini touch you. Resist her urgings to manifest for now. It may seem to cause problems in the Meddler scenarios, but you'll lose a powerful edge when Miklinn's little pawn-army comes for you if they know you can transform at any point before then.*)

(*. . . Right.*) Even without touching the timestreams for that moment, not all that far upstream from this one, Ia could see the difference that sort of advantage would make. (*Right, I know that particular possibility-scenario. I didn't think it was a strong enough probability, but if you say . . . er, if we say so, then I'll go for it,*) she agreed, gathering her wits. Hands still clasped, she let her older self help her to stand up on the bank. (*So, what's on that list aside from the hyperrelay?*)

It came across as a pulse of thought. Ia embraced it, as familiar in flavor as her own, and carefully secured it in a corner of her upper thoughts. Older-Ia nodded encouragingly. (*. . . Got it?*)

(*Yes. And we'll both resist the urge to linger in your . . . our . . . presence. This is going to take a lot of thought to come to grips with,*) she added, letting go of her other self's hand.

(*Get some more crysium and make some special wreaths out of it,*) Elder-Ia told her. (*You'll see the exact life-paths the new Rings of Truth should influence. You'll need to lose about a week's worth of sleep within a year, but the price isn't bad.*)

(*No, it wouldn't be,*) she agreed. Eyeing herself, a deep part of her mind wondered how this could happen. Another part prodded her into an impulsive move. Wrapping her arms around her older self, she hugged. (*Thank you,*) Ia sent. (*Thank you for all that you've done, and all that you're going to do.*)

(*Thank you yourself,*) she got in return, along with a squeeze, and a push back. (*Now get back to work. And don't forget to sleep, and all that other self-care* shakk.)

Ia peered at her future face, noting the shadows under her older self's eyes, the worry-frown beginning to crease her otherwise young brow. (*Don't forget that for yourself.*)

Amused, the older version stepped back into the waters and vanished. Bemused, the younger one stared at the rippling stream, then shook her head and started trudging back up the gentle slope.

That has got to be the weirdest . . . ! She stopped after a moment, taking the extralong span of seconds within the timestreams to just contemplate the awe of what had happened. *I just . . . I just* talked *with myself. I've broken the Time-barrier of . . . of vidshow versus reality . . . ! I never once checked the* time*plains for temporal anomalies. Just the streams themselves.*

"Slag me," she whispered, letting the winds of the prairie carry her stunned words across time. "Just freaking *slag* me . . ."

CHAPTER 16

Interstellar warfare isn't won in a single year. Hell, ground-based warfare is rarely over in a single year, particularly not when the two sides are fairly evenly matched. The Salik and the Choya did their best to smash our support infrastructure. We did our best to smash theirs. They tried to shatter our fleets while strengthening and rebuilding theirs. We tried to shatter and strengthen and rebuild as well.

Some of that was successful. Some of it was not. Lives were lost, prisoners taken and eaten, colonists and soldiers and cities were saved, while others were destroyed. The various militaries of the Alliance couldn't be everywhere, but neither could our foe. There was time to heal, time to repair, time to rebuild and build more. And time to be castigated for not moving faster, for not doing better.

The best I could do, however, was march along to the drumbeats of Fate.

~Ia

JULY 13, 2497 T.S.
ZUBENESCHAMALI SYSTEM

This time, she was still awake. Still clad in her grey slacks and paler grey shirt, too, though she had taken off her black ship boots and had her sock-clad feet levered up on the footrest of her easy chair. This time, Belini appeared in a set of black tights and tunic trimmed with red edging. At least, when she coalesced into a matter-based body, after popping into view like a silvery soap bubble in reverse.

". . . If you think your colormood choice will frighten me, I'm not intimidated by death, and I am not swayed by rage," Ia stated calmly, scrolling up through the text of her precognitive missive on the workpad screen. This one was a message to her family, requesting them to separate out a few more sprays for her to convert. She wouldn't get to see them for over a year, but she liked having things prepared in advance. A thought that amused her.

"Smile all you want; you are trying my patience," the not-pixie snapped. Hands on her hips, she strode across the carpet and stopped next to Ia's chair. "Why do I get the feeling you're not even *trying* to manifest?"

"I don't have to try," Ia told her. She sealed the message to her brothers and opened the next. "My ability to manifest will reveal itself in the right place, at the right time. In the meantime . . . I now have the politics of the Dlmvlan Queen High Nestors' court to redirect." She lifted the pad in her hands, tilting it briefly at the other woman to show the electrokinetically composed words filling the screen. She tipped it back her way and shrugged. "I'm not sure I've used enough of a mix of logic and illogic to sway them. I'm good at the logic part, and not too bad at drawing absurd analogies, but I'm not a poet laureate."

"I don't give a radioactive *fart* about the Dlmvlan High Nestor," Belini snapped. "That part of the Game isn't in my way. *You* are in my way."

Ia looked up from her notes. "I give you my word, I will manifest in the right place, at the right time."

"Ha! What good is your word?" the Feyori argued, and pointed off to one side. "Every day you fail to prove you are a player and not a pawn is a day that *I* lose face! Mcuinn and Gzikk are already positioning themselves to scoop up chunks of *my* plays."

Slanting her an annoyed look, Ia unclipped the datapad resting on the table next to her armchair. "Here is a list of instructions on how you can position your influences to outflank theirs by the rules of the Game. And *yes*, this will work by the rules of Feyori politics," she added, seeing the Meddler narrow her eyes in doubt. "Belini, when have I ever been wrong?"

That made the not-pixie snort with mirth. Hands on her hips, she surveyed the white-haired Human. "How short the memory span is in your mother's species. Private Sung? Private N'Keth?"

Sighing, Ia waggled the second pad, gesturing for her to take it. "When have I ever been wrong about something *I* can control? If you take this information, the only person after that who could screw it up is *you*. Are you a screwup? Or are you a Meddler, a galactic reshaper of lives and worlds?"

Belini snatched the pad from Ia's grasp, not noticing that Ia subtly tossed it upward a little, letting her hand drop to prevent contact. "If I *do* screw this up, I'm still going to blame you."

It was Ia's turn to choke on a laugh. Well, a chuckle. She let her humor fade as Belini raised her brows in surprise, then lowered them in a scowl.

". . . *This* is idiotic," Belini finally growled. "You have me giving ground, with these instructions! Concessions right and left, up and down, even helically spiraled . . . !"

"It does seem that way, but look at what they have to give up. It's in the fine print," Ia added helpfully.

Belini didn't have to scroll the screen to read it. Feyori were natural electrokinetics on a level above and beyond what Ia could do. She did blink twice, though, gaze unfocusing. "That's . . . That . . . would require . . . You're going to *Gather* us?" she asked, shifting her gaze back to Ia. "But the energy requirements . . . and that *you* are the party listed as the Summoner, to trigger these conditions? No.

"*No.* There's no way that *you* could pull that off! Not when you can't even manifest yet," Belini scoffed. She tossed the pad back into Ia's hands. "You may *think* you can manipulate energy just because you're an electrokinetic, but a Summoning is a manipulation of *hyperspatial* energies, on a scale your puny little meat-mind cannot grasp. That chance is so slender, it's see-through!"

Ia brought her knees up, bracing her sock-covered heels on the seat of her chair. She did so to avoid even the slight chance that Belini would touch her; once she did, the Meddler's greater telepathic abilities had an equally slim but dangerous chance of reading her subthoughts. The ones where she knew she'd already manifested. It was safer to avoid contact. That, and she'd been sitting in one position for too long. The sensors in the easy chair quietly folded the leg rest back into place as Ia spoke.

"Believe as you will. I have foreseen it. All you need to do is make those agreements and hold to them, so that *they* have no grounds to back down from their bargain when my prophecies come true. And for the record, my 'puny little meat-mind' has already grasped the fullness of Time in every direction I've ever cared to stretch. Hyperspatial manipulations are child's play by comparison."

That creased the not-pixie's brow with another frown, a skeptical one. "You may be able to *see* 'the fullness of Time,' but can you *understand* everything you see? *Can* you fully grasp it?"

Slightly sheepish, Ia shrugged. This was not something she could lie about, not without its coming back to bite her later on. "Mostly. I know enough to be able to do what I need to do—I don't have to understand how to create a hyperspace nose cone from nothing, like some engineering pioneer, in order to grasp the principles of how it works and how it is used. That'll take me one more lifetime," she added in a muttered aside to herself. At the pixie's frown, Ia shook her head, dismissing her words. "Luckily, I don't need to go that far in this life.

"And you don't need to, either. All you have to do is follow through on what I've told you to do." Gesturing with the returned datapad, Ia said, "I see, I plan, I act. That is enough for now."

Snorting, Belini took the device, finished absorbing the information on the smaller pad, then tossed it one more time to Ia. Not bothering to watch the heavyworlder catch it one-handed, she turned back toward her corner of the small living room. "Well. You'd *better* be right. I'll hold up my end of the bargain, even though it seems like I'm losing face . . . and I will be. If you fail, I will devour your life-energies myself."

"If I fail, it won't matter what you do. You'll be left trying to flee across the intergalactic void—good luck with that, by the way," Ia added. "Even if you glomp up *en masse*, the strongest clutch would only get about halfway before starving to death. And the Greys won't share their teleportive technology with you. They'll have already fled to the next galaxy, and they won't stop to pick up you. You're nothing but salt and lime juice with a chaser of tequila to their mental wounds."

"Don't knock the salt and lime juice. Margaritas are one of the few delights that a digestive tract can experience. That, and chocolate," Belini admitted. Sucking electricity out of the wall, she flashed into her true shape. (*Don't make me regret this factioning for you.*)

(*It's a factioning* with,) Ia corrected. (*My part of the payment just has a bit of a time delay on it, is all.*)

It shouldn't have been possible for a silvery ball of semireflective energies to snort. Snorting was sound, which usually required the collision of matter against matter to create, so a Feyori in its natural state rarely made noise. Still, the peculiar swirl on the center focal point of Belini's surface managed to re-create a visual snort, before she slid away.

Or possibly a visual raspberry. Amused, Ia went back to work.

NOVEMBER 15, 2497 T.S.
BATTLE PLATFORM *PLENITIA III*
MARS, SOL SYSTEM

"That's the last of the boxes, sir," Sergeant Halostein said, dipping his head at the hoversled being guided into their amidships storage bay. "I still don't get why we had to strip the bow sector of all the supplies and emergency cabinets but for the stuff on those lists, Captain. Care to explain?"

Ia shook her head. She had encouraged her crew to display the level of familiarity inherent in his question, but this was something she couldn't talk about. Feyori eyes were now focused on her in the timestreams. The strongest among them could only see a few months ahead, but a few months was enough to cause problems. At least, she couldn't mention the *real* reason.

"I'm about to be keelhauled, Sergeant, and I need those unused supplies shipped off to pad my hide instead of my bottom line—you do know what keelhauling means, don't you?" she added, glancing at him.

Halo frowned a moment, then scratched the fringe of pale blond stubble circling his head, freshly buzz-cut by one of the crew. ". . . Not really. The keel part refers to the bottom of a sailing ship. I know that much."

"It's a very old nautical term, yes," she agreed. "And an ugly form of punishment. A rope would be looped around under the hull of the ship. Usually from starboard to port, or if the offense was deemed truly heinous, from bow to stern. The sailor to be punished would then be lashed into the loop, and dragged under the ship.

"Since the hull would often be covered in barnacles and other forms of sea life by that point, he would either be dragged fast enough to scrape the flesh from his body, possibly even causing limb loss or decapitation, or dragged slowly enough that his weight *might* slacken the rope enough to avoid the barnacles and such, but at that low a speed, it would be more likely for him to drown."

He glanced at her sharply, blue eyes wary. "And you're about to be keelhauled?"

"Well, the alternative euphemism is raked over the coals, but I do believe my enemies would rather have me lacerated, decapitated, *and* drowned than merely burned. Scorching my hide under the pretext of discussing unpleasant subjects isn't nearly so evocative." She paused, dipped her head, and added, "Though if it makes you feel better, I will be trying to steer the conversation in that direction."

Halostein chuckled. "Well, if anyone can, you can, sir," he murmured. "If you'll excuse me, Captain, I'll disembark and seek out the dock officer so we can get this mess off our ship."

"Carry on, Sergeant," Ia agreed, gesturing for him to walk ahead. Her bracer beeped. She didn't have her headset on her, though. Unsnapping her left sleeve, she pulled up the unit's screen. "Ia, here. Go."

York's face filled the screen. "We've just received orders for you, Captain, from the Admiral-General. Transmitting them to your unit."

"Inform Lieutenant Commander Harper that he is in charge of the ship in my absence. Status quo until I return," she instructed. She checked her arm unit. ". . . Orders received."

"Aye, sir. I don't know why they keep sending you these things, when you already know," Private York muttered. Then rolled his eyes and corrected himself. "Well, yes, I *do* know;

they have to have a paperwork trail—please don't mind me, sir, it's been a long watch, and Private Teevie's slightly overdue. Said she was taking a head break before hitting the bridge."

"She'll be there in three more minutes. Ia out," she added, ending the link with a touch of the screen. Another tap opened up the file transferred to her. The paperwork in question— electronically written and about as far from wood-pulp sheets as they were from Earth—directed her to report to one of the *Plenitia III*'s briefing rooms immediately.

Flipping the lid shut, she rebuttoned her left sleeve, dusted off her Dress Grey jacket with its minimum glittery of rank and zone pins—now more than two years out of date since there was no ribbon bar designated to cover all of Alliance space—and headed for the airlock in Halostein's wake.

———————

The briefing room was a heavily guarded, scaled-down version of the one she had invaded just over two years ago. This time, her palm and bracer were scanned, her identity confirmed, and herself formally escorted in by two of the guards. Blank when she entered, the screens around the room stayed dark until the guards left, and the doors sealed behind them.

At that point, they lit up again with various data, some of it statistics from the Damned's various activities, some of it with surveillance footage. A part of her flinched away from the shot at the back left of the round, two-tiered chamber. It had been taken from someone else's helmet pickups from back when that one robot attempted to rip off her mechsuited arm. Her shoulder was long healed, but the memory of the pain was still there in her subconscious.

Focusing on the nine men and women seated around the lower of the two horseshoe-shaped tables, Ia searched for the face of her immediate superior. As she had foreseen, he wasn't there. Two others represented the Special Forces instead, both of them from the Psi Division. One of them was a middle-aged blonde, a lieutenant general who hadn't been at the previous meeting. Ia knew her name, Mercea Wroughtman-Mankiller. The other was General Jolen Phong, who had been there. Every Branch had two representatives, which suggested a formal review board.

Seated in their center, Admiral-General Christine Myang

returned Ia's respectful salute, laced her fingers together, braced her elbows on the table, and spoke without preamble.

"Tell me why we shouldn't throw you in the brig for Fatality One, Ship's Captain Ia."

"Let me guess," Ia returned, unfazed. "Lieutenant General Wroughtman-Mankiller is pressing the unspoken charges in question. Correct?"

Mercea leaned forward as well, though she didn't clasp hands. "These allegations are *very* serious, soldier. You have *failed* to undergo your yearly ethics examinations as a duly registered psychic. Your last one took place on January 19, 2496, as registered on your homeworld of Sanctuary . . . and yes, I *did* subpoena the Witan psi-priests in question for a face-to-face and mind-to-mind interview of all your past reviews."

"Are you aware, Lieutenant General Wroughtman-Mankiller, that at this point in time, you are acting under the influence of Feyori Meddling?" Ia asked, turning to face the blonde in the grey-striped black jacket. "I believe *that* falls under Fatalities Two and Six: Treason, and Subversion. Inadvertent or not, your accusations against me are intended by a Feyori named Miklinn to be counterproductive and subversive to the continued safety, operation, and success of the Terran United Planets Space Force and the government it supports. Those definitely qualify as both Treason and Subversion."

The Special Forces woman scowled. "I am a Rank 14 Xenopath, soldier. *More* than strong enough to sense the presence of a Meddler *and* keep it out of my thoughts."

"Not when you're making love." Her blunt rejoinder made the other woman blush. A few of the others did as well. Ia shrugged. "At that blissful moment of the orgasmic crux, a psi's mental defenses are lowered—I myself have suffered from the same phenomenon. Your longtime partner, Brad Blackburn, has unwittingly been tapped to be a conduit in those moments. As a Rank 4 telepath, he has just enough strength to be used to influence your mind but not enough sensitivity to notice he is being used to do it at such moments.

"The Feyori Miklinn, whose normal purview would be the Solarican military, has counterfactioned my efforts to ensure that this war progresses to the best possible ending for all the races of the Alliance," Ia continued. "He has received dispensation from the Feyori who normally controls all Meddling in the Terran Space Force to have an indirect influence upon your activities . . . hence using your moments of intimacy against you." Her mouth twisted in a wry imitation of a smile. "I'd tell you how to prevent it from happening again, but *that* would be an open counterfactioning of his efforts. An act which I am not prepared at this time to perform because it would spiral this mess out of control."

Wroughtman-Mankiller flushed again but did not argue the point. "That may or may not be the truth, but my own situation will have to be examined later. *You* are the point of this High Tribunal."

"This is not a High Tribunal," Admiral-General Myang countered. Then added in warning, "*Yet*. But the accusation is still there, Ship's Captain. *Have* you undergone a psychic ethics evaluation since January of 2495?"

"No, sir, I have not," Ia stated calmly. She continued before the nine men and women around her could do more than sit back in shock at such a free admission. "However, my lack of an ethics examination is completely covered by two words, rendering said examination unnecessary."

General Sranna of the TUPSF-Army tapped his finger on the surface of the long, curved desk. "I'm sorry, Captain, but 'Vladistad, *salut*' does *not* exempt you from being examined. In fact, it makes it all the more imperative that you *are* examined on a yearly basis."

She almost replied flippantly. Almost, except at the last second, the timestreams turned cold in her mind. As cold as the dread she had experienced over the Friendly Fire incident. Her subconscious doused her veins with ice-cold warning. Squaring her shoulders, Ia answered plainly instead.

"No, sir, Vladistad, *salut* does not exempt me from examination, sir. Two other words did that, sir," she stated, clasping her hands behind her back to hide their trembling. If she wasn't careful in the next few minutes . . . "It's good to see you again, General."

"Which two words would those be, then?" the other Army general asked her, his brow lifted skeptically.

"*Carte blanche*, sir. Two words that have been backed by my scrupulous filing of daily reports." She looked at Myang. "Everything I have done, everything I have shared with you, Admiral-General, I have conducted myself and guided my crew with the strict scruples and ethics required by the Terran laws regarding psychics and their abilities." Ia held her gaze for a moment more, then nodded at the information flickering on the screens. "Pick anything I have done and question me about it. I will give you the exact duty reports that cover each incident."

"You're a good enough electrokinetic, you could have tampered with those recordings at any point in time," Mercea countered wryly.

"But I'm *not* a good enough telepath to have tampered with the reports of your spies," Ia stated. She tipped her head to her right. "You've had plenty of reports from them corroborating everything I've officially sent. You've heard from me time and again in my reports explaining why *this* battle had to be fought instead of *that* battle. I've given you headcounts and ident files of the soldiers and citizens we've saved.

"My Company and I have filed more paperwork than a ship with nine times the crew complement, with our moves and our motives constantly displayed for you . . . and my crew has fought for you with so little free time in our schedule, we haven't had more than six days' worth of Leave in the last two years, sirs, because there *hasn't* been time for anything else." Ia shook her head. "What else *could* I do but keep fighting?"

"You were required to be examined anyway!" General Phong countered.

"If I had stopped to disembark long enough for an essentially redundant examination, sir, I would've risked thousands of lives being slaughtered because my crew wasn't in the right place at the right time." Ia looked at Myang. "Or should I have permitted unauthorized personnel on board my ship, sir, an act which by your own command would be considered an act of Grand High Treason? The only time I've had free that *was* long enough for an ethics review has been while my ship was in transit between battle zones—and the few times my ship *has* been in dock long enough for me to undergo an ethics review, I *still* had work to do.

"When would I have had time, without risking too many lives, sirs? My only recourse *is* to conduct my actions openly. Ethically and morally, openly. Word, thought, and deed are all one within me. How else can I prove myself to you yet still continue to save all these desperately needed lives?"

She surveyed each high-ranked officer in turn. None of them

looked away, but most didn't look comfortable. Only Myang met her gaze without changing her expression. Then again, the Admiral-General was an expert at displaying that flatly neutral look.

"I serve—*I act*—because I am here to save lives to the best of my abilities. And I have done so," Ia argued. "If you cannot see for yourselves the truth in my deeds, the *ethics* inherent in my actions, then unless you are a psychic yourself, and one strong enough to conduct a probe, then there is nothing I can do or say to convince you. So what *can* I do, given the constraints of my orders and of Time itself, that I have not already done?"

"Alright, I'll bite," one of the two Navy admirals stated, her voice as crisp as her blue-striped black uniform and her silvered crew-cut hair. "How about you explain to us how you can justify working for a foreign government? Your very first act was to haul *cargo* for some branch of the government back on your homeworld. Yes, by contract the military *can* deliver cargo to a colonyworld under our protection, such as I.C. Sanctuary, but those contracts must undergo military review for the best allocation of our limited freighting resources.

"And don't give me any *shakk* about that cargo being 'emergency military supplies,'" Admiral Nadine Nachoyev added dryly, slanting Ia a dark look. "We've received complaints from the Sanctuarian government that those supplies vanished the very day you left the planet, and that despite great efforts by said government, they have never been found in the two years subsequent. The only conclusion that can be drawn is that you were smuggling in supplies under the orders of subversive elements on your homeworld. That *you* were taking orders from a foreign power to do so. Fatalities Two and Six would therefore apply to *you*."

"My actions were neither a case of Treason nor of Subversion, Admiral," Ia returned calmly. This, she could handle. She had anticipated it among the possibilities of questions thrown at her in this session and come prepared with her answer. "Yes, I lied about the nature of those supposed military emergency supplies to the officials logging that complaint, but I *am* permitted to do so. That option exists under the rules and regulations stating that no Terran military officer may allow a foreign power to confiscate cargo under our protection, whether or not that cargo is of a Space-Force-assigned nature."

"So who did you transport the cargo to, if not to the government of Sanctuary?" General Sranna asked her, frowning softly.

"The Free World Colony, sir. It is its own, separate government from the Church-controlled elements currently running the rest of Sanctuary. They requested that the cargo be kept secret from those elements," Ia stated quietly.

Admiral Wroughtman-Mankiller pounced on that. "Then you *did* take orders from a foreign government!"

"No, sir, I didn't do that," Ia replied, tucking her hands behind her back. She looked over at the Special Forces admiral. "You see, I am not taking orders from them, and I never have."

That earned her several snorts. Freeing one hand, she snapped her fingers. Text appeared on the main screen behind her, with the top line enlarged so that the words were easily seen from all nine seats. The image zoomed to display the pertinent sections as Ia explained what they were now viewing.

"Before you is the Alliance-registered Charter for the Free World Colony of the Zenobian Empire . . . also known as the *other* half of Independent Colonyworld Sanctuary. As you can see for yourselves, Article I, Section A, paragraph 1—the very first law of the Free World Colony—clearly states: *The duly verified commands, precognitive missives, and orders of the Sanctuarian-born woman known as Ia, Prophet of a Thousand Years and soldier of the Terran Empire, supersede, supplant, and overrule all laws of the Free World Colony, its citizens, descendants, and successors, without exception to this rule, save by her own command.*

"*Legally*, meioas, they take their orders from *me*," she stated, defending herself neatly. "Which means I am not violating Space Force law because I am not under the influence of any foreign power."

"Yet you still are working for a foreign power," Admiral Nachoyev argued. "Your own crew members claim that you have admitted to not only using technology borrowed from the future, but that you have refused to share the results of that technology with anyone outside your own ship and have forbidden them to share it as well."

"*That* would be covered under Vladistad, *salut*, Admiral," Ia told the older woman, returning her hands to the small of her back in modified Parade Rest. "By its very nature as precognitively extracted information, that information is protected by the *Johns and Mishka* statute sheltering all precognitives within the Terran Government, and by extension the Alliance.

"Considering how much precognitively based information I *have* given to this military and its government, and the accuracy of all my various predictions, a court of law would rule that I do have the right to withhold that information, based on the fact that it would damage the future. And it would, sirs," Ia told them.

"*Enough.*" The solitary word silenced the others. Unclasping her hands, the Admiral-General studied Ia. "I think I am beginning to understand why your Priestess Leona used a modified format during your ethical scans. I suspect if we tried to dissect each and every one of your many actions over the last two-plus years, we'd be stuck in here for *ten* years at this rate."

"We don't have ten years, sir. I'm sorry," Ia apologized. "Mars will be attacked in three more days. You'll be busy with the system's defense, and my ship will be needed in the defense of one of the Solarican heavyworld colonies approximately three hundred light-years from here."

"*Thank* you for finally telling us about that," Admiral Nachoyev muttered darkly. "You *could've* done it sooner."

Ia tried to restrain her tongue. She knew she had to tread carefully, but Nachoyev's antagonism was rubbing her sense of patience raw. "I knew it would come up in here, and that three days is plenty of time to prepare. When else should I have told you? Five years ago, when I was still a lance corporal in the Marines? You wouldn't have paid attention to me back then. Three days is plenty of time to prepare."

"Enough!" Lifting a hand to her forehead, Myang rubbed at the bridge of her nose. "I will accept your constant stream—your *barrage*—of visual and written reports on all of your activities as your version of an ongoing ethical review. But understand this: if we *do* have doubts as to your actions, you will be called into a much more formal review, Captain. A tribunal review."

"Yes, sir. I know that, sir. It'll happen in a few more

years—but not for the reason you're thinking," Ia confessed. Myang blinked at her. "It will be instigated by the Alliance Council, not the Terran Space Force. As Admiral Viega will attest, I did warn the Salik that engaging in this war with us would lead to their destruction and advised them to abandon their ambitions.

"They chose to ignore my warning, and will eventually reap the seeds that they have sown. I already knew that I will be held accountable for that because I have not told anyone what those seeds are," Ia told the men and women before her. "I have been very careful to make sure there is no way the Salik can use that information against *us*, which *would* be an extreme case of Fatality Thirty-Five: Sabotage.

"Having had a taste this last year of the corporal punishments administered for Fatalities Five and Thirteen, I have no intention of enduring any greater penalties," she finished dryly. "Particularly not during a war when I myself as a precog could foresee and prevent them."

"I am quite sure," Myang murmured, studying her. "Ship's Captain Ia, I find you to be arrogant, boastful, irritating, and borderline subordinate more times than I'd care to count. You are the single biggest headache in this war next to the Salik themselves. You are a *problem* for me."

Her tone, mostly quiet and calm, now dripped with barely checked vehemence. Ia tried not to swallow visibly. She clung to her foresight-based faith that she would make it through this interview more or less intact, and waited stoically for the other boot to drop.

"Unfortunately, that borderline you tread is found within the edges of your *carte blanche* . . . and you have pulled off multiple miracles time and again despite your many abuses of it," Admiral-General Myang allowed grimly. "You look and talk like a loose cannon on a seafaring ship, but *somehow* you have managed to be the *right* loose cannon every damn time.

"Don't let the fact that we *do* still need you go to your head, though," she warned Ia. "There are some edges to your *carte blanche* out there, and if you cross over them, you will fall a very, *very* long way. And you *will* hit bottom, soldier."

"Whatever you may think of me, sir, arrogant or irreverent or . . . or mad with poetry and prophecy, as is your right, I do respect you and your authority," Ia murmured, holding the older woman's gaze. "So far, you have given me what I need to save lives. I will not forget how much I owe you for that."

Myang stared back for a long moment, then nodded slightly, blinking her dark brown eyes. "Alright. Before we move on to the subject you raised regarding Mercea's supposed, inadvertent contamination by outside forces, is there anything *else* you'd like to share with the Command Staff? One of your infamous 'one more thing' moments?"

Nodding, Ia fished out the datachip stored in her pocket. She floated it off her palm telekinetically, rather than tossing it, and set it gently on the table in front of Myang. "There's all the latest precognitive data I can give you for the next year— some of it becomes a little fuzzy on the Dabin question in half a year, but the rest of it's good for other parts of known space. I'll do whatever I personally can to help correct the Dabin issue. Is that all, sir?"

"No," Myang stated, picking up the chip and pocketing it. "*I* have one last thing. This meeting has also been called to review your performance as an officer. The DoI thinks you could handle a higher rank. They are also wondering, in the face of all the fantastical reports filed by your Company with us, why we haven't seen fit to grant you any awards or commendations. Do you know why that is, Ship's Captain?"

"I can make an educated guess, sir," Ia said.

"Go on," Myang ordered Ia, sitting back in her seat. "Enlighten me."

"It's because I don't give a damn about medals, or ranks, or commendations, and you know it," Ia said flatly. "I could finish out this war *and* the coming Grey War, remaining a mere Ship's Captain for the whole of it, and not care, so long as my goal of saving lives would still be met, and I'd be more than happy with that. I have no ambitions for anything higher."

"No. You don't," Myang stated dryly. Too dryly. Ia wanted to peek at the timestreams to see what that comment was about, but knew such a subtle thing would take more time—even accelerated on the timeplains—than she could spare right now.

Instead, she boldly stated, "Admiral-General, while we're on the subject of elevations in rank, I'd like to personally commend Lieutenant Commander Harper, and recommend that he be granted the rank of Commander. He's kept my ship and crew alive, and kept it repaired with the absolute minimum of supplies."

Admiral-General Myang rolled her eyes. Ia hadn't *said* "one more thing" but the implication was still there.

"At the moment, he is currently doing a series of sweeps across the *Hellfire* to remove excess supplies that we do not need but which will be needed elsewhere," Ia added. She did not mention, given Admiral Wroughtman-Mankiller's compromised presence, that Myang already knew those supplies were being packed off to her next ship in advance of its deployment. Instead, she kept the focus on Harper's readiness for promotion. "He has earned the complete confidence of my crew, and I feel he can handle the increase in rank to Commander."

"Didn't you tell the DoI you wanted him permanently assigned to you, the same as the rest of your crew?" General Phong asked, eyeing Ia. "What would be the point of elevating his rank if he's still assigned to you? Or do you mean to have him reassigned?"

"I do still need his ability to organize the repair of my ships, sir, throughout both the Salik and the Grey Wars," Ia admitted. "But at some point, those two wars will end, and he'll be free to move on to other posts. I believe—not just foresee, but believe—he will be capable of achieving even higher rank as time moves on, if that is what he chooses to do with his life once he is released from my crew. His presence at my side doesn't negate the fact that he has already worked hard enough to have earned it."

"We will consider your recommendation, Ship's Captain. But we will not make up our minds tonight," Myang stated. "Since the discussion of anything else would be a waste of *your* time," again, that odd, dry tone to the older woman's voice, "we might as well let you go. I do expect you to continue to act with the high level of effort and ethics you have displayed so far, if not more. If we find any discrepancies, understand that we reserve the right to haul you before a tribunal for breaking the law. Now, seeing how we have only three days to prepare for the next wave of attacks, you are dismissed, Ship's Captain."

"Sir, yes, sir." Saluting her crisply, Ia turned on her heel as soon as Myang saluted back and left the room.

And that is that. Once Mercea has her and her lover's minds purged and warded against further Meddling, Miklinn is going to be very upset with me. Which means everything is right on track . . . provided I can keep clearing the Hellfire *of "unnecessary" supplies so they can be shipped over to await being loaded onto the* Damnation.

In the meantime, she had only so many hours left before her current ship had to leave dock. They had already been here for almost two days, giving her crew a rare chance at a full day's worth of unrestricted Leave, with free boarding tickets to head down to the Red Planet and priority seating for coming back. It was a mild abuse of her *carte-blanche* powers, and one which could have been contested during this little interview, but her soldiers had definitely earned it.

The Solarican colony that was their next destination was just that, the next in a long line of engagements. As much as her crew needed this break, Ia herself couldn't take any. Her crew could take a day off, but she couldn't afford to slack off.

JANUARY 29, 2498 T.S.
SIC TRANSIT

The officers' mess wasn't always used because there weren't more than a handful of officers on board, spread out over three duty watches. But rank had its privileges when it came to requesting special birthday dinners. With a meal of her favorite foods—pasta, salad, and pastries—prepared by the talented Private First Class Philadelphia Benjamin, one would have expected the doctor's mood to be good.

Except the birthday girl, Jesselle Mishka, entered the cabin in the company of Glen Spyder, both of them arguing vehemently.

"—an' I say y' got yer 'ead on wrong!" Lieutenant Spyder snorted, glaring at her.

"Hiding heat signatures in bodies of water is a time-tested method. The squad should've ducked into the pond!" Jesselle argued, one hand on her hip, the other flipping at his face. "That's what the scenario called for!"

"Yeah, but we ain't dealin' wit' yer average alien, sweets," he retorted, leaning in closer rather than flinching away. His own hand lifted, all but poking her in the sternum. "We're goin' up against Salik, an' th' frogtopi have *sensitivities* f'r maneuvers in water, *includin'* current patterns. So yeah, th' water'd cut the squad's actual heat traces down, but the Salik'd still see th' bloody convection plumes!"

"Oh, and you think hiding the squad in the *trees* is any better?" she scoffed. She snapped her hand up, pointing at the ceiling. "Salik eyeballs point *up*! You'd think, with all those boarding-party missions you've led, you would've *noticed* the Salik viewscreens being posted overhead?"

"Human limbs'r at least *shaped* like most tree limbs," he countered, shifting even closer. "Which you'd know if you'd ever tried t' wrap yer limbs around sommat!"

For a moment, Doctor Mishka stared at him, cheeks flushed and eyes wide with anger, her lips slightly parted as she sought for something to say to that. Their faces—their noses—were mere centimeters apart, and there was barely enough room for a datapad between their bodies. Folding her arms across her chest, Ia bit back the urge to smile. Her plan to ensure that even their Company doctor was competent at thinking strategically, forcing the woman to attend Spyder's weekly tactical discussions, had just borne some unexpected fruit.

Amusingly, Jesselle also folded her arms across her chest. The movement brushed her forearms against Spyder's T-shirt-clad chest. "Are you offering me a target, Lieutenant?"

Even more amusing, Spyder blushed, tried to speak, swallowed, then tried again. "I . . . er . . . not in front 'f the troops, a' course. I mean, y' might be lousy at it. Wouldn't want t' shake their—"

"I might be *lousy* at it?" Jesselle demanded, glaring at him. "After all the training I've gone through on this ship, I can beat the pants off of you on *any* obstacle course—*and* make you *like* it!"

Ia decided she'd had enough entertainment for now. As interesting as this little drama was, they had bigger problems to focus upon. Her revelation to the Command Staff that Lieutenant General Wroughtman-Mankiller had been subtly compromised by a Feyori had drawn attention from the growing membership of Miklinn's little counterfaction against Ia. That meant she had to work with equal subtlety for certain plans, appearing to do one thing while in actuality aiming for something slightly but significantly different.

"Gentlemeioas," she stated just loudly enough to catch both their attention before they could either argue some more or kiss. They jumped a little and twisted to face her, the tension quelled between them, though not completely broken. "I have zero objections to the two of you fraternizing, since neither of you are in each other's immediate chain of command. I must, however, insist that the only thing thick enough to cut in this room be your birthday cake, Doctor. In short, Lock and Web the sexual tension between you two. At least until you can take it to one of your quarters."

Spyder blushed even more. Jesselle paled, then flushed. Interestingly, neither of them denied her labeling it sexual tension. *At least they're competent enough, I can foresee any relationship between the two of them not getting in the way of their duties.* Gesturing at the table, Ia changed the subject.

"Please sit down, both of you. Lieutenant Commander Harper and Lieutenant Rico will be joining us in less than two minutes, and Private Benjamin will be bringing out your birthday dinner in two more. Commander Benjamin will join us about ten minutes in. Her third-watch counseling session is running a little long. As for your argument, the obvious solution to your squadron dilemma lies in both planes."

Spyder frowned at her as he toed one of the chairs back from the table by its lever. He held it steady for the doctor, then selected one for himself across from her. "What d'y' mean, both planes?"

"The squad in question could just as easily submerge themselves in the pond for a minute or two to cool their infrared signature, then climb up the nearest trees along the waterline and hold themselves still," Ia said. "The Salik will most likely see the churned-up mud at the edge of the pond first, along with the thermal plumes still roiling the water, and waste their time searching beneath the surface for their prey. The foliage flanking a pond is always going to be thicker than the kind found deeper in the woods . . . or whatever passes for woods . . . so hiding at the pond's edge in the canopy is not as bad an idea as it sounds.

"You could even leave a couple brave souls down in the water with rebreather masks to lure the Salik down, and set up a flanking ambush from both below and above. At least, that's what I'd do," she stated, as the door slid open again. "Run it by the troops, Spyder, and see if they can strengthen that scenario or poke some serious holes in it."

The tall bulk of their intelligence officer filled the doorway. He was neatly dressed in grey shirt and slacks, his uniform crisp and clean, but his eyes were half-lidded, and a crease mark from his pillow could still be seen on his cheek.

"Good evening, Lieutenant . . . or technically, good morning," Ia greeted him.

Rico grunted and nodded. "Captain, Doctor, Lieutenant. Ah—Lieutenant Commander Helstead says the current watch is quiet, and wants to know if she can come share the birthday girl's supper—happy birthday, Jesselle," he added in an aside. "I told her I'd eat quickly and relieve her, if that's alright with you, sir. I know you don't like leaving a duty watch unmanned."

"You sound like you still need to wake up," Ia countered, watching the way he tried to stifle a yawn and almost succeeded. "I'll be the one to eat fast. That way, my three Platoon officers can have a nice, peaceful *discussion* with the good doctor, here, on various combat and reconnaissance scenarios for our upcoming trip to Dabin." Carefully, shaping and pushing her thoughts outward to catch each of the three of them, she added telepathically, (*Do not forget that you need to throw in false suggestions among the true, regarding what we'll be doing over the next few months. I'll remind you that the Feyori are now watching not only me in the near timestreams but also you. Be grateful they can only watch and cannot read your minds temporally.*)

"Understood, Captain," Rico muttered. Jesselle winced a little, none too happy at the unannounced telepathic projection, but she nodded.

Spyder shrugged and covered the birthday girl's hand. "Sorry t' argue on yer natal day," he apologized. "We c'n table it 'til tomorrow, if y' like."

"Or take it to my quarters," Jesselle muttered, glancing at the green-haired ex-Marine.

That earned her a sharp look from Rico, but he lost the opportunity to ask anything as the door to the corridor slid open once more, admitting their chief engineer.

CHAPTER 17

I pushed the Hellfire and the Damned as hard as we could go without risking our breaking point. Unique as we were, I did my best to utilize everything we could do in an economy of action. My goal was a frugal pursuit of our enemies—and I say enemies, plural, because it wasn't just the Salik and the Choya we had to face. The Meddlers were getting involved, jockeying for new positions, new powers. New plays in their great Game. But they weren't the only ones, either.

In the chaos of war, opportunities await the bold and the reckless. In the fringes, where attention has been turned from shepherding the masses in civilized behavior to defending the masses from a specific foe, certain elements flourish. Criminal elements, beings who wouldn't hesitate to form unholy alliances if it meant increasing their own power, prestige, wealth, or whatever.

They flourished, and they grew bold, and they seized opportunity after opportunity . . . until they grew just a little too reckless, listened to the wrong whispers, allied themselves with the wrong people, and stretched their resources trying to reach for what they wanted, when what they wanted lay within my protection. Some, I had already smacked repeatedly back on Oberon's Rock. Others tried a different tactic.

When the criminal undergalaxy joined in faction with
a certain group of Meddlers, laying plans to go after my
most prized possession, they stretched themselves past the
breaking point . . . and yes, I enjoyed breaking them.

~Ia

MAY 31, 2498 T.S.
BATTLE PLATFORM *SARATOGA JONES*
KUIPER BELT, CS 47 SYSTEM

Ia stared at the contents of the crate she had just unpacked.
Everything was there. Power cables to hook it up, Terran-
designed controls that no longer needed a sucker-hand on the
boxy body of the infernal device, and a jury-rigged trans-
mitter sphere. After pain-filled experimentation with the original captured machine and the ones salvaged from various
wrecked Salik vessels, the Space Force's Psi Division had
figured out how the Salik broadcasted the anti-psi field uni-
laterally over a larger area than an individual victim's helmet
could.

For the next twenty or so hours, this would be a literal
headache, if a necessary one. If it blocked all but the strongest
of psychic abilities, it would block attempts by the Feyori to
peek through the skin of her ship.

Sighing, she pulled the main box out of the crate, carried it
over to the workbench Harper had cleared for her, and secured
it to the surface. It felt a little heavy, but only because she and
her crew were now living and working in 1.8Gs Standard, just
about the right gravity to match their upcoming assignment.
She turned back to fetch the cable and the emitter, but Harper
had already grabbed those.

Bringing them over to her, he wordlessly helped her hook
them up to the ship's power grid. All of her orders in the last
few weeks regarding this day had been delivered telepathically
to her crew. She disliked touching people while speaking
telepathically—and had accidentally tripped herself and a few
of her members of the crew into the timestreams while doing
so, on those few occasions where she had to touch someone
to deliver a message—but it was imperative that the Feyori

watching her from their own version of the timeplains did not hear any actual orders regarding what they were about to do.

If they knew, they wouldn't walk into the trap she needed to set for one of them. A trap in which she hoped to snare many more.

Harper didn't spill the details, but he did make his displeasure known. ". . . Would it do any good to protest?"

"Not a single bit. I am turning on this machine and pointing this ship at your homeworld. We will wait about a light-month out from the system, then swoop in at the right moment and destroy the blockade currently in orbit." Webbing the emitter to the gridboard above the workbench, she glanced at him. "I know you're not happy about Dabin's falling to their forces. And I know you're *not* happy about the genetically engineered monsters they've let loose on your homeworld. But we will go there, and we will arrive in time to save it, and do so in such a way that my goals will be met."

He looked away. She knew that wasn't his real protest. Touching his shoulder, Ia sent, (*I will survive, I promise you that. You have my Prophetic Stamp.*)

. . . *Only because I gave you the tools to do so. Are you sure this thing will foil their vision?* Harper thought back. He couldn't project his thoughts, but he could form them clearly enough for her to read.

(*At the right setting, both machines will block their view of what lies inside each ship, without blocking their view of exactly where this ship will sit.*) Squeezing his shoulder, she lifted her chin. "You're lucky you're not a psi. This thing will hurt like a bite from one of your Dabin swamp rats, the ones you said clamp onto their prey and don't let go."

Releasing him, she turned to the machine and started it with just a few button pushes. The ache built quickly. Within seconds, her head from brow to nape throbbed. Another set of taps on the position-sensitive controls modulated that pain into a dull ache. An ache similar to the one already awaiting them on the ship docked one gantry up from theirs.

"You have your orders, Lieutenant Commander. Carry them out," she instructed.

"Sir, yes, sir." Unhappy, he turned on his heel, picked up the packing crate, and strode out, leaving her alone in the main engineering compartment.

Without the warmth of his personality and presence to fill it, the stripped-down compartment echoed. Every sector and cabin on the ship had been stripped to its barest necessities. Ia knew the Feyori stalking her took that as a sign that they would succeed in their coming attempt. That she intended to deny them every scrap of resources she could. To them, the coming nexus point was muddied, misted over, but there *was* a timeline where they very well could succeed. She didn't need to hide from the Feyori the fact her ship was empty; the anti-psi device was needed to hide that successful path from them.

Hopefully they would be blocked by the device from reading the timestreams, given their milder abilities. That nexus was still somewhat clear to her. Mild as its broadcast was— poisonous as it was to the Feyori—the machine was already starting to mist up the timestreams ahead. She hadn't seen any mists this strongly since manifesting. Not for the first time, Ia wondered why her half-breed life was so oddly immersed in such a vast ocean of prognostication when not even her father-progenitor could do a single percent of the things she could do.

She took her time leaving engineering and made sure to use the port side of the ship to return to the bridge. That permitted her to avoid everyone but Lieutenant Rico, the last person on duty. Ironically, for all that he would have been loyal to her anyway after his trip into the timestreams with her, he would have strenuously protested this plan right alongside Harper if it hadn't been for Private Sung's indiscretion.

But they were hers now. The Damned were solidly hers. If she said, "Jump," they paused only to ask, "How high?" then did their best to hit that exact mark, no more and no less. Even Hollick's replacement, Private Nesbit, was hers. He had asked plenty of questions among her crew, watched her actions and plans unfolding in combat after combat, and had developed a solid level of faith in his CO.

After more than two years of open war, two and a half if one counted their preliminary strikes, and after enduring three to four times as many fights as any other crew, they had lost only one soldier from their Company. There was no doubt that Ia's Damned were the finest fighting force available to the war. Two things made them that way: Ia's trust in them to be the right people for the right job at the right point in time, and their trust in her to let them know what the right job was.

Knowing all of that, believing in all of that, didn't stop Rico from giving her a dirty look as he left the bridge, though. Ia didn't have to read his thoughts to know why. As far as the tall Platoon officer was concerned, his CO was being an idiot for doing all of this on her own. Unfortunately, he had no way to escape along with her, and she wasn't about to waste his life needlessly. He knew all of that, but it didn't make him any happier with her.

Settling into the command seat, Ia levered the chair forward and buckled herself in. The harness straps had long since been replaced but were starting to show some wear and tear from their constant use. With nothing to do but wait, Ia pulled a trick out of both Helstead's and Spyder's bags and put her bootheels up on the console. Not near anything sensitive, of course. Then again, she didn't need to touch the controls to activate them.

Screens flicked to life around the bridge. With her primary screen blank and thus transparent, she read the distant displays monitoring the ship's statistics. The engines looked good, tiny little green bars indicating energy consumption was running low. The shields displayed their status in two levels, low on the starboard, toward the Battle Platform, high on the port side, standard wartime procedure whenever docked, in case of an unexpected attack. The *Hellfire*'s scanners were sweeping passively, collecting and collating data with the navicomp's help.

Lifesupport, however, was nothing more than a series of red lines and blanks, save for a few tiny green bars. Plants had been boxed up, fish bagged, hens crated, and all of it shipped out. Including her precious supply of carefully nurtured topadoes, with their beautiful dark purple and sky blue striped foliage, and their tasty aquamarine roots. The ship was running purely on mechanical reoxygenators now, with the air scrubbed chemically instead of biologically.

The emergency systems could easily reoxygenate the ship long enough to keep the original crew complement of five hundred or so alive for at least two months, though the air would start to smell a bit ozone-ish and stale after the first three weeks. With just Ia on board—well, her, and a last clutch of crew members slipping out the amidships starboard airlock with a few last-minute kitbags of belongings slung over their shoulders—the air supply could easily last a year. Food would be the biggest problem; all but the bridge galley had been stripped of everything, and even that one only had a few ration packets left.

The Salik had already tried several times to board and capture the *Hellfire*. Every single time, Ia had precognitively thwarted them. Missiles had breached their hulls, but not a single ostrich-legged flipper had landed on their decks. They weren't a concern, though. Even if they had, they'd never be able to use the Godstrike cannon.

The Feyori . . . were a different matter. All they needed was a bit of Ia's DNA and enough time to read her mind, and they could replicate her body and personality in the flesh of a volunteer, much as she and Belini had turned Private Hollick into Private N'Keth. Belini hadn't ever mentioned that possibility, but Ia knew it could be done. Once they had a duplicate clone of herself, they would be able to access the Godstrike cannon. It was debatable whether or not they would be able to replicate her psychic abilities, since even among identical twins such things varied, but the cannon did not require that much accuracy for access. All of these things, she had carefully explained to Myang in a message embedded in that latest datachip.

A glance at the chrono showed she had twenty hours and fourteen minutes to prevent them from trying.

When the airlock sealed shut behind Rico, the last of the Damned to leave, she unstrapped from the command chair and visited the head. Fixed herself a mug of water with a sipping lid. Brought it and a snack packet back to her station and redonned the safety harness. Tapping in a command manually, she shifted the view on her right secondary screen from blank nothingness to the dorsal view of the slightly oversized OTL courier parked one gantry up from hers.

Like her old Delta-VX from her time on the Blockade, it fell into the Harrier Class of ships, though it was a single vessel, not two mated together. It was also small enough; it could've fit into one of the hangar bays on board the *Saratoga Jones*. The captain had agreed to park it at a gantry instead, in order to make the short trip of her crew from ship to ship as inconspicuous as possible.

As she watched, sipping from her mug, the oversized courier finally detached from the Battle Platform. It drifted away, then gently turned and shimmered, activating its insystem thrusters. The insystem field was more primitive than FTL warp panels, yet more fuel-efficient at speeds below three-quarters Cee. With a pulse that fluttered and rippled the starlight along the Harasser's polished grey hull, the ship soared away from the Battle Platform.

Ia's yeomen pilots maneuvered their much larger ship with thrusters. FTL was tricky; milliseconds of misuse could literally translate to kilometers of travel at higher speeds. With her reflexes coupled to the timestreams, using FTL had allowed her to dodge laserfire from both enemy and allied ships. For instances where accuracy was vital, such as that Choya task force sent to Earth, she used the insystem method like a sane pilot would.

A simple maneuver such as leaving the *Saratoga Jones* was a lot saner than the madness of combat. Finishing her mug, she returned it to the galley, tossed the emptied plexi packet into the recycler—out of habit, not because she expected the material to be recycled—and used the head one more time. When she sat down at her station for the third time, she activated the comms.

"This is TUPSF Hellfire *to Battle Platform* Saratoga Jones, *requesting permission to undock and depart."* This was usually handled by the comm tech, one of the many operations that happened seamlessly, smoothly in the background of a well-run bridge. She waited for a reply, and got one within a few moments.

"Hellfire, this is Docking Control. You have permission to decouple and depart. Godspeed, and go smash some more of the enemy for us," the unnamed comptroller added. This was the first time they'd docked briefly at this particular Battle Platform. The reputation of the Damned, which she had painstakingly built over the last two years, had preceded them, however.

"Thank you, Saratoga Jones,*"* Ia acknowledged, smiling slightly. *"We'll do our best.* Hellfire *out."*

Flying the ship solo required several command overrides. It was an attempt by the Space Force at preventing their ships from being hijacked by their enemies, whether amphibious or criminal. Ia manipulated each one electrokinetically, decoupling the clamps that held them to their gantry. A gentle pulse of the thrusters drifted them away from the oversized hybrid of warship and space station. Another gentle pulse turned her ship onto a vector similar to the courier's.

Warming up the insystem thrusters, she set the *Hellfire* on a course that would take it away from the Battle Platform by a good thousand klicks. A slide of her fingertips over the helm controls brought the FTL panels online, trembling them forward by the pulsing of the fields that greased the palms of normal physics, making Newton and Einstein roll in their graves.

The Harrier-Class dropship carrying her crew vanished via OTL before she even reached one-quarter Cee, punching open a hole into hyperspace and sucking itself through. On the far side, Ia knew the ship would arrive somewhere near Dabin's outermost gas giant. At that point, her entire crew would climb into their mechsuits and await a short hop that would bring them skimming in close to Dabin's atmosphere. From there, it would be a matter of a short dip down to a low enough altitude to be air-dropped behind friendly lines.

The courier had a ninety percent chance of escaping the ensuing counterattack from the Choyan and Salik warships blockading the planet, if all went well. If it did not, and they were pursued, Helstead had carefully memorized a chunk of Dabin landscape from surveillance images captured a good five klicks up, and would teleport the ship to that zone so they could drop out. It would leave everyone on board nauseated from the jump, and possibly incapacitate the redhead for a few hours from the backlash of overextending herself in moving that much mass, but it was a viable means of ensuring everyone arrived where and when they needed to go.

Everyone except Ia. She had to get there the hard way.

The transition to faster-than-light happened smoothly. Dots burst as grey bubbles and collapsed into streaks of prismatic light. Setting the ship to fly on automatic, and for the onboard sensors to beep at her if anything went wrong—less than one-hundredth of a percent in probability, but still a possibility—she twisted a little in her seat, slouched, hooked her legs up over the left-hand console in as much comfort as the harness would allow, and settled in for a nap.

With the ship fully fueled, the trip from CS 47 to the edge of the Dabinae System wasn't going to tax the engines. It would just take her twenty hours to get there. Twenty hours of head-aching boredom. Her datapads had been packed up along with her other belongings and shipped off earlier. Some of the more time-sensitive stuff had been packed into Harper's last-minute kitbag, with the rest shipped off to meet up with their next ship.

Without even so much as her prophecies for distraction, and no interest in watching anything from the entertainment data-banks, there was nothing for Ia to do but nap and wait, nap and wait. Mostly nap. All those long, long days were beginning to catch up to her. Awkward as her perch was, as much as the device back in engineering made her skull throb, at least every-thing was secure enough that she could nap, for now.

JUNE 1, 2498 T.S.
ONE LIGHT-MONTH OUT FROM THE DABINAE SYSTEM

The ship's shields fluttered. Cracking open an eyelid at the first warning beep, Ia studied the screens. The navicomp had her main screen lit up, a tiny green-circled dot insisting that the approaching ship was an allied Terran vessel. She knew better. The signature codes were all fake, inserted into the Space Force's registry by clever electrokinetic pro-gramming.

The other vessel slowed as it approached. It also hailed the *Hellfire*. Activating the comm system, Ia gave them a pingback, waited for a response, and opened the requested link.

"TUPSF Zizka *to TUPSF* Hellfire, *boy are we glad to find you out here."*

Ia didn't bother to activate the vid half of the link. Adjusting her headset, which had slipped while she had caught up on far too many months of shorted sleep, she stretched, rubbed the bridge of her nose where that persistent behind-the-sinuses ache from the anti-psi machine continued to throb, and replied. *"Greetings,* Zizka, *this is the* Hellfire. *What brings you all the way out here?"*

"We have an urgent message from Vice Commodore Wil-liam Quan of the Special Forces Psi Division. The vice com-modore is a registered precog. He swears he's had a vision running contrary to what you told the Command Staff about the upcoming battle on Dabin and wishes to board so he can personally compare your version versus his. Do we have per-mission to dock?"

"TUPSF Zizka, *you have permission to grapple to the port-side amidships airlock. The Captain says she looks forward to chatting with your vice commodore,"* Ia added, suppressing the urge to smile. She didn't want it showing up in the tone of her voice. Apparently these criminals hadn't yet realized that they needed the Admiral-General's permission to board this ship legitimately. Myang had reluctantly permitted Ia's request to destroy the ship rather than let it fall into enemy hands, though the head of the Space Force undoubtedly thought this moment would come violently. Not peacefully. *"Let me ping you the navicomp link for a smooth docking."*

"Thank you, Hellfire.*"*

Unbuckling—since they were still at least five minutes away—Ia visited the head one last time. She could do nothing about the fact she was still clad in yesterday's clothes, just a plain, rumpled grey shirt and darker grey slacks, but she did finger-comb her white locks more or less straight in the mirror over the sink, rinsed her mouth with a plexi cup to get the fuzzy taste out, and took a few moments to close her eyes, center her mind, and calm herself. Her head still ached, but it was bearable.

Tossing the cup in the recycler, she visited her quarters. With that brief task handled, Ia returned to the bridge and resumed her seat. She did not reattach the harness. She did, however, flip up the little door built into the side of her console and grasped the two electrodes hidden within the little alcove.

As the two ships' navicomps chatted at each other, guiding the smaller courier-class *Zizka* into docking with the elongated needle of the *Hellfire*, Ia pulled on that conduit's juice. Pulled and pulled and pulled, balling it up inside her body. Every time her hair threatened to fluff, she sucked it in tighter, clamping down on the external signs. By the time the telltales for the portside airlock greenlit with a viable seal, the lines and angles of the bridge's stations were starting to glow.

The slightest nudge of her mind cracked a miniature bolt of lightning by mistake. Thankfully, the various bridge consoles had been built with capacitors; they functioned properly, absorbing the extra energy without overloading the command station. Using her hands instead of her gifts, Ia activated the interior surveillance pickups the old-fashioned way.

The courier had already disgorged several passengers. They

looked like TUPSF troops, were armed and lightly armored like Terran troops, but she knew each one was a career criminal who specialized in pirating and pilfering Terran military supplies. And it was the tall scowling woman in their midst who was really in charge, not the short Asiatic man pretending to be the vice commodore in question.

She rubbed at her brow as Ia watched, and snapped something to the dozen men and women accompanying her. Ia had to manually replay the scene to hear what she said. When she heard it, she activated the intercom. *"Attention, Zizka personnel. The nearest door into the main engineering compartment is located on Deck 8, aft-sector port side. The actual deck containing what you are looking for is in main engineering, Deck 8 starboard side . . . and once you get over there, you can't miss it. You are currently on Deck 12, amidships-sector port side. The nearest crossover point to starboard from your location is Deck 6."*

The tall blonde checked her stride. Still scowling in pain, she squinted up at the ceiling until she spotted the closest active camera. *"So you know why we're here?"*

"Who you are and why you're here . . . though I'm surprised you agreed to risk your sparks with this little trip, Janeal," Ia added. The Feyori blinked twice, but otherwise didn't react. *"Whatever Miklinn offered you, it won't be enough. I'm sorry."*

"You are nothing more than a pawn," Janeal stated, moving forward. *"You always have been, and you always will be. Prepare to be removed from the Game."*

Smirking, Ia quipped quietly into her headset pickup, *" 'I'm sorry, Dave. I'm afraid I can't do that . . .'* Only in my case, I'm definitely not Hal, and you're not the hero of this little vidshow. The bridge is located in the middle of amidships-sector Deck 6. I look forward to your arrival. Ia'nn sud-dha."*

Rubbing again at her aching head, the tall, blonde Meddler strode forward. Her accomplices accompanied her.

"Oh, one more thing. You might want to tell the others to head back to the Zizka right now and start running for the stars within the next minute," Ia added. *"I realize you're willing to sacrifice at least three of them to find and shut off the antipsi machine sitting in Engineering, Deck 8 starboard, but the others don't have to die. This is between you and me, after all."*

The back door slid open. An annoyed-looking, red-clad

pixie padded onto the bridge. Her frown deepened as she looked around the almost empty cabin. "What the . . . ? Where did everyone go?"

Her trip to her quarters to trigger Belini's summoning spot had once again worked. Her cofaction partner didn't look particularly happy to be here, but at least she had come when called. Ia lifted her bootheels back up onto the console.

"Welcome aboard, Belini. You're just in time," she greeted the petite Feyori, her tone light and cheerful. Mockingly so. Gesturing at the empty duty stations, Ia extended her meager hospitality. "Feel free to have a seat. I'd offer you something to eat, physical or otherwise, but I'm afraid we're almost out of time. Janeal and her thugs will be joining us in about a minute or so."

Blinking, Belini twisted to face her. "Janeal? The Feyori who plucks the puppet strings of the local undergalaxy?"

"The Queen of Predators and Piracy," Ia agreed. She fluttered her hand vaguely at the other stations. "Have a seat and enjoy the show."

"If you're expecting high tension and danger to tip you over the energy-to-matter barrier, I'm afraid Janeal isn't going to give you the time to build up that sort of momentum," Belini warned her. "The moment she steps inside, her thugs will shoot you dead, and that will be that. Not even you can dodge laserfire, half-breed. She also comes with too many cross-factions for me to counteract directly, if you were expecting me to save your hide. Since I now hold a very low and tenuous ranking, *in case you forgot?*"

Ia rolled her eyes and pointed at the pilot's seat. "She is not going to shoot me right away. She'll want to monologue first. *You* are here to observe my manifestation, and to stand witness to all that will follow. You won't have to lift a finger. My debt to you, in exchange for all your trust and faith in me, is about to come due. Have a seat; I'd hate for you to miss a single millisecond of it."

Still scowling, Belini studied her for a long moment, then padded over to the indicated chair and plopped herself into it. Only the narrowing of her eyes made her look dangerous; the rest of her looked like a pouting pixie. Squirming a little in her own seat, Ia slouched a little more comfortably and once again stuck her hand in the conduit hole. Some of her built-up energy had bled off during the miniature jolt. She replaced that and more, lounging in the command chair.

The portside door slid open. Janeal stepped through, projecting an air of command more successfully than the look-alike Human tapped to imitate the real-life Vice Commodore Quan. He in turn kind of looked like her old Drill Instructor, Sergeant Tae, Ia decided, looking him over. *Except he's in no way related to Harper. I should probably find a spare minute or two in the future to give the real Tae a call and see how he's doing. I know Meyun keeps in touch with him, but I haven't had a chat with the man since the third time he dropped by the Academy . . . A pity this fellow isn't going to survive this little encounter.*

"What, too lazy to meet your own fate, half-breed?" Janeal mocked. Her look of contempt was an excellent study of Human emotions. It also summed up the general Feyori mind-set toward the short-lived matter races succinctly, and she gave it to Ia with an added sneer of derision.

"Oh, I'm meeting it," Ia said—and kicked, shoving her bootheel hard against the plexi lockbox encasing the main cannon's switch.

That broke it with a *crack*, and an immediate flash of red lights. They flared every second, accompanied by an unnerving, atonal buzzing. Bright white numbers appeared on every screen, starting at 60 and counting their way down. The hyperrelay telltales over at the communications station lit up, hard-dumping the black-box recordings for the last hour in an encrypted broadband stream. It would continue to stream its previous reams of data to the Command Staff, too, all the way through to the last second of the *Hellfire*'s existence. Ia didn't bother to stop it.

"If your thugs ran right *now*, they *might* make it from the bridge to the airlock in forty-nine seconds," she stated, sitting up. Her mind snapped out, stabbing at the Humans on board her ship. They dropped with sighs and thumps to the deck, mercifully knocked unconscious, half-drawn weapons clattering to the deck. "But they'd only have a handful left to get through the airlocks, and would not escape in time. Unconsciousness is the only mercy I can give them."

"I can stop this!" Jeneal snapped, lifting her hand.

Ia shook her head, pushing to her feet. She could feel the woman probing electrokinetically at the controls, and knew better. "It's too late. It's *chemistry*, not electronics. The hydrocatalysts have already been released into every tank on this ship, and you won't stop more than a fraction of it. You have maybe thirty seconds to shift shape and survive."

"Shakk!" Grabbing the pilot's console, Belini ripped electricity out of it, popping from pixie to bubble in three seconds flat.

Ia planted her hand on her own station, drawing out the energy she needed more gently, but with the same result. In a flash, she floated instead of stood before the other two. Belini swirled in agitation, then clamped down hard on herself, blocking out all forms of radiation, turning a shining shade of mirror white.

Janeal grabbed for the gunner's station, changing as well. Between Belini's and Ia's efforts, there wasn't a large flow of energy available. It took the other Meddler ten full seconds to manifest. Even as she shifted, Ia noted to herself that Feyori in matter-forms stood out to their energy-form fellows like a glowing-hot iron on an infrared scanner. *I'll have to keep that in mind for when I'm on Dabin.*

For one moment, the pirate Meddler hung there in a swirl of confusion, then she turned brilliant white like Belini, the Feyori equivalent of holding one's breath by blocking out all incoming radiation.

So did the rest of the ship, when the countdown reached zero and the tanks exploded, turning the *Hellfire*, and by collateral damage the *Zizka*, into a tiny, bright nova. Forewarned by her trips onto the timeplains, Ia did not block off the inferno, like the other two. Instead, she embraced it, swelling outward as the energy rushed through her, using the part of her mind that dealt with, that comprehended, that controlled and manipulated Time itself to withstand the overwhelming flows.

Expanding and twisting, she snatched up the two Feyori with her thoughts, swirling them into her grasp. Ia watched them carefully as she spun them around her expanded sense of self. There, in the wake of the energies thrust aside by her vortex, were the little hyperthreads that attached each alien to their faction-allies, their favorite places.

Seizing those threads, Ia *pulled*. It was a variation on the summoning spark that alerted each attached Meddler that they were needed, a variation that could only succeed if the Feyori doing the summoning had access to a great deal of power. A solar flare, a massive thunderstorm, even the surface of a dying star could be used. Or an explosion caused by the catalytic conversion of tens of thousands of metric tons of purified water fused into a muddled, white-hot plasma of pure hydrogen and supercharged oxygen.

When each Feyori popped into range, dragged there by her summons, she grabbed *their* threads and yanked. Grabbed *those* threads and pulled. Grabbed the next set and tugged. Four degrees out was all the strength she had to spare for her task, and only with the first cycle's worth of Meddlers did she literally pull any of them through the aether of hyperspace.

But the others came out of alarm and curiosity and boredom as she summoned each clutch. They crowded around her, dozens, hundreds, then roughly two thousand strong, brushing through each other, bobbing in empty space. Demanding in pulses of energy and empathy and telepathy to know what was going on, even as they drank in the remnants of the explosion she had made.

Spun out to an almost tenuous level, Ia enveloped the last ones to arrive and *pulled* them all inward, spinning around and down, flipping everyone in, up, and out. Landing on the banks of the timestreams in her Human form, she looked at the mass of tiny silver beads clinging to her left hand. They huddled close to her skin not because they willed it, but because *her* will trapped them there. Ruthlessly, Ia forced them to see the verdant fields, the golden waters, the blazing-hot skies in her mind.

"Welcome to my *chessboard, gentlebeings. Welcome to* Time *itself,"* she warned them, letting the word roar across the plains like wind from a thunderstorm, letting the force of that word shift them forward by three centuries and a little more. *"And if you do* not *faction with me . . . welcome to the end of your precious little Game."*

I am not fully Human, no. I admit it outright. Half of my being was conceived by the usual earthly delights, while the other half was crafted by the meddling of purified will. But I was raised to be a Human, I have lived as a Human, and I fight as a Human. And I love as a Human. With compassion for more than just my own interests. For more than my own culture. More than my own kind. I have loved from birth every person you have ever seen, regardless of species, and I love the septillions more that you won't.

Because I am still Human, I swim in the frozen waters of my duty, lifting up others' lives so they do not drown in the tempest-tossed storm. I burn with the raging flames of my conscience and never divert from the embers underfoot on the dangerous paths I must tread. I walk through the hellish inferno to save others' souls, knowing that at the same time I slip down the ice-cold slopes of my lonely task with each condemned step.

I am the Prophet of a Thousand Years, the Changer of Worlds, the Meddler of Destinies, the Defender of Our Galaxy . . . and neither Hellfire nor Damnation will keep me from my task.

~Ia

After having a terrible vision of the future, Ia must somehow ensure the salvation of her home galaxy long after she's gone...

From national bestselling author

JEAN JOHNSON

AN OFFICER'S DUTY

THEIRS NOT TO REASON WHY

Promoted in the field for courage and leadership under fire, Ia is now poised to become an officer in the Space Force Navy— once she undertakes her Academy training. First, however, she travels back home to Sanctuary, a heavyworld colony being torn apart by religious conflict. Ia must prepare her family and followers for the hardships they will endure in order to secure the galaxy's survival.

Her assignment is to command a Blockade Patrol ship. Her goal, to save as many lives as she can. But at the Academy, she discovers an unexpected challenge: the one man who could disrupt those plans, the man whose future she cannot foresee. And time is running out for Ia, for the galaxy is on the brink of the Second Salik War...

"Reminiscent of both *Starship Troopers* and *Dune*."
—*Publishers Weekly*

facebook.com/AceRocBooks
jeanjohnson.net
penguin.com

M1289T0313